THE
13TH APOSTLE

A NOVEL OF
MICHAEL COLLINS AND
THE IRISH UPRISING

Dermot McEvoy

Skyhorse Publishing

This book is dedicated to five extraordinary writers from the old Lion's Head saloon on Christopher Street in New York City—Joe Flaherty, David Markson, Lanford Wilson, Frank McCourt, and Pete Hamill.

Thank you.

Skyhorse Publishing books may be purchased in bulk at special discounts for sales promotion, corporate gifts, fund-raising, or educational purposes. Special editions can also be created to specifications. For details, contact the Special Sales Department, Skyhorse Publishing, 307 West 36th Street, 11th Floor, New York, NY 10018 or info@skyhorsepublishing.com.

Skyhorse® and Skyhorse Publishing® are registered trademarks of Skyhorse Publishing, Inc.®, a Delaware corporation.

Visit our website at www.skyhorsepublishing.com.

10 9 8 7 6 5 4 3 2

Library of Congress Cataloging-in-Publication Data is available on file.

Print ISBN: 978-1-5107-1207-2
Ebook ISBN: 978-1-6287-3923-7

Printed in the United States of America

ACKNOWLEDGEMENTS

I want to thank all my Dublin cousins for their help in the writing of this book, as their knowledge of the city was invaluable: Maura and Gerry Bartley and their sons, Declan, Father Kevin, and Brendan; Terry O'Neill and his wife, Mary; and Monsignor Vincent Bartley on this side of the Atlantic.

I want to especially thank Collins's biographer, Chrissy Osborne, and her husband, David. I don't think anyone knows more about Michael Collins's Dublin than Chrissy. Her books opened new doors to me, and there's nothing more exciting than traveling with Chrissy to the houses Collins used around Dublin town to get a feel of what it must have been like to be a wary rebel in Dublin during the War of Independence.

A big thank-you to *Irish Independent* columnist Mary Kenny for her generous help on the Collins-Churchill friendship, which she portrayed so brilliantly in her play *Allegiance,* and for introducing me to the seduction of Black Velvet—Guinness and champagne—at the Horseshoe Bar in the Shelbourne Hotel in Dublin.

One of the characters in the book, Charlie Conway, was my great-uncle. I want to thank Seán Connolly of the Royal Dublin Fusiliers Association for finding Uncle Charlie's military records. I also want to thank Eibhlin Roche of the Guinness Archive, who was most helpful in obtaining Charlie's employment record at the brewery between 1902 and 1932. Their work breathed new life into Charlie, at least as a fictional character.

Thanks to my hardworking editor, Jenn McCartney, and publisher, Tony Lyons, who have always encouraged me in my insanely quixotic writing quests.

Special thanks to Rosemary Mahoney and Mike Coffey for their editorial suggestions.

And a heroic thank-you to the only two people who read the book as I wrote it: Marianne Fagan and Jack Hornor. Their suggestions and encouragement made my complicated task easier.

"You will not get anything from the British government unless you approach them with a bullock's tail in one hand and a landlord's head in the other."

—*Michael Collins*
Ballinalee, County Longford
October 7, 1917

AUTHOR'S NOTE

For seven hundred years the British occupied Ireland, stealing its land, looting its meager wealth, enacting extraordinarily punitive taxes, and imposing a famine on its inhabitants.

On Easter Monday, April 24, 1916, a handful of rebels commandeered buildings around Dublin City and fought the British army to a standstill for nearly a week.

Almost immediately after their surrender, fourteen of the leaders were shot in the breaker's yard of Kilmainham Gaol. Sixteen men in all were executed for their uprising against the British.

With the elimination of the 1916 leaders, another generation of revolutionaries rose to take their place.

This cadre was led by Eamon de Valera, a senior commandant who escaped execution because of his natural-born American citizenship, and Michael Collins, who would soon rise to hold the positions of Minister for Finance in the first *Dáil* and Director of Intelligence for the Irish Republican Army.

Collins's reign as a revolutionary was short—a lively six years, between the Easter Rising and his death in an ambush on August 22, 1922.

But during that short period of time, he led a bloody guerrilla war that is now textbook for all emerging revolutionaries, much studied by the likes of Mao Tse-Tung and Yitzhak Shamir, who would later become the seventh prime minister of Israel. (Shamir's *nom-de-guerre*, interestingly enough, was "Michael.") For the first time, the British became the hunted—and they did not like it. Michael Collins, against impossible odds, had beat the British at their own game of intimidation.

One of Collins's cohorts and co-conspirators was a fourteen-year-old Dublin boy he met in the General Post Office during Easter Week.

His name was Eoin Kavanagh.

This is their story.

Dermot McEvoy, Jersey City, New Jersey, 2014

"And David put his hand in his bag, and took thence a stone, and slang it, and smote the Philistine in his forehead; and the stone sank into his forehead, and he fell upon his face to the earth."

—1 Samuel 17:49

OCTOBER 2006

OCTOBER 2006

"Johnny Three," an ancient, gravelly voice said. "It's time to come get me. Now." Then the phone went dead.

Eoin Kavanagh III—known as Johnny Three to everyone—knew it was his grandfather's way of summoning him back to Dublin for the final farewell. "I have to go to Dublin," Kavanagh said to his wife, Diane. "I think I should go alone."

"I'm coming," his wife said, and Kavanagh was smart enough not to argue this time.

When the flight from New York landed, they headed to the old man's house in Dalkey. "I don't like this," Johnny Three remarked to his wife as their taxi swung to the southside of Dublin Bay.

"Why?"

"It's October 16th."

"So?"

"Michael Collins's birthday," replied Johnny. "You know the old man."

"He's picked his death day," Diane exclaimed, shocked.

"Yes, he has."

When they arrived at the house, Bridie, his grandfather's long-time housekeeper, opened the door. "I shouldn't have," she said, then repeated, "I shouldn't have."

"Are you alright, Bridie?" asked Johnny Three as Diane took the distraught woman by the arm.

Johnny Three heard a ruckus from the bedroom above. He knew that his grandfather, the original Eoin Kavanagh, would not go out quietly. "Bless my ancient HOLE," he heard his grandfather say.

"I shouldn't have called the priest," said Bridie as a curate, purple stole flying about him, came running down the stairs.

"He's incorrigible," the harassed man said as he removed the stole and kissed the cross on the back.

"Thank you, Father," said Bridie.

"Incorrigible," said the priest to Johnny and Diane.

"Contrary," corrected the grandson.

"Whatever!" the priest said as he exited the house.

Johnny chuckled at the priest's distress and hit the stairs, followed by his wife. "How are you, grandpa?"

The old man looked up, and his eyes brightened as he surveyed his only grandchild. "Not good," he said, motioning the couple toward his bed, which had a panoramic view of Dublin Bay and Dalkey Island.

The younger Kavanagh reached down and kissed his grandfather on the forehead. "Did you make your peace, grandpa?" he said.

"Peace my arse," said Eoin. "Bloody priests never change." The grandfather shooed his grandson away and motioned for Diane to come to him. "How are you, dear?" he said as he kissed her hand and then patted her gently on her round Presbyterian rump.

"Oh, grandpa," she said and started to cry.

"There, there," he said and patted her bottom again as he looked at his grandson and smiled. Johnny Three turned away so his wife wouldn't see *him* smile. Death was banging on the door, but the old rebel kept petting Diane's caboose.

The old man was crazy about Diane Kavanagh. Even after bearing three children, she was still a remarkably beautiful and fit woman. She had gorgeous brown hair, dancing blue eyes, and one of the most remarkable bottoms God had ever created. "How did an eejit like you end up with a woman of that caliber?" he liked to chide his grandson.

"She fell in love with you," he replied with some truth, "but she married me."

"Grandpa."

"Yes, son."

"Should I follow your wishes?"

"Yes," said Eoin. "To the letter." He looked intently at his grandson. "I have a surprise for you."

"You're leaving me the house?"

"Who else would I leave it to? You're the last *real* Kavanagh."

"How about the Church or the State?" A negative smile gave the answer. "What's the surprise?"

"You'll see." With that, the old man serenely laid his head on the pillow and closed his eyes.

"Is he?" asked Diane with concern.

Johnny Three was a little more cynical. "I wouldn't bet on it," he said.

Suddenly Eoin's eyes shot open, and he urgently motioned the grandson to his side.

"Yes, grandpa."

"Fook," he said, suddenly having trouble forming words.

"Fuck?" repeated Johnny.

"Fook Eddie de Valera."

The old man was defiant to the end. Then, by a blink of his eyes, he asked his grandson to come closer. "How did he do it?" he said in a whisper.

"Who?" said Johnny.

"How the fook did Mick Collins pull it off?"

"I don't know, grandpa."

"Neither do I, son." A single tear rolled down Eoin Kavanagh's cheek. "My God, I loved that man." His eyes slowly closed.

"Oh, Johnny, he's gone." Johnny took his wife in his arms and hugged her as hard as he could. "He's gone," she said again. With that, Diane heard the loudest laugh she had heard in a long time. Johnny Three was doubled over. "What are you doing?"

"I'm giving the old man," he said, catching his breath, "the sendoff he deserves."

EOIN KAVANAGH, TD, DEAD AT 105
WAS LAST SURVIVING GPO REBEL

Johnny Three read the *Irish Times* headline and smiled. He handed it back to the army officer the *Taoiseach*, the Irish prime minister, had sent over to set up the viewing in the rotunda of Dublin's City Hall.

Eoin Kavanagh lay in a simple box. He was dressed in his Volunteer's uniform. The man hadn't gained a pound since 1916.

"Can I have a moment alone?" Johnny asked the officer. He straightened the tricolor on the bottom half of the coffin and looked at his grandfather. The old man still wore a beard, and his head of Paul O'Dwyer-esque white hair—the closest thing to an Irish halo—was still full. He had insisted on being viewed in the City Hall because that was where his boss, Michael Collins, had lain in state after he was killed in 1922. You couldn't mention the name of Eoin Kavanagh without people saying that he was The Big Fellow's personal bodyguard—or perhaps something more. Sometimes, with an unsettling gleam in his eye, Eoin would refer to himself as "Mick's Thirteenth Apostle," never elaborating. The old man knew his place in history, and even in death, he wanted to be sure he got all he had coming to him—right down to the twenty-one gun salute at Glasnevin, where he would be buried in the army cemetery, right next to General Collins.

"I think I need a drink," said Kavanagh to the officer. "I'll be back in a while." Johnny went down the front steps of the City Hall into Cork Hill. He swung into Palace Street at one of the Dublin Castle side gates and headed down Dame Lane, which would take him across South Great Georges Street and into Dame Court. He and the old man had walked this narrow street many times as Eoin told him how he and Collins would often case English touts to the gates of the Castle itself, then retreat to the Stag's Head for a drink.

At night, the Stag's Head was a madhouse, but, in the daytime, it was serene—one of the most beautiful Victorian pubs in Dublin. Johnny Three was first brought there by his grandfather during his summer visits in the late 1960s and '70s.

The death of Jack Kennedy had taken a lot out of the old man—for a while. It was like losing Collins again. Eoin Kavanagh was the only member of Congress to travel with Kennedy on his trip to Ireland in 1963. They had sat with the *Taoiseach*, Seán Lemass, and regaled Kennedy with stories of 1916, the War of Independence, and being Michael Collins's personal bodyguard. Although Kavanagh and Jack Lemass had been on opposite sides in the Irish Civil War, they had remained friends, even after Kavanagh left Ireland in 1922 and went to America. During World War II, Congressman Kavanagh served as Lemass's personal intermediary with Eoin's long-time friend, Franklin Roosevelt, during Ireland's "Emergency." Kennedy had marveled at the close relationship between Lemass and Kavanagh and noticed that the Congressman never uttered a word to President de Valera, Lemass's mentor, who was sitting on the same dais. It brought a smile to Kennedy's face—he knew all about the Irish and their grudges.

After Kennedy died, Lemass had phoned. "Come back to Ireland," he told his old friend. And he did: Kavanagh ran for the *Dáil* as an independent in the South Dublin district he had been born in and ended up sitting in the opposition aisle to his friend, the *Taoiseach*. "You're nothing but a troublemaker," Lemass laughed after Eoin Kavanagh was sworn in as a *Teachtaí Dála* (TD): Deputy to the *Dáil*, the Irish parliament.

"Jack," Kavanagh deadpanned, "how could you t'ink such a thing?" (Eoin had known Lemass even before he Gaelicized his first name, for political reasons, to Seán. To Eoin, he would always be plain old Jack.)

And a troublemaker he was. In 1971, after Lemass died, Deputy Kavanagh began running guns to the North after internment without trial was instituted by the British government. When Liam Cosgrave became *Taoiseach* in 1974, he was indicted. He refused to resign his seat in *Dáil Éireann* and stood trial, where he proudly declared his guilt—and was found innocent by a jury of his delighted peers. "This is a great day for Ireland," Kavanagh declared on the steps of the Four Courts, where he and his wife of fifty-two years stood before the assembled media, "and a bad day for Liam Cosgrave and those other *Fine Gail* eunuchs who are trying to turn the Irish government into the subservants of the British imperialists! What a bunch of pussies! Mick Collins would be appalled!" When infuriated, the New Yorker in Eoin Kavanagh had a tendency to surface with a bang. Mrs. Kavanagh looked straight into the gutter, hoping her feminist friends back in New York would not see the smile on her face.

Johnny Three had been with him when he crossed paths with Eamon de Valera for the last time. It was at a function at the Gresham Hotel in O'Connell Street in June 1975, just months before Dev's death. The two old antagonists had literally bumped into each other at the reception. De Valera, blind as a bat, was as sharp as ever. "Eoin Kavanagh," he said, looking down at the diminutive Kavanagh, "I see young, respectable Cosgrave doesn't like you." Dev had had his own run-ins with the father, W.T. Cosgrave, during the Civil War.

"Well, Chief," said Eoin, "neither did his old man!"

De Valera laughed, enjoying his first conversation with Kavanagh since 1922. "God be with you, Eoin Kavanagh."

De Valera wasn't going to get off that easy. "Chief," Eoin said.

"Yes."

"Mick was right."

De Valera looked down with unseeing eyes through his thick glasses and sighed. "Perhaps," he responded. "Perhaps."

"God bless, Chief," were the last words Eoin Kavanagh said to his former antagonist.

De Valera slowly moved through the room on his way out. "Look," said Eoin to Johnny Three. De Valera had extended his supine hands to the side, like the Blessed Virgin Mary, so people could touch him. "Look at that old bastard work the room!" said Eoin with genuine admiration. "Goddamn it, Johnny, Jack Kennedy couldn't have done it better." Eoin Kavanagh appreciated political talent when he saw it.

——————

Diane joined Johnny Three at the Stag's Head. "Man, you look good," he said as he rubbed her hip, sliding his hands across the back of her black mourning dress.

"Poor grandpa," said Diane, "and you're feeling me up."

"Funerals make me horny," said Johnny. "It must be something to do with stiffs."

"You Kavanagh men are all alike!"

His cell phone rang. It was the City Hall. The *Taoiseach* had arrived for the trip to the Pro-Cathedral for the funeral mass. "Time to go, honey. Bertie's waiting for us."

Diane and Johnny retraced their steps back along Dame Lane to the City Hall. When he got to the coffin, Bertie Ahern, the *Taoiseach*, was waiting for him.

"My condolences," said Ahern in a flat Northside Dublin accent.

The old man never could stand Ahern. But like him or not, Eoin Kavanagh had insisted the *Taoiseach* and the American ambassador show up. He figured it was the least they could do. The Irish president and head of state, Mary McAleese, would also join them at the Pro-Cathedral for the funeral. Johnny Three introduced Diane, then told Ahern: "My grandfather would be proud that the *Taoiseach* of a free Irish nation had the time to attend his funeral. Let's get moving."

Johnny watched as they closed the lid on the old man for the last time. The soldiers hoisted the narrow pine box on their shoulders and slowly marched out of City Hall and down the front steps, then carefully lowered the casket and placed it in the old-fashioned, horse-drawn glass hearse for its short trip to the cathedral on Marlborough Street. The black horses snorted and snapped their heads, making their funeral plumes dance a spastic jig. The old hearse was Eoin's idea, perhaps remembering the Dublin of his youth, when his Mammy, younger brother, and infant sister had prematurely made this same, sad trip to Glasnevin Cemetery.

Johnny Three and Diane climbed into the trailing limousine with the *Taoiseach* and the ambassador. Slowly they followed the hearse as it made its way down Dame Street. Citizens stopped in their tracks, stood at attention, and removed caps as the old rebel began his final journey. Johnny looked around for a banshee, without success.

First they came to South Great Georges Street, and it reminded Johnny that his great-grandfather's barber shop, set up by Michael Collins himself, was only a few blocks away on Aungier Street. To the left, they passed Temple Lane, where his great-grandmother had lived before she married in 1900. Further up was Crow Street and building number three, where Eoin had worked in Collins's intelligence office, compiling the dossiers that would culminate in the assassination of the British Secret Service in Dublin in November 1920.

Suddenly there was a dry lump in Johnny Three's throat, and the color left his face. Diane asked if he was alright, and he shook his head. Then he knew what it was—the body of Eoin Kavanagh was slowly drawing him back to another time: a time of sickness, revolution—and freedom. As he followed his grandfather's casket, he was slowly, but ineluctably, being transported back to his grandfather's time—the terrifying rebel Dublin of 1916.

EASTER WEEK, 1916

...THEN...
...AND NOW

2

EASTER MONDAY
APRIL 24, 1916

The hacking cough of his mother woke Eoin Kavanagh from his holiday sleep.

Morning was Eoin's favorite time of the day. He knew it was the only time you could talk to God, and when He might have time to listen. But that persistent cough kept interrupting his conversations of late.

Another hack. Eoin winced.

The cough was getting worse by the day. He had seen his mother spit blood into a dish rag just the other day and then toss it in the dust bin, turning to see if anyone had caught her. She didn't know he'd been watching. She had lost so much weight—gone were the round hips and the full bust.

She was disappearing before his eyes.

It was the consumption, he had heard the neighbors whisper. Rosanna Kavanagh was being consumed by it, whatever it was. Although Eoin was only fourteen, he was no fool. He knew his mother was a goner, and it broke his heart.

It was his brother Charlie's fault. It really was. If he hadn't died last year, maybe Mammy wouldn't have gotten sick. Diphtheria was the word they'd used for Charlie when all was said and done. He died down the lane at the Adelaide Hospital. Dead as a doornail, and they had trouble breaking the Glasnevin turf in January as they laid Charlie in his lonely grave. But Eoin knew that Charlie would not be lonely for long.

The last couple of years had been hard on all the Kavanaghs. Gone were the happy, prosperous days at 40 Camden Row. Bad times had caused Da to lose his hairdressing business, and it was now a move a year as the finances continued to crumble. Handouts from the St. Vincent de Paul Society, neighbors, and relatives had barely kept the family afloat. His father prayed for the odd haircutting job, just to make a few bob. They had gone from the comfort of Camden Row to Golden Lane and the terrible, filthy Piles Buildings. More truth than mirth in that terrible name.

Eoin heard that the buildings had been named after a "Lady Pile." He didn't know if it was truth or only the locals having a laugh. "We're stuck at the bottom," was his father's joke, which always embarrassed his pious mother. But the joke was on them, with six Kavanaghs crammed into two small rooms. A cold-water scullery the size of a closet completed the flat. The water closet was outside on the landing, shared with neighbors. He learned early on that a piss-pot under the bed was often a boy's best friend.

When his frustration overwhelmed him and he couldn't take it anymore, Eoin's father would declare, "These buildings are a sore on the arse of St. Patrick's Cathedral!"

Eoin couldn't understand it either. There, just across the road, was the jewel of the Church of Ireland, St. Patrick's beautiful Protestant cathedral. He had seen all the fine carriages and automobiles arrive at Christmas carrying their precious cargo of handsome fur-lined women and top-hatted gentlemen. We are here, thought Eoin, and they are there. And there was no in-between. Eoin rose and wondered why it was so quiet. Usually there was roughhousing with his younger brother, Frank, and the screams of the kids, Mary and young Dickie. It was as if the children knew that Mammy needed quiet.

"Mornin'. How ya?" said Eoin to his parents. "Where is everyone?"

"Out in the street, playing," said his mother. "It's a beautiful morning."

Beautiful, indeed.

Eoin's father, Joseph, sat at the kitchen table with his empty pipe and yesterday's *Freeman's Journal*, musing over its contents. Joseph was a dandy. He didn't have a job to go to, but he was fully dressed, down to the turgid white collar he wore every day. Unlike Eoin, the senior Kavanagh loved good clothes. But now the threads were growing old and shabby, as if recording the downward economic spiral of the family. Toast fragments hung from his waxed handlebar mustache, and Eoin was forced to smile. "Bad days for the Brits," said Joseph with some satisfaction, commenting on the war news.

"Oh, Josey," said his mother, using her pet name for her husband. "Why do you enjoy the British and their misery so much?"

"And why shouldn't I?" came the quick reply.

Rosanna smiled but then remembered her brother, Charlie Conway, who was a corporal in the Royal Field Artillery over in France. "Charlie," she said softly.

For a moment, Joseph thought Rosanna was talking about their dead son, whom she had named after her favorite brother. "*Corporal* Charlie," said Joseph, shaking his head. "What was he t'inkin'?"

"I don't know," replied Rosanna.

They were talking about Charlie Conway's affinity for the Crown. He had served in the Boer War, then secured a job as a policeman at the Guinness Brewery upon his return to Dublin in 1902. But at the age of forty-six, he had joined up again and marched off to war in September 1914.

"I worry about him," said Rosanna.

"I do, too," said Joseph, "but what the hell was he t'inkin', especially at his age?"

"Love of country."

"England is not his country," Joseph said definitively. "Ireland is Charlie's country. Why doesn't he realize that?" He kept talking. "It will be conscription soon. The British are down, almost out, and what do they do when they are in that situation?" He didn't wait for the answer. "They turn to Irish bodies for sustenance and fodder!"

"No conscription," she replied, stifling a cough. "Seven hundred years. We've given enough. Especially in this family."

The conscription and the consumption. The big Cs of the moment.

"Where's Frank?" asked Eoin, wondering about his younger brother.

"Gone out," said his father. Eoin grunted. Frank was still marching to his own tone-deaf drummer. At least he didn't have to endure Frank's endless slagging this morning, either about his build—Frank was almost as big as he was—or his name. "Hey, *Ian*," he would yell out, purposely mispronouncing his name, purposely making it sound English and soft.

"It's *Eoin*," he would remind his brother. "Pronounced O-W-E-N. Irish for John." Eoin would pause before adding, "You got that, Francis of Assisi?" Frank didn't like to be called Francis of Assisi, especially when Eoin put the emphasis on "sissy." That usually shut Frank up.

Eoin was Frank's complete opposite, from looks to temperament. Eoin, Rosanna often thought, was a smaller version of his father. He had the Da's oval-shaped face, prominent Kavanagh nose, silent hazel eyes, and beautiful dark-brown hair. If he weighed eight stone, it would be a shock. Eoin, unlike Frank, was easygoing and respectful, almost to a fault. His sincerity, however, was punctuated by a sly sense of humor. Both Rosanna and Joseph knew they couldn't ask for a better son than their Eoin.

"Will you take the childer up to the Green?" asked the Mammy.

"Of course," replied Eoin, and he was immediately out the door looking for them. They were in Arthur Lane, a tiny patch of street that reminded all how omnipresent the Guinness family was to the city and to this neighborhood in particular. Young Mary, only seven, and baby Dickie, barely four. "Would you like to go up to the Green?" he asked, although he knew what the reply would be.

"Yes, yes," said Mary, and little Dickie jumped up and down, his curly locks animated.

"Wait," cried Dickie as he ran back to the house and returned, clutching a rock of bread in his little hand.

"Come on then," said Eoin as he took one in each hand and headed towards Peter Street.

"That's where Charlie died," Mary said, pointing in the direction of the Adelaide Hospital. The three of them stood in their tracks for a moment, quietly sandwiched between the majestic tower of St. Patrick's Cathedral behind them and the back of the dull, thick, concrete-gray Carmelite Church before them.

Eoin looked at little Mary Bridget. She reminded him of her twin sister, Mary Josephine, who had died at three months. No one in the family knew about little Josephine, except Eoin and his mother and father. Brother Frank was too young to remember her, and Charlie now occupied the same grave in Glasnevin with his baby sister. Eoin looked on the death of baby Josephine as the beginning of the breakup of his family. Everything had been good until Josephine up and died, and his parents had never been the same. Sometimes he would hear his mother sniffling and wiping a tear away, with a whisper of, "Poor Josephine, my beautiful, sweet lost baby." Now they called Mary Bridget "Mary," to honor both of the twins.

"Yes, that's where Charlie died," said Eoin finally, not wanting to dwell on it. Soon they were into Aungier Street and traveling up York Street by the terrible, high, dark tenements, until the bright sunshine of St. Stephen's Green rescued them.

They walked along the Green by the Royal College of Surgeons, where small cliques of Irish Volunteers in their green uniforms were already gathering. They crossed the street to the Fusiliers Arch, a memorial to the dead British of the Boer War and the official entrance to the Green.

"Traitor's Gate," said a pointing Dickie, getting it correct even at his young age.

There were more men in green uniforms blocking the gate, and their numbers spilled out to both sides of the Green. Something was up.

A man with a bucket, brush, and posters under his arm stepped up to the left wall of the gate and started splashing paste on the gray stone. "Hot off the presses from Liberty Hall," he shouted as he posted the declaration:

POBLACHT NA H ÉIREANN.

THE PROVISIONAL GOVERNMENT
OF THE
IRISH REPUBLIC
TO THE PEOPLE OF IRELAND.

Civilians and Volunteers rushed up to see the proclamation, pushing against each other to get the first glimpse. The man with the posters went to the opposite wall and plastered another proclamation. Eoin and the children followed him. "Can I have one of those?" asked Eoin.

"I don't see why not!" said the man as he stripped one off his arm and handed it to him. Eoin rolled his own personal copy up and began reading the posted one as others began crowding around him:

IRISHMEN AND IRISHWOMEN: In the name of God and of the dead generations from which she receives her old tradition of nationhood, Ireland, through us, summons her children to her flag and strikes for her freedom.

"Eoin, Eoin," said Mary, "what's it's all about?"

"Hush," said Eoin as he continued to read:

We declare the right of the people of Ireland to the ownership of Ireland, and to the unfettered control of Irish destinies, to be sovereign and indefeasible. The long usurpation of that right by a foreign people and government has not extinguished the right, nor can it ever be extinguished except by the destruction of the Irish people.

Dickie kept pulling at Eoin's arm, wanting to get to the lake to see his ducks and swans. Eoin skipped to the end of the proclamation:

We place the cause of the Irish Republic under the protection of the Most High God, Whose blessing we invoke upon our arms, and we pray that no one who serves that cause will dishonour it by cowardice, inhumanity, or rapine. In this supreme hour, the Irish nation must, by its valour and discipline and by the readiness of its children to sacrifice themselves for the common good, prove itself worthy of the august destiny to which it is called.

As both kids pulled at him from opposite sides, Eoin read the signatures:

Signed on Behalf of the Provisional Government,

THOMAS J. CLARKE,

SEAN MAC DIARMADA,	THOMAS MACDONAGH,
P.H. PEARSE,	EAMONN CEANNT,
JAMES CONNOLLY,	JOSEPH PLUNKETT.

By now, the crowd around the two proclamations was getting rowdy, some cheering and others cursing the insurgents. A man went up to a Volunteer and shouted in his face, "Ya Fenian gobshite!"

The Volunteer pulled his rifle off his shoulder and clubbed the man with the butt end. "Any other words of wisdom for me, mister?" he demanded as the man scrunched on the ground, holding his head in case there were other blows coming, but there weren't.

"This is great," said the young lad next to Eoin.

"What's happening?" asked Eoin.

"Rebellion!" came the gleeful reply.

Eoin smiled, intrigued by the boy's enthusiasm. "I'm Eoin Kavanagh," he said, putting out his hand.

"Vinny Byrne," came the quick, cheery reply, along with a strong handshake. "There will be a hooley in Dublin this week!"

Vinny was diminutive, with reddish blond hair and a pink complexion. He was dressed in a Volunteer's uniform, his only show of rank being his Pioneer's pin, which was stuck above his left breast pocket.

"I'm from South Anne's Street," Vinny said, pointing.

"Golden Lane," replied Eoin, "over by St. Patrick's Cathedral."

"The Piles?" Eoin nodded. "God help ya," replied Vinny, without malice. "I've got to get moving now," said Vinny. "We're going to take Jacob's Factory for the Republic. Will you come with us?"

Eoin was taken aback. "I can't," he stammered. "I have my brother and sister with me," pointing at the children.

"Fair enough," said Vinny. "But the invite stands!"

Eoin nodded and took the children away from the chaos and into the Green. "Swans!" Dickie tore his stale bread apart to feed his favorite birds. "Here, here," he said, tossing the bread into the water, where it was quickly scooped up, the swans beating a hasty retreat. Soon Mary handed him two pamphlets she had found and asked her big brother to turn them into paper sailboats. Eoin dutifully made two boats, saying, "This one is the *Lusitania*, and that one is the *Titanic!*" The kids didn't understand his black sense of humor and rushed to the "lake" to set sail. With that, Eoin took a seat and watched them playing joyfully with their ships by the pond.

Eoin was still thinking about the proclamations posted to the front gate. Was it more empty Fenian talk, or was this the real thing? The war in Europe was getting closer to Ireland, he knew, and he had heard his parents talking about him eventually being conscripted into the British army. They were against it, he knew, because they considered themselves Irish, not British, like Uncle Charlie. Both his parents' families had managed to live through the famine because they lived in Dublin City and were not subjected to the utter devastation of the countryside. Still, old memories—and hatreds—died hard in the Kavanagh and Conway families. They would cut the British no slack.

Eoin unrolled his copy of the proclamation and read the top again. His Irish was miniscule, but he knew that *Poblacht Na Éireann* meant "Irish Republic." He then looked at the names of the signatories but recognized only two, Pearse and Connolly.

Pearse was famous because of the oration he had given at the grave of the old Fenian Jeremiah O'Donovan Rossa last summer at Glasnevin Cemetery: "The fools, the fools, the fools!—They have left us our Fenian dead . . ." The whole episode had made an impression on Eoin because Rossa had died on Staten Island in New York City, but the Volunteers had dug him up and brought him back to Ireland. His father had even brought him to the City Hall to see Rossa, lying in state in his open coffin. It always impressed Eoin that Rossa had been dead for more than a month, and he didn't stink, even at the height of summer. Could Rossa, Eoin thought, be Ireland's Lazarus?

Eoin knew Connolly because he was Jim Larkin's successor at the Irish Workers and Transport Union. A lot of people said he was a trou-blemaker and a rabble-rouser because he was a socialist and for the working man. He was also considered dangerous because he had his own militia, the Citizen Army. At the beginning of the Great War, he had hung a sign on the front of his headquarters at Liberty Hall: "We Serve Neither King Nor Kaiser, But Ireland." Eoin had heard his father say that if there were more men like Connolly in Ireland, the Kavanaghs wouldn't be living in the putrid, godforsaken Piles Buildings.

Soon it got noisier near the front gate, and Eoin's curiosity got the better of him. He fetched the children and headed back to where the action was. The first person he bumped into was young Byrne, who was howling his eyes out. "Vinny," Eoin said to his new friend, "what happened?"

"Lieutenant Shiels sent me home," he said, tears pouring uncontrol-lably. "He said I was too young to take Jacob's."

"What's going on here?" said one of the Volunteer officers. Vinny explained his demise. "Sure, come along out of that, and don't mind him," reassured the officer.

"Yes," interrupted Major John MacBride, impeccable in his sartorial splendor and beautifully coiffed hair and mustache. "We need all the men we can muster. Sure, I just volunteered meself. Everyone should volunteer for Ireland!" MacBride had been on his way to the Wicklow

Hotel to attend a luncheon for his brother, who was getting married, when he ran into the Volunteers assembling on Stephen's Green for revolution. The temptation was too great, and he couldn't resist an "invitation" to take Jacob's for the new Republic. Eoin knew him from the newspapers. He was always in them because of something, usually a scandal involving a woman other than his wife, Maud Gonne, who was often referred to around Dublin City as "Gone Mad" because of her nationalistic and suffragette endeavors. MacBride's hatred of the British was also legendary—it had carried him as far as South Africa to fight against them in the Boer War. "Will you join us?" he asked of Eoin.

"I can't," replied Eoin, again pointing. "The children."

"Well," said MacBride, "at least you can march with us to Jacob's." Eoin could and would. Soon the brigade was mustered into shape. MacBride and Thomas MacDonagh, the commandant in charge, led them down to the Harcourt Street side of the Green to Cuffe Street, where they made a smart right. They marched the short distance to the rotunda of Jacob's Biscuit Factory, where Bishop and Aungier Streets met. There they came to a halt. The air was heavy with tension as concerned citizens came out of their tenements to see what all the fuss was about.

Eoin had a feeling in the pit of his stomach that he was about to miss one of the greatest moments in Irish history. "I'll be buggered," he said under his breath, took then took Mary and Dickie in each hand, and walked them back up Aungier Street, just a block from home.

"Mary," he said to his sister, "take Dickie by the hand and bring him home to Mammy."

"Where are you going?" she asked.

Eoin was conflicted. But it was time to stand and deliver. Finally he blurted out, "Jacob's Biscuit Factory." He paused. "Tell that to Mammy and Da. Here, take this proclamation, which will explain it to them. Now hold onto Dickie's hand, and go straight home." He watched them go down Whitefriar Place by the side of the Carmelite Church, holding their paper boats in their little hands.

"I'm back," Eoin said to Vinny at the back of the column.

Vinny smiled, his tears now just a memory. "It's going to be a grand adventure," reassured Vinny.

Eoin fell in line, and the only thing he could think of was the sentence from the first paragraph of the proclamation: *"Ireland, through us, summons her children to her flag and strikes for her freedom."* He looked at Vinny and some of the other young lads, and, with a shiver running down his spine, wondered how Vinny's grand adventure would play out.

3

The two children burst into the tiny scullery, Mary dragging Dickie by the hand. Instinctively, Rosanna knew something was wrong. "Where's Eoin?" she asked tentatively.

"He's gone with the others to Jacob's," replied Mary, breathlessly.

"Why?"

"Jacob's has been taken over by the . . ."

"Fookin' Fenians," interjected Dickie, parroting what he had just heard in the street.

Joseph looked at Rosanna and didn't know whether to laugh or cry. "Now, now, son," he finally said, "we shouldn't be using that dirty word."

"Fenian?" replied Dickie.

"No, the other one," interrupted Rosanna. She turned to Joseph sternly. "You better go out and get that boy. I don't know what's happening. I thought the maneuvers were canceled."

"So did I," replied her husband, putting on his jacket and grabbing his cap.

Before he could go through the door, Mary held the proclamation out. "Eoin says this will explain all." They unrolled the proclamation, and, as soon as they saw

POBLACHT NA H EIREANN.

their hearts sank. The signatures told the tale.

"Jesus, Rosanna," said Joseph. "Pearse, Clarke, and MacDiarmada. It's the bold Fenian men themselves!" Rosanna sank into a chair in

23

despair. Joseph tried to reassure her. "I'll be back with the boy in a few minutes." But it was not a few minutes—he didn't return for nearly an hour.

"Well?" asked Rosanna.

"No luck," replied Joseph. "The Volunteers have the street cordoned off. They wouldn't let me through. The fellow I spoke with said he didn't know any Eoin Kavanagh."

"What in God's name is going on?" asked Rosanna.

"Revolution, my love," said Joseph, gently taking his wife's hand. She stifled a cough and looked intently into her husband's eyes, as the words of her youngest son echoed in her ears.

"Fenians, fookin' Fenians."

4

"*I hope me Mammy won't be cross with me.*"

Those were the first words in the rebel diaries of Eoin Kavanagh. The "diaries" were notebooks, school ledgers, and assorted pages. The material covering April and May 1916 was now spread before his grandson on the bed where the old rebel had died the week before. *So this is the surprise,* thought Johnny Three. He was indeed surprised. Although his grandmother was a well-known author in both Ireland and America, he had no idea the old man liked to scribble as well. There were nine cardboard boxes in all. Johnny went about taking the diaries out of the boxes, dusting them off, and trying to form a chronology of events.

"You're very quiet," said Diane.

"I wonder why he left them to me?"

"Well, you *are* the writer in the family."

Johnny shook his head. "No, my grandmother was the writer in the family. I'm just a glorified hack."

"Though well reviewed."

"Through friends in the business."

"He left them to you because he trusted you," Diane responded. "He didn't leave them to the state archives or some university."

"Probably because he didn't trust them," agreed Johnny. "The old man didn't trust anyone, which may be the reason he lived so long."

"They may also be worth something," she added. "Did you think of that?"

"I did, indeed. He always admonished my poor father: 'money on trees does not grow!'" Diane laughed with him. "Listen to the first line: *'I hope me Mammy won't be cross with me.'*" Johnny shook his head. "He was a typical Irish lad, he was, influenced by the matriarch of the family."

"Poor boy," said Diane as she took hold of the page. "What beautiful penmanship."

"The nuns and the Christian Brothers," said Johnny. "Big emphasis on penmanship back then, so you could get some low-paying job as a clerk." Johnny shook his head and re-read Eoin's first sentence. He became pensive. "He deeply loved his Mammy, my great-grandmother," he said to Diane. "She was dying of consumption—tuberculosis—at the time of the rebellion. You know, the British used to call TB 'the Irish disease.'" He gave a bitter laugh. "What a poor, fucked-up family."

Diane shook her head sadly.

Johnny continued to read aloud: "'*Mammy asked me to take Mary and Dickie up to the Green for a walk this Easter Monday holiday. The rebels were gathering, and I got carried away in the excitement. They were on the way to Jacob's to liberate the biscuits, so when we got to Aungier Street with the battalion, I sent Mary home with Dickie and went along for the adventure in Bishop Street.*'"

"He has a way with words," said Diane.

"He was a great storyteller, wasn't he?" added Johnny. "Look at these," he said, holding pieces of paper up for Diane to view.

"What?"

"They're genuine."

"Wow!" said Diane. "I'm surprised he kept these papers so secret."

"He probably had his reasons," replied Johnny, "and I'm sure we'll find out what they were in due time."

"This is bothering you, isn't it?"

"I don't feel comfortable with this stuff. I'm afraid there may be family skeletons that I don't want to confront in these boxes."

"What could be the big secret?"

"I'm not sure, but I suspect there was a lot more to grandpa than being Michael Collins's bodyguard. He kept himself to himself. I have a feeling that, in America, it was politically correct to be an Irish rebel, but not one with blood on his hands. I think he didn't want to scare the electorate." Johnny smiled. "Grandpa knew how to collect a pension."

"How many?"

"Let's see. The Irish Army. The U.S. House of Representatives. *Dáil Éireann*. Plus Social Security and the Irish Old Age Pension. Five. Not bad!"

Diane took Johnny's arm, drew him close, and kissed him. Johnny laughed; then he kissed his wife full on the lips and slid his hand down the back of her capris, running a finger into her beautiful crack. Even after thirty years together, they were still awesomely horny for each other. "Not now, dear," admonished Diane.

"Ah," said Johnny, "how Presbyterian of you!"

Diane was used to the slagging about her being the only Protestant in a mad Irish-Catholic nationalist family. (In her defense, she had taken to listing off Protestant patriots, such as Wolfe Tone, Robert Emmet, Lord Edward, and Charles Stewart Parnell, to keep the "Papists," as she fondly referred to her family, in their place.)

"Behave yourself," she said to her husband, "or I'll hide your dick pill!"

"Ah, 'The Vee-ag-gra!'" said Johnny. "The Pfizer Riser! The County Cork pecker elixir! You've got to look out for those four-hour erections."

"If you get a four-*minute* erection, I'll alert the media!"

Johnny looked at his wife and decided that his friend Frank McCourt was right about Irish men's attraction to Protestant women. They were indeed a step up in class—and in sex—and dating one was a way of thumbing one's nose at Holy Mother Church. "Time to look at grand-pa's diaries," she said. "I'm sure he wouldn't have left anything to upset you." But Johnny knew that the last thing Eoin Kavanagh worried about was the comfort level of his only grandson. Then Johnny laughed.

"What?"

"You've just reminded me of one of grandpa's favorite sayings: 'Comfort the afflicted—and afflict the comfortable!'"

And it was working, because with a poke from the grave, Eoin Kavanagh III was getting less comfortable by the minute.

5

5

EOIN KAVANAGH'S DIARY
WEDNESDAY, APRIL 26, 1916

General Post Office
Sackville Street
Dublin, Ireland

What a day! My wound is bandaged and I have dry clothes on at last. Safe—if you can call it that—in the GPO. It looks like a bloody disaster here. Nothing but wounded men and broken glass. It was safer over at Jacob's.

After we took Jacob's, we were very busy the first few hours. Commandant MacDonagh and Major MacBride had us fill up the windows with sacks of flour to guard against snipers. We were covered in flour, swiftly moving white ghosts on a mission. "Keep your bloody head down, boy," MacBride warned me with a wink, "and welcome to the fight!" We also unwound the fire hoses just in case of fire. Most of our rifles were aimed at the Ship Street army barracks near the Castle. After we had our fill of biscuits, it got quite dull. We knew the British army was out there, but they didn't make a rush to take us. The only excitement was caused by Vinny Byrne, who was sent out on patrol and had a ruckus with the fine citizens of the Blackpitts. Apparently they don't care if Ireland is free or not. Anyway, some eejit tried to take Vinny's gun away from him, and someone was shot—and it wasn't Vincent Byrne.

Tuesday the skies were dark, and it was pouring bucket after bucket without any sign of letting up. It was like the heavens were weeping for poor old Ireland. We ate more crackers and patrolled the factory. We'd filled up every available vessel with water in case the city water supply was interrupted or tampered with by the British. The only grousing from the men is because we're not allowed to smoke for some reason. Still, some go off and hide for a quick puff.

Jacob's must be a nice place to work, clean and not too many mice around. They have an employees' canteen, and there is plenty of tay for everyone. Their bathrooms are cleaner than anything we have at the Piles. You could eat your dinner off the floors here. They are even cleaner than the toilets under Tommy Moore's arse in Westmoreland Street. And unlike the public toilets on the quays, I don't have to watch some wrinkled old priest waving his willie at me.

During the night, Commandant MacDonagh had a few of us lads brave the elements to place empty biscuit tin boxes outside the factory as noise booby-traps so that we would know if the British were sneaking up on us. A cunning stunt on the commandant's part, I think. He also explained to us the importance of Jacob's in the fight. He said that we now controlled Dublin because we held the GPO, the Four Courts, Stephen's Green, and the South Dublin Union. The British army would probably land at Kingstown and march on Dublin. We at Jacob's were in a position to cut them off, depending on where they crossed the Grand Canal. Commandant de Valera, he said, would probably have first shot at them at Boland's Mills. We could also block any advance by the British, MacDonagh explained, from Portobello Barracks just to our south and Richmond Barracks to the west. We were right in the middle of it all. Commandant MacDonagh is a good egg, and it's surprising to me that such a quiet, gentle man like him would sign such a bloodthirsty proc-lamation. But the British war with their first cousins, the Germans, is beginning to grate on the Irish. Even gentle folk are threatening sedition.

But revolution is boring! We sat around all day—as the British surely did—waiting for the rain to let up. I thought I would die just sitting around and eating more crackers. Finally Commandant MacDonagh asked for a volunteer to go to the GPO, because the phones are dead. I stuck up my hand and told him I was his man. The commandant was doubtful because of my age, but I insisted I knew Dublin City and this neighborhood in particular better than any man in Jacob's that evening. Sure, wasn't I born just blocks away in Camden Row, off Wexford Street?

The commandant asked me what my plan was, and I told him that I doubted there would be many men out on either side this terrible night. I would head for the River Liffey and see if I could get over one of the bridges and make my way to the GPO. I told him my youth was an advantage—how could the British think that this innocent boy was with the rebels? My face was fresh and eager, and MacDonagh, thoughtfully scratching his curly hair, finally agreed, adding, "Just be careful, son." I promised him I would.

Commandant MacDonagh wrote out a note on Jacob's stationery and sealed this in an envelope. "Take this to Commander-in-Chief Pearse."

I exited on Peter Row and went down the side streets. I actually went by my mother's house, and our paraffin lamp was alight. I was tempted to go in and tell them that I was alright, but I couldn't take the chance. I had that letter to Commander-in-Chief Pearse, and I had to get it through. I couldn't take the chance that Mammy and Da might try and stop me. And as luck would have it, when I got to the Ha'penny Bridge, there wasn't a sinner in sight, not even the toll man. I ran up the steps and started to make my way across when there was a terrible burning in my lower back that dropped me to the footpath of the bridge. It took me a minute to realize I had been shot in the high hole of me arse. I didn't know where the shot came from, but there was noise from up Sackville Street way. I crawled the rest of the way over the bridge as bullets hit the metal bridge above me. I kept crawling down the steps on the north side and jumped up with a fright to get past the old Woolen Mills and up Liffey Street. There wasn't a soul to be found on the streets, and I dashed, my arse dripping blood, to Henry Street and banged on the first door I came to in the GPO. No one answered at first, and the looming presence of Lord Nelson atop his pillar staring down at me began to frighten the shite out of me. Finally the door opened a squeak, and I told your man that I had a communiqué from Commandant MacDonagh for C-in-C Pearse.

After a quick look up and down, he saw that I was no threat to the revolution. They let me in and brought me to a young officer named Collins. I handed over the letter to Captain Collins, and, after that, I felt faint. The next thing I knew I hit the deck in front of Collins, out for the count.

6

Collins picked the boy up and called out for Róisín O'Mahony. She was a nurse and a member of the *Cumann na mBan*, the women's auxiliary of the Irish Volunteers, and she was all business: "Where's he hit?"

"Looks like his back," said Collins, the boy's blood all over the arms of his impeccable uniform.

O'Mahony rolled the boy over and felt his back from the shoulders down. No blood. She was puzzled. "Help me with his pants," she said to Collins.

"Yes, Countess O'Mahonyevicz," said a mocking Collins, knowing that Róisín was a fervent admirer and follower of the real Countess Markievicz.

"Come on, ya big git," shot back O'Mahony. "Come on, big fella, for once show you have a set of brains." Collins first instinct was to retort, but one look at the determined O'Mahony quickly put that thought out of his mind. The nurse wondered why she had to put up with such testosterone-fueled eejits. She looked at the gangly twenty-five-year-old Collins and figured his actions were dictated by his bollocks, not his brains. By right, she should have been with Markievicz over in Stephen's Green, but she was urgently needed at the GPO. Collins undid Eoin's belt, and O'Mahony pulled the britches down, displaying Eoin's long-johns. She unbuttoned the arse trapdoor and exposed the wound in the right buttock. "He's lucky," she said. "A clean flesh wound. Just nicked him. All the blood makes it look worse than it is."

Eoin opened his eyes and looked at Collins and then at O'Mahony, who was swabbing his arse with disinfectant. "Am I dying?" he asked, the sting of the medication bringing him further into consciousness.

"You'll live to be a hundred," said Collins.

"I gave me only arse for Ireland," said Eoin, which forced both Collins and O'Mahony to smile in rare unison.

"What's going on?" said Commander-in-Chief Padraig Pearse. He was surveying Eoin's bare butt with interest, perfectly framed by the longjohns' trapdoor. But it was never easy to tell what direction Pearse was actually looking in because of that cast eye. The right one was straight on, but the other was heading off in the direction of Belfast.

"Messenger from Jacob's," said Collins, leading Pearse away from the boy. "He has a dispatch from Commandant MacDonagh for you."

Collins handed him the blood-smudged envelope, and Pearse opened it and read aloud. "'All quiet on Bishop's Street. Phones are dead. Rain has quenched the British. Jacob's well cracked. The men are ready to fight. MacDonagh's doing his best to help de Valera over at Boland's Mills.'" Collins nodded, and Pearse went back to the command center, which was in the front of the building where they sold stamps.

O'Mahony was bandaging Eoin's aching, stinging behind. "That's one penny-ha'penny bottom you have there," said Nurse O'Mahony. By now Eoin was wide awake and covering up his privates, as his mother called them. O'Mahony smiled at his modesty, and Eoin felt his willie getting hard.

"Yeah," said Collins to O'Mahony, "he has an arse on him just like you—that of a skinny thirteen-year-old boy."

"I'll be fifteen in October," corrected Eoin.

"Get away from me," shouted O'Mahony to Collins, her voice rising. "You're nothing but a Cork culchie, a ruffian, a bogman, and a Nighttown guttersnipe."

Eoin looked around at O'Mahony and saw that she was beet-faced. Beet-faced but beautiful, with long brown hair, exquisite eyes, and a smile stolen from the Irish Madonna. He didn't mind this beauty patting him on his bare arse at all. In fact, he felt that Collins somehow envied the attention his bottom was receiving from O'Mahony.

"You alright, boy?" asked Collins.

"My name is Eoin Kavanagh."

"Are you alright, Eoin?"

"I'm fine." He paused a second before adding, "I hope you two will make up."

"Make up!" hissed O'Mahony. Collins didn't say a word, just turned on his heel and headed back to the front of the GPO. He knew he had met his match. "Fookin' men," said O'Mahony.

"How old are you?" asked Eoin.

Róisín was taken aback by the freshness of the question. "Too old for you, sonny boy."

Eoin was quiet for a second. "We'll see," he said with enough cheek to match his patriotic arse.

7

EOIN'S DIARY
FRIDAY, APRIL 28, 1916

General Post Office
Sackville Street
Dublin, Ireland

M e arse is sore, but I'm recovering. Róisín says I'll live, and she's awful busy with all the wounded, including Commandant-General Connolly, who has a severe leg injury. Connolly is in terrible pain from being hit in the ankle by a shell. Besides the rest of the wounded, Commandant-General Plunkett is very sick. By right, he should be in hospital. They say he has consumption of the neck glands. I wonder if his disease is related to me Ma's. Captain Collins seldom leaves his side.

Collins has put Jack Lemass in charge of me. Jack's a couple of years older than I am and is from Capel Street. Jack was supposed to be with Commandant de Valera over at Boland's Mills, but with all the disarray caused by the countermanding of maneuver orders, it looks like the Volunteers are going to the nearest location they can get to. Collins has told me to stay out of the way and to keep my head down. He ordered Jack to go up to the roof and bring down the tricolour. I have a feeling we are coming to the end. As soon as Collins left, Jack asked if I was well enough to help him.

We got up to the roof, and, from the parapet, the scene in Sackville Street shocked me. Total destruction on the east side of the street. Right opposite the GPO, at the entrance to North Earl Street, there was a burnt-out tram. I counted at least two dead horses. The Dublin Bread Company building, the tallest on the thoroughfare, was totally gutted. Commander-in-Chief Pearse had sent men out earlier in the week to stop the looting. The women from the neighborhood had their way with Clery's. The poor children from Tyrone Street and Greg Lane enjoyed Christmas in April as they did their mischief in Graham Lemon's Sweetshop. The wreckage is a lot worse than I ever imagined. I had a feeling someone was looking at me, and, as I looked up, I realized it was Lord Nelson atop his pillar, just as he had peered down at me when I first gained access to the GPO with my letter for Pearse. Mammy once took the first three boys—me, Charlie, and Frank—to the top, and it was like we were on top of the world, looking down on the Dublin Mountains. Why a British admiral is in the middle of an Irish street is beyond me. I look down on Dan O'Connell's statue at the foot of the Liffey and see Charles Stewart Parnell's monument at the Rotunda end of Sackville Street. Nelson's Pillar is an insult to these two great Irishmen.

I have yet to meet an Irishman who gives a shite about Trafalgar. Just another battle in endless English wars. Maybe someday, someone will blast the admiral's stone arse into the sky, the closest the adulterant hoor will ever get to heaven. As Jack and I got close to the flagpole, we had to hit the deck because of the sniper fire. I think it's coming from the D'Olier and Westmoreland Streets area. Maybe from the top of Trinity College. It was hard to say with all the smoke and soot in the air. "Fook this," said Jack, and we left the poor tricolour to fend for itself.

All the lads have been very kind to me. One of the Volunteers, Arthur Shields, came over and asked if there was anything he could do for me. He told me he was an actor over at the Abbey Theatre. He's another of the misdirected. He told me that when he heard the rebellion was on again, he went to the Abbey to get his rifle, which he had hidden under the stage, and then joined Connolly around the corner at Liberty Hall. That's how he found the GPO.

Arthur is about six or seven years older than I am. He asked me where I was from, and I told him I was born on Camden Row. He said we were from the same neighborhood because he was born in Portobello, down by Harrington Street. He asked about my people, and I told him my mother's people, the Conways, were from Temple Lane. It's turning out to be a small world, because Arthur said he lived on the next block, Crow Street, as a child. I feel a little bit more comfortable now, having a neighbor for company in the GPO.

Arthur was chatting with me when the Angelus bells rang about the city, revolution not stopping devotion. I blessed myself, but some of the Volunteers dropped to their knees, starting banging their craws, hugging their rosaries, and began reciting: "The angel of the Lord announced unto Mary." Looking around, Shields said: "I wonder if I'm the only Church of Ireland man in the GPO this week?" Then be added with a wink and an actor's flair: "Pray for us, O Holy Mother of God!"

We were joined by a comrade of Arthur's. "You may be the only Church of Ireland man here, Arthur," he interrupted, "but I know I'm the only Jew."

Arthur then introduced me to Abraham Weeks, just over from London. "My God," I said, "what are you doing in Dublin?"

"I'm avoiding conscription," he said defiantly. "I will fight for the working man, but not for the corrupt bourgeois." I had no idea what he was talking about.

"He's devoted to Jim Connelly" Arthur helpfully added. "Abraham is a dedicated trade unionist."

"That's a unionist I can deal with!" I said, getting a laugh out of the two of them.

The men were still working on the Angelus when Captain Collins came by. "Jaysus," he said dismissively as he observed the kneeling men. "Will these people ever learn?"

Seán MacDiarmada, one of the big shots who signed the Proclamation, has also come over to say hello. He is from the North and is strikingly handsome. He has a stiff leg and walks with a cane. I asked him if he was wounded. He smiled and said no, that he had a bout of what he called poliomyelitis a few years ago. It seems to me that there are more unpronounceable diseases to fight in Dublin then there are British soldiers. It looks like we're in an awful fix.

The shelling has finally stopped. The men are running around with buckets and pots of water, trying to put out fires. With all the fires we're roastin' inside the GPO, it can't be much hotter than this in hell. They say there is a gunboat on the Liffey, and that's where the shells are coming from. All in all, our spirits remain high. There's been plenty of grub for us all. Some of the *Cumann na mBan* women are manning a makeshift kitchen, and there is enough commandeered bread and butter, spuds, and meat to go around. I wonder how long we can hold out. I'm sure the British aren't finished with their shelling yet.

Yesterday I was bored, so I quietly went to the front of the GPO to see what the bosses were doing. It was quite remarkable. Several of them—Pearse, old Tom Clark, the newsagent from Parnell Street, MacDiarmada, even Collins—were sitting where the postal tellers usually sit. I didn't tell anyone, but those teller cages, with the bars in front of them, did not seem to foretell a bright future for them—or for myself either, now that I think of it.

I can't stop thinking of me Mammy. I hope I haven't broken her heart, and I hope I don't get sent to prison, because the strain just might kill her, with the delicate condition she's in. But I didn't get a lot of time to dwell on Mammy. Jack Lemass came over to me and said, "We're off."

"To where?" I asked.

"To Moore Street," said Jack, without fear. "We're going to make a break for it." Jack must have been thinking of the Moore Street fishmongers when he added: "Alive, alive Oh!"

Alive, alive Oh, I thought. At least for the present.

8

The great escape began. Eoin, Abraham Weeks, Jack Lemass, and about ten others, one by one and under heavy fire, headed for a building just opposite the GPO on the east side of Moore Street at Henry Place. Eoin kept low, like a sprinter on the blocks, only moving. He could actually hear bullets whizzing by his head. He thought that if he could only get to Moore Street, he might be safe. Then he heard an awful howl and turned to see Abraham down, with blood draining out of his back. Abraham's terrified eyes beseeched him for help, and Eoin backtracked to help his new friend. He put his hand under Weeks's arm and tried to pull him into Moore Street, but Weeks was too heavy. Then Jack Lemass came up and put his hand under Weeks's other armpit, and, together, they managed to pull the poor man to safety.

Once inside Moore Street, they forced their entrance at the first building. They propped Weeks against a wall, and many of the men immediately started digging. Abraham just sat there, his eyes open, not saying anything. "Abraham," asked Eoin, "are you alright?"

"Don't," said Lemass as gently as he could. "He's dead, Eoin." Eoin couldn't believe it. "Leave him, Eoin. We can't help him anymore. Let's get to work and save the living."

The plan was to secretly get down Moore Street—burrowing building to building—as far as they could and see if there was any chance of regrouping to fight, or, at the worst, escape. "Jaysus, Jack," said Eoin, "they've turned us into fookin' navvies!" Lemass kept on hacking at the brick wall with his hammer, trying to get into the next house. Eoin pulled the brick and mortar debris away from Jack and tossed it to the rear. Other Volunteers searched for any makeshift tools they could find. Spoons and forks were plentiful, and a garden spade was considered a major discovery. Pretty soon all the men were assaulting the wall in shifts, as Eoin continued to clean up after them, blood now seeping through the seat of his pants.

It was exhausting work, and, by early Saturday morning, they had made their way through several buildings and into 16 Moore Street. Finally, out of exhaustion, both Eoin and Jack had fallen asleep in the corner of a strange bedroom. Eoin was covered in soot and blood, and Jack had begun to take on a sinister look because of his five-day growth of beard. Eoin wished he could shave also. At daybreak, they were awakened by others coming into the room. Eoin opened his eyes and saw that they had been joined by Padraig Pearse and his brother Willie, Tom Clarke, the sick Plunkett, the stiff-legged MacDiarmada, and Connolly, who was in agony from the gangrene that had infected his ankle wound. He was also heartened to see that Captain Collins—his fancy uniform now singed from the GPO's fires—had accompanied the leaders and about a dozen other men. As Eoin looked around, he realized that five of the seven men who had signed the Proclamation were now in this room. He didn't know if he should be thrilled or terrified.

The leaders were huddled, trying to figure out what to do. One of the GPO nurses, Miss Elizabeth O'Farrell, was sent out to meet the British and discuss terms of surrender. She was a friend of Róisín's from the *Cuman na mBan*. Róisín said that she was a midwife over at the Hollis Street Maternity Hospital. She was keeping a close eye on Connolly. She returned and took Padraig Pearse with her on her next sortie to Parnell Street. She returned alone and spoke to Clarke and MacDiarmada.

"Alright, men," said MacDiarmada to us all. "This is it. We're going to get Jim Connolly out first, and then the rest of us will surrender. Commander-in-Chief Pearse has made all the arrangements with the British. You men will be treated as prisoners of war."

MacDiarmada's words were met with curses and shouted shibboleths reminiscent of the North: "No surrender!" There was discontent in the ranks because the men didn't want to yield, especially the London Irish, who had traveled from England for the Rising and were afraid of being conscripted if they gave up. Collins, London Irish himself, was brought in to mediate and then huddled with MacDiarmada for a few minutes.

MacDiarmada, dragging his stiff leg, walked to the center of the room, and Collins raised his hand for quiet. "We're hopelessly beaten," he began. The men were attentive as they listened to MacDiarmada, who was widely admired by one and all. "We haven't a prayer of fighting our way out of here. You've already fought a gallant fight, every one of you. You gain nothing, you lose everything if you try to continue. You think you'll be killed, do you, if you surrender? Not at 'tal. Some of the rest of us will be killed, but none of you. Why should they kill you? And why should they put you in the British army? You'd be no good to them. They'll send you to prison for a few years, that's the worst. But what does it matter, if you survive? The thing you must do, all of you, is survive, come back, and carry on the work so nobly begun this week."

"What will happen to the leaders?" Arthur Shields demanded. MacDiarmada did not immediately answer, which upset the men. "Those of us who are shot can die happy," he finally said, "if we know you'll be living on to finish what we started. I'm proud of you. I know also that this week of Easter will never be forgotten. Ireland will one day be free because of what you've done here." There was still grumbling in the room. "No," said MacDiarmada. "For the sake of Ireland, for the future of Ireland, you must obey Commander-in-Chief Pearse's orders. We did our job. We held Ireland for a week, and by doing that, we've saved Ireland's soul."

The men were still growling their discontent, but they slowly came to realize it was over. Small groups gathered together to share a smoke. Some said their final rosary before capitulating.

Connolly was carried out first, and then Willie Pearse went out into Moore Street, door to door, calling out, "Any Volunteers here?" Slowly, doors opened, and men came into the street in twos and threes. When all the Volunteers had mustered, they started walking back up the street under a white flag, led by Willie Pearse and Clarke. Plunkett and MacDiarmada, due to their infirmities, tried to keep up in the rear. There, they were joined by Collins, Eoin, and Jack Lemass. They then marched into Henry Street and out into Sackville Street, surrendered their weapons, looked at their beloved Dublin in ruin, and wondered if it all was worth it. Silently, Eoin said a prayer for the lost London Jew, Abraham Weeks, who had somehow managed to become an Irish patriot as a member of the Irish Citizen Army.

9

EOIN'S DIARY
SUNDAY, APRIL 30, 1916

Thank God we survived the night. The British have us on the march, and the rumor is that we're on the way to Kilmainham Gaol.

Last night was the most terrifying night of my life. After the surrender, we were trooped up to Parnell Square and forced to quarter for the night inside the Rotunda Hospital grounds. It was cold and damp, and there was no food, water, or sanitation. Men were pissing and shitting on the grass.

Captain Collins kept an eye on Jack and me, and the British Tommies were decent enough. Things changed when the fellow in charge of the troops showed up. He was one of those British officers with a thin pencil mustache and a riding crop, the kind you'd see going out to the RDS in Ballsbridge for the Horse Show in August. Stiff upper lip and all that. Then the Dublin Metropolitan Police showed up.

"Oh, Jaysus," said MacDiarmada to Collins. "The G-men. And they've got Superintendent 'Butt' Brien with them. We're done for."

"Who are they?" I asked, innocent enough.

Collins looked annoyed at me, but MacDiarmada smiled and said, "This is part of your education, Eoin. Those are detectives of 'G' division of the Dublin Metropolian Police. Those are the boyos who are paid to keep an eye on lads like us." MacDiarmada turned to Collins and said, "Next time, Mick, eliminate them." MacDiarmada paused before adding, "Just like they'll eliminate me." I knew what he meant by "eliminate," and it frightened me. Collins nodded that he would.

Mick was about to slip me a malted milk tablet when it was knocked out of his hand by the crop of the British officer in charge. "No food here, Fenian scum."

Collins stood his ground. "He's only a boy."

"And what would that make you? The fucking Fenian Pied Piper?" The officer struck Collins on the shoulder with his crop, knocking his lone captain's insignia away. Collins was silent, but he did not cower. I thought I was going to pee in my pants. The officer passed Collins and me by, but he pulled MacDiarmada out of our group. "Is this one of the leaders?" he asked Butt Brien, who seemed to know Seán by sight. I don't know why they called him "Butt," but I had an idea. He was just over five foot tall and must have weighed fifteen stone. He looked like a walking arse.

"John McDermott," replied Brien, resplendent in his trench coat. "IRB organizer from Belfast, and signer of the proclamation."

"Come here," the officer said, using his crop to turn MacDiarmada around. "Up front, big man," he said, and gave him a good push with the crop to get him going. The officer continued pushing the limping MacDiarmada along. "Here," he said, "let me help you." He pulled Seán's walking stick from him and threw it away. "Now move!" I could see he had Willie Pearse, Clarke, and now MacDiarmada. The officer then made a great show of tormenting Tom Clarke. "This old bastard is the Commander-in-Chief. He keeps a tobacco shop across the street. Nice general for your fucking army."

He started pulling Clarke's clothes off him. First the jacket and then the shirt and the pants. I couldn't look anymore.

"Who is he, Tommy?" I heard Collins ask a British soldier who was guarding us. The poor Tommy was also embarrassed and turned his eyes away. "Who is he? You can tell a fellow Londoner."

"You from London?"

"I am," said Collins. "Who is he?"

"Captain Percival Lea Wilson," was all the soldier said and then turned and marched away. Out came Collins's notebook, and down went that name.

"What are you going to do?" I asked. But Collins did not respond; he just turned his back on me. For the first time, I saw a different Collins— no more strut; all his energy had suddenly evaporated. For some reason,

I had never felt more alone. I went to the end of the yard, almost underneath the entrance to Vaughan's Hotel, and huddled by myself in the cold. Then everything went silent as sleep took me away for the rest of the night.

In the morning, I saw the spire of the Findlater's Church at the corner of North Frederick Street begin to materialize at first light. I looked at all the sleeping rebels. They were packed like sardines; the only sign of life was the occasional snore or cough. Wilson had left. So had Clarke and MacDiarmada. The only rebel I saw standing was Captain Collins. "What are you going to do?" I said, again asking the question of hours before.

This time, Collins was more talkative. "Someday," he said, "I am going to even the odds. Now the English terrorize us. Someday I will terrorize them."

"How will you do that?"

"I think, Eoin," said Collins as he placed a hand on my shoulder, "Seán MacDiarmada has already told us how that will be done."

"But that would be a sin," I finally said.

"It would be a mortal sin not to," said Collins, and I knew a new page was about to be turned in Irish revolutionary history.

10

They marched the rebels out of the Rotunda grounds, along Parnell Street to Capel Street, over the Liffey, and along the southside quays toward Chapelizod. As they came to Kingsbridge Railway Station, the "separation women" came out to jeer them. Their husbands were in French trenches with the British army, and, because of the rebels, there would be no separation allowance this week—or for many weeks to come, for that matter. The torching of the GPO had taken care of that.

"Jack," said Eoin to Lemass as the Tommies fought to keep the citizens away from the rebels, "do you t'ink they'll let us go?"

As a rotten tomato sailed over his head and landed in the Liffey, Lemass gave the only sane answer. "Jaysus, I hope not!" They kept marching right past Kilmainham and ended up in Richmond Barracks.

They were paraded into a huge gymnasium, and the G-men of the DMP started sorting them by importance. Eoin and Jack ended up on one side of the room while the big shots—Clarke, MacDiarmada, the brothers Pearse, Plunkett—were on the other. Eoin saw that Collins's dandy uniform, now full of soot and Eoin's own blood, had landed him with the leaders. "I hope Captain Collins likes Australia," said Jack to Eoin, referring to the place where the British put the "penal" in penal colony.

The G-men were organized. Tables had been set up, and two or three to a group sat waiting for the rebels, cards and pencils at the ready.

"Name and address?"

Eoin supplied the answers.

"Where were you fighting?"

"Jacob's," said Eoin and then paused. "And the GPO," he added, for good measure.

"Why?"

"To free Ireland."

"Are you in the Volunteers or the Citizen Army?"

"No."

The detective looked up in surprise. "How old are you?"

"I'll be fifteen in October."

"Fourteen," said the cop aloud, as if to shame Eoin. "In a few years, you can join the British army," he added.

"I'm Irish, not British," said Eoin. "Why should I want to join the British army?"

"Next!" the detective said, shaking his head.

Eoin was marched to the other end of the room, where Lemass had preceded him. "Jaysus, I'm hungry," said Eoin.

Lemass smiled. "Me, too."

Eoin looked across the room and saw that Collins was staring at the two of them. Collins was also happy to see that the G-men were busy with their interrogation cards, crossing their Ts and dotting their Is. It was turning into bloody clerical chaos. Collins knew that the English were a nation of glorified clerks. In a blink, Collins walked across the room to where Eoin and Jack were standing. "Captain Collins!" exclaimed Eoin.

"Jaysus, boy, call me Mick." Collins silently thanked Percival Lea Wilson for batting away his captain's insignia.

"Hey, mate," said a Tommy to Collins.

"Yes, sir."

"No funny business. No talking. Get in line and give your particulars to the detectives."

"Yes, sir," said Collins, as he winked at the boys, aware that he had just torn up his ticket to Kilmainham Gaol and a possible firing squad.

Eoin and Jack ended up in a billet with about fifteen other teenage boys. Collins was long gone, segregated away from the leaders, but earmarked for prison in Wales with most of the GPO rebels. The floor was the boys' bed, and the only food was three war ration biscuits each. That night, Eoin dreamed of Jacob's chocolate Gold Grain crackers.

The man in charge of the rebel children was Sergeant Martin Boyle. He was fat and red and had trouble closing the collar of his tunic. "Jaysus," said Eoin, "the only reason he's in Ireland is that they couldn't find a French trench big enough to fit him into." Lemass suppressed his laughter.

"Listen up, boys," said Boyle as he stood in front of them. The young rebels knew from experience with this type of man that the most important thing to Sergeant Boyle was his forthcoming pension, which he had to be pretty close to receiving. "The rules will be followed meticulously," barked Boyle. "Violators will be severely punished. Follow the rules, and all will be well. Any questions?"

One lad in the back stuck up his arm. "What does 'meticulous' mean?"

Sergeant Boyle ignored him. "Okay boys, fall out."

It wasn't long before a priest was allowed in to see them. He introduced himself as Father Patrick O'Flanagan and said he was from the local parish of Inchicore, and that he was also one of the Catholic chaplains at the barracks. "Any complaints?"

It was unanimous—everybody was hungry. "I'll take that up with Sergeant Boyle," said the priest.

"Good luck with that one, Father," said one of the boys.

"Ah, old Boyle is alright," said O'Flanagan. "Sure he's a Kerryman and has ten boys of his own."

"What's he doing in the British army?" asked Lemass.

"The same reason some of you have relatives in the British army—it's a job." The priest smiled. "Go easy on Boyle, and you'll see he's a decent sort."

The boys were dubious. The priest talked to each boy and even heard a few confessions. Eoin and Jack passed on the confession, because they believed they were still in a state of grace from Easter mass. Near the end of his visit, the priest gathered the boys around and gave them his blessing. Then the sergeant returned. "Sergeant Boyle," said O'Flanagan.

"Yes, Father."

"These poor boys are hungry. Look at this little fellow," he said, putting his hand on Eoin's shoulders. "Could you find some cakes and tea for the lads?"

"We'll see," said Boyle, and Eoin lost hope, because whenever his mother didn't want to give him a negative answer, she would only answer, "We'll see."

"I'm leaving now," said Father O'Flanagan, "but I'll be back to see you tomorrow."

Eoin found incarceration boring. The highlight of the day was going to the toilet. They would be taken by a Tommy across the yard, where they would be left to do their business. "Why did you want to kill us?" asked the young Tommy guarding Eoin. He couldn't have been more than eighteen himself.

"Why are you in *my* country?"

The soldier ignored the jab. "Are you hungry?"

"What do you t'ink?"

"If you come back tomorrow morning, I'll see if I can get you something."

"Thanks," said Eoin.

And the Tommy was good to his word. On Tuesday, he brought a half loaf of bread and a big lump of butter. "Don't eat it all at once," advised the Tommy. Eoin had no intention of doing so—he brought back the bread and butter for Jack and some of the other boys. It only amounted to a small slice each, but it was better than nothing.

That evening, another boy was added to the teenage battalion— Vinny Byrne, lately of Jacob's Biscuit Factory. Eoin introduced Vinny to Lemass and the other boys, and Vinny brought as much news from the outside as he knew, which wasn't much. "I t'ink the citizens are still cross with us," said Byrne slyly.

Tuesday evening Sergeant Boyle showed up with cakes and a bucket of tea. "Behave yourself, lads, and there will be more," he said. The lads agreed that old Boyle wasn't a bad sort at all and that Father O'Flanagan had been right.

Wednesday, May 3rd, just before dawn, Eoin's uneasy sleep was shattered by shots. Jack and Vinny were wide awake also. "What is it?" asked Eoin.

"The executions at Kilmainham," said Lemass somberly. "They've begun."

Half an hour later, there were more shots, and more a half-hour after that. Three were dead before the sun rose in the sky. The three boys didn't say a word. After a breakfast of more army rations, Eoin went to the bathroom. His Tommy was there with more bread and butter for the lads, and although Eoin didn't say a word, the Tommy knew what he was thinking. "Those were the first three," he said.

"Do you know the names?" asked Eoin.

"Patrick Pearse, Clarke, and MacDonagh."

Eoin felt like he had swallowed his heart. He returned to his billet and told the rest of the boys. "Commandant MacDonagh," said Vinny, tears filling his eyes.

Eoin remembered MacDonagh's concern for him when he sent him to the GPO. He could still hear him telling him, "Just be careful, son." Lemass felt the same way about Pearse and Clarke, whom he had dealings with through de Valera. The rest of the dreadful day was only unusual because of the silence that had overcome the raucous rebel boys. The only light in their day was when Sergeant Boyle again brought them cakes and tea in the evening.

It started again as a volley of shots rang out on Thursday at 3:45 a.m. Half an hour later, the process was repeated. Another half-hour, again. And then again one more time. Eoin made his way to the bathroom. As he peed, the Tommy simply said, "Willie Pearse, Plunkett, Daly, O'Hanrahan." Eoin accepted his bread and butter and dutifully relayed the information to the rest of the boys. On Thursday evening, the boys settled down to an uneasy sleep, dreading what their deadly alarm clock might bring early Friday morning.

11

EOIN'S DIARY
FRIDAY, MAY 5, 1916

bout 3:30 a.m., my eyes flew open, and I awaited the inevitable. A quarter-of-an-hour later came the terrible noise of death. Jack and Vinny were awake, propped up against the far wall from me. We never thought of speaking.

We waited a half-hour and braced ourselves for the next volley, but it didn't come. Another half-hour passed, and still no shots. The dawn broke bright, and still no shots. The Christian Brothers over in Synge Street used to tell us that everything was relative, and today I believe it—only one rebel executed, and I'm happy there wasn't more.

I was dying to go to the toilet to pump my Tommy for information, but I never got the chance. A soldier came into the room, ordered us up, and told us to collect our belongings. We were marched out single-file into the room where we were marshaled that first day and ordered to the tables, where they reviewed our information cards. Then we moved down the processing line, where we were fingerprinted like common criminals. I'd never been out of Ireland before, but I had a feeling we were headed for the North Wall and a trip on a cattle boat to England. All I could think of was my Mammy, God protect her.

"Come on, get ready," said our sergeant, the appropriately named Boyle. We were brought out into the yard and told to look sharp. "Right turn," he called out, and I had to remember which was my left or right before I turned the correct way. "Quick march," sang out Sergeant Boyle as he drove us toward the front gate of the barracks. The gates were opened, and we strode through them. Then we heard a clang as the gates slammed behind us. There were no more marching orders. We looked around and discovered there was no Sergeant Boyle, no DMP detectives. There was no one to tell us what to do. It took us a minute, but we soon realized we were, indeed, free.

Vinny, Jack, and I couldn't believe our luck, and we were all jokes and laughter as we headed back toward the city centre. We had no money, so a tram was out of the question. We kept looking behind us to see if we were being followed, but there was no one to fear. We were giddy with delight.

It does seem strange not to be taking orders, though. Not from MacDonagh, MacBride, Collins, Pearse, or MacDiarmada. It's even odd not to be following orders from some British officer, or even an odd one like Sergeant Boyle. I don't know if I like taking orders, but I think I now know the meaning of chain-of-command. With all the leaders being shot, what will the new chain-of-command be? Will it be the likes of Collins? I also wonder how the people are reacting to the shootings. Are they still cross with us? Or do they now think we're not as bad a lot altogether? I sense a change in the air. As we marched away from the Richmond Barracks, we've been greeted with a few friendly "Good mornin's," and there hasn't been a rotten tomato thrown in our direction yet. I think the British may have overplayed their hand, but only time will tell.

It was around noon when I entered our flat. Everyone was jammed into our wee scullery, and, for a second, there was only shocked silence. Finally, Mammy, looking gaunt, rose slowly and said, "Eoin, my darling son." Da embraced me, Mary and Dickie pulled at my pants, and even Frank looked like he was happy to see me.

"We've been looking all over for you," said Da. "No one knew anything about you. We didn't know if you were alive or dead, ya little scoundrel."

"What's this?" asked Mammy, looking at the dried blood on the seat of my pants.

"I got shot in the arse on my way to the GPO."

"Weren't you in Jacob's?" asked Frank.

"Yes, until Commandant MacDonagh sent me to the GPO with a communiqué for Commander-in-Chief Pearse."

"God bless their memories," said the mother, blessing herself. "But your bottom?"

"I got shot on the Ha'penny Bridge getting across the Liffey. Róisín says I should be alright."

"Who's Róisín?" Mammy demanded.

I told her she was the *Cumann na mBan* nurse in the GPO. "She's beautiful, Mammy."

Mam coughed and stared at me. "And she saw your bare bottom?"

"Rosanna," said Da. "The most important thing is that he's back with us, safe 'n sound."

"Promise me you'll never leave us again," said Mammy. "Never leave your Da and me ever again."

I was about to say, "We'll see," but thought better of it. "I'll never leave you again, Mammy." Then I saw the paper on the kitchen table with the STOP PRESS on the front page of the *Freeman's Journal*: MACBRIDE EXECUTED. And I started crying. Suddenly the horror of the early-morning shots came back to me with full force.

"What son?" said my Daddy.

"They murdered Major MacBride. He was my friend."

"Your friend was very brave at the end," said Da. "He refused a blindfold. His last words were: 'I have been looking down the barrels of rifles all my life.'"

"The British are ruthless," stated Mammy.

"Buggers!" said Frank, cocksure with all the wisdom of his eleven years.

"Francis," said Ma to him. "Your language." Frank's language was always bad, so I was not shocked in the least.

Although my eyesight was blurred by tears for Major MacBride, I could see that Mammy and Da had stuck the proclamation up on the far wall of the kitchen. I went over to it and saw that they had drawn a line through the names of Clarke, MacDonagh, Pearse, and Plunkett.

I picked up a pencil and drew a line through the names of MacDiarmada, Ceannt, and Connolly. "Now, why did you do that?" my father demanded. "They're still alive."

"Not for long," I replied. I was ashamed of what I had just said, but I told them the truth as I saw it.

"When will all this awfulness end?" asked my Mammy.

"When the British leave Ireland," I said. Mammy looked me in the eye and brushed my hair out of my eyes. She knew Ireland had been changed forever—and so had her eldest son.

12

Eoin couldn't wait to go to work in the morning at Sweny's Chemists over on Lincoln Place, down the street from the Westland Row railroad station. He was only a messenger boy, delivering Christmas gifts, but he was the only one in the family bringing home any money. He was also happy to go to Sweny's in the morning to escape the depression of the flat in the Piles Buildings. His mother was bedridden now, and his father was lost, not knowing how to earn a living or even take care of his children.

Eoin was keeping a close eye on the comings and goings over at Westland Row, because a lot of the rebels in the Frongoch prison compound in Wales had been granted amnesty for Christmas and were arriving home in Dublin. He had run into Arthur Shields the other day, and it had been a grand reunion. Arthur was picked up by his brother Will, also an actor over at the Abbey, who went by the stage name of Barry Fitzgerald. Eoin was about to make a run over to tip-rich Fitzwilliam Square with a delivery when he saw the solitary figure in the early winter twilight standing in front of the depot, his cheap cardboard suitcase—which a good soaking would disintegrate—at his feet. He was a big man, and Eoin's heart began to pound as he ran up the street to see if it was who he thought it was. "Captain Collins!" he called out.

The man turned quickly and searched for the source of the voice calling his name.

"Eoin? Is that you?"

"Welcome home!" said Eoin as he shook Collins's hand and was surprised by the hearty embrace.

"I don't believe my eyes," said Collins, surveying the youngster. "You're beginning to look like a man."

"You've gained weight," lied Eoin, poking Collins in his flat belly. "Looks like the Brits overfeed their Irish rebels in Wales!"

"You must be jokin'," said Collins, clearly delighted to be in Eoin's company. "How's the arse?"

"The envy of all the girls!" replied Eoin. "I'm in fine shape." He looked at the lonely suitcase. "What are you doing for Christmas?"

"Going to see my family in West Cork," said Collins. "Unfortunately, I think I missed the last train at Kingsbridge Station. I'll try for the first one in the morning."

"Why don't you stay with us tonight, and then you can catch the first train in the morning? We're not that far from Kingsbridge."

"I'd be delighted," said Michael Collins, happy to be back in Dublin and itching for action.

13

EOIN'S DIARY
SATURDAY, 23 DECEMBER 1916

"*I'm famished," Captain Collins said to me as we headed for home. "I could do with a fry up," he said, dragging me into a butcher's shop in Cuffe Street. He ordered up sausages, eggs, rashers, black and white puddings. He paid for it with a crisp pound note, taken from a roll of pound notes. It was obvious that Mick had a knack for making money.*

We burst into the scullery and took the whole family by surprise. I introduced Captain Collins to everyone, and he insisted they all call him "Mick." "Jaysus," said Mick, looking around, "it's colder in here than outside." He surveyed the water running down the kitchen wall. "You," Collins said, tossing a half-crown at Frank, "go find some coal." Then he added, "Get some paraffin oil, too." Frank snatched the horse figure of a coin out of the air and held it in his fist by the side of his leg, as if mesmerized by Collins. "Quick!" commanded Collins, and Frank scooted out the door.

Mammy heard the commotion and left her bed. As she stood in the doorway, bracing herself on the doorframe, she meekly said, "Hello." I told her that Mick—it's still strange calling Captain Collins "Mick"— was my boss in the GPO. "Thanks for taking care of my dear son," she said, moving closer to Collins. She looked deathly, but that didn't stop Collins. He embraced Mammy, calling her "Mum," and gave her a big hug. "This is the kind of man who will make Ireland free some day!" he said, ruffling my hair.

"I've asked Mick to stay the night with us so he can catch the first train at Kingsbridge station in the morning."

"And I've brought provisions!" said Collins, hoisting the rashers and sausages into the air like a trophy as Frank returned with the coal and paraffin. "Where's me change?" he asked Frank. Frank drove his hand into his pocket and came up with the lone half-crown. "How did you pay for these?"

"I put them on the family tab at the grocery," said Frank. "Old Man Dockerty says this is the last time."

"So you were going to pinch the half-crown on me?" Collins paused to let it sink into Frank's obstinate brain. "Hand it over." Frank meekly complied.

"We'll talk about this later," said Da.

"I don't like people who cut corners," said Collins.

"And neither do I or your mother," seconded Da.

With the business done, Collins said, "You all sit down, and Eoin and I will do the cooking."

"That really wasn't necessary," said Da, but Collins would hear nothing of it.

"It's Christmas," said Collins, "and if we can't feast this time of the year, when can we feast?"

I'm expert with the coal stove, and, within fifteen minutes, Mick and I had a hearty Irish breakfast under production. "How do you like your oiges?" he asked. Suddenly there was absolute quiet in the kitchen. "Your oiges?" Mick repeated. No one had a clue what he was talking about.

"Eggs!" screamed little Mary.

"Yes, oiges!" repeated Mick triumphantly. I guess they pronounce "eggs" differently down in County Cork. "I hope you like them fried with the sunny side up because that's all I know how to cook," he said, waving the spatula at us. Mick generously cut the black and white puddings down the middle, length-wise. The Mammy always cuts it into half-inch slices so there'll be enough for everyone. This was definitely turning into a feast.

Dickie and Mary got stuck into the sausages, and Frank was soon dipping his bread into his egg yolk. Mick, the big man he is, devoured the black pudding. I love the white pudding, and, after a while, I saw Da getting familiar with the thick, hairy Irish rashers. Mammy played with a lone sausage.

Afterwards, as Mick was washing the dishes—he ordered me to do the drying—Da told him of our financial troubles and how we ended up in this fix. There was talk of my brother Charlie's death last year, and then Collins blurted out, "That's a pretty severe cough you have there, mum."

Mammy looked up and smiled a deadly smile. "I'll be alright, Captain Collins. It's getting better by the day." Mick nodded and left it at that.

I slept on the floor that night and gave Mick my bed. Before sunrise, he shook me awake and said it was time to get moving. The house was quiet, with only the snoring of Da and the desperate gasping for breath of Mammy making a sound. Just before we left, Mick put his hand into his pocket and pulled out a pocketful of change. He left three half-crowns on the kitchen table and asked me for a piece of paper and pen. I delivered a pad, and he scrawled "To Mary, Dickie, and Frank—Happy Christmas!—Uncle Mick." "I hope Mary and Dickie get here before Frank," said Mick, and with a jolly wink, we were off for Kingsbridge Station.

We went down by the Liffey, and the December wind was penetrating. Inside Kingsbridge, we warmed up around a stove, and Mick went to look at what trains were leaving for Cork City this morning. Mick returned, saying he would be taking the 7:00 a.m. train. "I want to be sworn in," I blurted out.

"What?"

"I want to be sworn into the Irish Republican Brotherhood."

"The IRB?"

"Yes. I think it's time."

"You haven't been active since Easter?"

"No, I thought it was more important to take care of my family and my Mammy."

"You made the right decision," said Collins. "Come on," he said, pointing in the direction of the toilet. Mick looked around to make sure the bathroom was empty and then took me into a toilet stall and closed the door, Mick on the left of the toilet and me on the right. Collins raised his right hand, and I followed suit. "I, Eoin Kavanagh," he began, and I repeated. "Do solemnly swear, in the presence of Almighty God, that I will do my utmost, at every risk, while life lasts, to make Ireland an independent Democratic Republic; that I will yield implicit obedience, in all things not contrary to the law of God to the commands of my superior officers; and that I shall preserve inviolable secrecy regarding all the transactions of this secret society that may be confided in me. So help me God! Amen."

"Amen," I said.

"Remember, once you're in," added Collins, "you're never out."

"Understood."

"Well," said Collins, "it's time to catch that train." I walked him to the platform, sorry to see him leaving Dublin again.

"It seems you know that oath by heart," I said.

"I've sworn in my share," said Collins, and then he added with a laugh, "but you're the first I did in a toilet." He paused before saying, "I'll be running the Brotherhood soon." It was not a brag, but a fact, the way he said it. We came to the train, and Mick said, "I'll be back after the first of the year. I'm up for several jobs, and we'll be in touch." Before he left, he reached into his pocket again and dragged out that wad of bills. He peeled off five one-pound notes and a fiver and said, "Get a goose for Christmas." Then he added, "And pay off that grocery bill."

"That's not necessary," I said, somewhat echoing the sentiments of my Da the night before.

"Think of it as compensation," said Collins. "We take care of our own in the IRB!" He climbed onto the train and, with a big smile, said, "*Nollaig Shona Duit!*—Happy Christmas and a glorious 1917 to you, Eoin Kavanagh. 1917 is going to be a great year for Ireland—and you're going to be a part of it." He waved to me as the train pulled out of the station. I had to go to Sweny's for work, but I couldn't take my mind off 1917 and what Michael Collins had in mind for Ireland and, it seemed, for me.

1917

1917

14

Eoin's mother died on February 23, 1917. The wake was held in the family flat in the Piles Buildings. Rosanna Kavanagh was laid out in a brown habit that had been secured from the Carmelite Church on Aungier Street. As Eoin looked at what remained of his emaciated mother, he still couldn't believe this was happening.

Eoin looked around the room and wondered where the term "wake" came from. He had heard it was a form of watching over the deceased, a kind of defending of the body. He liked to think that it was an effort to "wake" the dead, so they would be wildly alert when they hit St. Peter's Gates. Eoin's first wake was only two years ago, when his brother Charlie died of diphtheria. It was at dinner on Friday night, and, at first, they thought Charlie had caught a fishbone in his throat, but that was not the case. The diphtheria had actually choked poor Charlie to death. It was strange seeing his own flesh and blood, just two years younger than him, dead and gone, lying in a cheap pine box. Charlie's death was like a warning from Dublin City itself—that it would devour those who could not stand up to her. A Fair City indeed, thought Eoin Kavanagh.

It was bad enough that Charlie and the Mammy had been taken from them, but now they had to sit and look at them, forced to remember them dead, not alive. Eoin remembered how his parents grieved over Charlie. His mother had barely left the coffin that contained the fruit of her womb, and his father had embraced her, hardly ever leaving her side. Now Joseph sat on the far side of the room, looking straight ahead but not seeing anything. Eoin knew that if Mammy hadn't died, they would have somehow pulled out of this financial abyss. But she was dead, and every day, Eoin knew that, if anyone was going to get this family going again, it was going to be up to him. He was just fifteen, but he knew he was the man of the family.

The first visitor of the day was Vinny Byrne. "Sorry for your troubles," Vinny told him; he went to the coffin, knelt beside Rosanna, and prayed for her immortal soul. When he finished, he got up and sweetly touched Rosanna's hands, which were wrapped around her rosary. He was surprised by how cold they were. Vinny then went over to Eoin's father and sat down beside him. He spoke to him in a low voice, and Eoin could see his father nodding his head in agreement. The condolences given, Vinny headed over to Eoin. "How are you?" he asked.

"I'm numb," replied Eoin. "We're devastated. I don't know what will happen now, especially with the children." Eoin motioned towards Mary and Dickie, who were sitting with Rosanna's sister, their Aunt Nellie, over from Temple Lane. He looked around for his brother Frank, but the little cunt had snuck out on him and the family. Eoin vowed then and there that if the father wasn't going to straighten out Frank, he would.

"I have something for you," said Vinny, pulling an envelope out of his inside jacket pocket. "It's from the boss."

The handwritten note began, "Dear Eoin, I'm sorry I could not attend your mother's wake, but I had to go out into the country on business. I am praying for you and your family. At your convenience, could you drop by my office at 10 Exchequer Street for a chat? God bless you, Mick Collins." Inside the note there was a crisp ten-pound note. Eoin was stunned.

"Jesus Christ," he said, fingering the oversized bill. "At least now I won't have to pass-the-black-sugar-bag to pay for the box. Will you go out and get some grub for the wake?" he asked, turning the ten-pound note back over to Vinny.

"I will indeed. And I t'ink maybe a bottle of whiskey would do no harm, here and now." Eoin looked at Vinny's Pioneer pin and smiled. Vinny was "a cute hoor," as they liked to say around Dublin. His mild appearance betrayed his street smarts, his feel for people and situations.

"You're right, Vin." The rare tenner in Vinny's hands turned Eoin pensive again. "I wonder what he wants?"

"Who?"

"Collins."

"Whatever it is, I'm sure it will be a grand adventure," replied Vinny. *Vinny and his grand adventures,* thought Eoin. His last great adventure had him locked up in Richmond Barracks for a week.

"Do you know?"

Vinny put his left index finger to his lips and winked. The IRB oath immediately came to Eoin's mind. "Once in, never out," Collins had said, and now Eoin wondered what Michael Collins had in mind for him and what remained of his broken family.

15

The day after Eoin Kavanagh buried his mother, he met with Michael Collins in his office at 10 Exchequer Street. The office was on the top floor, and Eoin quickly ran up the four flights of stairs. He looked at the door, which had "National Aid and Volunteers Dependents Fund" newly painted on it in gold letters. Eoin's fist gave the door three knocks.

"Come in," said a male voice, and Eoin entered the office to see Collins seated at a desk, surrounded by papers. When he saw Eoin, Collins jumped out of his chair and embraced the boy. "Oh, Eoin, I'm so sorry for your troubles," he said. He pointed Eoin towards an empty chair and said, "You still working at Sweny's?"

"No," said Eoin. "That job died after Christmas."

"I hope the money that Vinny Byrne gave you helped with the funeral arrangements."

"It did."

"Well, are you ready to go to work for me?"

"What's the job?"

"Do you care?" Collins said with a laugh. Eoin didn't care at all and laughed along with his new boss.

"What's the National Aid and Volunteers Dependents Fund?"

"It's a bloody long name, isn't it? In the NAVDF, we take care of veterans of Easter week who need some help. Kathleen Clarke—Tom's widow—hired me. You were one of the first on the list. That's why I authorized the ten quid for you."

"Charity?"

"Compensation," replied Collins. Eoin nodded. "How's your handwriting?"

"I won the prize."

Collins smiled. "Can you type?" he said, pointing at the typewriter on the spare desk.

"No."

"Then you'll learn."

"When do I start?"

"After you get some decent clothes."

"What?"

"You can't be wearing rags like those and working for me." Collins sat down and scribbled some words on a piece of paper. "Here, take this over to Fallon's in Mary Street and get yourself a suit. I'll pay for it. You signed up with Vinny's battalion, right?"

"Second battalion, Dublin South."

"Good—get yourself a Volunteer's uniform, too. Do this right now."

"Why are clothes so important?" asked Eoin, who had no sense of fashion at all.

"Clothes aren't all that important, but people think they're important." Eoin looked confused. "Let me put it this way. If you wear a suit and tie, you can get away with a lot of things. Society respects clothes but for all the wrong reasons. We start early around here, so be here at eight tomorrow morning. Alright?"

Eoin was so overwhelmed by Collins's whirlwind performance that he didn't even ask what his salary was. "Remember," added Collins, "we're in this together!"

Together indeed, thought Eoin, as he headed over to Mary Street to pick up his new clobber.

16

EOIN'S DIARY

Mick *taught me how to type today. Well, not exactly. He told me to use the middle keys on the typewriter and to keep my hands astride of the G and H and go up and down. He told me to forget the numbers. He calls it being a "touch" typist. He said I'll practice for a half-hour every morning until I become expert.*

The first day, he looked me up and down in me new suit. "Very nice," he said. I had my sleeves rolled up, and he asked me why. I told him for some reason the cuffs didn't have any buttons to hold them together.

"That's because you're supposed to use cufflinks." I shrugged because I didn't have a clue. "Here," he said, removing his own cufflinks, "take these. I'll commandeer another pair during the day. There's no point in wearing French cuffs if you don't display them—and that's that." I asked Mick if they were named for Lord French, the failed Great War British field marshal who helped to suppress the Rising. Mick just gave me a vicious smile as his own French cuffs stiff with starch, stood at attention without the aid of a cufflink.

We get all types here at the office. Weeping widows, crying children, men down on their luck. Apparently half of Dublin was in the GPO Easter week. Word is spreading about the free money. Mick is very circumspect when he's interviewing people. Very solicitous. Sometimes he gives a stipend, sometimes he doesn't. The ones who don't get any money don't realize it until they're on the street, Mick is so smooth with the talk.

At the end of this first day, Mick locked the office door and had a heart-to-heart with me. "Eoin," he said, "there's more to this office than meets the eye." I nodded. "We're a legitimate organization," he added, "but we're here to do more than be the Fenian St. Vincent DePaul Society." I nodded again. "We'll be doing the work of the Republic here. Do you understand?" I nodded for the third time. "Are you a fucking mute?" said Mick as he leapt out of his chair, grabbed me by the arms around the shoulders and lifted me to the ceiling. That made me howl and got a big laugh out of Collins. He then put me down.

"The British have just three rules," he said. "One, they make the rules. Two, they want you to play by the rules. Three, they never play by the rules." Mick looked me dead in the eye before adding, "We're going to make a new rule—we make our own rules!"

"Fook 'em!" I exclaimed, leaping out of my chair, immediately ashamed that a dirty word had escaped my lips.

Mick didn't say a word. Only a smile told me he approved of what I had said. I had a feeling we would be getting out of the charity business shortly.

"How's your arse, Eoin?"

Young Kavanagh was sitting on the open top of a number-19 tram. He turned around to see a smiling Róisín O'Mahony. She was standing in the aisle with her arms crossed and a big smile on her face. When the woman across from Eoin heard what Róisín had said, a cross look darkened her face, and Eoin turned puce in embarrassment. The woman was about to say something when Róisín cut her off. "He was wounded in the GPO, fighting so ignorant people like you could have a better life!" Róisín took one look at the woman and could tell that she was the kind of busybody she loathed. You could bet the house that her strained, pinched face was constantly relaying moral indiscretions as fodder to the local parish priest. Your typical ecclesiastic informer, thought Róisín.

"Well," said the woman, standing up. "I never!"

"Yes, and I'm sure you never will! Hurry up, or you'll miss your novena!" added Róisín as the woman fled with alacrity. "Well, how *is* your arse, Eoin?"

This time Eoin laughed and said, "You want to see the scar?"

"Cheeky lad!"

"High and low!" Róisín slid in beside him and gave him a peck on the high cheek. She could see he was growing up. He wasn't much taller, but he had put on a quarter-stone.

"Now you look like a young man," she said. "Where'd you get this beautiful suit?'

"Mick Collins."

Róisín's mouth dropped open as the tram passed opposite Trinity College and turned left onto Westmoreland Street. "That gobshite?"

"He saved my family."

"How?"

"He gave me a job so we could eat and pay the rent."

"What do you do for him?"

Eoin hesitated. "I can't tell you."

"He's running the relief fund, isn't he?" Eoin nodded. "I know everything!" Róisín said with good humor as she wagged her finger in front of Eoin's nose. Eoin smiled at her because all she knew was what Mick Collins wanted her to know.

"I'd like to know something," said Eoin.

"What?"

"What you wouldn't tell me in the GPO." Róisín didn't remember and had a blank look on her face for once. "How old are you?"

"That again!"

"Well? After all we've been through."

Róisín laughed at that. "Well," she said, "I guess it isn't a state secret. I was born on January 28, 1899."

"So you're eighteen."

"And that makes you what? Twelve?"

Eoin wanted to punch her. "I'm almost sixteen. October 10, 1901."

"I remember."

"You do!" Eoin felt thrilled that she would remember anything about him. Then a small smile crossed Eoin's face. "I guess that makes you one of those 'older women.'" Eoin's small smile turned into a hearty guffaw.

At first Róisín looked cross but then broke into laughter of her own. "You're as cheeky as ever, Eoin Kavanagh." She gave him another peck on the cheek, which surprised the young rebel. Eoin blushed, and the tram slowly passed the ruins of the GPO. "I can't believe it's a year already," said Róisín quietly.

"A year come and gone," said Eoin. He looked at the men clearing the rubble on the other side of Sackville Street. "Finally, jobs for Dublin!" Róisín snorted at the dig. "Revolution equals jobs! We start the revolution, the British bomb us, we get jobs clearing the destroyed buildings. Justice for the working man!"

Róisín could see that Eoin was growing up in more ways than one. "You sound like Jim Connolly."

"I'd settle for Jim Larkin," replied Eoin.

"A couple of good Jims," declared Róisín. "Where are you going?"

"Going to see me Ma and brother Charlie."

"Where are they staying?"

"Glasnevin."

Suddenly Róisín realized what Eoin was talking about. "Oh, Eoin, I'm so sorry. I didn't know that your mother died. You told me in the GPO that she was sick."

"She died of the consumption."

Róisín was silent for a moment. "They say that the consumption is the disease of a highly sexed person."

Eoin stared at Róisín, his mouth agape. He wasn't comfortable talking about such things—especially with a female. "I wouldn't know about that," Eoin finally replied.

Róisín bit her lip. "I didn't mean to upset you. I'm sorry."

"I don't know how to talk about such things."

Róisín, feeling like a month-old rotten tomato, took Eoin's hand and squeezed it. "You in the organization?"

"Second battalion."

"South Dublin," confirmed Róisín. "Did they jail you after the Rising?"

"I spent a week in Richmond Barracks, but they eventually let us go. I was wondering about you. Did they lock you up? I heard Elizabeth O'Farrell was put away for a while."

"The bastards," spat Róisín. "Poor Elizabeth. She did right, and the Brits treated her like shite. Luckily, I made my escape. I went down Henry Street and took refuge in Jervis Street Hospital. Brits took me for staff."

Suddenly, out of the blue, Eoin asked, "Why do you always wear britches?"

The question left Róisín momentarily speechless. "Because I like to," she retorted, somewhat defensively.

The tram headed north, passed Parnell Square, and approached the appropriately named Black Church. "I like them on you."

"I know what you like," said Róisín in a cross voice. Then she smiled. "Thank you."

The tram came to Mountjoy Street, and Róisín got up to get off. "Where are you going?" Eoin asked.

"To my job at the Mater Hospital. It was nice seeing you again, Eoin."

"Would you like to have tea after mass next Sunday?"

"I don't go to mass."

"Then we should meet at the Traitor's Gate. Noon?"

"Noon," said Roisin; she bent down and gave Eoin another peck on the cheek. She bounded down the winding stairway at the end of the tram and then scampered off to the Mater, a few blocks away on Eccles Street, turning once to see if Eoin was still watching her. Eoin sat atop the tram, marveling in the glory of *her* superb arse.

18

"Sometimes it skips a generation. Love, that is."

That's what the old man wrote about his relationship with his son, Eoin Jr., Johnny Three's father. Now, as Johnny sat alone at the dining-room table, Diane and Bridie started packing away his grandfather's earthly possessions. Dishes rattled and pots clanged, as if wondering where their old master was.

"Git rid of the house as soon as possible when I'm dead," the old man had told Johnny on his last visit to Dublin in the summer of 2006. "The hoors in the *Dáil*, the banks, and the real estate industry will be swimming in shite over their heads very shortly." Johnny was heeding the old pol's advice, because Eoin Kavanagh had learned the facts of economic life from Michael Collins himself. The old man had looked at the "Celtic Tiger" and was fond of quoting Joseph P. Kennedy, the president's father, who pulled all his money out of Wall Street two months before the 1929 crash. "This is too good to be true," Kennedy had said, and he was right. Deputy Kavanagh, TD, felt the same way about the Irish economy. "I'm watching 30-year-old imbeciles," Eoin had commented, "a generation removed from some fookin' bog, referring to themselves as 'real estate entrepreneurs!' Holy Jaysus protect us!" Eoin had winked at his grandson. "They'll soon be trading in their iPods for iHods!" Deputy Kavanagh was the hippest centenarian in the world. Johnny would feel better when the cash from the house sale was in his pocket.

"*Sometimes it skips a generation. Love, that is.*"

In amongst all the papers about the revolution, Collins, and his grandfather's time in America, Johnny had found these handwritten notes about his father. Eoin Kavanagh and his only child, Eoin Jr., were complete opposites. Eoin kept his nose to the ground and ground it out. Young Eoin—somewhat like his Uncle Frank—thought of himself as a playboy, romping around New York and Washington with young Jack Kennedy and FDR Jr. The three were Navy veterans of the war and liked to drink and chase skirts. At least Joe Kennedy set Jack up in Congress, while young FDR drifted, never making much of his life. "I kept telling my son that I am not a millionaire," he told friends. "I actually live on my congressman's pay. Unlike Jack Kennedy and young Frank Roosevelt, my son does not have a trust fund to fall back on."

"*I almost curse the day Eoin was born,*" wrote the old man. "*He has done nothing but break the hearts of his mother and me. The only good thing to come out of his conception was Johnny Three.*"

Diane heard a groan and peeked in from the kitchen. "Are you okay?" Johnny nodded, and Diane went back to her packing. He knew Diane tried, but she just couldn't understand the Irish. *Christ*, thought Johnny, *the Irish don't understand themselves.* There's an old New York joke: Italian first cousins are closer than Irish identical twin brothers. And it's true. The innate suspicion bred into the Irish over centuries of domination and poverty is not easy to eradicate. There is always that need to be suspicious—even of the ones you love. It's not purposeful.

After a rocky early childhood, his grandparents had been Johnny Three's salvation. By the time he was put in his grandparents' charge at age ten, his father was on his third wife, and his mother had run off with her Mexican gardener. Both would be dead within five years from the drink. "Conceived in Ireland," Eoin would lament, "and murdered by America."

His grandparents had treated Johnny as if he were their own. They lived at 45 Christopher Street in two large apartments pulled together. The flat overlooked Sheridan Square and Christopher Park, and it was the liveliest street in Greenwich Village. The Stonewall riots happened just next door, the Lion's Head writer's saloon was just down the block, and on the corner were the offices of the *Village Voice*.

Eoin Jr. loved that his father was an influential congressman, but he wanted nothing to do with the process. In the beginning, Eoin dragged young Johnny to his Sunday political meetings at churches, synagogues, soup kitchens, and senior-citizen centers. Eventually these pilgrimages became a vital bonding ritual between Johnny and his grandfather. They wandered from the Village up into the Upper West Side—the full length of the congressional district. Johnny loved to watch Eoin work the crowd. He noticed that his South Dublin accent grew more pronounced the closer it got to Election Day. The old man knew how to pour it on, especially in the Irish-packed Village, Chelsea, and Hell's Kitchen.

Of course, his grandfather's congressional seniority had its perks. Any day of the week, there might be a visitor like Senator John F. Kennedy or a very elderly Eleanor Roosevelt, who came over from her home on Washington Square for dinner one Sunday night. In the 1960s, you might have seen Norman Mailer, Pete Hamill, and Joe Flaherty, fresh from the *Voice* office, arguing over drinks, or you might be serenaded by the Clancy Brothers and Tommy Makem before they got down to some real drinking at the Lion's Head. And it was a treat watching Eoin and union leader Mike Quill swap lies over Irish coffee.

His grandmother had her own clique. She worked for years as a nurse at St. Vincent's Hospital and gained some notoriety for her first book, *GPO Nurse*, which de Valera had banned in Ireland because of its deadly portrait of him and the Church. Dublin Archbishop John Charles McQuaid had denounced her from the pulpit of the Pro-Cathedral, making *GPO Nurse* the premiere souvenir that the Irish brought back with them from England and America.

Her next book, *Fenian Woman*, had become an early feminist manifesto on both sides of the Atlantic and, by the late 1960s, had attracted a coterie made up by the likes of Germaine Greer, Kate Millet, Betty Friedan, and Gloria Steinem.

As Eoin's legend had it, he first came to America on a diplomatic passport from the Irish Free State. Eoin did not agree with the policies of W.T. Cosgrave, the Irish President, and Kevin O'Higgins, the Minister for Justice, who, together, had taken draconian measures against those who opposed the Treaty. Eoin believed that they were murdering hundreds of Ireland's future leaders and opening political wounds that would take more than half a century to heal. Róisín was already working as a nurse at St. Vincent's when Eoin resigned from

Ireland's American delegation and, being an unemployed revolutionary, found himself working as a "super" in the Village, cleaning houses and taking out people's garbage. For someone who had been working at Collins's elbow at 10 Downing Street only a few years before, it was a strange beginning to an American political career.

Eoin knew the Village inside and out. On nearby Gay Street, he would point out building number 12 to the school-aged Johnny and remind him that his first American political mentor, Mayor James J. Walker, lived there. He was shoveling snow early one morning in 1924 opposite Walker's house when New York City's future mayor returned from a night on the town after dropping off his girlfriend, Betty Compton, just across the street. (Mrs. Walker, by the way, was safe and sound in her brownstone over at 6 St. Luke's Place. Beau James was a master at domestic bliss.)

"Good mornin', Senator," said Eoin to the president pro *tempore* of the New York State Senate.

As Walker descended from his chauffeur-driven black Dusenberg, decorated with an embarrassment of chrome, he jerked his head at the sound of the Irish brogue. "Good morning to you," he said with a big smile and a tip of his top hat before slamming his front door behind him. Suddenly the door to number 12 opened a peek. "Would you like a cup of tea—or perhaps a wee drop of the *crather*?" Walker called across the street. It was a little early in the morning for drink, but Eoin was not about to pass up such a prime opportunity. He slammed his shovel into a snow bank and bounded into the senator's small townhouse. Walker poured Eoin a teacup full of Irish whiskey and then one for himself. "Bottoms up," he said.

"*Sláinte mhaith*," replied Eoin, as he dropped the whiskey in one gulp. The warmth settled snugly in his chest. "It protects against the New York City winter."

Walker laughed. "So what do you think of our fair city?"

"What kind of a country is this that would deny a man a drink?"

"Rule one," replied Walker. "New York City is not America. Rule two, New York City is the world. America the country still celebrates the Puritans!"

"Puritans and Prohibition. They must love bootleggers!"

Walker laughed. "A most humorless group—the Puritans I mean. What do you like most about America?"

"Modern dentistry," replied Eoin, and Walker laughed harder, knowing the Irish and their bad teeth. "Where do you fit in?" Walker raised an eyebrow. "I haven't seen many of those in New York," Eoin said, pointing at the mayor's spats.

Walker realized this was not your ordinary Village super. "Are you a registered Democrat?"

"I'm not even a citizen yet."

"We'll take care of that," said Walker.

"I was a Republican in Dublin," laughed Eoin, "but I guess I'll be a Democrat in New York."

"What did you do in Ireland?"

"We were in the same racket," Eoin replied.

"How so?"

"I worked for Mick Collins." A smile brightened Beau James's rogue of a face, and a beautiful friendship was born.

"*Sometimes it skips a generation*," said Johnny aloud. "*Love, that is.*"

"What's that, dear?" asked Diane.

"I think the old man loved me."

"Of course, he loved you."

Johnny laughed. "You still don't know anything about the Irish, do you?"

"Don't start," Diane said, suddenly mad. "Don't start pulling any of that Irish crap on me."

"John Millington Synge!" shouted Johnny, teasing her about being the only Protestant in the whole family.

"William Butler Yeats!" she screamed in reply and laughed heartily, her anger dissipating. In reply, Johnny hissed his three-name Catholic response: "Patrick Henry Pearse! Oliver St. John Gogarty! Joseph Mary Plunkett!" He paused for a moment, guffawing. "Come here," said Johnny, and he stood and kissed her.

"What are you reading?"

"About how Congressman Kavanagh hated my father."

"No, he didn't."

"I think he did," said Johnny. "But there's a silver lining."

"What?"

"45 Christopher Street."

"Where we met!"

"Yes, where me met and fell in love." They embraced and kissed for the longest time, embarrassing Bridie, who pretended she did not see or disapprove of such behavior. even though Diane and Johnny had been married for thirty years.

"I'll never forget meeting Grandpa for the first time," said Diane.

"In the elevator at 45?"

"Yes, I was visiting my brother, and Grandpa said to me: 'My God, who is this beautiful woman?'"

"Grandpa could really shovel it, couldn't he?"

Diane stuck her tongue out at her husband and then pretended to ignore his comment. "Soon he was telling me about his Purple Arse and his 'eejit' grandson."

Johnny laughed with delight. "The old Purple Arse! Now that was brilliant politics."

The "Purple Arse" was Eoin's way of telling his constituents about his GPO arse wound, a clever way to let the district's Irish know that he was in the GPO and had been wounded, while at the same time playing on the prestige of America's Purple Heart.

"I don't think your grandmother approved of the Purple Arse." Diane paused. "And what's so funny?"

Johnny thought of another famous Dubliner, Samuel Beckett. A foreign interviewer had once asked Sam the innocent question, "You are British, correct?"

"*Au contraire!*" Beckett had replied.

Johnny had always loved Beckett, a great heroic figure and the bridge between Collins's time and the modern Dublin. "*Au contraire!*" said Johnny with relish. "After all, it was the Purple Arse that brought Róisín and Eoin together in the first place."

19

EOIN'S DIARY

"**P**ut Him In to Get Him Out."

That's the slogan Mick came up with to win the Longford election. I had to put Róisín off, and I think she's cross with me. I went up to the Mater to tell her I had to go out of town on business with Mick for a few days, and, before I could explain, she blurted out, "So, you'd rather spend time with Mick Collins than with me?"

I told her she knew better, but Mick is all excited about this County Longford election. There's an open MP seat at Westminster, and Mick feels it's important to "show the flag" and prove to the British that we're serious about taking back our country. He's determined to put our reluctant Sinn Féin candidate, Joe McGuinness, in there, whether he likes it or not. Róisín eventually came around and told me she would meet me at the Traitor's Gate next Sunday. I finally coaxed her address out of her. She lives on Walworth Road in Portobello, in the heart of Little Jerusalem. I'm already beginning to see that her bark is definitely worse than her bite!

I met Mick and Harry Boland at the office, and we took a taxicab up to the Broadstone Station—a rare treat for me, riding in a taxi. I know Harry because he's always popping into the office on business or just to say hello. I'd say that he's Mick's number-one mate. Harry's a right man, always on top of it and ready for bedevilment.

The train ride to Longford was raucous, with Harry and Mick trading barbs, left jabs, and headlocks. It's what Mick calls getting his "piece of

78

ear." Mick is obsessed with this election. He's spent a lot of time in Longford in the last month, and Election Day is just around the corner.

Our biggest problem is our candidate, Joe McGuinness. Joe is still locked up in Lewes Prison in England because of his 1916 activities. Mick calls him his "felon candidate." De Valera doesn't want him to run. He sent a note to Mick saying he "considers it unwise."

"Fookin' eejit," Collins said to me after reading Dev's letter. "I don't care what Dev thinks, because this is not going to be a *Sinn Féin* operation—it's going to be all IRB." Mick is always careful to separate the business of *Sinn Féin* with the business of the Brotherhood. "I admire Arthur Griffith, but where he came up with that Hungarian monarchy shite as a model for Irish independence is beyond me."

As soon as we got off the train in Longford, we went to a rally in the town square. Mick gave a rousing speech for the silent candidate and the crowd went wild. Harry and I were sent out into the crowd to urge them on. I was shouting, "Up *Sinn Féin!* Up *Sinn Féin!*" I should have been yelling "Up the IRB! Up the IRB!"

Afterward we retired to the Grenville Arms Hotel, which is run by the Kiernan family. At night, we sat around and had a few drinks and a sing-song. There are many Kiernan daughters, all of them very handsome. I don't know a lot about women—in fact I don't know anything about girls, as I'm sure Róisín will vouch for—but both Harry and Collins seemed to have their eye on Kitty, who is lovely.

Everyone was made to sing, and Mick and Harry were jeerin' me so much that I got up and sang "Dr. John," one of my Da's favorite songs:

> *Oh, doctor, Oh, doctor, Oh dear Dr. John*
> *Your cod liver oil is so pure and so strong*
> *I'm afraid of me life I'll go down in the soil*
> *If my wife don't stop drinkin' your cod liver oil*

The song was well received, and I got a big loud clap from the folks when I finished. Then it was Mick's turn, and he sang "The Virgin, Only Nineteen Years Old." There was quiet in the room as Mick described a young man's wedding night, as he watched his bride undress—then begin disassembling every part of her anatomy—from popping an eye out to unscrewing her wooden leg! The mood of the room soon went from apprehension to laughter as the folks realized the song wasn't as dirty as they thought it might be. By the end, Mick had the whole room, including the modest Kiernan sisters, belting out the chorus:

> *Singin' hi-yi-ye the Virgin only nineteen years old*
> *Only nineteen years old, only nineteen years old. . .*

Election Day dawned full of tension. The Irish Parliamentary Party's candidate is Patrick MacKenna. Collins believes we have to make an example out of the IPP and their leader, John Redmond. Mick is still cross at Redmond for promising Irish lives for Britain's adventures in France. "Who the fook does he think he is?" Mick has asked several times about Redmond.

I told Mick that a Mr. Molloy, a friend of my father's, said he would "go to hell and back" with John Redmond.

Mick didn't miss a beat. "I'd not trouble about the return portion of the ticket!" he said with a wink.

We spent the day getting people out to vote. Reinforcements in motorcars arrived from Dublin so we could get some of the old folks to the polls. Mick personally went into the pubs and promised free drinks to anyone who would vote. He said they should vote and get a drink voucher from the *Sinn Féin* man after the polls. Collins knows how to buy a vote from the common man.

We had dinner at the hotel, and then Mick and I walked down to the City Hall, where the votes were being tabulated. "Doesn't look good," Harry told us. "I think we're short."

"We will not be short," said Collins coldly, before adding, "Bring me to the tallyman."

The three of us entered a small room in the back, and Collins gestured to me to shut the door and block it. Your man had just finished his counting and was about to declare the IPP candidate the victor. Mick said to him, "Can I have a word with you in private?"

"Certainly," your man said.

"My name is Mick Collins, and I run the National Aid Society Association in Dublin. May I ask your name?"

"Thaddeus Lynch" was the reply. He was a little man with a wee mustache, and he wore the same old-fashioned winged collar that my own Da was so fond of. Tiny wire spectacles were perched on the end of his nose.

"Mr. Lynch, I represent the *Sinn Féin* candidate, Joe McGuinness, who is still in jail for being a patriot."

"Yes," said Lynch, oblivious. "Put him in to get him out."

"Exactly," said Collins. "What's the tally?"

"Bad news for Mr. McGuinness," said Lynch. "He won't be getting out of the gaol anytime soon. It's the IPP by 25 votes."

"You miscounted," says Mick.

"No, that's the correct count."

Mick then pulled a revolver out of his coat pocket and said, "You don't understand, sir. You miscounted." He then pulled the hammer back. Lynch got even smaller, and I thought he was going to faint. "Harry, do you have those 'missing' votes?" Harry handed them over. "Start counting!" says Mick.

"37 new votes for *Sinn Féin*!"

"Nice work," says Collins. "Now go out front and announce it. And that's that." Mr. Lynch was only too happy to comply. I can hardly wait to see the papers in the morning, with the headlines declaring a *Sinn Féin* victory.

"You cheated," I said to Mick later, as we enjoyed a drink before bed. Mick eyed Harry, who was chatting up Kitty Kiernan on the far side of the room.

"No, Eoin," said the big fellow, with a tight grin. "Sometimes you have to help democracy along a little bit." He took his eyes off Kitty and looked at me. "You think the British fight fair?" He raised his glass of whiskey and clinked mine, smiling. "Always remember, Eoin, the old Fenian adage: 'Vote early, vote often.'"

20

Eoin paced back and forth nervously in front of the Traitor's Gate, waiting for Róisín. She was five minutes late, and he wondered if he had been stood up. The nervousness left his face as soon as he saw her coming down the side of the Green.

"Did you t'ink I forgot you?" was her greeting.

"I didn't know," said Eoin honestly.

"Don't worry, I didn't forget you," and she punctuated the remark with a peck on the cheek.

"Come on," said Eoin, gently taking her by the elbow and heading into the park.

"So how was your trip with Collins?"

"Don't you read the papers?"

"What?"

"Jaysus, Róisín, the bloody Longford election."

"That was yours?"

Eoin wanted to say yes, but he decided to tell the truth. "It was Mick's project."

"So the Big Fella is finally earning his pay!"

"Mick earns his pay every day," said Eoin, defending his friend and boss, turning red in the process.

Róisín looked at the boy and smiled. "Great work in Longford—you and Mick!"

"Thank you," said Eoin. "Would you like an ice cream?"

"I'd rather have a bloody drink," she replied.

"I know where we can go." Eoin grinned as he took her hand and reversed course, leaving the Green and heading towards Grafton Street.

"You know a place where they'll serve a woman in this goddamn town?" Róisín queried.

"I do."

"On a Sunday?"

"Always on a Sunday!"

They walked in silence until they bumped into Vinny Byrne. "Eoin," he said, "great work in Longford!"

"Jaysus, Vin, don't tell the world!" Vinny vigorously shook Eoin's hand and then spotted his companion. "Vinny, this is Róisín, who took care of me in the GPO."

Vinny bowed gallantly, getting a laugh out of Róisín. "Nice to meet you, ma'am. Where are you two off to on this beautiful spring day?"

"For a fookin' drink, I hope," replied Róisín, shocking the innocent Vincent Byrne. "Would you like to come along?"

Eoin was worried that he might have competition, until he spied Byrne's Pioneer Pin. "Sorry, ma'am, I'm a follower of Father Matthew."

"A miser man, God help ya," said Róisín, but it flew right over Byrne's head. Róisín obviously had no time for the man she would one day refer to as "Ireland's patron saint of Prohibition."

"I'll see you, then," said Vinny, clapping Eoin on the shoulder. "Say hello to the boss man for me."

Róisín looked at Eoin and didn't say a word. "*What?*" he finally said.

"You really like Vinny, don't you?"

"Yes, we were in Jacob's together and then in Richmond Barracks. He's the one who got me into this mess." Eoin allowed himself a small laugh.

The couple continued down Grafton Street until Eoin stopped at Weir's Jewelry Shop on the corner of Wicklow Street. "I wish I could buy you something beautiful, Róisín."

"Why would you want to do that?"

"Because you saved my life." Róisín blushed, and Eoin squeezed her hand tight. Their eyes locked on each other.

"What the fook is this?" roared a voice as it came out of the Wicklow Hotel, right next door to Weir's. "Alert the clergy—there's tomfoolery going on here!" It was Collins at his jeering best, and the young couple wanted to disappear into the ground. Even Róisín was silenced. "Róisín," he said, "it's so good to see you." There were no taunts about "Countess O'Mahonyevicz" this time, and he seemed genuinely pleased to see her. "Eoin tells me you're working at the Mater."

"I am."

"Keep your eyes open," he said. "Can I depend on you up there?" Róisín nodded mutely, shocked at the notion of working for Collins. "I'm off to a meeting now," he said, before adding, "but don't you two do anything I wouldn't do!" His hearty laugh was his goodbye, and he was soon lost in the crowd.

Eoin took Róisín's hand and headed down Wicklow Street in silence. "Mick's a great mate," he finally said.

"He's alright," conceded Róisín.

"Alright?" said Eoin, voice rising. "He's the best!" They were into Exchequer Street now, and Eoin pointed out number ten. "That's where my office is." He then walked Róisín down Dame Court until he came to the Stag's Head. Silent Peadar Doherty, the barman who knew all and said nothing, was behind the stick, and Eoin pointed to the back room. Doherty nodded. Róisín took a seat and lit up a Woodbine, the stinkiest cigarette in Ireland. "You smoke?" a shocked Eoin asked.

"You don't?" Róisín replied, as she blew smoke upwards towards Eoin.

"My Mammy wouldn't allow it," said Eoin.

"Your Mammy's dead," said Róisín. Eoin turned white. "Oh, Eoin, I'm sorry. I didn't mean to sound so cruel. You're an angel and I'm so cruel. Come here." Eoin moved to sit next to Róisín, and she took his hand in hers.

"How about *your* Mammy?" he finally asked.

"She's dead, like yours," replied Róisín, surveying the floor.

"How?"

"I was a baby. She died of influenza."

"Your Da?

"My father is a piece of shite!"

"Sorry," Eoin mumbled in embarrassment.

"Don't be," replied Róisín, picking her shoulders up. "The lump of shite put me in an orphanage and joined the British army. Haven't seen or heard from him since. If it wasn't for my mother's spinster sisters, I would have rotted in that goddamn place with those bloody nuns. My aunties got me educated, gave me a future." They looked at each other, and neither said a word for the longest time. "God forgive me," Róisín finally spoke, "but I hate that gobshite father of mine."

Eoin finally smiled. "Do you check out the Tommies to see if the old man is in Dublin?"

"Every fookin' day!" replied Róisín.

"No luck?"

"Luck! It will be his unlucky day if I spy him." Róisín finally laughed. "He's too old to be an active soldier by now. I'm eighteen, and he was twenty-five when I was born. So he's in his forties. Too old for the trench."

"But not too old to torment the Irish," said Eoin cryptically.

Róisín looked at Eoin and realized that he was beginning to think like Collins. "You sound like a pint-sized Mick Collins." Eoin smiled and nodded, proud of the compliment.

"Would you like a sherry?" Eoin said, coughing a bit from the smoke of Róisín's cigarette. Eoin knew that respectable women always drank sherry.

"How about a pony of whiskey and a pint of porter?" Róisín replied, and Eoin Kavanagh knew he was falling in love.

21

EOIN'S DIARY

Mick *is fond of the Jew-man.*

    Before going to work for Mick, the only Jew I had ever met was poor Abraham Weeks in the GPO. But Mick has two of them working for him, a merchant named Robert Briscoe and a lawyer called Michael Noyek. I asked Mick how the Jews came to Ireland. "They first came to Ireland in 1062—did you know that? Same way the Normans, the Vikings, the Celts got here—they were waylaid!" Some priests call Jews "Christ killers," but Mick doesn't care what a man is, just as long as he believes in one thing—removing the British from Ireland. I think Mick gets fed up with the "usual," the monotony of the everyday. All the Irish look alike, down to the freckles. Some of the Jews, the very religious ones, are very different, with their black hats and their side-locks and their beards. I think that's why he likes having Jews in the movement. Unlike a lot of the Irish, he is not afraid of the different or exotic.

    Briscoe has just returned from New York, where he was living when the Uprising took place. He's devoted to Eamon de Valera. In fact, he worships him. He's always saying, "Dev believes this," or "Dev believes that."

    "Puppy love," Collins said with a laugh, and I'm not sure exactly what he meant.

    Briscoe has a tailor shop over on Aston Quay, but it's really a front for *Sinn Féin* business. He also has a safehouse over on Coppinger's Row, just off Grafton Street. He was sent to Mick by de Valera, who just got out of prison this summer. "Do you belong to the IRB?" asked Collins at the first meeting. I was sitting at my desk and observed everything.

"Oh," says Briscoe, "Mr. de Valera doesn't believe in secret organizations." I thought Mick would fall out of his chair, because he now runs the IRB. But he didn't give anything away and simply sat mute.

Briscoe has shown some talent for securing guns and munitions from various sources, including the police and the British Army regulars who are stationed here. Mick will pay up to five quid for a handgun. "I am building this army one gun at a time," he said to me as soon as Briscoe left the office. I don't know if Mick likes Briscoe or not. I think there's something about him he doesn't trust.

On the other hand, you can tell Collins likes Noyek, whom he calls "Mike." Noyek is kept busy representing our lads when they get pinched by the Crown. He's very businesslike but friendly. He always has time to say hello to me and ask me how my family is coming along. He lives down on Clanbrassil Street, near the South Circular Road in Little Jerusalem, like a lot of the Jews.

Mike also does a lot of Mick's real estate transactions. When he arrived at the office this morning, Collins called us into conference. "We'll be expanding our operations soon, and we'll need more properties to do it right." Collins turned to me and said, "Mike has a few properties under consideration, and I want you to go with him and see if they will work for me. I'll need an office with a view"—that meant he didn't want to get trapped or caught by surprise—"and a storefront. Go with Mike, and report back to me."

We came out of the office, walked to the corner of South Great Georges Street, and headed for Aungier Street, a few blocks away. We crossed over to the other side, and Noyek stopped me when we were opposite number thirty-one. "That's it," said Mike. "What do you think?"

"Good shop room," I said. "Is the whole building for rent?"

"Yes," Noyek confirmed. "I think Mick wants to put a front business on the ground floor and have room for offices upstairs."

"I think it will work," says I. "What's next?"

"Bachelors Walk," Mike said. I was ready to hike over there when Noyek stopped me. "I think we'll take a tram. I'm not as young as you."

We got off the tram in Sackville Street and came around to 32 Bachelors Walk. There was a bookstore on the ground floor, and we went up to see the office on the second level. It had a panoramic view of the River Liffey and O'Connell Bridge. "Mick will love this," I said, and Noyek agreed.

"There will be no sneaking up on your man in this place," he said. "I have to go to court. Go back to Collins, and give him the low-down on these places. Call me if he'll go for them." And, with that, I headed back to the office on Exchequer Street, a real estate expert after a quick lesson from Mr. Noyek.

22

The telephone rang, and Collins and Eoin sat looking at it. They were mesmerized by it because it didn't ring for days on end. It was still a fairly new contraption around Dublin town.

"Better answer it," Mick finally said.

"It's Róisín," said the voice at the other end of the line.

"Róisín!" said Eoin, excited, and Collins went back to the work on his desk.

"I have to talk to Collins," she said. "We have big trouble up here."

Collins face darkened as he spoke with his favorite Mater nurse. "Alright, Róisín, I'll be up there as soon as I can." Eoin remained silent, dying to know what was going on. "It's Tom Ashe," Collins finally said.

"He still on hunger strike in Mountjoy?"

"He's in the Mater. They force-fed him, and the food went into his lungs. Róisín thinks he's dying. I'm going up there."

Ashe—along with de Valera—was the only surviving commandant of Easter week. He was five years older than Collins, and both were devout members of the IRB. They had first met in the months leading up to the Rising, and both had been interned at Frongoch Prison in Wales. Being Munster men, their friendship was immediate. Ashe had done a remarkable job protecting the northern flank against British reinforcements during Easter Week. His small battalion of only sixty men outmaneuvered the British and won a major battle in Ashbourne, County Meath. His death sentence commuted, he ended up in Lewes

Prison in England, along with the likes of de Valera and Collins's reluctant candidate, Joe McGuinness. He was a master at employing the hunger strike as a weapon of defiance. Collins put on his trilby hat and was out the door in a flash. Eoin went to the window and saw him set off on his trusty high nelly bicycle—called "The Clanker" by one and all because of the unique sound that emanated out of its protesting chain. His gallop indicated that he would beat any tram to the Mater.

At the Mater's front desk, Collins asked for Nurse O'Mahony. Róisín, stunning in her white nurse's uniform, came out. "I have to get in to see him," he said.

"You can't," she said in a whisper. "They have guards from Mountjoy watching the door."

"Get me in!" Collins insisted.

"Come on," Róisín whispered, and Collins followed her into the doctors' lounge. "There," she said, pointing at a white coat hanging on a rack. Collins did not hesitate in putting it on and pulled a stethoscope out of one of the pockets. With a tip of her head, Róisín indicated that he should follow her. In front of the Mountjoy guards, she cleared her throat. "This is Dr. Collins. He's here to examine Thomas Ashe."

"No one is allowed in, ma'am."

"I'm a specialist," Collins said as he rushed by the two guards. Ashe was in a coma, and his breathing was shallow. "Tom," said Collins. "Can you hear me?" There was no answer from Ashe. Collins looked at the nurse on duty, and she shook her head.

"What's the meaning of this?" said a doctor in his own white coat. "Who are you?"

"I'm Mick Collins," came the curt reply. "Tom Ashe is a colleague of mine."

"How did you get in here?"

"I didn't see any harm in it," said Róisín, suddenly realizing she was in major trouble.

"I'll have your job for this," said the doctor to the young nurse.

Collins stepped in front of Róisín and went face-to-face with the doctor. "If you do anything to Miss O'Mahony, mister, *you'll* need a doctor." The color left the doctor's face at the threat. "Understood?" The doctor meekly nodded his head and retreated to the door.

Then Thomas Ashe, as though he had held on just to witness Collins's histrionics, let go of his last breath and exited this life, forever a martyr in Ireland's fight for freedom.

The phone rang back at Exchequer Street. "Thomas is gone, Eoin. Go over to Fallon's in Mary Street and get me a commandant's uniform. Tell them it's for Ashe, and they'll know what to do. Bring it to the mortuary at the Mater."

Eoin arrived shortly after with the uniform and its trappings, and the only two people in the room were Collins and Tom Ashe, lying naked on a slab, a towel covering his midsection. "They have to do the autopsy," said Collins, listlessly. "Then we'll dress him for his funeral." Collins brushed the hair back from Ashe's forehead, and Eoin thought he was going to break down, but he remained resolute.

The two of them retreated to a waiting room. Eoin had now known Collins for almost a year and a half, and he marveled at the man more each day. Collins paced up and down the short room, his trilby cocked over his forehead. He pulled a pack of Greencastle cigarettes from his coat pocket and shook one out of the packet. Collins now chain-smoked about two packs a day, and the only redeeming feature of the Greencastles was that they didn't smell as bad as Róisín's stinky Woodbines. He pointed the pack perfunctorily at Eoin, who declined. He knew Eoin didn't smoke, but the gesture was out of habit. The strike of the match filled the room with smoke as Collins continued to pace nervously.

He was nearly six feet tall and weighed about thirteen stone, but he looked taller because his body could easily hold more weight. He had the build of an athlete, and he knew how to use it. He would often stand in front of a seated person and loom over them. He knew the power of intimidation. Energy just seemed to explode out of him.

Their time in Exchequer Street had made them close. Eoin viewed Collins as the big brother he never had. Although they worked long hours, Collins always had time for some horseplay. Out of nowhere, he would leap up, grab Eoin, and commence a wrestling match. "No fair!" Eoin would scream. "You're twice my size."

"Too bad," would come the reply.

Collins shared all with Eoin; his contacts, his plans, his fears. He made sure he knew as many people in the organization as possible, from de Valera and the other ministers to Dick McKee and Richard Mulcahy, the guys who ran the brigades. It was only after Collins died that Eoin realized that he probably knew more about the operations of Collins and the IRA than anyone in British intelligence. It made him shiver with trepidation.

"They're done," said Róisín, breaking the silence.

"Will you help us?" asked Collins.

"I will indeed," replied Nurse O'Mahony, and the three of them went to the mortuary to dress Thomas Ashe for his funeral.

23

EOIN'S DIARY
FRIDAY, SEPTEMBER 28, 1917

I got to wear my Volunteer uniform for the first time today. It was for Tom Ashe's funeral. Collins has taken care of all the arrangements. Ashe is lying in state at the City Hall just down the lane. Collins has planned every detail of the day. "If a Fenian has to die," he said, rather coldly, "he might as well be used as a recruiting tool."

After a pause, Collins muttered, "Syncope."

"What?"

"Tom died of syncope," he said, reading from the newspaper.

"What's that?"

"According to Professor McMeeney, 'death was due to syncope, arising partly from heart trouble and partly from an intense congestion of the lungs.'"

"Congested by porridge," says I.

Mick shot me a look. "God, you can be blunt."

"He's Number Seventeen," I noted.

"Seventeen?"

"Seventeen. Sir Roger was Number Sixteen."

"I never thought of that," admitted Collins. "The seventeenth rebel 'executed.' The Brits took thirteen months after hanging Casement. There will be more." He became pensive. "We're going to have to step up. Our intelligence is pitiful. We have to start targeting the ones who are crippling us, the RIC, the G-Division of the DMP, their touts." I didn't say anything, and Mick was again quiet for a minute. "It's going to be brutal," he finally said.

We left for the City Hall and escorted the coffin to the Pro-Cathedral for the funeral mass. After the mass, we marched behind the box all the way to Glasnevin. It seems I've spent more time in Glasnevin in the last year than I have in the Phoenix Park. It's always a sad journey for me because I'm thinking of me Mammy and Charlie, who I miss a lot. Me brother and I were only two years apart in age.

The crowds were amazing. Some were saying it was the biggest funeral since Parnell's. Others agreed it was even bigger than Jeremiah O'Donovan Rossa's funeral in August 1915, where Padraig Pearse gave his famous speech: "The fools, the fools, the fools, they have left us our Fenian dead."

After the priest blessed the remains, three shots were fired over the grave by Volunteers. Mick stepped forward, resplendent in his new Vice-Commandant's uniform, with its smart Sam Browne belt. As Mick was getting set to speak, I saw that there was a movie camera to record the event. All we need is Mick's face in every cinema in Ireland for the next couple of weeks, making the G-men's job easier. I left the grave and walked over to where the cameraman was. It said "British Pathé News" on the equipment. Your man was cranking the camera away at a furious pace as Mick stepped up to the grave. The camera was resting on a tripod. Mick was just about ready to speak when I grabbed one of the tripod legs and gave it a merry heave, sending camera and operator to the ground.

"Nothing additional remains to be said," Mick began. "That volley which we have just heard is the only speech that is proper to make above the grave of a dead Fenian." As we headed back to the city centre, I watched Mick weep for the first time.

Yes, Mick is right. It's going to be brutal.

24

As Michael Collins crossed Golden Lane with Eoin, he saw the dank Piles Building. Inside, Joseph Kavanagh was happy for the company. "Good to see you, Mick. I just wet some tay. Would you like some?"

"I would, indeed," said Collins, pulling up a chair at the small kitchen table. "How's the family?" he asked, although he already knew the answers from Eoin.

"I had to put the babies, Mary and Dickie, in orphanages. They're too young, and I couldn't handle them."

"How about Frank?" said Collins, looking in Eoin's direction.

"He's staying put," said the father. "I'm having trouble keeping him in school. He's a bit wild."

"Break him."

"Easier said than done," replied Joseph.

Collins grunted. "Your son and I have a proposition for you." Joseph looked up as he poured the tea into Collins's cup.

"Proposition?"

"You need a job, and I need a barber."

"Simple as that?"

Collins laughed. "Nothing is ever simple. I have a shop over in Aungier Street that would do nicely."

"What would I have to do?" asked Eoin's father.

"Besides cut hair?" Collins laughed. "You know what I do."

"I do," replied Joseph, "and I approve."

"Thank you," said Collins. "Let me be frank with you. Part of my job"—he then pointed to Eoin and added—"part of Eoin's job too, is intelligence. If we are to best the British, we must have sound, up-to-the-minute intelligence."

"But I'm not an intelligence agent," protested Joseph, "I'm a hairdresser." He paused for a moment before adding, "a *master* hairdresser."

"A hairdresser with *ears!*"

"Ears?"

"To listen to British agents and soldiers."

Joseph perked up. "I see, the barber shop as front."

"And right down the street from Dublin Castle," added Collins. It was all becoming clear, and Eoin could see some light in his father's eyes for the first time in a long time.

"We'll need a good name for the shop," Joseph declared. "How about Crown Hairdressers?"

Collins almost spat out his tea, and started laughing. "Joe, no, no." He pulled out his handkerchief so he could clear his throat. "That's too obvious. We need something more subtle." Joseph nodded.

"How about Castle Barbers?" asked Eoin.

"Castle Barbers," repeated his father.

"That's it, Eoin," said Collins. "Castle Barbers. Is it a deal?"

"It is, indeed," replied Joseph.

"Eoin will take you over to 31 Aungier Street tomorrow morning. The shop is totally vacant. Lay it out as you want. Make a list of equipment, and give it to Eoin; we'll have this place up and running within a fortnight. We'll meet before you open and go over things. Also, there are lodgings on the second floor so you, Frank, and Eoin can get the hell out of this fookin' place. I'll keep an office on the top floor. Is that alright with you?"

"I must be dreaming," said Joseph, ready to turn the page on the nightmare his life had become.

1918

1918

25

C ollins had just returned from an IRA recruiting trip to Munster and decided to check on his latest investment. He came out of the Exchequer Street office and walked towards his new barbershop. As it came into view, he noticed a crowd gathering around the barber pole right next to the front door. Collins couldn't get by the crowd, so he tapped one of the men on the shoulder. "What's going on?"

"Free shaves for Castle personnel."

Collins almost swallowed his tongue. "What?"

"Free shaves, but this week only!"

Collins pushed his way to the front of the phalanx and read the sign in the window:

SHOW CASTLE ID

GET FREE SHAVE

THIS WEEK ONLY

There was Joseph Kavanagh in his striped barber's shirt, wrapping a steaming towel around one of His Majesty's Castlemen. Frank Kavanagh, similarly attired, was shaving another. Eoin was checking IDs and writing down names. He looked up and saw Collins, now almost purple, staring at him from the window.

"It's about time," said one of the men to Collins.

"What?"

"It's about time Dubliners showed us the respect we've earned," said the man. "Since the Rising, all you hear are catcalls from the local guttersnipes. This is a welcome respite."

Collins nodded. In the window was a poster of Lord Kitchener doing his "I Want You" pose, which was soon to be mimicked by Uncle Sam. Next to the poster was a Union Jack. Inside on one wall was a portrait of the King, on the other a picture of homely Victoria, the Famine Queen. Collins again caught Eoin's eye and this time was greeted with the happiest wink he had ever seen.

Eoin came into the office an hour later. Collins was still steaming. "Who the fook came up with that brilliant idea?!"

"I did," said Eoin. "You interested in these signatures?" He threw them on Collins's desk, and Collins looked at them quickly, realized their importance, and carefully went through the thirty-four names on the list. "That's a day's work," Eoin added.

"Fookin' brilliant," said Collins. Before him he had names, addresses, and occupations of Dublin Castle insiders. "How did you get this stuff out of them?"

"A free shave."

"Did you hold a gun to their heads?"

"No, I just asked them if they would like to be on our mailing list for future free events at Castle Barbers."

"You're a brilliant fookin' rascal, do you know that?" said Collins as he ruffled Eoin's carefully combed hair. "But be careful."

"Careful?"

"Yes, you know I can't intervene if there's any trouble from the neighbors. That would give the whole job away. It's a rebel neighborhood. You may have some ruffians throwing bricks through the front window."

"I understand."

"How do you like your new lodgings?"

"Supreme," said Eoin. "We've never had such comfort."

"The office on the top floor will be occupied shortly," said Collins. "I'll be keeping my distance. We're beginning to branch out. The days of feeling our way are over. It's time we start confronting the British both here in Dublin and in the countryside." Collins paused. "But Dublin is the key, Eoin. Whoever controls Dublin holds the fate of the Irish nation in their hands." Eoin nodded, thinking that the climate in Dublin City might be getting a wee bit tropical in the months to come.

26

EOIN'S DIARY

I met Róisín at Nelson's Pillar, and we took the tram out to Sandymount where my sister Mary is living in the Star of the Sea convent. Sunday is orphanage day for Róisín and me. Last Sunday, we went up to Cabra to visit Dickie, and it broke my heart.

I brought Dickie sweets and some coppers and introduced him to Róisín, whom he took an instant liking to. By the time we had to leave, he was holding onto Róisín's trousers, and his howling had me in tears as well. He says he's lonely, and some of the boys and staff are cruel to him. When Róisín heard that, she wanted to know all about it. Finally, Dickie spit it out: "Father Murphy caned me." He's such a sweet boy, he didn't want to snitch, even on his tormentor.

"He did, did he?" said Róisín. "He didn't touch you in your genitals, did he?" Both Dickie and I looked at her blankly. "Your genitals," she repeated in exasperation, pointing below my belt. "Oh," I finally said. I whispered into Dickie's ear, "Did he touch your willie?" Dickie looked at the floor and shook his head no. I couldn't believe what was going on. After we said goodbye to Dickie, we went looking for this Murphy fellow. We caught up with him on his way to the chapel. "You Father Murphy?" Róisín asked.

"I am indeed," he said with cheer, resplendent in his flowing cassock and hard white dog collar. His biretta was cocked at a jaunty angle.

"This is Eoin Kavanagh, Dickie Kavanagh's brother," Róisín said, leaving the rest up to me.

"What can I do for you?" said Murphy.

101

"Well," says I, "first, you can keep your cane off my brother. Is that understood? This is unacceptable behavior on your part." I must have looked preposterous, looking up to lecture this giant of a man, well over six feet tall.

"That was a cowardly act on your part," Róisín interjected. "The act of a bully."

"Young woman," began Murphy, rather highhandedly, "we have discipline here."

Róisín turned red. "Don't patronize me with that 'young woman' crap. I know all about your so-called 'discipline.' A nice word for cruelty." You could see in his eyes that Murphy wasn't used to being spoken to in such a way, especially by two young people. I thought the priest was going to swallow his Adam's apple.

"Is it understood, then?" I asked.

"You don't understand," said Murphy, suddenly apologetic. "This whole thing has been blown out of proportion."

"Look," says I, "Dickie is here because our mother died of consumption last year. She never laid a finger on any of us. And I won't allow it to happen here. The lad has been damaged enough already."

"Well," said the priest, playing the ever-reliable guilt angle, "if you're not happy with us here, you can always take him back." He paused before adding, "You're nothing more than a boy yourself."

"Father Murphy," I said, trying not to lose my temper, "taking Dickie out of here right now is out of the question for many reasons. Believe me, if I could handle him myself, I would."

"So you have more important things on your mind than your little brother."

I had had enough. "I was in the GPO Easter Week. So was Róisín. I was not afraid of the British, and I'm not afraid of a priest who likes to cane five-year-olds. What gives you the right to hurt innocent children?" I paused to calm down. "If I hear any more of this nonsense, someone will have to pay up here—and I won't be using a cane!"

"Got that?" added Róisín. Murphy didn't say a word, his jowly face flushed with indignation. He just turned and walked swiftly into the chapel. "That's the way to handle those bullies," said Róisín, giving me a hug. "I know all about their so-called 'discipline.' It may take another hundred years, but the Church's time will come to an end in Ireland." I am respectful by nature, willing to avoid confrontation if possible, but Róisín wears her edge without shame.

"This brings back memories of your time in the orphanage, doesn't it?"

"Fookin' clergy," she said bitterly. "I have no time for the Church and its nonsense."

"Really?" I teased. With that, she gave me a terrific punch in the arm. "Hey," I protested.

"And I don't have much time for fookin' eejit men, either!" I was still rubbing my arm when she added, "But I'll make an exception in your case." It was her way of making up.

It was a beautiful day, and we took Mary out for a walk on Sandymount Strand. We passed the old Martello Tower on our way to the beach. The gulls were swirling above us, and the familiar smokestacks of the Pigeon House were close by. We could see clearly all the way to Howth. We walked down by the surf, daring it to catch our feet. Mary and Róisín were frolicking and laughing, holding hands as they skipped near the water's edge. Róisín looked beautiful, the sun raising freckles on her face. I tried to keep up with them, but Róisín turned toward me and gestured she wanted to be alone with Mary. I quickly discovered that one into two won't go.

After we had an ice cream lunch, we brought Mary back to the convent. Unlike Dickie, she seems happy enough. I told her that Da would be up to see her next Sunday. "Well," I said to Róisín, "did you get all the information you needed out of her?"

"I was just checking up on her," said Róisín. "You know women are different than men."

"I've heard."

"Well, she'll be a woman soon, and I just wanted to see how she was doing."

"She's only nine."

"You know nothing about women and their bodies," said Róisín, speaking to me like I was some kind of imbecile.

"I don't," I admitted.

"Well, someday, maybe I'll teach you something." She lit up a Woodbine and exhaled mightily. "Let's get the tram back to town," she said, taking me by the hand. "I could do with a pint of porter at the Stag's Head."

27

"God bless David Lloyd George," said Collins.

"Since when are you a supporter of the prime minister?" asked Eoin.

"Since he went totally daft and wants to implement the conscription laws. Do you know what it means?" Collins didn't wait for an answer. "It's a dream come true for us. More recruits. More anti-British sentiment. Look, even the clergy is backing up the *Sinn Féin* agenda. I couldn't have plotted a better plan myself."

They were sitting in Collins's new office at 32 Bachelors Walk, the one with the view of the Liffey and O'Connell Bridge. The new office was beginning to have a lived-in look. On bookshelves were green membership cards and copies of *The Irish Volunteer Handbook*. On the wall behind Eoin's desk was a map of Ireland with red arrows shooting out from Dublin, indicating Collins's recruiting drives across the country.

The papers this April 2 were full of the "Conscription Crisis," as they referred to it. Even with America now in the war and the first Doughboys already in the trenches, Lloyd George was revving up his call for Irish bodies. The estimation was that the British were looking to recruit 50,000 Irishmen for their disastrous adventure. The law, known as the Man-Power Bill, was set to pass Parliament within two weeks. Everyone thought that, with the Americans in tow, the British would come to their senses and let conscription drop out of the political dialogue. They were wrong.

"I'm going up to 6 Harcourt," said Collins. "We're having a meeting on how to best exploit conscription. I hear the archbishop is even sending a representative." He paused for a second. "Jaysus, I just hope the British don't come to their senses! Even the Orangemen are against this."

With that, he was out the door, and Eoin could hear his heavy feet hitting the stairs. He began cleaning up his desk. It was strewn with rail and bus timetables. In the last year, Collins had taken on the job of travel coordinator for the rebels, whom were either returning from jail in England or coming up to Dublin from the country on business. Collins soon discovered that, as the man with the tickets and the money, he could meet and greet all the men in the movement. The first person a rebel met in Dublin was none other than Michael Collins himself.

Collins may have been the travel agent, but Eoin did all the work. He knew he could get a job as a clerk at Cook's when all this was over. Eoin needed to stretch. He got up and went to the window. It was a beautiful spring day. He could see a Guinness barge sputtering downriver under the Ha'penny Bridge, while a seagull scooped up its dinner. The rush hour had begun, and people were queuing up to catch their trams home.

Out of the corner of his eye, Eoin could see a kerfuffle going on in the middle of O'Connell Bridge. It was Collins being accosted by two men in trench coats. Eoin's guess was that they were G-men from the DMP. Collins was resisting, but the two detectives had a firm grip on him. Then he spotted Joe McGrath, a friend of Collins, moving to intervene. McGrath's presence seemed to calm Collins down, and the four of them eventually started walking across the bridge, headed for D'Olier Street. "Jaysus," said Eoin aloud, "they must be on their way to the DMP HQ in Great Brunswick Street."

Eoin's first reaction was to search Collins's desk for a gun. He opened all the drawers, but there was no gun to be found. Eoin was out the door and soon charging across O'Connell Bridge. As he turned into Great Brunswick Street, he saw Collins, McGrath, and the two cops enter the DMP's grey stone building. Eoin came to a stop, trying to catch his breath. He decided to cross the street and take up a position opposite the police station while he tried to figure out what to do. As he leaned against the Trinity College fence, he became very agitated. What would the movement do without Mick? What would *he* do without Mick? Dread filled Eoin Kavanagh.

This is no way to act, Eoin thought as he tried to pull himself together. What should he do? He had to let someone know about this. Should he head back up to Vaughan's Hotel in Parnell Square to see if any of the lads were around? Maybe head over to Harcourt Street to see who was at that conscription meeting? Dick McKee, Dick Mulcahy, or one of the other big-shot commandants might be there. He kept thinking, hoping that Mick would come walking out of the station at any minute, joking away with Joe McGrath. But it was not to be. All of a sudden, it became clear—Mick needed a solicitor. He had to find Michael Noyek.

In a quick trot that was almost a run, Eoin rounded the front gate of Trinity and headed up Grafton Street towards Noyek's house on Clanbrassil Street. He knew vaguely where Noyek's house was because he had once been there with Collins. It was near the South Circular Road, so he walked in that direction. Suddenly he spotted the sign: Michael Noyek, Solicitor. Eoin rapped hard on the door, which was soon opened by Noyek himself. "They pinched Mick," Eoin blurted out.

"When?"

"About twenty minutes ago."

"Where?"

"They nabbed him on O'Connell Bridge, and they brought him to the police station in Great Brunswick Street. He was with Joe McGrath."

"Do you have a contact there?" Eoin was silent. "Well, do you?"

"I know someone, but I don't know if I should tell you. Mick might be cross with me."

"I'll be cross with you," Noyek replied, "if you don't tell me. We've got to find out what's going on."

"Mick calls him his 'carbon copy man,'" said Eoin. "Detective Sergeant Ned Broy of the G-Division."

Noyek immediately picked up the phone. He told the operator the number he wanted and waited for someone to pick up. He then told them to whom he wanted to speak. "Detective Sergeant Broy? Mike Noyek here. I'm Michael Collins's solicitor. I hear you have him in custody. What's the charge? Making seditious speeches? You're jokin'? You're not. Alright, I'm on my way." He hung up the phone, and he and

Eoin headed towards the door. As he went out the front door, he kissed his hand and then placed it on a small object in the doorway.

"What's that?" asked Eoin. He had noticed that a lot of the houses in Little Jerusalem had these little cylinders attached to the right side of their doorjambs.

"That's a *mezuzah*," replied Noyek as he again touched his fingers to his lips, then to the *mezuzah*. "It contains parchment from the Bible, and it serves to protect and consecrate the home."

Eoin, imitating Noyek, touched his fingers to his lips, then to the *mezuzah*. "God bless all here!" he said, eliciting a smile out of Noyek. They got into Noyek's car and headed to the Dublin Metropolitan Police Station in Great Brunswick Street. The apprehension showed on each of their faces. Life without Collins was unthinkable to both of them.

28

The hot young rebel, much to the amusement of the Royal Irish Constabulary, was cooling his heels in Sligo Gaol.

Michael Collins was arrested in Dublin for making a speech "likely to cause disaffection" in Longford and imprisoned in Sligo while he awaited bail from Dublin. If nothing else, the British knew how to use Irish geography to slow up the rebel machine.

For most of his stay in Sligo, Collins had the company of other rebels before they either made bail or were moved to another jail. It was all harassment by the British. They knew they didn't have anything on these men, but they enjoyed disrupting the lives of the rebels and thus disrupting the movement itself.

If nothing else, the time in Sligo had given Collins the time to think about what had to be done, and done immediately, when he got out and back to Dublin. He had already started organizing the Irish Republican Army in the countryside, but he knew the war would be won in Dublin. It would be brutal and dirty, and, for the first time in Irish history, Collins was going to take the battle to the British and their spies. In the country-side. he would begin eliminating the RIC as an entity of authority, and, in Dublin City, he would systematically begin dismantling the G-Division of the DMP. They would be warned, and, if they did not leave, they would be erased as brutally and efficiently as possible.

The other thing he knew he needed was money. Collins was still figuring out how to do it, but he would have to float some kind of national loan right under the nose of the British. As Tip O'Neill, one of

Eoin's protégés in the U.S. House of Representatives, would say generations later: "Money is the mother's milk of politics." O'Neill was half
right: Money is also the mother's milk of revolution. Collins knew this,
and he planned to protect the money of the new nation with the same
tenacity and brutality that he would turn on the RIC and G-men. There
was so much work to do, and here he was, stuck in gaol in the arse-end
of Sligo.

"Would you like a fag?" asked a young fellow dressed smartly in an
RIC uniform.

Collins got up from his bed and looked the lad up and down. "I would
indeed," he said. He walked over to the bars, stuck his hand between them,
and pulled a Woodbine out of the package. He stuck it in his mouth, and
the young Peeler applied the fire. "*Go raibh maith agat*," said Collins in
Irish as he blew blue smoke into the face of his nicotine benefactor, hoping
to embarrass the young man.

"*Tá fáilte romhat,*" replied the copper, piquing Collins. "How do you
like our fair jail?"

"Jail is for criminals, not patriots," Collins said, and the young fellow
smiled, as if to provoke him. "What's your name?"

"Brendan Boynton."

"What are you doing," demanded Collins, "working for these fookin'
English hoors? A nice job you've got, spying on your countrymen. What
sort of a legacy will you leave to your family, looking for blood money?
Could you not find some honest work to do? You should be ashamed
of yourself."

"Maybe I am," replied Boynton, capturing Collins undivided
attention.

"So, what are you going to do about it?"

"Well," said Boynton, "I'm transferring to Dublin next week. I'll be
going to work for G-Division of the Dublin Metropolitan Police. I was
hoping to meet you when I got to Dublin, but you were nice enough to
make the trip up here."

The sweet words did not seduce Collins. "Why should I believe you?"

"Because I'm telling you the truth."

"You're telling me what I want to hear. For all I know, you're nothing
more than a cheap British tout."

"How can I prove that I'm sincere?"

"Go to Dublin," said Collins, "get embedded with the rest of the G-men gobshites, and then get in touch with me."

"How can I do that?"

"You have a piece of paper?" Collins wrote down a name and a number.

"Ask for Mr. Kavanagh?"

"He'll be expecting your call."

"You can depend on me."

"I hope so," said Collins, hoping against hope that he would not have to eliminate the G-Division's fresh, young Officer Boynton.

29

*"*onscription pricks at my conscience—what's left of it, anyway," Eoin
wrote in his diaries.

"What's this conscription stuff?" asked Diane. The two of
them were in bed, Johnny Three naked and Diane topless. Johnny did
not move in response to the inquiry. Diane's well-placed elbow made
the difference.

"Jesus," said Johnny.

"Pay attention to me," she demanded.

Johnny turned towards his wife and grunted out: "It's the draft. The
military draft."

"Oh."

Johnny looked up and spied his wife's beautiful breasts. He liked to
call them his "Criminal Pair." They were not large, but firm and round.
What made them special was that Diane's nipples were as large as a
child's pacifier. A quick suck doubled their size. "Any milk left in those
trophies?" he asked.

His query was met with another elbow. "They've been dry for years—
as you well know, Johnny Kavanagh! For God's sake, our kids are all in
college. Of course, they're dry."

"I never give up hope!" He wasn't going to give up that easily. "Would
you like a mercy suck?"

"No! Don't you think about anything but sex?" Johnny looked like
a little boy whose adventure in pursuit of the "nookie jar" had gone
awry. Diane had begun going through Eoin's diaries herself, and she

had many questions about Irish history and the many nuances that she didn't understand. She was completely mystified by the Irish Civil War. "You mean the rebels finally get the British out of Ireland, and then they go to war with each other? But why?"

Johnny smiled. "Because they're Irish!"

"Very funny."

"It's true." Diane looked skeptical.

"Why does conscription prick at Grandpa's conscience?"

"Because, in Ireland, he was against it, but, in America, he was reluctantly for it. Mostly, he was for Roosevelt."

The lives of FDR and Eoin had been intertwined for nearly two decades. They had met for the first time in 1928 when FDR, Governor Al Smith, and Mayor Jimmy Walker were all present at the dedication of the new Tammany Hall on Union Square. All the Tammany pols were resplendent in their mourning coats and top hats. Eoin felt that the only thing missing from the ceremony was the corpse. Still adhering to Collins's sartorial rules, Eoin was dressed in his usual three-piece blue suit. Eoin knew he was surrounded by Tammany anachronisms. If things were to change, Tammany would have to change—or become extinct.

Roosevelt couldn't stand Tammany, but it was an election year— Smith running for president, FDR for governor—so it was time to politically kiss and make up. Eoin was there as the precinct captain of the Ninth Ward, and Walker had introduced him to FDR. "Jimmy thinks the world of you," beamed Roosevelt, his left hand leaning on a cane and his right hand clutching his son Jimmy's arm in what looked like a death grip. Eoin could see the pain and discomfort of Roosevelt—it reminded him of another polio victim, the crippled Seán MacDiarmada—and when he saw that million-dollar FDR smile, his admiration for the man grew. "We'll have some 'adult' soda pop over at the Old Town on 18th Street after this is over," said Roosevelt. "Won't you come and join us?"

And join FDR he did. In the back room on the first floor of the sacred saloon, they had placed a heavy curtain for privacy. FDR was sitting there in a wheelchair, holding court, a huge martini in front of him. "Eoin," he said with a wave of the hand, "would you like some lemonade?"

"How about a cold beer?" Eoin replied as he loosened his necktie.

"Done!" said FDR as he waved Eoin to a seat next to him.

So much for Prohibition, thought Eoin. Over the next hour, they talked local and state politics. FDR wanted to know Eoin's opinion on everything.

"It's going to be a Republican year," he told Roosevelt, not missing the irony of the statement.

"And Governor Smith?" asked FDR.

"He's going to get killed." Roosevelt was used to hearing facts sugar-coated, but Kavanagh shot straight from the hip. "The country's not ready for a Catholic yet—and I doubt it ever will be."

"How about me?"

"You'll sneak by."

Roosevelt laughed. "How will Greenwich Village's Ninth Ward go?"

"The votes are counted already," said Eoin, with a sparkle in his eye, and FDR roared in delight.

"I hear you're an expert in vote counting."

"I learned from the best."

"Michael Collins?"

"Like I said, Mr. Roosevelt, the best."

After Roosevelt's election in November, Eoin was summoned to meet the new Governor in Albany. He returned to the Village as FDR's eyes and ears on the ground in Tammany territory. It was a sticky situation for Eoin politically, but he had been in worse jams in Dublin. The year of 1929 brought the stock market crash, and, by the following year, the Democrats were beginning their takeover of government. In 1932, FDR ran for president. One of the unpleasant duties Eoin had during that hot summer was greasing the skids for his old friend, Jimmy Walker. The mayor was in hot water, and FDR had no intention of losing a race for president because of Jimmy Walker's expensive lifestyle.

"Jimmy," said Eoin, "it's time to go."

"But Eoin, I made you. You can't do this to me."

"I already did, Jimmy. Do yourself a favor and take a vacation in France." It killed Eoin, this dirty side of politics, but it had to be done.

Beau James heeded the advice and waved *au revoir* to New York for several years.

With Walker out of the way, FDR came to power heading a ticket that swept one Eoin Kavanagh into office as the representative of Manhattan's Seventh Congressional District, running on the west side from the Battery to just below Harlem. After so many years of railing against the establishment, Eoin found himself in the odd predicament of *being* the establishment.

In August 1940, Congressman Kavanagh was summoned to the White House for cocktails. The President gave him a cold beer and cut directly to the chase: "Eoin, I need your vote on the draft bill."

"I have problems with that one, Mr. President."

"Because of conscription in Ireland?"

"Yes, Mr. President, because of conscription in Ireland."

"This is different, Eoin," the President insisted. "The British were drafting Irishmen out of their own country. We are Americans conscripting Americans. We must be prepared. Hitler is ruthless." Eoin nodded, not giving anything away. "Do you think if Hitler invaded England that it would be good for Ireland?"

"Not at'tal," replied Kavanagh. "We saw what the Nazis did to Poland and Belgium. How long would Eire be free? As you know, we have our own Nazi problem with the Blue Shirts. Whatever color their shirts, their politics are always pornographic."

"Very perceptive," agreed the President. He reached into his desk and pulled out a folder. "Unfortunately, Eoin, I have some bad news for you about Ireland. Take a look."

The cover label was stamped TOP SECRET, and the title of the document was *UNTERNEHMEN GRÜN*. "What's this all about?" asked Eoin.

"We got this from our military attaché in Berlin," said the president. "It's the Nazi invasion plans for Ireland."

"It's in German. What does it mean?"

"The English translation is OPERATION GREEN."

A chill ran through Eoin as he flipped through the pages. "What's the gist of all this?" he asked the president.

"The Nazis will land in the southeast of Ireland, in Wexford, head north, and then try and cross the Irish Sea into Britain."

"When will this happen?"

"As soon as the Battle of Britain comes to a conclusion," FDR replied.

"Is this a diversion to throw the British off?"

"We don't know," the president, admitted. "But we know the purpose of the Battle of Britain is to eliminate the RAF. That done, they should have a free hand invading Britain or Ireland."

"That's an insult to the Royal Navy," said Eoin.

"Do I hear a bit of a rooting interest for the sudden success of the Royal Navy?" laughed the President.

"This is terrifying," said Eoin. "I still have family there." Then he went silent. "And so many of my Jewish friends would be murdered." He thought of Bob Briscoe and Mike Noyek and shook his head. "I know what these Nazi bastards are up to since *Kristallnacht*. Thank God Rabbi Herzog went to Palestine," he said absently.

"What?"

"Nothing, Mr. President. I was just t'inking of my Jewish friends in Dublin."

"The Germans," FDR continued, "will use 50,000 troops. They will commandeer their supplies from the gentry, be it food, livestock, fuel. Listen to this: They even have the addresses of all the gas stations throughout the province of Munster."

Eoin shook his head. "I don't know what to say."

"I think you should be rooting for the RAF and Winston Churchill."

Eoin gave that a knowing, empty laugh. The conversation had drifted away from the purpose of the meeting, the draft bill. "What do I get for my vote?"

The president was momentarily stunned and then threw his head back and laughed. "You drive a hard bargain. What do you want?"

"Input on Ireland," Eoin said. "Remember, I *know* Churchill. I was there when Collins negotiated the treaty in 1921."

"Yes," said FDR. "I had forgotten."

"I just want some input into what Churchill has in mind for Ireland. I don't want Ireland invaded by the Germans—or the British. Churchill hates de Valera, and vice versa. He could deal with Collins because Mick was fearless and would make a deal. De Valera likes to let other people make the hard decisions and then play Pontius Pilate."

"Pontius Pilate!" roared the president, sticking a cigarette in a holder and lighting it. "I will seek your input, Congressman—you can be sure of that."

"I can be more helpful than that," reminded Eoin. "I still have friends in the Irish government. Jack Lemass, de Valera's minister for supplies, is an old friend and the smartest man in the cabinet. I can find out what's really going on. I just want to keep Ireland neutral—and unoccupied."

"Yes, Congressman," replied the president, "neutral and unoccupied by either side, in this case, at this time, is helpful."

On August 12, 1940, the House of Representatives voted 203-202 to pass the Selective Training and Service Act of 1940. Representative Eoin Kavanagh (D-NY)—thinking that this conscription bill might actually save both the independence of his birth country, his adopted country, and even his erstwhile enemy, Britain—cast the tie-breaking vote.

"So that's what all of that conscription stuff is about," said Diane to her husband.

Johnny laughed as he draped his left arm around the small of Diane's back. "Nothing with the Irish or this family is *ever* simple! Come here, you gorgeous woman." Johnny's hand deftly slid Diane's underwear down her legs, and they held together in a long, sensuous kiss.

"Do you want to take a Viagra?"

"No," said Johnny, "I don't think I need it tonight."

"Grandpa would be so proud of you!" Diane exclaimed, as she worked her way on top of her husband. Johnny hung on to her buttocks for dear life.

"I feel like I'm being conscripted," he said.

"You are."

30

EOIN'S DIARY

"Are you some kind of fookin' eejit?"

Collins looked up at me in surprise. He was looking out the window, watching the countryside go by as the train made its way to Dublin. "What's bothering you?"

"You are," says I.

"Why?"

"Because of your recklessness."

"Recklessness?"

"You had to take a victory lap, didn't you? You couldn't go straight back to Dublin after I bailed you out of jail in Sligo. You had to go to Longford to rub it in the Brits' noses."

"I wasn't . . ." began Collins, but I cut him off.

"Yes, you were," says I. "You had to act the big fellow, didn't you?" Collins was silent, which in itself was a victory for me. "Do you know that the organization in Dublin came to a standstill while you were in prison? Do you realize that when they passed the conscription bill last week, everyone was turning to you to know what they should do? You keep acting like this, and you'll end up the new de Valera."

Collins laughed. "The new Dev?"

"Yeah," says I. "You'll be back in gaol, happy and contented as a clam—just like Dev. Dev would rather have a good protest in prison than change things on the outside. In fact, half the dunces in Dublin thought you shouldn't post bail—just there sit there in jail to show the Brits you didn't recognize them."

"Ridiculous."

"Ridiculous," I agreed, "but that's the kind of *Sinn Féin* thinking we're dealing with here. We're not dealing with IRB here."

I was sitting across from Mick, and I stared at him hard. Finally he spoke. "You're right, Eoin. I should be more careful. Things are about to get rough shortly, and I have to keep my arse out of the lockup."

"And for fook's sake," I added for good measure, "will you stay away from bloody cameras? They're poison. That's why I tripped up that British newscamera at Ashe's funeral. For all we know, those lads could be working for the G-men. Don't make their work any easier. If you want to be Charlie Chaplin, go to America!" That got a laugh out of Mick, who said, "You are a fine observer of humankind, Eoin Kavanagh, but there was another reason I wanted to go to Longford."

"What?" I asked.

"I wanted to chat up Kitty Kiernan."

"You have a lot of energy."

"Funny," he said with a straight face. "That's what Róisín says about you!"

"She didn't!" I exclaimed and then realized he was codding me. Collins laughed with delight. "Fook you," I said, and he laughed even harder.

When the train pulled into the Broadstone Station, the same two G-men who arrested Mick on O'Connell Bridge were standing waiting for him. They weren't going to arrest him, but they were in a harassing mood. Mick looked at me and smiled. "Don't you dare," I said to him. Mick nodded at me, and we strode right past the G-men without uttering a word.

31

"That fookin' Long Hoor!"

"I see you've seen the morning papers," deadpanned Eoin, quietly amused at Collins's nickname for de Valera. The day at 32 Bachelors Walk was getting off to a lively start.

"No, I haven't, but the newsboys are having a field day out there. I don't know why I waste my time on him," said Collins. "I warned him last evening he was going to be lifted, and what did he do? He let them lift him."

Eoin held up the front page of the loyalist *Irish Times*: DE VALERA ARRESTED: "GERMAN PLOT" REVEALED.

"Where'd you stay last night?" Eoin asked.

"Over on Exchequer Street. I slept on the couch. I'm avoiding Vaughan's and the Munster Hotel these days. Too obvious, too dangerous." Collins paused. "Who else did they get?"

Eoin scanned the paper. "Griffith, Cosgrave, Count Plunkett, the Countess Markievicz . . ." Collins broke the recitation with a sigh. "They also lifted Kathleen Clarke, Tom's widow."

"That poor woman," said Collins. "What grief her whole family has gone through. People forget she lost not only her husband but also her brother Ned, who was in charge of the Four Courts during the Rising. And her children are so young." He snatched the newspaper out of Eoin's hands and gave it a perfunctory glance. "'German Plot,' my arse."

"What is it?"

119

"Doesn't exist," said Collins. "They're making shite up again. Fookin' Huns can't help themselves. You think they worry about the bloody Irish?" Collins was quiet for a few seconds before he blew up. "Fook this shite," he said, his voice rising. "No more of this shite. No more. They know everything about us. They know where we work, where we live, what churches we attend. I bet they even know who prefers black pudding to white pudding." Eoin had never seen Collins this angry, and it frightened him. "This shite is going to change."

"Well," said Eoin, finally finding the courage to speak up, "look on the bright side."

"The bright side!" roared Collins. "What's the fookin' bright side? They basically lifted the whole *Sinn Féin* Executive. It may only be an *ad hoc* government, but, for now, it's the government of the Republic."

"Exactly," said Eoin coolly. "They've lifted the politicians, not the soldiers. Griffith, Plunkett, Cosgrave, Dev—all bloody politicians. Not a soldier among them." Collins was about to defend his compatriots but kept mute, absorbing Eoin's young sagacity. "Let Boland run *Sinn Féin*. You run the Volunteers. Remember, whoever runs the Volunteers, runs Ireland." Eoin paused to let it sink in and then said, "Looks like *you're* in charge now."

The slot in the door opened, and the morning post hit the floor. Eoin got up and retrieved it. He checked each envelope. All were addressed to Mr. Kavanagh, 2nd floor, 32 Bachelors Walk, Dublin. He checked the postmarks on the front and separated the letters between local Dublin mail and mail from the country, and those from England and America. He made sure there were no return addresses on the back. Security mattered most. He held the Dublin mail up. "Broy's carbon copies."

Collins nodded and then turned turned to look out the window at the Liffey below. "Thank God for Broy," he said as he turned away from the window and faced Eoin. "I need more Broys. I need more people inside G-Division and inside Dublin Castle." Then Collins remembered. "Did you hear from a fellow named Boynton?"

"No," said Eoin.

"I met him up in Sligo," said Collins. "He's in the RIC and was transferring down to the G-Division and wanted to help."

"Do you trust him?"

"I don't know." Collins absently rubbed his unshaven chin. "If he calls, get his information, but keep him at a distance. We'll check him out before we do anything. We have to get more information."

The morning mail was sorted out in front of Eoin, and he systematically started opening letters and sorting them into folders. "How about all that information my father got at the barber shop?"

"Yes," said Collins. "I want that stuff put on index cards. When all that information is compiled on the cards, we'll start finding out just what is happening at the Castle. There's got to be some interesting telephone information there. We'll have a who's who before we're finished."

"How about this stuff?" said Eoin, holding up a stack of letters. Collins punched his fist into the air in delight. "What?"

"That's it, Eoin."

"That's what?"

"Where are the British sorting the mail?"

"Up in the yard of the Rotunda Hospital."

"Exactly," said Collins. "How's the security?"

"I don't know," said Eoin. "But I certainly haven't seen any extraordinary measures taken."

"There's hardly any security," said Collins. "They have a few shell-shocked Tommies standing around. I've seen them from the windows at Vaughan's up on Parnell Square."

"They lifted our people . . ." Eoin began excitedly.

". . . Now we're going to lift their bloody mail," said Collins, finishing Eoin's sentence. "Let's see exactly what Dublin Castle is being told by the RIC in the country and the big shots in London." Collins slapped his hand on Eoin's desk. "Let's see how they bloody like getting their bloody arses whipped by the rebels."

"That be ripe shite," deadpanned Eoin, and Collins lifted him out of his chair and gave him a bear hug that hurt.

32

Never accused of lacking initiative, the next morning Eoin was up with the May dawn and crossed Aungier Street, awaiting the first Glasnevin tram of the day. Eoin usually walked to work or sometimes took his bicycle, but, today, he was going to reconnoiter, from above, the rink at the Rotunda, where the British were sorting the Royal Mail. The tram arrived, and Eoin skipped up the back winding stairs to the top saloon. He was followed by the conductor. "Parnell Square," said Eoin, and paid his fare.

The tram bell clanged, and it began its slow journey towards the heart of Dublin City. It seemed that Eoin knew every nook and cranny of Dublin. They were now into South Great Georges Street, and, as the tram made its steep turn into Dame Street, he strained to see if he could see his Aunt Nellie outside her abode at 26 Temple Lane. It was funny how life was. Aunt Nellie and her family all remained healthy and alive—no disease, no revolution. It must be the bad luck of the Kavanaghs to have brother Charlie and his Mammy die within just two years of each other. Eoin allowed himself a chuckle. Rosanna Conway had once told her firstborn that there had been a great competition between herself and Nellie over the hand of his father, who was deemed a fair catch of a bachelor. Aunt Nellie had even lied about her age—subtracting three years—to entrap the enticing Joseph Kavanagh. Eoin understood, because "spinster," spit out by acerbic Dubliners, could be the cruelest of words. In the end, Rosanna, the younger and more beautiful of the two sisters, had won out. Eoin often wondered how his life would have been different if Aunt Nellie had ended up as his mother. It was a pretty stupid idea, he decided, because then he would be a totally different person.

Leave it to the British to pick the Rotunda to sort the mail. He was beginning to dread the sight of the old hospital and its terrible grounds. The movement had buildings all over Parnell Square, especially on the west side. Years later, Eoin would tell his grandson that if the British had a neutron bomb and dropped it on the Square in 1920, they would have wiped out the entire Republican movement, including Collins. That's how concentrated the Square was with the Fenian hierarchy. Eoin hated the Rotunda because of his night there at the end of Easter week but also because the Rotunda was the beginning of the end of his mother, Rosanna. All the children had been born at 40 Camden Row, except Dickie. Eoin was only twelve when Dickie was born, but he remembered his mother not being well during the pregnancy. She went to the Rotunda to have the baby, and it seemed her health was never the same after she returned home. So the Rotunda had become a sign of loss to Eoin, but if he could figure out a way to pull off this mail hoist, perhaps things would change.

The Rotunda Hospital was now dead ahead. Eoin nodded to Charles Stewart Parnell atop his monument and began to eyeball the Rotunda site as the tram turned left into Parnell Street. At Parnell Square West, it turned right, and Eoin stood up so he could get a better angle on the grounds as he passed the hospital buildings. In the area where the rebels were billeted after the Rising, Eoin could see temporary sheds and two horse-drawn mail vans. Eoin hopped off the back of the tram and went to the Gaelic League building at number forty-six. He banged on the door, and Conor, the porter, let him in. He scooted up the stairs to the top floor to see if he could get a better view of the rink below, situated behind the hospital buildings. He could see soldiers guarding the mail, but they did not seem very attentive to their posts. Eoin then walked down the street to Vaughan's Hotel, nodded to the desk clerk, and went up to one of Collins's offices on the third floor. From there, he had a straight view of Parnell Square North and the two mail carts. He saw that they would be exiting on the far side—the east side of the Square. Eoin commandeered a bicycle from the hotel and got ready for the chase.

"Hey, Eoin," came the shout as he exited Vaughan's. It was Róisín, and she was cycling to work at the Mater. "What are you doing up so early?"

"I'm always up early," Eoin replied.

"Or Mick will roast your arse, right?"

"Right," Eoin agreed with good humor. He looked at Róisín, but she did not seem right. "Are you alright?"

Róisín blew out an exhausted breath before saying, "I'm okay. Just tired. We've been swamped at the Mater with influenza. The damn thing killed me Mammy, and it will probably kill me."

"Don't say that," said Eoin, before adding, "What else is wrong?"

"I'm upset that they arrested Connie."

"Connie?"

"The Countess Markievicz."

"Oh," said Eoin, finally figuring out how the *Cumann na mBan* ladies addressed their leader.

"She was lifted with Mrs. Clarke and the others."

"I know." Eoin tried hard not to smile, because Róisín was truly upset. And he had no intention of telling her what Collins had said about Markievicz and Maud Gonne MacBride, who was also lifted with the others: "Poor tee totaling Kathleen Clarke, locked up with those two boozing snobs of the Ascendancy!"

"I haven't heard anything about Connie. She's been terribly ill with measles. I'm worried."

"Don't be."

"What?"

"She's alright," assured Eoin.

"How do you know?"

"I know," said Eoin, not revealing Broy, the source. Eoin put his index finger to his lips. "She's on her way to London. She should be there by now. She'll be at Holloway Prison, along with Mrs. Clarke and Maud Gonne." Eoin paused to chuckle. "That's a trio that might bring the British prison system to a standstill."

"Don't be jeerin' me friends!"

"I wasn't jeerin' them. I was congratulatin' them!"

Róisín could see the concern in Eoin's eyes and smiled. "I know you were. We're all overworked, that's all. This war gets harder by the day."

"Come on," said Eoin. "I'm working on something for Mick." They walked the length of the north square with their bicycles and stood in front of the Findlater's Protestant Church.

"What are you looking for?"

"The mail."

"The mail?"

"Yeah," said Eoin. "I'm trying to steal it. Want to help?"

"Sure," replied Róisín. "I'm early for work. I have time."

"There are two mail vans down there," he said, gesturing towards the rink, "and I want to see what time they leave at and where they're going."

"What's so important about them?"

Eoin smiled. "Sometimes you ask too many questions." Róisín looked annoyed but liked the way Eoin was beginning to speak his mind.

"There!" she said as the first cart, drawn by two horses, pulled out into Parnell Square East.

Eoin took out his notebook. "What time is it?"

Róisín opened her nurse's cape and read the time off an upside-down clock on her left breast. "Ten after seven."

Eoin jotted the information down and noted that there was a driver and a mail handler in the back with the bags of mail. He also noted that there was no military escort.

"There's the other one," said Róisín, and Eoin saw it follow the first, which was about fifty yards ahead of it.

He stepped out into North Frederick Street and saw that both vans turned right onto Parnell Street. "I bet they're headed for Capel Street."

"Dublin Castle!" exclaimed Róisín.

"Tell the world!" laughed Eoin.

"Why do you always jeer me?"

"I'm only defending myself!"

"From who?"

"The Great Róisín O'Mahony!" Róisín reached out to punch Eoin, but he was too quick. "Which one do you want?"

"What?"

"Why don't you take the first one. Follow it until it crosses the Liffey at Capel Street, see which way it goes, and then wait for me at Parliament Street."

Róisín saluted. "Yes, sir!" Then she hopped on her bike and tore after the first mail van. Eoin mounted his bike and casually peddled after the second. The vans were now into Parnell Street, and their only possible destination was to go down Capel Street and then head for the Liffey. Róisín was so far in front of him now that Eoin couldn't see her. As Eoin passed Dominick Street, he thought that it would make a perfect place for an ambush. The carts were soon into Capel Street, and their mystery would be revealed by which way they went when they met the River Liffey.

Eoin's van was in no rush, so he decided to catch up to Róisín. He sped to the top of Capel Street, and he could see Róisín waiting at the foot of Parliament Street on the south side of the river. "There she goes," she said of her cart. "All the way to Dublin Castle."

"Let's see where this hoor is going," said Eoin. "What do you t'ink? Richmond Barracks, Kilmainham, or Arbor Hill?"

"None!"

They stood astride their bicycles as the second cart crossed Gratton Bridge, did not turn, and headed straight up Parliament Street. "Damn!" said Eoin. "I would have sworn only one was going to the Castle."

"Well," said Róisín, with superiority, "you were wrong!"

"That's lots of fookin' mail there, Róisín." Then he turned serious. "Not a fookin' word about this to anyone, understood?"

"Yes, my little man," said Róisín. "I understand."

"And stop calling me your 'little man.' I'm not that little."

Róisín smiled and kissed Eoin on his forehead. "I'll take you at your word—until I know otherwise."

Eoin blushed, and then he heard the distinctive sound of the high nelly "Clanker." The kiss hadn't even dried when a voice rang out: "Hundreds of Hail Marys, dozens of Our Fathers, and bushels of Acts of Contrition!" The penance was punctuated by laughter as Michael Collins bicycled by on his way to another twenty-hour workday.

"I don't know why the British can't find him," said a flustered Róisín. "We can't seem to avoid him." Then, as if to earn Collins's penance, she gave Eoin a deep kiss, pushing her tongue against his teeth. It was obvious that Róisín's hormones were ahead of Eoin's terrified teenage ones. Eoin didn't know what it all meant, but like the *Sinn Féin* executive a few nights ago, his willie was suddenly lifted.

33

EOIN'S DIARY

I'm fed up with Collins.
 And I'm also up to my sore Irish arse in the Royal Mail. I have
three bags here in Bachelors Walk, and there's another three bags over
in Exchequer Street. Now Mick is talking about renting more offices,
but I'd prefer more hands to open all this stuff. Liam Tobin, Mick's main
intelligence man, is going through every piece of paper with me as I
open them. Liam finally said he was going to bring in a few *Cumann na
mBan* women to help us out. As we go through the letters, they are catalogued and put into individual folders, depending on importance. I am
jotting every name down on index cards for future reference. About an
hour into the operation, Liam turned to me and simply said, "Eoin, this
is a bloody gold mine." I guess we hit the jackpot with my little scheme.

But I'm still fed up with Collins. He won't let me do anything except
shuffle papers around. "I want to have fun," I told him.

"Shooting people is not fun," he replied.

After casing the mail carts with Róisín, I went back to the office,
and Mick was there with Tobin and Dick McKee, who runs the Dublin
Brigade. I told them of my plan, and McKee thought it would be an
easy steal. Tobin thought the information might be priceless in that it
was coming not only from the countryside but from London as well.
"Won't Lord Johnny French be surprised when he sees 'CENSORED
BY THE GOVERNMENT OF THE IRISH REPUBLIC' stamped on
his mail!" chirped Collins.

The next morning, McKee had several of his men—Vinny, Mick
McDonnell, Paddy Daly, and Jim Slattery—head off the mail carts. One

by one, they drove them into Dominick Street and transferred the bags into a waiting lorry. Vinny told me that he stood over the mailmen with his Mauser and said, "If you want to collect your pensions, lads, just lie there and watch the floor." They then had some of the young lads from one of the Dublin North battalions drive the carts off in the direction of the stockyards. It was, as the saying goes, like taking candy from a baby.

It was my plan, and I begged Mick for permission to go on the ambush, but he said no-go. I guess I sulked, and he told me curtly to shape up and just do my job. Dick McKee came by the office later in the day. Dick is a native Dub like myself, hailing from the Finglas area on the North Side. He is in his late twenties and wears a handsome black mustache. He was in the printer's trade before taking over command of the Dublin Brigades. After congratulating me on the mail coup, he told me I had been promoted to sergeant in the South Dublin battalion. I said, "That's nice, Commandant, but I've never even drilled with the battalion—Mick won't let me out of the bloody office!"

Dick laughed but then turned serious. "Could you kill a man, Eoin?"

The question caught me off guard. "I don't know," I replied.

Dick pulled his Webley revolver out of his pocket and held it out in front of him, pointing at the floor. "Eoin, could you do this? Imagine a man on the floor there. Could you point this gun and blow his brains out? Then put another into his skull for good measure?"

I swallowed hard. I didn't know. In the GPO, all the shooting was long-range. There was nothing personal about killing a man. I guess it was anonymous murder.

"Could you?" McKee repeated.

"I don't think so," I said. "I guess it's against my religion."

"It's against my religion, too," replied McKee, "but someone has to do it and do it well, or Ireland will never be free."

"I understand," I replied meekly.

"Congratulations on the promotion, Eoin. We're all proud of you." McKee headed for the door and opened it. "Mick, too!" he added.

That brought a smile to my face, and I said, "Thanks." The door slammed, and McKee was gone. I guess Mick is right—shooting people is not fun. And I know in my soul that murder is still a mortal sin, no matter what Dick McKee says.

34

The telephone rang in the office at Bachelors Walk.

"Mr. Kavanagh?"

Whenever they asked for "Mister" Kavanagh, Eoin knew it was serious business. It was Collins's way of protecting him and alerting him at the same time.

"This is Mr. Kavanagh."

"This is Brendan Boynton. I'm with the DMP."

For a second, Eoin was panicked by the mere mention of the DMP, but then he remembered Mick's Sligo jailer, who was supposedly eager to help the rebels.

"Yes, Mr. Boynton, what can I do for you?"

"I'd like to meet with Michael Collins."

"Wouldn't we all," said Eoin with a small, fake, humorous laugh. "Mr. Collins is very difficult to get in touch with, but I'd be glad to meet with you. Would that be convenient?"

"Sure," said Boynton. "Should I come to your office?"

This guy is eager—too eager, thought Eoin. "No," he said, "that wouldn't be convenient at the present. Do you know the Stag's Head, near the Castle?"

"I do indeed."

"Well, could we meet there about half-five?"

"Sure," said Boynton, "but how will I recognize you?"

"I'll be sitting in the last snug of the bar."

"Fine. See you at half-five."

"One other thing," added Eoin. "Could you bring a Castle phone directory along with you?"

"A phone directory," said Boynton. "I don't know if I can get my hands on one on such short notice."

"Oh," replied Eoin, "you'll find a way. Until half-five." He dropped the phone into its cradle before Boynton could say another word.

"Now I have to find Vinny," Eoin said aloud. He had no intention of meeting Boynton without bringing along a little artillery, as he liked to call it.

Eoin was still smarting from not being allowed to participate in the hoisting of the Royal Mail. Mick was out in Connaught "organizing," as he liked to call it, so Eoin was on his own. This time, he was going to have some fun.

Eoin found Vinny at his home in South Anne Street, and they walked over to the Stag's Head to wait for Boynton. Eoin took the last snug at the bar, and Vinny was behind him, sitting at a table, a bottle of lemonade in front of him, as he eyed the afternoon newspaper.

Eoin sipped at his first pint of porter of the day when a hand clamped down on his shoulder. "Mr. Kavanagh, I presume?"

Boynton had caught him by surprise. He expected him to enter through the front door, but he had come in through the back door on Dame Lane. Eoin looked at Vinny, but Byrne didn't even look up from his paper. It was Eoin's show, so far without the fun.

"Yes, I'm Kavanagh," said Eoin.

"I'm Brendan Boynton."

"I *presumed*," said Eoin snidely. "Would you like a drink?"

"I'd like a pint of that gorgeous porter," Boynton said with humor.

Boynton was well dressed and pristinely groomed. Collins, Eoin knew, must have been impressed with his impeccable preening when they first met up in Sligo Gaol. Boynton threw a few coins on the bar and then mused, "So you're Mr. Kavanagh." He was surprised that "Mister" Kavanagh was little more than a boy.

"I am," said Eoin in a low voice. "Do you have my directory?"

"Right here," said Boynton, as he handed the directory to Eoin in a manila envelope and passed his first test.

"What's your extension over there?"

"Extension 103," said Boynton, and Eoin wrote it on the envelope.

"I'll be in touch," said Eoin.

"Is that it?" said Boynton, surprised.

"That's it for now."

"But what about Collins?"

"When the time is right." Boynton was about to say something when Eoin added, "Just stay here and finish your drink. I wouldn't like you to follow me."

"I understand."

With that, Eoin scooted out the back door of the bar, Vinny Byrne and his Mauser watching his back.

The Castle telephone directory was a godsend. It was totally up-to-date and conveniently listed the name and number assigned to each division. Eoin was intensely interested in the notation "G-DMP,"

35

The Castle telephone directory was a godsend. It was totally up-to-date and conveniently listed the name and number assigned to each division. Eoin was intensely interested in the notation "G-DMP," which he took to mean G-Division of the Dublin Metropolitan Police. He immediately began the time-consuming work of checking and cross-checking each name he had at Dublin Castle, from both the material he had gathered at his father's barbershop and from the mail the lads had hoisted from the Rotunda rink. It all went on index cards, and they were filed alphabetically in a small black box.

When Collins finally returned from his trip, the first thing Eoin said to him was, "Your Detective Boynton finally called."

Collins flung his hat into a chair. "When?"

"When you were out west. I met with him."

"You met with him? Who gave you fookin' permission to meet with him?"

"I thought you appreciated initiative."

"I think we're developing a love-hate relationship, Eoin," said Collins calmly.

"What's that?"

"That's when someone's a pain-in-the-arse, but you still love them."

"Like *you*?" deadpanned Eoin.

Collins charged at the boy. "You little imp!" he said, messing his hair up again and giving him a mighty tickle that left the boy howling. "What do you think of him?"

"I didn't have much to say to him," said Eoin. "He was well-dressed, well-spoken, and I also got this out of him." Eoin held up the Castle phone directory.

"Good work!" said Collins, flipping through the pages.

"Some of the Castle boys are up to more than they make out to be."

"I'm still not sure about Boynton," Collins said, obviously troubled about his Castle windfall.

"Vinny followed him back to the Castle, so everything seems to be on the up-and-up with him. He's very eager to meet you."

"So you had Byrne in on this, too." Collins realized that young Kavanagh didn't miss a trick. "Well, I guess we should set up a meeting."

"Where?"

"How about Castle Barbers?"

At first Eoin was thrilled, but then he thought of the danger to his father and brother. "Will it be safe?" asked Eoin, with concern.

"No one is safe," said Collins matter-of-factly, and Eoin began to realize that there was no fun to be had in Michael Collins's revolution.

———————

Collins and Vinny Byrne arrived at Castle Barbers at half-five. Collins, after some protest, sent Frank Kavanagh on his way and out of danger. Vinny replaced his coat jacket with Frank's striped barber shirt and slid his Mauser into his belt. They closed the door and turned the sign to "CLOSED." At 5:45 Eoin, at the Exchequer Street office, phoned Dublin Castle and spoke to Brendan Boynton. "Go to Castle Barbers immediately. Be there by six. Get a shave." Before Boynton could reply, Eoin hung up the phone.

The church bells around town announced the Angelus. Vinny Byrne sat in the last chair and camouflaged himself with the evening newspaper. Collins waited in the back room. Suddenly the doorway was darkened by a well-dressed figure. He looked confused at the "CLOSED" placard, but Joseph Kavanagh opened the door anyway. "Yes? Can I help you?"

"Could I, get a shave?" he said. Vinny nodded to Kavanagh, and Boynton entered and removed his jacket. Vinny visually checked for bulges and holsters, but there were none apparent. "Have a seat," said Kavanagh, and Boynton took the first chair by the door. As soon as he sat down, Kavanagh draped him with a barber's sheet and lowered the back of the chair to an almost horizontal level. He went to the steamer and plucked a hot towel. As soon it was on Boynton's face, Collins entered from the rear of the shop.

"Mr. Boynton," said Collins. Boynton tried to rise from his prone position, but Collins gently pushed him back into the chair.

"Collins?"

"Who else?"

"You're a hard man to meet."

"Not really," said Collins. "How's the new job coming along?"

"Pretty boring," replied Boynton. "All I do is type up reports."

"Excellent."

"Excellent?"

"From now on, put another piece of carbon paper in your typewriter. At the end of your workday, put the carbons in plain envelopes, no return address, and mail it to Mr. Kavanagh, 32 Bachelors Walk. Got that?"

"Yes," replied Boynton. "Do you want me to do anything else?"

Collins was looming over the G-man. Boynton was looking up at Collins, who was upside down in his vision field. "I want *everything*! Are you up for it?"

"I'll do anything you ask."

"One," said Collins, "I want the home addresses of every man in the G-Division who works in Dublin Castle. Two, I want, *immediately*, any roster changes that occur within G-Division. Three, I want to know any big shots who are sent down here from Belfast or London. Four, I want to know everything and anything G-Division has on the rebels."

"What are you planning?"

Collins laughed. "Mayhem, Mr. Boynton. Mayhem."

The conversation was punctuated by Joseph Kavanagh noisily, mixing shaving powder in a cup. "How will I contact you?"

"You won't," said Collins. "I'll contact you. You're on probation. One slip-up, and I'll be sending your body back to your mammy in a box. Understood?" Boynton, bug-eyed with fear, remained mute. "Never come back to this shop again." Collins turned and spat a wad of saliva halfway across the room and dead-on into a spittoon. Byrne tore off his striped barber shirt and replaced it with his jacket. "Relax," said Collins to Boynton. "Have a shave on us." With that, Joseph Kavanagh flung open his straight razor and put it to Boynton's throat as Collins and Byrne, their work done, exited into Aungier Street.

36

EOIN'S DIARY

I can't believe what I did to Frank last night.

    After Collins met Boynton, he and Vinny came back to the office in Exchequer Street for a recap. Collins was pleased and thought all had gone well. He loved telling me about my father holding the straight razor to Boynton's throat so he and Vinny could make their escape. If this is what Mick does to his friends, I don't want to be his enemy!

I went home, and Frank returned, stupid with the drink. Apparently Mick gave him a shilling to get his arse out of the shop, and Frank spent it on pints. If I ever find the barman who serves children, I'll have his head. I was fagged out from the day when Frank, all thirteen years of him, barged into the shop and started berating Collins. "That cunt," he said, "is trying to get us killed, and you think of the world of him!"

"Shut up," says I, in a whisper, but Frank would have none of it.

"He's a cunt, Eoin," he said. "A goddamned cunt."

"You've had enough to drink," says I. "Get to bed."

"Fuck bed—I'm going to Dublin Castle to turn your mate in."

"You go to bed, or I'll lay you low."

"With what, little man?"

Frank was bigger than me—and I'm not braggin'—but I'm a lot smarter. "Just shut the fook up, and go to bed," says I.

"Meet me at Dublin Castle, you Fenian cunt."

I had had enough. Mick won't let me carry a gun, so I've taken to "wearing" a pipe in me inside jacket pocket. One foot long, and it does the trick.

"I've got you!" Frank laughed like he actually had me.

I went up to him, pulled the pipe out of my pocket, and laid him out with one blow to the side of his head. Blood was gushing on the floor when my father rushed out of the back room. "My God," said Da. "What happened?"

"Frank had an accident," I told him, as I got a towel to wrap around Frank's thick head.

"But why?"

"He was talking treason. Do you understand?" My father nodded. "Take him to the Meath—get him stitched and sobered up."

"Will you help me?"

"No," I said with sorrow. "He's your problem now." I paused for a moment. "Don't make him Collins's problem."

Frank, holding the towel to his head, looked at me in stunned disbelief. My father looked at me with dread, and I knew that Mick's revolution had already poisoned my family, perhaps forever.

37

"I never knew a girl who was ruined by a book."

That was Mayor Jimmy Walker's response to a call for censorship. When Eoin Kavanagh's wife first read it in the *New York Daily News*, her face broke out in a big smile. "Eoin," she called to her husband, "I like your Mayor Walker. Finally a politician who's against censorship." She paused for a second. "Censorship is the rancid juice of government and the Church."

Eoin smiled. "You're becoming a rabble-rouser."

"I want to write what I want to write, and no one is going to tell me what I can write and what I can read. Censorship is the tool of the ultimate insecure coward!"

As a congressman's wife, she remained in New York while Eoin spent the week in Washington, returning to the Village on weekends. She continued to work as a nurse at St. Vincent's Hospital, and Eoin Jr. went to high school at LaSalle Academy on the Lower East Side. It was a happy domestic scenario, but the wannabe writer in the family was restless.

She first got into the writing business working for First Lady Eleanor Roosevelt. Eoin was with other congressional leaders at the White House right after the Nazis invaded Belgium in May 1940. The meeting was grim, but the president remained ebullient, even though his outlook for the invasion was not rosy. For the first time since the Great Depression, Eoin felt fear and uncertainty in the Congress.

As the meeting broke up and the congressmen were leaving the Oval Office, Eoin heard the president call him aside. "Eoin," FDR said, "do you have a minute?" As soon as the others were out of the office, he asked, "How's Congressman Johnson from Texas coming along?"

Eoin laughed. "You mean LBJ?"

"LBJ?"

"Lyndon Baines Johnson."

"But LBJ?"

"You're responsible, Mister President."

"*Moi?*" asked the president innocently, sticking a Lucky Strike into a cigarette holder and lighting it.

"Yes," said Eoin. "He figured if Franklin Delano Roosevelt is FDR, then Lyndon Baines Johnson has to be LBJ."

The president threw his head back and let out his wonderful laugh. Then he looked at his watch. "I think that story deserves a martini. Cocktail hour has commenced!"

"I never disagree with my president," said Eoin, taking a seat next to FDR's desk. The president often called members of Congress—including LBJ—to the White House to have drinks. Eoin thought that he was probably lonely. It seemed that Eleanor was everywhere—except Washington, D.C.

In due course, the drinks were brought in. It was a hot and humid Washington day, but the Oval Office was air-conditioned to help minimize the president's allergies. The condensation on the martini glasses made them more inviting than ever, and the two friends clicked glasses.

"How bad is it, Mister President?"

FDR shook his head. "You don't give me a break, do you Eoin?"

"You forget I've been through a war myself."

"I never forget that," said the president, "and the situation is not promising."

"Can't the French and British stop the Germans?"

"I don't know," replied FDR. "My General Marshall is not optimistic."

"George Marshall is the smartest man in Washington," said Eoin. The president cocked his head to the side. "Present company excluded, of course." Eoin was always amused by the egos of politicians, and FDR was no exception. "So, Mister President, are you running?"

"What do you think?"

"I think you now have no choice, with another war on the horizon. And I think you're about to win your third term in November."

"Just between us," the president said in a conspiratorial tone, "I agree!"

"You'll kill Wilkie."

"It won't be easy, but the 'Barefoot Boy from Wall Street' is about to see his first big league pitching." That got a laugh out of Eoin. "And how's the beautiful Mrs. Kavanagh?"

"Typically restless," said Eoin. "I think she's tired of the nursing. She's been at it now for well over twenty-five years. She wants to be a writer."

"Funny enough," said FDR, "Eleanor is looking for someone to help her out with her newspaper column. It might be a good pairing. Eleanor spends much of her time in Greenwich Village these days—heaven forbid America should hear about that!—and, of course, you two live there, too."

"And my son is going to college in the fall," said Eoin, "so the house will be empty. I think it might be the right opportunity at the right time."

The congressman's wife walked over to 20 East 11th Street, just off Fifth Avenue. She rang the bell labeled "Esther Lape" and was buzzed in. The apartment belonged to a friend. When she got to the door, there was a Secret Service man seated outside. "Mrs. Kavanagh? Go right on in."

She was greeted by Mrs. Roosevelt, who offered her tea. "As you know," Eleanor said in that high-pitched voice famous to all America, "I write the 'My Day' column six days a week, and, frankly, my dear, I need help. As you can see from the events in Europe over the last week or so, things may be getting a little more hectic."

"I'd love to help you, Mrs. Roosevelt. It's time for a change in my life. I've been nursing since I was a girl in Dublin."

"Nursing is such a fine profession."

"I know it is, Mrs. Roosevelt, but there are times of change in every woman's life, and I think I'm at that threshold."

"How did you meet Congressman Kavanagh?"

Róisín laughed. "In the General Post Office during the Easter Uprising. He was one of my patients."

"How romantic!"

"He had a hole in his arse!"

"Don't we all." The two women first blushed in unison and then laughed heartily together.

"Oh," said Róisín, "I didn't mean it like that. He was wounded in his bottom. We fell in love over a number of years. He's a wonderful husband and father."

"That's wonderful, Róisín—may I call you Róisín?"

"Of course, you may, Mrs. Roosevelt."

"And you might as well call me Eleanor." The First Lady turned serious. "This is my 'hiding house,'" she confessed. "I can't stand Washington. I much prefer the Village. So it would be convenient to have someone in the neighborhood here to work on my columns and the occasional book. What are your qualifications?"

"Well," said Róisín, "I'm Irish."

"That does seem to be a literary advantage, I must admit."

"I'm well read. I read almost all the New York papers every day and I love books—and, in a way, the people who write them."

"Have you written anything?"

"No," said Róisín honestly, "but I want to. I've lived in such exciting times, and I think I have something to say."

"Good for you! How are your politics?"

"A lot more radical than my revolutionary husband!"

Mrs. Roosevelt howled. "We share the same dilemma." She turned pensive. "I don't know what I shall do with Franklin. He could be a much better, more progressive president." Róisín was amused that they both thought their so-called "liberal" husbands weren't that liberal at all. Eleanor liked this Dublin woman with the wide smile, freckled nose, and dancing, intelligent eyes, still marvelously youthful at forty-one. "You come with a very high recommendation from my husband. He thinks you're 'swell,' as he likes to say. Tell you what, Róisín. Can you get a leave of absence at St. Vincent's?"

"I think I can."

"That way, if it doesn't work out, you can return to nursing. But I think we'll be fine, you and I. You are obviously a highly intelligent woman. Well, then, Róisín, should we give it a try?" And, like they say in the movies, it was the beginning of a beautiful friendship.

38

EOIN'S DIARY
TUESDAY, NOVEMBER 12, 1918

Thank God it's over.

The papers are full of the news that the Great War ended last night on the eleventh hour of the eleventh day. What that will mean for Ireland I'm not sure, but I am thrilled the carnage in the trenches is over.

The carnage in the trenches may be over, but the carnage in Dublin may just be beginning. Not surprisingly, there were great celebrations at Trinity College yesterday, with the students hoisting the Union Jack to the top of the entrance and carrying on in their usual obnoxious behavior. There were lots of jeers from regular Dubliners and quite a few scuffles around town. Róisín phoned this morning to tell me that the Mater was filled with dozens of injured Unionists and policemen. She said there were a few fatalities. And that's only one hospital. I haven't heard anything from Jervis Street, the Meath, or the South Dublin Union.

Mick came bursting into the Bachelors Walk office in high spirits. He was also glad the war was over—but for a different reason. "Now our work really begins!" he shouted.

"What are you talking about?"

"Elections, Eoin, elections!"

I told him Róisín had called about all the injuries that had come into the Mater. "Great work by GHQ," said Mick. He said that most of the injuries were inflicted by Volunteers on direct orders by Dick McKee and Dick Mulcahy. "Great work by my two Dicks!" crowed Mick.

I was about to say, "Yeah, two Dicks, and you're one big prick," but I thought better of it.

"According to reports," Mick went on, "there have been more than a hundred injuries and a few fatalities. The Volunteers came out without a scratch."

But the main thing on Mick's mind this morning were the elections. "This is the time to split from the British Empire. We're going to have our own parliament. We'll no longer sit with those hoors in Westminster."

"Yes," says I, "now we can sit with our own hoors right here in Dublin." That got a big laugh out of Mick, but I've never seen him looking so happy, looking forward to the new challenge. In my bones, I have an uneasy feeling. It looks like we'll be playing politics for a while, but I know the reality of the situation—and that reality will, eventually, be brutal.

39

As Collins climbed the stairs to the Bachelors Walk office, he could hear a female voice on a rampage.

"Fookin' British!" said Róisín in the loudest voice she had ever used on Eoin.

"I can't argue with that," said Collins, as he opened the door and threw his trilby hat on his desk and began taking his overcoat off. "With all that screechin' I heard on the stairs, I thought yer man was pleasurin' some Nighttown hoor." Róisín turned beet red and was about to let Collins have it when the Big Fellow put his hand up in surrender. "Only, jokin', Róisín," he said, then gave her a playful faux punch on the jaw. For once, Eoin was speechless in front of his boss.

"They are so unfair," snapped Róisín.

"Of course, they're not fair," said Collins. "That's what makes them British. What, exactly, is your complaint?"

"I can't vote in the general election."

"And what's the general consensus of the *Cumann na mBan*?"

"Connie is all upset. She wrote us from prison in England that we should make as much noise as possible."

"Poor Connie," said Collins in a voice that was not exactly rattling with confidence in the Countess Markievicz.

"What?" snapped O'Mahony, until she realized that Collins was needling her. With that, both Collins and Eoin burst out in laughter. "You're a big jeer, you are, Mick Collins."

"Róisín, love, I can't help it. You're too easy." Eoin didn't like the "Róisín, love" stuff, but he kept it to himself.

"Well," replied Róisín primly, "I guess I am."

"She's a suffragette, without the suffrage," offered Eoin.

Róisín was still peeved. "Who decided a woman has to be thirty in order to vote?"

"Probably some man," said Eoin, helpfully.

"You bet it's some fookin' man."

"How old are you, Róisín?" asked Collins.

"I'm almost twenty."

"Nineteen," corrected Collins.

"How old are *you*?" Róisín shot right back.

"Twenty-eight," said Collins.

"If you had my genitalia, you wouldn't be allowed to vote either." *Genitalia*, thought Eoin, *there's that word again.*

"If I had your genitalia, I'd be in a different line of work!" replied Collins, getting a great laugh out of the room. "Róisín?"

"Yes?"

"Why vote once when you can vote twenty times?"

"Twenty!"

"I'm not jokin'," said Collins. "We can get the *Cumann na mBan* ladies working all over the country. The victims of the famine will be voting this year!"

"We shouldn't have any problem with this election," opined Róisín. "The country is with us right now."

Collins looked down at the young couple and added a dose of reality. "One, things change. Two, take nothing for granted. This is our chance. We are going to *crush* the British in this election, and we are going to work hard to do it. We will leave no stone unturned." The intensity on Collins's face was almost frightening. "This time, my young friends, Ireland will not be denied! And that's that!"

Róisín and Eoin, paralyzed by Collins's little speech, knew the British had, indeed, met their match.

40

C ollins was a natural at electioneering. Although he liked to portray himself as only a humble "soldier," he was, as he would prove in the years to come, a master politician.

With Eoin in tow, he hit the towns and fields of South Cork on market days, chatting up anyone who would talk with him, whether they were selling livestock or sitting in a pub. In one hamlet, he found a bunch of "ould wans," as he called them, sitting on a bench in front of a general store. "Ah," said Collins to Eoin, "the Banshee Brigade!" They were ancient, dressed in black from head to toe; only their wrinkled faces peeked out of their shawls. As he approached them, they were very quiet— until Collins turned on the charm.

"How are ya, missus?" he asked every one of them. "Aren't we having fine weather, even for this time of the year?"

"We are, indeed," one of them replied. "And what is your name?"

"I am Michael Collins, and I'm running for the Irish parliament— not in London, but in Dublin. It's time we took control of Ireland's future."

"Yes," the woman agreed. "*tUasal Ó Coileáin*," she added, addressing "Mr. Collins" in the Irish, "a real Irish parliament would be a great victory for poor ould Ireland." Collins shook her hand vigorously at the smart reply. He was sure he had the people behind him.

"I'm glad you agree with me," he said, bent over her like a question mark and still holding her hand from the shake, their eye contact intense. "Now, remember to vote for me on December 14th. Vote for the whole *Sinn Féin* slate, and we'll be rid of these British hoors in no time!"

There was, at first, silence, and Collins looked horrified that he had let the word slip by his lips. Then the women began to laugh, and, since they were enjoying his indiscretion, he burst out with his own guffaw. "You're the bold *garsún*," the old woman finally said.

"I am indeed, missus," he said, tipping his hat as they moved on. "There's three votes there," he said to Eoin.

"You think?" said Eoin, with a gentle tweak. Collins gave him his famous "look," and Eoin smiled.

Eoin enjoyed these weekend trips to Cork with Collins in November and December, for it gave him a chance to view his mentor in his natural environment. It seemed Collins knew everyone around Clonakilty. It was a pleasure meeting Michael's sister Mary and brother Johnny, and he enjoyed their immense hospitality. Michael was the youngest of the family, and his siblings loved telling stories of the naughty Michael and his youthful misadventures. The suddenly important revolutionary tried hard to turn the conversation around but with little success. It was easy to see how much love was spent on Collins-the-boy by his adoring family.

Back in Dublin, a lot of the politicking fell on Eoin's shoulders. Candidates had to be found and put on the ballot. Voting rolls had to be reviewed to spot strengths and weaknesses. *Sinn Féin* reinforcements had to be sent from Dublin to troubled precincts throughout the provinces.

Collins was particularly interested in inflicting heavy casualties on the Irish Parliamentary Party. Its leader, John Redmond, had died earlier in the year, so the IPP was rudderless. But Collins had never forgiven Redmond for offering Irish support in Britain's war without securing the enactment of Home Rule. And to compound the felony in Collins's eyes, the IPP could do nothing to stop the conscription bill from passing. When conscription was passed, the IPP walked out in protest. Collins wanted to turn that walk into a full running retreat. From now on, he pledged, Irishmen would not be fodder for England's international adventures. His plan for the IPP was annihilation.

Eoin, working out of the Bachelors Walk office, was inundated with telephone calls and telegraphs from all over the country. Collins had attached a sign to the wall: VOTE EARLY, VOTE OFTEN. This time, it was no joke.

Sinn Féin volunteers were dispatched to check the parish death rolls going back to 1915. With all the confusion of the general election, it would be very difficult for local officials to keep up with who was dead and who was breathing. Collins saw nothing wrong with the dead voting to bring democracy to Ireland.

Men of voting age were told not to shave for the next month. A good beard was worth at least four votes. First, there was the full beard (vote one); then just the mustache and goatee (vote two); then the mustache (vote three); and finally the clean-shaven face (vote four). Poll watchers who didn't go along with Collins's plans could be neutralized by showing them a Mauser bulge. This policy was particularly important in "swing" districts where *Sinn Féin* would have to fight for votes. Collins was leaving nothing to chance.

When the votes were counted, it was an overwhelming victory for *Sinn Féin*. They won seventy-three of 105 seats and swept the country, except for four counties in Ulster. The IPP was reduced from eighty seats to six.

"Now," said Collins to Eoin, "the fun begins."

41

"Look what I found."

Johnny Three held Eoin's pocketwatch, dangling from its fob, in front of his wife. "Where did you find it?" asked Diane.

"In the last suit he wore," said Johnny. "It was in the vest, or the 'waistcoat,' as he always called it."

"Boy," said Diane, "that's an antique. It might be worth something."

"It's priceless."

"Priceless? Why?"

"Look." Johnny held the watch in front of Diane and opened its lid. "Look at that."

Diane took the watch into her hand and strained to read the inscription. "I can't see it," she said. "Let me get my glasses."

"You're getting old."

"And you're getting close to big trouble." Diane dropped her spectacles to the end of her nose and read:

> *Eoin Chaombánach, a chara,*
> *Do chara, Mícheál Ó Coileáin*
> *Nollaig, 1918*

"What does it mean? It's in Gaelic."

Johnny took the watch and squinted to see the engraving. Then he read:

> "To Eoin Kavanagh, My Friend
> From Your Friend, Michael Collins
> Christmas, 1918."

"That's beautiful," said Diane, getting tearful.

"That's a beautiful piece of history," agreed Johnny. "No one knew about the secret to this watch but me and my grandmother. Did you know that?"

"No, I didn't. What was the big secret?"

"I think it was kind of the old man's love bond with Collins." Eoin paused. "He always carried it with him to remind him of Collins's relentless tunnel vision."

Diane took the watch back from Eoin, closed the lip, and kissed it. "I wish we'd never found that damn diary."

"Why?"

"Because it's just too heartbreaking for me."

"Geez," said Eoin, "I doubt it went down to easy for Grandpa, either."

"I didn't mean that," said Diane, wiping an eye dry. "I just wish they all didn't have to suffer so much."

And suffer the Kavanaghs did. Christmas 1918 was to be their last holiday together as a family. Collins had headed to Cork for the holidays, and Eoin and Róisín decided to put together a Christmas dinner for the family. Da was delighted that the two of them were "courting," as he liked to say. Mary and Dickie were brought home from their orphanages, and the barbershop at 31 Aungier Street came alive with children's laughter, if only for a week. On Christmas Day, Róisín sent the entire family off to mass at Saints Michael and John's down on Wood Quay, while she stayed home and cooked a fat goose. Róisín could do without the cooking, but any excuse to avoid mass was good enough for her. She had gone to midnight mass on Christmas Eve, she fibbed when they asked. Mary and Dickie were delighted that Father Christmas had brought them toys, but Frank was still his morose self. "Cheer up, grumpy," Róisín had said to him, but he remained stale.

The whole clan sat down around the table in the flat above Castle Barbers. Before he carved, Joseph Kavanagh said grace and thanked the Lord—and Michael Collins—for rescuing his family from desperate poverty. Then, almost as an afterthought, he said, "Please, Lord, protect this family in 1919," as if he knew of a terrible foreboding.

Johnny laughed as he wound the old pocket watch. "What's so funny?" asked his wife.

"Grandpa was the only man I ever knew who wore a wristwatch *and* carried a pocket watch. What an eccentric!"

"He sure was a stickler for time," said Diane. "Nothing would piss him off more than people who were late."

"And guess where he got that from?"

"Mr. Collins?"

"I'd *hate* to be late for the Big Fellow. You could be made permanently 'late' for being late."

Diane laughed and then turned serious. "1919 will be bad, won't it?"

"Diane, my love," said Johnny, as he took his wife's hand, "it won't be nice." He paused. "And what comes after that will be even worse."

1919

1919

42

"Let's buccaneer the hoor!"

Michael Collins's 1919 actually started during the last week of December, when the newly minted MP-elect traveled to London. He was there to meet with the "hoor" he wanted to buccaneer—Woodrow Wilson, President of the United States of America.

There was only one problem—the president had no intention of meeting with the Irish delegation, as it would be insulting to his host, British Prime Minister David Lloyd George. It turned out that all the talk about the integrity of small nations was just that—talk. With the Huns out of Belgium, promises were being forgotten.

"That constipated-faced Presbyterian," said Collins of Wilson. "We'll take him, hold him for an hour, and present our agenda to him. He can't ignore us." But ignore the Irish Wilson did. Cooler heads finally prevailed, and the young MP-who-would-never-be returned to Dublin.

The first *Dáil Éireann* convened in the Mansion House on January 21, and Collins was not there. He was back in England "on business," as he liked to say. Eoin was in the gallery when the new Republic's first *Teachtaí Dála*, Deputies to the *Dáil*, or TDs, were sworn in. Twenty-five—including the missing Collins—were "*i láthair*," or "present." Forty-three, including Eamon de Valera, were not as lucky. In their absence, they were described as being "*fé ghlas ag Gallaibh*," or "imprisoned by the foreign enemy."

Eoin was dressed in his Sunday best, and his breast swelled with pride. The results from all the hard work he had done were now right

153

before his eyes. From his bloody arse, to stealing the Longford election, to setting up the intelligence bureau—it had all been worth it. Eoin was so proud of his new infant nation.

The whole session took place in Irish, and Eoin could pick out only single words or the odd phrase now and then. There was no Gaelic taught in the schools, as the English continued to try to delouse the Irish of every vestige of their culture. All the pidgin Irish Eoin knew he had picked up from his granny, Mary Anne Conway, Rosanna's mother. She was born during the Great Famine and loved to tell the youngster tales of old Dublin. Eoin was her first grandson, and he spent many a happy Sunday afternoon in her flat over on Temple Lane. Granny Conway told him that, in the olden days, Temple Lane used to be called "Dirty Lane." And in Eoin's mind, until the day he died, he couldn't think of Temple Lane as anything but his granny's "Durty Lane." Then suddenly, in 1909, his granny was no more. He remembered the funeral mass at Saints Michael and John's down on Wood Quay, only blocks from Temple Lane. He knew this church well, because his mother always reminded him that she had married his father there in 1900. It seemed the church and the neighborhood were Eoin's womb, and now an important part of that had been taken away from him. He knew, too, that his granny would take pride in this important day in Irish history.

But the real work on this twenty-first day of January was being done in the Soloheadbeg quarry in County Tipperary. There, Volunteers led by Seán Treacy, Séamus Robinson, Seán Hogan, and Dan Breen had hijacked a cart containing a hundredweight of gelignite, and in the process shot two RIC policemen dead.

The next morning, the phone rang in the Bachelors Walk office. "You've been preempted, Deputy Collins," said Eoin. "Have you seen the morning papers?"

"No," said Collins. "What happened?"

"The big, black headline says TIPPERARY OUTRAGE!"

There was a shout on the other end of the line. "For fook's sake, what happened?"

"Some of the boyos lifted a ton of gelignite from the Soloheadbeg quarry in Tipperary. Two RIC shot dead."

"God bless them!" said Collins, with joyful fire. "Finally," he added, "I've found men who will fight!"

"There's a rumor on the streets that this is your job."

"I wish it were. I can't be in two places at once."

"Do you know who did it?"

"I'll bet Seán Treacy, Dan Breen, and company," said Collins. "Do you realize that these are the first two Brits killed in Ireland since the Rising? Great, great fookin' work."

"The papers are against this kind of conduct," said Eoin. "You should see this morning's editorials."

"Fook their editorials," said Collins. "These hoors have been lifting us, imprisoning us, harassing us, and I haven't heard a word out of the fookin' papers or fookin' priests about that! Eoin, we're at the beginning of something big. We now have our own parliament, and soon we'll have our own army."

"You'll have to find bodies," replied Eoin. "With the Great War over, the lads are leaving. No conscription, no Volunteers. I've seen the reports from the countryside."

"Yes, we're in trouble in the country," Collins admitted. "But Tipperary will fight. Kerry will fight, and I know my own Cork will fight."

"Rebel Cork!" Eoin yelled into the phone with delight.

"Rebel Cork, indeed!" Collins echoed back across the line. "But it all starts and stops in Dublin. Dublin is the key. We will control the city. We will control it with the only thing that the British understand—fear and blood." Collins went quiet for a second, and Eoin thought they had lost their connection. "Are you with me, Eoin? Or will you desert me like the rest of those conscription hoors?"

"I'm with you to the death—whoever goes first!"

Collins laughed but then turned serious. "Don't worry, Eoin. It won't be you. You'll survive. Men like me? Ireland eats them up and spits them out. All you have to do is look at our history."

Eoin was sorry he had even mentioned Collins's possible death, but he knew one thing in his heart. He would never desert the Big Fellow, even if it meant following him to the grave.

43

EOIN'S DIARY

Before Mick rang off on me from England, he said, "Watch the mails."
When the post arrived this morning, I sorted it in my usual
way: Dublin, Irish Countryside, England, America. In the
England pile was a bulky package. There was no return address, but the
postmark said "Manchester." I opened it, and for a minute I didn't know
what to make of it. The note simply read: "Make two. Check with Gerry
Boland. Be quick. I'll be in touch."

It was Mick's scribble. I knew Gerry because he was Harry's brother.
But the contraption in the box was, at first, a mystery to me. Finally, I
figured out what it was—a key impression depressed in wax.

I immediately got on my bike and started the ride up to Gerry's
house on St. Vincent's Street, which is not far from the Mater Hospital.
When I got there, Gerry answered the door and took me into the parlor.

"What's up, Eoin?" he asked.

"You tell me, Gerry," I replied. "I just got this from Mick in Manchester.
I know he's there with your brother, but I'm in the dark otherwise. Do
you know?"

Gerry took the key mold from my hand and shook his head. "I guess
they're going to go ahead with it."

"With what?"

Gerry was silent for a moment, then said, "I guess it would be alright
to tell you."

This sounded serious, and I finally let out an exasperated, "What?"

"Gerry and Mick are going to spring de Valera from Lincoln Gaol in Lincolnshire," he explained. "This is the key to the gate Dev's supposed to dance through. Looks like he made the impression from the stubs of old candles."

"Mick could have told me," I told Gerry.

"It was all hush-hush," he replied. "I just kind of stumbled on it myself from Harry. You know what this means?"

"Fookin' big," says I. "I knew something was up when Mick missed that first meeting of the *Dáil*. What we need is a Fenian locksmith."

"Dinny Doyle, down in Henry Street."

"What's Doyle's story?" I asked.

"He's in the Volunteers. Part-timer. Helps out when he can."

"Let's go," I said, and the two of us hopped on our bikes for the quick ride into the City Centre. We found "Henry Keys" and entered the premises.

"Dinny," says Gerry, "we have a job for you."

"Jaysus, Gerry," says Doyle, "not today. I'm up against it."

I threw the mold down on the counter and said, "I need two keys made from this today."

"I can't."

"You can't," says I. "What do you mean 'you can't?' I need those keys by this afternoon." I slammed my hand on the counter, and I could see the dust rise.

"Who is this bloody kid?" says Dinny.

Gerry looked uncomfortable, but then he caught my eye. He turned to Dinny and said, "He works for Mick Collins."

The color left Doyle's face. He didn't say a word. He picked up the mold and went into the back of the shop. I followed him. "How long will it take?"

"A couple of hours."

"I'll wait."

I told Gerry I could handle it from here. Dinny was good to his word, and I returned to Bachelors Walk to wrap the keys and await Collins's instructions. The phone was quiet. I kept taking my pocket watch out and looking at it. The quiet was killing me. Finally, at half-three, the phone rang. "Mr. Kavanagh," I answered.

"Mr. Kavanagh," said a voice with a West Cork accent, "did you get my bloody keys yet?"

"Fook you, Mick!" says I. "You could have told me."

My insult provoked only laughter out of Collins "I take it you're ready to go to the post office?"

"I am. Give me that address." I jotted the information down. "When's the big day?"

"I can't tell you that, Eoin," said Mick. "Just keep this one under your hat. Keep an eye on the newspapers. If we pull it off, the newspapers will be printing EXTRAs all over Dublin and England."

I addressed the package and tied it strongly with twine. Then I walked to the post office over on St. Andrew Street, clutching it to my breast like the keys were made of gold. I was thrilled to be the "key man" and helping get Dev out of jail—and embarrassing the British in the process.

44

"*The divil pulled it off!*"

So wrote Eoin in his diary on February 5, 1919. Mick was right about the newspaper EXTRAs. Dublin was in a state of frenzied celebration. You could hear the laughter and see the delight on the faces of the citizens. De Valera was free, and the Brits were red-faced.

On the night of February 3, Collins and Harry Boland went to Lincoln Gaol with one of the keys Eoin had made in Dublin. The other key—smuggled into the prison in the much clichéd cake—was in the hands of de Valera on the other side of the prison door. At the precise time of the rendezvous, Collins stuck his key in the door—and snapped it in half! "Jaysus, Dev, I broke the fookin' hoor in the fookin' keyhole," said Collins.

"Michael," replied de Valera through the door, "your language!" Collins didn't know who he wanted to kill more—the bloody key or de Valera. Dev stuck his own key in the door and, in a stroke of luck, pushed Collins's broken key out, turned the lock, and was free.

"I can't believe Collins," said Diane, after reading Eoin's rendition of the Lincoln Gaol caper. "This guy is like James Bond—only worse!"

"You mean 'better,'" responded Johnny Three. "James Bond had nothing on Michael Collins, believe me." They were sitting in the kitchen of Eoin's house, having their morning coffee.

"But how did he do it?" asked Diane. "Here's this country boy going up against Lloyd George and Woodrow Wilson, and he's not awed by it at all."

"I think," said Johnny, "that was his big advantage. The British underestimated him. You know their attitude: 'The Irish wouldn't *dare* do such and such.' Well, *this* Irishman said, 'Fuck them, I'm doing it!'"

"What would have happened if he didn't get de Valera out?" Diane asked as Johnny poured another cup of coffee for himself.

"A very interesting supposition," said Johnny, laughing.

"What's so funny?"

"You know what Dev did when he got out of jail?"

"What?"

"He went to America for a year and a half."

"You're kidding!" Diane exclaimed, and Johnny let out an amused, knowing laugh. "You mean Collins—and Grandpa—went to all that trouble, and he up and left them high and dry?"

"Dev was difficult."

"No wonder Mick called him the 'Long Hoor,'" Diane said, showing agitation for the first time. "Why, that's like George Washington crossing the Delaware and heading off to France for a two-year vacation!"

"Not a bad analogy, my sweet," said Johnny.

The conversation was interrupted by the ringing of Diane's telephone. "Hi Róisín," Diane said to her eldest daughter, named after her great-grandmother. "We're both fine. We're planning on being home for Thanksgiving. The house is on the market, and we're trying to get rid of it ASAP." Johnny gestured for the telephone, and Diane handed it over.

"How's our number-one daughter?" Johnny asked.

"Oh, Daddy," said Róisín, "you're such a sweet talker!"

"I am, indeed," said Johnny. "You keeping up on your studies? I want you out of that college next June. You're costing me a fortune!"

"You sound just like Great-Grandpapa. Always worried about money."

"On trees. . . " began Johnny.

". . . It does not grow!" shouted Róisín into the telephone, and Johnny could see the personality of both his grandmother and his wife in the spunky child.

"Alright," said Johnny, "you still going with that creep Dylan you brought home last summer?" Johnny was firmly of the belief that most of the problems in the modern world were caused by old hippies naming their progeny "Dylan."

"We might be in love," said Róisín.

"Well," admonished Johnny, "keep your knickers on!"

"Too late for that, Daddy!"

Johnny was about to blow a gasket when Diane said, "Give me that" and pulled the phone out of Johnny's hand, leaving him with his mouth agape.

After the call ended, Johnny said, "She's still going with that Dylan bastard."

"He's a nice young man," said Diane.

"He just wants to get into her knickers."

"So unlike what you were up to with me thirty years ago!"

"That was *different*," protested Johnny.

"Sure it was," said Diane, and Johnny knew he had lost another battle with his wife and daughter.

"I wish they would call more."

"They text me all the time," said Diane.

"I don't do texting."

"They're lucky you answer the phone," Diane said, exposing the true Luddite inside her husband. Johnny was quiet. "Are you sorry we never had a son?"

"Never," said Johnny. "I much prefer the girls. I couldn't stand some son of mine repeating the same stupid testosterone mistakes I made in my life." Johnny shook his head. "I can't believe the way men treat women sometimes. If I were a woman, I'd become a lesbian because of all the macho nonsense."

"Oh, thank you, Alice B. Toklas!" added Diane with a hearty laugh.

"I'll smoke to that, Gertrude," was Johnny's reply.

"Alice B. Kavanagh, I love you!" laughed Diane, as she kissed her Johnny on the top of his head.

Johnny was being truthful, for he loved all three of his girls. After being married for seven years, working hard on their careers, and having fun drinking at the Lion's Head at night, Diane had drunkenly demanded of Johnny, "I want babies, and I want them now!" So Johnny fucked her on the kitchen floor in the family apartment at 45 Christopher Street, and, nine months later, Diane got her wish. Róisín was the first, and Aoife and Ashling were his "Irish twins"—Aoife born in January and Ashling born in December of the same year. All three were born within a two-year period. "You damn near fucked me to death those two years," Diane used to kid her husband.

"I damn near fucked my bank book to death," was Johnny's response.

"We were saved by my IUD!" exclaimed Diane.

"We were saved by your IUD—and the creative use of other sophisticated orifices!"

Diane got up and kissed Johnny on the top of his head again. "And I enjoyed it too, darling," laughed Dirty Di.

"Whatever," said Johnny, his face flushed. "We did okay."

"We did more than okay!"

Johnny again began wading through Eoin's diaries. "So?" said his wife.

"So?"

"So," said Diane, taking a bite of toast with lots of creamy Irish butter, "what's up with de Valera's obsession with America?"

"Collins didn't want him to go," said Johnny. "He figured the head of the fledgling Republic should stay and fight."

"A novel idea."

"But not for de Valera," said Johnny, as he continued to pore through Eoin's papers. "Dev thought he could be of more use in America, gaining recognition for the Republic and raising funds. Look at what Collins said to Grandpa: *'You know what it is to try to argue with Dev. He says he thought it all out while in prison, and he feels the one place where he can be useful to Ireland is in America.'*"

"That is so bizarre," said Diane.

"But it was for the best."

"Why?"

"Because when Dev left, Collins won the war," explained Johnny. "If de Valera had stayed, I'm sure there would have been disagreements over Collins's methods. And you know who went to America with Dev?" Diane shook her head. "Harry Boland."

Diane laughed. "So the Big Fellow began to put the moves on pristine Kitty Kiernan."

"My, you have a suspicious mind!"

"I have a dirty mind," said Diane, "and I *know* men. Remember, all's fair in love and war."

"For when the cat's away, the mice will play."

"Yeah," said Diane with a twinkle in her eye. "At all times, ya got to keep an eye on the Pulchritudinous Pussy."

"Pulchritudinous Pussy!" guffawed her husband. My, how Johnny Kavanagh loved his Dirty Di.

45

The *Dáil* met for the second time on April Fool's Day. De Valera was appointed *Príomh-Aire*, or First Minister, and Collins was selected to be the Republic's first Minister for Finance, *an Aire Airgid*.

With the politics of the day out of the way, Collins, with vehemence, got back to his primary task—intelligence. He summoned Ned Broy to the Bachelors Walk office. "How about a peek at those intelligence reports?" Collins asked.

Broy looked at Eoin and shook his head, "The boy."

"That's the boy," said Collins, "who reads your intelligence reports."

"Mr. Kavanagh?" said Broy with surprise.

"The one and the same," said Collins.

"Nice to meet you, Mr. Broy," Eoin added.

"Call me Ned."

"You can call me Eoin," said the imp, and the three of them laughed.

"Now that we're all grand pals," said Collins, cutting to the chase, "how about me looking at those delicious files on the filthy Fenians."

"I can't take them out of Brunswick Street," said Broy.

"Who said anything about taking them out?" responded Collins. "I'll go in."

"To Brunswick Street? You're daft!" said Broy, and Eoin nodded his head in agreement.

"There is no place as quiet as the lion's den when the lion is sleeping," said Collins.

"Meaning?" said Broy.

"Meaning how about next Monday night? What's that? April seventh."

"Mick . . ." began Broy.

"Next Monday, Ned. I'll be there at the wishing hour."

"Bring candles," said Broy. "And a gun."

At midnight, Broy let Collins in through the back entrance on Townsend Street. "Did you bring the candles?" he asked Collins, as he unlocked the door to the DMP's "Fenian Room."

"I thought you were jokin'," said Collins.

Broy looked exasperated. He exited the room and returned with a few old stubs of candles. "Do you at least have matches?" Collins fished in his waistcoat pocket and displayed his pack. "And gun?" Collins gave him a smile, indicating Broy didn't have to worry about that. "Then," said Broy, "you're on your own!"

"Come back for me in three hours' time," commanded Collins, and a chill ran down Broy's spine out of fear. In front of Collins was a treasure trove—all the files on all the boys in Ireland, England, the U.S., Canada, and even Australia. Never before had a Fenian had such access to such secret information. "These bastards," said Collins, beginning to steam at the arrogance of the British. He took his notebook out and jotted down information. The British knew everything. Collins couldn't believe that the rebels had even got this far with all the intelligence the British had collected on their organization.

Then he came across it—the file marked "Michael Collins." They knew all about him, going back to his IRB days in London. It was all there, from the GPO to his incarceration in Sligo. "He comes from a brainy Cork family," he read, and was finally forced to smile. Then he heard a ruckus out on the street. A window in the building had been broken, and some drunken soldier was shouting at the top of his lungs. Collins blew his candle out and sat there in the dark. The coppers went out and took the drunk inside, and Collins gave a sigh of relief. He lit the candle again and went back to his file. They even had a picture of him. Luckily it wasn't very good. He put it in his pocket, a souvenir of his night in Brunswick Street.

He heard a key at the door. Collins blew again, and the room went dark. It was Broy. "Time's up. Get the hell out of here." As Broy let

Collins slip out into Townsend Street, he asked, "Well, what do you think?"

"I think we've been fooked," said Collins. "But I'll promise you one thing, Ned. From now on, we're going to be doing the fooking." And with that, Michael Collins disappeared into the Dublin night.

46

The post on the morning of April 9 brought some much-needed fear to Dublin Castle:

CEASE AND DESIST FROM ALL POLITICAL ACTIVITIES
BEFORE IT'S TOO LATE.
YOU'VE BEEN WARNED

"I'm not letting any young scuts," said Detective Sergeant Sebastian Blood as he read Eoin's perfectly typed letter, "tell me how to do my duty!"

"What's the matter, Sergeant?" asked Detective Constable Brendan Boynton.

"Who do they think they are!" Blood spat. "Threatening the Crown!"

"You got one of those letters, too?" said Boynton, holding up his own copy.

"Guttersnipes," said Blood. "We'll teach them!"

"Calm down," Boynton soothed. "The boyos are just trying to show us they're in the game."

"This can't be allowed."

Blood had just been sent down from Belfast to harass the Fenians. He had all the qualifications that a smart, young RIC G-man going places should have: Presbyterian, the proper lodge, and, of course, a deep hatred for Catholics. This was the kind of man, they thought in London, who would eventually bring the nationalists to their knees.

Like Boynton, Blood was young for a job in the G-Division, but the British were rapidly discovering that they needed young men to keep up with the infant IRA. Blood—Boynton had learned from the few weeks that the two had worked desk-to-desk in Dublin Castle—was full of indignant bristle. His hatred of the nationalists was matched only by his love of clothes. He was impeccable from head to toe, and he liked to punctuate his Orangeman shibboleths by pounding his brass-handled walking cane into the floor *twice*. To Boynton, he was just the first in what was sure to become a long line of pompous Belfast RIC eejits sent to disrupt the rebels.

"It starts now," Collins told Eoin the morning after his Brunswick Street adventure. Collins quickly dictated the two-sentence letter to Eoin. "Send a separate letter to every G-man in Brunswick Street and Dublin Castle."

"How about Broy and Boynton?"

"Them, too," said Collins. "We've got to keep their cover. I want to see the reaction. We'll start roughing them up if they don't resign. And we'll eliminate them if they continue their intelligence work. We mean business," said Collins, slamming his hand down on his desk to punctuate the word "business." "Look at the shite I found," he said holding up a typewritten telephone log.

"What is it?" asked Eoin.

"It's a log of every telephone message that the RIC got during the Rising."

Eoin went down the list line-by-line, then slowly looked up. "We know some of these people. They're supposed to be on our side."

"This is why we have to move now and move fast," said Collins. "It's the same old story—we plot rebellion, and the informers do us in. Well, that shite is going to stop, and that's that. Remove their eyes and ears, and they're impotent. Dead men don't make telephone calls!"

At Dublin Castle, Blood continued his diatribe. "Who do they think they are? First a Rising, now a so-called *Dáil*." Blood pronounced it "*Dale*."

"*Doyle*," corrected Boynton.

"What?"

"It's pronounced '*Doyle*.'"

"I don't bloody well care," shouted Blood, "how it's bloody pronounced! It's an illegal assembly, and we have to put an end to it."

"Easier said than done," answered Boynton.

"We should imprison their leaders immediately."

"We tried that," reminded Boynton. "It didn't work."

"Shoot them!"

"Tried that, too."

"Well," Blood insisted, "we have to make an example out of *someone*!"

Boynton turned his head away and was forced to smile. Collins would know about Blood's reaction shortly and how he wanted to make an "example" out of someone. Boynton looked at the red-faced Blood again and almost felt sorry for him, for he didn't know who or what he was up against—the newly appointed Minister for Finance of the Irish Republic, one Michael Collins.

47

EOIN'S DIARY

I *have just spent the oddest week of my life with Eamon de Valera.*

Late last week, Mick came into the Bachelors Walk office and informed me that Dev needed an office for a short period, and he was going to give him the lend of the Exchequer Street one. He also informed me that I was going to go along with the office and be at the disposal of Mr. de Valera. I know it's an honor to work for the First Minister, but I really wanted no part of it.

My "But Micks . . ." were ignored.

"Shut yer gob and keep yer ears open," Collins said. "Is that understood?" I nodded. "Nothing about this office, your father's shop, the Lincoln Gaol keys, or our intelligence gathering." I thought it was a little odd, but I think Mick wants to keep everything close to the vest.

I was at the office on Monday at 7:00 a.m. to await Dev's arrival from Greystones. I kept looking at my pocket watch, but there was no sign of him. Finally, at a quarter after eleven, the door opened, and this immensely tall, gaunt figure stood in the dark doorway. For a minute, my imagination ran away with me, and I thought it was Abe Lincoln, of all people. "Eoin Kavanagh?" the deep voice said to me.

"*Príomh-Aire!*" I said, referring to him as the First Minister of the *Dáil.*

"Yes, Eoin," he said, examining me and the office all at once, "Minister Collins said I could use this office for a week or so."

"Yes," says I, "Mick—eh, I mean the Minister—told me you would be coming." I still can't get it in my head that Mick is the Minister for Finance.

"Very well," he said. "Is that my desk?"

"Yes, *Príomh-Aire*," says I, "that's your desk." I showed him to his chair, where he sat down without taking off his coat jacket and began going through a briefcase. He didn't say a word to me for the next half-hour. I went about my usual business.

"Eoin," the deep voice broke the silence.

"Yes, *Príomh-Aire*."

"What exactly do you do for Minister Collins?"

"Oh," I said, as innocently as possible. "I do Mick's—I mean the Minister's—messages. Just the regular stuff. Make his tea. Go to the post office for him. Run his errands all over town."

"I see," said the First Minister.

"Would you like a cup of tay?" I asked hopefully.

"No, thank you. Are you still in school?" he asked, in a way that made it clear that he was a schoolmaster through and through.

"No," says I, "I haven't been to school in years."

"I see," he said, rather coldly, I thought.

"How long have you worked for the organization?"

"Since Easter Monday." I saw that I had piqued the First Minister's attention.

"Where?"

"Jacob's and the GPO."

"I see," the First Minister said. "Do you see yourself going into politics?"

I was about to say, "Well, maybe, after Mick and I get the British hoors out of Ireland!" but I thought better of it. "Maybe someday," I simply replied.

"If you are a young man," said the *Príomh-Aire* as if he were lecturing a calculus class, "going in for politics, I will give you two pieces of advice—study economics, and read *The Prince*." I nodded. "Do you know what *The Prince* is?" I shook my head. "It is a political science work by Niccolò Machiavelli. Have you ever heard of him?"

"No, I haven't," I replied honestly, thinking that he sounded like an I-talian chipper I knew down on Cork Street.

"He was a political scientist. He has no peer."

I nodded numbly, and, with that, the First Minister rose and went out to his lunch. I jotted down some items in my notebook to relay to Mick later. *Príomh-Aire* returned after his dinner and went to work on the phone, sometimes speaking in Irish so I wouldn't know what was going on. Over the next couple of days, many of his cronies came to see him. Seán T. O'Kelly, our man in Paris for the Versailles Peace Conference, stuck his head in the doorway and called out, "Chief!" They huddled together for an hour, whispering so low that I could not make out what they were saying. Cathal Brugha also stuck his head in, looking for "The Chief." I was even surprised to see Robert Briscoe, Mick's gun purveyor, pop in, looking for "My Chief."

"He's right over there, Mr. Briscoe," I said.

The only man I knew more than casually was Harry Boland. He's like Dev's aide-de-camp or something. There was a lot of talk about America when Harry visited, and I have a feeling the *Príomh-Aire* won't be hanging around Dublin much longer. Harry bade me goodbye and said, "I'm off to America to scout the Chief's trip."

"Harry," admonished de Valera, like it was a big secret that he couldn't wait to get out of Ireland and get to America.

"How's Miss Kiernan?" I asked.

"She well," said Harry. "I hope that Mick will take good care of her while I'm in America."

"I'm sure he will," I said, with more vehemence than I should have. Harry looked like he was going to say something but then just smiled.

"Harry," de Valera said again. I think he was getting upset with all the talk of America.

"Ah, Chief," said Harry, "you can trust Eoin. He's the Big Fella's Little Fella!" I blushed at the compliment, but *Príomh-Aire* looked at me suspiciously.

That was the first time Dev had heard the term "The Big Fella." Several of Collins's mates stuck their heads in during the week and said, "Is the Big Fella about?" "Where can I find the Big Fella?" "Will the Big Fella be at Vaughan's tonight?" I discreetly directed them away with as little information as possible.

"Eoin," de Valera said to me.

"Yes, *Príomh-Aire*."

"Who is this 'Big Fella' that everyone seems to be looking for?"

I was dumbfounded. "Why, that's Mick," I said, and Dev looked confused. "Minister Collins," I corrected myself.

"I see." De Valera was quiet for a moment. "So Minister Collins is 'The Big Fella.' He must make quite an impression on people. A Napoleonic nickname!"

I was tempted to tell him that Mick had a Napoleonic nickname for him too: "The Long Hoor." But I thought this might not be the time and the place.

On his last day at the office, he told me that I didn't have to call him *Príomh-Aire* or "First Minister" anymore. I was thrilled. Was it going to be "Eamon," or perhaps "Dev," or maybe even "Eddie," as I've heard some of the men refer to him?

"Eoin," he said, "you can call me 'Chief'!"

"Geez, *Príomh-Aire*," I said. "I mean, thanks, Chief!" And, with that, the Irish First Minister got up and left the building, obviously hot for America.

48

Eoin was already at work at the Bachelors Walk office when Collins and Liam Tobin arrived. "Good mornin' to ya," said Eoin. "Would you like a cup of tay?"

Collins grumbled something into his chest, and Tobin said "Yes, Eoin, that would be grand." Eoin made the tea and opened a tin of Jacob's Biscuits, which made him smile in irony.

"I'm a wanted man," Collins finally said.

"On what this time?" Eoin asked anxiously.

"Bench warrant from Sligo," said Collins. "Didn't show up for my trial."

"Like you had any intention to," added Tobin.

Collins grunted. "Fook 'em. They were looking for me up at the Munster Hotel last night."

"Better steer clear of number 44 Mountjoy Street," said Eoin.

"I'll never have me own bed to sleep in," lamented Collins, but then he brightened. "So how was your week with *Príomh-Aire*?"

Eoin looked at Collins and could see that he was having a hard time concealing a smirk. "I learned three things," said Eoin. "He can't wait to get out of here and to America."

"Common knowledge," said Tobin.

"He says I'm allowed to call him 'Chief.' And that I should read *The Prince* by Niccolò Machiavelli if I want to go into politics."

"Machiavelli!" roared Collins. "You've got to hand it to Dev. England has the Prince of Wales. Hamlet was the Prince of Denmark. Ireland has the Prince of Hoors! Machiavelli has nothing on Eddie de Valera."

Collins was still shaking his head in total amusement when Tobin said, "Mick has something to tell you, Eoin."

Collins immediately cut to the chase. "You're going to work for Liam," said Collins. He could see misapprehension in Eoin's eyes. "You're not being sent to a penal colony in Australia," Collins added, trying to soften the blow.

"Eoin," said Tobin, "you've done such a good job here at Bachelors Walk that we're going to move the whole operation over to Crow Street."

"We're finally getting down to serious business," Collins threw in.

Tobin was a tall, gaunt man who always had a sad look on his face. Eoin always thought he'd look good in a top hat working for Fanagan's, the Aungier Street undertakers. But he was a good sort, Eoin knew, and Mick trusted him implicitly. "Our plan is," said Tobin, "to channel all intelligence through the Crow Street office. Mick is now *officially* Director of Intelligence, and I'll be his adjutant."

"I feel we have to have a much more sophisticated operation," said Collins. "For starters, we need to know everything about every man in the G-Division. Then we have to separate the bad apples from the good."

"Good?" interjected Eoin.

"Yes," said Collins, "there are good ones. Broy and Boynton, for instance. There are also men who do us no harm, so I don't want to touch them."

"And we want to leave the regular DMPs to themselves," added Tobin. "If they don't bother us, we won't bother them. In fact, they can be helpful to us."

"That's Broy's idea," said Collins. "He says there are more nationalists in the peelers than any of us think. Our goal is to castrate their intelligence network here in Dublin."

"Castrate?" said Eoin, feeling it in his bollocks.

"Intelligence is mostly in the brain," said Collins. "Even stuff on paper is not that all that important. The brain is what we aim for."

"If we eliminate the brain . . ." said Tobin.

". . . They cannot process the intelligence," finished Collins.

Eoin was beginning to see what they were trying to do. "How is this 'castration' going to come about?"

"From your work," said Collins.

"You're going to shoot them, aren't you?"

There was a moment of silence in the room. "If we have to," Collins finally said.

"Are you alright with that, Eoin?" asked Tobin.

"I am," he responded thoughtfully, almost in a whisper.

"Well, in that case," said Collins, "start packing."

Eoin was packing up the files that were going over to Crow Street when the telephone rang. "Mr. Kavanagh," he answered.

"Ned Broy here, Eoin. Is Mick about?"

"He's over at that special session of the *Dáil* at the Mansion House. There are some important Yanks in town, and they're winin' and dinin' them."

"I have to get in touch with him," said Broy. "They're about to lift him on that bench warrant from Sligo."

"Shite," said Eoin. He hung up the phone quickly and headed out to Dawson Street.

When Eoin got to the Mansion House, he found the Minister for Finance sitting at his appointed desk, drumming his fingers on the surface as someone at the podium droned on about something. "Mick," he said, tapping Collins on the shoulder.

Collins spun around as quick as a top and began reaching into his pocket for what Eoin assumed was his trusty Colt pistol. "Jaysus, boy," he said, flustered. "Don't do that!"

"Sorry, Mick," Eoin apologized. "But this is an emergency."

He whispered into Collins's ear what Broy had told him and was surprised when Collins said, "Is that all? Let's have lunch first."

After lunch with several Irish-Americans—they were going on to the Paris peace conference to lobby President Wilson into recognizing the Irish Republic—Collins had a brainstorm. "Go over to Exchequer Street, and bring me my uniform," he told Eoin.

"Your uniform?"

"My new uniform," repeated Collins.

"Mick," said Eoin. "Don't."

"Get movin', lad," commanded Collins. "The G-men will be here soon!"

With his stomach churning, Eoin made his way to Exchequer Street and returned to the Mansion House with the uniform, only to find the place surrounded by the British Army, 250 strong, with G-men standing about waiting for their quarry to be hauled out into Dawson Street. But nothing happened. Fifteen minutes after Eoin arrived, the Brits left, apparently *sans* Minister Collins.

Eoin entered the Mansion House and saw that the place was in a frenzy. "Where's Deputy Collins?" Eoin asked Count Plunkett, the new Foreign Minister and father of Joseph Plunkett, executed in 1916.

"He's disappeared," said Plunkett, spittle landing on his beard in his excitement. Men were animatedly talking to each other about the British raid and the sudden disappearance of the Minister for Finance.

Eoin headed for the basement with the uniform box still under his arm. There he saw Collins calmly reading the *Irish Times*. "Give me that," said Collins as he started undressing in front of Eoin. Soon Collins was adjusting the collar on his new Commandant-General's uniform. "How do I look?" he asked.

"Like Lord Fookin' French!"

"Johnny French never looked this good," winked Collins. "Come on," he said, "let's give the Yanks a show!"

Collins strode into the chamber, strutting like a peacock, and stopped at the podium. "Was anyone in here looking for me?" he said to the assembled deputies and guests. Applause broke out, and cheers filled the room. "By this time," spoke up Collins, "everybody should know that it is by naked force that England holds this country." The Yanks, in awe of the audacious Irishman, looked on, slack-jawed.

At first, Eoin was cross, but, then, watching Mick work the room, he couldn't help but admire his boss. It was just Collins being Collins. It wasn't really conceit. It was Collins trying to prop his country and his people up against the British. He was like the little street imp with his thumb to his nose, wagging his fingers at the local bully—then sticking his tongue out at the same time for good measure. The Irish were just as good as ould Britannia—and Collins would personally prove it to his downtrodden people. But it still bothered him that Mick could be so reckless on a moment's notice, be it by allowing his picture to be taken or taunting the British up in Longford. In his heart, Eoin knew that Collins's relentless—yet systematic—recklessness would eventually free Ireland. But, conversely, it might be the death of him yet.

49

etective Sergeant Sebastian Blood needed a haircut and, being new in town, asked around the office at Dublin Castle for a recommendation. It was unanimous—Castle Barbers was the place to get tonsured.

Blood made his way down Aungier Street and had no problem finding number thirty-one. He entered the shop and felt right at home seeing Queen Victoria looking down on him. "Can I help you?" asked Joseph Kavanagh.

"Could I get a trim?"

"Take a seat." Blood stuck his cane in the umbrella bucket, placed his arse in the chair, and Joseph threw a sheet over him. Frank was shaving a customer in the adjoining chair.

Joseph started both clipping and small-talking. "Nice weather for this time of the year," he commented.

"It will be better weather when we rid this town of its Fenian element." Blood wore his heart on his sleeve, and Joseph's ears perked up. "How did a loyalist like you end up in this Fenian neighborhood?"

"I have a great reverence for authority," said Joseph, and Frank bit his lip to keep from laughing. "Did you hear about us up at the Castle?"

"Yes, indeed," said Blood. "You're well thought-of up there."

"We try to please," said Joseph. "You can sign up for our specials, reserved only for Castlemen."

"I'd like to do that," said Blood. "Do the locals give you any trouble?"

"Only the occasional catcall," replied Joseph. "The DMP on the beat keeps an eye out for us."

Blood reached under his sheet and presented Joseph with his card. "If any of the Fenian scum ever threaten you, give me a ring."

Joseph took the card and simply said, "Thank you."

"It won't be long now," said Blood as Joseph removed the sheet. Blood stood tall and preened for himself in the mirror.

"What won't be long?" asked his barber.

"We're winning this war," responded Blood. "It will all be over soon."

"That might be news to Mick Collins," said Frank, sorry as soon as the words escaped his lips.

"Collins?" said Blood.

"The Fenian guttersnipe," said Joseph, before Frank could dig himself in deeper, "who's always shooting off his gob in the papers."

"Yes, Collins," Blood mused.

"Thanks for the card," said Joseph, holding it up for show. "I'll put your name down. The first one is always on us."

"Thank you," said Blood. "What's your name?"

"Joseph Kavanagh, and this is my son, Francis."

Blood nodded and gave Joseph a two-bob tip. "Thanks again," Blood said, tapping his cane twice before he exited into Aungier Street, an unsteady thought already beginning to percolate in his brain.

50

It was meticulous work, gathering intelligence. Three Crow Street had J.F. Fowler Printers on the ground floor. One flight up was the "Irish Products Company." In reality, it was Michael Collins's main intelligence office. Eoin always started his day with every Dublin newspaper. He was interested in the general news of the day—what Inspector So-and-So of Dublin Castle had to say about the latest rebel atrocity—but he found his meat-and-potatoes in, of all places, the society pages. Who got engaged? Who was getting married? What child was being christened? What happened at that Church of Ireland charity gala at the Gresham Hotel last night? How did the annual meeting of the retired veterans of the Boer War go at the Shelbourne? There, in those mundane items, was where the intelligence nuggets were found.

Sergeant Joe English of the RIC attended his cousin's wedding out at Foxrock Monday morning. Who was Sergeant English? Check the cards. Joe English was supposed to be down in Tipperary. What was he doing in Dublin? Crosscheck the Tipperary cards. Get in touch with Broy or Boynton. What was Sergeant English *really* doing in Dublin? Keeping an eye on Fenian fugitives? It's not that long a way to Tipperary, Eoin Kavanagh was learning. A man out of his element, Eoin knew, was a dangerous man.

"If we ever win this war," said Eoin to his coworkers, "I'm getting a job as a gossip columnist." He knew more about Dublin high society than anyone else in the movement.

His most important weapons in this job were his scissors, paste, and index cards. If the British knew who was buying up all the index cards in Dublin City, they could easily crack this intelligence operation in a morning.

His phone number had been transferred from over in Bachelors Walk, and he was still Collins's "Mister Kavanagh." And he still visited number thirty-two every day to pick up his post. It was getting more complicated, but Collins and Tobin liked it that way. If it was confusing to the men running the intelligence scheme, it might be nearly impossible for the British trying to crack what was going on about them.

Like some of the other lads working in Crow Street, Eoin had his own portfolio. Eoin's was transportation. Trains, buses, Dublin taxis, ambulances, even hotel doormen fell into his domain. He spent an immense amount of time bicycling around Dublin, meeting relatives and friends of men and women in the movement. So-and-so has a cousin who's a doorman at the Shelbourne Hotel, and he wants to help. Eoin would meet your man and instruct him to keep an eye out for Englishmen and visitors from the North. They would check the registration book, and Eoin would know that Dublin Castle had an important visitor in from London or Belfast.

Taxi drivers reported who was arriving at Kingsbridge Station and what hotel they were staying at. Province bus drivers were keeping an eye on well-dressed gentlemen visiting some bog in Connaught, and the local boyos were alerted. It was frustrating work, but it was all coming together, piece-by-piece.

The phone rang, and Mr. Kavanagh answered it. "This is Minister Collins," shouted the voice on the other end of the line. "Get your arse over to number six pronto." Eoin threw on his hat and started the quick walk up to Harcourt Street. Number six was the HQ of *Sinn Féin*, but it was more than that. Collins kept several independent offices there, and now he was about to start one of his biggest. He found the boss on the top floor.

"What's my title?" asked Collins.

"Director of Intelligence, Director of Organization, TD, President IRB, Commandant-General of the IRA. Did I miss anything?"

"Minister for Finance," said Collins. "This will be my most important job—after intelligence. A nation without a treasury is a fraud. We cannot be at the mercy of any new *gombeen* men."

The *gombeen* men were the notorious monetary predators of the famine years. They were Ireland's Shylocks, despised by all. One hundred years after Collins, they would be replaced by banks and credit card companies. The human obsession with greed was dangerous, and Collins would be meticulous in protecting Ireland's money—which he had yet to raise.

"Where's it going to come from?" asked Eoin.

"From you, from me, from America, England, Canada, Australia—wherever Irishmen roam."

"How?"

"In the form of a national loan," replied Collins. "The Republic will sell bonds, and, when they mature, the holder will collect interest."

"Will this work?"

"It better," replied Collins, slightly annoyed. Collins had started out working in the British postal system in London in 1906, so he knew about the mails, but, more importantly, he knew about communications, for the postal system also included the telephone and telegraph exchanges. Communications were changing rapidly in the early twentieth century, and it was important for the movement to keep up with them. If they could compromise Britain's communication system, it would be a masterstroke for Collins's intelligence network.

After working in the post office, Collins moved on to the Guaranty Trust Company of New York's branch office in London. He studied banking and accounting and had even attended an economic seminar given by Vladimir Lenin in London in 1915. "For a communist," Collins told Eoin, "the man could count!"

Collins was still perplexed by Eoin's "Will this work?" comment. "Look," said Collins, "I've been authorized by the *Dáil*, as Finance Minister, to float £1,000,000 in bonds—£500,000 to be immediately offered to the public for subscription at 5 percent—and you're going to help me."

Eoin was flabbergasted by the immense figure. "Where do we start?"

"Well," said Collins, "I finally have the prospectus written—but I'm not happy with it."

"Why?"

"I wanted to guarantee the Fenian loans of the 1860s, but I couldn't get Dev to go along with it. Dev is one of those people who agonizes over every dotted 'I' and crossed 'T'—so nothing ever gets done!"

"Well," replied Eoin, "he's in America now."

"Thank God!" laughed Collins.

Eoin looked at Collins intently and was disturbed that he could read him so well. "You don't like this job, do you?" he finally asked.

Collins looked up, surprised. "I don't have a good feeling about this, Eoin. You know that old Bible saying, 'For the love of money is the root of all evil'? Well, it is, but without money, Ireland cannot exist as a nation. I'll just have to keep a sharp eye out for avaricious bastards disguising themselves as patriots!"

"Avaricious?"

"Greedy, Eoin, greedy."

Eoin smiled, already feeling pity for the eejit who might be thinking of playing the *gombeen* man with Michael Collins's money.

51

"Have you ever been to Castle Barbers?" Blood asked Boynton.
Boynton was about to lie but thought better of it. "Only once. I had a shave."

"They're a curious little couple," said Blood. "The father and the boy."

"Only met the father," said Boynton.

"The boy is very handsome," said Blood, and Boynton raised an eyebrow. "He's also opinionated. I said something about cleaning up this Fenian mess in short order, and he said that it would be 'news to Mick Collins.' What do we have on Collins?"

"Your Belfast roots are showing," said Boynton matter-of-factly. "He's the *Dáil's* Minister for Finance."

"Is that all he does?"

Boynton suppressed a smile. "He's also a TD."

"That's their MPs, right?"

"You're learning."

"Where's the file on him?"

"Over at DMP headquarters in Brunswick Street."

"I'll have to check it out," said Blood.

"Why the big interest? He's just another ruffian."

"But why did that kid in the barbershop think he was so important?"

"He's only a bloody kid," said Boynton. "What does he know?"

"Out of the mouths of babes, Boynton," replied Blood. "Out of the mouths of babes."

Boynton shrugged his shoulders. He didn't like it. It was time to keep a closer eye on Detective Sergeant Sebastian Blood.

52

EOIN'S DIARY

"Would you like to go to the moving pictures tonight?" I asked Róisín when I got her on the telephone at the Mater.

"I thought you weren't talking to me," she said in her gruff manner.

"Jaysus, Róisín," says I, "Mick is killing me with work."

"I've heard that before."

I explained to her that I was working in two offices and traveling all over the country checking on the local commandants. Mick likes to send me out to the countryside with communiqués and money because, apparently, I am a very innocent-looking lad, and he thinks the British won't be suspicious of me. He laughingly calls me his intelligence "lamb," whatever that is supposed to be.

"It's been two months," Róisín reminded me.

"And I think about you every day," I told her truthfully.

"You do?"

"You know how much you mean to me."

"I don't," she said, "because you never tell me."

"I forgot," I said sincerely.

"Well, then," she said sweetly, "you can tell me at the picture show."

Mick is having terrible problems publicizing the national loan. The British have just outlawed the loans, and we can't even place ads in the newspapers because the British will shut the papers down. What he did was against my better judgment, but I have to admit that Mick, God love him, is fookin' brilliant at times.

One morning, he rang me on the phone in Crow Street and said, "Meet me at Exchequer Street. We're going to spend the day out at Rathfarmham." He was waiting for me in front of number 10, and we hopped a tram to Patrick Pearse's old school, St. Enda's, where he had gathered a lot of the relatives of the Fenian hierarchy—everyone from Pearse's mother, Margaret, to Erskine Childers, Count Plunkett, Arthur Griffith, Grace Gifford Plunkett, and Kathleen Clarke—to make an advertisement to help sell the loan.

Mick was in one of his more mischievous moods as we got on the tram and headed to the open top. "Well," says he, "are ya ready to spend the day at the home of the creepy Pearse brothers?" My jaw dropped. I was shocked, because Padraig and Willie Pearse are spoken about only with great reverence. But Collins merely laughed. "Patrick Pearse," he said, eyes twinkling, "would have made a wonderful Mother Superior!"

"You better not say that in front of Mrs. Pearse," I said, with great scorn.

"Why not?" said Mick, who burst out laughing at my discomfort. "Ah, don't worry, Eoin. I'll be a good boy today for the all the family celebrities of our martyred dead." We traveled through Rathmines and Tenenure, and it was like we were a hundred miles from Nelson's Pillar, it was so rustic. I felt I could reach out and touch the foot of the Dublin Mountains. "Now can you imagine being stuck out here in the country with Mr. Pearse?" Collins asked. "Studying the Erse and hearing tales of the heroic Cuchulain? Do you think they liked girls—other than their mammy?"

"What in God's name has gotten into ya?" I asked Mick.

"Bedivilment, Eoin. Absolute bedivilment. Without it, I would be howling tears."

We were the first on the scene, and Collins and I roamed around the empty school. "I bet you'd freeze your arse off here in the winter," said Collins, as he surveyed the dorm. "I hear ould Pearse was tight with the coal." He gave a filthy laugh that said I didn't understand something.

We went to the front of the school, and there was the block where they chopped Robert Emmet's head off on in 1803. "Beheaded," pronounced Collins, "and his head went a-rollin' all the way down Thomas Street!"

"Oh," says I, "stop it!" Mick thought my displeasure was hilarious.

"And maybe we'll see the ghost of the courtin' Robert Emmet at the Hermitage," Mick added, not wanting to miss a chance to throw mud at another Irish patriot.

A fellow with a camera showed up, and Mick began bossing him around like he was D.W. Griffiths and this was the Irish *Birth of a Nation*. I have a feeling that the only thing missing will be those lads in the white sheets; the Ku Klux Klan eejits. Mick told me to sit down at Emmet's block and pick up a pen. "Now, don't lose your head!" I was disgusted, and he could see it. He sat next to me and said, "You don't like this, do you?"

"I don't," I told him directly. "It's too dangerous."

"It'll be more dangerous if we don't raise money for the nation. No money, no Ireland." He saw how I was worried about his safety. "It's alright, Eoin," he said, punching me hard in my arm. "I'm going to make you a movie star!"

"Me and fookin' Charlie Chaplin," I said. Mick looked fearsome for a moment, but then he laughed and began ordering people around. One by one, the Fenian celebrities came up and pretended to buy National Loan bonds from Mick or me. Mick was chatting them up and smiling for the camera, while I kept my head down. We filmed for about a half and hour, and then we were done.

"We'll edit this down to five minutes," Mick told me, "and put in some information on how to purchase the bonds, and then we'll hit the cinemas."

The reason I'm so against making this film is that I don't want Mick's face in front of the public. The newspapers always make the British out to be so smart, but they're not. And we shouldn't be helping them. They were in such a rush to execute and imprison us in 1916 that they lost control of themselves. My own circumstances were very similar to the rest of the rebels. All they know about me is that I used to live in the Piles Buildings, and they have my fingerprints. Everyone loves to talk about the importance of fingerprints, but unless I turn into a cat burglar, those fingerprints aren't going to help them much. What they didn't do, in their rush, was take pictures of us. They don't have my mugshot, and they don't have Mick's. In fact, I'm told that they didn't even take photos of the rebels they shot. So, with Mick lifting his photo from the DMP HQ in Brunswick Street, the British are completely in the dark—and we should keep them that way.

So last night was the tryout. I met Róisín in the lobby of the Volta Cinema in Mary Street. She gave me a big smooch and brushed the hair off my forehead. "You look wonderful," she said to me, and I kissed her as my hand found its way to her hip. She didn't brush my hand away, and the ould willie was about to speak out. Then I heard coughing behind me. It was Vinny Byrne and Paddy Daly.

"Sorry to interrupt," said Vinny, blushing. "Róisín," he said, "nice to see you again." He turned to me and said, "Do you have it?" I handed the big, bulky bag containing the reel of film over to Vin, and he and Paddy disappeared into the crowd.

"What are they doing here?" she asked.

"They're big Lillian Gish fans," I lied.

We bought some sweets and then sat in our seats, waiting for the feature to begin. The lights went down, and I was wondering how the boys were doing with the projectionist. I was told by Mick to sit out here and see the reaction of the audience. The boyos with the artillery would do the heavy lifting. The Gish film, *Broken Blossoms*, began, and I kept fidgeting in my seat. "What's wrong with you?" asked Róisín, but I couldn't tell her what was bothering me. I knew Paddy and Vinny were "persuading" the projectionist to put on the Collins film, and my heart was pumping in excitement.

All of a sudden, the screen went white, and the next thing on it was big block letters that declared FREE IRELAND—INVEST IN THE NATIONAL LOAN. Then there I was on the screen, sitting next to Collins, and the house went wild. "It's Mick Collins!" someone yelled out, and the foot-stomping began in earnest.

All of a sudden, the piano player started a rousing rendition of "A Nation Once Again." I couldn't believe it. I looked over and was shocked to see that the pianist was Dilly Dicker, one of Mick's agents. She had a big smile on her face, and I thought I was going to die.

"Jaysus," said Róisín in shock, "it's you and Mick!" She put her hand inside my arm and squeezed me tight. "This is amazing! You're a cinema star!" she said as I sank lower in my seat.

"I'm a fookin' eejit," I said, hoping no one would recognize me. "Let's get the hell out of here." I had to pull Róisín out of her seat, she was so mesmerized by the screen. We trekked to Capel Street and then across the Liffey, heading for the Stag's Head.

"Why didn't you tell me?"

"I said I was busy."

"This is fantastic," Róisín said. "This will put you on the map."

"I'm a revolutionary. I don't want to be on the fookin' map," I said. "It's dangerous enough, the work I do. I don't need to be recognized."

When we got to the Stag's Head, I asked her what she wanted. "You know what I want," she said, crinkling the freckles on her nose as she broke out in her gorgeous smile.

"For now," says I, somewhat wearily, "you'll have to settle for a whiskey and porter."

53

D ETECTIVE SMYTH DIES, mourned the headline in the loyalist *Irish Times*.

"It's about fookin' time," said an irritated Michael Collins, as he threw the paper on his desk at Bachelors Walk. Eoin was gathering the intelligence mail and about to return to Crow Street. "We fooked the whole job up," said Collins.

After sending letters to G-men telling them to cease and desist from all political activity, the more eager ones—the true believers—were often taken aside and given a physical warning. Some were roughed up or tied to fences as a final warning that there would be no further warnings. Detective Sergeant Patrick Smyth continued steadfastly in his work. His testimony put Collins's friend Piaras Beaslaí behind bars for a longer sentence than his political offense called for. Collins had had enough. He assigned a group of Volunteers to go to Drumcondra and shoot Smyth dead as he headed home from work. Armed with .38s, the Volunteers did shoot Smyth, but he managed to live for weeks before expiring.

"No more .38s," said Collins. "We'll have to acquire more .45s. We need man-stoppers! No more body shots. Just head shots from now on." They were on a learning curve, but they were learning fast.

"He leaves a big family," said Eoin.

"Fook him," snapped Collins.

"His son said we were cowards to shoot him in the back."

Collins turned white in anger, his blue eyes sharp as darts. "That fook Smyth has been playing with us since the rebellion began. He made sport of pointing out IRB men after Easter Week. He was warned by letter. He was warned in person, but he persisted in putting Piaras away for a long time. That bastard got what he deserved." Eoin sat quiet. "Do you feel sorry for him?" Collins suddenly quizzed.

"No," said Eoin, "but I feel sorry for his family."

"Feel sorry for your own family," shot back Collins. "Do you think Smyth cares about your family, or my family, or Vinny Byrnes's family? Like shite he does. Mark my words," continued Collins, "Patrick Smyth is the first—but he won't be the last."

"You're right," Eoin finally agreed. "We have to be more effective."

"Let's get a meeting together," said Collins. "Check with McKee and Mulcahy. Let's get some men who can do some *real* heavy lifting." He paused. "This is the rough stuff I've been promising you, Eoin. It won't be nice."

"I'd like to be a part of it."

Collins raised his eyebrows, slightly surprised at young Kavanagh's response. "I'll give you that opportunity," said Collins, throwing on his trilby. He was about to go through the door when he stopped. "I will give you a chance, Eoin, but God help you, that chance may end up destroying your life."

54

EOIN'S DIARY
FRIDAY, SEPTEMBER 19, 1919

*E*arlier this evening, Mick called a meeting at the Gaelic League at 46 Parnell Square. I met Mick at Vaughan's Hotel with his daily intelligence brief, and then we walked down the street to number forty-six. "Take notes," he said to me. This was heavy stuff. Mick's two Dicks, McKee and Mulcahy, were there, and all the lads carried artillery: Vinny, Mick O'Donnell, Paddy Daly, Joe Leonard, Tom Keogh and Jim Slattery, among others.

"One week ago today," he began, "the British proscribed our *Dáil*." Mick paused for effect. "They have also proscribed our National Loan." Mick paused again. "Now we are going to proscribe them!" Mick said that he was forming an elite Squad to carry out "special assignments." He said the Squad would take orders directly from him or, in his absence, from McKee and Mulcahy.

"Under no circumstances whatsoever," he began, "are you to take it on yourselves to shoot anybody, even if we know he is a spy, unless you have to do it in self-defense while on active service." He paused. "Remember, not all of the G-men are our enemies, and indiscriminate shooting might result in the death of friends. And believe me, we have more friends in the peelers than you might think.

"To paralyze the British machine, it is necessary to strike at individuals," he continued. "Without her spies, England is helpless. It is only by means of their accumulated and accumulating knowledge that the British imperialist machine can operate.

"Spies"—Mick spat the word out—"are not so ready to step into the shoes of their departed confederates. And even when the new spy has stepped into the shoes of the old one, he cannot step into the old one's knowledge. We will strike at individuals, and by doing so, we will cut their lines of communication and shake their morale."

Mick paused and then asked, "Are there any questions?" There was stunned quiet in the room. "Very well," he said, "let's get to work." With that, he gave me a nod and headed for the door. All the men in the room surrounded McKee and Mulcahy to get more information. We headed back to Vaughan's Hotel. On the street he said to me, "Well, Eoin, are you ready to have some of your 'fun,' as you like to put it?"

"I don't know, Mick," says I.

Mick saw I was distressed. "Come on up into my office." Once inside Vaughan's, Mick was blunt in his questioning. "What's bothering you? The shooting part?"

"I'm a Catholic, Mick."

"So am I."

"It's the worst mortal sin. My mother would never forgive me."

Mick snorted. "Your mother!"

"You knew her."

Mick suddenly changed his tone. "I know it's hard, Eoin. But we're in a desperate situation. You know we can't put an army on a battlefield against the British. You know we're desperate for a few used revolvers and some rounds of bullets to put in them." He went quiet for a moment. "You know we only have about eighteen months! If we do not free Ireland in that time span, she will remain a British colony forever!"

"Forever" sounded very frightening.

"You're under no obligation," Collins finally said. "Go back to Crow Street, and do your intelligence work. Keep helping me out on the National Loan in Harcourt Street." He put his arm around my shoulders and gave me a hug. "You'll know when your time to join the Squad is ripe. Until then, don't desert me."

I was shocked that he would say such a thing to me. "Never!" says I.

Collins smiled and without saying a word, fled the office. Within seconds, I could hear his clanker of a bike outside on Parnell Square, off in the Dublin night, like a whaling banshee in search of a G-man's funeral procession.

55

"I'm so glad Grandpa didn't join the Squad," said Diane to her husband. Johnny gave a knowing grunt. "What's that supposed to mean?" she demanded.

"Nothing."

"Nothing, my ass!" Johnny smiled at the mention of her delicious derriere, and Diane caught his sexual drift. "Don't start!" she scolded.

"Remember "Afternoon Delight" back in the '70s?" Johnny suddenly said, referring to a hit song that was an ode to matinee fucking.

Diane laughed. "Johnny, you're incorrigible! I haven't thought of that dirty song in thirty years. As Maurice Chevalier used to say, 'Yes, I remember it well!'"

"So do I," said Johnny, turning nostalgic. "*Skyrockets in Flight!/ Afternoon Delight!* I remember it playing on the radio while the sun shined in on us as we were screwing in that old rocking chair of yours."

"Down, boy!" admonished his wife. "You're quite the romantic—probably just like Róisín's young Eoin."

"Okay," said Johnny, blushing, knowing he had been clearly caught in sexual hypocrisy. "You win."

"Let's get back to Grandpa. I'm glad he didn't join the Squad, because he might have gotten himself killed."

"No member of the Squad," replied Johnny, "ever died in action. They were pros."

"But it was still safer sitting in some office."

"No one working for Michael Collins," said Johnny, "was ever safe, especially working intelligence and finance like Grandpa did."

"Anything is better than being in the Squad. Being a murderer."

"You think?" said Johnny.

"What are you saying?"

Johnny let a breath out. "There are defining moments in history. You know, George Washington at Valley Forge in 1777, Napoleon versus Wellington at Waterloo in 1815, General Grant at Vicksburg in 1863— and Michael Collins and his Squad in Dublin in 1920."

"You're making me nervous. Will you just spit it out?"

"My grandfather had a unique sense of history, be it here in Ireland or in America. He also had a determined sense of duty. Those two instincts, plus his total dedication to Michael Collins, might make him change his mind about the Squad."

"Do you know this as fact?" asked Diane.

"No," replied Johnny. "The old man only hinted at things. I remember meeting the *Taoiseach*, Seán Lemass, when I was a teenager. Grandpa was openly fond, even affectionate towards the *Taoiseach*, but, as we were leaving, he said to me, "Johnny, I love Jack Lemass, but, when I go out to do a job, I go with Vinny Byrne.""

"Meaning?"

"What was Vinny's job?"

"Collins's enforcer."

"Shooter," replied Johnny. "Vinny was the supreme shooter. He killed more people than cancer."

"Do you have anything else you want to share with me?" asked Diane, and Johnny shook his head. "Would a little 'afternoon delight' perhaps stimulate some other recollections?"

Johnny silently took his wife by the hand and headed for the upstairs bedroom. "*Skyrockets in Flight!* . . ." he began, as he started to climb the stairs.

"*. . . Afternoon Delight!*" sang Diane in reply, adding her own deliciously dirty laugh to set the mood.

56

C amden Street was turning into a British highway. Day by day, hour after hour, British military lorries, Crossley tenders, and armored cars came rambling through the old neighborhood, honking their horns, frightening children playing in the streets, drenching pedestrians with splashed rainwater—which would always evoke howls of derisive laughter from the Tommy in the driver's seat.

They were coming from the Portobello Barracks, down past the Grand Canal, and their destination was Dublin Castle. They would range unmolested through the long, twisted thoroughfare that started out as Camden Street, then turned into Wexford, Aungier, and South Great Georges Streets. At Dame Street, they would make their safe left turn and find the front gates of Dublin Castle.

Unmolested.

The Second Battalion of the South Dublin IRA wanted to change that word.

It started with one hand grenade. The pin was pulled, and the grenade was tossed into a lorry, and soon the ambulances began arriving from the Meath Hospital.

There would be no more free passage down the middle of Camden Street for the British Army. There would be no more laughing at the locals—only nervous glances at the citizens in the street, wondering which one had a deadly grenade in his pocket.

The attacks became a daily occurrence. The British, so used to dealing with their local savages around the world, improvised. Soon the tops of lorries and tenders were covered with chicken wire. A grenade now bounced off and was returned to sender with a bang.

But the British weren't the only ones who knew how to improvise. A fishhook made a nice catch on the wire mesh, and more ambulances would arrive from the Meath. The hunters had become the hunted.

Now, as they entered Camden Street, the proud British Army could hear the heckles of the street urchins: "Welcome to the Dardanelles, ya fookin' English hoors!" Listen to the children, and you'll know what the parents are thinking.

On other occasions, they would be serenaded by the same street kids, with the anti-British Great War ditty called "The Grand Ould Dame Britannia:"

> *What's the news the newsboy yells?*
> *What the news the paper tells?*
> *A British retreat from the Dardanelles,*
> *Says the Grand Ould Dame Britannia*

The British just did not do well in the Dardanelles—Winston Churchill's disastrous Great War misadventure—be it in Turkey in 1915, or in Dublin in 1919. The new Battle of the Dardanelles had begun, and the next move belonged to the Crown.

57

S ebastian Blood couldn't get Castle Barbers out of his head.
He found himself taking walks over to Aungier Street to see what was happening in the shop. There was nothing suspicious going on, but it just didn't feel right. Blood saw the local DMP constable on the beat, flashed his badge, and asked about the family that ran the shop. Constable O'Shea was nearing his pension, and the last thing he needed was some eager Orangeman RIC eejit fucking up his said retirement. "Good loyal men," was all O'Shea offered. "And your name, sir?"

"Blood. Detective Sergeant Sebastian Blood."

"Good evening to you, Detective Sergeant," said O'Shea, making a note to tell his nephew, Matty O'Shea, Second Battalion, South Dublin, IRA, about this nosey RIC detective.

Blood's other obsession was this Mick Collins fellow, the one the kid in the shop seemed to think was so smart. Boynton told him the Collins file was over at the DMP station in Brunswick Street. Blood called for an appointment and was met at the front desk by Ned Broy. He took Blood to his office. "Tell me all you know about Michael Collins," was his first demand.

"Michael Collins," began Broy, "is the *Dáil's* Minister for Finance."

"What's his background?"

"Cork farm boy," Broy said, ticking each item off on his outstretched fingers. "Worked in the postal system in London between 1906 and 1915, fought in the GPO in 1916, served time in Wales, and has been

involved in running candidates for the *Dáil* in the past couple of years."
That was enough, thought Broy. *Let Blood figure the rest out.*

"Could I see his file?" Broy took Blood to the same Fenian room where Collins had spent the night and unlocked the door.

"Be my guest," said Broy. "His file is in here someplace."

"Not very efficient," offered Blood.

Broy grunted. "You're in Dublin now, not Belfast."

Blood was left alone in the room, and he finally came across Collins's file. He saw there was a warrant out for his arrest for jumping bail in Sligo. He was dismayed that there was no photograph of the mysterious Minister for Finance.

Blood returned to Broy's office. "Why hasn't this bench warrant been enforced?"

"Collins is elusive," said Broy diffidently.

"Or maybe you Dublin boyos are incompetent."

There was a stony silence between the two men. "Have a good day," said Broy, as he returned to examining the papers on his desk.

It was rush hour as Blood started heading up Grafton Street on his way to his lodgings at the Ivanhoe Hotel on Harcourt Street, off Stephen's Green. Just before he was to cross Cuffe Street, he decided to take one more look at Castle Barbers before he called it a day. It was nearly half-six, and he could see Joseph Kavanagh sweeping the floor and tidying up for the next day's work. Joseph finally pulled the shade on the door and went outside so he could enter his flat from the doorway on the left, and Frank was right with him. But Frank said something to the father and started walking down Aungier Street. At the corner of York Street, he entered the Swan Bar.

Blood couldn't believe his luck. A fourteen-year-old kid going for a drink. The barman pulled the pint of porter and placed it in front of Frank. Blood threw a coin on the bar and said, "That's with me."

Frank looked up to see who his benefactor was. He was shocked to see that it was Detective Sergeant Sebastian Blood. Flabbergasted, all he could muster was, "Thanks."

"I'll take one of those, too," Blood said to the barman, suddenly full of camaraderie. When his pint was delivered, he lifted it and clinked Frank's glass. "To the Crown!" he said softly, in a conspirator's tone.

"The Crown," Frank feebly replied as the barman walked away casually. But the man was as alert as a parish priest hearing a mortal sin in confession, so he perked his ears up to catch all that was going on.

Blood pulled the porter silently into his mouth before saying, "Francis, can I have a word with you?" Frank nodded, but he was annoyed that a stranger would call him "Francis." Blood lowered his voice. "There's much Fenianism in this neighborhood. Can you help me out here? It's like the Dardanelles out there. No one is safe."

Frank's pint sat untouched before him. He wished that his father or his brother were here. What he really wished is that Mick Collins was here to tell him what to do. "I don't know anything," he finally said. "You know too much in this neighborhood, you could end up in a box with a rosary wrapped around your hands."

Blood gave a tight smile. "Well," he finally said, "think about it. Any help you can provide will be appreciated and compensated."

Frank didn't understand the word. "Compensated?"

"There's money in it for you and your father." Frank, stunned at the offer, numbly nodded his head. Blood smiled and put his hand on Frank's arm. "Remember," he said delicately, "there'll always be an England."

Just then, there was a terrific blast as another hand grenade of the Second Battalion found its mark in the middle of a British tender. Blood leapt up and headed out the door. Frank finally picked up his pint and dropped it in one long gulp. He nodded at the barman, who looked at him warily. Outside the bodies of three British soldiers lay in Aungier Street, dead. Blood was leaning over them, too late to help. The pint hit Frank nicely in his teenaged brain, and he smiled woozily. He suddenly realized that he had been saved from Detective Sergeant Blood's touch by the bold citizen soldiers of Michael Collins's IRA.

58

October 10, 1919, was Eoin's eighteenth birthday, and he was going to celebrate by having dinner with Róisín. He picked her up at the Mater Hospital at 6:00 p.m., just as the Angelus was ringing about Dublin. "Jaysus," she said. "Those fookin' church bells depress me."

"Maybe I should save your soul," said Eoin, "by thumping your craw for you!"

"I can thump my own craw, thank you very much." Róisín looked cross but then broke out in a big smile. "Happy birthday, Eoin," she said as she gave him a nice wet kiss, then immediately cut to the chase. "Where will we eat?"

"How about Vaughan's Hotel?"

"Is it safe enough?"

"For now," said Eoin.

They soon found themselves on Mountjoy Street, crossing in front of the Black Church en route to Parnell Square, when they ran into Dilly Dicker, who was coming from her red-brick, two-story home at number thirty. "Dilly," yelled Eoin, "how are ya?"

"Eoin," said Dilly with equal enthusiasm as she embraced her colleague.

"How are the mails?" inquired Eoin.

"Hush!" said Dilly laughing. "The Big Fella will kill us!" Dilly had been on many a mail-lifting caper with Eoin, even traveling to Holyhead on the night mail boat disguised as a man to lift important Dublin Castle posts.

"Dilly, this is my friend Róisín."

"Hello, Madeline," said Róisín coolly. "I think it was that job out in Donnybrook the last we met."

Eoin didn't know that Madeline was Dilly's real name. Collins had come up with "Dilly" as a term of affection. What was amazing to Eoin is how much Dilly and Róisín looked alike. The two 20-year-olds could have been sisters.

"Yes," said Dilly, "it was Donnybrook. Hiding the guns in Batt O'Connor's house."

Róisín nodded. "It was an interesting adventure," she finally said.

"I didn't know you two knew each other," said Eoin.

"We do," said Róisín, without enthusiasm.

"You and Mick were great in that National Loan film," said Dilly, turning her attention to Eoin and changing the subject.

Before Eoin could answer, Róisín said, "We liked your rendition of 'A Nation Once Again' on the piano."

"I got carried away," admitted Dilly. "Eoin and Mick looked like such businessmen on the screen. The crowd really got into it. It was a grand occasion."

"Well," said Róisín, "we're off to Vaughan's for supper."

"If you meet up with Mick," said Dilly, "give him my love."

"Oh," said Róisín, "we will, we will!"

As they continued their walk to Vaughan's, Eoin said to Róisín, "You weren't very nice to Dilly."

"I was polite enough," said Róisín, before adding, "Have you ever noticed that the Munster Hotel is right across the street from Dilly's digs? Cozy arrangement."

"What are you talking about?"

"Dilly at number thirty, Mick at forty-four."

"What are you saying?"

"You know what I'm saying."

"I don't."

"Do you think Mick is shaggin' Dilly?"

"What?"

"You know, dickin' Dicker." A gleam came into Róisín's eye. "I think they don't call it Mountjoy Street for nothing!"

"What's wrong with you?" asked Eoin in exasperation.

"I'm sorry," Róisín said, flushed. "It's just my time of month."

"What time is that?" asked Eoin, confused.

"You are an imbecile," snapped Róisín. "No, you're worse—you're an Irish imbecile!"

Eoin was clueless as to what he had done. "What's gotten into you? What did Dilly or I ever do to you?"

"You and her seem to be *really* good friends."

"What do you mean by that?" Róisín shook her head. "You," said Eoin belatedly, "are a mortal sin waiting to happen!"

Róisín stopped in her tracks and kissed Eoin roughly on the mouth. "You bet I am!" She took Eoin by the arm, and they continued on their way to Vaughan's. They found a table for two in the dining room and ordered their supper. Afterward, as they were preparing to leave, Collins and Kitty Kiernan came in. "Well, well," said Róisín.

"Well, well, what?" said Eoin.

"Oh," said Róisín, "don't be naïve."

As they were exiting, they stopped at Collins's table. "Hello, Mick," said Eoin. He paused for a second before adding, "Mick, there was a man in my room when I woke up this morning."

"Who?" said Collins, concerned.

"Me!" crowed Eoin. "It's my eighteenth birthday today."

"Well, happy birthday, Eoin lad," said Collins laughing. "You remember Kitty from Longford."

"I do, indeed," replied the lad. "How are ya, Miss Kiernan?"

"Happy Birthday, Eoin," said Kitty.

"And Róisín," said Collins. "You look lovely tonight. Kitty, this is Róisín O'Mahony, who does great work for us at the Mater."

Kitty nodded and Róisín gave a tight smile. "Nice to meet you, Kitty." She turned to Collins. "We bumped into Dilly Dicker on our way over here, Mick. She asked us to send her love if we ran into you."

"That's very nice of you," said Collins evenly, a bit baffled by Róisín's tone.

"Well," Eoin cut in, "good night. See you tomorrow, God willing."

The "good nights" were liberally exchanged between the four of them, and Collins added a hearty "Happy Birthday!" Eoin and Róisín found themselves walking towards Sackville Street in silence. "Do you think Mick is doing Kitty?" Róisín finally asked.

"Róisín! What's in God's name has gotten into you?"

"Well," she said coyly, "they do call him the Big Fella."

"Mick does nothing but work, for God's sake. Why are you, all of a sudden, so interested in that dirty stuff?"

"Isn't it obvious?"

"No, it isn't."

"I'm afraid for you."

"For me?"

"What if something happens to you?"

"If it happens, it happens."

"But what about me?"

"You're young and beautiful. They'll be sniffin' around you before I'm cold in the Glasnevin ground."

"I don't want to be sniffed about," said Róisín. "I want *us* to be happy."

"We'll be happy when Ireland is free."

"I can't wait another seven hundred years," snapped Róisín.

Eoin took her by the hand, and they turned into Bachelors Walk so he could pick up the late post at the office. "I can't wait that long, either," Eoin said. "But for now, we'll just have to muddle through."

"I think I'm beginning to hate this country," said Róisín, wondering if their love would ever have a chance to truly blossom in this Dublin City, now so ripe with revolution that it was beginning to rot.

59

E oin was a notoriously early riser, so he was surprised when he was woken out of his sleep by Frank. "Eoin," he said solemnly, "I have to talk to you." Eoin couldn't imagine what Frank wanted to talk to him about. "We had a customer in the shop from Dublin Castle," said Frank. "A detective named Blood." Eoin was silent, just taking it all in. "He bought me a drink last night at the Swan."

"What did he want?"

"He wants me to inform on the neighborhood," said Frank. "He said he'd pay. Apparently all those bombings are having an effect on Dublin Castle."

Eoin got out of bed and started dressing. "Don't mention a word of this to anyone else—even Da," he told his brother. "Keep yer gob shut until I find out what's going on."

When Eoin arrived at Crow Street, he told Liam Tobin about his conversation with Frank. "I've never heard of this fellow," said Tobin.

Eoin immediately went to his index cards and pulled out the one with Blood's name on it. There was nothing but his rank and Dublin Castle phone extension on the card. "We don't even know where he lives," said Eoin.

"I want a report on this as soon as you know something," said Tobin. "Check with Broy and Boynton."

Eoin went to the Bachelors Walk office to pick up the first post and returned with it to Crow Street. He sorted the letters in the usual way. Besides the usual carbons from Broy and Boynton, there were also notes

204

on Blood. Boynton said that Blood had a special interest in Collins, and Broy reported that Blood was over in Brunswick Street snooping around Collins's file.

Eoin went back to Tobin. "That's three reports—Frank, Broy, Boynton—about this Blood in one morning."

"Type it up," said Tobin, "and put it in Mick's intelligence pouch for the day."

Eoin met Collins at Vaughan's at nine o'clock that night and gave him his intelligence update, with a special emphasis on Detective Blood. "Hmmm," said Collins, "this boyo has the nose of a bloodhound." He laughed at his own joke. Eoin was so tired from the long day that he just looked ahead blankly. "He's somehow tied to you and the barber shop," said Collins. "I'm concerned for you and your family, but I also have an office there on the third floor." Even Eoin had no idea what was going on over his head in Collins's latest office. "We've got to know *all* about him," said Collins thoughtfully. "Find out from Boynton where he lives, what he likes, his vices, his quirks. I want this done yesterday. Do you understand?" Eoin nodded. "By this time tomorrow, we'll know what we're up against."

Eoin was about to leave when he turned and asked Collins, "Do Boynton and Broy know that they both work for you?"

Collins gave a tight smile. "Not yet!"

Eoin nodded his head. "I thought so." He paused before adding, "I guess I should keep me gob shut."

"Yes," said Collins. "We'll introduce them to each other at the proper time. Remember," he said, as he looked Eoin intently in the eye, "never let one side of your mind know what the other is doing."

Heeding that advice, Eoin discreetly met with Boynton at the Stag's Head the next day and got as much information as he could on Blood, including the gem that he lived at the Ivanhoe Hotel over on Harcourt Street. Eoin reported back to Collins that night at the Wicklow Hotel. "Who is this hoor?" he asked. "Dick McKee told me he was questioning the local DMP on the beat—one of our 'good policemen'—about your family. That's report number four on this hoor. This is not a man we can ignore." Collins went over the limited information that Eoin, with Boynton's help, had compiled. "All we know," Collins added, "is that he's a Belfast man, an eager beaver, and a general pain-in-the-goddamned arse." Collins stood up and paced the room for a good minute without speaking. "Let's let him know we know."

"Is that wise?" asked Eoin.

"It's worth a try," replied Collins. "He may be a freelancer, trying to impress his bosses with his initiative. Let's rough him up and see how he likes it."

"If that doesn't work?"

Collins grunted. "We'll cross that Ha'penny Bridge when we come to it. Tell Mick McDonnell to get a few of the lads from the Squad to say hello to Detective Blood."

If Sebastian Blood wanted to get Michael Collins's attention, he had succeeded spectacularly.

60

S ebastian Blood's snooping around 31 Aungier Street was beginning to pay off.

He found that number thirty-one had two lives, one during the week and another on the weekends. During the week, there was Joseph and Frank—no surprise—occupants of the shop and the second floor. But he learnt that there was also a mysterious tenant working on the third floor, where Collins kept his newest office. On the weekends, he discovered there was a thin young man who came and went. He was always dressed conservatively in a blue three-piece suit and seemed to be in a rush, often with a briefcase in hand. Blood wondered if this was another son of Joseph's, because he often sat in the shop and talked to the older Kavanagh. He had never seen this young man during the week, probably because he was never there early or late enough. All the activity was beginning to pique Blood's fertile imagination.

But Sebastian Blood wasn't the only one with an imagination. Unknown to him, he had been "tagged" by the Squad—and he was "it." Their orders were to stake him out and then rough him up. While he was staking out number thirty-one, he was being watched by members of the Squad, standing down Aungier Street in front of William Fanagan's Funeral Establishment. For days, they patiently followed Blood around Dublin. After a full week, they knew his routine. Up early at the Ivanhoe Hotel—located right next to *Sinn Féin* HQ on Harcourt Street—he always headed over to Cuffe Street to check out the barber shop before he proceeded onto his office at Dublin Castle. He spent an extraordinary amount of time just observing the shop, probably throwing together a couple of hours a day at various times.

The Squad had been working on their "methodology," as Collins called it. Depending on the job, they would send out two to four men as the main attack column, covered by a backup team of the same number. The first group did the job, and the backups made sure the first group got away and were not interfered with by police or "innocent" bystanders.

Two teams from the Squad were waiting for Blood when he left Dublin Castle just after 6:00 p.m. They expected him to head over to Aungier Street before he returned to his hotel. But Blood had other ideas. He walked straight down Parliament Street, crossed the Liffey, and started heading up Capel Street. Blood was on a mission, and the four Squad members looked at each other as Blood forced them to quicken their steps to match the frantic tapping of his walking stick.

Blood made a right onto Mary Street. "He's heading to the Volta," said Paddy Daly to Vinny Byrne, the number-one team who were going to do the roughing up. The four Squad members broke into a trot in an attempt to get ahead of Blood. Byrne and Daly did just that, leaving their two comrades to trail Blood. Byrne and Daly bought tickets and went into the lobby. "He's after the film," said Vinny. Daly nodded. Somehow Blood had been tipped that the Volta Cinema was cooperating, showing Collins's National Loan trailer at every showing. Byrne and Daly waited until Blood entered the lobby, then turned discreetly until he passed them. The movie had already begun, and they watched Blood go down and grab an aisle seat. Right in the middle of the movie, the screen went white, and Collins and Eoin appeared.

Sebastian Blood stood up and started talking to himself. "That's the bloody kid from Aungier Street," he said aloud, waving his cane in the air. "So that must be Collins!" He said it loud enough that Byrne and Daly could hear him, because they were seated right behind him. "This," Blood called out to the theatre, "is an illegal film." That was the last thing he said before Daly threw an abandoned overcoat over his head and Byrne hit him a vicious blow with a policeman's black-jack, forcing Blood to drop his cane. Vinny liked to refer to his baton work as "Paddywacking" someone. He gave him a couple of shots in his upper arms, and Blood's body began to go numb. Byrne and Daly pulled Blood into the aisle. The backup team stood guard, discouraging any "help" from arriving. "Stay out of politics, yer hoor," warned Daly, "or we'll take yer fucking head off the next time." They rolled him over and took his badge, notebook, wallet, and more importantly, his Webley revolver. As an afterthought, Daly also retrieved Blood's walking stick. The four Squad members left Blood barely conscious on the floor as Collins and Eoin continued to sell the National Loan on the screen.

61

EOIN'S DIARY

I was with Mick giving my daily intelligence brief in Joint Number One, as we now call Vaughan's, when Paddy Daly and Vinny Byrne arrived. Vinny dropped a reel of film on the desk. "What's that?" asked Collins.

"The National Loan film," said Vinny.

"Why's it here?"

"Because of Blood," said Daly, reaching into his pockets and emptying the detective's wallet, notebook, Castle ID, badge, and gun onto the desk.

Collins picked up the Webley. "Good pickup," he said, and placed it in the top drawer of his desk for safekeeping. Mick and I noticed that Daly looked particularly morose. "What's wrong, Paddy?" he asked.

Paddy is a tough man and is rapidly becoming one of the leaders of the Squad. He's from just down the way on Parnell Street. He's tall and lanky with a great shock of hair and a ready smile. He's so genial-looking that you wouldn't know how tough and brutal he could be when it came to his duties. "Blood has made the Aungier Street connection."

"How do you know?" I said.

"We were off to warn him this evening," began Daly, "when he suddenly takes off for the Volta Cinema in Mary Street. Someone must have tipped him off that the Volta was playing the Loan reel at every showing."

Collins grunted in discomfort before adding, "Shite."

"Because just before Vinny clubbed him he said, 'That's the bloody kid from Aungier Street.' Then he added, 'So that must be Collins!'"

Collins was quiet, and I was nervous. "That fookin' film," Mick finally said. Then there was nothing but quiet between the four of us.

Mick picked up Blood's notebook. "Let's see how good a detective he is," he said as he flipped through the pages and then began to read aloud. "Here it is: '31 Aungier. Castle Barbers. Alleged Loyalist. Joseph Kavanagh, son Francis, about thirteen. Two strangers come and go. One might be another son. About eighteen or nineteen. Three-piece suit. Who is he? The Collins connection?'" Mick stopped and looked up. "He's guessing."

"He's close enough," I said.

"He still doesn't know your name?"

"We hope."

"Look at this," Paddy finally said, handing Blood's walking cane over to Mick. "Look at the handle."

Mick ran his hand over the brass knob before looking at it intently. He held it out for all to see. "The 'All-Seeing Eye,'" he said with a wicked laugh.

"A bloody Freemason," Vinny chimed in.

Paddy, Vinny, and meself were seemingly mystified by the stick, which Mick moved around like a magic wand. "Secret organizations!" whispered Collins, before bursting out in another great laugh.

"What's so funny?" demanded Vinny, who attends mass daily. "The Church is wary of secret organizations. You can be excommunicated for joining one."

"Ah, yes," said Mick, "the evils of 'secret organizations'!" The three of us stood with our mouths open. "You bloody eejits!" He laughed again. "You're all in the Brotherhood. What's that?"

"A secret organization," said Daly meekly.

"But that's different," I insisted.

"I'm sure it is," added Collins, with a very dubious look on his face. "Paddy," he finally said, "I want you to deliver Mr. Blood's stick back to him at his residence."

"And the message?"

"No message necessary," Mick declared. "He'll get the message—one way or the other."

"What are we going to do?" I finally said, but I really meant: "What am I going to do?"

"There's no immediate danger," Mick replied. "Maybe he'll take the warning and go the fook back to Belfast."

"If he doesn't?" asked Daly.

Mick looked annoyed. "Then we'll 'box' him up and send him back to Belfast."

"When will we know?" I asked.

"Soon," said Mick. "But I'm worried about my office on the third floor over in Aungier Street."

"I'm worried about me father and Frank," I shot back.

Mick looked suddenly weary. "I know, Eoin," he said quietly. "I know."

"That bloody film," I said.

"It had to be done," said Mick. "The money is beginning to come in. And we had to warn Blood. We will not play rebellion by their rules any longer. We will not be intimidated by shites like Blood or anyone else. From now on, there will be consequences for the British."

"Right you are," echoed Paddy Daly, but Vinny remained quiet, as if he could read my mind, which was riddled with sudden, unrelenting fear. There would be consequences—and I wondered how hard they would come down on me and my family.

62

After spending the night at Jervis Street Hospital and the next two days in his room at the Ivanhoe Hotel, Sebastian Blood finally showed up for work at Dublin Castle. He looked a mess. His head was still bandaged, with a spot of blood bleeding through. He looked like the flutist in A.M. Willard's painting, *The Spirit of '76*.

"What happened to you?" asked Brendan Boynton, as if he didn't know.

Blood groaned. "Fucking Fenians," was all he managed.

"You look awful," commiserated Boynton, feigning concern and trying not to show how much he was enjoying the whole thing.

"I shouldn't have come in today," said Blood.

"Good thing you did," said Boynton. "Lots of brass around. Military and G-Division meeting to see what we should do about the Dardanelles."

The military contingent was led by the Viceroy, Lord Lieutenant of Ireland, and Supreme Commander of the British Army in Ireland: Lord John French. French was one of those people who physically matched his occupation. If you were to say to a Hollywood casting director, "Send over a Great War British Field Marshal," Johnny French would appear, pressed and shined up. He was also one of the first people to define what would become known as the Peter Principle: "In a hierarchy, every employee tends to rise to their level of incompetence." A failure in the trenches in France, he was sent to Ireland to put down the rebels, eventually becoming Lord Lieutenant of Ireland. He was also known as Viscount French of Ypres. The ultimate incompetent, he had more titles than battle victories.

The quiet in the detective offices was broken by a shout: "Everyone to the Day Room. Now!" Blood and Boynton looked at each other, and Boynton shrugged. In the huge room, around the long table, were RIC commissioners, superintendents, and inspectors, along with Johnny French and his merry men. Boynton noticed Ned Broy from Brunswick Street, who he knew by sight but had never been introduced to. Broy noticed Blood in the companion of a young detective and wondered if the kid was another Protestant eejit from Belfast.

Perfunctory introductions were made to the G-Division detectives. French rose to speak first. "We have to suppress what is happening on the streets of South Dublin."

Good luck to ya, thought Boynton, but he kept his mouth shut and his ears open.

"In the last week alone," said French, "the Shiners have bombed five lorries, completely destroying three of them, and killed four soldiers. And last week was an average week compared to the last month. This has to stop." French looked around the room, apparently expressing his *gravitas*. "I now want to introduce you to Derek Gough-Coxe, who just arrived this morning from London."

Gough-Coxe was dressed in civilian clothes and wore an old-fashioned, high hard-collar which made his head appear to jump off his shoulders. "I, would just like to correct the Viceroy," began Gough-Coxe. "I, unfortunately, haven't been in London in two years. I am *en route* to London from the Middle East, where I have just concluded my business there."

The Middle East, thought Boynton, getting it all down in his head for Collins and realizing that the British were showing their first signs of desperation. Across the room, Broy was thinking the same thing.

"I am not up to speed yet," Gough-Coxe continued, "and I will not be returning here until the first of the year, but I wanted to sit in and meet all of you and see what thoughts you had on this problem with the terrorists. Is there anything anyone wants to say about the Camden Street chaos?" There was quiet in the room. The G-men didn't know who this Gough-Coxe fellow was, but they would not be surprised if he showed up as their new boss in January 1920. "No comments?" said Gough-Coxe again.

A few throats were cleared, and feet shuffled. Finally Blood had had enough. He tapped his cane twice. "We should be making the rules in the Dardanelles," he spoke up, "not playing the victim. Let the Fenians play the victims."

Gough-Coxe looked at Blood and could see from his bandage that he had been to the fight. "Your name?" Gough-Coxe asked.

"Detective Sergeant Sebastian Blood. G-Division. DMP."

Gough-Coxe could hear the Belfast accent. "You're not from here."

"Neither are you or Lord French," Blood snapped, before adding, "And believe me, that's a good thing, because things tend to get very cozy in Dublin town." Boynton began to realize that Blood hadn't quite gotten the message the Squad had tried to convey to him a few nights ago. In fact, he seemed more ambitious than ever.

Lord French was not impressed, but Derek Gough-Coxe was. "What is *your* solution to the Camden Street problems?"

"The reason the rebels are succeeding in the Dardanelles is that they have the people behind them," said Blood. "If the people want to support the Fenians, there should be a price to pay."

"Such as?" asked Gough-Coxe.

"Let's make the citizens put their lives on the line, not our soldiers and policemen."

"How would you do that?"

"Hostages."

A murmur swept across the room. "That is a simple solution," said the equally gormless Lord French.

"Simple," shot back Blood, "but effective." The room went quiet. "You will not beat Fenian terrorists without radical thinking," stated Blood, now cocksure. Broy suppressed a smile, because he realized that Blood and Collins thought exactly alike about their enemies.

Gough-Coxe liked this man Blood. All the other detectives seemed to be followers; this man was a leader. "Detective Blood, you seem to have all the answers."

"Better than that," replied Blood, beginning to enjoy the attention he was getting in the room, "I have a candidate."

"A candidate for what?" asked French.

"Our first Dardanelles hostage."

Broy and Boynton looked at each other across the room, and their eyes locked for a second. They both felt isolated and alone among all the brass and the other G-men, many of whom had been recently brought in from the North. They couldn't wait to tell Collins what was going on in this room.

"Gentlemen," said Lord French, "I'm happy that we could have this meeting. We will consider this problem, and I think we will have a solution shortly. Thank you for your time." He paused. "God save the King!"

"God save the King!" the room shouted in unison as they all jumped out of their seats like Pavlovian jack-in-the-boxes. Broy was still staring at Boynton, aware that his lips did not move and had risen slowly, even reluctantly. He made a mental note to see who this young G-man was.

Derek Gough-Coxe kept his eye on Sebastian Blood as the detective left the room, easy to spot with his head bandage and tapping cane. He was the man with the plan, and Gough-Coxe wanted to know more about him and his plan. "Detective Blood," he called out. Blood stopped in his tracks to see who was calling his name. He was delighted when he realized it was Gough-Coxe. Blood stuck out his hand to shake, and Gough-Coxe suddenly realized that Blood's knuckle was brushing the back of his hand. It was the Freemason's secret handshake. "You are a man of many surprises," said Gough-Coxe. Blood held the knob of his walking stick up so Gough-Coxe could see it. Gough-Coxe saw the Freemason's "All-Seeing Eye" engraving and smiled. "Detective Blood," Gough-Coxe said, "come and tell me all about your hostage candidate and the situation in the Dardanelles."

63

On Collins's orders, Eoin called both Broy and Boynton and told them to meet the bossman after work at 32 Bachelors Walk. Collins and Eoin were going over the daily intelligence brief when Broy arrived. "How's it going, Ned?" asked Collins.

Broy threw an envelope on Eoin's desk and said, "I thought I'd save the postage this time." Broy hung up his overcoat and then asked, "What's up?"

"We're still waiting for someone," said Collins. With that, there was a knock on the door. "Come in," he called out.

Brendan Boynton entered, and Broy jumped to his feet. For a second, Boynton thought he had entered the wrong office and was in the process of turning around to get out when Collins said, "Detectives! I thought you lads should meet each other." This statement was followed by a loud Cork laugh. "Detective Sergeant Broy, meet Detective Constable Boynton." The two men stood looking at each other for a second. "You can shake hands if you like," Collins finally said, and the two men gave a rather reluctant and suspicious shake.

"I saw you across the room with Blood," said Broy. "I thought you were his mate."

"God save the King!" laughed Boynton, which prompted a smile from Broy. "Blood and I do not get along," he said. "He's interested in your man here," Boynton said, pointing at Collins, "so I sent him over to you to check out the file." Boynton paused for a second before adding, "I wish I had known about you before. I could have been more effective."

"Well," cut in Collins, "you know now. The time is now right for you two to know about each other. I had to be sure I could trust both of you."

"Are there any more of your men in G-Division?" asked Broy.

Collins smiled. "Let's get down to the business of the day—Detective Blood. What are we up against?"

"He's a persistent prick," said Boynton.

"Even after the beating he took the other night?"

"More so," said Boynton, and Broy nodded in agreement.

"You should have seen him in that meeting with Johnny French," said Broy. "Had a grand idea about how to clog up the Dardanelles."

"His solution?" asked Collins.

"Civilian hostages," said Boynton.

"Jaysus, Mary, and Joseph," snapped Eoin. "He's thinking of my family."

"How do you know?" asked Collins.

"Who the fook else in Dublin does he know?" said Eoin. "He hasn't been in town more than six weeks, and, from reports, he's obviously obsessed with that fookin' barbershop. What can we do?"

"For the moment, Eoin, nothing," said Collins. "We have to see what he's up to."

"He's got the ear of the new man in town," said Broy. "An agent named Derek Gough-Coxe."

"Gough-*Co-shay*," laughed Collins. "Another fancy-name eejit. How do you spell that?"

"G-O-U-G-H-hyphen-C-O-X-E."

"Cocks!" roared Collins.

"*Co-shay*," corrected Broy.

Collins rolled his eyes. "I don't believe it. What's this eejit's story?"

"Don't know much about him," said Boynton. "Just in from the Middle East."

"Middle East," spat Collins. "When they start bringing people in from the Middle East and India, you know they are getting ready to give us a good royal fooking." Collins got up from his chair. "Eoin, let's find out about this Gough-Coxe, and let's find out quick." Collins turned to Broy and Boynton. "Find out all you can about this shite. A full rundown. Coordinate with Eoin." The detectives nodded affirmatively. "Eoin, buckle down. We'll have to see how this develops. Don't tell your Da or Frank. A warning to them will only make things worse. Right now, innocence is their best weapon." And, with that, Collins got up, threw on his overcoat and hat, and left the room, leaving his three intelligence agents to themselves.

Innocence is their best weapon, thought Eoin, rehashing Collins's departing words, knowing full well that innocence was in short supply in a dank Dublin City awaiting what would surely be an exceptionally cold winter.

64

The Crossley tender pulled up in front of Castle Barbers, and two British soldiers entered the shop. "Joseph Kavanagh?"

Joseph, unthreatened, looked up from his customer in the chair and said, "That's me."

"Come with us." Each soldier grasped the diminutive barber by an arm and frog-marched him out the front door, dressed only in his striped barber shirt against the November cold. The two soldiers lifted Kavanagh into the back of the tender, then joined him. Frank Kavanagh came to the door and stood mute, his mouth agape, as the tender pulled out and headed down Aungier Street in the direction of the South Circular Road.

Joseph Kavanagh was flummoxed by what was going on. "What's wrong?" he asked the Tommies, but got no reply. The tender continued into Camden Street, opposite the Bleeding Horse public house, and crossed the Grand Canal by Davy's Pub at the Portobello Bridge. As they headed into Rathmines, Kavanagh guessed that they were heading towards the Portobello Barracks, and he was right. Once there, he was marched into an office where a number of military types were milling around at their desks.

"Mr. Kavanagh," boomed a deep voice. Joseph turned around to see Detective Blood enter the room. *Maybe*, Kavanagh thought, *he can explain what's going on.* But there was no explanation forthcoming, only a righthanded blow to the side of Kavanagh's head, which sent the barber reeling across the floor. Several soldiers tentatively started to come to the aid of Kavanagh, but stopped short after Blood rushed to the fallen man.

"Where's your fucking Fenian son?" Blood demanded as he grabbed Kavanagh by the front of his barber's shirt, straightened him up, and blasted him again, sending him flying over a desk and landing in a lump in a corner. He again rushed to Kavanagh, spun him around, then battered him in the face with his walking stick, cutting his lip and sending blood flying spasmodically onto the wall. "Where is he?"

"Francis is not a Fenian," said Kavanagh, having trouble forming words because of the blood in his mouth. "He's only a kid."

"Not Francis," yelled Blood, "Your other son. I want to know where this Eoin character is. The one who works for Michael Collins."

Michael Collins. And with that, it became clear to Joseph Kavanagh what had happened—and what was about to happen to him and his family.

———

After his father's removal, Frank Kavanagh didn't know what to do, so he continued working in the shop. But there were no customers, and he found himself staring out the window onto Aungier Street. Then the honking started. It was long and persistent, and he'd never heard anything like it before. Frank opened the front door and looked to his left. There was a long convoy of British tenders and lorries advancing from the Portobello Barracks, obviously on their way to Dublin Castle. They were making themselves known to the neighborhood with all their honking horns. It was like they were inviting someone to throw a hand grenade. *They're asking for it*, thought Frank. But he noticed that something was queer with the lead lorry. It had the one necessity that the Dardanelles demanded—the bounce-back chicken wire was firmly in place. Then he saw it. On top of the cab of the truck, there was a man strapped into a makeshift, haphazard chair. He was there for a purpose—to tell the neighborhood to lay off this convoy, or your man would pay the consequences. As the lorry slowly passed Castle Barbers, the man turned his head to the right and stared straight at Frank.

That's when Frank realized that the hostage in the chair was his father.

"Da," he called out, stepping out into the street. His father shook his head violently, blood spitting out from his cut lip. Then Frank saw his father deliberately mouth one word: "E-O-I-N." He said it once, then a second time, and a third. As the lorry moved on down Aungier Street, Frank could hear laughter and realized it was coming from the right side of the lead lorry, where RIC Detective Sergeant Sebastian Blood was behind the wheel.

Frank ripped off his barber shirt, got his coat, and locked up Castle Barbers. He had to find Eoin but was clueless as to the whereabouts of his brother because Eoin was very secretive about where he worked. He knew, however, that Eoin often met up with Collins at the Wicklow Hotel, right off Grafton Street. He paused before going into the hotel, but he had no choice; he had to find his brother.

Frank stopped at the front desk and asked if Eoin Kavanagh was around. "Who's asking?" spoke up Willie Doran, the hotel's porter.

"I'm Eoin's brother, Frank. It's important I see him."

"Wait here," said Doran as he went into the back.

He returned within the minute and took Frank to an office where Joe Leonard, a member of the Squad, was alone. In front of Doran, Frank explained the situation with his father, and Leonard listened intently. Leonard was a fearless young man with an innate daring that had captured Collins's heart. Although only in his twenties, he was beginning to bald, and with his prominent beak of a nose, he had the intent look of a furious eagle. "Eoin's with Collins over in Harcourt Street," Leonard said. "I'm supposed to meet them here within the hour. Let's wait." Leonard turned to Doran. "When the Big Fella arrives, send him right back here."

"Will do," said Doran as he left the room.

"I'm sorry for your trouble, Frank," said Leonard. It was the kind of talk you would hear around the coffin at a wake, Frank thought, and he was getting more nervous by the minute. Suddenly, Leonard stood up. "I don't like this," he said.

"What?" said Frank.

"Come on," said Leonard. "Let's scoot!"

Within seconds, they were swiftly walking up Grafton Street, heading towards the Green. "What's wrong?" asked Frank.

"My bones," said Leonard.

"Your bones?"

"They tell me something isn't right." Within minutes, they were inside 6 Harcourt Street. "Where Mick?" Leonard demanded of one of the secretaries.

"He's over at number seventy-six."

Leonard, Frank in tow, flew out the door, across Harcourt Street in the direction of number seventy-six. "Where's Mick?" he demanded.

"Upstairs," came the reply.

"Wait here," Leonard told Frank, then climbed the stairs two at a time. Collins and Eoin were going over the National Loan books when Leonard burst in. "Let's go," he yelled at the two men.

"What's up?" asked Collins.

"We're about to be raided," said Leonard.

"How do you know?" said Eoin.

"My bones, lad," said Leonard, "my bones." It was always in the bones with Joe Leonard. "Let's get the fook out of here." When Eoin and Collins came down to the main floor, they were shocked to see Frank. Eoin looked his brother in the eye. Neither spoke, but Frank slowly shook his head.

"Let's go," said Collins, realizing what was happening. Out in Harcourt Street, he hailed a taxi coming down from the railway station at the end of the road. "Vaughan's Hotel," he told the cabbie. As they approached number six, they could see the first tenders arriving for a raid. The taxi continued down Stephen's Green and into Grafton Street. There was a commotion at the corner of Wicklow, as British soldiers rushed the Wicklow Hotel. "Get around that fookin' tram," Collins told the cabbie. The taxi swerved around a dormant tram and burst into Westmoreland Street. Within minutes, they were at Vaughan's.

"I knew there was something wrong," Leonard marveled. "Two raids simultaneously."

"As if they knew," said Eoin.

"They did," Collins replied grimly.

65

Brendan Boynton looked up from his desk when he heard the commotion. Flying through the office door was a disheveled Joseph Kavanagh, followed immediately by Sebastian Blood.

Boynton stood up as he recognized the prisoner but couldn't place him. "What's going on?" he demanded of Blood.

"We're getting close to Collins!" Blood stated with delight.

Kavanagh looked up and, for the first time, spoke to Blood: "In your fookin' dreams!" Then the striped shirt revealed the secret, and Boynton realized who the prisoner was—it was the barber who held a razor to his throat while Michael Collins made his quick exit over in Aungier Street.

Blood wound up his cane to strike, but was stopped when Boynton slammed a flat hand into his chest. "That's enough," Boynton said calmly. "We're not savages here."

"Here's the savage," protested Blood, his voice rising.

"You're both right," Derek Gough-Coxe cut in as he marched into the room. He walked up to Kavanagh and looked him up and down like he was surveying a Nighttown whore on the make. "So this is your solution, Detective Blood?"

"It is."

"Pathetic," said Gough-Coxe, shaking his head as he looked at Kavanagh. "But we'll know shortly, won't we?"

"How?" said Boynton.

"If the bombs stop going off in the Dardanelles, that might be a clue as to how successful Detective Blood's little plan is." Gough-Coxe paused. "The proof of the pudding is in the eating." With that, Gough-Coxe spun and left the room, late for his boat back to England.

"Well," said Boynton, "he doesn't exactly sound cocksure." He kept his poker face as Blood looked at him with disgust.

"Get ready for your trip back to the Portobello Barracks," Boynton finally said to Kavanagh. "For the foreseeable future, the Dardanelles will be your regular beat. Rain or shine, you'll get the British Army through!" With that, Blood grabbed Kavanagh and brought him down the hall to a holding cell. Brendan Boynton, trying hard to conceal his terror, put on his coat and hat and went to look for Michael Collins.

Boynton didn't know what to do. He had to get in touch with Collins, and he knew his best chance was through Eoin. He marched out of Dublin Castle and headed into Temple Bar on his way to the Ha'penny Bridge so he could cross the Liffey. He headed over to the Bachelors Walk address, where he sent his reports and met with Collins and Broy. But when he got there, the office was closed. Collins had been meticulous in keeping Boynton in the dark, and now he cursed that secrecy. Boynton stood in front of the office and briefly thought of contacting Broy but thought it too risky. He finally decided his only other option was to head to the Stag's Head, where he'd had his first meeting with "Mister Kavanagh."

At the Stag's Head he was relieved to see that the same barman, Silent Peadar Doherty, was still behind the stick. Boynton slid into an empty snug and leaned over. "Do you know how I can get in touch with Eoin Kavanagh?" he asked.

Doherty looked Boynton up and down and then finally said, "And who would like to know?"

Boynton didn't know if he wanted to tell him he was a Dublin Castle detective or not, but he felt he didn't have much choice. He reached into his pocket and presented Doherty with his business card. Doherty read it but said nothing. He walked into the back room and spoke to his shopboy in a low voice. "Get on your bicycle and take this card up to Eoin Kavanagh at Vaughan's Hotel. Ask him what we should do."

Boynton sat in the snug without a drink. It seemed like he was there for hours, but it was only twenty minutes later when the lad returned and spoke to Doherty. The barman came over and said, "Go to Bachelors Walk" and turned and went back to his business.

Within minutes, Boynton was there and was relieved to see not only Eoin but also Collins. As Boynton entered the office, he instinctively felt Collins's rotten mood. "I've been trying to reach you, and it hasn't been easy."

"It's not supposed to be fookin' easy," exploded Collins. "I put you in your box, and you'll stay in your box. No one will break the cell!"

Boynton was red-faced with embarrassment and more than a bit tongue-tied. There was a heavy quiet in the room until Eoin came to the rescue. "What do you have to tell us?" he said in a very calm voice.

"They've brought your father to Dublin Castle."

Eoin nodded calmly. "How is he?"

"Blood roughed him up, but he's alright."

"What's Blood's game?" interrupted Collins.

"Convoy hostage," said Boynton. "His grand idea is to use a neighborhood hostage in front of the convoy so the lads won't blow up the lorries."

"Very simple," said Collins.

"But effective," added Eoin.

"What are we going to do?" asked Boynton.

"For the moment," said Collins, "nothing. I have to work this out."

"Be fast about it," shot Eoin at his boss.

Eoin's admonishment caught Collins squarely and forced him to smile at his young acolyte, releasing the tension in the room. Collins turned to Boynton. "Brendan," he said, "you did well. But you should not contact me directly except in dire circumstances. I agree, this is a dire circumstance. I never sleep in the same place two nights in a row, and there's a reason for that. Avoid Broy, and the only place you can poke your head in is this office. You can leave a message through Peadar Doherty at the Stag's Head. But other than that, steer clear of me—and Eoin, for that matter."

Boynton stood up. "Thanks, Mr. Collins."

"Make it simple and call me 'Mick' from now on."

With that, Boynton was out the door. "Now what?" Eoin asked.

"I wish I knew," Collins replied with a sigh.

66

EOIN'S DIARY

I wonder what I have gotten my family into?

Mary and Dickie are in orphanages, Da is a pawn of the British, and Frank is about to be shocked into the reality of the movement.

I feel dejected, lost—like my world is spinning out of control. This revolution gets more demanding by the day, and I'm beginning to feel it's only a matter of time before it completely devours us all.

Before Mick left for business in Munster and the West, he assigned Vinny Byrne and Joe Leonard from the Squad to come to 31 Aungier with me. He's very worried about his office on the top floor and wants Vinny and Joe to get the files out of there. Mick also wants Frank to take a "vacation," as he puts it. He's worried that the British will not stop with harassing Da, and that Frank might be their next target. Frank was turned over to the Second Battalion, South Dublin, and will be moved to the Dublin Mountains to begin his "run."

We got to the house after midnight and entered through the back entrance. As we were heading towards the stairs, a muffled voice called out, "Who's there?" Vinny and Joe pulled out their guns.

"Don't shoot!" says I, because I knew it was Da, even though his voice was queer.

He was sitting in his big chair, fully dressed. His lip was swollen full. "Daddy," says I, "what have they done to you?"

"I'm alright, son," he said. "Where's Frank?"

I told him that Frank was under the care of the IRA, and he nodded that he understood.

"Mr. Kavanagh," said Joe Leonard, "who did this to you?"

"Fellow by the name of Blood," Da said and gave a little laugh at the irony. "I'm their ticket to Camden Street. They'll be back in the mornin' for me. I can handle it, Eoin, but I want you out of here. It's not safe for you or your mates." I told him we were here to get Collins's files. He nodded. "Good," he said. "Then get the hell out of here. They'll be back here at 6:00 a.m. for me."

"Why don't you come with us?" asked Vinny. "We can protect you."

"I don't want to be a burden to you or Mr. Collins," said my father. "They'll get tired of me after a while and go on to something else. I can take it."

"You're a brave man," said Vinny in admiration, and Leonard nodded his head in agreement.

We went upstairs and boxed up the files. I don't know what's in them, and neither do the lads. If it was important to know, Mick would have told us. We have a car, and we'll move them over to Bachelors Walk. As we were leaving, I went to my father. We are not a demonstrative family. We don't hug and kiss, and we never even think of saying the word "love," but I felt it was important to show Da how proud I am of him. I went over and kissed him on top of his perfect hair. "I'll keep an eye out for you, Da. And you can be sure that the boys in the street know what's going on. So you're not alone."

"I know that, son," he said. "I know I'm not alone. And believe me, the British know that, too." He paused. "But stay out of this place. If they find you, they'll do anything to get information out of you about Mr. Collins. So steer clear."

We loaded the files into the boot of the car and left 31 Aungier Street with dread in our hearts, not sure that my father could survive the interrogation methods of Detective Sergeant Blood.

67

Róisín came out of her flat in Walworth Road and rode out into Harrington Street on her bicycle, late for work. As she was about to turn into Camden Street, she was stopped by DMP Constable O'Shea as a military convoy came over the Portobello Bridge and moved on through. She thought of riding over to Clanbrassil Street to avoid the traffic but decided it wasn't worth the time. She would stay put and follow the convoy—at a distance, for safety's sake.

As she waited, she was shocked to see Eoin's father in his throne sitting atop the cab of the first lorry. He was tied to the chair nice and tight. "Mr. Kavanagh!" she called out, getting Joseph's attention. "Take care of Eoin," he shouted back, before the truck accelerated and moved on down Camden Street.

Constable O'Shea still had his hand up to stop traffic. "Get out of me way, ya fat eejit!" shouted Róisín, as she pushed her bicycle around him and went in hot pursuit. Róisín pedaled at a furious pace and soon caught up to the lead lorry. "You gutless cunts!" she shouted into the cab at the two Tommies. "You should be bloody ashamed of yerselves. Cunts!" The lorry accelerated to get away from Róisín, but she was up to the challenge. And the faster she pedaled, the more angry she got. "Get out of Ireland, ya fookin' hoors!" she screamed at the laughing Tommy nearest her. In total frustration, she propelled a large wad of saliva at the riding Tommy, hitting him solidly on the left side of his face.

"Jesus Christ!" came the Tommy's response.

"English cunt!" spat Róisín.

"Irish cunt!" The Tommy turned to the driver and said, "Let her have it, Nigel!"

With that, the lorry swerved left and drove Róisín toward the sidewalk, where she landed with a bone-shaking thud.

"Róisín! Róisín!" Joseph called out, but Róisín didn't hear him; she was seeing stars.

The lorry continued down the Dardanelles and made their left turn into Dame Street and found the safety of Dublin Castle. The two Tommies grabbed Joseph and took him directly to Detective Blood. "How was the trip?" he asked.

"They're not throwing bombs anymore," said Róisín's Tommy.

"That's good!" said Blood.

"They've got their ladies involved. The bombs have been replaced with fucking spit," he added, as he continued to wipe the side of his face clean of Róisín's spittle.

Blood was outraged. "So now you have Fenian cunts doing your dirty work," he said to Joseph. "Not man enough to do your own filthy deeds! Well, little man, you'll be paying for that." Blood hit Kavanagh squarely in the lip with a powerful right hook, ripping open the old wound and spattering blood around the office. Kavanagh hit the floor, and Blood went right after him, giving him a vicious kick to the lower back. Then, holding his walking cane like a shovel, he drove the brass handle with the All-Seeing Eye into Joseph Kavanagh's left kidney.

The two Tommies looked at each other in disbelief. "Hey mate, it was *only* spit," the one protested, before adding, "He had nothing to do with it."

Blood grimaced at the soldier as he lifted Kavanagh by the collar and led him to a cell down the hall. He threw Joseph into the cell, and the helpless barber fell face-first on the floor. For good measure, Blood went over to Kavanagh and gave him another kick in the kidney. "This will stop only when you tell me where your son is and where I can find Collins." With that, he slammed the cell door shut. "I will get that Fenian bastard if it's the last thing I do."

When Kavanagh regained consciousness some time later, he had to pee. He released into the chamber pot. His piss streamed blood red, reminding Joseph who he was up against.

———

Róisín's head felt wet, and her touch revealed blood. She dabbed it with a handkerchief and saw that it was only a superficial cut. "Are you alright, ma'am?" Róisín looked up to see Constable O'Shea, who put out a hand to help her rise. She ignored the help and continued to sit on the sidewalk, still trying to get her bearings.

"Get away from me!" she said to O'Shea. "Shame on you, working for those snakes."

"Ma'am," explained O'Shea patiently, "appearances can be deceiving." O'Shea extended his hand again, and this time Róisín took it, confused.

"Deceiving, eh?" she said, rubbing her bruised bum.

"You know what I mean," said the Constable.

"Yes, I think I do." Róisín checked out her bicycle, which was fortunately unharmed. She had to get to work at the Mater. She hopped on and continued her ride down Wexford Street.

"Miss," called out O'Shea. Róisín stopped and turned around. "Be careful!"

Róisín was forced to smile at the rotund DMP, feeling better knowing that she had a friend in the most unlikely place.

———

Róisín arrived at work, and her appearance shocked her co-workers. "Róisín," gasped Sister Aloysius, the supervising nun. "What happened to you?"

Róisín was about to say, "The fookin' British" but caught herself. "I had a little trouble with a lorry, Sister."

"We'll have to get that fixed," said the nun. Peroxide made the wound sting, but she considered herself lucky. She knew she should keep her temper under control, but sometimes she couldn't help it. As she changed from her trousers into her nursing attire, Róisín saw that she was bruised from her arse all the way down to the top of her knee. *My God*, she thought, *how I hate the British!* Then she thought of Mr. Kavanagh and Eoin, and she could feel her blood pressure rise and her face redden. There would be no simple relief, she knew.

On her way home that night, she made a quick stop at Dinny Doyle's key shop in Henry Street. "Dinny," she said, "could you make me a copy of one of these?" She held out her latchkey. New key in pocket, she continued on to the quays and Bachelors Walk. She went into number thirty-two and knocked at Eoin's office door, but there was no reply. She knew Eoin always picked up the late post, so she sat on the landing and waited. About fifteen minutes later, Eoin arrived, surprised to find the landing blocked by Róisín.

"How are ya?" she asked as their eyes met.

He saw the bandage on the side of her head and replied, "How are *you*?" He touched her face gently, kissed the top of her head, and helped her to her feet.

"I saw your daddy this morning."

Eoin slid his key in the lock, picked up the afternoon post off the floor, and threw his hat on his desk. "How was he?"

"He was on top of a British lorry in Camden Street."

"He's their hostage."

"For how long?"

"A few days. They're trying to stop us from bombing their convoys." Eoin paused before adding unconvincingly, "He can take it."

Róisín noticed that Eoin had a little stubble on his chin and above his lip. "You're growing a beard," she said with a smile.

"I didn't shave today."

"Why not?"

"Because I'm homeless. Mick and Da don't want me returning to Aungier Street. I slept here last night. I'll survive." Róisín reached for her handbag and winced. "What's wrong?" asked Eoin.

Róisín smiled. "The lorry your Daddy was riding in drove me to the ground. I have an awful bruise." Róisín undid her belt and lowered her britches to show Eoin her bruise. He moved her bloomers aside so he could see the full extent of the bruise, running from her left buttock all the way down her leg.

"You have a beautiful arse, Róisín," Eoin said quietly.

"And you have a dirty mind," came the response, punctuated with a laugh at the end. She pulled up her knickers and her pants and reached again for her bag. "Here," she said, turning over Dinny's brand-new key. "You're not homeless. You can always stay with me."

Eoin pocketed the key with a simple, "Thanks."

"Be sure to stay away from Aungier Street," Róisín said. "Mick is right. The Brits are looking for you. You're their key to finding Collins."

"That fooking film," said Eoin.

"Yes," agreed Róisín, "being the new Douglas Fairbanks wasn't worth it."

"Is anything worth anything?"

"Love is worth something," said Róisín. She smiled at her Eoin and then kissed him gently on the lips. "Take it from an older woman, a woman of the world!"

"Well," Eoin joked, "you are *older!*"

"You little imp," exploded Róisín, pushing Eoin onto Collins's couch. She was on top of him, and he wasn't moving.

"You weigh a ton!" he protested in a teasing voice. Róisín planted a wet kiss on Eoin, and the struggle ceased. Eoin could feel his willie move, and they settled into each other's arms. "Thank you," said Eoin.

"For what?"

"You know what."

68

Like a thief in the bleak, dank, and damp December night, Eoin approached 31 Aungier Street via the back alley. The house was dark, and he wondered if his father was home. He let himself in through the back door and dared not turn on the light. He made his way to the second floor and could see the silhouette of his father sitting in a chair by the front window. The gas street lamp, which his Uncle Todd had lit, lent just enough light to the room. "Da," he said quietly, but there was no response. "Da," he said again, and the only response was an exhale of a breath. "Da!" he said a third time, more urgently, touching his father's arm. Joseph opened his eyes, and, at the sight of his oldest son, he gave a quiet smile.

"Eoin, lad," he said. "I'm glad you came. I wanted to see you."

"Why?"

"I wanted to see you before I died," he said quietly, and a chill ran through his son.

"You'll be fine," he said as he brushed his father's hair off his forehead. Joseph groaned in pain. "What's the matter?"

"My back is sore," said Joseph. "They kept kicking me there. They're looking for Frank and you." He paused to catch his breath. "They're especially looking for you, because of Mr. Collins." Joseph winced as he tried to readjust himself in his chair. "I want you to do something for me."

"Anything."

"I want you to promise me you'll take care of your brothers and sister. I'm not long for this world. You must take my place."

"Da," said Eoin, "what in God's name are you talking about?"

"I'm done for, son," Joseph said as he closed his eyes. "I'm done for." He opened his eyes one more time. "Will you tell Mick something for me?"

"Yes, of course."

"Tell Mick Collins that I said thanks."

His father suddenly went quiet. Eoin shook his arm, but there was no response. "Daddy," he whispered desperately, but the old man didn't move. Eoin decided, despite the risk, that he had to do something. He went to Collins's abandoned office on the third floor to use the telephone. He asked the operator for the Mater Hospital. When they answered, he asked for Róisín O'Mahony.

"Eoin," Róisín said, sounding surprised. "What is it?"

"I need an ambulance at home. Da is very sick. I think the British overdid it with him today. Send an ambulance quick."

"Eoin, get the hell out of that house. If the British know you're there, they'll fry you."

"I'll go as soon as the ambulance arrives. Here's the number you can reach me at," said Eoin, as he gave her the phone number for the Dump, where the lads in the Squad would often "dump" their hot revolvers after a shooting.

Eoin sat quietly with his father for forty-five minutes until the ambulance arrived. Joseph was unconscious, breathing shallowly. He let the ambulance crew in the front door and directed them to his father on the second floor. As they passed him to get to his father, Eoin let himself out the back door and silently began to make his way to the Dump in Abbey Street.

Eoin navigated the back alleys and unmapped pathways and came out on St. Stephen's Green. He pulled his cap over his eyes and yanked the collar of his trench coat up as far as it would go. He prayed that no one, friend or foe, would recognize him.

The British had touts everywhere, ordinary Dubliners who lusted after their thirty pieces of English silver. During the famine, they took the soup. In revolutionary Dublin, they took the cash. Collins and Liam Tobin were catching on to them, but until they could be identified and eliminated, they were the eyes and ears of the British in Dublin. Eoin kept walking right into Grafton Street, and, on his left, he passed the Cairo Café, which was becoming a British hangout.

As he walked along, he suddenly realized that Christmas was upon Dublin. Although the war was escalating, you wouldn't know it by looking in the windows of Brown Thomas and Weir's, all decorated merrily for the Yuletide. *Yeah*, thought Eoin to himself, *this is really going to be a fookin' Happy Christmas.*

Vinny Byrne and Paddy Daly were in the Dump when he arrived. Eoin got himself a hot mug of Bovril and waited for the phone to ring. The Dump was on the corner of Abbey and Sackville Streets. It was an office like any other office in Dublin, but it contained Collins's assassins, the men who were making this an even fight. It was here that they rested and awaited orders on who next to shoot. As he thought of his father, he was sorry he had turned down Collins's offer to join the Squad.

The phone rang, and Paddy, one of the leaders of the Squad, answered it. "Eoin," he said, "it's for you. The Mater."

"Róisín," he said into the phone. "How is he?" There was quiet on the other end. "Róisín?"

"Eoin dear," she finally said. "I have some bad news for you." There was quiet again.

"He's dead," said Eoin flatly. "Isn't he?"

"Yes, Eoin. I'm so sorry. Your dear daddy is dead."

"Eoin," said Vinny, when Eoin failed to respond. "Are you alright?"

"Me Daddy is dead, Vinny. Me Daddy is dead." Tears flooded from Eoin's eyes, and he dropped heavily to the floor, the phone still in his hand.

"It's alright, lad," said Vinny, embracing his friend. "*Misneach,*" he said in Irish, the word for "courage."

"Eoin, Eoin," he could hear Róisín's voice say distantly.

"Yes, Róisín," he said, replacing the receiver to his ear, suddenly dry-eyed. "I'll be up there in a few minutes."

"For God's sake," said Róisín, "stay away. If they find out your father's dead, they'll be watching for you."

"I'll be there in a few minutes," said Eoin, his soul as cold and empty as the winter night outside.

When he arrived at the Mater, he asked for Róisín. When she came down, she hugged Eoin as hard as she could. "Take me to my Daddy," was all he said. She took him to the mortuary where his father was lying naked, covered only by a sheet. It was the same slab that Thomas Ashe had occupied. It seemed that history was repeating itself, only this time it was his family on that cold slab. Eoin pulled back the sheet that covered his father's head and just looked. Róisín stood by him, holding his left arm with both of her hands. "So it all comes down to this," he said, not really talking to Róisín, but to his father. "This time, Da, we will not be denied. And I swear on my immortal soul that I'll find out who did this to you, and they will be paid back in kind."

With that, the door opened, and Michael Collins walked into the mortuary. He had a big box under his arm, and he immediately went to Eoin. "I'm so sorry, Eoin," he said. "But I promise you, we'll get the scum that did this."

"Don't bother," said Eoin coldly. Collins shook his head, confused. "*I'm* going to get the gobshite, and I'm going to get him good." He finally looked at Collins. "How did you know?"

"Róisín sent a message over to Vaughan's for me."

There was silence among the three living and the one dead. "Let's dress the body," said Collins. He opened his big box and took out a Volunteer's uniform. He had woken Mr. Fallon of Fallon's of Mary Street so that he could procure the uniform.

"But my father wasn't in the Volunteers," protested Eoin.

"Yes, he was," said Collins forcefully. "Your Da did more work for the movement than a lot of the IRA brigades around the country. He was a Volunteer through-and-through." For a moment Eoin was touched, but the moment didn't last long.

"I want to examine the body," Collins said. "Look away," he commanded Eoin.

"No," said Eoin firmly. "I want to see what they did to my Daddy."

"Róisín," said Collins, "will you help me?" They removed the sheet.

"We come into this world naked," said Eoin absently. "And I guess we leave it the same way."

Collins and Róisín looked at each other and grimaced. There were no marks on the front of the body until they came to the legs, and they saw ugly sores on both calves and ankles. "Ulcers," said Róisín. "Very, very bad nutrition," she added, in diagnosis.

"He starved himself for years so his family could eat," said Eoin. "He sometimes survived on one egg a day and cups of watered-down tay."

"One miserable oige," said Collins, shaking his head. He turned Joseph over, and his back revealed his demise. It was all black-and-blue, from his shoulder blades to his buttocks. The British had slaughtered his kidneys.

"I hope they note this in the autopsy," said Róisín innocently.

"There won't be any autopsy," snapped Collins. "The British don't want any more inquests."

"Why?"

"Because the juries keep returning 'death by murder' against the Crown."

In deadly silence, they dressed Joseph Kavanagh in his Volunteer's uniform. Eoin noted that he looked sharp, still keeping his sartorial splendor, even in death. As a final act, Eoin made sure the curl of Joseph's handlebar mustache was perfect. As they prepared to leave, Collins said, "I'll send a coffin over in the morning. No wake. The mass will be tomorrow and then the burial. The quicker, the better."

"I'll be there," said Róisín.

"So will I," said Eoin.

"No, you won't," said Collins, and the boy looked shocked. "I'm sorry, Eoin, but Saints Michael and John's will be crawling with G-men hoors. It's not safe. I can't go, either."

"But I will," interjected Róisín.

Eoin dropped his head. "I understand, Mick." The British were still robbing the Kavanaghs of their dignity. Suddenly, Eoin turned to Róisín. "Did he receive the last rites?"

"No," said Róisín, somewhat baffled. "He didn't. I didn't think it was safe to draw any more attention to him then I had to. I don't know who I can trust anymore."

"Smart move," agreed Collins.

"Then there's one more thing we have to do before we get out of this terrible place," said Eoin. "He deserves—demands—a Perfect Act of Contrition." With that, Eoin bent down to his father's ear and said, "*Oh my God! I am heartily sorry for having offended Thee, and I detest all my sins, because I dread the loss of heaven and the pains of hell. But most of all because they offend Thee, my God, Who art all-good and deserving of all my love. I firmly resolve, with the help of Thy grace, to confess my sins, to do penance, and to amend my life. Amen.*"

"Amen," echoed Róisín and Collins, and, for one last moment in time, the four Fenians were united as one.

1920

1920

69

Eoin decided he had to see Collins. He began the trek from Crow Street, over the Ha'penny Bridge, and up Liffey Street, unconsciously retracing his steps to the GPO that rainy Tuesday night of Easter Week. He walked blindly, as if on auto-pilot. He was thinking about what he had to say to Mick. He found himself in Moore Street and then continued on his way to Parnell Square. He knew the boss would be in Joint Number One, Vaughan's Hotel, at the top of the Square.

Eoin banged his open hand on the reception desk, and Christy Harte, the porter, nodded and shot his eyes upward to indicate that Collins was in.

Eoin knocked on the door. "Come in," Collins called from inside.

He was alone in the room doing paper work. Eoin didn't mince words. "I want to join the Squad," he said without hesitation.

"I want you at Crow Street," returned Collins.

"I think I can do both jobs."

If nothing else, Collins liked his ambition. "What made you change your mind?"

"My Da."

"Simple as that?"

"Yes."

Collins looked down at the papers in front of him. "I don't like revenge as a motive. The man who holds revenge in his heart is not fit to be a Volunteer."

243

"I can handle it," came the defiant answer.

"Revenge gets you in trouble."

"Tell the truth," snapped Eoin, "and shame the devil." Collins stared at Eoin, remaining mute. "Sometimes revenge is necessary. When will Percival Lea Wilson get his?" Eoin said, referring to the tormentor of Tom Clarke and Seán MacDiarmada that damp Saturday night on the Rotunda Hospital grounds, just across the way. Little did Eoin know that Collins was already planning the demise of Captain Wilson, who thought himself safe and sound in Gorey, County Wexford.

"You have a way of making your point, Eoin," conceded Collins.

"You think I want to live this vindictive life?" said Eoin. "I was not brought up that way. You know my parents."

"You do realize that joining the Squad is equivalent to a 'calling'?"

"A 'calling'!" snapped Eoin. "What are you looking for? A priest of sanctified murder?"

"Fair enough," said Collins, allowing a smile, and not wanting to rile the boy any further. "The Squad has taken to calling themselves 'The Twelve Apostles.' Imagine that."

Eoin could. "I guess that makes you Jesus Christ." Collins laughed out loud before Eoin cut him short. "Beware of Judas." The smile evaporated from Collins's face.

Collins stood up and towered over Eoin. "You jeerin' me, boy?"

Eoin became deadly serious. "I need this job. This country, this city has destroyed my fooking family. My parents are dead. My brother Frank is on the run in the Dublin Mountains. Mary and Dickie are in orphanages. I have to make a better tomorrow for this country, or my family is done for." Eoin paused. "For now, you and the movement are my family."

Collins sat down again, his hands calmly on the papers in front of him, deflated. He finally opened the top drawer of the desk and pulled out a Webley. "Here," he said, placing the gun on the desk near Eoin. "This is Blood's. The one they took off him at the movie house. Get Vinny to show you how to use it. Go out to the country and make yourself an expert. You will continue to work in Crow Street, and I will use you only when I have to. You will supplement the Squad."

"The Thirteenth Apostle."

"The baker's dozen," said a suddenly weary Collins. Eoin picked up his gun, slid it into his coat pocket without saying another word, and left. Collins rose, stretched, and went to the window, which had a straight-on view of Parnell Square North and the grounds of the Rotunda. One thought kept pricking at Collins's conscience—who was his Judas?

70

EOIN'S DIARY

I was on me way to meet the boss at the Stag's Head. I had his daily intelligence brief for him. I knew I was in trouble as soon as I stepped out of 3 Crow Street and walked into Dame Street.

The British had dropped the net.

Since we've been pushing back, I think they are getting a little frightened. They are expert at this, but I was surprised they did it this close to Dublin Castle. Usually they do it away from the Castle, in hopes of snatching a big fish off the street. What they do is cordon off four to six blocks with Crossley tenders and send in the troops. They stop one and all and check IDs.

I thought of turning back to the office, but thought better of it when I saw a Tommy advancing towards me up Crow Street. I turned towards Trinity College, but it was chaos that way, with the army stopping and boarding trams. Thinking quickly, I turned into Temple Lane and headed to Turner & Kelly, Watchmakers & Jewellers. I went by their window, and everything looked normal as a man sat concentrating his eye-loupe on the guts of a sick watch. I banged on the door next to the shop. It was the home of the Gallaghers.

"Who's there?" my Aunt Nellie asked.

"Eoin," says I. "Let me in." I barged in and slammed the door behind me.

"Eoin, what's the matter?"

"Aunt Nellie," says I, "the Brits just dropped the net on Dame Street."

"God bless us, save us," replied my mother's older sister.

"Don't worry—you'll be safe enough," I reassured her.

"Who's that, Nell?" called my Uncle Todd from the next room. He was getting ready for work. When he came in and saw me, he turned white. "What's the matter?"

Didn't even ask how I was. "The Brits dropped the net on Dame Street." Todd nodded, hitching up his suspenders in the process. He looked very uncomfortable. "I'll only be staying a few minutes." He mutely nodded again.

"Would you like a cup of tay?" asked me auntie.

"I would, indeed." Both Todd and I sat down as my young cousins, Mary, Richard, and Dan, came bounding out of the back room. It seems a lot of the cousins share the same family names. Mary Anne and Richard Conway were my mother's parents, and my grandmother lived in this very flat until the day she died. I thought of the happy Sunday afternoons I had spent with me Granny Conway and me Mammy here in Granny's "Durty Lane," and suddenly the British army didn't seem as fearsome anymore.

Auntie Nellie poured the tea. "What are you doing now?"

"I work for a loan society," I said, not really lying.

"I see you going into that building on Exchequer Street," said Uncle Todd, letting me know he knew my business. He never says anything, but he knows I'm in the movement. Todd and I do not see eye-to-eye. He was born in England of Irish parents, and he proudly admits that his father was a warder in a prison back in England. This is one occupation that Dubliners loathe, and I'm surprised that Todd would admit to such a degenerate ancestry. "Leave it to Nellie," me Daddy always used to say, "to end up living with a screw's son." For some reason, this always upset me Mammy, who would say "Hush!" and slash at Da with a dish rag.

Todd, of course, doesn't think much of the rebels. He has forbidden my cousins from getting involved in any way with the movement. I quietly tried to feel Todd out for Collins because of his occupation. He's a lamplighter and works both ends of the night. I don't see much of a future in that job, but he's allowed to wander the Dublin streets after curfew and would be the perfect agent to be moving papers around town. But he wanted nothing to do with the Shiners, as he called us. I was lucky he allowed me to stay in the house for a few minutes.

I'm not trying to get anyone in trouble, but if I know someone in the family could be of help to the movement, it is my duty to ask. And sometimes they come to me. I was coming out of the Bachelors Walk office with the intelligence post, on my way to Vaughan's to deliver it to Collins, when I ran into my Uncle Charlie Conway, my mother's older brother, in front of Knapp and Peterson's Tobacconists at Kelly's Fort. Charlie works as a brewery policeman down at the Guinness factory in James Street. He's been there since just about the time I was born. Charlie is a kind soul, and I think he was my Mammy's favorite sibling, because she named my brother after him. I haven't seen him since my Da's funeral last Christmas.

"I saw the film" were the first words out of his mouth to me. I could see he was concerned. "I went by the house in Aungier Street, and it was abandoned. What happened to Frank?" I decided to take him up to the office so we could talk.

Once inside I said, "Frank's on the run in the mountains. Would you like some tea?"

"I don't know what's going to happen to this poor family," he said, downhearted.

"Whatever happens, happens," I replied coldly. "I will fight to the end."

Charlie suffered his own tragedy in 1918 when his wife, Margaret, died of influenza while he was away with the Royal Field Artillery during the Great War. I could never figure Uncle Charlie out. He had fought in the Boer War, and as soon as the war in Europe broke out, he re-enlisted, despite his advancing age.

"He's gone daft," my Da had said to Mammy, and, this time, she offered no disagreement. I have to be careful with Charlie because of his loyalist leanings, but I don't think he would ever do me any harm.

"How are you coming along without yer Da?" he asked.

"I'll survive," I replied, before adding, "How are things in Stoneybatter without Aunt Margaret?"

Charlie was quiet, thinking. "I should have been there for her."

"Yes, you should have," I added quickly, with maybe a little with a little too much vigor. "You should have been there when my Mammy died, too. She was asking for you at the end."

"I had my priorities."

"They were wrong."

"I love my country."

"England is not your country. Ireland is. When will you realize that?"
Charlie was quiet again. Then he smiled. "You are young."

"But that doesn't make me stupid."

"No, it doesn't."

I was about to pour the tay when he held his hand up. "Do you have
a strainer?"

He wanted to block the tea leaves. I smiled. "Sorry," says I. My
Mammy used to love to "read" the tea leaves—she could see the future
in them, she swore—in the bottom of an empty cup, but I think Charlie
is a little superstitious about the whole thing. I don't care one way or the
other. "So," says I, "what did you think of the movie?"

"That was you with Michael Collins," he said. I nodded my head.
"I'm worried for you if the authorities find out."

"No one will find out, Uncle Charlie, if everyone keeps their big, fat
gobs shut."

Charlie nodded. "You don't have to worry about me, son." He paused
and looked me directly in the eye. "I'll ask you no questions, so you
won't have to tell me any lies."

"I appreciate that," I said honestly.

"I've been thinking about this, and I have something for you or Mr.
Collins." He paused, then added, "I have a few guns I took back with
me from France." Charlie, being a Catholic, probably got his job at
Guinness because of his military service to the Crown. As Mick often
tells me, it doesn't hurt to have police friends in any organization. Mick
is quite proud of his brother Paddy, who is a policeman on the force in
Chicago.

"We're desperate for guns, you know," I said. "If you can rouse up
any more, we'd appreciate it. The heavier the caliber, the better."

"I'll see what I can do," said Charlie, standing up.

"Why?" I asked.

"Things are not right in this country," Charlie began. "I fought in the
war to protect small nations. Charity begins at home, here in Ireland."
He paused, maybe disturbed at what he had just said. "How can I reach
you?"

"Ask for me at Vaughan's Hotel in Parnell Square," I replied. "They can get a message to me." I looked him directly in the eye. "Forget about this place."

He nodded. Uncle Charlie put his empty cup on my desk and stood up to leave. I picked up the cup and stared into the leaves. "What do you see?" he asked, with some apprehension.

"I think I see a gun," says I, with a small smile.

"You are your mother's son," returned Charlie, with his own quirk of the lips.

———

Charlie was on my side, but Uncle Todd remained adamant against the rebels. In Aunt Nellie's kitchen, my ears were pricked for outside gunfire, but everything was quiet. His tay finished, Uncle Todd went to get his coat, and I took Collins's papers out of my coat pocket and slid them under Aunt Nellie's apron. "I'll be back in a few minutes. Please. Do this for me." Nellie nodded, and I realized how much she looked like my mother.

"Ready?" asked Todd, letting me know he wanted me out.

We both walked out the door together and turned left into Dame Street. The dragnet was over; it was business as usual. I said goodbye to Todd and watched him head down South Great Georges Street with his lighting pole, which he used to turn on the gas lamps in the neighborhood.

When he was out of sight, I returned to my auntie's flat. When she saw me, she gave me a sweet smile and handed me Collins's daily intelligence package. "I didn't peek," she said impishly.

"I'll tell that to Mick Collins," I said.

"Mick Collins!" she said, flushing like a young girl.

"I'll give him your regards," I said, and her blush brightened.

"God bless him," Aunt Nellie said as she closed the door, showing that Fenian blood could flow in the most unlikely households in Ireland.

71

"I should have done better by the boy."

Collins, feeling guilty, was sitting in the back room of Kirwan's Pub on Parnell Street—now known as Joint Number Two—with Mick McDonnell and Paddy Daly, the leaders of the Squad, along with McKee and Mulcahy. Since Eoin had barged his way into the Squad, Collins wondered what had gone wrong in the Dardanelles. His instincts told him Sebastian Blood was not that dangerous, but the corpse of Joseph Kavanagh on that slab at the Mater told him he was wrong.

"What's the latest with the hostage situation in Camden Street?" asked Collins, wearily.

"Kavanagh has been replaced by the local butcher," replied McDonnell.

"When they're not using the local baker," added Daly.

"I just hope there's no fookin' candlestick-maker in the neighborhood," said Collins. "Do these fellows work for us?"

"Not at 'tal," replied McKee. "They're just local merchantmen."

Collins turned to McDonnell. "How's Eoin coming along with the gun?"

"I asked that very question of Vinny yesterday," replied the balding McDonnell, cracking a rare smile. "He says, 'there are no bad shots at one-foot range'!"

"So he's ready?" asked Collins, and McDonnell nodded that he was. He paused. "What do you men think about Blood?"

"He's gotta go," said Daly without hesitation, and McDonnell nodded in agreement.

"So be it," said Collins. "Let's start tagging him. I can't allow this to go on. No more hostages. We will take Blood out, and then we'll take out the convoys, no matter what hostage they stick up there. Is that understood?" Collins stood up and walked around the small room. "I want to send a message to the G-men that this sort of harassment is out of bounds. I want to take Blood out in spectacular fashion. I want Dublin Castle to know that this is not just another assassination. This is personal."

"Right you are, Mick," said Daly.

"The Squad will do Blood. Then McKee's lads will take out the convoys."

"Grenades again?" asked Mulcahy.

"Drivers," replied Collins. "If their drivers are dead, who will drive the lorries?"

"What do you mean?" asked McKee.

"I want a lad from the country, a marksman, who can kill a racing jackrabbit at two hundred yards," said Collins. "I don't want some Dublin city boy. Half the men in Dublin couldn't hit their mate's arse at point-blank range."

"A culchie sniper?" asked Dublin native McKee.

"The best you can find, you bloody Jackeen!" said Collins, giving a great laugh. "Find him and get him into Dublin as quick as you can." Collins rubbed his cold hands together and smiled at the four men. "It's going to be grand." He slapped his hands together hard. "Bloody grand."

———

Eoin was working in Crow Street when he got a call telling him to report to the Dump over in Abbey Street. When he arrived, the only men in the office were McDonnell, Daly, and Vinny Byrne. "Collins has signed Sebastian Blood's death warrant," said O'Donnell. "He wants you in on the job. We're tagging him now. We'll hit him in another couple of days. The four of us will be the primary team, and, of course, we'll have another four in the backup." McDonnell paused for a minute. "Are you ready?"

"Yes," said Eoin. "Just tell me what I have to do," he added, quietly terrified at what was about to happen.

72

Sebastian Blood was a creature of habit, which delighted the Squad members tagging him. Every morning, like clockwork, he would emerge in the dark from the Ivanhoe Hotel in Harcourt Street at seven and start his trek over to Dublin Castle, always via Aungier Street. He made it a point to go by the empty Castle Barbers, as if he was reliving, daily, one of the great moments of his life.

Normally, the Squad would have shot Blood dead in front of his hotel. It would be quick, and the getaway would be certain. But Collins wanted to telegraph this one to Dublin Castle, and Blood's monotonous routine was only going to help them. "Let's be on our toes," reminded Paddy Daly. "The last time we hit this bastard, he broke his routine and we had to chase him to the movie house in Mary Street. Be sharp."

The Squad cleared Blood's calendar with Brendan Boynton, and it was decided to hit him on Monday, January 26. The morning dawned clear and cold, with a hint of dawn appearing over the east side of St. Stephen's Green. Blood did not disappoint as he headed down Cuffe Street and turned into Aungier Street. As he walked by Castle Barbers, he was shocked to see the shop lit up in the early morning darkness. A man was standing in the back, dressed up in a striped barber's shirt.

It couldn't be Joseph Kavanagh, thought Blood. *He's dead.* And Blood didn't believe in Fenian ghosts—at least not yet. He rubbed his eyes to clear his head and saw that the barber was too young to be Joseph Kavanagh. Then it hit Blood—this was Collins's kid, the barber's missing son, the one in the film, the one he had been searching for all over Dublin. Blood went to the door, and his hand stiffened in anticipation before he turned the knob and entered. Blood knew in his gut that this was the perfect conclusion to the Joseph Kavanagh caper. It had all been worth it.

"Eoin Kavanagh?" he said.

"Detective Sergeant Sebastian Blood," came the reply.

"Kavanagh," Blood said, as he tapped his walking stick twice for emphasis, "you're under arrest for sedition."

Blood was so focused on Eoin that he did not see McDonnell and Daly coming up behind him. Blood stood in his tracks until he saw Vinny Byrne come out of the back room. Instantly he realized that he was trapped, and he reached for his revolver. Daly hit him in the back of the head with his Luger, and Blood dropped to the floor, groggy, but conscious. Eoin retrieved Blood's newly reissued gun, ID, badge, notebook, and wallet. Daly and McDonnell picked Blood up and put him in the first chair by the window. Vinny Byrne came up to their prisoner with a cup of cold water and threw it in his face.

"Wake up, ya gobshite," said Vinny, and Blood's eyes flew open in terror. He looked out into Aungier Street hoping for some help, but all he saw was the backup team.

"I have a message for you from Michael Collins," said McDonnell, who went face-to-face with Blood while Daly held him in the chair by the shoulders. "You've been convicted of the murder of Joseph Kavanagh, soldier of the Republic, and other high crimes against Ireland. Your sentence is death. Say your prayers."

Blood couldn't think of any prayers to say. He was so frightened, and his heart seemed to leap out of his chest with each beat. "I was only doing my duty," was all he managed to say.

"Was your duty tormenting my Da?" said Eoin, cold as the Webley in his right hand. "Who the hell do you think you are to come into my country and tell me and my family what to do?"

"I'm sorry about your father," Blood meekly replied, his solipsistic pomp gone flaccid.

"No, you're not," said Eoin, as he positioned himself on Blood's right. "There's nothing really to you, is there?" Blood made no reply in his defense. "May the Lord have mercy on your immortal soul," said Eoin as he raised the gun, which had once belonged to Blood, even with the detective's head. Daly released Blood's shoulders and stepped back, as did the two other Squad members. Without hesitation, Eoin shot Blood once in the right temple. The detective's blood splattered onto his barber's shirt. Eoin walked away as Byrne came around and finished Blood off with a shot into his left ear. To complete the job, Daly pinned a note to Blood's coat:

G-MEN
BEWARE!

McDonnell made sure to snugly position the Freemason walking cane between Blood's stiffening knees, as Collins had instructed. Daly wished he had a camera, because this corpse was worth a thousand words to the British—it was dead proof that the gamesmanship was over, and the war had begun in earnest. Eoin stripped off his barber's shirt as two cars pulled up in front of the shop. The primary team jumped into the first car, and the backups took the second. Detective Sergeant Sebastian Blood sat in Joseph Kavanagh's barber chair, as dead as he could be, with Queen Victoria looking down on him, a slight hint of dissatisfaction on her homely face.

———

Timmy O'Farrell was down the street on the roof of a four-story building on the corner of Aungier and Digges. He was a long way from his home in Coolshannagh, County Monaghan. In his hands he held a British-issued Lee-Enfield rifle—known as the "Sniper's Friend" by the British army during the Great War—which he had been practicing with in the Dublin Mountains for the last two days. His orders from McKee were simple—take out the driver of the lead lorry of the first British convoy coming into the Dardanelles that morning. He was then instructed to take out the soldier in the passenger seat. He was also told to be sure to avoid hitting the hostage, sitting in his chair above the cab, at all costs.

He had heard two shots behind him on Aungier Street and knew that the first job of the day had been done. Now it was his turn. He carefully took aim as the truck came through Wexford Street and sweetly pulled the trigger. The bullet hit Private Alphie Constance in the mouth and traveled through to his spinal cord, killing him instantly. The lorry jerked to the side of the road. His mate, Corporal Ian Stamp, leaned over his friend in terror and never felt the bullet that ripped off the top of his head.

Out of the doorways of Wexford Street came members of the Second Battalion, South Dublin Brigade of the IRA, to untie the hostage and haul him to safety. Soldiers were shot as they sat in their lorries, and hand grenades devastated all eight lorries in the convoy. And, as swiftly as they has descended, the IRA vanished, leaving nothing but destruction in their wake.

Timmy O'Farrell left his post on the roof, impressed with the Lee-Enfield, and wondered who Dick McKee wanted him to shoot next. This was easier, he decided, than shooting jackrabbits in the Monaghan countryside.

73

EOIN'S DIARY
MONDAY, JANUARY 26, 1920

A fter the job, the car dropped me off in Dame Street, as they thought I was going to the Crow Street office. But on impulse, I decided to catch the 8:00 a.m. mass at Saints Michael and John's. I don't go to mass much during the week. It's strictly a Sunday thing with me. I think I went there because I wanted to be near my parents, who were married there in 1900. I needed their support after the awful events of the morning.

At the beginning of the mass, I felt nothing. I didn't feel happy about killing Blood, but I didn't feel particularly bad about what I did, either. I didn't even feel a sense of revenge—just the satisfaction of doing my duty.

I love the mass, and I know the Latin by rote. I was an altar boy down at St. Kevin's in Harrington Street, and, out of habit, I still mouth the responses to the priest. The Church, like my Fenianism, runs deep in my gut.

I was fine until the *Confiteor* intruded on my numb reverie:

"Confiteor Deo omnipoténti, beátae Maríae semper Virgini, beáto Michaéli Archángelo, beáto Joánni Baptistae, sanctis Apóstolis Petro et Paulo, ómnibus Sanctis, et tibi, Pater: quia peccávi nimis cógitatióne, verbo, et ópere."

"I confess to Almighty God, to Blessed Mary, ever Virgin, to Blessed Michael the Archangel, to Blessed John the Baptist, to the Holy Apostles Peter and Paul, and to all the Saints, and to you, Father, that I have sinned exceedingly in thought, word, and deed."

And, suddenly, it hit me that I had, indeed, sinned exceedingly in thought, word, and, especially, deed. It struck me particularly hard when he mentioned *Michaéli Archángelo*, and I realized that I had basically begged my own Michael for this job, and now I think I regret it. I don't know if I can do this again.

"*Mea culpa, mea culpa, mea máxima culpa. Ideo precor beátam Mariam semper Vírginem, beátum Michaélem Archángelum, beátum Joánnem Baptistam, sanctos Apóstolos Petrum et Paulum, omnes Sanctos, et te, Pater, oráre pro me ad Dómiunum Deum nostrum.*"

"Through my fault, through my fault, through my most grievous fault," said I, as I hit me craw three times hard. "Therefore I beseech Blessed Mary, ever Virgin, Blessed Michael the Archangel, Blessed John the Baptist, the Holy Apostles Peter and Paul, and all the Saints, and you, Father, to pray to the Lord Our God for me."

My Most Grievous Fault.

What would my dear, gentle Mammy think? Would my Da approve, even though I did this awful shooting to give him some kind of awkward justice? What kind of a son did they raise?

Now I am just lost, and I wonder if I should even be doing this intelligence work, which will only cause more death and destruction.

The priest ended the Confiteor by saying: "*Misereátur vestri omnípotens Deus, et dimíssis peccátis vestries, perdúcat vos ad vitam aetérnam.*"

"May Almighty God have mercy on you, forgive you your sins, and bring you to life everlasting."

Mercy, forgiveness, life everlasting.

I wonder if God will have it in his power to bestow these sacred, precious gifts on me, a sinner of the worst kind.

I picked up the newspapers, including the British Sunday papers, on my way back to Crow Street. Only Liam Tobin was in the office. "How did it go, Eoin?" he asked gently, and I told him Blood was dead, efficiently, with the use of only two bullets. Without asking, he brought me a cup of tay, and patted me on my back when he put it down in front of me. My conscience was still pricking at me when I started to go through the classifieds of the London papers. It didn't take long to be brought back to reality by the neat little advertising box:

EX-OFFICERS WANTED. Seven pounds a week,

free uniform and quarters. Must have first-class records:
to join Auxiliary Division, Royal Irish Constabulary:
12 months guarantee—apply, with full particulars,
service, age, to R.O., R.I.C., Scotland Yard, London S.W.

"Jaysus, Liam," says I, "come look at this!" Tobin was reading over my shoulder in seconds. "Scotland Fookin' Yard! What does it mean?" I asked.

"It means we're in for the fight of our lives," said Tobin. "They're going to send a boatload of Sebastian Bloods to Ireland. That's what it means."

"A boatload of Sebastian Bloods to Ireland."

My melancholy began to lift as my blood began to boil.

"Make sure Mick sees this in his intelligence brief tonight," Liam said.

Yes, it was important that a certain Irish *Michaéli Archángelo* saw what the British had in mind for Ireland in 1920. And I began to wonder how long it would be before the Squad needed my services again.

74

"Welcome to the Dardanelles!"

Diane and Johnny were standing in front of Whelan's Pub at the corner of Wexford Street and Camden Row.

"So, this is it," said Diane.

"Yes," said Johnny. "It runs all the way to the Grand Canal in the south and up to Dame Street in the north, connecting the Portobello Barracks to Dublin Castle. You can see how important it was to the British back then."

"And important to Michael Collins."

"And Grandpa, too," said Johnny. He took Diane's hand and walked a few paces into Camden Row. "That's number forty."

"So?"

"That's where Grandpa was born. That's where his father's barbershop was between 1894 and 1910—before his finances went south."

"So this is Grandpa's neighborhood."

"Deep to his gut," replied Johnny, "he knew every inch of it. He also represented it in the *Dáil* until the day he died. Come on," he said, taking his wife by her hand. They started walking north, entering Aungier Street. He pointed out a derelict building on the corner of Digges Street. The only clue to its past was the battered Smithwick's sign hanging above, indicating that it was once a pub. "That's where Dick McKee's Monaghan sniper worked—great view down into Wexford and Camden Streets."

They walked past the Dublin Institute of Technology, and Johnny continued his dissertation. "Do you know what that once was?" Diane shook her head. "That was Jacob's Biscuit Factory, where it all began for Grandpa."

Johnny could see that Diane was beginning to get overwhelmed by it all. "I can't believe how intimate it all is," said Diane. "History on almost every corner."

"And 'intimate' is a good word," said Johnny. "The one thing people forget about the Dublin street war is how close-quartered it was. Basically, Collins was picking a fight with the British Secret Service in what would be the size of New York City's Greenwich Village and Chelsea, combined, and daring them to destroy him. This was hand-to-hand combat!"

Soon they were standing directly across from 31 Aungier Street, which was now a Polish grocery store, another sign of the times. "I can't believe it's still there," said Diane.

"The only tenement to survive on the block," added Johnny. "Pretty creepy, eh?"

"Grandpa had mystical powers."

The day started on a sour note when Diane had confronted Johnny with a hearty, "You lying sonofabitch!"

"What did I do now?" demanded Johnny.

"You knew about Grandpa."

"Knew what?"

"That he was a murderer."

Johnny turned angry. "Grandpa was not a murderer," he said. "My grandfather was a soldier and a patriot, who helped established the Irish nation. What he did was entirely within the rules of war."

"But you knew," Diane insisted.

"I didn't know for sure," said Johnny. "Grandpa was always circumspect about the whole thing. Not even in America, where it might have gotten him votes, did he reveal he was in Collins's Squad. He didn't even give a witness statement to the Irish government when they were soliciting histories back in the 1940s and '50s. It was his secret, and although I was suspicious, I respected his privacy." Diane gave him a kiss to make up. "Come on," said Johnny, "we're going to town. I want you to know how it felt to walk in Grandpa's shoes."

___

After arriving at the Westland Row DART station, Johnny walked Diane to St. Stephen's Green, shot down Montague Street from Harcourt Street, and began his little tour.

"It's a remarkably unremarkable building," said Diane.

"Would you believe it's eighteenth-century Georgian architecture?" Diane shook her head. "It's been made a 'protected structure' by the Dublin Corporation—basically, a historic building. They can't tear it down. I'm sure my great-grandfather would be impressed!" said Johnny, laughing. "It's been remade over many, many times, of course." The bricks were covered by a cream-colored, stucco-like surface. Johnny figured the fragile house remained standing only because of the strength of its latest coat of paint. "When it was built, both King George III and George Washington were alive. Think of that! I get a lump in my throat when I look at it," Johnny said, and Diane squeezed his hand hard, "because that's where my great-grandfather was murdered, and that's where, I know now, my own grandfather avenged his death."

"This little city has our family in its grip, doesn't it?" asked Diane. "Even after almost a hundred years."

"It does, indeed," said Johnny. "Come on—let's go for a walk." They held hands as they walked down Aungier Street. At the Carmelite Church, they made a left and walked down to Golden Lane. "This is where the Piles Buildings were. As you can see, nothing exists of them anymore. Everything was torn down around 1980. It must have been a horrible eyesore by then."

Then Johnny laughed. "What's so funny?" asked Diane.

"I was thinking of the Duke of Clarence."

"Who was he?"

"Queen Victoria's grandson."

"Oh," said Diane, now laughing herself, "this has to be good."

"Well," said Johnny, "the young Duke and his father, the Prince of Wales—who would later become King Edward VII—were visiting this very site in 1885. It was one of those annoying visits where royalty meets and greets the great unwashed. Anyway, they were shaking hands when some ould wan tossed the contents of a chamber pot on top of the Duke's pristine head. The Dublin poor had spoken!"

Diane laughed out loud. "Oh, that's wonderful!"

"The Duke was quite a guy," added Johnny. "Do you know he was suspected of being Jack the Ripper?"

"No!"

"Yep," replied Johnny, with some satisfaction. "Died of syphilis. Always looked a little light in the boots to me, if you know what I mean."

"Oh," said Diane, "you're so bold! And you get such satisfaction from such information."

"The only duke I ever liked," said Johnny, sincerely, "was Duke Ellington."

Johnny led her up Stephens Street, and they emerged on South Great Georges Street. At Dame Street they crossed and turned left. Before they came to the City Hall, they turned down Cow Lane. At the bottom, they found what remained of Saints Michael and John's RC Church.

"This is where it all began," said Johnny. "My whole family is linked to this dead church."

"It's closed?"

"For a long time," replied Johnny. "It's a shame. It's the oldest Catholic Church in the city, and it was the first Catholic Church to ring its bells after Catholic emancipation. Now it's waiting to become a theatre or something."

"You really hate change, you do!" laughed Diane. "You're nothing but a historical stick-in-the-mud!"

"Go ahead, mock me," sighed Johnny, "but our family history was made in this church. And," he added, "this is where Grandpa visited on the morning of Blood's assassination—and maybe the reason he had such mixed feelings about the church."

"Did he? I thought Grandpa liked the clergy," protested Diane. "He once told me that he always kissed the Cardinal's ring on St. Patrick's Day because it was worth a thousand votes!"

"Yeah," said Johnny, "I can just see him now, kissing Francis Cardinal Spellman's ring on the steps of St. Patrick's Cathedral. They hated each other. The Cardinal thought Grandpa was too liberal, and Grandpa thought Spellman was an old queen, which he was. They were both right!"

"I love it when you talk dirty, filthy sex," teased Diane.

"They didn't call Spellman 'Aunt Franny' for nothing," replied Johnny, with relish. They walked around the old church, hoping that a ghost from the family's past might want to reach out, but it was quiet. "That assassination of Blood had a traumatic effect on Grandpa," said Johnny. "I think he was probably in shock when he came here that morning. It must have been awfully disturbing for a man like Grandpa, a straight-shooter if there ever was one."

"No pun intended," interjected Diane.

"That must have been a Freudian pun, don't you think?"

"Wouldn't be the first time old Sigmund came between us!"

"You know," said Johnny, turning serious again, "he never took the sacraments ever again. Not even matrimony."

"You mean your grandparents never married?" said Diane, looking shocked.

"I hate to disappoint you," Johnny said, laughing, "but my father was not a bastard."

"That's a relief—considering the stuff I've heard about him!"

Diane realized she had been too flippant about the subject of Johnny's father. It seemed that no one in the family wanted to discuss Eoin Jr. The old man and Róisín never talked about him, because they never got over the loss of their only son. And Diane thought Johnny didn't want to discuss him because he felt his father had abandoned him. "My father," said Johnny, unconsciously dropping his voice a full octave lower, "was the unfortunate offspring of two exceptional people. He had a hard time living up to the standard his parents had set. Sometimes people find this world such a terrible place that they can't handle it." Johnny paused and then smiled gently at his wife. "My father may have been a bastard, but he was no bastard! My grandparents were married in a civil ceremony by the State of New York at the Municipal Building, down by City Hall. I'm sure it was a mutual decision. Róisín wasn't crazy about the church, either."

"I don't get this whole thing with the church," said Diane. "He's always going into churches, but he wants nothing to do with the church."

"Remember Grandpa chasing away that priest the day he died? He was going to give him Extreme Unction. What euphemism do they use today? The Sacrament of the Sick? Grandpa didn't want any part of it. Tough old bird to the end."

"See! That's what I don't understand," said Diane. "But he insisted on having a funeral mass at the Pro-Cathedral."

"I think Róisín had a lot to do with it," said Johnny. "I think she was abused as a child by the nuns and wanted nothing to do with them. And, of course, she had great influence over Grandpa. She was in the movement, the *Cumann na mBan*, before 1916. Remember, Grandpa was an accidental revolutionary! He was also a suspicious old cod anyway. There was a lot of politics going on back then. Some bishops were excommunicating Volunteers. Excommunication became certain bishops' choice of ecclesiastical terror. Apparently, it was alright for the British to murder Irishmen but not okay for Irishmen to defend themselves. Many, including Collins and Grandpa, resented it. Collins actually thought that some of the bishops were collaborating with the British against their own people. They never fully trusted Holy Mother Church again."

"It's so, so complicated," confessed Diane.

"I think the shooting of Blood—and others—had a lot to do with it," said Johnny. "In his own way, I think Grandpa didn't feel he was worthy enough to receive the sacraments. When you think of it, he was purposely starving himself of God's love, a love I think he deeply craved."

"What a remarkable way to put it," said Diane, clearly moved by the thought. "In effect, he was penalizing himself."

"We Kavanaghs are a remarkably bad lot of Catholics," confessed Johnny. "But we were all born Catholics, and we will all die Catholics." He looked intently at his Protestant wife. "Why, even Róisín had a Catholic burial."

"Bloody Papists!" said Diane, laughing before turning serious. "You think there are more killings to come?"

"The Squad was *very* busy in 1920."

Diane shook her head. "It's so frightening," she said. "It's like learning your favorite Grandpa was in Murder Incorporated."

"You're close," laughed Johnny easily, as he took her hand and walked her through the winding back streets of Temple Bar, circling back to Dame Street. "Here it is," said Johnny. "It's still here, but it's gone."

"What?"

"The entrance to 26 Temple Lane. That was Rosanna's home, where Aunt Nellie ended up living. The building's the same, but the façade's been altered. Come on, I've got something to show you." They walked to the corner and made a left at Nico's Italian Restaurant and walked a block towards Trinity College. Johnny turned left into Crow Street and stood with Diane in front of number three. "This is it," said Johnny. "The IRA's CIA office in 1920. Second floor. Irish Products Company was the cover. That's where Collins's intelligence office was," he continued, "although he almost never visited it."

"He didn't?"

"Too dangerous," said Johnny. "Collins didn't visit in case he was being watched by the British. This office was too important to give away. That's why Grandpa was always running his daily intelligence brief to him around the city. The British never discovered this office. The building's been altered, but, as you can see, it's just three blocks from Dublin Castle. Oh, how the Brits would have loved to know about this place!"

Diane shuddered. "It's spooky, even eighty-six years later."

"Yeah," said Johnny. "I'm scared stiff." Johnny pulled Diane to him and gave her a serious, sensuous kiss.

"That's good," she said softly. Johnny ground against Diane, and she could feel his arousal. "Revolution has an uplifting effect on you, I see," she teased.

"Reminds me of my yute!"

"Yeah," laughed Diane. "Erection-on-demand!"

Johnny adjusted his trousers and walked Diane to the edge of Dame Street. "See that alley over there?" Diane looked across Dame Street and could see a narrow alley almost directly opposite from them. "Let's go!" Johnny pulled Diane by the hand, and they jumped into Dame Street, dodging traffic in both directions. In New York, jaywalking was sport; in Dublin, it could be suicide. They came to a halt in front of the alley. Johnny pointed at the ground.

"The Stag's Head," Diane read from the tile in the sidewalk.

"It's time for a drink," said Johnny. They walked through the alley, emerging in Dame Court. Johnny pointed up the street. "See that doorway just to the left of the Dunne's Store? Well, that's 10 Exchequer Street, Collins's and Grandpa's first office. They did a lot of their conferencing right here," Johnny said, turning to his left, where the Stag's Head front door was. "I love this fucking place," he said, as he secured a snug for himself and his wife at the end of the bar. They sat down and ordered a couple of pints of stout. "This was Collins's favorite snug," Johnny revealed. "Grandpa said he liked it because he could scoot out the back door in a second."

The bar was quiet this time of the day, so different from what it was at night. "If these walls could talk!" said Diane.

"I don't think you'd want to know!" responded Johnny. "Collins drank here so much in the early years that they had a keg known as 'Mick's Barrel.' Must have been a hell of a whiskey."

"I never think of Collins as a drinker," said Diane.

"He liked a sup, but as time went on, he didn't drink or even smoke. He needed all his strength for the revolution."

"What are you expecting out of Grandpa's papers next?"

Johnny took a sip of his Guinness and sighed. "Vicious brutality."

"You're being redundant."

Johnny smiled weakly. "You're right. But it will take 'vicious brutality' to finally make the British redundant."

Diane gave an involuntary shiver, as she remembered that she was sitting in Michael Collins's favorite snug. Then, suddenly, she knew what was eating at her—the horror of 1920 had *finally* penetrated her bones during her visit to Dublin's Dardanelles.

75

All the participants rose as Prime Minister David Lloyd George entered the conference room at 10 Downing Street. "Please be seated, gentlemen," he said, as he took his place in the middle of the table. "Our agenda today is the tragedy that Dublin has become." He paused, brushing aside his shoulder-length white locks. "Winston, the floor is yours."

Winston Spencer Churchill, Secretary of State for War, stood to speak. "Gentlemen, you are all aware of the outrages that occurred recently on the streets of South Dublin, where military convoys were destroyed and a detective sergeant of the Royal Irish Constabulary was brutally murdered." He paused for effect. "The time for dillydallying with the Shiners is over!"

The Churchill of 1920 was light-years away from the iconic Churchill of 1940. Although now occupying another cabinet position in Lloyd George's government, he was still fresh from a string of Great War failures, which had branded him as a politician of mostly unrelenting failure. From the sinking of the *Lusitania* under his watch as First Lord of the Admiralty in 1915, to his disastrous Gallipoli adventure in 1915–16, Churchill had shown he had the Midas touch—only in reverse.

Around the table were Johnny French, Field Marshal Henry Wilson, General Sir Nevil Macready, and Derek Gough-Coxe. "It is time," said Churchill, "for a shake-up in Dublin. General Macready will become the new Commander-in-Chief for Ireland. Lord French will remain as Viceroy, and we will be sending help for the embattled RIC."

"About time," Wilson proclaimed. "The rebels have had the run of us."

"We are undermanned," said French, "as General Macready will soon find out."

"There will be no more excuses," the Prime Minister reassured them.

"We have begun to recruit—on the recommendation of Field Marshal Wilson—some temporary constables to supplement the RIC," Churchill continued. "And I am proposing a Special Emergency Gendarmerie, also to supplement the RIC as auxiliary cadets. The quicker we can get these brigades organized and shipped to Ireland, the better."

"What is your estimated time of arrival?" asked the Prime Minister.

"The temporary constables should be in Ireland by March," replied Churchill. "The auxiliaries, a little later in the year."

"It's going to be a hot summer in Ireland," laughed Wilson.

"But not hot enough for you, Henry, I surmise," snapped Churchill. Churchill was anti-nationalist, but Wilson was an outright bigot in his disdain for the mostly Catholic rebels.

"Perhaps this time, Winston," replied Wilson, his martinet piqued by Churchill's comment, "you will not be befuddled by these Dublin Dardanelles, as you were by the Turkish Dardanelles."

Churchill ignored the jibe and responded evenly: "We have shot the rebels. We have imprisoned them. We have deported them. We have harassed them. What would *you* want us to do?"

"More," replied the succinct Wilson.

Gough-Coxe laughed. "Field Marshal, you sound just like Sebastian Blood!"

"Who the blazes is Sebastian Blood?" demanded Wilson.

"Our detective/martyr from Aungier Street," replied Gough-Coxe, "whom Mr. Churchill was just discussing." Wilson looked ambushed by Gough-Coxe's remarks, and Churchill suppressed a smile.

"Besides the military," said Lloyd George, interrupting the high-level pissing match, "what can be done at the local level in Dublin?"

"The intelligence unit of the Dublin Metropolitan Police—that's the G-Division—will be reorganized," said Churchill, pointing to Gough-Coxe. "Our new Deputy Commissioner of Police Derek Gough-Coxe has had a remarkable career, recently in the Middle East during the Great War. Without his help in the region, we might have lost the Suez

269

Canal. A great part of his success was due to him 'going native' to inspire and captivate the local Arab chieftains. We worked closely together, and I expect he will be able to supply equal expertise to our problems in Dublin City. I expect him to become our Fenian *savant.*"

"And what exactly, Deputy Commissioner, do you see as our problems in Dublin City?" asked the Prime Minister.

Gough-Coxe stood and surveyed the men around him. He felt confident that the trouble in Ireland would be over by this time next year. He felt secure that, with the backing of Churchill—whose father, Lord Randolph Churchill, was the first to play the "Orange Card" and originated the phrase, "Ulster will fight, and Ulster will be right!"—and the likes of the Catholic-hating Wilson, who had the ear of the Prime Minister and the MPs from the North of Ireland, that the problems in Ireland could be soon overcome.

"The problems in Dublin come down to two words," said Gough-Coxe, pausing for effect. "Michael Collins."

"And," said Lloyd George, "who is Michael Collins?"

Before Gough-Coxe could commence his carefully prepared presentation, Lord French cut in: "Collins is a murderer who has become a folk-hero on the streets of Dublin," he said, his voice rising. "According to the local legend, he is the Fenian Pimpernel, supposedly fearless, conniving, cunning, and ruthless." French stood up. "He has attempted to assassinate me several times without success."

"He has to succeed only once, Field Marshal," said Gough-Coxe, and French returned to his seat. "Michael Collins," Gough-Coxe continued, "is the *Dáil's* Minister for Finance—but he's more than that. He is a Commandant-General in what is becoming known as the Irish Republican Army. He is also the president of the terrorist Irish Republican Brotherhood. Many think he is behind the string of assassinations we have been experiencing in Dublin since last September."

"Think?" teased the Prime Minister.

"He is quite the mysterious figure," said Gough-Coxe.

"A bounty may remove the mystery," interjected Wilson.

"He sounds like a street thug to me," offered Macready.

"Nothing more, nothing less," agreed the smug Johnny French.

"It's not as simple as that," said Gough-Coxe. "I suspect that Michael Collins is the equal to anyone here in this room." Gough-Coxe had suddenly caught everyone's undivided attention, as four pairs of eyes targeted him.

"What do you propose to do?" asked Lloyd George.

"I propose to smoke him out," said Gough-Coxe. "Not only will G-Division be reorganized, but I propose we start sending a series of *agent provocateurs* to draw Mr. Collins out of his shell."

"Why don't you just arrest him?" asked Wilson.

"We don't even have a good photo of him," replied Gough-Coxe. "Detective Sergeant Sebastian Blood was getting close to Collins when he was murdered. Collins is ruthless."

"As ruthless as we are going to be?" taunted Wilson.

Gough-Coxe laughed at the Field Marshal. "How ruthless should we be?" he asked, tossing the ball back into Wilson's court.

"Disgustingly brutal," came the reply.

"I can do that," said Gough-Coxe calmly. "I know how to handle opponents of the Crown—as my record indicates."

"So when do you propose to begin?" asked the Prime Minister.

"Immediately," said Gough-Coxe. "I'll be leaving for Dublin on the mail boat tonight. My *agent provocateur* will be joining me shortly." He laughed again.

"And what amuses you?" asked Churchill.

"The name of my agent—a name the Irish will surely embrace."

"Yes?"

"Jameson."

There was laughter around the table as the builders of the disaster in Ireland felt sure they had found the right man to lead them out of their Irish quagmire in Derek Gough-Coxe, the new Deputy Commissioner of Police for the G-Division of the Dublin Metropolitan Police.

76

Róisín was on her way to work, cycling by the Black Church at Mountjoy Street, when a voice called out her name. She stopped and turned around, surprised to see Collins standing in front of the Munster Hotel at 44 Mountjoy Street. He was carrying a pillowcase, weighed down with its contents.

"What in God's name are you doing here?" she demanded, stopping her bike right in front of the inauspicious-looking hotel.

"Picking up my laundry," replied Collins.

"Your laundry!" Róisín couldn't imagine that the most wanted man in Ireland was fetching his laundry in front of her very eyes.

"I don't wear dirty knickers, like someone told me you do!"

"Who told you that?" Collins smiled mischeviously, and Róisín realized her goat had just been captured by the Minister for Finance.

"You're daft to even be close to the Munster," Róisín lectured. "The British are always looking for you here."

"No," replied Collins, "it's alright. I leave my clean clothes at Vaughan's and change there."

Róisín noticed that Collins' face was puffy from fatigue. "Are you getting any sleep?"

"Oh, the hours wasted in sleep! I'll sleep when I die."

"The headlines have been gruesome," said Róisín. "Especially the news from Camden Street. I see the boys finally got that clown, what was his name? Blood?"

"He's the one who murdered Joseph Kavanagh," said Collins.

"Go way!"

"Eoin plugged him," Collins said matter-of-factly.

"No, he didn't!"

"Yes," said Collins, wearily, "he did."

"How could you let him?"

"It was his decision."

"You bastard!"

Collins put his laundry bag down on the sidewalk and took Róisín by the hand. "It's getting serious now, Róisín. This is the year."

"The year for what?"

"The year we drive the British from our shores."

Róisín shook her head violently. "We'll destroy the British, and we'll destroy ourselves!"

"Eoin needs your attention."

"I never see him. He blames you, the amount of work you put on him."

"He's telling the truth," admitted Collins. "I work the lad to death. He's the best I have. I hate to admit this, but I've come to depend on the cheeky little bastard." Róisín smiled, and Collins added, "He's about the only one who will tell me the truth and challenge me."

"Eoin is a great kid," said Róisín.

"Do you love him?" Collins queried, out of the blue.

Róisín stared at the ground before finally looking up. "I might," she finally said.

"Then keep an eye out for him. He's homeless right now. One night sleeping in the Bachelors Walk office, the next night in Vaughan's, the night after that on someone's sofa. It's a tough life."

"I can't even get in touch with him. He gave me a number over in Abbey Street but told me not to call it."

Collins knew it was the phone at the Dump, but said nothing. He pulled a notepad out of his pocket and jotted a number down. "Eoin never breaks the cell," said Collins, "but I do! You can reach him at this number. Ask for 'Mr. Kavanagh.' If he gets annoyed at you, tell him you got the number from the Minister for Finance."

"Thanks, Mick. I will call him."

"This week?"

"Promise."

"Grand lassie ya are!" he said, as he gave her a peck on the cheek.

Róisín mounted her bike and continued on her way to the Mater Hospital. Collins looked up at the appropriately named Black Church, which cast an intimidating shadow on this cul-de-sac part of Mountjoy Street. The local legend says that if you run around the Black Church three times at midnight, the devil himself will appear. Collins smiled, for the Church and all its blackness would not win out today. The chat with Róisín had revived Collins's spirit, and her touch reminded Collins how lonely he was for female companionship. Kitty was still up in Longford, and Collins was glued to Dublin. As Róisín cycled out of sight, Collins picked up his laundry bag and walked straight across the road to 30 Mountjoy Street, hoping that Dilly Dicker might offer him some breakfast.

77

Liam Tobin and Eoin arrived at the Bailey Chop House for an intelligence briefing with Collins. The Bailey, on Duke Street right off Grafton, was one of the Big Fellow's favorite places. He never used the bar, but management always kept a private room on the second floor available for his meetings.

When the two Crow Street agents entered the room, they were surprised to see that besides Broy and Boynton, Collins had also invited his two Dicks, Mulcahy and McKee. When the army was brought into it, you always knew that something was up.

"What's this?" demanded Tobin. Eoin thought that his immediate boss was suddenly looking even more morose than usual.

"What?" asked Collins, defensively.

"You're taking a lot of risk here," the Adjutant Director of Intelligence replied sternly to his boss. "These four men," he said, waving his hand at the G-men and the army men, "should not know each other. You've broken the cell."

"Sit down and have a drink," said Collins.

Collins pulled two new packs of Greencastle cigarettes out of his coat pocket. He opened one and began to light up. He offered the fags around the table, and they were greedily snapped up by everyone except Eoin.

"I thought you gave those up," said Eoin.

"Only for tonight," replied Collins, "so I can get through this bloody meeting." He tore open the second package of fags and started carefully placing them in a silver cigarette case, oblivious to the looks he was receiving from the rest of the room.

A shopboy knocked at the door and took the drink orders. Usually, Collins ran drink-free meetings, but tonight he waived that rule. When the kid left, Collins stood up and addressed the room. "I'm aware that the cell has been broken, Liam. But we are moving on to another level, and I think it's time that my trusted lieutenants knew each other. It's only going to get more complicated from here on out. We will have to work intimately if we are to succeed at anything before this year is out."

"It's February already. We're down to ten months," said Mulcahy. "It will be almost impossible to succeed before the year is out."

"If we don't succeed within this year," said Collins, "Ireland will never be free." He looked around the room and added ominously, "It's now or never."

The shopboy knocked at the door again and brought in the drinks. The fag fog was so dense in the room by now that he could hardly see the faces of the men. Eoin's pint of porter was placed before him, Collins had a small pony of sherry, and the other men had glasses of Jameson Irish whiskey, neat. When the shopboy left the room, Collins spoke up. "It's time we go over the new Deputy Commissioner of Police for the G-Division of the Dublin Metropolitan Police, Derek Gough-Coxe." Collins pronounced it "Cocks."

"*Co-shay*," meticulously mouthed Broy.

"I may be only a culchie in your eyes," said Collins, "but I think I know a 'cocks' from a 'Co-shay!' " The room erupted in laughter, the tension broken. "Liam and Eoin have compiled, over the last couple of weeks, a complete dossier on your man Gough-Coxe." Collins began passing the newspaper clippings around the table. In the middle of almost every story was a picture of Gough-Coxe in full Arab regalia, right down to his puşi headdress. Headlines heralded "Derek of Suez."

"Jaysus," said McKee, "'Derek of fookin' Suez.' I can't believe they put this gobshite's picture in the paper. That's insanity on their part."

"Hubris," said Collins, as he turned to Eoin. "That's a fancy word for pride or conceit."

"Ah, you'd be knowin', Commandant-General," replied Eoin with a straight face. No one laughed, but knowing smirks filled the room.

"I'm a little uncomfortable here," said Mulcahy, the army Chief-of-Staff. "Is this in Cathal's territory?"

Although Cathal Brugha was the Minister for Defense, Collins constantly poached his portfolio. In Dublin City, in particular, the duties of the army, now known as the IRA, and Collins's many projects in finance, IRB, and intelligence were constantly blurred.

"What about Brugha?" Mulcahy asked a second time.

"Let Cathal know what he needs to know," said Collins cryptically. "Let's get back to the Sheik."

"The Sheik!" laughed Broy. "Oh, the boys in Brunswick Street would love that one!"

"Don't you dare, Ned," said Collins. He thought for a minute. "The Sheik. I like that. That will be our *nom de guerre* for Gough-Coxe. It fits so well." He paused and looked intently at Tobin. "Liam, tell us all about our Sheik."

"The Sheik is Eoin's domain."

Eoin opened up his folder and began reciting the facts. "He was born in 1888."

Before he could continue, he was interrupted by Collins. "He's two years older than me."

Eoin ignored his boss and continued. "He was born in Wales. He is illegitimate."

Eyes opened wide around the table. "Who's the bastard's mother?" interjected Collins.

"His father's children's nanny." Collins grunted. "His father is Anglo-Irish and was the late Baronet of Roscommon. Grew up in Oxford. The rest is the usual, Eton, etc. Did post-graduate work at Oxford."

"Not your usual British thug," said Boynton.

"War record?" said McKee.

"Largely responsible," continued Eoin, "for rallying the Egyptians away from their Muslim Ottoman brothers. Is credited with keeping the Suez Canal in British hands, thus his nickname. 'Went native,' the press likes to say, dressing up in Arab clothing. Speaks the language. That's the thumbnail sketch on your Sheik," Eoin paused before adding, "Awarded the Companion of the Order of the Bath, Distinguished Service Order, and the *Chevalier de la Légion d'Honneur*," said Eoin, butchering the French.

"Jaysus," said Mulcahy.

"Oh," said Eoin, "I forgot the *Croix de guerre*."

"*Croix de guerre*, my arse," spat Collins, standing up. "Don't get overwhelmed by this eejit. He isn't here to go native in a Paddy-cap, hobnailed boots, and speak the Erse! He's here to destroy us. This man is going to try and take out every man in this goddamn room." He looked around the room, which was duly impressed with the Sheik's resume. Too impressed, thought Collins. Collins voice went near a shout. "Is that understood? He is a master colonist. He knows how to treat the native. In Egypt, it was the carrot. In Dublin, it will be the stick. We underestimate this man at our own peril."

Eoin continued to read in a monotone. "He's a charmer, apparently. The press's favorite word for him is 'charismatic.'"

"Should we send a message and eliminate him right away?" spoke up McKee.

"No," said Collins. "For now, he's more valuable to us alive than dead. We will monitor him closely. We will not 'tag' him. That won't be necessary. Ned and Brendan will see him daily. Let's see where he leads us. Why run down the hill to fook one cow when we can walk down the hill and fook the lot of them?" The men looked around at each other, wondering what, in God's name, had seized their master bull. "Where is he living?"

"38 Upper Mount Street," said Eoin.

"Nice neighborhood," replied Collins.

"He's not the type, I think," said Eoin, "to embrace the rebel Liberties!"

"Or Monto," said McKee, to a roomful of laughter.

"Alright," said Collins. "We now know what we're up against. McKee and Mulcahy are here because the Sheik, in one way or another, will eventually become their problem. But not right now. Right now, Gough-Coxe is my problem. He's Broy's and Boynton's problem. He's Crow Street's problem." Collins picked up his small glass of sherry, thought about drinking it, then replaced it, untouched, on the table. "The Sheik is not really a problem," Collins said to disbelieving ears. "In fact, the Sheik may be the man we've been waiting for. He may be the answer to all our prayers." With that, the meeting broke as Collins put on his hat, grabbed his overcoat, and hurried out the door. Slowly the men stood and left. Eoin realized that he hadn't touched his pint of porter. He sat down by himself and sipped slowly, wondering what Collins's Sheik was doing right now, this minute, in his abode at 38 Upper Mount Street, an address that would soon change Eoin's life—and the destiny of his nation—forever.

78

EOIN'S DIARY

M y phone rang and I picked it up. *"You evasive bastard!"* was the greeting, and I knew immediately who it was.

"Who gave you this number?" I demanded.

"Cupid Collins," she sang, and I knew I was in trouble.

It was Róisín's way of telling me that we should get together for the weekend. I tried to tell her that I had to work, but she shot back, "Even those bloody Presbyterians in Dublin Castle take Sundays off!" She said she had it all planned out. We would take Mary and Dickie out of their orphanages for the weekend and bring them to the Zoological Gardens in the Phoenix Park, and then we could all sleep at her flat Saturday night before taking the children back to the orphanages on Sunday evening. I really miss my kiddies, and I was happy to go along with her. She had it all planned out like a Squad hit. She would pick Mary up in Sandymount, I would fetch Dickie in Cabra, and we would all meet up at the zoo.

I picked Dickie up, and, since it was such a nice day—a teaser of spring, it was—we decided to walk up to the park. He told me all was going well at the school, and, since my last visit there, he's had no problems with Father Murphy. He even says that Murphy has been exceedingly nice to him. "Father Murphy's my friend now," said Dickie, and I smiled knowingly.

We caught up with Róisín and Mary. My sister has become quite the little young lady. She looks a lot like Mammy, with that long line of a Conway mouth. Her hair is so dark a brown that it appears black.

Dickie and Mary embraced and took off together, the two playmates separated by terrible luck now reunited.

"Mary's a woman now," Róisín said to me. I was quiet, because every time I open my mouth about womanly functions, Róisín tells me what an eejit I am. "Do you understand what that means?"

"Yes," I finally said, clearly exasperated.

"Good," replied Róisín and, thank God, she didn't bring up any more female mysteries for the rest of the weekend.

We had a wonderful time at the zoo, watching the monkeys and the tigers and the elephants, and we stuffed the kids with sweets and ice cream. We took the tram back into town and went to have a light tea at the DBC on Stephen's Green. Then it was back home and bed. Mary and Dickie jumped together into Róisín's bed, and she said she'd join them later. We then went into the parlor to talk.

"What's bothering you?" Róisín asked when we were alone.

"You know what's bothering me," says I.

"Blood."

"The late Detective Blood."

Róisín came over and sat down next to me on the sofa. "You were doing your duty."

"Duty?"

"To your country—and your father."

"It was terrible," I told Róisín, and she took my hand. "I hope I never have to do that kind of thing again."

There was an awful quiet for well over a minute before she finally said, "I hope you won't let Mick down."

I exhaled mightily and then got up and went over to stoke the fire. Róisín stuck her head into the bedroom and told the kiddies to go to sleep. When she came over to me, she had a pony of whiskey in her hand for me. "Drink this," she said.

"Why?"

"Because it might loosen you up."

"Why?"

"So I can take advantage of you, you thickheaded Jackeen!"

With that, she gave a great laugh. "The children!" I said. She took my hand and put it on her breast. "Róisín," I protested, as we sat down on the sofa. I suddenly realized that me arse was down, but me willie was up.

"It's about time you knew a little more about me," she said. "Not a lot more, mind you, but a little more."

I thought I heard giggling from Róisín's bedroom, as if the children knew what was happening and were mocking me. But my throbbing willie made me ignore the phantom jeers. *I'm beginning to learn about women*, I thought. I shut me gob and did as I was told.

Sunday morning, I stuck me head into Róisín's bedroom. She was still fast asleep between two wide-awake children. "Hush," I whispered. "Let Róisín sleep."

"How do you expect me to sleep with all these noisy kids around me?" she barked and started tickling them in a furious manner. The screams—for once—were screams of pure joy.

"It's time for mass," Mary said, and I told them to get dressed. As they were getting ready, I looked at Róisín, and she gave me a look that indicated she had no intention of going to any mass. As we were getting ready to head out to St. Kevin's in Harrington Street, the kids asked her why she wasn't going with us.

"Someone has to cook your breakfast," she said. "Now, scoot!" As she let us out the door, she said, "Don't forget to say a prayer for me!" Róisín is full of surprises.

St. Kevin's was where I was baptized and where I went to mass every Sunday. It's a grand old church on the edge of my dead parents' neighborhood. The two children were very attentive, especially Mary. They knew all the responses, and when communion was given out, Mary devoutly received. "You?" I said, pointing at Dickie. He shook his head "no," and I realized that he hadn't made his First Holy Communion yet.

"You?" he pointed.

I shook my head. "Not today," I said, and I was happy when Dickie didn't persist.

We landed back at Róisín's, and the smell of rashers, sausages, black and white pudding, fried tomatoes, fried eggs, and beautiful bread and butter overwhelmed us. Róisín poured tea for us all, and we chatted away. Suddenly, Mary asked, "Eoin, what do you do for a living?" Mary had succeeded in gaining our undivided attention.

"I work for an insurance company," I replied, barely lying.

"Who wants to know?" asked Róisín, getting right to the interrogation.

"Oh, the sisters at school," said Mary. "They were just curious." I bet they were.

We spent the rest of the day walking along the Grand Canal and playing in St. Stephen's Green, just like we had on that Easter Monday nearly four years ago. We watched children sailing boats in the pond and that, too, brought back memories of the day that changed all our lives. Soon, it was time to head back to their orphanages. Departing was such sorrow, none of it sweet, for me and Dickie. Once again he got all teary-eyed, and I promised him that Róisín and I would see him soon again.

"Why doesn't Frank visit me?"

It was the first mention of Frank all weekend, strangely enough, and I told Dickie that Frank was away on holidays.

"Where?" asked Dickie.

"In the mountains," I replied, without lying.

I met Róisín back at her flat in Walworth Street. "I thought it went well," she said.

"Dickie finally asked about Frank. I told him Frank was taking a mountain retreat." Róisín laughed. "I wonder why they didn't ask about him before."

"They don't want to get attached to someone who will desert them, like your parents did."

"Desert?"

"You know what I mean," said Róisín. "They are afraid to love someone who will leave them forever. Children are fragile."

"So unlike adults, like you and me."

"We're barely adults ourselves," said Róisín, and there was more truth to the statement than she realized. I wanted to go out and see if the Sunday papers from Britain had arrived. "You're going nowhere," she said. "Come with me." She brought me to her bedroom and announced, "I think you have earned the right to sleep in my bed with me."

"Róisín!"

"You will be chaste," she said seriously, "as I will."

"I don't think that's a good idea."

"We will wear night garments. There will be no tomfoolery," she said sternly. "Do we have an agreement?"

"No tomfoolery?"

"No tomfoolery."

And, true to her word, there wasn't, but it was nice to have someone to embrace during the long Dublin winter night.

79

"Need any more guns?" Mulcahy asked Collins.

"Does a religious fanatic collect rosaries?" replied Collins. "What kind of a fookin' question is that? We never have enough guns."

"Well, there's a fellow over from England looking for you. He says he has some guns for us."

"Sounds too good to be true," said Collins. "Where did this good fellow come from?"

"Artie O'Brien sent him to us," said Mulcahy, speaking of the *Sinn Féin* leader in London. "Do you want to meet him?"

"Why not? What do we have to lose?" Mulcahy gave Collins a look, which drew a laugh out of the Big Fellow. "Don't worry, Dick, I'll be careful." Mulcahy was still apprehensive about the whole thing. "Look," said Collins, "the only person I have consistently supplying me with guns is Bob Briscoe. If Bob wasn't doing business in Germany, we'd have no guns at all. Set up the meeting with this fellow. What's his name?"

"John Jameson."

"You're jokin'," said Collins. Mulcahy's face was made of stone. "You're not jokin', are you?" Mulcahy shook his head. "What's his background?"

"He's making out that he's some sort of labor organizer, maybe even a communist or a revolutionary," said Mulcahy. He paused. "If you can believe that."

"And he just dropped into our laps," said Collins. "How convenient."

"My point exactly."

"Set it up for tomorrow at the Home Farm produce shop in Camden Street," said Collins. "Get Tobin to come along."

"Bad idea. I don't think our two intelligence directors should be in the same room with this stranger."

"You're right," conceded Collins. "Tell Eoin I want him there."

"Why Eoin?"

"Because Eoin has the 'sniff,'" said Collins.

"The 'sniff'?"

"He can smell the enemy."

"I hope you're right."

John Jameson showed up in the Camden Street grocery and introduced himself to the young clerk behind the counter. Eoin Kavanagh wiped his hands on his apron and directed the Englishman to the back room, where Collins and Mulcahy were waiting for him.

"Mr. Jameson," said Collins.

"And you must be the bold Michael Collins," replied Jameson. He shook hands with the two men, and Collins offered him a cup of tea. "This is so exciting," the Englishman proclaimed, dropping three spoons of sugar into his tea.

"Exciting?" asked Collins.

"One hears such exciting things about you in London," said Jameson.

"Really?" said Collins.

"Like what?" queried Mulcahy.

"Oh, the general stuff," said Jameson. "You know, how you've turned Camden Street into a hellhole for the British."

Collins remained quiet as he scratched the beginnings of a new mustache. Kitty didn't like facial hair, and now she was back in Longford, so Collins thought he'd try out the hairy lip. Eoin came into the room, feigning work. "Excuse me," he said. He went to the back on a phantom search, then surveyed the earnest Jameson, who was animatedly telling all how important the great Collins was.

Mulcahy cut to the chase. "The guns?"

"I can get you what you need," replied Jameson.

"We need revolvers," said Collins. "Heavy caliber. We also need rifles for the army. Can you help us?"

"I can do that," said Jameson. "But it'll cost money."

"We have the money," said Collins.

"Let me see what I can get my hands on," said Jameson.

"That's grand," said Collins. "Can I ask you something?"

"More tay?" interrupted Eoin, as he brought a fresh pot over to the table. All three men declined, and Eoin looked Jameson right in the eye. "You sure?"

"I am," said Jameson. "Thank you. You were saying, General Collins?"

Collins was taken aback; seldom was his rank referred to, if it wasn't Eoin jeering him.

"Yes," said Collins, "my question is simple—why do you want to help us?"

"Because I hate the British," said Jameson. "How's that for a starter?"

"And how does that manifest itself?"

"I have been trying to organize the police in London and Manchester," replied Jameson. "I have been trying to foment strikes where I can. I believe in the people, not the capitalists."

"Good for you," said Mulcahy, and Collins almost smiled.

"Alright," said Collins, "see what you can dig up for us."

"I will," said Jameson, with enthusiasm. "But how will I get in touch with you?"

"We'll get in touch with you," Mulcahy replied. "Where are you staying?"

"The Gresham Hotel."

"Fine."

"But I may have to travel back to Britain to pull this off," Jameson protested. "How will I get in touch with the General when I return to Dublin?"

"Don't worry," Mulcahy reassured him, "we'll come to you."

"You got the city covered," laughed Jameson, "don't you?"

"Like a tight sheet," Mulcahy replied, with a small smile.

Jameson stood up from the table and shook the hands of Collins and Mulcahy. He turned and walked through the shop, nodding at the young clerk, and exited into Camden Street. Eoin immediately went into the back room. "How did it go?" he asked.

Collins shrugged. "What do you think, Eoin?" asked Mulcahy.

"Mister Whiskey stinks."

Collins laughed and nodded. "When you get back to Crow Street, tell Tobin to start tagging him. First thing tomorrow morning."

"Pretty bad?" asked Mulcahy.

"I don't believe in philanthropic revolutionaries sent on angel wings from England who only want to help poor, ould Ireland," replied Collins. "Do you?"

80

Every G-man was called to Dublin Castle to meet their new boss, Deputy Commissioner of Police Derek Gough-Coxe. Boynton bumped into Broy, who had walked over from Brunswick Street, as they headed towards a small auditorium. "I see you're here for the coronation," teased Boynton, which elicited a quiet smile from Broy. For security reasons, they seated themselves on opposite sides of the room. They did not want to be known to their fellow officers as friends.

Boynton observed that there were now around thirty-five G-men on active duty. That number had been going down over the last few months, with the help of Collins's threatening letters and selected harassments and killings. There was a small hum in the room, which went silent as Gough-Coxe approached the podium.

"Good morning, gentlemen," he began. "My name is Derek Gough-Coxe, and I have been sent to Dublin by the Prime Minister to reorganize the G-division of the Dublin Metropolitan Police." There were a few claps, but a full round of applause did not materialize. "We are at a crossroads in Ireland, and here in Dublin in particular. He who controls Dublin, controls Ireland." He paused for effect. "From here on out, the G-division will control Dublin, not a bunch of ragtag Fenian murderers. And murder is where we'll start. We are going to find the murderer of Detective Sergeant Sebastian Blood, who was killed in cold blood in Aungier Street last month."

Boynton gave a small grunt as he shifted in his chair and re-crossed his legs. Gough-Coxe's use of "in cold blood" was beginning to make him boil.

"Who murdered Detective Blood?" Gough-Coxe asked rhetorically. "We don't know who pulled the trigger, but we do know who ordered the assassination. One Michael Collins, Minister for Finance for the so-called *Dáil Eireann*. We will apprehend both Collins and his gunmen. I have read Collins's file, and it is a beauty. There was only one piece of valuable information missing—his photograph. Apparently, the combined Secret Services of the British Empire have been unable to come up with a single photograph of the most wanted man in Ireland."

Broy, the man responsible for the missing photograph, fixed his eyes on the floor before him. Gough-Coxe moved from behind the podium and began walking up and down. "I spoke with Detective Blood when I was last here in Dublin. At that time, he told me he was working on a connection between Collins and the man who owned the barber-shop where he was killed. That man's name was Joseph Kavanagh, who expired himself just before Christmas. How will we find out about Joseph Kavanagh? Detective Blood believed that his son—named Eoin—worked for Collins. He saw both of them in a film soliciting funds for their National Loan. Unfortunately, copies of this movie have disappeared." Gough-Coxe laughed. "Believe you me, gentlemen, the National Loan is item number two on my to-do list, but we must decipher Detective Blood's Kavanagh riddle first. How will we do this?" The response was silence. "Gentlemen, let's go backwards. Who was Joseph Kavanagh?" Boynton's arm shot into the air. "Yes, detective, please identify yourself, if you would."

"My name is Detective Constable Brendan Boynton, and I was Sebastian's partner. Our desks were side-by-side."

"What do you know about this character, Kavanagh?"

"We know very little," replied Boynton.

"And why is that?"

"Because Sebastian didn't share his information. He thought he was on to something big and, perhaps, wanted to keep the information to himself for security reasons."

"Gentlemen," said Gough-Coxe, "this nonsense will stop. *All* information will be indexed and shared from this moment on. If I lose an agent, I don't want to lose his information. We shall pursue Collins from where Detective Blood left off. As I said before, by going backwards." Gough-Coxe went back behind the podium. "We'll start at that barbershop in Aungier Street. And Detective Boynton, being Detective Blood's professional next-of-kin, will pick up the investigation where it ended—with Blood's death. You will report directly to me, and I expect results." And with that, the new Deputy Commissioner of Police left the stage without speaking another word.

On his way back to his desk, Boynton bumped into Broy again. "You're in for it now," laughed Broy, "but Mick will love you to death for it." Boynton nodded, suddenly wondering how being loved to death by Michael Collins would feel, which forced a smile. Either way, he knew he was fucked.

81

J ameson had Crow Street flummoxed. He was nowhere to be found in their carefully indexed cards. Boynton and Broy could find out nothing about him, either. They finally got Artie O'Brien over in London on the telephone, but he knew nothing more about Jameson other than "he wanted to help."

"There's not a trace of this fellow," Eoin told Liam Tobin.

"Maybe he's been out trolling in the Empire," replied Tobin.

"Maybe he's legitimate."

"You think?"

"No, I don't," replied Eoin. "Maybe we'll know more when the tag-team reports back."

"We'd better, or we're putting Mick and the rest of us in jeopardy."

Suddenly, the door opened, and Vinny Byrne burst in. "Grab your guns, lads. Mick sent me for you."

"Vin," said Tobin, "what's up?"

"One of Mick's touts told him that Johnny French is at Trinity College, and he will be leaving via Suffolk Street shortly. Mick has sent an SOS out for all available Squad men in the area."

"Where's Mick?" asked Tobin.

"I just left him at the Wicklow Hotel. He said he'll meet us in front of Hogan's public house in Suffolk Street. Come on!"

Eoin grabbed Detective Blood's Webley out of his desk drawer and shoved it in his jacket pocket. He followed Tobin and Vinny out the door. They crossed Dame Street and ran up the alley that led to the

Stag's Head. They then ran along Dame Lane, parallel to Dame Street, which was usually deserted, to give them cover. At Trinity Lane, they shot up towards St. Andrew's Church of Ireland and crossed the road to where Collins, Daly, Dan Breen, and Joe Leonard were waiting for them. They stepped down into narrow Church Lane, and Collins briefed them quickly.

"One of my informers has sent word that French is at a conference at Trinity College, and he'll be making his way back to the Castle through here momentarily. Let's spread out. He may try to go down Dame Lane and right into the Castle side gate. He'd want to avoid Dame Street because of the traffic." Collins checked his pocket watch. It was half-eleven. "This time," he admonished "let's get the shite."

This was unfinished business for Collins. Twelve attempts had been made on French in the last three months of 1919 alone. The last time the Squad had a shot at French, it turned out to be a disaster. In December 1919, Collins pulled together eleven Volunteers and Squad members—including Daly, Leonard, Byrne, McDonnell, and the Tipperary contingent of Breen, Treacy, and Seamus Robinson—and sent them to ambush French as he returned to Dublin by train from Roscommon. French was supposed to get off the train at Ashtown and proceed by automobile to the Viceregal Lodge in the Phoenix Park. The Squad knew it would be a two-car convoy, and they also knew that French always traveled in the second car. A roadblock was put into position. They let the first car through and planned to ambush the second. Unfortunately, French was in car number one, which they had allowed to proceed. A gun battle ensued with the second car, and Volunteer Martin Savage was killed. Breen was severely wounded, and two DMPs were also hurt in the skirmish. It appeared that French had a sixth sense, because that was the first time he changed routine and rode in the first car. He was not only good—he was lucky.

The men spread out to various points around St. Andrew's Church with four of them—the still-limping Breen, Collins, Byrne, and Eoin—planted down at the end of Trinity Lane, where Dame Lane starts. They waited for Paddy Daly's sheer whistle, but none came. Collins pulled his pocket watch out and saw it was a quarter to twelve. "I think the hoor got lucky again," said Breen.

"We'll wait," said Collins, his eyes revealing that he knew he had been stood up.

Eoin walked up to the Church and looked for Leonard, Daly, and Tobin. They were loitering in front of the pub, and Daly shook his head "no." Eoin went back to Collins and Breen with the bad news. "We're fooked, I think."

"We are indeed," said Collins, letting out a breath. He took out his pocketwatch and saw it was just noon. "Let's get the hell out of here. Something's not right." Eoin signaled the other men, and the Squad disappeared into the narrow streets of Dublin.

Eoin and Tobin walked together up Dame Street on their way back to the ADOI office. Suddenly, three British tenders came roaring down Dame Street from the Castle, heading in the direction of Trinity College. They stopped short in College Green and cut into Trinity Lane. "Mick was right," said Eoin, as he observed the British soldiers scrambling about where the Squad had been just moments before.

"Coincidence?"

"I don't believe in coincidences," replied Eoin.

"Neither do I," said Tobin.

John Jameson had spent a busy day running around Dublin town. He left the Gresham Hotel and went shopping in Grafton Street before lunching at the Shelbourne Hotel. In his wake went young Charlie Dalton, who did a lot of the legwork for the Squad. When he was relieved at six o'clock, he scampered over to Crow Street to report.

"Nothing special to him," said Dalton. "He acted more like a tourist than a commie agitator."

"Maybe that's what he wants us to think," said Tobin.

"When is he leaving Dublin?" asked Eoin.

"I heard him tell the clerk at the Gresham that he would be checking out tomorrow evening and taking the boat from the North Wall to England."

"Who did he have lunch with?" asked Tobin.

"A woman," said Dalton. "A real lady, if you know what I mean."

"Maybe he fancies himself a Romeo," Eoin sneered.

Tobin smiled. "You have a very suspicious mind for a young man, Eoin." Eoin grunted, and Dalton laughed. "Charlie, keep an eye on him all day tomorrow, up until he steps on that boat. Whatever you do, don't lose him, or you'll drive Collins mad."

"Yes, sir," said Dalton, who—unlike Eoin—was still awed by the great Collins.

Eoin threw papers in his attaché case and headed out the door for his daily intelligence briefing with Collins. He walked up to Stephen's Green and headed in the Baggot Street direction before turning into Ely Place, just east of the Green. At number fifteen, he stopped and knocked on the door. A maid in a black uniform and white apron answered the door. "Is Dr. Gogarty in?"

"Whom shall I say is calling?"

"Eoin Kavanagh."

"Mr. Kavanagh," said the maid, "we've been expecting you."

Eoin was shown into a parlor, where Collins and Gogarty were enjoying a drink. Both men rose as Eoin entered the room, and Collins introduced Eoin to the good doctor. "Mick tells me you're quite the man," said Gogarty.

Eoin didn't know if his leg was being pulled or not. "Thank you, Doctor," he finally said.

"Oliver will suffice."

"Thanks, Oliver."

"I'll leave you men alone so you can do your business," Gogarty said, as he left the room.

Eoin placed his attaché case on the table, and Collins queried, "What's the news?"

"Today," said Eoin, "the news is all about Jameson—or should I say the news is all about the lack of news on Mr. Whiskey."

"Did you tag him?"

"Charlie Dalton had him under his eye all day. Says he acted like a tourist. Had luncheon with a fine lady at the Shelbourne and then went back to the Gresham."

"Shite," said Collins.

"We do have one bit of information," said Eoin. "He'll be leaving us tomorrow night at the North Wall."

"Maybe he's going to get our guns in England," said Collins, hopefully.

"Maybe he's planning your demise," returned Eoin.

"Maybe we should tag him to England."

"I have a better idea," Eoin said, pausing.

"Well," Collins said impatiently, "maybe you'd like to share it with me?"

"He seems to like the ladies, I think."

"So?"

"Why don't we tag him with an attractive female?"

"Like who?"

"How about Dilly?"

"That's dangerous."

"Not for Dilly, it isn't," Eoin countered. "She's stolen the mail on the Irish Sea many times. She knows her way around. Maybe she can chat him up on his way to Liverpool. Have a couple of drinks with him."

"Smile sweetly," said Collins. "Offer a little female companionship for the long crossing."

"Exactly."

Collins laughed. "You have a very wicked young mind, Eoin Kavanagh—but it's a fookin' brilliant idea." And with that, he said goodbye to Gogarty, hopped on his clanker, and headed up to Mountjoy Street to do a little sweet-talking of his own to his pal Dilly Dicker.

82

C harlie Dalton met Dilly Dicker at the North Wall and handed off John Jameson to her. Dilly, carrying a cheap cardboard suitcase with one change of clothes, boarded the boat, never letting Jameson out of her sight.

He immediately headed for the bar, which posed a problem for Dilly, because ladies weren't usually served in such male bastions. Dilly had no intention of traveling the whole way to England and coming up empty. She charged into the bar, bellied up right next to Jameson, and asked for a pony of sherry.

"Ma'am, I'm sorry," said the barman. "I can't serve you at the bar."

"Why not?" demanded Dilly, creating a mini-scene.

"You know very well, ma'am," said the shocked barman.

"Tell you what," interrupted Jameson. "What if I got a sherry for the lady, and she drank it in the traveling lounge?" The barman nodded his head, just hoping to avoid confrontation. "Problem solved," said Jameson, triumphantly. Dilly went directly to the lounge, and Jameson followed with her sherry. Dilly accepted her drink and took out her purse to pay for it. "I wouldn't think of it," said the chivalrous Jameson.

"You are so kind," Dilly gushed.

"But not as kind as you are beautiful."

Dilly smiled sweetly at Jameson, thinking all the time, *Boy, does this fellow work fast!*

"My name is John Charles Byrne," Jameson said, allowing the first crack.

"My name is Madeline," said Dilly, telling the truth. Her last name would remain a mystery.

"Madeline, are you traveling back to England to visit family?"

Dilly's smile drooped. "Me poor ould granny is awful sick, and I'm on my way to Liverpool to take care of her."

"What a dedicated child," Jameson praised her.

"Yourself?" asked Dilly innocently, as she sipped her sherry and batted her eyelashes at her prey.

"Myself?"

"Why are you traveling to England?"

"I'm returning to England on business."

"And what kind of business are you in?" queried Dilly, again pretending innocence.

"I'm in the insurance business."

I'm sure you are, thought Dilly, but instead she said, "That must be interesting work."

"I'm taking a beating in Ireland."

"Are you now, Mr. Byrne?" Dilly asked. "Now, why is that?"

"All the deaths around town," said Jameson.

"So you insure the locals?"

"Mostly I insure the British army," Jameson admitted, before adding, "God bless them."

"Their work is legendary," replied Dilly.

"It's tough work," added Jameson, standing. "Can I get you another sherry?"

"No, thank you," said Dilly. "I want to read my newspaper, if you don't mind."

Jameson headed back to the bar and did not return. Dilly did not take her eye off him the whole trip. As they came closer to Liverpool, she went into the ladies' room and got to work. First she scrubbed all the makeup off her face. Then she combed her hair tight and wound it into a bun. She opened her suitcase and took out her outfit, which she last used when she robbed the mail boat out in Kingstown. She slipped off her dress and pulled on her britches. She also wore a bulky sweater to cover up her bosom. Lastly, she pulled a cap over her hair and frowned at herself in the mirror. She was ready.

Jameson had had his fill at the bar, and Dilly stuck close to him as he made his way to the London train. He rode in the first-class carriage, and so did Dilly. He dozed most of the way to his destination. At Euston Station, Jameson got off the train and hailed a cab. Dilly jumped in the next cab and said, "Follow that taxi!"

"Bloody hell!" said the hackie. Dilly waved a ten-pound note under the cabbie's nose. "Yes, sir!" came the reply.

The cabbie was good at his game and damn near tailgated Jameson's taxi. "Not so close," barked Dilly in her deepest voice.

"Yes, sir!"

Jameson pulled up in front of Whitehall Place and entered Scotland Yard. Dilly didn't get out. She gave the cabbie Artie O'Brien's address and relaxed for the first time in nearly a day. Dilly knocked on O'Brien's door, and Artie was surprised to see a young man in front of him. "Yes?" he asked, confused.

"I'm Dilly Dicker," she said. "Mick Collins gave me your address."

Dilly pulled off her cap, and O'Brien realized it was a very attractive young woman standing in front of him. "Yes," he said, "I've heard Mick speak about you."

"You have?" asked Dilly, surprised.

"Yes," said Artie, "he says you're a bonnie lass!"

"I'm here to use your phone. I have to report back to Dublin."

O'Brien watched her with some bewilderment as Dilly waited for the long-distance connection to go through. "Mr. Kavanagh," the voice on the other end of the line said.

"Eoin, it's Dilly."

"What have you got?"

"He says his name is John Charles Byrne, and you can reach him at Whitehall-1212."

"Scotland Yard!" said both Eoin in Dublin and O'Brien as they recognized the famous phone number.

"Good job!" added Eoin, and Dilly hung up the phone.

"You should be more careful about whom you recommend to Mick Collins," Dilly admonished O'Brien. "You've helped create a mess in Dublin."

Artie was the head of *Sinn Féin* in London, but London pulled no rank in Dublin. He was dumbfounded by this beautiful agent from Ireland. "Can I get you a cup of tea?"

"Get me a taxi," said Dilly curtly. "So I can get back to Euston Station and get the hell out of this bloody country."

Fearing the wrath of Michael Collins, Artie O'Brien did exactly as he was told, praying that the taxi would arrive swiftly.

83

EOIN'S DIARY
SUNDAY, FEBRUARY 29, 1920

*I*t's a leap year, and Mick is leapin' all over me today.
   "Have you seen these fookin' hotel bills from New York?"
   I think Mick is cross with Dev, but he's taking it out on me.
   "Have you seen these bills from Devoy in New York?" Mick repeated, now stuttering, as he got red in the face. "I can't believe them!"
   John Devoy is a favorite of Mick's. We've been getting a lot of mail from him since Dev went to America. I'd never heard of him before, and when I innocently inquired into who he was, I was berated by Mick for my ignorance. He informed me that Devoy was one of the greatest of the Fenians. He had fought in the uprising of 1867, did time in Kilmainham, and went to America, where he organized *Clan na Gael* into an organization that brought attention to the cause of Irish freedom. He also got Fenians out of an Australian penal colony on a daring rescue mission, employing an American ship called the *Catalpa*. As the Royal Navy bore down on the *Catalpa*, with the escaped Fenians on board, the captain hoisted the stars and stripes, frightening away the British. I think Mick likes Devoy so much because he is like an older version of Collins himself.
   "Ten thousand fookin' dollars!" shouted the Minister for Finance. "He's trying to bankrupt the Republic at the Waldorf-Astoria in New York!"
   I had to suppress a smile at all this. Mick is going daft trying to buy a few guns and bullets off a shady character like Jameson, and Dev is

parading around America like a king. But there's something about the names of the hotels that digs at Mick. His main target is the Waldorf-Astoria in New York City, but the Copley Plaza in Boston, the Bellevue-Stratford in Philadelphia, the Blackstone in Chicago, and the Wardman Park in Washington, D.C., also get a rise out of him. "Isn't a B&B good enough for the First Minister?" he asked me.

"Well," says I, innocently as I can, "he's not the *Príomh-Aire* anymore. He's now the august President of Ireland!" That's how he had signed the register at the Waldorf upon his arrival in New York, which Devoy had duly informed us about. I loved that Dev had invented a new title for himself, and I knew just the mention of it would drive Mick to distraction.

"He thinks he's Brian fookin' Boru," said Mick, as he tossed the hotel bill into a pile of other American bills de Valera and Boland had run up.

"What should we do with Dev's bills?"

"Pay them." Mick picked up one of the bills again and ran his finger down the charges. "I see we're paying for Kathleen O'Connell all these months." I told Mick that Kathleen was only Dev's secretary, and that he had a dirty mind. "Indeed I do," he bragged. "With poor Mrs. de Valera slavin' away, taking care of the kiddies out in Greystones, and Dev gallivanting around America. Maybe I should have a chat with Mrs. D and see if she'd like to join Dev in America? He's already renting a suite big enough for ten." Mick gave me a laugh and a devilish wink.

It was getting too hot in the Harcourt Street offices, so Mick has rented another office at 22 Mary Street. This is where we now do most of the business of the National Loan. Like he had turned a page, Mick instantly forgot about Dev's largess and turned to more deadly matters. "The British have been snooping around the banks," said Mick. "I was in the Munster & Leinster Bank in Dame Street yesterday, and the manager told me his books had been summoned to the Police Court at Inns Quay by someone named Alan Bell."

"What does it mean?"

"They're beginning to examine the books. They're looking for the National Loan money." We have National Loan money hidden in bank accounts all over Ireland, and in England and America, too.

"What can we do?"

"Dead men don't count," snapped Mick at me. "Get a dossier on this fellow. The manager said he was in his mid-60s, so he's been around. Check with Broy and Boynton. This takes priority—do you understand?"

"Even over Jameson?"

"Even over Jameson," replied Collins. "After all the trouble I've gone through with this money, no old English bastard is going to snatch it away from me."

"Jameson is due back in Dublin tomorrow," says I. "Joe Leonard and Charlie Dalton went over to England to tag him."

"Good move," said Mick. "Make an appointment so I can meet with him on Monday."

"Isn't that dangerous? This fellow works for Scotland Yard, maybe one of the British Secret Services. Maybe he's a double-agent?"

"Don't be getting too excited about all that Scotland Yard stuff that Dilly discovered," he said matter-of-factly. "He told us he was organizing the police into a union. Maybe that's what he was doing there."

I just shook my head. Sometimes I think Mick is naïve, but I never think that for long. I think he secretly loves danger, whereas it terrifies me. I think Mick gets a rush from it. "Do not underestimate Jameson," I finally cautioned. "Or I'll be reading an oration over your grave at Glasnevin."

"I know that, for fook's sake," snapped Mick, looking at me with disgust. "But if he has some guns, maybe I can get them off of him before we send him on his way."

"We have our hands full," I conceded, wondering what would happen next to gum up the works.

"First Jameson," said Mick, "now Bell. I don't believe in coincidences. I bet these guys are connected somehow. You're right. Whatever we do, we cannot let either of these men out of our sight."

I don't believe in coincidences, either. I think it's time I carry me Webley with me at all times.

84

A knock came at the door of John Jameson's room at the Gresham Hotel. He opened the door to see Liam Tobin standing on his threshold. "Michael Collins wants to see you immediately."

"Oh," said Jameson, "I have to make a phone call before I leave."

"No call," said Tobin. "Let's get going, now."

There was a taxi waiting in Sackville Street for them, and it took a left at North Earl Street and headed in the direction of Amien Street Station. At Amien Street, it pulled up to the J&M Cleary public house. Tobin got out of the cab and held the door of the pub open so Jameson could enter. "Upstairs," he said, and was right behind Jameson as he climbed the stairs to the private room on the second floor. Inside the room sat Collins, alone at the large round table in the middle of the room. Paddy Daly sat in a chair to the right of the fireplace.

"Mr. Jameson," said Collins.

"General," returned Jameson, as he shook hands.

"I don't have a lot of time," Collins said. "I just wanted to check to see when you'll have my guns."

"I can deliver the revolvers tomorrow."

Collins looked surprised. "Grand man, ya are!" he said, with genuine delight.

"Where do you want to meet?"

"Liam here will contact you and tell you where to bring them," said Collins. "Don't leave your room at the Gresham. You'll be hearing from us." Jameson gave a small laugh. "What's so funny?"

"Your mustache," said Jameson. "It's beginning to fill in." Collins did look kind of ridiculous when he grew a mustache. "Are you trying to disguise yourself from the British?"

This fellow doesn't know when to shut up, thought Collins but simply said, "Not at 'tal." He grinned mischeviously before adding, "I do it for the ladies!" With that, he stood up and started showing Jameson to the door. "How much will it cost?" added Collins.

"One hundred pounds should cover it."

"Cheaper by the pound," Collins joked. "I'll be in touch."

Collins closed the door on Jameson and turned to his two cohorts. "If this gobshite has any guns, take them and pay him for them. Let's see what happens after that. Maybe you should put out a little milk for the cat, Liam," said Collins mischievously. "What do you think of him?"

"I don't know," Tobin remarked, thoughtfully. "I wanted to meet him so I could get a feel for him. He's as smooth as aged whiskey."

"And well-named, too," said Collins with a laugh. "Let's get the hell out of here in case he's ambitious." Soon Collins was on his clanker, heading in the direction of Vaughan's. Daly headed for the Dump in Abbey Street, while Tobin decided to return to Crow Street to catch up on his intelligence work.

John Jameson was walking down Talbot Street, heading in the direction of Sackville Street and his hotel. He could see Nelson's imposing pillar right in front of him, dead ahead. He thought that the old one-armed, adulterous admiral would be proud of him and his seduction of Michael Collins. Jameson was beginning to enjoy Dublin City, and he walked leisurely, in no hurry. Charlie Dalton and Joe Leonard were in no hurry, either, as they discreetly tagged him from the opposite side of the street, under strict orders from Collins not to let Jameson out of their sight.

85

Brendan Boynton had a new desk mate. His name was Alan Bell, and he had been in and out of Ireland since the days of the Land League and Parnell. His specialty was catching Fenians. "I've outlived more Fenians than any man in the RIC," he joked to Boynton.

Bell was a dapper, jolly little man with a tightly trimmed white mustache and an affinity for bowler hats. He was so common, so benign-looking, but so dangerous. He looked like a grandfather or a favorite uncle, but he was the kind of poison the British had been putting in the Irish well for seven centuries. He had been brought to Dublin to find the National Loan money, but there was more to this fellow than being a bank examiner. Boynton noticed that Gough-Coxe seemed very reverential to Bell and often sought his advice on matters. The lines were blurring at Dublin Castle. All of a sudden, here was Bell, a Resident Magistrate, First Class, sharing a desk with G-division detectives. Something was awry here, Boynton knew, and it frightened him.

The big office was now occupied by the new bossman, Gough-Coxe. He was very hands-on. He was beginning to reshape the G-division in his own image—he had brought new men in, mostly from the North, and he had shipped detectives out. If you didn't cut the mustard, you might end up walking a beat in the arse-end of some misbegotten fishing village in Donegal. He would frequently come out to the bullpen area and check with his detectives. Of late, he was manic with anticipation, because he thought he had caught a sniff of the elusive Collins.

"Gentlemen," he told the detectives as they sat at their desks, "why can't *you* find Collins? I will not rest until we get him. Getting Collins is the most important job this office is doing right now." He paused and then resumed his tirade. "You are a bright lot! Not one of you has been able to get on to Collins's track for a month. Is it clear to you yet? You were supposed to be looking, relentlessly, for Collins. You have been after him for months and never caught sight of him, while a new man, just over from England, met him and talked to him after just two days."

There was absolute quiet in the room, and Boynton wondered if they could hear his heart pounding away in his chest. "Resident Magistrate Bell," said Gough-Coxe, pointing out his elderly colleague from England, "has an undercover agent who was in contact with Collins as recently as last evening." Gough-Coxe surveyed the look of amazement on his detectives' faces. "Our agent even reports that Mr. Collins is now wearing a mustache!

"There is only one way we are going to get Collins—we have to hit the streets, ask questions, and pump up our touts. Collins is walking around Dublin every day—unmolested! Unmolested, do you hear me? Now get out of here. Get off your arses and hit the streets. NOW!"

The room emptied in a matter of seconds. Boynton came out the side gate of the Castle and walked straight down Dame Lane, headed across South Great Georges Street, and went into the Stag's Head. Silent Peadar Doherty was behind the stick, methodically shining glasses. Boynton leaned over the empty bar. "I need to get in touch with Eoin Kavanagh." Doherty resisted his impulse to say, "Again?" He left the bar and went to the office in the basement. There, he called Eoin a block away in Crow Street and told him his young detective was looking for him again.

Eoin arrived at the Stag's Head within five minutes. The look on Boynton's face told him that there was a disaster in the making. "Gough-Coxe says they have an agent who has been in contact with Collins within the last twenty-four hours," Boynton began. "This guy is over from England. Works for a Resident Magistrate named Alan Bell, down from the North to find the National Loan money. They think they are close to both Mick and the money."

Eoin looked at Doherty and said, "What do you think, Peadar?"

"You know what I think," said the barman, a devoted IRB member and veteran of Easter Week.

"We think alike," replied Eoin calmly, adding a small smile.

"Well," said Boynton with some desperation, "what are you going to do?"

"We'll handle it."

"You don't seem too concerned."

"I'm not."

"Be careful with this guy, whoever he is. I'm betting he's MI-6. All of a sudden, everything is out of sync at the Castle. MI-6, Secret Service, Resident Magistrates, all milling about G-division. They're upping the ante on Collins."

"We've graduated," said Eoin.

"From what?" asked Boynton.

"From being harmless guttersnipe hooligans," said Eoin. "We've gotten their attention."

"One other thing," added Boynton. "Their agent says that Collins is now wearing a mustache."

Eoin raised his eyebrows in acknowledgement and then turned and walked out the front door without saying another word.

86

"The Sheik knows Mick has a mustache."

Liam Tobin, looking more glum than usual, finally said, "Tell me more."

"Boynton says the Sheik was bragging that one of their Secret Service agents just over from England met Mick last night. The agent is being run by Resident Magistrate Alan Bell. Talk about killing two birds with one stone."

"Fucking Jameson."

"Fucking Bell," said Eoin. "Mick will be delighted."

"Don't bother with Bell for now. It's Jameson who is the immediate threat. We have to neutralize him somehow."

"Do you really think he has the guns we need?"

"My guess would be yes," replied Tobin. "If he doesn't have the guns, he knows we would drop him immediately—and he'd never get to Collins again."

"He's not going to let us keep the guns—if he does, indeed, have them," said Eoin. "If we meet him, he could be trying to trap us."

Tobin rubbed his lugubrious chin. "Why don't we trap him?"

"How?"

"Easy," said Tobin, as he picked up the phone and got the Gresham Hotel on the line. "Mr. Jameson," said Tobin, easily. "Do you have the guns?" Tobin nodded to Eoin in the affirmative. "That's grand. I have the money. Meet me at the New Ireland Assurance offices at 56 Bachelors Walk. That's right on the corner of Sackville Street, in the building where Kapp & Peterson have their tobacconist shop. I'll meet you there in a half-hour." Tobin hung up the phone and said to Eoin, "Let's go. Bring your gun."

They charged out of Crow Street and headed for the Ha'penny Bridge. They crossed the Liffey and headed straight towards Bachelors Walk. At number thirty-two, Tobin turned to Eoin and said, "Go up to the office and wait for me. I shouldn't be long." Eoin did as he was told. Tobin continued to the end of the quay and went up to the offices on the third floor. The New Ireland Assurance offices were another Collins front. They had been frequently raided, but there was nothing of importance there. Tobin pulled up a chair and waited for Jameson.

Jameson was lugging a portmanteau of Webley revolvers down Sackville Street, and they were heavy. The leather case was so burdensome with the twenty guns that he never saw Joe Leonard and Paddy Daly trailing him. He led them to Bachelors Walk, and they let him enter number fifty-six. "Must be on his way to sell the guns to Liam," Leonard observed, and Daly nodded in agreement.

In the office, Jameson proudly opened his suitcase and showed the Webleys to Tobin. They were in mint condition, and Tobin was secretly delighted. He counted out the one hundred pounds and took the guns, placing them in a secret hiding place in the back of a broom closet. "They'll be safe here," he told Jameson.

"It's a pleasure doing business with you," Jameson replied. "I hope I can be of assistance to General Collins in the future."

"The General," said Tobin, "may want to meet with you later today. Will you be available?"

"I will, indeed," said Jameson. "I'm going back to the Gresham, and I'll stick close to the phone for the rest of the day."

"Grand," Tobin said. "I have some paperwork to do now, but I'll relay your regards to General Collins." With that, Jameson turned and left the office. Tobin listened as his steps descended to the street. He then went to the closet and retrieved the bag of guns. He dropped the three stories two steps at a time and rushed out into Bachelors Walk, turned right, and walked the few paces to number thirty-two. In seconds he was in Collins's secret office. "Let's hide these things," he said to Eoin. The two of them moved a couch, and Eoin pulled up a secret trap door that had been built by Batt O'Connor for such a contingency. The guns fit snugly. They replaced the sofa. "Come on," said Tobin, "—let's see what happens next."

The two of them went out and headed back to the Ha'penny Bridge. When they got to the south side of the Liffey, they headed back towards Aston Quay, which gave them a panoramic view of all the buildings on Bachelors Walk. Tobin pulled out a cigarette and lit it. The two intelligence agents leaned on the parapet of the wall running off O'Connell Bridge. Eoin played with the balusters, trying to wedge his shoe into them. Neither man spoke as they kept an eye on number fifty-six.

Forty-five minutes into their wait, two British army lorries pulled up, and the Tommies charged into the building.

"The cat took the milk," said Tobin.

"And licked the saucer dry," Eoin replied gleefully. "That's the final nail in Jameson's coffin."

"Let's get back to the office," Tobin decided. "I have to tell Mick to shave that bloody mustache off."

87

At six o'clock, Collins met with Tobin, Eoin, Daly, and Leonard in the second-floor parlor of the Stag's Head. He had just returned from a shave in Capel Street, and his upper lip was as pristine as a baby's bottom. Tobin relayed the events of the day as Collins silently listened. "That's it," the Big Fellow finally said. "He's got to go. Tonight." He turned to Daly and Leonard. "Tell him I want to see him. Then take the shite out and shoot him."

"Should we leave a message?" asked Daly.

"Pin a note on the shite," said Collins. He paused, thinking, for a few seconds. "I think all of you did a terrific job on Jameson," he praised them. "Our intelligence was superb from Dilly to Dublin Castle, to the work of Crow Street. The Squad did a great job keeping an eye on him. Now let's finish it up. Let's not fook it up at the last minute!"

Collins got up and went on his way, but the other four men walked across the road to the office in Crow Street. Tobin picked up the phone and called Jameson at the Gresham Hotel. "General Collins wants to meet you tonight. He'll send a car for you at eight o'clock."

"Vinny Byrne is tagging him," said Paddy Daly. "I think the three of us can handle him without a backup team. We don't want Jameson to get suspicious."

A taxi driven by a Volunteer pulled up in front of the Gresham Hotel, and Jameson came bounding out, full of good cheer. Leonard got out of the back seat and allowed Jameson to pop in. Daly was on the extreme left, and, when Leonard got back into the car, they made a nice sandwich out of Jameson. Vinny got into the front seat alongside the driver.

"Great day, today," Jameson said to Daly, whom he knew from his meeting with Collins in Amien Street. "I hope General Collins will put those guns to good use." Just then, Joe Leonard began searching Jameson. "Gentlemen," said Jameson with a chuckle, "I am unarmed."

"You won't be seeing Mick Collins tonight," said Daly. "Or ever again, for that matter."

"You have been found guilty of spying against Ireland," said Leonard. "The sentence is death."

"Gentlemen," protested Jameson, suddenly nervous. "There must be some misunderstanding. I've been helping General Collins. I delivered the guns to his agent this morning."

"And then you sent the British army to take them back," replied Daly. Finally, there was silence as the motorcar headed up Parnell Square, past Vaughan's, on their voyage north. Vinny Byrne drew his Mauser and held it steady on Jameson. "By the way," said Daly, "Collins shaved his mustache off this afternoon." Jameson realized that they had him. "Who are you working for in Dublin Castle?" asked Daly.

There was no answer.

"What branch of the Secret Service do you work for?"

Again, there was no answer as the car sped into the dark Dublin night, on its way to a lonely cul-de-sac in Grangegorman. After another ten minutes, the car came to a dark spot and stopped. Vinny got out first and covered Jameson as he came out of the back seat. Both Daly and Leonard had their guns drawn as they led Jameson down a narrow path. "Say your prayers," said Vinny.

"I don't believe in God," replied Jameson. "I was only doing my duty."

"As are we," said Leonard.

"I know," replied Jameson, letting out a deep breath. "God bless the King. I would love to die for him."

With that, Vinny Byrne came around and shot him once in the right temple. Jameson dropped to his knees with a thud, as if in prayer, his eyes frozen open. Leonard came around and shot him right between his unseeing eyes. Daly made sure with a shot to the heart. Leonard then pinned a note to his coat:

SPIES BEWARE!

"Lucky bastard!" said Byrne.

"Lucky?" asked Daly.

"How many of us," said Byrne, "get our dying wish fulfilled *immediately?*"

"You're a twisted one, ya are," Leonard said, wryly.

The three Squad members jumped back in the taxi and were driven home to the Dump, their filthy, but essential, work finished for another day.

88

John Jameson, aka John Charles Byrne, was found early the next morning by a man walking his dog. The "stop press" in the *Irish Times* proclaimed ATROCITY IN GRANGEGORMAN. Collins read the headline from the hand of the Blackpitts Terry O'Neill, known to one and all as "Black Terry" on his paper route, which stretched from the top of Grafton Street all the way to Parnell Square. Terry, stationed in front of Bewley's Oriental Café in Westmoreland Street at high noon to catch the dinnertime crowds, was one of Collins's army of urchin newsboys. They served Collins and his intelligence staff as touts, often pointing out and physically detouring Secret Service who patrolled the streets of Dublin. As he passed Black Terry, Collins was delighted that the *Times* had another one of their ATROCITY headlines, which they were so fond of. "Mr. Mick! Mr. Mick!" the twelve-year-old, red-haired, freckled kid yelled as Collins took a paper and gave the lad two bob. "Keep the change, Terry," said Collins, as he laughed and patted the top of the newsboy's Paddy-cap. "Me t'inks they're having conniptions in D'Olier Street," Terry said, referring to the location of the *Times'* offices. "Just got out of the 'Joy!" Terry proudly declared.

Collins stopped and looked concerned. "What for?"

"Wouldn't pay the license fee," said Terry, as he held up his wrist to show Collins his leather and tin vendor license. "Fook the hoors!"

Collins reached into his pocket and pulled out a sovereign. "Next time," said the man who was still out on bail from the Sligo Gaol, "pay the fine! I have enough good men in the 'Joy."

"Will do, Mr. Mick," said Terry, as he hopped on a tram heading up Sackville Street. "But the peelers are still hoors!" Terry ran up the winding back staircase of the tram, happily yelling, "Atrocity in Grangegorman! Read all about it! Atrocity in Grangegorman!"

One of the reasons Collins could walk around Dublin in relative safety was because of the staunchness of everyday Dubliners. Newsboys all over the city knew Collins by sight, as did many ordinary citizens, tram conductors, and even DMPs on the beat. It was the Irish at their best—eyes open and mouths shut. Apparently everyone in Dublin City knew Mick Collins, except the G-men in Dublin Castle.

At Dublin Castle, the mood was somewhat stifled. Gough-Coxe and Bell were huddled in the Sheik's office, talking intently. Boynton looked up and was surprised to see Ned Broy standing next to his desk. "What are you doing here?" he inquired.

"He sent for me," Broy explained, cocking his head in the direction of the bossman.

"I wonder what's up?" Boynton said, beginning to feel uneasy.

Gough-Coxe stepped out of his office and waved at Broy and Boynton. "Men," he said, "step in." On his desk he had the same *Irish Times* headline that had so delighted Collins. He picked it up and waved it in the air. "You've seen this, I take it? This is a catastrophe!" Gough-Coxe exclaimed. "This is the man who had the track on Collins, gunned down as we were beginning to make our move. It's as if Collins had inside information."

"Everyone here hates Collins," put in Broy, for good measure.

"We are tired of his bullying tactics," added Boynton.

"He was one of our best Secret Service men," added Alan Bell, referring to the deceased Jameson. Bell suddenly looked very old, and he seemed down in the dumps.

"Look at this," said Gough-Coxe. He held Joe Leonard's piece of paper up for all to see: SPIES BEWARE! "The cheek on them!" He was silent for only a second. "Jameson's gone now, and we're going to have to pick up the pace. That's why I've called you two here. You will be working together with Magistrate Bell as we try to one, get Collins, and two, find the National Loan money." Gough-Coxe went to the corner of his office and picked up a walking stick. He let it drop out of his hand, and it hit the floor, bouncing back up into Gough-Coxe's hand as if it were a yo-yo on a string. "I've just gotten off the phone with Mr. Churchill in London, and he has authorized a £10,000 reward for information leading to the arrest of the murderer or murderers of Jameson."

"As you might suspect," Bell cut in, "it's really a £10,000 bounty on the head of Michael Collins. We'll see how protective Dublin City will be of this murderer when they see all those nice round zeros." Churchill, Bell, and Gough-Coxe were obviously hoping to test the Fenian mettle of the likes of Black Terry O'Neill and his impoverished family. Broy and Boynton looked at each other with surprise and knew that the British were really becoming desperate, trying to patch the leaking Irish roof any way they could.

"Broy," Gough-Coxe said.

"Yes, sir!"

"I hear you're the keeper of the Collins file over in Brunswick Street."

"That job seems to have fallen to me."

"I want all the material you have on Collins brought over here to the Castle," commanded Gough-Coxe. "I want it catalogued and copied. We have to have all information at our fingertips. We will meticulously go over the information to glean what we have so far missed.

"As for you, Boynton," said Gough-Coxe, "you are our missing link." Gough-Coxe had taken a particular interest in the young detective. Boynton was his connection to the late and much-lamented—to Gough-Coxe, at least—Sebastian Blood. Gough-Coxe, as he stated, liked to "work backwards." He knew Joseph Kavanagh and his son, Francis, had been in touch with Blood. It was the missing son, Eoin, whom he wanted to meet. According to Blood, the son was the connection that would lead to Collins. "I want to find this boy," Gough-Coxe. "That will be your assignment, Boynton. Find the missing Kavanagh boy."

"I'll do my best," Boynton promised.

"Do better than that," snapped Gough-Coxe.

"There are, many ways," said Magistrate Bell, an old detective himself who had risen to the rank of District Inspector in the RIC.

"There are, indeed," interrupted Broy. "The public records, newspapers. There are many ways to glean information."

"Yes!" Gough-Coxe exclaimed. "That's the spirit, Broy. Detective Sergeant, why don't you help young Detective Boynton find the missing

Kavanagh boy? You are my B&B Boys!" Gough-Coxe took his walking stick and held it out, handle first. He pointed it at Broy and Boynton. "I'll be keeping my eye on you." The two detectives looked at the "All-Seeing Eye," and suddenly realized it was Sebastian Blood's walking stick. They knew they were in for it.

89

Collins called a meeting at 22 Mary Street, the latest National Loan office, and everyone was there: the army was represented by McKee and Mulcahy, the Squad by McDonnell and Daly, G-man Broy, and Crow Street in the personages of Tobin and Eoin. One look told everyone in the room that Collins was in a foul mood.

"I have just discovered," began Collins, "that the National Loan is short more than £18,000, seized by the British government out of several of our bank accounts in Dublin in the last week. Although it is a minor sum compared to the total sum of the Loan, this has to stop. The financial health of the Republic is at stake."

"Magistrate First Class Alan Bell is your man," said Broy. "He's practically walking around Dublin Castle with a sandwich board that says, 'I'M LOOKING FOR THE NATIONAL LOAN MONEY!'"

"He's been a bad lad," added Tobin, "going back to the 1870s. Fooked with the Land League and even Parnell. I can't believe he's lived this long."

"Neither can I," shot Collins. "And there's no reason he should continue to breathe."

"This sounds like a job for the Squad," McKee said, gleefully.

"The sooner, the better," added Mulcahy.

"This man has to disappear by the middle of this month," Collins insisted.

"Beware the Ides of March," laughed McKee.

"I don't think we can plug him that quick," McDonnell said, slowly. "A week won't matter."

"He's stealing *my* money!" erupted Collins.

"It's not *your* money, Michael," corrected Mulcahy, gently.

"Yes, it is!" barked Collins. "Nobody gives a shite about the nation's money. The *Dáil* authorizes it. Dev leaves for America, collection plate in hand. And I'm here in Dublin doing all the bloody work. I have been entrusted with the coppers of Irish peasants and the dollars of Boston charwomen. I have an obligation to these wonderful people—and no fookin' bank-examinin' shite is going to take that money away from *me*—and the Republic."

"If we don't do it right," Daly said, calmly, "he'll continue to steal the Loan money." Collins cleared his throat in agitation as Daly continued. "This guy has been fucking Fenians longer than anyone at this table has been alive. He is not an amateur. Let's take our time and get it right."

"I agree," said McKee.

"Alright," said Collins, irritation still in his voice. "We'll start tagging him tomorrow. Where does he live?"

"Monkstown," Broy answered.

"I want Eoin on the tag team," Collins insisted. "My ministry will be represented!"

"Done," said Eoin.

"This is priority number one for the Squad," declared Collins. "Any other business?"

"We have a problem at the Castle," said Broy. "With Eoin."

"With Eoin?" said Collins. Eoin looked up, interested, but not shocked.

"The Sheik believes that the secret to finding you," Broy said to Collins, "is to find Eoin. He's heard all this stuff from Blood about the National Loan movie and Eoin's father and brother and, of course, Blood was killed in the family barbershop. He's a big believer in 'working backwards,' as he likes to say. So, he has Boynton and me trying to track down your man here," he finished, pointing at Eoin.

"Why don't we just tell him what he wants to know?" Eoin suggested.

"You'd be putting yourself at risk," Broy cautioned.

"Not at 'tal," replied Eoin. "They don't know who I am or where I live."

"But they do know your first name."

"Then I'll change it to Charlie."

"Why Charlie?"

"He's my other brother."

"Won't that put him in danger?"

"There is no danger in Glasnevin."

For the first time that evening, Collins smiled. Then said, "How anxious is the Sheik for this information on Eoin?"

"Very," said Broy. "He wants Boynton and meself to have some information quickly."

"Feed him a piece at a time," said Collins. "Couple of items a week. Work it out with Eoin. When we get rid of Bell, he won't be thinking about Eoin—or is that Charlie?—anymore."

"One more thing," said Broy. "Mr. Churchill has authorized a reward of £10,000 for the apprehension of Jameson's murderer." Broy let it sink in and then added, "Bell says it's really a £10,000 bounty on Mick's head."

"Not a bad figure," conceded Collins, duly impressed.

"Don't you think it's a bit inflated?" asked Eoin, which made the room roar with laughter. The meeting broke up, and, as the men were heading for the door, Broy said, "By the way, he's got Blood's Freemason walking stick, the one with the 'All-Seeing Eye.'"

Collins burst out in cynical laughter. "Now that's a stick with luck in it, isn't it?" And with that, the clock started ticking on the remaining days of Magistrate First Class Alan Bell's service to the Crown.

90

EOIN'S DIARY

The Squad has started tagging Alan Bell.

He lives out in Monkstown at 19 Belgrave Square North. We have been watching him every morning. He travels alone, taking the Dalkey tram into Nassau Street, and is met by a detective from Dublin Castle. Then he walks over to the Castle for his day's work. We know this for a fact, because Broy and Boynton have been alternating picking him up in Nassau Street. Some would say it is the act of a courageous man. I say it is the act of either hubris—to use one of Mick's favorite words—or someone who is a fool. And no one thinks Bell is a fool. He's been getting away with playing with Fenians for over forty years, and he thinks no one is going to harm him. But this time, he is about to learn that he's dealing with Michael Collins's Fenians!

This morning, McDonnell told me and Vinny to go ride the tram and see what the daily routine is. I will be on the backup team, and Vinny will be part of the shooting team. We are leaving nothing to chance.

We went up to the top of the open tram, and Vinny and I began examining the connection to the electrical wire that powers the tram. My assignment is to unhook the connection, which will stop the tram, and then go downstairs and join the backup team. It's a flimsy connection, and I should have no problem with the unhook.

We were heading back to town when the British army dropped the net on us just outside of Ballsbridge. It was only Vinny and meself and a few other people on top. "Shite," says I. We were both packing artillery, and I was getting very nervous. I didn't think we had a chance in a shootout.

The conductor was up top collecting fares when the Tommies pulled us over. "Here," commanded Vinny, pulling out his Mauser and gesturing at the frightened conductor. When the conductor came over, Vinny opened his change purse, which hung in front of him, and tossed the Mauser in. I looked at Vinny, and he seemed a little downcast as he planted his beloved Mauser C96 pistol—he called it his "Peter the Painter" ("Peter" for short), after the famous London anarchist siege of 1911—in the conductor's purse. Vinny loved that gun. Vinny bit his lip and said to the conductor, "Mum's the word!"

"What am I supposed to do?" I asked.

"Give me that yoke," said Vinny. The conductor's pouch was full, so Vinny crept down to the front of the tram and dropped me gun discreetly into the destination box. "NELSON'S PILLAR" was the new home of me Webley. "Now be good citizens," said Vinny to one and all, "and everyone will live to see another day." With purpose, Vinny added, "Everybody understand?" He sat down and we quietly, but nervously, waited for the Brits to board the tram. "Be respectful, but firm," he advised me.

Two Tommies came marching up the back circular staircase and surveyed us customers. They told me and Vinny to stand up. I immediately knew we should have split up. As one Tommy kept a close eye on us, the other Tommy frisked Vinny down, then did the same to me. "What's your name?" the Tommy demanded.

"Vincent Byrne."

"What's your business?"

"I'm a cabinetmaker," says Vince.

"Where do you work?"

"Duffy's in Leeson Street."

The soldier pushed Vinny away and said, "Sit down." Then he turned to me. "What's your name?" I hesitated for a second, wondering if the Sheik had put the word out on me. "Well?"

"Charlie Kavanagh," I said meekly. Vinny had a look of shock on his face.

"Where do you work?"

"Irish Assurance, Bachelors Walk."

"You lyin' to me, boy?"

I stared him right in his face. "No, sir!" He placed a hand on my shoulder and pushed me down into the seat. The two Tommies looked over the other passengers, saying nothing, and then went down the narrow stairs. Vinny and I sat silently, looking at each other across the aisle. Vinny kept looking at the destination box, and I knew he'd love to get his hand on my Webley and let one of the blackguards have it. Suddenly, the tram came alive and pulled ahead, heading to the city centre. Vinny immediately went to the destination box and retrieved my Webley, handing it back to me. He then flew down the stairs and got his "Peter" back from the conductor.

"What's all that 'Charlie' stuff about?" asked Vinny.

"The Sheik is looking for Eoin Kavanagh," I said, and Vinny nodded his head.

As we approached the Grand Canal, we decided to get off. "Thank you," Vinny said gallantly to the customers as we headed down the back stairs. When he came to the conductor, he said, "Thank you. Good job!"

"Heart-stopping," replied the conductor, who could have ended up in Mountjoy for collaborating with us if the British had found Vinny's gun.

As we walked down Leeson Street, Vinny turned and said to me, "If he thinks that was heart-stopping, wait until he sees what we're up to!" Vinny was exhilarated with the morning. As usual, I was terrified. I couldn't wait to get back to my index cards in the precarious safety of Crow Street.

91

E oin burst into the Crow Street office and blurted out, "Vinny and I just had a close call!"

"Come on," says Tobin, in a rush, "We're going to have a close call if we don't meet Mick over at the Stag's Head, pronto."

The two of them charged across Dame Street and ran up the alley to the Stag's Head, racing upstairs to the private parlor. Collins was there with Daly and Mulcahy, and he was in a piss-ugly mood. "About time!" he snapped at the two of them. "As you know, Tomás MacCurtain, the Lord Mayor of Cork City, was murdered in front of his wife and child four days ago by a gang of intruders." Collins continued pacing as he spoke. "Now, we've come to expect this type of thing from the British, but there's something different here. We don't know if it was the RIC or some auxiliary branch that did the actual murders. Also, the British are circulating rumors to the loyalist press that Tomás was done in by his fellow Fenians. As evidence, the Crown has produced forged threatening letters to poor Tomás. The letters were written on *Dáil* stationery."

"Where the hell did they get that?" asked Tobin.

"They could have gotten it in a raid," said Collins. "Christ, there're boxes of *Dáil* stationery in our two buildings in Harcourt Street."

"Diabolical," added Daly.

"I feel so bad about poor Tomás," said Collins. "We became good friends when we were doing time in Frongoch together. It's our duty to keep the pressure up."

"We have reports," added Tobin, "that the new RIC Auxiliaries have begun arriving in the country. Maybe it was those boyos who did Mac-Curtain in."

"And I have reports from Limerick City," said Mulcahy, "that some Crown ruffians shot up the city centre the last couple of nights."

"What's so special about British troops shooting up some Irish city?" asked Collins.

"These blackguards," replied Mulcahy, "weren't regular British army. They weren't wearing regular British army uniforms. They were ragtag. Tunics didn't match trousers, or vice versa."

"This is not our day," said Collins, pensively.

Collins looked like he was getting depressed, and Eoin knew it was time to pump a little bravado into the Corkman. "Have you gone over those British tax figures I got for you?" he asked Collins.

Fire shot into Collins's eyes, and he roared, "The fookin', thievin' hoors! Do you know how many pounds the British have taken out of this island since the Act of Union went into effect in 1801? Over four hundred million fookin' pounds!"

"Jaysus," breathed Mulcahy. "that's almost half-a-billion pounds!"

"A half-billion pounds," emphasized Collins, "from one of the poorest fookin' countries in the fookin' British Empire."

"It's financial rape!" added Daly.

"This is not rape," said the Minister for Finance, "this is sodomy—the out-and-out buggery of the Irish nation!" Eoin looked at Collins and suppressed a smile. "Speaking of buggers," said Collins, without missing a beat, "what's the situation with Magistrate Bell?"

"We're ready to go," Daly said. "We've been tagging him all week. Friday morning will be the day, if you give the go-ahead."

"You have my permission," said Collins, standing up. He was about to go out the door when he stopped and turned around. "Don't disappoint me," he warned. "Ring up Bell so loud that the sound will reverberate all the way to Dublin Castle."

92

Friday, March 26, 1920, dawned bright with the promise of a beautiful early spring day. Magistrate First Class Alan Bell came out of his house in Monkstown and went in search of the tram that would take him to the city centre. As he waited with the other commuters, he didn't notice Eoin Kavanagh waiting with him or Charlie Dalton sitting on his bicycle across the road. When the tram came along, Bell got on, as did Eoin, who immediately went upstairs and took a seat in the rear of the open-top. Dalton jumped on his bike and pedaled ahead of the tram, bringing the news, two stops forward. "He's on the next tram," Dalton confirmed to Daly, McDonnell, Byrne, and Tom Keogh.

As the tram pushed along Simmonscourt Road in Ballsbridge, Eoin got up and disconnected it from its electrical line. Down below, the primary Squad team entered the cab and sought out Bell. He was sitting between two women, wheezing and coughing away from a spring cold. "Come on, Mr. Bell," Daily announced. "Your time has come." Daly and McDonnell grabbed Bell by each of his arms and pulled.

"No, no," said Bell. "You've got the wrong man! The wrong man!" Bell, with a strength that belied his years, pulled himself free from McDonnell's grasp, grabbed a pole, and held on, literally, for dear life.

"Come on, ya shite," said Vinny Byrne, as he slammed Bell on the arm with his Mauser. Bell let go of the pole, and Daly and McDonnell pulled him, shoulders first, out into the road. Then Bell began kicking like a showhall chorus girl. He would not go quietly.

"Look what they're doing to the poor ould man," exclaimed one of the female passengers who had been sitting next to Bell. "Well, come on!" she told the other passengers in the cab. "It's our moral duty to help the poor man!"

Eoin came down the back stairs of the tram, his Webley in hand. Two women and a man were about to go to the rescue of Alan Bell. Eoin held the gun out in front of him, easy for all to see. It was important for them to see the gun, because then they always remembered the weapon, not the face of the man holding it. "Mind your own bloody business!" Eoin snapped. "Sit down, or you'll need coppers for your eyes!" The rescue party moved tentatively backward. Joe Leonard, gun in plain sight, hopped on the tram and shouted, "Move! Now!" The three shrunk back into their seats. "God bless us, save us!" intoned the man as he made the Sign of the Cross and then blessed himself again to be sure.

Bell was still fraying about, trying to kick his abductors. Byrne had had enough. He took one shot and hit Bell right in the bollocks, blood flooding onto the street. Bell screamed and hopped about as he grabbed his groin with both hands. "You castrated me!" he screamed.

"That's the least of your problems," Daly said, as he shot him in the chest, which drove Bell to the ground. McDonnell came from behind, stuck his Colt under Bell's chin, and pulled the trigger, the bullet exploding out of the top of Bell's head. Keogh made sure he was dead with one more head-shot.

"Let's go!" shouted Daly to both teams. The two teams, eight in all, started run-walking back to the city centre. Here they were, out in the open, with no means of escape except their legs.

"Break up," said McDonnell to the men. "Go your separate ways. Scoot!"

Eoin found himself on a solitary walk back to the city, moving as fast as he could, trying not to draw suspicion to himself. As he got closer to the Grand Canal, he saw ambulances coming from St. Vincent's Hospital, charging out Ballsbridge way. Then the Crossley tenders came bolting from the city, full of Tommies.

Eoin felt bad that he'd had to shout at the passengers to keep them in line, but there was no other way. He smiled as he thought of the man blessing himself, which he knew would surely amuse Róisín. But mostly he was surprised how innocuous-looking Alan Bell had been.

Here was a man who had been gumming up the works of the Fenians for over forty years, and he could have passed for an ordinary haberdashery clerk. But he was anything but ordinary. His man Jameson had gotten close to Collins, and Bell himself had sniffed out the National Loan. But Eoin was surprised at the fuss Bell made at the end. He had been expecting the famous British "stiff upper lip," but the little man only displayed sheer panic. And Eoin was surprised with himself— surprised that he had taken such keen satisfaction when Vinny gelded Bell, causing a bloody mess. Eoin smiled as he crossed the Grand Canal into the city, for he knew that Alan Bell's Spotted Dick would be on the menu that night at Dublin Castle.

93

Boynton was showing Gough-Coxe what he had found out about Eoin Kavanagh. They were going over Eoin's arrest card from Easter Week. The fingerprints were still pristine. "Where are the mug shots?" the Sheik asked.

"No mug shots," replied Boynton. "Things were so rushed and chaotic that week that few, if any, of the rebels were photographed."

"Bloody bad luck," Gough-Coxe sighed.

Broy had left his office in Brunswick Street and walked the several blocks to Nassau Street, where he would pick Alan Bell up near Grafton Street. Bell was usually on the nine o'clock tram, and then the two of them would walk over to Dublin Castle, via Dame Lane, favored by both the British and the rebels because of its anonymity. But there was no number-eight tram from Dalkey this morning. After waiting half an hour, Broy discovered that there were no number-eight trams coming through at all. Then it hit him. This must have been Magistrate Bell's morning. Collins purposely didn't tell Broy and Boynton what he was up to. Collins kept to his own time schedule; everybody else adjusted. Broy was suddenly filled with joy—and fear. He realized that he would be the one bringing the bad news to the Sheik up at the Castle.

"What we need is a photograph of this boy," Gough-Coxe said.

What you need, thought Boynton, *is a photograph of bloody Michael Collins.*

Just then, Broy busted in the door. He was in a huff. Gough-Coxe took one look and said, "Where's Magistrate Bell?"

"There are no number-eight trams this morning," Broy said, breathless. "Something must have happened."

Gough-Coxe stood up and began pacing. Not a word was spoken between the three men. The Sheik picked up the receiver on his telephone and then replaced it with a sigh. There was really no one to call. He would just have to wait.

He didn't have to wait long. The phone soon rang. "Yes," he answered and listened for a moment. "Thank you," he replied, as he slowly replaced the receiver into its cradle. He looked up at the two G-men. "Alan Bell was murdered this morning out in Ballsbridge. He was pulled off the tram by fifteen or twenty men and murdered in the street." After pausing for a few seconds, he added, "This is a disaster for us. First Jameson, then his handler Bell."

Boynton held up Eoin's fingerprint card from Richmond Barracks. "About young Kavanagh," he said.

"Fuck young Kavanagh!" snapped Gough-Coxe. "We don't have time to dance around Dublin looking for some kid who may or may not know where Michael Collins is. We are in a very precarious situation here. We are at the tipping point. London has no clue how bad the situation is here. We need more help. The Auxiliaries are arriving, but we need more. We need intelligence help. This Collins is not your typical Fenian—he's *good* at what he does!"

Gough-Coxe called his secretary into the room. "Get me a reservation on the mail boat this evening. I have to travel to London to straighten this mess out."

Boynton slid Eoin Kavanagh's fingerprint card back into its folder. Collins had been right about Bell's demise. Young Kavanagh wasn't important to the Sheik anymore. What *was* important was Michael Collins—and *only* Michael Collins. And Gough-Coxe knew that he would never catch Collins using only the G-division of the Dublin Metropolitan Police. He had to convince London that it was now time to bring in the cream of the British Secret Service from throughout the empire. He hated to admit it, but the Cork farm boy was more than he could handle.

94

EOIN'S DIARY

I let meself into Róisín's flat in Walworth Road and sat down at the tiny kitchen table. Out of me pocket, I retrieved both of Sebastian Blood's notebooks, collected by the Squad at the Volta Cinema and meself the day of his execution. Blood was not a great note-taker. Mostly there were scribbles about the Kavanagh family and the notation, "Eoin/missing son." That, for some reason, made me smile. I keep going through these books because I think I'm missing something. The notes are so rudimental that I'm wondering what kind of detective Blood really was. He was either fookin' brilliant, or he was a dunce. My gut tells me that Blood could not have cut the Colman's at Crow Street. There's nothing in them, except for one quizzical notation: "williewick."

What the fook is a williewick?

Also on the same page was the entry "vchrist."

Williewick and vchrist.

Something to do with candles and church?

I was just sitting there looking at the books when Róisín let herself in, just off work. "Jaysus!" she exclaimed. "You gave me an awful fright!" She punched me playfully in the shoulder and added, "Don't scare me like that! What are you doing?" I don't stay with Róisín that often. I find it safer to keep moving. Last night I slept at Dr. Gogarty's over in Ely Place; tomorrow it will probably be the Bartleys up in Phibsborough. And there's always the couch over in Bachelors Walk.

I told her I was trying to figure out what a "williewick" was. She blurted out, "Isn't that the thing between your legs?"

I looked up and shook my head. "You have a durty mind," I said to her. "Do you know what a 'vchrist' is?"

"Maybe a victory for Christ?" Róisín suggested. "Maybe playing with your williewick is somehow a victory for Christ."

"You're a big help," I told her.

"Williewick," she whispered in my left ear, then did the same into my right ear, adding a diabolical laugh.

Now my willie was getting hard. "Róisín," says I. "Do you know what you're doing to me?"

"I do, indeed!"

"You're a terrible tease," I acccused, as I stood up from the table and pushed her against the sink. I ground my hips into hers, and she could feel my banger. "I'm hungry," I said.

"A fry-up?"

"How about bangers and mash?"

She laughed and pushed me away. "You know the rules."

"No tomfoolery."

"No tomfoolery," she confirmed. "Not yet, anyway."

She guided me back to the table and Blood's two notebooks. I looked down at the pages. "Williewick" still didn't mean anything to me. Róisín threw her black frying pan on the stove and pulled some sausages from a cooler box on the windowsill. "Eoin," says she. I turned and saw she was holding a banger by its tip, letting it hang out for me to see all its glory.

"That's about the size of it," says I.

"You wish!" Róisín said, laughing. She took me by the hand and led me to the bedroom, where I knew my frustration would continue to grow—Blood's "williewick" now driving me mad at both ends.

95

Eoin's diaries were having an effect on Diane and Johnny's relationship. The more brutal 1920 became, the less they spoke to each other. Their long marriage was often like that—*quiet*. While Johnny was writing, he was often uncommunicative, stuck in his book for long periods of time. Diane had come to accept the behavior of her husband, which she noticed he had inherited from his grandmother, Róisín. Diane knew Roisin during only the last decade of her life, but she was writing and publishing books—and causing controversy—until the day she passed.

"Is there any good news coming out of those diaries?" asked Diane, as the two of them sat in their Dalkey living room watching the RTE news.

"Good news!" said Johnny. "Mayor Walker has returned to America, and, thanks to Grandpa, he has a job."

Diane brightened. "Now that's what I want to hear! I do like Mayor Walker."

"So did Grandma," said Johnny. "I think Grandpa could have stayed away from Jimmy Walker, but Róisín insisted he get him a job."

"How did it happen?"

"Well, they were living at 45 Christopher Street, and, according to the diary, one Sunday night, Grandpa went out to get the *Daily News* at eight o'clock in the evening and bumped into Jimmy as he was hailing a cab to take him home."

Walker was returning from the Tamawa Democratic Club that Carmine De Sapio had just opened on Seventh Avenue South. "Mr. Mayor!" said a surprised Eoin.

"Congressman Kavanagh!" returned Walker, genuinely happy to see the person who had issued him his walking papers.

"What are you doing down here in sinful Greenwich Village? I heard you were strictly an uptown man since your return from Europe."

"Sinister Carmine," laughed Jimmy, "wanted me to launch his new club with a speech to inspire."

"Thinking of making a comeback?" nudged Eoin.

"You never can tell!"

Eoin grabbed Walker by the elbow and walked him across Grove Street to Jack Delaney's saloon, a former speakeasy. "I'm calling Róisín," Eoin declared, and, five minutes later, the three of them were bellying up to the bar.

"Mr. Mayor!" said Róisín, as she kissed Walker on his cheek.

"My lovely Róisín," charmed the Mayor, "you get more beautiful by the year!" Walker took her hand and kissed it, and Róisín blushed in his admiration.

"Funny," intoned Eoin, "when I say that kind of stuff to her, she wants to know what I did wrong!"

Walker laughed. "Well, Eoin, *everyone* knows the sins of Jimmy Walker!" Walker, of course, was right. He had returned to New York in 1935, when the Justice Department decided they had nothing on him. He and his new wife, Betty, had tried many business schemes and had come up short. "For a guy who was supposed to have stolen City Hall," said Walker, "I'm flat broke."

"Have you heard from the president?" asked Eoin.

"Not a whisper."

"Well," Eoin said, "he told me he was delighted by your defense of him against grumpy Al Smith during last year's election."

"The president could have called Jimmy," insisted Róisín.

"Busy man, the president," added Walker. The Mayor finished his drink and put on his hat. "I have to get going."

"It was great seeing you again, Jimmy," said Eoin.

"Pass my regards on to the president," Walker replied.

"Will you and Betty come down to dinner at our home?" asked Róisín.

"I will, indeed," Walker agreed. "If your cooking can match your beauty, it will be a gourmet feast!"

"Where'd you find that shovel, Mr. Mayor?" Eoin teased, and the three of them roared.

Walker made his way to the door, glad-handing patrons on his way out. "He's one of a kind," Eoin remarked.

"Why don't you ask FDR if he has a job for Jimmy?" pushed Róisín.

"You never give up, do you?" responded Eoin.

But knowing that the motto, "Happy Wife, Happy Life," was true, he did ask FDR the first chance he got. "I'll see what I can do," said the president. "Maybe Fiorello has something for him."

"Why would Mayor LaGuardia want to help Jimmy Walker?" asked Eoin of the president.

"Because, Congressman, he's Jimmy Walker!"

Eoin arranged for Walker to meet the president and then brokered a meeting with LaGuardia. As Walker emerged from his meeting with the Little Flower, reporters asked what they had talked about. "We were trying to find out if Diogenes was on the level!" replied Beau James.

And it wasn't long until LaGuardia came up with a job: "Czar" of Industrial and Labor Relations in the Women's Coat-and-Suit Industry, one of New York's signature commerces. FDR signed off, and Walker found himself making a cool $25,000 a year. Not bad in 1938. Asked exactly what he did in his new job, Jimmy quipped, "They are always buttonholing me!"

"That's a wonderful story," Diane marveled.

"Jimmy Walker must have been quite a guy," Johnny agreed. "Even his enemies loved him. They figured he did his penance, so why not reward him?"

"Róisín could be quite feisty, I see," said Diane.

"Eoin and Róisín were separate moons, rotating around the same planet," said Johnny.

"In what way?"

"Well," Johnny explained, "even as a kid, when I moved in with them, they led separate lives. Grandpa would be in Washington, and Grandma would be writing books in New York and running salons for all her crazy women friends."

"Watch your step, Mr. Kavanagh!" warned Diane.

"Well," said Johnny, "they were all crazy. It was a *Who's Who* of the feminist movement running through that apartment. Half of them thought I had no right to live there!"

"Oh, you poor thing," said Diane, gently touching Johnny on his chin. "You seemed to survive."

"As did their marriage," said Johnny. "Even after Eoin retired from Congress in 1964 and went to Dublin to serve in the *Dáil,* they remained close. Grandpa wore out Aer Lingus flying back and forth between Dublin and New York."

"Why didn't Róisín go to Dublin and live with him?"

"Well," said Johnny, "to be honest with you, Róisín wanted nothing to do with Dublin—or Ireland, for that matter. She felt it was a century behind the times, and she thought there was something special happening in New York in the 1960s and '70s. She was also pissed that they banned all her books!"

"She held a grudge!"

"Of course, she did. She was Irish, wasn't she? That's why Grandpa and I were always running around Dublin alone together when I was a teenager. He taught me so much."

"I wish he were here again," Diane remarked wistfully. "There is so much I want to ask him now. You only think about stuff after people die."

"What did you want to ask him?"

"Oh," said Diane, "why he quit Congress and left America. It seems to me that that was a very outrageous thing to do for a man in his mid-sixties."

"As outrageous as joining a revolution on the spur of the moment?"

"*Almost* as outrageous," laughed Diane.

"I actually know the answer to that," said Johnny. "You know Grandpa was mentor to a generation of Democratic politicians in the House for nearly thirty years. Guys like JFK and LBJ. He liked all of them, especially JFK. And when Kennedy got shot, it took something out of Grandpa."

"It might have also reminded him of his job in the Squad—and of Collins," said Diane.

"Absolutely," Johnny agreed. "Then the civil rights movement came along under LBJ, and Bobby Kennedy was still Attorney General. Grandpa had to marshal those votes in the House because he was a whip. He saw how divisive the whole thing was and, of course, there was the Vietnam War coming down the chute. Grandpa had a great sense of history, and he knew it was time to get out, to go back to Ireland and maybe finish Collins's work in some way."

"He was a truly amazing man," Dianed said. "But this shooting stuff really gets to me. I can't believe Grandpa could do something like that." Diane paused and then quietly asked, "Did he shoot anyone else in 1920?"

"No comment!" laughed Johnny. "Let's just say, for now, he helped send several on their way!"

"It's not funny." Diane took Johnny's hand. "Now don't lie to me. Did you have any clue that Grandpa was a gunman?"

"In all my years with Grandpa and his cronies," said Johnny, "I only heard one story, and that was from Speaker O'Neill, another of the old man's protégés."

"What happened?"

Johnny began the tale of Big Haley Bourbon, the Democratic congressman from Biloxi, Mississippi. Haley was six-feet-four and 325 pounds. He always wore white linen suits that looked like they had been purchased from Sidney Greenstreet's estate. Bourbon had rotted Bourbon's insides—he even got red in the face peeing. The odds of him bursting his guts were running three-to-two against his guts. He was great pals with Mississippi Governor Ross Barnett and Alabama Governor George Wallace. He was staunchly against the civil rights movement, saying, "The negras of Mississippi never had it so good!"

"Well," said Big Haley—a liquid lunch making him feel invincible—as he spied the diminutive congressman from Greenwich Village, "if it isn't the nigger-loving, homo-loving Democratic whip from Nude Yawk Shitty!"

It had been a hard week for Eoin Kavanagh, counting LBJ's votes and trying to get the Civil Rights Act of 1964 through the House. He had had enough.

The color drained out of Eoin Kavanagh's face. He walked up to the southern congressman, who towered over him. He grabbed Haley by his necktie, and as he jerked it, he kicked the congressman's leg from under him. The thud of the congressman hitting the marble floor could be heard throughout the Cannon House Office Building. Eoin was still holding Haley's tie as he bent over him and whispered in his ear, "You've heard that stuff about me being a gunman in the IRA? I was. Don't fuck with me. One more at my age won't make any fucking difference. You understand me, shithead?" With that, he let the Mississippi congressman slump to the floor and walked away, Tip O'Neill in tow.

"That's unbelievable," said Diane.

"Not really," said Johnny. "Grandpa was such an even-tempered man that people are always shocked at the idea that he could be tough or even violent. He had his boiling point—and God help the individual who brought him to that boiling point."

96

EOIN'S DIARY

My briefing with Collins took place tonight at the Wicklow Hotel. I arrived about half-six, and Willie Dolan, the porter, indicated to me that the Big Fellow was in his back room on the first floor. I had just settled down at the desk and opened my attaché case when Joe Leonard came bursting through the door. "Get up!" he shouted. "The G-men are on the march along Exchequer Street." We jumped up and ran out into the lobby. "Follow me," said Joe, and we all went up the stairs, two steps at a time.

When we got to the top floor, we headed straight for the skylight. Collins hopped on a table and went first. I got up on the table, tossed my attaché to Collins, then went through the skylight with a boost from Leonard and Mick pulling me through. Joe was next, and, with a leap, Mick and I pulled him through. "This way," said Joe. This was Joe's escape plan, which he had planned well in advance. Anywhere Collins frequents has an escape plan.

Mick went to look over the edge of the roof. "For fook's sake," said Joe, "come on!"

"There're two cars of G-men down there, and a tender of Tommies," said Collins, chuckling. I think Mick loves this stuff, but I was about to wet me pants. Joe began to lead us up over the roofs of Grafton Street. "Where are you going?" asked Collins.

"Away from them," said Joe. "To Suffolk Street."

"Oh, fook that," said Mick. "I want to go out on Wicklow Street."

"You're daft!" spat Leonard.

"Come on this way," said Mick, pointing to the roofs along Wicklow Street. "Let's have some fun!"

Joe, looking like he wanted to take a dive into the street, took us along the buildings until we were about five buildings down from the hotel. We followed him down the stairs and came out on Wicklow Street. As we hit the street, a limousine of G-men pulled up. Mick calmly surveyed the scene, then took out his silver cigarette case, withdrew a fag, and lit it. He went right up to one of the detectives and asked, "What's going on here?"

I spied Boynton, and, as soon as he saw Collins, he started staring into the ground. "We're after Collins!" replied the G-man.

"Smoke?" said Collins to the G-man.

"No thanks," came the reply.

"I hope you get the gobshite Collins!" Mick said heartily, as he winked in Boynton's direction. Then, with a great laugh, he said, "Let's go to the Stag's Head." As we walked along Exchequer Street, he asked, "Who knew you were coming here tonight?"

"Tobin," I replied. "Who did you tell?"

"No one."

"Well," said Leonard, "someone bloody well knew."

We went upstairs to the Stag's Head parlor and tried, for the second time, to get down to business. "Tonight, we were lucky," Collins admitted.

"We've had tough luck at the Wicklow Hotel recently," I added quietly. "Vaughan's is much safer."

Collins stared at me. "You're like me, Eoin. You don't believe in 'tough luck,' do you?"

"You make your own luck," I finally said.

"What bothers you about the Wicklow?"

"I don't know."

"But something does?"

"Yes."

"Well," said Collins, "work it out. I'm tired of climbing through skylights."

97

After his meeting with Collins broke up, Eoin returned to Crow Street and retrieved Sebastian Blood's file, took out his photograph, and placed it in his coat pocket. He then headed over to Exchequer Street, where he spent the night sleeping on the couch, still dreaming of his father's tormentor.

The next morning, Eoin phoned Dublin Castle. "Meet me at the Palace Bar in Fleet Street at five o'clock," he told Brendan Boynton.

As soon as Boynton joined Eoin in the snug at the end of the bar, the questions began. "How did you find out about Collins being at the Wicklow Hotel last night?"

"One of the Sheik's tipsters called him," said Boynton.

"What time?"

"About half-six."

"That late."

"We were all about to go home when Gough-Coxe rounded us up, called the army, and scooted to Wicklow Street. I almost shit when I saw Collins."

"I beat you to it," said Eoin, as he took the first sip of his porter.

Eoin didn't say a word as he stared straight ahead. The crowd was beginning to drift in from the *Irish Times* in D'Olier Street, and the bar was beginning to fill up. "What's bothering you?"

"I'm worried about the Wicklow Hotel."

"Why?"

"Too many 'coincidences,'" said Eoin.

"And you don't believe in coincidences."

"Exactly."

"What can I do?"

"Find out the Sheik's tipster."

"You don't know?"

"I might," said Eoin, "but I'm not sure. Let's work on this from both our sides. Whoever the tout is, he's very, very dangerous." With that, Eoin took one more gulp of porter and hit the door.

Eoin took the direct route to Vaughan's Hotel, right up Sackville Street to Parnell Square. He decided that he was going to check all the hotels that Collins was known to frequent. Vaughan's was still Joint Number One, and it drew G-men to it like flies to shit. When he went through the lobby door, he was greeted by Christy Harte, the hotel's porter. "Can I have a word with you?"

"Sure."

"In private." Christy Harte was IRB, and he was trusted implicitly by Collins and his comrades. He managed a very ticklish situation at Vaughan's, leading the G-men and their touts on a merry goose chase searching for Collins and his cronies. They went into a back room, where suitcases were stored, and Eoin pulled out his picture of Sebastian Blood. "You ever see this boyo?"

Harte looked at the photo and laughed. "Indeed," he said. "Just another eager G-man."

"Another?"

"Oh, they come around here all the time, snooping for Mick and the other lads. I can handle them."

"What did this guy want you to do?"

"Oh, he wanted me to be his snitch," said Harte. "To call him when Mick or the other big shots came in. Offered me pounds and pounds."

"What did you tell him?"

"I told him that Mick was hanging out at the Munster Hotel over in Mountjoy Street."

"Which he wasn't."

"Not for a while, at least," laughed Harte.

Eoin took out Blood's notebook. "Does this mean anything to you?"

" 'Williewick'? Not at 'tal."

"How about this one?" Eoin said, pointing out "vchrist."

Harte laughed. "Well," he said, "would that be me?"

"You?"

"Vchrist. Christy at V. V for Vaughan."

"Jaysus," said Eoin, it all becoming clear.

"Was I of any help?"

"More than you'll ever know."

"I think I know who 'williewick' is."

"Then you're a better man than I am, Eoin," said Liam Tobin.

Eoin placed Sebastian Blood's notebook on the desk. "Vchrist is Christy Harte up at Vaughan's. Christy identified Blood from his photograph. He said that Blood tried to recruit him to inform on Mick and the lads."

"Christy's smarter than that," said Tobin.

"The G-men, and many an eager freelancer, are always hanging around Vaughan's," Eoin explained. "Christy knows how to sort them out."

"So how does that help you with the Wicklow Hotel?"

"If 'vchrist' is Christy, who do you think is 'williewick'?"

Tobin paused. "Willie Dolan?"

"Of the Wicklow Hotel."

"Unbelievable."

"I think Blood passed Willie onto the Sheik."

"What does Boynton say?"

"He knows nothing about anything. The Sheik is keeping this one to himself."

"What now?"

"Let's set a trap."

"Maybe we should get Mick's approval?"

"Not yet," said Eoin. "Let's talk to the Big Fellow after the trap is sprung."

"When?"

"Tomorrow," Eoin decided. "I'll set it up with Boynton. Tell Mick to steer clear of the Wicklow and the whole area from there to the Castle."

98

Eoin caught up with Joe Leonard and Vinny Byrne at the Monico Pub on Exchequer Street. The pub was a favorite of Collins's, who had another office around the corner at 3 Andrew Street.

"What's so important?" Leonard demanded, impatient as ever. Eoin had called both Leonard and Byrne to the meeting because they used the Wicklow Hotel more than any other members of the Squad.

"Remember Blood's notebooks?" Eoin asked. Leonard nodded. "I figured out who 'vchrist' and 'williewick' are." Leonard looked intensely at Eoin. "'Vchrist' is Christy Harte up at Vaughan's."

"A sound man," chimed in Leonard.

"And 'williewick'?" interjected Vinny.

Eoin paused before answering. "I think it's Willie Dolan at the Wicklow."

There was a moment of silence. "That's hard to believe," Leonard said slowly.

"But the perfect cover, isn't it?" put in Vinny.

"There have been three close calls there in the last six months," began Eoin. "First, there was the time Frank came looking for me. You thought something was fishy."

"I did, indeed," replied Leonard.

"Then there was that time we tried to get Johnny French coming out of Trinity College. He never showed up, but the G-men and the army did. Mick's tout turned out to be Willie Dolan himself. And then there was the incident the other day."

"How can we be sure?" asked Leonard.

"We'll set a trap. Remember how they almost got Collins the other night? I'll tell Willie that I'm going to meet Mick at two o'clock, and we'll see if the G-men come a-prancin'. There is no danger to anyone here. Mick is steering clear of the area. If Willie doesn't call the Castle, he's in the clear."

"Ah," said Vinny, "but what if he calls?"

"Then this becomes a job for the Squad."

Very casually, Eoin went into the lobby of the Wicklow Hotel at half-one and buttonholed Willie Dolan. "Get the back room ready, Willie, the bossman will be here at two o'clock for a meeting with the lads."

"Mick?"

"Himself, indeed," said Eoin. "I have to fetch some papers up in Harcourt Street, but I'll be back in plenty of time." With that, Eoin walked out of the hotel and headed up Grafton Street. Half a block later, he backtracked and stationed himself with a good view of the hotel and Wicklow Street. Then he waited. As the clock ticked closer to two o'clock, he noticed a car stop at the corner of Duke Street. Four men in trench coats sat inside. In the distance, he could see another limousine on Exchequer Street. Same thing. Four trenches without movement. Eoin pulled his pocket watch out of his vest by its fob and saw that it was almost two. He inched back into the doorway and continued watching. Neither car moved. Two o'clock came and went. He kept an eye on the automobile at the corner of Duke Street. He pulled his watch out again. It was two-fifteen. The car in Duke Street started up quickly, and the other car down on Exchequer followed suit. They both pulled up with a screech, making an inverted V at the doorway to the Wicklow Hotel. All eight G-men jumped out and headed inside. Eoin noticed one of them was Brendan Boynton. Willie Dolan had signed his own death warrant.

99

Róisín was reading a book on her sofa when she heard the key go into the lock and turn. The door opened, and there stood Eoin. "I thought you'd be showing up."

He kissed her on the forehead and gave her a tired smile. "How did you know?"

"Because of what happened at the Wicklow Hotel on Tuesday," she replied, as she went into the kitchen to retrieve the *Irish Times* from earlier in the week. She held it up for Eoin to read: SLAUGHTER AT THE WICKLOW HOTEL. "This your handiwork?"

Eoin grunted. "Yes and no."

"That's like saying Willie Dolan is only a little bit dead."

"He had it coming. He was informing for Dublin Castle."

"Did you shoot him?"

"No," said Eoin in a quiet voice. "I just set it up." He took the newspaper out of Róisín's hand and looked at the headline that everyone in Dublin was still talking about. "The next boyo I'm going to shoot is the eejit who keeps writing these headlines!"

He plopped down on the sofa. Róisín sat down next to him and took his hand. "Are you alright?"

"No, I'm not alright. How'd you like to make a living by murdering people?"

When Eoin and Tobin told Collins about Willie Dolan, he was livid. "I'm going to kill him myself—with me bare hands!" he said.

"Now, Mick," said Tobin. "Just let the lads handle it."

Collins calmed down and finally said to Eoin, "How did you know he was the snitch?"

"Blood's notebook. When I discovered Christy Harte was 'vchrist', I knew 'williewick' was Willie Dolan. Too many problems at the Wicklow Hotel."

"Yes," said Collins, turning to Tobin. "Call up Paddy Daly and tell them to shoot Willie *immediately*."

The next morning, Willie Dolan was taking suitcases out of the boot of a taxi when Joe Leonard walked up behind him and dropped him with one shot to the head. Paddy Daly finished him off on the ground with another bullet, again to the head. Then Daly and Leonard mixed into the morning rush-hour crowd on Grafton Street as Dolan bled to death on the pavement.

At Dublin Castle, Brendan Boynton heard the Sheik slam his phone into its cradle and then start pounding his desk with his fist. "Damn! Damn! Damn!" he heard Derek of Suez shout.

"Sir," said Boynton, "is there something wrong?"

"Something wrong!" shouted Gough-Coxe. "Something wrong! Are you a fucking imbecile?" Boynton stood mute as Gough-Coxe plopped helplessly into his desk chair. "I've just lost Blood's last contact with Collins." Then he added, "We're back to square one." Gough-Coxe spun in his chair and stared out the window that overlooked one of the court-yards of the Castle. "This is the straw that broke the camel's back," he said. "Maybe this will get those politicians in London off their soft asses."

"Are they giving you trouble?" asked Boynton.

"When Magistrate Bell was murdered, I pleaded with them for more help," Gough-Coxe said. "I asked for some of the men who worked for me in the Middle East to be reassigned to Ireland. But they wouldn't go for it." The Sheik looked up and locked eyes with Boynton. "With this murder, maybe I'll get my way."

"Your way?"

"It's about time some of my friends from Cairo joined me," Gough-Coxe said, finally breaking a smile. "I think Michael Collins will enjoy these boyos."

"Why?"

"Because they're just like him—they don't play by the rules."

———————

"What's bothering you?" Róisín finally asked.

"Willie's family," said Eoin. "He had a wife and kids."

"Like Willie Dolan was worried about you and Collins and the rest of the lads in the Squad. Don't believe all those human-interest stories they like to run in the *Times* about the poor ould 'victims.' 'Victims,' my arse!"

"That's easy for you to say, Róisín. You don't have to set these guys up and then read the headlines."

"What are you more upset about? The informers or the headlines they create?"

Eoin went to his attaché case and opened it. He took a piece of paper out of it and handed it to Róisín. "Read this."

She read the letter and then started laughing. "You're jokin'!"

"I am not."

"Willie Dolan's wife asked for a pension for herself and the kiddies? What did Collins say?"

"He gave it to her."

"He gave it to her! You're kiddin'. He gave her a fookin' pension?"

"Mick said he didn't want the family to know Willie was a snitch. He said, 'The poor little devils need the money.'"

"I'll say this for Mick Collins," Róisín said, grudgingly. "He'll *always* surprise you." Eoin plopped down on the sofa again, dejected. She put her arms around him and gave him a great hug. "You'll be fine, Eoin. Mick will be fine. And Willie Dolan's family will be fine."

"Why do you think that?"

"Because we're growing a bizarre brand of revolutionary this year." Eoin looked Róisín in the eye, and she gave him her dazzling smile.

"You know, Róisín, this life is supposed to be about love, not hate and death. That's what my parents taught me. What do I love? Ireland. Who do I love? My brothers and my sister. That's it, and that's not saying much."

"How about Mick?"

"Yeah, Mick."

"Anyone else?"

Eoin hesitated. "You—but I shouldn't have told you that."

"Why not?"

"Because."

"Because why? Because you're a thick young Irishman?"

"Maybe."

"I think we might make a match—eventually."

"You can do better than me."

"Of course I can, Eoin dear. But I think you might be worth the try."

"I'm liable to be dead by this time next year."

Róisín smiled and then said gently, "Mr. Fatalistic, that's you."

"You can joke all you want, but it's the truth."

"I'll take my chances."

"Do you really think we could make a go of it?"

"All depends," said Róisín, "on what your definition of 'go' is!"

Eoin chuckled. "*You* have a dirty mind!"

"Just as dirty as yours."

"Can I stay the night?"

"Yes," Róisín teased, "but no tomfoolery."

"We've never had any tomfoolery," Eoin said, exasperated. "In fact, I wouldn't know tomfoolery if I tripped on it."

Róisín laughed. "Believe me, you'll know tomfoolery when I perform it!"

Eoin, for the moment, was glad he was alive.

100

"We're almost done with the National Loan," Collins said to Eoin. They were going over the books in the Mary Street office. "I'll have to write up a report for the *Dáil* shortly, but at least we can put this behind us and concentrate all our energy on intelligence."

"What should we say is the official final tally?"

"Let's mark it as £355,500."

"Impressive!" Eoin said, before adding slyly, "That should cover Dev's American expenses."

Collins grunted. "I think of the Chief every goddamn day I do this bloody gruesome work." He stood up and stretched. "The National Loan will certainly break my heart if anything ever will. I never imagined there would be so much cowardice, dishonesty, hedging, insincerity, and meanness in the world, as my experience of this work revealed."

"But you got the job done," Eoin said. "That's all that matters."

"Come on, Eoin," Collins replied. "Let's go for a walk. I got some interesting news from England this morning. I want to show you something."

They bounded out into Mary Street and walked in the direction of Nelson's Pillar. They passed the burnt-out GPO and made the turn into Sackville Street. At Abbey Street, they passed the brand-new Eason's Bookstore, which concealed the location of the Dump on the top floor, right on the corner. Standing in front of the building was a DMP on the beat. Eoin eyed him warily. As they went by the copper, he snapped off a sharp salute, which elicited a laugh out of Collins. "A queer thingeen!" he said to Eoin. They walked down the south side of the street, past the Abbey Theatre and into Beresford Place, where they stood in front of the bombed-out Liberty Hall. Collins surveyed the building, which looked like it just might fall down upon itself. "What a fookin' mess," he finally pronounced, then added, "God bless Jim Connolly."

Eoin was getting impatient. He hated standing around in the open, especially with the notorious Michael Collins. "You wanted to show me something?" he prompted.

"Yes. We're waiting for Fergus." Eoin nodded, for he knew that "Fergus" was Dick McKee's nickname. Passersby came and went, paying no attention to the Big Fella and his little friend. Finally, McKee showed up. "You're late," Collins chastised him.

McKee gave him a look of desperation before saying, "I see you brought the Lieutenant along."

"Yeah," said Collins. "We're handing out officer commissions like communions on Easter Sunday morning."

Eoin was quiet for a moment, and then it hit him. "Lieutenant! What are you talking about?"

"Congratulations," said McKee with a laugh. "The Commandant-General thought you deserved a pay raise."

"But why?" asked Eoin. "I've never even drilled with the Second Battalion. I can't believe it."

"Believe it," said Collins. "You've done everything I've ever asked of you—and more." Collins, as he liked to do, immediately shifted gears. "Let's go," he said, and the three of them crossed to the Customs House and walked along the quay. "What are those reports from Limerick and Cork saying, Eoin?"

"Irregulars have arrived and are brutalizing the citizenship."

"How are they dressed?"

"Their uniforms are throw-togethers. They don't match. Tunic and britches are different colors. They're topped off with a Tam o'Shanter."

"And what are the citizens calling them?" demanded Collins.

"The 'Black and Tans,'" said Eoin and McKee in unison.

"Let's go meet them!"

The three of them walked down the quay to the North Wall. There they saw the first Tans, destined for Dublin, disembarking from the channel boat. They were all business as they hopped into lorries. "Where are they going?" asked McKee.

"The garrison in the Phoenix Park," replied Eoin. "That's the rumor, anyway."

"I want you to meet the enemy, Dick," said Collins to McKee. "You are to do everything in your power to murder these bastards—before they murder us!"

"A rough-looking crowd," Eoin commented.

"Fook 'em," Collins scoffed. "This is a present from the Prime Minister. Lloyd George has no idea what he has done. He's put the match to the Irish dynamite. If you think the country's united now, give these bastards six months, and the country will rise up and act as one!"

"This," said McKee, pensively, "isn't going to be easy."

"No, it's not," replied Collins, "but your boys can handle them."

"They can, indeed," McKee agreed, coldly.

"Dick," Eoin said suddenly, "how's my brother Frank?"

The question caught McKee by surprise. "He's fine. I have him working in . . ."

Eoin held up his hand. "I don't want to know. God knows what Blood told the Sheik about Frank. The less I know, the better. Just as long as he's alright."

"He is," replied McKee.

"Well, Dick, don't let me hold you up," said Collins, brusquely letting McKee know that he was finished with him. Dismissed, McKee spun and headed west along the quays towards O'Connell Bridge.

"I better be getting back to Crow Street," said Eoin.

"Not yet," Collins objected, and the two of them headed for Butt Bridge. They crossed over to Tara Street, along Brunswick Street, and around Westland Row until they found themselves in Baggot Street. They crossed the Grand Canal and entered Mespil Road, stopping in front of number five. "Batt O'Connor just acquired this place for me. No one—do you hear me?—*no one* is to know about this place, not even Tobin."

"But he's my boss," protested Eoin.

"And I'm his boss," shot back Collins. "I want you to know because you'll have to meet me here once in a while with the daily intelligence brief. But this place must be kept a secret. I can't get any work done with everyone wanting a piece of me. The finance department, Crow Street, IRB, IRA—they're driving me daft. I need quiet so I can concentrate. That's where this place comes in. Understood?" Eoin understood perfectly. "Fine," said Collins. "Now you can go back to Crow Street."

And newly minted Lieutenant Eoin Kavanagh did exactly that, via Leeson Street and St. Stephen's Green.

101

EOIN'S DIARY
AUGUST 15, 1920

J *ust got back to Dublin after a heart-wrenching twenty-four hours in Gorey, County Wexford. Captain Percival Lea Wilson is no more.*

I took the late train down there last night and was met by Mickey Coffey, who was my classmate at the Christian Brothers School in Synge Street when I was a lad. Mickey was the class poet, and all the neighborhood lassies were mad for him. We went to Coffey's house and met up with dapper, mustachioed Seán Mellor, the local IRA commandant, and Big Neil O'Granger, some local IRA muscle who has a simple, homely mug that only a mother could love. The sight of the three did not fill me with confidence. I explained to them that Collins wanted them to do the job, since this was their territory. I didn't tell them that Collins thought they were a bunch of slacking shites because things were too, too quiet in Wexford. The Commandant-General wants action.

Wilson is now a district inspector for the RIC. He's come a long way from that night in the Rotunda grounds when he made sport of humiliating Seán MacDiarmada and old Tom Clarke. The boys have been tracking him for months and have his routine down pat. I explained the set-up to them—that we'd work in two teams, two men apiece. Mellor and O'Granger will be the shooters, and Coffey and I will be the backup team, making sure no eager, pain-in-the-arse, innocent civilians come to Wilson's rescue and interfere with the business of the shooters.

Today dawned beautifully. We have an old Ford motorcar as a ruse and getaway vehicle. A local IRA lad, Rory, will be the driver. Wilson, who dresses in civilian clothes, walks from his RIC barracks every morning. We parked the car halfway on his route, near the railway station, and opened the bonnet to make it appear that we were having engine trouble. Rory poked around inside the engine as the rest of us kept an eye out for Wilson.

Just before half-nine, the lads pointed him out about two blocks away. He was walking with an RIC man. "What if the constable gets in the way?" asked Coffey.

I thought of how Collins would react, and I had no intention of being battered by Mick for being timid. "We'll shoot both bastards," I replied, and Coffey looked terrified.

"Jesus, Mary, and Joseph," he whispered under his breath.

Luckily for the RIC man, he left Wilson before they reached us. Wilson, however, continued right towards us, reading a newspaper as he walked, oblivious to everything around him. He was getting closer.

"Is that him?" Mellor asked, wanting me to make the definitive identification. There was no doubt. The four years since the Rotunda had not improved Wilson's looks.

"That's the bastard," I confirmed. "He's all yours."

Mellor and O'Granger immediately started walking towards Wilson. I pulled my Webley out of my pocket and got ready. Coffey looked on with his mouth open. "Get your gun out," I told him, but he was stiff with fear. "Come on," I said, more urgently. Coffey pulled his old Luger out and held it out in front of him. "By your side, you bloody eejit," I hissed, and he lowered it by his pants' leg. "Let's go," I said, and we started tracking the gunmen about ten yards behind the shooting team. My knees were stiff with apprehension. It didn't help that Coffey had started reciting The Act of Contrition: "Oh my God, I am heartily sorry for having offended Thee . . ." *Coffey will need a Perfect Act of Contrition if he keeps this up*, I thought. I knew there would be no contrition from Collins if we missed this bastard. There wasn't another person in sight, thank God.

"Captain Wilson," Mellor called out, and Wilson looked up from his newspaper. O'Granger brought his gun shoulder-high and fired, hitting Wilson in the upper torso. Mellor shot and missed. He fired again and hit Wilson in the leg this time, blood spouting all over the street and splattering Mellor and O'Granger as they lowered their guns and observed their prey.

Suddenly Wilson was up and limp-running down the street. "For fook's sake," I complained to Coffey. It looked like the son-of-a-bitch Wilson was heading right back to the RIC barracks. "Fook this," I spit out, and ran at full speed towards Wilson, easily overtaking him. "Fook you, Wilson" I yelled. He turned to look at me, fright in his eyes. I shot once and hit him in the jaw, dropping him to the road. He was bleeding profusely, but he was still alive and alert. "You should have let me have that malted milk tablet," I said. His eyes were wide, and I think that, with the mention of the malted milk tablet, he recognized me as the kid in the Rotunda Garden. "That was for Tom Clarke," I said. "This is for Seán MacDiarmada." I pulled the trigger and hit him in the forehead. Then I bent down and shot him solidly in the back of his head. The job was done.

The motorcar drove up, and the four of us piled in, buzzing by the barracks before anyone knew what had happened. "Good job," I lied to the lads. We headed north, and I caught a province bus for Dublin.

The bus pulled up to its terminus in Aston Quay, and I looked out the window to see what was going on. We were only a few blocks from the DMP barracks in Brunswick Street, and I could see that several of the G-men were watching the people getting off the buses from the country. I had my Webley in my attaché case, and I was tempted to get it out and put it in my jacket pocket. But I pulled my trilby hat over my eyes, adjusted my necktie, straightened my waistcoat smartly, and got off the bus like I did it every day. I walked right past the G-men and headed up Bedford Row and into Anglesea Street. Collins was right—you could get away with murder if you wore the right suit. I made my way to Grafton Street, turned right at the corner of Wicklow Street, and walked into the lobby of the Wicklow Hotel, now safe with the demise of Willie Dolan. I asked the new porter— a trusted IRB man this time—if the boss was around. He shot his eyes towards the back room. I didn't even knock, I was so revved-up. Collins was inside with Joe Leonard.

"How was Gorey?" asked Collins, anxiously.

"Gory," I replied. "But it's done."

Mick slapped his hand on the table and crowed, "We got the bastard, Joe!"

"*I* got the bastard," I corrected, annoyed. "He almost got away."

"You're sure he's dead?" asked Collins.

"Three in the head from me alone."

"Don't waste bullets!" snapped Collins.

I couldn't believe he said that. I felt like a pricked balloon. "Fook you, Mick!" came out of my mouth. He had cut me to the quick.

Mick got up from the table and came over to me. He embraced me, and my head fell onto his chest. "You did well, lad. Well." It was his way of making up to me. "How were the Wexford lads?" he finally asked.

I didn't want to get them in trouble, but I had to be honest with Mick. "Next time, send the full Squad." Collins nodded that he understood. He looked down at the cuffs of my trousers, which were covered in Wilson's blood.

"You've blood on your trousers," he noted. I could hardly see it against the dark blue material. It was pure luck that I had escaped from the G-men over on the quay. "Go over to Fallon's and get yourself a new suit. On me."

And that's what Captain Percival Lea Wilson's death was worth to the Republic. A new suit from Thomas Fallon & Company, Republican haberdashers, over in Mary Street.

102

"**E**ggs!" shouted the Sheik.
　　"Eggs?" replied a confused Brendan Boynton.
　　"Eggs! He can't pronounce eggs!"
"Who can't pronounce eggs?" put in Ned Broy.
"Collins!"
"Who told you that?" asked Boynton.
"Willie Dolan."
"You mean the *late* Willie Dolan, don't you?" highlighted Broy.
"I wonder why Collins can't pronounce 'eggs'" Boynton remarked. "Maybe . . ."
"Maybe he's an eejit," cut in Broy, just in time. Boynton was about to let slip that maybe the gap between Collins's two front teeth was the reason the Big Fellow had trouble pronouncing "eggs." With that precious piece of information, Broy was sure that the British army would be going around saying, "Smile!" to every male in Dublin.
"What are you two doing here?" demanded Gough-Coxe.
"We have a gift for you."
"What?"
"How about a photograph of Michael Collins?"
Broy threw the photograph on the desk in front of Gough-Coxe. The Sheik scanned it. "Eamon de Valera, Arthur Griffith, Count Horace Plunkett," he said, rattling off names, strutting his expertise. "Which one is Collins?"

Broy put his right index finger under the chin of the Minister for Finance. "That's the hoor," he said. "Right next to Cathal Brugha."

"Sonofabitch!" Gough-Coxe exclaimed, and Boynton looked on in silent amusement.

"God, this is a tremendous coup," Gough-Coxe marveled. Then he laughed. "He even looks like a thug!"

Little did he know that he had just been hoodwinked by what Liam Tobin called "a bit of Crow Street prestidigitation." The Sheik had been after Broy and Boynton to come up with a photograph of Collins for weeks. Tobin and Eoin decided that it was safe to let them see a photo of members of the first *Dáil*. They already knew what de Valera, Plunkett, Griffith, Brugha, and the rest of the big shots looked like. What made this photo so appealing was that Collins was at his chameleon best—mouth shut, lips scowling, head cocked to the left. The photo revealed nothing—except what a superb actor Collins could be when he wanted to be. Tobin, Eoin, and Collins all agreed the photograph would make for a grand detour for the British.

"Let's get copies made, pronto," said Gough-Coxe, all of a sudden filled with good humor. "Great job, men," he added. "Now it's only a matter of time until this Fenian shit is dead. His time is limited."

Standing in front of the Sheik, both Broy and Boynton thought exactly the same thing: *But not as limited as yours.*

103

EOIN'S DIARY
WEDNESDAY, AUGUST 25, 1920

Something is going on. Mick has restricted me from the Squad *indefinitely and assigned me exclusively to Crow Street.*

It's been a tough month for us. On the twelfth, Lord Mayor Terence MacSwiney was arrested. He's presently in Brixton Prison in England and has started on a hunger strike. It's obvious that Mick's very concerned about his fellow Corkman. And just last week, the British introduced the Restoration of Order in Ireland Act. Already the good citizens of Dublin's fair city are referring to it as the "Coercion Act." Now the newly arrived Tans and Auxiliaries are beginning to flex their muscle around Dublin. The Tans have taken to shooting up the Dardanelles daily. They are sending a message, and Mick has heard it loud and clear.

McKee is trying to find a strategy to deal with the Tans, but Mick doesn't seem to care that much. He is most concerned about the agents that the Sheik has started importing from the Middle East. We have started to refer to them as "The Cairo Gang," and by happenstance, they like to hang out at the Cairo Café at the top of Grafton Street. It might be a coincidence, but Mick doesn't believe in coincidences, and he thinks they are doing this to flaunt and jeer at us.

Tobin has me checking the manifest of every boat that has arrived in Dublin during the month of August. Charlie Dalton and I have been checking the registration cards of Dublin hotels that have guests over from England and who are planning on an extended stay. Tobin has even started to tag the Sheik, when he is not at the Castle under the watchful eyes of our own G-men.

As I was giving Mick his intelligence briefing tonight in Mespil Road, he said to me, "They are getting close, Eoin." He paused for a minute, and I could feel the terror in the pit of my stomach. "But we are getting close, too."

I think this is the battle Mick has been planning for the last four years. It's going to come down to him and the Sheik. Funnily enough, it kind of reminds me of those American Cowboy & Injun movies that are so popular over here. I went to see one with Róisín last week at that cinema in Camden Street, just around the corner from the house I was born in. Somehow I always find myself rooting for the Injuns, because they are the underdogs. It was their land, and the Yanks went in and stole it from them—just like the British did to us.

Well, the British cavalry has arrived in Dublin in the guise of the Tans, the Auxies, and the Cairo Gang, and I'm waiting to see just how crazy our own Crazy Horse, Michael Collins, TD, will be when the conclave finally convenes.

104

"Spokes!"

Derek of Suez had become obsessed with the reinvention of the wheel. "Work backwards" was obviously last month's mantra. He had convinced himself that the secret to the capture of Collins laid in the structure of the bicycle wheel. Collins was at the hub, and all spokes led to the elusive Minister for Finance.

Boynton's spokes—along with Eoin Kavanagh—included Dan Breen. Broy's was Seán Treacy. Each G-man had been assigned several rebels, and their jobs were to bring rebel heads on a platter to Derek Gough-Coxe at Dublin Castle.

"I will not be defeated by Collins," the Sheik told his detective minions softly. "I have had it up to here," he continued, "and I will not be made a fool of by Collins, McKee, Mulcahy, Breen, Treacy, and the rest of the murdering lot." He paused, before adding, "We are getting close again. Our reinforcements have arrived, and more help arrives from the Middle East by the day."

Collins was most interested in this Middle Eastern help, and he had both Boynton and Broy monitoring how Gough-Coxe was orchestrating his special agents. All information was passed onto Liam Tobin, who had it counter-checked against the data that Eoin and Charlie Dalton had collected at hotels and rooming houses around the city. Boynton and Broy could see the stress on Gough-Coxe—his face had broken out in a rash. Bell's assassination still tormented the Sheik, because it had basically put an end to his search for the National Loan. Collins had been right—bank examiners in both Britain and Belfast had not been lining up to come to Dublin to look at the books. Alan Bell's corpse revealed their unhealthy future. The Loan was history to Gough-Coxe, but getting Collins would make everything right.

Now the Sheik was concentrating on certain fugitives from the country who were close to Collins. And none were closer than Breen and Treacy. Their reputations on the streets of Dublin had strangely protected them, for the Tans and the G-men knew that the Tipperary duo, the heroes of Soloheadbeg, were armed and had no intention of being taken alive. They would fight to the end, and certain G-men were rethinking just how important their pensions were to them. Boynton had Breen's pug of a face taped to the wall in front of him. Through Eoin, Boynton had been able to warn Breen away from certain "safe" houses that were about to be raided. Broy had warned Treacy, through Eoin, to get rid of his high riding boots, but Seán had resisted, because he was so fond of them. It was things like boots and the way Collins pronounced "eggs" that the British were counting on and that, by the day, brought them closer and closer to the fugitive rebels.

"Your spokes will lead you to Collins," the Sheik had reassured. What he didn't realize is that spokes could work both ways. For Collins was now concentrated on the Sheik's spokes, which were leading him to the most dangerous men in Ireland: the elite of the British Secret Service, Derek Gough-Coxe's Cairo Gang.

105

MONDAY, SEPTEMBER 20, 1920

I t was to be a busy day for the University College Dublin student. He was up early cramming for his pre-med exam at UCD that afternoon. After mass, he met up with a few of the lads in Bolton Street and was briefed on their raid, which was to take place outside Monks' Bakery on North King Street. They had done this many times before, and there shouldn't be any trouble pulling this one off. They knew a lorry full of British troops stopped by the bakery every day to bring bread back to their base in Collinstown. Today, members of Auxiliary C Company of the First Battalion of the Dublin Brigade would relieve them of their weapons. What could go wrong?

Everyone was in position when the troop truck arrived. Instead of a swift lift-and-retreat, a firefight broke out. The UCD student was firing away with his .38 when the gun jammed. He managed to unjam it and continued firing, only for the Parabellum to jam again. The fire was heavy, and the young man hit the deck and crawled underneath a nearby lorry for cover. He was so preoccupied with his faulty gun that he did not see the rest of IRA lads retreat. The next thing he heard was someone shouting, "There's a man under the lorry!"

The game was up. The British had their man—an eighteen-year-old Volunteer named Kevin Barry.

365

106

After Collins, Dan Breen was the most wanted man in Ireland. Unfortunately for Breen, he had none of the chameleon-like qualities of the Big Fellow. While Collins could physically be all things to all people, Breen was terrifyingly distinctive: five-foot-seven inches tall, over twelve stone, and with a block of a head that could not be mistaken for anyone else in any part of the world. His "wanted" poster was in every government office in Dublin, touting his "sulky bulldog appearance." It had gotten too hot for Breen in Tipperary, and he hoped the relative bigness of Dublin could save him. The G-men, the Tans, the Auxies, and the local Tipperary RIC patrolled Dublin in search of Breen and his buddy, Seán Treacy. For these two rebels, there would be no arrest and detention. Their warrants read DOA.

Breen was leading the typical life of an "on-the-run" rebel—a different, strange bed every night, which guaranteed only a half-sleep as the eyes closed and the ears stayed on alert, a loaded revolver sleeping on the chest. Breen's life on the run was more difficult than that of Collins or Eoin. At least they had friends and family in the city whom they could rely on. Collins also had many offices that could offer a couch when the pinch was on. For Breen, it was one strange bed after another, night.

Of all the rebels Eoin dealt with, the only one who frightened him was Breen. He was a great rebel, but Eoin hated being seen in public with the second-most-wanted man in Ireland. Collins would often have Eoin meet Breen, to give him either orders or money. They would usually meet up in pubs around the city; the Stag's Head one time, and Kirwan's, Collins's "Joint Number Two," on Parnell Street at other times. Another favorite of Breen's was Shanahan's on Foley Street in Monto, Dublin's red-light district, Nighttown.

On Eoin's nineteenth birthday—October 10, 1920—he was sitting in Shanahan's with Breen when a couple of DMPs stepped into the pub for a midday drink. Eoin reached into his coat pocket to get ahold of his Webley, but Breen slowly put his hand on Eoin's arm to calm him. Both rebels looked straight ahead, their eyes steady on their drinks.

The coppers placed their spiked helmets on the bar and ordered a couple of pints of Guinness. One then turned to the two rebels. "Is that me bould Dan Breen?" Breen, who had his hand in his own gun pocket, smiled tightly. "Well, what sort of a gun are you using at present?" the cop insisted.

"I like the Colt best of all," said Breen, as he pulled the gun out of his pocket for show.

The DMP nodded. "You're in luck, then; these will suit," he replied, pulling bullets out of his tunic and dropping them on the bar.

"Thanks," Breen said, as he scooped them up and put them in his trouser pocket.

"I have to be going," Eoin said, standing up, but keeping his eyes glued on the two policemen. He headed for the door.

"Young man," the DMP called out, and Eoin froze in his tracks and slowly turned around. "Say hello to the Big Fellow for me."

Eoin stared at the copper and realized it was the same one who had saluted Collins in front of the Dump on Abbey Street. Eoin nodded and then slipped out the door. He had a rendezvous with Róisín to celebrate his birthday and was looking forward to an evening away from revolution in her quiet flat on Walworth Road. It would be the last quiet night the two of them would enjoy for the next two months.

107

EOIN'S DIARY
TUESDAY, OCTOBER 12, 1920.

It's been a murderous two days.

After meeting Breen on Sunday, I spent the day with Róisín as we quietly celebrated my birthday. We had a few drinks at the Stag's Head, picked up some grub at the local chippers, and spent the rest of the night at Róisín's place. I was expecting big things after we got through with the cod. I thought that maybe Róisín might give me a special present on my nineteenth birthday, but it was all a cod—the cold kind. There was no tomfoolery of any kind. Róisín said it was her time of the month, and that I was lucky that she shared her fish and chips with me. I am mystified by Róisín's behavior. One day she's hot, the next day she's not. As for me, I am always hot. I just don't understand women. Happy Birthday to me!

I left her in the morning, picked up the papers, and headed over to Crow Street. I got there just after half-six, and Liam Tobin was already on station. I knew something was wrong.

"Breen's been shot," was the first thing he said to me.

I put the papers down on my desk and took a quick look. There was no STOP PRESS. "Nothing here," says I.

"It was late, after curfew."

"How's Dan?" Tobin was quiet, which disturbed me. I was forced to pop the awful question. "Is he dead?"

"Not yet," replied Liam. "He's badly shot up. He was with Treacy, but there's no sign of Seán. Maybe the British have him. Breen's in a safe house on the North Side. If we don't get him into a hospital soon, he's going to die."

"The Mater Misericordiae."

"You'd better have a word with your girl."

Róisín's shift started at eight o'clock, so, at half-seven, I waited for her to come out of South Great Georges Street on her bicycle. She was right on time and was shocked to see me standing on the corner of Temple Lane, waiting for her. I pulled her into the alley, and we huddled in front of my Aunt Nellie's house. I cut to the chase. "Breen's been shot up. He's badly wounded. We're going to get him into the Mater somehow. Be on your toes." Róisín didn't say a word—she just gave me a very serious, wet kiss.

Just then the door to my aunt's house opened, and me first cousin Richard Gallagher stepped into the lane. He took one look at Róisín and me, and his eyes grew large. I didn't say a word to Róisín—I just gave her the high sign, and she hopped back on her bike and continued up Dame Street without saying a word.

"How are you, Richard?" Richard was one of those names that kept reoccurring in the family. The original Richard Conway was our grandfather, who died before I was born. He was a talented cabinetmaker, my Mammy told me. And Mammy said that her daddy taught her how to be a French polisher, finishing off his workmanship. It seems furniture was the Conway family business. My Mammy loved her daddy and called our youngest brother Dickie, after her dead father. And Aunt Nellie added to the Richards with her own son. But Richard Gallagher was always "Richard," never "Dick" or "Dickie." He was a couple of years younger than me, but he was already much taller and gangly. A really handsome boy, the lassies would say.

"How are you?" Richard asked me. He really wanted to know how I was doing in the IRA.

"The usual," I replied, noncommittally.

"I really want to join, you know?" I stood mute. "I want to die for Ireland."

I looked at him like he was daft. "I don't," I replied.

"But me daddy won't let me."

"Die for Ireland?" He nodded. "Your daddy is right."

Richard stood there awkwardly, and I wondered what was going through his head. He had the body of a man and the mind of a child. He was having a childhood crush on ould *Cathleen Ní Houlihan*. Hide the Yeats and save the child. I knew the feeling, and I felt sorry for him. He has no idea what's going on in the streets of Dublin. Our odd conversation was interrupted by the honking of an automobile horn. I looked around, and it was McKee, motioning to me to get into the car. "Richard," I said, "I gotta go."

There were several Volunteers in the car, including Charlie Dalton. "We've got to move Dan and get him to hospital," McKee said, and I immediately knew it would be a tricky job. As I got into the car, I watched Richard solitarily walking down Temple Lane, in the direction of the Liffey. Maybe, I thought, he'll find another way to serve Ireland.

We arrived at the house in Drumcondra, and Dan was a bloody mess. He was shot up from head to toe. The lady of the house, a Mrs. Holmes, had saved Dan's life by taking him in. When Dan knocked at the door, Mr. Holmes wanted to send him away. Mrs. Holmes told her husband, "If you do, I'll report you to Michael Collins." That did the trick, and they brought Dan in and called a neighbor who was a nurse. Dan was wounded seven times, the most serious being in his lung and spine. He even broke his big toe trying to escape, and that was the one wound that was giving him the most pain. Dan is a tough old bastard.

McKee had brought clothes with him, because Dan's had been shredded in his escape. We dressed him with great care and got him into the car for the short ride to the Mater. When we arrived at the hospital, the place was swarming with British soldiers. They were probably looking for Dan.

"We can't chance bringing him in there," said McKee, turning to me. "Eoin, I'm going to take Dan to a safe house off Mountjoy Square—you know the place. You go in and talk to your girl. Get her to call you when the coast is clear, and then come up and get us."

I found Róisín and pulled her aside. I told her we had to get Breen into the hospital as soon as possible, and that she was to call me in Crow Street as soon as the British cleared out. As I talked to her in the lobby, I saw a bunch of trenchcoated G-men milling about. One of them was Boynton, and he caught my eye. He came over to me and made like he was interrogating me. "They're looking for Breen," he said.

"Big surprise," says I.

"I was just down in the morgue with a Sergeant Comerford, RIC tout from Tipperary. He says the man on the slab isn't Breen. Comerford said he'd 'know Breen's ugly mug anywhere.'"

"He's not here yet," I told him. "We're waiting for you guys to clear out."

"It will be a while."

We were interrupted by another copper. "Can I be of any help here, Constable?"

"No, Sergeant Comerford. I can handle this ruffian," said Boynton, as he pushed me in the chest for emphasis.

Comerford left, and Róisín joined us. "You know what to do," I said to her. "Call me."

Two hours later, the phone rang in Crow Street. I hopped on a bike and made my way to Mountjoy Square, cycling up Gardner Street. When I got there I received a great surprise—Seán Treacy! He had escaped untouched and had been saved by another citizen, who took him in for the night. His riding boots were as shiny as ever. We lifted Dan into the car and headed back to the Mater. We went to the loading platform in Eccles Street, where they brought in medical supplies. We carefully unpacked Dan, placed him in a wheelchair, and rolled him inside, where Róisín and the doctors were waiting for him. Dan was white as a ghost from all his blood loss, but he was grateful that he was finally in medical hands.

"Be careful," I told Róisín. She nodded and then came to me and kissed me gently on the forehead, leaving me starry-eyed.

McKee pulled at the sleeve of my jacket. "Don't let it go to your head, Lieutenant," said the commandant, with a laugh.

"You're a lieutenant?" asked Róisín, embarrassing me. "You never told me!"

"You mean our Eoin kept his mouth shut?" said McKee. Róisín nodded. "I'm not surprised."

I just wanted to get out of there. We finally left, sure that Dan Breen was in loving hands.

108

E oin was going over some intelligence papers, and Róisín was placing the hem on a dress, when there was a bang on her Walworth Road door.

"Shite," Eoin swore, scooping the papers up. He wanted to throw them in the fireplace, but the fire had grown cold. Eoin finally pulled up the cushion of the couch and planted the papers underneath. The banging became louder. Eoin went to his coat and pulled out his Webley.

"For fook's sake," someone called from outside. "Open the door!" Another bang, before the voice added, "It's Mick." Eoin opened the door, and there stood the Minister for Finance. Eoin waved him in with his gun. "What are you doing with that thing?" Collins said.

"I was going to shoot you. You scared the shite out of us."

"Ah," said Collins, "the lovebirds." His laugh made both Róisín and Eoin blush. "Can a man get a cup of tay around here?" The three of them headed to the kitchen, and Róisín began to wet the tea. "I'm actually here to see you, Róisín," said Collins. Eoin looked at his boss and felt a ping of jealousy in his craw. "But I'm glad Eoin's here, too," added Collins, sensing the boy's discomfort.

Collins envied Eoin and Róisín their young, contrary love. In the dark Dublin of 1920, at least they had each other. His Kitty was in Granard, County Longford. Not that far away, but it might as well have been Timbuktu, because Collins could not leave Dublin. He didn't want her in Dublin because it was so dangerous, but he still longed for her. He wondered how Harry Boland could give up the lovely Kitty for

Eamon de Valera and America. The thought of that exchange always made Collins smile. But he knew Harry and his sense of duty, and admired him for it. Even if it had made pursuing Kitty a lot easier. There was a lot to that old saying, "Out of sight, out of mind." It was true. He looked at Eoin and Róisín and promised himself that the first break he got, he would be on the train to Granard and Kitty.

"How's Dan Breen coming along?" he asked Róisín.

"He's struggling, but he's tough as nails."

Collins laughed. "Well, at least you didn't say he was 'holding his own.'"

"The only people I see 'holding their own' at the Mater Misericordiae Hospital are those old priests who are always playing with their old dead willies, trying to get a rise out of the poor nuns!"

Collins and Eoin looked at each other, trying not to smile as the anti-clerical Róisín started to redden in anger. "Yes, Nurse O'Mahony," was all that Collins could muster. He put his hand in his pocket and pulled out a small package. "Give this to Breen when you see him tomorrow." Róisín took the package, and Collins said, "Just some medicine for the bold Daniel." Róisín looked inside and found Breen's favorite tobacco, Mick McQuaid, along with a baby bottle of Jameson's Irish whiskey. "That should hold him until I can sneak in there."

"That's not a very good idea right now," said Eoin, as the three of them sat down at the kitchen table and Róisín poured the tea. She cut several thick pieces of her own soda bread and threw a tub of butter on the table.

"I know," said Collins quietly. "It's a hard time to be alive in Dublin City the past two days." Collins seemed down in the dumps over Breen, and Eoin suddenly realized that the great Michael Collins was, like anyone else, capable of loneliness and doubt. "Well, Róisín," said Collins, brightening, "where are you hiding Dan?"

"We move him around when the British come a-calling," she said. "He's a regular in the maternity ward."

"And the ugliest one of the bunch!" said Collins, with a laugh.

"Any news on Kevin Barry?" asked Eoin. Eoin knew Barry casually and, like the rest of Dublin, was very concerned about his fate.

"I think the British are planning to make an example out of him," said Collins.

"In what way?" asked Róisín.

"At the end of a rope," replied Collins, matter-of-factly, the coldness of his statement chilling the kitchen.

"And only eighteen years old," added Eoin.

"Listen to the old man!" said Collins, as he realized Eoin was only a year older than Barry. *My God*, thought Collins to himself, *I'm running an army full of children.*

"What's the word on Lord Mayor MacSwiney?" asked Róisín.

"Not good," replied Collins. "He can't go on much longer. Maybe a couple more weeks."

"Did you see what Churchill said at that dinner the other night?" said Eoin.

"No."

Eoin got up and retrieved a paper from the sitting room. "He said: 'It was during the silly season the Lord Mayor of Cork announced his determination to starve himself to death. After six weeks' fasting, the Lord Mayor of Cork is still alive.'"

"That sonofabitch." Then Collins grew quiet. "We'll have to start planning the funeral." Both Eoin and Róisín looked horrified, as if Collins was purposely tempting the devil with his statement. Collins looked at them and said, "What?"

"The man's not dead yet," said Eoin.

"You should be ashamed of yourself," shot Róisín.

Collins grunted. "No opportunity will be missed to worship our Fenian dead! We did it for Rossa. We did it for Ashe. They will do it for me."

Silence fell on the three of them, and the only sound was teaspoons swirling tea. "Don't talk like that, Mick," said Róisín finally.

"It will come to that," said Collins. "I know it in my bones. That's why I'm in such a hurry. I don't have much time left, and neither does Ireland." Eoin reached out his hand for Collins's, but then pulled back. Collins noticed and smiled. He took a slice of the soda bread, lathered it with the daisy-yellow butter, and chopped off a chunk, showing the split between his two front teeth. "Hmmm. Delicious, Róisín. You can cook, too!" Róisín didn't know if Collins was jeering her or not, so she remained quiet. "God, I wish I had a battalion of Dan Breens and Seán Treacys. I'd win this war in a week. What's the intelligence saying?"

Eoin got up and went to the couch to gather his papers. "It's coming together now," he began. "From what I can piece together from the morgue and Boynton at the Castle, Breen and Treacy took out thirteen."

"Thirteen!" said Collins, delighted. "That's more than the papers said."

"Don't always believe what you read in the *Irish Times*," Eoin chided him. He would remain suspicious of the media until the day he died. "I don't think their propaganda machine wants anyone to know what Breen and Treacy did—and then got away scot-free to boot."

"Jaysus," said Collins, "it was a slaughter! Who were the dead? Mostly Tans?"

"Tans, regular British army. Also, some of the Sheik's friends from Cairo," said Eoin.

"Tell me more."

"One fellow was Major G.O.S. Smyth."

"Any relation to that Smyth we shot up last September?"

"No. It's worse than that."

"In what way?"

"This fellow," said Eoin, "is the brother of Colonel Smyth."

"The hoor from Listowel?" Eoin nodded. "That's some fookin' family tree."

Lieutenant Colonel Bruce Smyth was the notorious RIC Divisional Commissioner for Munster, who knew exactly how the rebels should be handled. His advice to the RIC was infamous: "If persons approaching carry their hands in their pockets, or seem to be suspect characters, shoot them down. You may make mistakes occasionally, and innocent persons may be shot, but that cannot be helped. The more you shoot, the better I shall like you, and I assure you that no policeman will get into trouble for shooting a man."

Smyth's words turned into his own death warrant. He had the tables turned on him when a Cork IRA volunteer caught up to him in the street: "Your orders were to shoot on sight. You are in sight now. So make ready."

"And gunned down in my own County Cork," Collins bragged.

"This is serious stuff," Eoin insisted.

"It's all serious stuff," replied Collins.

"No," said Eoin, "this is *very* serious stuff. I'm working with Boynton and Broy on what all this Cairo stuff means."

"Tobin says you are tagging quite a few," said Collins.

"They are living among the people," said Eoin. "They stay in by day and go out by night."

"These men are more dangerous than the Tans and Auxies combined," Collins agreed.

"Our Major Smyth is a friend of the Sheik, Boynton and Broy report. He came to Ireland to avenge his brother's death. Smyth and the Sheik kicked the ball around in Egypt. Now they are kicking the ball around in Dublin."

"I'm tired of my balls being kicked," Collins said, not trying to be funny. "I think it's time we kicked back. These bastards come into our country, persecute the impoverished gentry, we kill them—and they take affront! Well, fook them. Those days are over. We won't kick back until we have all the facts, all the names, all the addresses. Everything." Collins stood up, drained the tea from his cup, and said, "I'd better get going. I still have to find a bed for myself."

"Stay here," said Róisín.

"And disrupt the love nest!"

Róisín reddened, until she realized that Collins was teasing her goat. She smiled. "You're welcome any time."

"I appreciate that, Róisín. And I'll remember," said Collins. "But I think I'll stay with Dr. Gogarty tonight. He's got a better liquor cabinet than you do," he teased, with a chuckle. "It's only a short walk across the Green." As Collins went out the door, he said, "I can't believe how bad it's gotten."

Little did he know that it was about to get a lot worse—and as soon as the next day.

109

D erek Gough-Coxe slammed the phone onto the receiver and raced to his office door. "Broy, Boynton! A man wearing riding boots was just spotted entering the Republican Outfitters in Talbot Street. Move your arses!" Boynton and Broy sprang to their feet and, followed by a half-dozen other G-men, charged out the door. Seán Treacy's boots had caught the attention of a Dublin Castle tout.

The funeral for Major G.O.S. Smyth—compliments of Dan Breen— was scheduled for Thursday, October 14. There was a rumor that Johnny French, and maybe even General Macready, would be showing up for the grand sendoff. They were scheduled to have a procession down the quays as they prepared to return their martyred dead to England.

Dick McKee, Peadar Clancy (the vice commandant of the Dublin Brigade and McKee's adjunct), Seán Treacy, and members of the Squad met at the Republican Outfitters, located at 94 Talbot Street, just a short jog from Nelson's Pillar. It was Clancy's place of business. It was also a place that Eoin liked to avoid if he could. He thought it was insane to declare to one and all your sympathies above the door in three-foot letters. He thought the same thing about all those British Secret Service agents over from Egypt who were hanging out at the Cairo Café on Grafton Street. He wondered if either side was retaining any common sense anymore.

Collins and Tobin had kept Eoin glued to his seat in Crow Street, but, with Dublin heating up, Eoin often found himself hitting the streets again, Webley in hand. Tobin told Eoin to meet McKee at the Outfitters for the quay job and to deliver some intelligence papers to Treacy. They drank cups of tea in the rear of the shop as they waited for word about whether the big shots would be showing up for the funeral. Word finally came that the desirable targets would not be making themselves available for assassination, and the men dispersed. Eoin was walking towards the Pillar when the first shots rang out.

Instinctively, he pulled his gun and headed back towards the shop. He knew Treacy was still there when he left, and he was concerned for Seán. As Eoin headed back down Talbot Street in the direction of Amien Street Station, he saw that a lorry of Auxies had pulled up in front of Outfitters. Eoin went to the north side of the street so he could see what was going on. All of a sudden, out of nowhere, Treacy came running towards Eoin, his gun at his side. A burst of fire came from the Auxies' lorry, and Seán spun into a crouch to return fire. Eoin saw one Auxie fall as Treacy continued to fire his Luger.

Eoin ran back up the street and was within feet of Treacy when he heard the dull, rapid *pop-pop-pop* and saw bullets rip into Treacy's torso. Eoin knew immediately that he was mortally wounded. All Eoin could think about now were the intelligence papers he had just delivered to Treacy. Returning his own fire, Eoin advanced to the fallen Treacy and pulled the papers, now bloodied, from Treacy's inside jacket pocket. Eoin could hear bullets buzzing by his head as he advanced to the south side of the street and ran as fast as he could for Sackville Street and the safety of its crowds.

The G-men from Dublin Castle finally pulled up. Dead civilians were lying in the gutter, along with Auxies and the fallen Treacy. Broy, gun out, went to Treacy and turned him on his back. He was dead. Boynton arrived right behind him and asked, "Is it Treacy?" Broy nodded a "yes." Boynton looked down at his secret comrade, and all he could say was, "Those fucking boots."

When Eoin got to Nelson's Pillar, he was shocked to see Charlie Dalton commandeering a car right in front of the GPO. "Get in!" Dalton shouted, and Eoin did as he was told.

"What's going on?"

"The British have surrounded the Mater," replied Dalton. "I've been ordered to get up there quick. Breen's in danger."

Charlie was jamming the driver in the ribs with his revolver. "Faster!" he commanded.

"For God's sake," said the terrified driver, "take the car and drive it yourselves."

Eoin looked at Dalton, and, even in this terrible situation on this terrible day, he was forced to suppress a smile—neither of them knew how to drive a car. "Just keep driving," said Dalton. "Get us up to Eccles Street."

When they arrived down the street from the Mater. they jumped out. Dalton warned the driver to keep his gob shut, and the reluctant chauffeur drove off as fast as he could. Eoin and Charlie saw some other Volunteers and ran to them. They could see the British in front of the hospital, standing by their tenders. An armored car was circling the block every five minutes. The Volunteers decided they would be safer in a pub, and they were soon joined there by Dick McKee.

"Seán Treacy has been shot," he told one and all.

"He's dead," confirmed Eoin. "I took the intelligence papers off him."

"This is a fucking disaster," said McKee. They looked out the window of the public house in despair, as the British continued to clog up the other end of Eccles Street.

"Why don't we rush them?" asked Charlie Dalton.

"No!" snapped McKee.

"But—"

"No," McKee repeated, this time more quietly. "We've lost enough good men today." Eoin took a sip of his porter, and, at that very second, the British came out of the Mater, empty-handed. He looked at McKee and, for the first time that day, saw some hope in his comrade's eyes. "Eoin," he finally said, "go visit Róisín."

Eoin wiped the suds off his mouth and headed for the hospital. Inside he found Róisín, who had a look of exhausted terror on her face. "Dan's fine," she said. "He'll be ready to give birth any minute now."

"Thank God," Eoin breathed.

Róisín could sense something was wrong. She said the first thing that popped into her mind. "Treacy?"

"Shot dead in Talbot Street less than an hour ago."

"This can't go on, Eoin. It has to stop."

Eoin knew she was right. It was now October, and Collins had said throughout the year that they had only until the end of 1920 to win Ireland's freedom. They were down to ten weeks.

110

"They are determined to make an example out of Kevin Barry," Collins said.

"I would say they are doing a good job of it," replied Dick McKee.

In the office at 3 St. Andrew Street, Collins had assembled Dick McKee, Liam Tobin, Paddy Daly, and Mick McDonnell of the Squad, along with Eoin.

"Is there a chance of negotiations with the British for Kevin?" asked McKee. "Can't Griffith do anything with his English contacts?"

"They are not in a negotiating mood, apparently," replied Collins. "I asked Arthur, and the back door has been shut on us. They think they have the upper hand now."

"But Barry's only eighteen years old," McKee exclaimed indignantly.

"As was one of the British soldiers who was killed in that ambush," said Collins. "In fact, he was younger than Barry." McKee fell silent. "I know he's one of your lads, Dick, but we've got to be realistic here. The British are not going to let Barry live. That would send the wrong message." Silence permeated the room. "It's only a question of who will go first—MacSwiney or Barry."

"Well," said Paddy Daly, breaking another long silence, "what will be our response to this shite? We're getting nowhere. We kill them and kill them, and nothing ever changes. I don't see a way out of this cycle."

381

"That's why we're here tonight," said Collins. "Crow Street is beginning to get a grasp on the Sheik's friends from the Middle East, the expanding Cairo Gang."

"What do we know about them?"

"We know," said Collins, "where many of them live. We are tagging them right now. Within weeks, I hope we can strike."

"What would be the purpose of striking these bags of shite?" asked Daly. "All our strikes are getting us nowhere."

"These guys are special."

"In what way?" asked McDonnell.

"They are special because they are here to do a specific job. They were not sent here for the purpose of tracking Breen or Treacy—although they were in on those jobs—but to bring the leadership of the movement down. To kill me, McKee, Mulcahy, Brugha, Tobin here. The lot of us, TDs, ministers, army chiefs. To put it simply, they were sent to Ireland to cut off the head of the duly elected Irish government. I'm not going to let that happen."

"Where do we come in?" asked Daly.

"When Liam and Eoin finish compiling their information—hopefully within the next fortnight—we are going to take them out in one fookin' morning. This is going to be a *big* job, and I mean *big*. It's much too big for the Squad alone. I want Mick and Paddy to coordinate with McKee and Mulcahy and get more teams together so we can effectively take them all out at the same time. Timing will be of the essence. Start now," continued Collins. "Tell the Volunteers that these are going to be close-shot executions, and if they can't handle that, get someone else. I want cold-stone murderers for this job. There will be no fuck-ups on this job."

"How many?" asked McKee.

"Plan on fifteen to twenty execution teams. The Squad itself can handle only about four, so recruit your best men out of the Dublin Brigade, Dick. I want no culchies for this job." Collins—a proud culchie himself—was surrounded by Dubliners, and his comment caught the men by surprise. "I want Jackeens who know this city inside out. After this job, the city will shut down. I need men who know the streets and can get back to their homes without detection." Collins paused. "I expect the retributions to be horrific."

"What's the exact message here?" asked McDonnell.

"I am telegraphing and telephoning this operation to the British government. The exact purpose is twofold," replied Collins. "To cut off the head of British intelligence in Ireland—thus blinding the British—and to put the fear of fooking Jesus into the British, right up to their Prime Minister in London. He thinks he can terrify us. Well, we are going to fooking terrorize him and the British like they've never been terrorized before!"

111

EOIN'S DIARY
MONDAY, NOVEMBER 1, 1920
ALL SAINTS' DAY

A terrible day in Dublin. A terrible week in Ireland's history.

They hung Kevin Barry this morning at eight a.m. On a Holy Day of Obligation. It was almost as if the British were trying to rub salt in the Irish wound. Are they that blind? That vengeful? That dense?

Collins is beside himself. For the last few days, he has been pulling at straws, trying to figure out a way of getting Barry out of Mountjoy Prison. He has been all over McKee and Mulcahy, looking for the answer. He was hoping to resurrect the successful escapes of de Valera in England and Robert Barton here, but luck was not on his side this time. I have seldom seen Mick like this. He is fit to be tied. When he realized that escaping was futile, he even started planning Barry's funeral. But the British were ahead of him on that one, too. There would be no funeral. The British had learned from the funerals of Rossa and Thomas Ashe that these funerals are nothing but recruiting tools for the IRA, and they weren't about to allow Barry's burial in Glasnevin to turn into a thousand new recruits for the Dublin Brigade. Kevin's resting place is the inside yard of Mountjoy. A sad, lonely, unjust place for a heroic Fenian.

Barry's death was made even worse by the death earlier in the week of Terence MacSwiney. The Lord Mayor of Cork City died on October 25 in Brixton Prison in England. After seventy-four days, he had starved himself to death. Mick wanted to bring MacSwiney's body through Dublin on its way to Cork for burial. But again, the British had preempted him. They brought the Lord Mayor home to Cork in a British navy warship, bypassing Dublin and the great publicity show.

MacSwiney was buried yesterday, on All Hallows' Eve, a spooky, mystical time of the year. Mick wanted to go to Queenstown to meet the coffin but was talked out of it. "Don't be a bloody fool," McKee had snapped at him, and the commandant was right. Broy and Boynton also reported that G-men had been dispatched to Cork to see if a foolhardy Collins would turn up at the funeral. Thank God, they were disappointed.

So, for now, we all sit here in Dublin, among the gloom and doom of this terrible day in Irish history, and wonder what is next. We know the other shoe has to drop. I look at the calendar and see that tomorrow is All Souls' Day, and I wonder who will get the honor of being the next martyred dead.

112

D ublin had fallen into a depression. You could just feel it. When de Valera was sprung from Lincoln Gaol, you could feel the ecstasy in the streets. Now, the wounding of Breen and the deaths of Treacy, MacSwiney, and Barry had seemingly taken the air out of the city. Dublin was choking on gloom.

The darkness had penetrated even the ranks of the movement. Eoin noticed that Liam Tobin, always saturnine, looked like he was about to burst out in tears any moment. Dick McKee was deeply affected by the death of Treacy and now walked around listlessly. And the scowl never left Collins's face. He was beginning to actually look like that picture that Crow Street had supplied the Sheik with. Every intelligence briefing with the Big Fellow was gruesome. No one could do anything right—especially Eoin. Why didn't he have the information? This paper? That photograph? Eoin could do nothing right for the Commandant-General, and he wished there was an end in sight.

But depressed or not, the filthy work of the revolution continued. Collins and Tobin had decided who among the Castle elite would be the first to go—and Derek Gough-Coxe caught the short straw. They decided that the main shooting team would be led by Vinny Byrne, and that Eoin would be his number-two man. The two immediately began to tag the Sheik. They picked him up from his lodgings in 38 Upper Mount Street in the morning, followed him to Dublin Castle, and caught him again at night. If Gough-Coxe went out during the day, Boynton would call Crow Street, and Eoin or another agent would be dispatched to watch him. The whole purpose was to get Byrne and Eoin as familiar as possible with the Sheik's schedule.

As Eoin stalked the Sheik, he realized that his housekeeper was Rosie Deasy, a friend from his childhood. Eoin and Vinny were standing on the corner of Merrion Square when they saw Rosie enter the premises at seven a.m. That morning, Vinny tagged Gough-Coxe to the Castle alone, while Eoin walked across the street and knocked on the front door of number thirty-eight.

"Rosie?"

"Is that you, Eoin Kavanagh?"

"It is, indeed, Rosie. Can I come in?"

"You can't, Eoin," said Rosie. "There are gentlemen getting ready for work."

"What time do you get off at?"

"I have a few hours off after luncheon."

"Could we meet for a cup of tay?"

"Sure," said Rosie, smiling sweetly.

"How about the DBC Tea Room on the Green? Half-two?"

"I'll see you there."

True to her word, Rosie was right on time. Eoin bought her a cup of tea and a sweet cake, and they talked about old times on Camden Street. They were both the same age and always seemed to have a connection, either eyeing each other at Sunday mass or playing hide-and-seek in the alleys behind the Meath Hospital. After some small talk, Eoin finally asked, as casually as possible, who the men were living at the Mount Street address.

"They are English gentlemen," said Rosie.

"What exactly do they do?" persisted Eoin.

"They are quiet gentlemen," she said. "They spend most of their time writing."

"I'm sure they do," replied Eoin, a little too cynically for Rosie's liking.

"What?"

"Oh," said Eoin, "I was only thinking out loud."

"They are very good to me, especially Mr. Gough-Coxe."

"Who else lives in the house?"

"Oh, several friends of Mr. Gough-Coxe, although most have moved out in the past few weeks."

"What did they do?"

"Oh, they looked like military officers," said Rosie, "but they don't wear uniforms. They never go out during the day, but always at night, after curfew."

"Isn't that rather queer?" prompted Eoin.

"Yes," said Rosie, finally thinking about it. "It is rather queer."

"Do you know where these other men went?"

"Yes, they went to other rooming houses in Baggott and Pembroke Streets."

"Do you have these addresses?"

"Yes."

"Could you give them to me?"

"Sure," said Rosie, with a laugh. "What's so important about these gentlemen? They seem like good sorts."

Eoin could see he was getting into a bit of a fix. "If you bring these addresses to me tomorrow, I'll tell you why these men are so important."

"It's a date," said Rosie, truly delighted at the prospect of seeing Eoin again.

"It's a date," repeated Eoin, praying that the rebels' luck was about to change.

113

WEDNESDAY, NOVEMBER 10, 1920

The Prime Minister was feeling his oats.

At the Lord Mayor's Banquet in London yesterday evening, David Lloyd George—perhaps relishing in the deaths of Treacy, MacSwiney, and Barry—was feeling confident enough to proclaim that, "Unless I am mistaken, by the steps we have taken, we have murder by the throat."

He paused for effect and then repeated, "Murder by the throat, I say!"

"The men," he continued, "who indulge in these murders say it is war. If it is war, they, at any rate, cannot complain if we apply some of the rules of war."

After being interrupted by cheers, the Prime Minister continued, "But until this conspiracy is suppressed, there is no hope of real peace or reconciliation in Ireland. Why? They were afraid. They were intimidated. You must break the terror before you can get peace. Then you will get it."

As might be expected, the Prime Minister's words about having "murder by the throat" caused a sensation in Dublin. Men in the Dublin Brigade movement were beside themselves with vituperation, but Collins had suddenly turned serene, his demons seemingly abating as he continued to plan. Every day, he met with Tobin and Eoin and went over every detail of where the Sheik's Cairo Gang were living and working.

"There has to be more," Collins said. "These will do, but I want more."

"I've been tagging the Sheik with Vinny," Eoin began. Collins shrugged his shoulders. "I know his housekeeper from the old neighborhood."

"Have you talked to her?"

"I have."

"What did she say?"

"She is reluctant to help us."

"You're jokin'!"

"She says the Sheik treats her very decently. That he's very kind to her."

"What have you found out?"

"There were other agents living in the same house with the Sheik, but they recently moved to other rooming houses in Baggott and Pembroke Streets, and Earlsfort Terrace. They go out by night, stay in by day."

"What do you make of this, Liam?"

"We are expanding our list," said Tobin. "Some of these characters we didn't even know about until Eoin chatted up the housekeeper."

"Rosie needs a little encouragement," offered Eoin.

"Who's Rosie?" questioned Collins.

"The housekeeper," said Eoin.

Collins thought for a moment. "Set up a quick meeting tomorrow morning with Rosie, right after the Sheik heads out to the Castle. In Merrion Square Park. I'll chat her up, but good." The Big Fellow got up and walked out of the room.

114

Collins sat alone on the bench inside Merrion Square Park. The weather for late autumn had been extremely moderate, and he looked snappy in his three-piece suit with his trilby cocked over his eyes. As he saw Eoin and Rosie approach, he stood up and put on that dazzling, gap-toothed Collins smile that the ladies found so irresistible.

"Rosie," said Eoin, by way of introduction, "this is Mick Collins."

Collins bent down to the young woman and shook her hand. "Are you *the* Mick Collins?" she asked, a little breathlessly.

"He's the one with TD after his name," said Eoin, annoyed.

"You," Collins said to Eoin, "shut up! Now, Rosie, I hear you want to help Ireland."

"Oh," said Rosie, sitting down on the park bench. "I'm so conflicted."

"Well," said Collins, "that's good, because it means you are a sensible and thinking woman. I want to thank you for the information you've supplied to us already. I hear that Mr. Gough-Coxe has a very busy rubbish basket."

"Oh, Mr. Collins . . ."

"Call me Mick."

"Oh, Mick, he does an awful lot of writing. I wanted to bring you some, but I felt guilty."

"Now, Rosie," said Collins, "you know we're at war with the British. This is a very important moment in Irish history, and you can become a part of that history if you help us." Collins took Rosie's hand and placed it in the palm of his right and then closed the left on top of it. He looked her intently in the eye. "Will you help us, Rosie? Will you help poor ould Ireland?"

Eoin was thinking that Mick could shovel the shite without the aid of a shovel, when Rosie opened her purse and pulled out a wad of papers. "Here, Mr. Collins. Take these. I've been saving them for a while. I don't know why. Something just told me to."

Collins looked through the papers quickly, then glanced at Eoin with a look that told him there was something special here. "God love ya, Rosie. Thank you." He stood up, and so did Rosie. "Now, don't mention this meeting to anyone. Just go about your business as you always do. You've been an immense help."

"God protect you, Mr. Collins," Rosie said and gave him a small curtsy, as if he were some kind of royalty. She turned and headed back in the direction of Mount Street. "We may have hit the motherload," Collins said to Eoin. "Let's go to Mespil Road and sort this out."

They headed towards the Grand Canal and were in the Mespil office within ten minutes. Collins threw his hat off and started to go through the papers. Eoin looked over his shoulder and said, "Jaysus, Mick, look at all these fookin' names and addresses."

"Go," said Collins, pointing to the typewriter on the other side of the room. "I'll dictate, you type." Eoin put a sheet of paper in the typewriter. "No," said Collins. "We'll need carbons. Five, plus the original. For Tobin, McKee, Mulcahy, Daly, and McDonnell. You are to deliver this memo personally."

"How about Brugha?" said Eoin, mentioning the Minister for Defense.

"Fook Brugha," replied Collins. "If we let Cathal know about this, he'll be telegraphing Dev in America to know if we should be doing anything about it. Dev will think about it for a month or so, and nothing will get done."

"Got it," said Eoin.

Collins got up from his chair and began to recite:

"One: Number 28 Upper Pembroke Street. Major Dowling, Grenadier Guards; Leonard Price, M.C., Middlesex Regiment. These two are the main targets. There's also a Colonel Woodcock, a Colonel Montgomery, and a Captain Keenlyside residing in the house. Take them out if they get in the way.

"Two: Number 117 Morehampton Road. Lieutenant D.L. McClean of the General List, late of the Rifle Brigade. It says he's now the Chief Intelligence Officer. He's gotta go.

"Three: Number 92 Lower Baggot Street. Subject: Captain W.F. Newbury of the Royal West Surrey Regiment.

"Four: Number 38 Upper Mount Street, the Sheik's house. Alright, in addition to the Sheik, we have Lieutenant Peter Ashmunt Ames of the Army General List, which could mean anything."

"Shite," said Eoin.

"What?"

"We know him. He's Cairo Gang."

"Make a note. He will not live. You and Vinny are going to have your hands full.

"Five: Number 28 Earlsfort Terrace. Subject: Captain Fitzgerald. Take him out.

"Six: Number 22 Lower Mount Street. Subjects: Lieutenant Angliss and Lieutenant Peel."

"We know Angliss," said Eoin. "His real name is McMahon. He was just recalled from Russia to organize intelligence in the South Dublin area."

"Well," replied Collins, "he's going to die in South Dublin."

"Seven: Number 119 Lower Baggot Street. Subject: Captain G.T. Baggelly, barrister and Courts-Martial Officer. Oh," said Collins suddenly. "This fook prides himself in prosecuting IRA men. Well, he's guilty. Sentence is death."

"He's the one," added Eoin, "who shot John Lynch at the Exchequer Hotel in Parliament Street."

"Fook him," said Collins. "He was after me Loan money."

"We better tag these guys as soon as possible," said Eoin.

"Also," added Collins, "case the houses. Get craftsmen—you know, plumbers, porters, carpenters, telephone repairmen, whatever—to get inside these addresses starting today, if possible, so we know as much as can about the lay of the land. We don't want to be going in blind if we can possibly avoid it."

"Noted," said Eoin.

"Alright," said Collins. "Get back to Crow Street and get Tobin up to speed on this information, and then deliver the memos to the rest of the group." Collins put his hat back on. "We'll see who has murder by the throat. By God, we will."

115

WEDNESDAY, NOVEMBER 17, 1920

Collins's memo to McKee: "Have established addresses of the particular ones. Arrangements should now be made about the matter. Lt. G is aware of things. He suggests the twenty-first. a most suitable date and day, I think. M."

116

SATURDAY, NOVEMBER 20, 1920

D ick McKee was restless, and Shankers Ryan was on the prowl. Collins had called a meeting at Vaughan's Hotel to go over the final details for Sunday. Eoin thought they were insane to even venture near Vaughan's. Tobin had been detained there by the British the previous week and was lucky to get away after being questioned. Vaughan's was poison, but it didn't stop Collins from going there.

When McKee arrived, he stopped by the front desk to say hello to Christy Harte. Christy was engaged in conversation with a young man but looked up when he saw McKee. "Are you expecting Piaras Beaslaí tonight, Fergus?" he asked, using McKee's nickname in front of the stranger.

"I don't know," replied McKee. "I'm here for the meeting with the Big Fellow. Why are you asking?"

"This lad is looking for him."

"I'm Conor Clune," the young man replied. "I'm up from Clare to meet Piaras about some Gaelic League business."

"Sorry, son," said McKee. "I don't know if Piaras will be here tonight." He turned to Harte. "Where are the boys?"

"Upstairs."

There he found Collins, Tobin and Peadar Clancy of the Republican Outfitters, along with Frank Thornton from Crow Street.

"Are we ready to go?" asked Collins.

"All have been vetted by Frank," said Tobin.

"They are all accredited British Secret Service," said Thornton. "We've covered each of them from the day they were born."

"Good enough," said Collins. "I'm particularly interested in the Sheik and Ames in Upper Mount Street. These bums are on the top of the list. Eoin and Vinny will do the job."

"I hope they're up to it," put in Thornton.

"They're a good team," cut in Collins. "They'll do the job."

""They'd better," replied Thornton.

Collins gave him a glare, which immediately cut off any further negativity. "I'm also hot for Baggelly in Baggott Street. He's the hoor who was after that £23,000 in National Loan money that Lynch delivered to me just before they murdered him in Parliament Street."

"We have information that this was definitely Baggelly's job," said Tobin.

"Good work," replied Collins. "Who gets this one?"

"Jack Lemass and Charlie Dalton."

"They don't miss," said Collins.

Christy Harte stuck his head in the doorway. "Tans on the street. I think, sirs, ye ought to be going."

"Come on, boys," said Collins, "quick!"

The five men rushed out of the room and headed for the skylight on the fourth floor. A ladder was already in place, and they went up, led by Collins. The last man, Clancy, pulled the ladder after him, rendering the group safe. They traversed the roofs along Parnell Square and dropped down into number thirty-nine. Collins wanted to have a final word with the Crow Street men, Thornton and Tobin. McKee and Clancy hit the street and sought beds for the night.

Outside, people were queuing up for trams, because it was getting close to curfew. Standing in line was John "Shankers" Ryan, Dublin Castle tout. As the Tans and G-men were rushing into Vaughan's, Ryan was watching the rest of the block, assuming that the boyos would get away again. He was not to be disappointed. When he saw McKee and Clancy coming out of number thirty-nine, he started imagining how he'd spend the reward money.

McKee and Clancy headed towards Parnell Street and started walking east. They turned into Sackville Street for a block before turning left into Gloucester Street. They were close to home for the night.

Shankers Ryan shadowed discreetly behind them. The two Fenians may have been close to home, but this was home to Shankers. To most, it was the forbidden Nighttown, Monto, or the Kips—Dublin's Red Light District. Here, whores serviced the high and mighty—the Prince of Wales, and later King Edward VII—and the lowly, like a young student/ writer named James Joyce and his friend, Oliver St. John Gogarty, now one of Collins's agents over in plush Ely Place.

As they walked further into Nighttown, Ryan felt no danger. He knew every street and dead-end alley in these parts. He knew every whore in the Kips, and why shouldn't he? Wasn't his sister, Becky Cooper, one of the great Madams of Nighttown? Becky and her talking parrot were known to one and all in Monto. And business had been very good of late, with the British army pouring more and more men into Dublin. "God bless the rebels," Madam Becky was often heard to say. "They know the importance of commerce in the streets of dear ould durty Dublin." There was a touch of the bard in the dirty bawd.

Yes, Shankers Ryan was in his comfort zone. He watched as McKee and Clancy went into 36 Lower Gloucester Street, home of another rebel, Seán Fitzpatrick. The door slammed, and Shankers walked another block to Becky's whorehouse in Railway Street, where he used her telephone to call Dublin Castle. It was now early Sunday morning, November 21, 1920.

117

EOIN'S DIARY
SUNDAY, NOVEMBER 21, 1920

*S*aturday night, we decided to stay at the Dump.

We went next door to the Oval Pub, had a nightcap, and then hit the hay. In the morning, Vinny Byrne and I went to eight o'clock mass at St. Andrew's on Westland Row. As we went into the church, we saw Jack Lemass, and the three of us sat in a pew together. We were subdued, thinking about the terrible work we had to do this morning.

"*Introibo ad altáre Dei,*" the priest began the mass, and the three of us, by instinct, replied, "*Ad Deum qui laetíficat juventútem meam.*"

But I am really paying no attention. The mass is rote to me this morning. My mind is on the business of the day, which will start in just an hour. St. Andrew's is a wonderful old Church. It was built right next to Westland Row railroad station, and I think about meeting Mick on the street that Christmastime while I was working at Sweny's Chemists down the way. Sometimes it is hard to hear the priest, as the rumble of a train drowns out his chants. We are sitting near the mortuary chapel, where Willie Pearse's sculpture, Mater Dororosa, Christ's sorrowful mother, rests. It reminds me of the Pearse brothers, who lived just a few paces from here on Great Brunswick Street. They were baptized in this church and probably made their First Communion here, too. I can still see them that Saturday morning of Easter Week, when they came into our dwelling in Moore Street and then went out to surrender. It didn't take the British even a week to murder both of them.

And this morning, I can't get me Da out of me mind. I can see him in my mind's eye, as if he were here before me. I can see him as the British returned him to the barbershop in Aungier Street, beaten and broken from a day riding around the city in one of their tenders, the perfect solution to their ambush problems. I remember that he was beaten and tortured for seven straight days, and, on the seventh day, he died, sitting in his big chair, trying to get some warmth from a few pieces of coal.

I can see me Mammy and my brother Charlie, too, killed by this whore of a country, stolen from its own people by a mercenary race, the most selfish race in the world. They are all before me this morning, as if I am at the Fenian Resurrection Day—the Pearses, MacDonagh, MacBride, Plunkett, Connolly, Clarke, and dear MacDiarmada. The list seems endless, but, today, there will be a sense of revenge, a sense of renewal—for, this morning, we will even the playing field in a way the British never imagined.

"*Credo in unum Deum,*" the priest began, "*Patrem omnipotentem, factórem coeli et terrae, visibílium ómnium et invisílium . . .*"

"I believe in one God, the Father Almighty, Maker of heaven and earth, and of all things visible and invisible." I couldn't help but smile, because this very morning our little rebel army, until this day invisible to the British, will rise up and show them the brutality they have unthinkingly reigned on the Irish nation for seven hundred years.

"*Lavado inter innocentes manus meas: et circúmdabo altáre tuum, Dómaine.*"

"I wash my hands in innocence, and I go around Your altar, O Lord." My hands have not been innocent since the elimination of Detective Blood, but if I must surrender my soul, I will give it for my country and the memory of those who loved and nurtured me, in the hope that this terrible day will give birth to a new generation of free Irishmen.

"*Agnus Dei, qui tolis peccáta mundi, miserére nobis.*"

"Lamb of God, You Who take away the sins of the world, have mercy on us." I patted the Webley in my coat pocket. I think maybe it hit us all at the same time, the terrible things we must do. I check my pocketwatch and see that it is going on twenty to nine, and we must get moving—Vinny and I to Upper Mount Street, and Lemass to Lower Baggot Street, only a block apart. "Nine o'clock sharp," Collins had commanded. "These hoors have got to learn that Irishmen can turn up on time." We get up, step out into the aisle, and genuflect to our God, who is sitting just a few yards in front of us.

As we head for the door, we hear: "*Sancte Míchael Archángele, defénde nos in proelio; contra nequítiam et insídias diabolic esto praesídium.*"

"Holy Michael, the Archangel, defend us in battle; be our safeguard against the wickedness and snares of the devil."

The three of us looked at each other and shivered. Collins's Apostles, on our way to meet the divil himself.

118

The three gunmen dipped their hands in Holy Water as they came out of St. Andrew's, slipped by Sweny's into Lincoln Place, and stood in silence on the mitre of Merrion Square, where the north and west sides joined. There wasn't a soul in sight, and not a word was said. Lemass continued towards Baggot Street, while Kavanagh and Byrne entered Merrion Square Park, using the green to camouflage their route to Upper Mount Street.

They emerged from the park on Merrion Square East, where their backup team was waiting for them—Rory Doyle, Jamey Holland, and Bobby Malone, all of the Third Brigade, South Dublin IRA, personally chosen by Vinny. "This is Lieutenant Eoin Kavanagh," Vinny said, introducing Eoin to the team.

Eoin felt even more nervous—his backup team was younger than he was. "How old are you, Jamey?" he asked the youngest-looking.

"Fifteen, sir, Lieutenant, sir," Holland replied.

"Jaysus!" said Eoin, turning on Byrne.

"How old were you in Jacob's?" returned Vinny, with a tight smile.

Eoin nodded wearily. "And forget that 'lieutenant' stuff," Eoin told the group. "Vinny's in charge here. Is that understood?"

The five of them crossed the road swiftly and turned into Upper Mount Street, a wide, handsome Georgian thoroughfare. It was quiet, as only a Sunday morning in Dublin can be. The lone sound on the street was the occasional squawk of a passing seagull, on its glide path away from Dublin Bay. At the end of the street was St. Stephen's Anglican

Church, which was known fondly by Dubliners as the Pepper Canister, because of its nifty dome. They had been warned by Daly, McDonnell, and Collins to get in and do their business swiftly, before the first Sunday service at St. Stephen's began at ten o'clock. They didn't need any innocent bystanders getting in their way or calling the authorities.

"Are ya ready, lads?" Byrne asked, and the wide-eyed returning stares showed how terrified everyone was. The clock of the Pepper Canister struck nine, and Byrne banged on the door. "Are Mr. Gough-Coxe and Mr. Ames in?"

Katherine Farrell, the scullery maid, opened the door and said, "They're still asleep."

She was about to close the door in Vinny's face when Byrne stuck his foot in, and Eoin pushed the door wide open with the flat of his hand. "It's alright," said Vinny, "we're friends of theirs." The five men entered the building and shut the front door. Vinny held his gun up for show and asked, "Where is Gough-Coxe?" Katie Farrell thought she would faint, and the blood drained out of her face. She pointed to the door directly to the right, and the backup team pushed her to the side.

"Up!" Vinny shouted, as he entered the room. Gough-Coxe began reaching under his pillow for his .45 Colt automatic, but Byrne was on him too swiftly. Vinny put his Mauser to the Sheik's head. "Now be a good lad, Deputy Commissioner."

The Sheik looked at the two teenagers in his room and was forced to give a small smile. Any concern he may have had evaporated. Just a couple of mammy boys playing soldier. He thought he was protected by the authority that was the Crown. He thought wrong, for this morning, Michael Collins had changed the rules of the game forever.

"Get up," Byrne told Gough-Coxe. The Sheik was wearing beautiful pajamas, his initials—DG-C—embroidered on the left breast pocket. "Where's Lieutenant Ames?" Gough-Coxe pointed to a room at the back of the first floor. The Sheik slowly rose and nonchalantly picked up a stick that was propped against the bedpost. "Give me that," said Vinny, as he snatched the cane out of Gough-Cox's hand. Then he saw it—the "All-Seeing Eye." "BeJaysus," he said to Gough-Coxe, "where did you get this?"

"It belonged to a friend of mine."

"Detective Blood?"

"Yes," said Gough-Coxe, and his face turned ashen in a second. These boys, he suddenly realized, were not amateurs. They had done this before—and probably to Blood.

Vinny held the stick out for show and then tossed it to Eoin, who caught it with his right hand. Eoin shook his head in disbelief and then pushed the Sheik out of the room. With the aid of Blood's cane to the back, he violently guided the Sheik to the back of the house. One of the backup team kept an eye on the maid, and the other trailed the two gunmen to the rear. Byrne pushed open the door and said, "Wake up, me sleepin' beauty," as Ames slowly opened his eyes, still groggy with sleep. Eoin pushed the Sheik into the room.

"Faces against the wall, the two of you," said Eoin, adrenaline pumping insanely. Ames, still half-asleep, tried to peek at his abductors.

"Eoin!" said Vinny in warning.

Eoin roughly stuck the gun in the small of Ames's back and said, "Look at the fookin' wall!"

"Eoin?" asked Gough-Coxe. "Eoin Kavanagh?"

"Shut the fook up," Eoin snarled.

"So we finally meet," said the Sheik, seemingly amused by the whole episode. Now, it all became clear. He had "worked backwards" to his own death.

"Where are your papers?" Eoin demanded.

"What papers?"

"Your intelligence papers, eejit," said Byrne, as he cuffed the Sheik with his gun on the back of the head.

"In my bedroom."

Vinny and his backup covered the two men as Eoin retrieved Gough-Coxe's papers from the man's briefcase.

"Got them," Eoin said, as he returned to the back room.

"You men are guilty of spying and have been sentenced to death," said Vinny. "May the Lord have mercy on your souls."

"Save your Papist shit for someone else," the Sheik spat.

They were to be his last words, as Byrne raised his gun and shot him in the back of the head once, dropping him in a heap to the floor. By this time, Ames was sobbing, and his knees were buckling. His terror was short-lived as Byrne floored him with a single shot, also to the back of the head. Eoin came around and leveled another round into each of them. He was reminded of what Tom Keogh of the Squad once said while administering the *coup de grace*: "For luck!"

Eoin quickly looked around the room to see if Ames had any other papers and found nothing. Vinny made sure to retrieve the guns of both victims, a bonus for the Squad. "Let's go!" Eoin said, and they headed for the front door. But before he left, he turned and hurled, in an act of exorcism, the "All-Seeing Eye" through the back window and into the yard, like it was a javelin. By this time, Katie Farrell was crying, and Byrne gave the distraught woman one final warning: "You've been a great help, miss. Now keep ya gob shut!"

With that, Eoin and Vinny were out the door. Their backup team headed towards Merrion Square, while they headed in the direction of the Pepper Canister before turning right at the corner into Herbert Place. Their orders were to get out of sight for the rest of the day and sit tight. Vinny would report the results to Crow Street from the phone at Kehoe's, the spirit-grocer public house across from his place in South Anne Street.

As they raced towards Baggot Street, they were surprised to see Jack Lemass and Charlie Dalton hustling towards them, at a full run. "Eoin," Lemass panted, "take these. We've got to get the ferry across the river." Eoin obligingly took both guns, which were still hot from being fired. He was weighed down with artillery.

Eoin rushed in the direction of the Grand Canal, while Vinny headed for his digs in South Anne Street. Eoin turned onto the Adelaide Road, walking as fast as he could to Róisín's flat. As he advanced on Harrington Street, he pulled out the pocketwatch Collins had given him for Christmas a few years ago. It was exactly half-nine.

119

McKee and Clancy sat on a bench in the guardroom of Dublin Castle as the Tan officer interrogated them. "You might as well tell me," he said, "because things won't get any easier when Commissioner Gough-Coxe gets here."

McKee wondered what time it was. He couldn't look at his watch because he was handcuffed from behind.

"What time is it?" he asked his guard.

"What?" said the Tan, confused.

"The time?"

"Too late for you, matey," said the Tan, laughing. McKee stared straight at him. Finally, his guard sobered and looked at his watch. "Half-ten."

McKee smiled.

"What's so fucking funny?"

"Nothing at 'tal," said McKee. "Nothing at 'tal."

So far, things hadn't been that bad for McKee and Clancy. They had been pushed around and took a couple of punches, but, overall, they had experienced worse in the past. This late on Sunday morning, they knew that the day had been saved by Seán Fitzpatrick's adopted sister, Florrie. As the British banged vehemently on the Gloucester Street door—thanks to Shanker Ryan's tout—Florrie's modesty became the paramount concern. "Let me put some clothes on—I'm in me nude!" Florrie's procrastination began. Upstairs, McKee and Clancy were burning the papers that Eoin had typed from Collins's dictation. By the time the British gained entrance, the memorandum was ash.

McKee and Clancy spent the night in a cell. By eleven a.m., it was apparent something was wrong. Important men, like the Sheik, couldn't be reached. Reports were coming in from the DMP that bodies were arriving at hospitals around the city, many from the residential areas adjacent to St. Stephen's Green. McKee and Clancy could hear the murmurings of the G-men and some of the Tans and army men. They looked at each other and nodded.

Abruptly, the door swung open, and the kid from Clare, Conor Clune, also cuffed, was thrown into the room. "Sit down and keep your gob shut!" snapped the G-man, before leaving the room. Young Clune was clearly terrified.

"How did they get you?" asked McKee.

"They came into Vaughan's and arrested the lot of us," replied Clune. "They think I'm in the IRA. They're adamant about it."

"Well," asked Clancy, "are you?"

"I am," admitted Clune, "but I'm more interested in the Gaelic League."

McKee looked at Clancy and rolled his eyes. "Stick to your story," Clancy advised the kid.

As the morning wore on, the atmosphere of the Castle began to change. McKee and Clancy could see the looks of concern on the Crown personnel, and they knew the Squad and the Dublin Brigade had been successful. The stink of fear had permeated the Castle.

At noon, the door flew open, and Auxiliary Captain Simon Hardy pounced into the room. McKee and Clancy immediately recognized Hardy. When he had first arrived in Dublin, the Squad had attempted to assassinate him, but they ended up only wounding him. Today, he would exact his revenge. Hardy knew the famed Secret Service had been destroyed. Many were dead, and the survivors would be of no use; they were all too frightened. Collins had rendered him—and the Crown—completely impotent.

"Who are they?" asked Hardy.

The Tan pointed at each of three and identified them: "Woods, Cleary, and Clune."

"Wrong," corrected Hardy. "Dick McKee and Peadar Clancy, how are ya?" Both sat mute. "Commandant and vice-commandant of the Dublin Brigade."

"The kid's from Clare," spoke up McKee. "He has nothing to do with us. He's just a Gaelic Leaguer."

Hardy laughed. "I guess this is his unlucky day. *Slán agat*," he said to the terrified Clune. McKee and Clancy knew the game was up.

120

Róisín's day was horrific. By ten a.m., they'd started bringing in the first casualties from the Gresham Hotel in Sackville Street, a Captain McCormack and a fellow named Wilde. There was no rush; they were dead on arrival. The Mater was soon swarming with British soldiers, DMPs, and Tans rushing about in a near panic. Rumors began to fly about mass killings of British agents, most of whom lived in the area just east of St. Stephen's Green—the neighborhood, Róisín thought, where the money was.

At six p.m., as the Angelus bells lugubriously rang throughout damp, dark Dublin, Róisín mounted her bike and started heading back to her flat in Portobello. Eoin had suggested that maybe she should take this Sunday off, and now she thought she knew why. As she came down Parnell Square, she could see that the British were stopping and searching every tram, car, and cart. Traffic in Sackville Street was at a standstill. There were throngs of soldiers around the front entrance to the Gresham Hotel. Róisín didn't like the look of things and decided to go down Parnell Street all the way to Capel, then make her way across the Liffey from there. She was stopped at the bridge by a soldier who made her open her coat and her pocketbook before waving her across to Parliament Street. She was shocked to see a panicked phalanx—they looked like families, to her—queuing up with their possessions at the front gate, trying to get into the Castle. The terrified look on their faces told Róisín that gaining access to the Castle was a matter of life and death to these people.

Róisín was tired from the long day and winded from her bike ride, and she couldn't wait to settle down and have a cup of tea. The flat was dark when she entered. As she lit the paraffin light in the small sitting room, she was shocked to see Eoin there, sitting quietly, his Webley in his hand, resting on his left leg. She leapt with fright. "Jaysus, Mary, and Joseph!" she yelped.

"How are ya, Róisín?"

"Were you trying to frighten me to death?" Róisín looked at Eoin and immediately realized he was in shock. He had been sitting in that chair for nine solid hours. On the table before him were the guns of Lemass, Dalton, and the two dead Secret Service agents. "Are you alright?" Eoin gave a crooked smile and shrugged his shoulders indifferently. Róisín went to him and saw the blood on his jacket. She quietly removed the gun from Eoin's hand and put it on the table with the others. "It's over," she said.

Eoin shook his head, and tears began to drop one by one from his eyes, so slow you could count them. "I'm nothing but a fookin' murderer," he said. "A fookin' murderer." Róisín cupped his head to her breasts and held him tight as her own tears dropped onto his beautiful dark-brown hair. "I'm supposed to be on the side of the angels," he said, "but how can that be?"

After a long time, Róisín bought Eoin into her bedroom. "We've got to get those clothes off," she said. "You're covered in blood."

Eoin grunted. "Crown evidence," he said in a small voice, not without humor. "That's the second suit I've ruined with blood."

Eoin's left arm, his shooting arm, was covered with the victim's blood, right down to his French cuffs. "Off with the clothes. We've got to get rid of them, or you'll be swingin' in Mountjoy by the end of the week." Róisín stopped in her tracks. Suddenly, her own safety popped into her mind. "Does anyone know you're here?" Eoin shook his head.

"How about Mick? Vinny?"

"No one."

Soon he was down to his longjohns. The chill began to seep into him, and he started to shiver. "Jaysus," Róisín said, as she headed for the fireplace. Eoin plopped down on the bed as Róisín started throwing pieces of coal into the fire. Soon there was a bit of warmth in the November room.

Róisín went to the kitchen and poured a glass of Jameson's into a tumbler. "Here," she thrust it into his hand, "drink this." Eoin did as he was told and downed the whiskey in one gulp. Róisín, fully dressed, slid into the bed and pulled the eiderdown up over them. Sleep soon overtook Eoin, but Róisín remained awake for a time. It wasn't long before Eoin shot up in the bed, eyes wild, shouting, "Don't miss him, Vinny!"

Róisín soothed him in a calm voice: "It's alright, Eoin. It's over. Vinny got him."

"Thank God," said Eoin, as he slid back, calm and relieved, into a deep sleep.

"Yes," repeated Róisín, "thank God."

When Eoin awoke later that evening, he was alone in the bed and momentarily didn't know where he was. Then Róisín entered the room, fresh from her bath, with a towel wrapped around her body as she dried her hair with another towel.

"How are ya?" she asked, as if it were any Sunday of the year. "I just had a grand wash. It seems I can never get that hospital antiseptic smell off me."

"It was awful," was all Eoin could muster.

As Róisín dried her hair, her towel dropped to the floor. Eoin's eyes grew as hot as the burning coals in the fireplace. Róisín looked at him and could only laugh. "It's a hairy ould oyster, isn't it, Eoin dear," she said, without embarrassment.

"I didn't know."

"Know what? The hair? Did you think I had a cauliflower down there?"

"Could I see . . ."

"See what?"

"Your bottom."

"My *derriere!*" Róisín laughed, turned around, bent over, and stuck her rump out. "Best arse in Dublin City!" she called over her shoulder.

"I know," said Eoin.

Collins was wrong. In the GPO, he said Róisín had an arse on her like "that of a skinny thirteen-year-old boy," but it wasn't small and boney at all. In fact, it was very shapely, with plenty of buoyancy to it.

Eoin's willie approved. "Come here," he said, the staccato of his voice showing his nervousness. "My Mammy always said, 'Modesty is the best policy.'"

"Your Mammy was *wrong*," she replied, and, this time, Eoin agreed. "When I'm naked," continued Róisín, "it's the only time I really feel free." She stood there, in her glorious nude, her arms defiantly on her hips. "Everyone on this terrible planet deserves one special person they can be naked with." She then went to Eoin and pulled his willie free of his longjohns. "Ah," she exclaimed, "the elusive Parnell! Little Big Fellow! Or is it Big Little Fellow?"

"For once," replied Eoin, "leave Collins out of it." This elicited a laugh from Róisín. She moved in and kissed Eoin full on the lips. "You're my Big Fellow now, and you always will be." Then Róisín was on top of Eoin, passionately kissing him. "I've wanted your shoes under me bed for a long time now."

"Why didn't you tell me?"

"The time had to be right."

"Is this a sin?" asked Eoin, uncomfortably.

Róisín was about to say, "Believe me, this is the least offensive sin you've committed today," but this time, she caught herself. The boy had been through enough. "Only if you don't get me off!" she laughed. Eoin gave a feeble grin as his newly christened Parnell stood at attention, climbing over his belly button, waiting for her. "Now, I want you to sin like you mean it," whispered Róisín, as she prepared to end Eoin Kavanagh's day in love, so far removed from the hate in which it had begun.

121

MONDAY, NOVEMBER 22, 1920

Eoin dressed in the dark as quietly as he could, all the time keeping his eyes on the sleeping Róisín. Amidst all the chaos that his life had become, he was calmed by her love and her beauty. When everything seemed hopeless, the mere thought of Róisín kept him moving for another day.

"Come back to bed," she said.

"Got to get going," Eoin replied quietly, as he leaned down to give Róisín a kiss. "I've got to see what's going on in Crow Street. I've kept my head low long enough." Róisín pushed herself up in the bed with her elbow and exposed her breasts. The biggest surprise to Eoin was how full and round they were. Róisín had done a neat job of keeping them tucked in. Another surprise was how brown and big her nipples were. He began to feel his Parnell move and repeated, "I've got to go." Róisín sighed, turned over, and went back to sleep for another hour.

Eoin came out into Walworth Street and made his way to Camden Street. He stopped in a tobacconist shop and picked up the newspapers from both Dublin and London. "Terrible, terrible day," the newsagent commented.

"Yes," said Eoin, absently. He knew all about it.

"Terrible carnage in Croke Park," continued the man. "Fourteen dead, including a footballer."

"What?"

"The murders in Croke Park."

"Croke Park?" Eoin was befuddled.

"Look at the headline."

DEADLY HAIL

THOUSANDS OF FOOTBALL

SPECTATORS UNDER FIRE

FOURTEEN KILLED

INDESCRIBABLE SCENES OF

PANIC AT CROKE PARK

MICHAEL HOGAN, TIPPERARY PLAYED, KILLED

The British had enacted their always-inarticulate revenge on Dublin for the elimination of their Secret Service. All the papers were crying out about the twenty-eight deaths in Dublin on what they were now calling "Bloody Sunday."

"Oh, my God," said Eoin, paying up. He came out of the shop and began a steady jog for Crow Street. It was still dark out when he arrived. When he entered the office, Liam Tobin was already at work. "What the fuck is going on?" he asked Tobin. Liam looked at Eoin and shook his head. "Where's Mick?"

"McKee and Clancy are missing," he said, not answering the question. "Mick has Boynton and Broy searching Dublin Castle for them. They were lifted late Saturday night."

"Mick?"

"He's gone mad," said Tobin. "I just got off the phone with him. He's beside himself over McKee and Clancy."

413

"But you don't know where he is?"

"I only have a phone number."

"Let me see it," said Eoin. It was Collins's number at the secret office in Mespil Road. "I've got to go see Mick," was the last thing Eoin said before he bolted out the door.

Years later, Eoin said the date he hated the most in the calendar year was November 22nd.

In 1963, he was on the floor of the House of Representatives, bullshitting with Republican Congressman Gerry Ford of Michigan and Congressman Tip O'Neill from Boston, when he heard the warning bell of the AP ticker go crazy in the Democratic Cloak Room. Something big had happened.

PRESIDENT KENNEDY SHOT. STOP.

Eoin ripped the paper out of the machine. "Good Jesus," he said to his fellow congressmen.

The bell on the UPI machine, sitting side-by-side with its AP mate, rang up ten bells, signaling a "flash" message.

THREE SHOTS WERE FIRED AT PRESIDENT KENNEDY'S MOTORCADE IN DOWNTOWN DALLAS. STOP.

The AP bell began manically ringing again, as if in competition with its UPI rival.

DALLAS-AP-PRESIDENT KENNEDY WAS SHOT TO/DAY JUST AS HIS MOTORCADE LEFT DOWNTOWN DALLAS. STOP.

A small crowd began to form, and all eyes were glued to the teletype machine.

The bell rang yet again.

AP PHOTOGRAPHER JAMES W. ALTGENS SAID HE SAW/ BLOOD ON THE PRESIDENT'S HEAD. STOP.

Eoin knew all about head wounds, and his heart sank into his gut. He was haunted, as if God were never going to let him forget the Dublin of 1920, now being recreated in Dallas in 1963.

The bell on the teletype machine rang once more, and this time it didn't stop.

DALLAS-AP-KENNEDY 46 LIVED ABOUT AN HOUR/ AFTER SNIPER CUT HIM DOWN AS HIS LIMOUSINE/LEFT DOWNTOWN DALLAS. AUTOMATICALLY THE MANTLE OF THE PRESIDENCY/FELL TO VICE PRESIDENT LYNDON B. JOHNSON . . .

"God help Lyndon," Eoin murmured as he quietly broke off from the crowd around the teletype machines and went back to his office. He closed the door and called Róisín in New York. "Have you heard the news?"

"Walter Cronkite is on the TV, crying," she said.

"I've known Jack Kennedy since 1947, when he was just a skinny kid with a bad back and a brand new congressional seat brought for him by his rich daddy. He couldn't even give a speech properly. He was awful on the stump." Eoin laughed for a minute, the way the Irish laugh when one of their own dies. "I got to get the fuck out of here," he told her over the phone.

"Now, honey, don't do anything rash."

"Remember the last November 22 like this?"

There was quiet at the other end of the line. "Forty-three years ago," said Róisín.

"To the day."

"You're thinking of McKee and Clancy."

"I hate this fucking world," said Eoin, and Róisín couldn't argue with him.

———

Eoin marched through St. Stephen's Green and continued up Lower Leeson Street. He crossed the banks of the Grand Canal and found 5 Mespil Road. He turned the key in the door and, as a precaution, pulled out his gun. He found Collins in the office, quietly reading the papers, his Colt revolver on the desk in front of him.

"I figured you would be here," said Eoin.

"A fookin' catastrophe," Collins replied. "They got fourteen in Croke Park at the match yesterday afternoon. I tried to call it off, but it was too late."

After what Tobin had told him, Eoin expected to find Collins in one of his frenzies, ready to strike out, but he was calm, as if it were any other morning of the revolution.

"And we got our fourteen," replied Eoin.

"How did it go with the Sheik?"

"Quick."

"Who did the shooting?"

"Vinny. And I made sure." Collins nodded. Eoin took the paper from Collins and read about his exploits:

SHOT IN COLD BLOOD

OFFICERS KILLED IN THER BEDROOMS

ATTACKERS ESCAPE

"What happens now?" asked Eoin.

"We wait."

"Wait?"

"To see what London wants to do."

"Liam says McKee and Clancy are missing."

"They must have them at the Castle," said Collins. "Rumor has it they were lifted very early Sunday morning."

"What are you going to do?"

"I have our two G-men looking for them. Until then, I have a wedding to go to."

"Don't be a bloody fool," snapped Eoin. "Do you want to end up like McKee and Clancy?"

"What does it matter?" Collins looked at his young acolyte. "Anyway, I promised I'd be there."

"For fook's sake," Eoin swore, red in the face, as he turned and went to the kitchen to wet some tea. He returned in a few minutes with two cups. "Who's getting married?"

"Michael O'Brien."

"Where?"

"Tenenure."

"I'm joining you."

"You're not."

"If you want to get yourself killed, I'm going to be at your side."

"Please yourself," surrendered Collins.

They traveled to Tenenure by taxicab, and when they arrived, Eoin was relieved to see that Gearoid O'Sullivan, Collins's cousin and a commandant-general himself in the IRA, was also a member of the wedding party.

When it was time for the wedding photograph to be taken in the backyard, Collins told Eoin to call Tobin and find out the latest on McKee and Clancy. Eoin dialed Crow Street: "Himself wants to know if there's any word on Fergus and Peadar?"

"We found them," replied Tobin.

"Good."

"Dead. In Dublin Castle."

The guests were lining up for the photographer when Eoin signaled to Collins, who excused himself and joined the huddle with Eoin and O'Sullivan. "They're dead. Dublin Castle."

Collins pursed his lips and turned to his cousin. "We'd better take that picture."

Eoin watched as Collins and O'Sullivan took their place in the back row, Collins second from the left and O'Sullivan next to him. As the photographer said, "Watch the birdie!" Collins turned his head down and to the left, showing not much more than the top of his head to the camera. Even in his grief, Collins was determined to best the British.

With the photograph done, Collins and O'Sullivan walked over to Eoin. "What now?" asked O'Sullivan.

"The task at hand," said Collins, "is our fallen comrades. Eoin, get some lower-ranking types and send them to Dublin Castle for the bodies. Work it out with Boynton and Broy if you need to. Bring the bodies to me at the Pro-Cathedral. I'll handle it from there."

Collins rejoined the wedding party as they prepared a toast to the success of the newly pledged nuptials. Eoin watched as Collins mingled and laughed, and he marveled at how Collins could compartmentalize his emotions—yesterday was war, today is a wedding, tomorrow are the funerals—as he mourned his friends, McKee and Clancy.

122

The Prime Minister stood alone in the conference room at 10 Downing Street and stared at the headlines of the same morning papers that had stunned Eoin Kavanagh. "Not a pretty picture," interrupted Winston Churchill, as he entered the room.

"Just awful," responded the PM. "So much for your Derek of Suez." Lloyd George laughed before turning back to the newspapers spread on the conference table. "Your Auxiliaries also did a bang-up job at the Croke Park, Winston. Or was it Henry Wilson's Tans, as the Irish call them, who did the filthy job?"

Churchill ignored the PM's jabs. "State funeral on Thursday for Gough-Coxe at Westminster Abbey," said Churchill, as he studied the Prime Minister, who was meticulously perusing the papers. "You're expected to attend. Honoring our martyred dead and all that." Churchill paused. "I imagine this puts the tin hat on any negotiations, at least for a while."

"Not at all, Winston. They got what they deserved—beaten by counter-jumpers." Even at 10 Downing Street, no one loves a loser.

"Talk like that will upset Henry Wilson. He's very proud of his modern-day Hessians, you know."

"Hessians," muttered Lloyd George. He raised his eyebrows and grunted. "Too bad," he said.

The two wiliest British politicians of the twentieth century had a symbiotic relationship. Whenever Churchill should have been sacked from a cabinet post because of his adventurism, Lloyd George could always find him a job. Right now, he was Secretary of State for War, and his war was in Ireland.

Both were cunning, cutthroat realists. What separated them was Churchill's sense of morality. It may not have been perfect, but it was there, albeit sometimes only in vapor form. The 1930s did not see Winston Spencer Churchill traveling to Berchtesgaden, hat in hand, to bathe in the glow of the Nazi *Führer*, as David Lloyd George did. As he aged, Churchill progressed; Lloyd George retrogressed.

Although Churchill owed a chunk of his career to Lloyd George, it did not keep his sharp wit from savaging the Prime Minister. (After they both left office, Lloyd George and Churchill were out one night. "Can you lend me a penny so I can phone a friend?" the former PM asked.

"Here's tuppence," replied Churchill, "call *all* your friends!")

"I want you to get in touch with Arthur Griffith," said the Prime Minister to his Secretary of State for War.

"That should be no problem," said Churchill. "We've just arrested him."

"Why? What were they thinking?" snapped Lloyd George. "We'll get nowhere without Griffith's help. He's our back door. This can't go on indefinitely. Ireland is tired of it, and this country—more importantly—is tired of it. *I'm* tired of it. Hell, I'll talk to anyone to get out of this mess."

"Anyone?"

"Anyone."

"De Valera—or maybe even Collins?"

"Collins," sniffed the Prime Minister. "You mean the Irish Houdini? I thought you said that £10,000 would deliver his body to us." Churchill looked at the floor. "You were wrong, Winston. The Irish are not like us—they take care of their own." The situation was now desperate in Ireland. And the two architects of that failed policy had been painted into a corner.

Churchill thought it was time to pique the Prime Minister. "You have your choice—the Irish pontiff, or the Fenian devil."

"I'll take the Fenian devil any day," responded the Welshman, as he brushed his long, white hair behind his ear. "I never did like Rome, you know. Too self-important." Narcissus couldn't have put it better.

It must take a pontiff, thought Churchill, *to know a pontiff. His Holiness, Pope Lloyd George I.* He suppressed a smile as the Prime Minister turned and left the room.

123

Eoin returned from the wedding in Tenenure, and, as soon as he walked in the door of Crow Street, Liam Tobin could see that he was distressed. "How's Mick?"

"Quiet."

Tobin smiled. "If he's so quiet, why do you look so downhearted?"

Eoin looked at his boss and shook his head. "You know what happens when the quiet ends?"

"There will be a hell of an explosion."

"If we're not careful, Mick will end up in a box like McKee and Clancy. You know how he is."

Tobin opened the bottom drawer of his desk and pulled out a shoulder holster. "I have a gift for you. Let's see how it fits." Eoin took his coat off and tried on the contraption. He looped the strap around his back, under his necktie, and fastened it. He took his Webley out of his coat pocket and stuffed it in the gift holster, where it found a snug fit. "I finally got rid of that thing," said Tobin. "We don't have a lot of lefthanders in the intelligence division."

"I like it," said Eoin, as he put his jacket back on. "I have a feeling it may turn out to be useful in the next couple of days."

Tobin sat on the edge of Eoin's desk and spoke quietly to his young colleague. "Now, what exactly did Mick say to you?"

"He wants me to get a couple of low-ranking Volunteers and go get McKee and Clancy's bodies from Dublin Castle and bring them to him at the Pro-Cathedral."

"I see."

"I was thinking that we have a few men down at the City Morgue in Store Street who could help."

"I don't think so," said Tobin.

"Why not?"

"Don't you think they just might be a wee bit busy today?"

"Oh, yes," said Eoin, realizing the irony. "I didn't think about that."

Tobin gave one of his lugubrious smiles. "We're not going to put *anyone* at risk on this caper."

"How can we avoid that?"

"We're going to let Fanagan's of Aungier Street handle this," Tobin said, speaking of the undertakers.

"I know them," said Eoin. "They took my whole family up to Glasnevin." Tobin thought Eoin had a strange way of talking about the funerals of his brother, mother, and father. It sounded like a family holiday excursion. "I'll make the call." After talking to Boynton at the Castle, Eoin called the people at Fanagan's. They agreed to take the bodies from Dublin Castle and hand them over to Eoin at their Aungier Street premises, just across the street from the building his father had died in.

Eoin was sick to the bone of dealing with dead Volunteers. He had dressed enough of them, including his own Da, and he wondered when it would all end. He was so tired and depressed that his brain had turned to tepid porridge, a skull of mush that couldn't think straight anymore. He wanted to take Róisín and get the hell out of Dublin—get the hell out of Ireland. But he couldn't. As long as Mick Collins stood fast, he would stand right behind him.

They didn't tell Eoin about the extra body. He was sitting in Fanagan's offices, looking out the window at his father's old shop across the way, when he was interrupted by one of the undertakers. "We have three," he said.

"Three?"

"McKee, Clancy, and Clune."

"Who's Clune?"

"I don't know, but the British were insistent I should take 'the little shite,' as they called him."

Eoin picked up the phone and called Tobin. "I have three," he said.

422

"Three what?"

"Bodies."

There was silence on Tobin's end of the line. "What's his name?" he finally asked.

"Conor Clune."

"Never heard of him."

"Taken at Vaughan's."

"Sit tight."

Fifteen minutes later, the phone rang at Fanagan's. "Christy Harte says he's a Gaelic Leaguer from Clare." Tobin paused. "Let Fanagan's pack him up and send him home."

In a strange way, Eoin Kavanagh envied his newfound ward, the late Conor Clune, Gaelic scholar from County Clare.

124

It took nearly thirty-six hours, but Eoin managed to get the three bodies to Fanagan's without being pinched by the British. Eoin left Conor Clune at Fanagan's, while he took McKee's and Clancy's coffins to the Pro-Cathedral in a lorry late on Wednesday evening. They parked in Cathedral Street and brought the boxes in by the side entrance. The church was eerily quiet and empty, except for several Volunteers.

Collins was waiting, the scowl on his face showing his disposition. "About time," he snapped at Eoin.

Kavanagh looked Collins straight in the eye and replied, "Yes, Commandant-General." Collins stared at his young lieutenant. Whenever Eoin referred to him as "Commandant-General," Collins knew that the needle was being applied, either in humor or as a jeer.

"Let's get to work," said Collins, as the coffins were carried to the mortuary chapel.

By now, the British propaganda machine was in high gear. If you believed everything in the papers, all fourteen British agents were choir boys who spent their spare time looking for old ladies to help cross Sackville Street like the good Boy Scouts they were. And of course, McKee, Clancy, and Clune—now part of a legendary, historical Fenian Trinity—were psychotic murderers whom they were reluctantly forced to shoot.

"Open the boxes," commanded Collins. The coffins were opened, and, at once, it was obvious from the battered faces that there was more to it than a mere "shot while trying to escape" going on here. "Strip them," said Collins. Eoin helped remove the clothes from Clancy and McKee, revealing bullet holes and bayonet jabs.

"Jaysus," whispered Eoin, shocked.

"Jaysus indeed," echoed Collins. "Enough. Let's get them properly dressed." Two Volunteer uniforms were brought out, and the time-consuming work of dressing the two corpses began. "Let's leave the coffins open for all the world to see," said Collins.

"No," said Eoin, "don't do that."

"And why not?" snapped Collins. "Why shouldn't the world see what the British did to these brave soldiers?"

"Think of their families," said Eoin, softly. "If they were your brothers, would you want to see them this way? Let's remember them at their best."

Collins knew Eoin was right. "Alright, close them up!" Eoin helped Collins place two tricolours on the caskets.

Eoin was exhausted. He had barely slept for the past three days. But he had no time for fatigue now—he knew how important these days were to the survival of the fledging Republic. He watched as Collins knelt in front of the two boxes and prayed. Finally the Big Fellow got up and took a seat in a nearby pew. Eoin went over and sat down next to his boss. Collins ignored him and stared straight ahead. "Time to get some sleep?" Eoin finally asked.

"Not tonight," replied Collins.

"You have to sleep."

"Not tonight. They can't be alone. I must keep watch."

"Well," said Eoin, "I'll keep watch with you."

Collins turned to Kavanagh. "Please yourself." Not another word was said between the two of them until sleep finally took them where they sat.

In the morning Eoin, felt the terror reach all the way to his groin—his Parnell retreated into its foreskin shelter, while his balls hid snugly inside him. He didn't dare stick his head out the front door of the cathedral into Marlborough Street, for fear of being seen by one of the G-men. As they prepared to wheel the caskets from the mortuary chapel

425

back into the cathedral for the funeral mass, Eoin pulled out his Webley and checked to see that it was in working order. If they tried to take Collins, he would be ready.

Eoin stood in the back of the church as the mass went on, keeping a lookout for any eager G-men or surviving Cairo Gang members hot for revenge. He was joined by Vinny Byrne and Paddy Daly of the Squad, which made him feel better.

At the end of the funeral mass, Collins got up and advanced on the coffins. Eoin saw him pin a note on the lead box, McKee's. Later he would learn that it read: "In memory of two good friends—Dick and Peadar—and two of Ireland's best soldiers."—Mícheál Ó Coileáin. They then wheeled the caskets down the aisle towards the front door. To Eoin's amazement, Collins hoisted McKee's coffin on his shoulder and started marching out of the cathedral.

Eoin leapt ahead of him and shoved his left hand inside his jacket, ready to pull his Webley out if necessary. Right in front, at the bottom of the cathedral steps, there was a brilliant flash and an explosion. At first Eoin thought someone had fired at Collins. But before he pulled his gun, Eoin saw that it was only a photographer from the *Evening Herald*. Eoin moved in his direction, but before he could collar him, the squirt dashed away, going full-blast, camera in hand, in the direction of Abbey Street. "Curse of God on ya," spat Eoin. He wanted to get the photo man, but Collins's safety was his first priority.

The crowd was packed around the cathedral gates. It was a dangerous situation. There were many of the locals from the Kips and Summerhill. This was great entertainment to them—a celebrity funeral. Eoin knew that somewhere in the crowd, hidden by the local Dicey Reillys, were G-men and touts. He was right. Shankers Ryan was hiding behind that stout one over there to the right.

Eoin pushed his back against the crowd, trying to hold them back. Paddy Daly was doing the same on the opposite side. Collins was front and center, his vision still blinded by the bright explosion of the photographer's flash. "BeJaysus, look," said one of the ould ones from the neighborhood, "there's Mick Collins!"

Collins jerked his head away from McKee's coffin, caught the woman's eye, and through the rictus that had become his mouth said, "You bloody bitch!"

He pushed the box into Fanagan's glass hearse, and, as soon as Clancy's body was placed in its own hearse, the procession began up Cathedral Street to Sackville Street, bound for the Republican Plot at Glasnevin Cemetery. Collins hopped in a car, and Eoin was right behind him. "What are you doing here?" Collins demanded.

"Keeping an eye on you, Commandant-General."

Collins almost smiled at his cheeky lieutenant, finally seeing some humor in this awful day. "Please yourself," he said.

125

After dinner at Batt O'Connor's house in Donnybrook, Collins and Eoin found themselves back in the city centre as darkness fell and bodies on the streets of Dublin became scarce. It was if the city were exhausted and numb from the events of the week. Only the insane were out on a night like this.

They walked in the front door of the Stag's Head, and Peadar Doherty jerked his head at them, indicating that they should head to the back room. As they passed him, he threw a copy of the *Evening Herald* at them.

"You take a lovely picture," said Doherty.

Collins looked at the photo of him carrying McKee's box and simply muttered, "Shite."

"I'm going to knee-cap that bastard the next time I run into him in Abbey Street," said Eoin, referring to the photographer.

Collins read the headline and then looked at Doherty. "A large Jameson for me, and a pint of porter here for my new bodyguard."

LAID TO REST

BURIAL OF PEADAR CLANCY
AND RICHARD MCKEE

IMPRESSIVE SCENES

The drinks were brought, and Doherty, his own Jameson in hand, joined them for a toast. "To Dick McKee and Peadar Clancy . . ." Collins began.

". . . And Conor Clune," Eoin interrupted.

". . . And Conor Clune," Collins agreed. "Three superb Fenians."

Eoin looked at the paper and asked, "What are we going to do about this picture?"

"A gang of the lads," replied Doherty, as he readjusted his white apron, revealing the outline of a revolver under it, "have already visited the *Evening Herald* and smashed the plates. Black Terry and the other newsboys are also going around, along with some Volunteers, rounding up any available copies."

"Black Terry," said Collins appreciatively, as he sipped his Jamey. Doherty went back to his bar, which had only a few customers in the snugs.

"I may never get over this week," said Eoin, before adding, "or my guilt from Mount Street."

"Forget your guilt about Mount Street," snapped Collins. "You acted as a soldier and did your duty."

"But I still feel guilty."

"By their destruction, the very air is made sweeter," Collins said testily. "That should be the future's judgment on this particular event. For myself, my conscience is clear. There is no crime in detecting and destroying in wartime the spy and the informer. They have destroyed without trial. I have paid them back in their own coin."

"You make it sound like it's over," said Eoin.

"It *is* over," replied Collins. "I know it's over. Lloyd George knows it's over. No one will admit it until next summer, but it's over. It will take that time to birth the new nation, but when we do, there will be an Irish nation until the end of time." Eoin gave a small laugh as he swiped the suds off his lip with his coat sleeve. "And what's so funny?"

"Dev will be back from America soon."

"How do you know?" asked Collins.

"Because it's over."

"My God," said Collins, "you have a twisted vision."

"I learned from the best."

"I," said Collins, finishing his whiskey, "am going to try and get a good night's sleep. You should do the same."

Eoin shook his head. "I still have work to do."

"What?"

"I'm going back to Fanagan's down the road."

"Why?"

"Because I have to take Clune down to the Broadstone Station in the morning for his train back to County Clare, and I don't think he should be alone tonight."

Kavanagh got up to leave. "Eoin, do you mind if I watch with you?"

"Please yourself, Commandant-General." And with that, the two rebels went out of the Stag's Head together, anxious to keep the hapless Conor Clune company on his last night in Dublin City.

1921

126

"He's either a liar or a fantasist."

"He's neither," replied Johnny to his wife. "He's telling the truth."

"He can't be," said Diane, "because that truth would be too gruesome."

"It's true," said Johnny. "It's all true." Diane Kavanagh was having trouble believing her beloved grandfather-in-law was the dedicated revolutionary of his diaries. "There was no shadow to this gunman," added her husband.

"I still can't believe it," said Diane. "What happens now?"

"It's the beginning of the modern Irish nation—an inchoate Irish nation, but nevertheless, an Irish nation. Unfortunately, it's also the beginning of the end for Michael Collins, I'm afraid."

"I hate to so readily admit this," said Diane, "but I do love Michael. He's so. . ." she paused, looking for the right word, ". . . romantic! I could see Errol Flynn playing him in a movie."

Johnny roared with laughter. "Errol Flynn! No way! I love Flynn, too, but he's too light to play Collins. All I can see in my mind's eye is Collins in green tights!"

"You know nothing about romance," protested Diane. "You're just a typical Irish donkey!"

"Don't be redundant," said Johnny. "But you're not unique—all women think Michael Collins was romantic. Remember what Mae West once said? 'Is that a gun in your pocket, or are you just happy to see me?'"

"In Michael Collins's case," said Diane impishly, "I think he had *both* things in his pocket!"

"Right you are. I think sometimes that he was the first Irish sex symbol of the twentieth century. Pierce Brosnan has nothing on the Irish James Bond. Neither does Liam Neeson. Michael Collins was the real thing."

"Especially when you compare him to de Valera," said Diane, "who was a sexual ascetic."

"'A sexual ascetic,'" laughed Johnny. "That's an interesting way of saying ould Dev didn't have any sex appeal."

"I know he had a lot of children, but God, he was so dreary-looking, almost asexual."

"Yeah," said Johnny, "I can just see Christmas dinner at the de Valeras now—'pass the potatoes to *it*.'"

"Eamon de Valera is so sexless," said Diane, "he makes Barry Fitzgerald look like Sean Connery!"

"Enough already!" said Johnny. "You're beginning to make me feel sorry for old Dev."

"Alright," conceded Diane, "but Michael and Grandpa did have an interesting relationship."

"Interesting is not the right word," said Johnny. "I would say their relationship was 'intense.'"

"Where are we now?" asked Diane. "What will be the repercussions from 1920?"

"It's a difficult time for Collins, which made it a difficult time for Grandpa. The shooting of the Secret Service had the desired effect. It's the most unique moment in the history of the Irish nation—and the way it's treated is very interesting."

"How so?"

"Well," said Johnny, "there's a sense of shame to it."

"Shame?"

"Maybe because Ireland was such a Catholic country. And it's still a Catholic country, although it seems no one goes to church anymore. This is something people have trouble discussing, even today. I think Bloody Sunday was viewed as murder—no matter how you dress it up— to most Irishmen. But Michael Collins was not Terence MacSwiney, who said, 'It is not those who inflict the most, but those that suffer the most, who will conquer.'"

"Those are the words of a victim," said Diane.

"Exactly," replied her husband. "And Mr. Collins was no victim. But his acts on Bloody Sunday had all kinds of ramifications that exist even to the present day in Irish history. You know Seán Lemass was involved in the shootings?"

"Of course, on Baggot Street."

"Right," said Johnny. "But he was once asked about what he did that day, and do you know what his response was? He said, 'Firing squads don't have reunions.'"

"What a great line!"

"I think Jack Lemass was protecting himself in two ways. One, he didn't think the *Taoiseach* of Ireland should be bragging about a shooting done more than forty years ago. And, two, being a de Valera man, it was good politics not to be associated with Dev's bête noire, Michael Collins."

"It's so strange," mused Diane, "that Lemass would shun the memory of Michael Collins."

"I don't think that's the case at all," Johnny disagreed. "As far as I can tell, Lemass and Collins did not have a close relationship. They were in the GPO in 1916, and Lemass was an assassin on Bloody Sunday. That's it. Lemass was basically drafted to do this shooting. The scope of Bloody Sunday was just too big for the Squad to handle. That's why Collins and McKee brought in men from the Dublin Brigade. So Lemass didn't really have an option in this. As a soldier, he had to follow orders. But, on the other hand, Lemass's loyalty was to de Valera, not the dead Collins. Dev treated Collins poorly, but he also treated Lemass shabbily. Because of Dev's ego, Lemass became *Taoiseach* probably ten years later than he should have. I think Seán Lemass is one of the top three Irishmen of the twentieth century."

"The stain of de Valera is everywhere!"

"Now that's a great way to put it," said Johnny, laughing. "What did Jack Nicholson say in *The Shining*? As he broke down the door? 'I'm hooome!'"

"Who's home?"

"De Valera's home. Just before Christmas 1920."

"Oh," said Diane, "poor Michael!"

"Poor Michael, indeed."

"How's it going to be?"

"It's going to be hell for Michael Collins—and for Grandpa, too."

127

With the arrest of Arthur Griffith in the aftermath of Bloody Sunday, Michael Collins became the Acting President of *Dáil Éireann*. Making a prophet out of Eoin, Eamon de Valera returned to Dublin two days before Christmas Day, 1920. Tom Cullen and Batt O'Connor met him at the boat. He was all business. "How are things going?" he asked.

"Great!" replied Cullen. "The Big Fellow is leading us, and everything is going marvelous."

"Big Fellow," spat de Valera. "We'll see who's the Big Fellow now!"

O'Connor duly reported the incident to Collins. "Jaysus, Batt, we're in for it now," replied Collins, seemingly placing the British on the back burner as he prepared to deal with the robust prodigal President, who had evolved from the humble *Príomh-Aire* of 1919.

Not too long after Bloody Sunday, rumors of peace feelers from 10 Downing Street began to circulate. They were only rumors, but Collins knew it wouldn't be long before the British came to their senses and started negotiating seriously. They were now in a war of attrition, and Collins was concerned because he knew his little army could not go on indefinitely. For the time being, he planned to keep up the pressure and hope for the best. He doubted the IRA could last out the year.

Although they met face-to-face many times on official government business, de Valera was not one to be confrontational with Collins. He liked his message to get through from others, and the fog of obfuscation was always his friend. His reading of Machiavelli hadn't gone to waste.

"Ye are going too fast," de Valera told a shocked Mulcahy. "This odd shooting of a policeman here and there is having a very bad effect, from the propaganda point of view, on us in America. What we want is one good battle about once a month, with about five hundred men on each side."

Mulcahy told Collins the story in front of Eoin at the Bachelors Walk office. Collins's face began to redden, and Eoin caught himself biting his lip. "That fookin' dilettante of a revolutionary!" shouted Collins. "Sitting on his royal arse for two years in the Waldorf-Fookin'-Astoria in New York City, while we risk our lives daily on the streets of Dublin. He has no concept of what has been happening here. Is he insane? Battle the British on equal ground?" Collins lowered his voice. "I guess he wants to wash his hands of my methods. Good ould Pontius Pilate de Valera!"

Eoin took the bite off his lip and solemnly said, "*Lavabo inter innocéntes manus meas.*" It was from the *lavabo* of the mass, when the priest cleanses his hands, saying "I wash my hands in innocence!"

Both Collin and Mulcahy burst out in laughter. "*innocence!*" my arse!" roared Collins. "Not our august President!"

"So, Mick," said Mulcahy, "I hear you might be making a trip to America soon." Mulcahy had a sly look on his long equine face. He was not known for his blazing wit, but he was testing how far he could stick the needle in Collins before the Big Fellow exploded.

"That Long Hoor won't get rid of me as easy as that!" said Collins defiantly. "Over Kitty Kiernan's knickers!" Eoin opened his eyes wide in shock. It was the first time he had heard Collins mention Miss Kiernan's knickers. Quickly, he realized that, with de Valera back in the country, Harry Boland wouldn't be far behind. This was no time to abandon the prize.

"So it's true?" returned Mulcahy.

"Yes, Dev broached the subject."

"Aren't you going to go?"

"I've come this far," said Collins, "and I plan to finish the job. I'm staying in Ireland."

With that, both Mulcahy and Collins got up and left Eoin alone in the office. Eoin walked to the window. It was getting dark now, and he watched the lights of the city reflect off the Liffey. "Pontius Pilate de Valera," Collins had called the President. *Only one thing is certain,* thought Eoin. *Someone is eventually going to be crucified*—and he knew it wasn't going to be President de Valera.

128

Dublin was still in the terror grip of the aftermath of Bloody Sunday when Collins gave the order to Tobin and Eoin: "Find out who informed on McKee and Clancy. Report back to me." Eoin immediately volunteered to handle the investigation personally, because of his great affection for Dick McKee, his commandant and friend. There were lots of rumors about who the snitch was, and all roads led to the sordid streets of Nighttown and its whorey inhabitants.

Dubliners are separated into two categories: Northsiders and Southsiders. And never the twain shall meet. Eoin was a proud Southsider, born on Camden Row, at the meeting of Wexford and Camden Streets. His parents both hailed from the neighborhood—his father from Lower Stephen's Street and his mother from Temple Lane, devoted parishioners of Saints Michael and John's on Wood Quay. He had to go back to his grandfather, Richard Conway, to find any Northside roots. For a few years, the family had moved away from the Dame Street area and lived on Upper Dorset Street, just north of Parnell Square. In fact, his mother had been born on Dorset Street in 1875.

Family legend had it that his maternal great-grandmother, Marianne Conway, lived and died on old Montgomery Street, which had given Nighttown, Dublin's Red Light district, one of its alternate nicknames, "Monto." Montgomery Street had been rechristened Foley Street, in the hope that a name-change would cleanse away its mortal sins of carnal delight. He couldn't help but wonder what his great-granny had been doing in the middle of Nighttown. Sometimes, he thought, it was better to let family secrets lie dormant, for tormenting them to life could lead to disturbing discoveries.

In reality, the line to McKee and Clancy's Castle tout was rather simple. It led from Vaughan's Hotel to Gloucester Street and ended back at Dublin Castle. Eoin met with Brendan Boynton and told him that the boss wanted the tout's name, pronto. The G-man reported back that the main snitch-man in Monto was Corporal John Ryan, known to one and all as "Shankers." From there, information about Ryan became blurred. He was a "corporal," but a corporal in whose employ? Did he serve the Dublin Metropolitan Police or the British Army, or was he just an eager freelancing spotter? No one really knew, and Shankers liked it that way. An interesting note on Ryan's resume was that his solid connection to Monto was through his sister, Becky Cooper, one of the legendary Madams, whose ladies had serviced the high-and-mighty and the low-and-downtrodden with equal enthusiasm these many years. Shankers had the stink of the neighborhood on him, and he was Eoin's prime suspect.

"I t'ink Ryan is your man," Eoin told Liam Tobin.

There was something in Eoin's voice that disturbed Tobin. "Something's bothering you. What is it?" Eoin mused for a minute before admitting that something about Ryan's CV troubled him. "It is odd," admitted Tobin, when Eoin laid out Ryan's background.

"You know, I wouldn't be surprised if he was deep undercover for the Dublin Metropolitan Police. A hidden G-man. So deep that even Boynton didn't know about him." Eoin finished.

"That's your job to find out," replied Tobin, with a smile.

"That's the other problem. How do you infiltrate Nighttown to get the goods on this guy?"

"Maybe you should go 'undercover?'" replied Tobin.

Liam was not known for his dazzling rapier wit, so Eoin continued on as if he hadn't heard him. "This is a closed neighborhood. Everyone knows everyone else, and there's only two reasons for being there—you either live there, or you're there on business."

"And what 'business' would that be?" asked Tobin, cheekily.

"The devil's business!" replied Eoin, with surety.

Tobin shook his head. "No, Eoin, *we're* in the devil's business. So is Ryan."

"It's just the neighborhood," said Eoin. "I don't know it, and I don't like it."

"We have lots of friends there," replied Tobin. "Some of the whores have been very good to us." Eoin shot Tobin a look. "What does it matter where a Webley comes from?" asked Tobin. "Out of the hand of a dead Tan, or out of the pocket of a drunken British Tommy getting his willie wonked?"

"You're right," Eoin finally admitted.

"You should talk to Deputy Shanahan," Tobin said. "He knows where all the bodies are buried in the Kips."

Eoin hit the pavement and was on Foley Street within fifteen minutes. Before entering Shanahan's Pub, he looked around. This had been his grandfather's neighborhood—and his great-granny's, too. Both had died before he was born, but he felt a close kinship to them because they had given life to his dear Mammy. No ghosts appeared for support, so Eoin decided to shun the January frost and find Phil Shanahan.

He hadn't been in the pub since his birthday the previous October, when he'd met up with Dan Breen and the friendly DMP. He asked for Shanahan, and the barman curtly asked, "And who might be asking?"

"A friend of Tipperary Dan."

The barman disappeared and returned a few moments later with Phil Shanahan, TD for Tipperary. "Eoin, lad," said Shanahan, "how are you?"

"Fine, Deputy Shanahan."

"Call me 'Phil.'"

"Fine, Phil. How's our bould Daniel?"

Shanahan put his left index finger to his lip and said, "Shush!" He looked around at the mostly empty bar. "He's recovering well—and well hidden! He thinks the world of the group that Dick McKee put together to save his life."

"This is about McKee," said Eoin. "Rather, it's about his murder." Shanahan's eyes grew wide. "He was murdered at the Castle, but the murder really started here, in this neighborhood. We t'ink a 'John Ryan' is the snitch."

Shanahan chuckled. "It wouldn't surprise me at all. The last time Shankers said 'No' to British blood money, he didn't understand the question."

"Does he come in here?"

"Oh, no," said Shanahan. "He's barred. I wouldn't allow a shite like that to come in here. If he entered that door right now, I'd shoot him dead," he added, patting his waist where his revolver rested.

"What's the word on the street around here?"

"Is this for Mick?"

Eoin nodded. "He wants the tout."

"I hear it's Shankers," confided Shanahan. "I hear he was shooting off his mouth around the corner at Hynes Pub, over on Gloucester Place."

"So you t'ink he's good for this?"

"He's your man," said Shanahan. "He lives with his wife at 15 Railway Street. He's a bastard." Shanahan paused for a minute, before adding, "Even if he didn't betray McKee and Clancy, he has it coming for some of the other stuff he's done. If you know what I mean."

"I know exactly what you mean," replied Eoin.

129

The day was bitterly cold, and Eoin was happy to learn that his evening intelligence briefing would take place at Dr. Gogarty's home. At 15 Ely Place, one could always depend on the good doctor's hospitality and that of his generous liquor cabinet. When Eoin arrived, Collins was already there, chomping down cakes and drinking sweet tea. Before he could ask, a hot toddy filled almost entirely with brandy was presented to Eoin.

Collins rubbed his cold hands together. "Alright, Eoin lad, let's get down to business." Gogarty got up to leave the room but was intercepted by Collins. "Oliver! Sit down, for fook's sake. If I can't trust you, who can I trust?" He turned to Eoin. "What's the news of the day?"

"Shankers Ryan is the news of the day," Eoin replied.

"That cunt," Collins said.

"Our boy at the Castle—and Phil Shanahan—says he's the one who snitched on McKee and Clancy."

"Well," said Collins, "he's got to go! Where's the best place, do you think?"

"In his comfort zone," replied Eoin. "Right in the middle of Nighttown."

"Work it out," commanded Collins, before adding, "Nighttown won't miss another hoor."

"Ah," said Dr. Gogarty, "the hoors of Nighttown. Reminds me of my misbegotten youth!"

"Do you know Becky Cooper?" asked Collins.

"I do, indeed," laughed Gogarty. "Intimately!"

"Well," interjected Eoin, "Shankers Ryan is the brother of Miss Becky."

"Go 'way!" said Gogarty, shaking his head. "Twenty years ago, she was something to look at. We had to fight off the British army to get to the hoors!" Gogarty was having a wonderful time remembering his sordid past. "What was the ditty from that time?

> *Italy's maids are fair to see*
> *And France's maids are willing,*
> *But less expensive, 'tis to me,*
> *Becky's for a shilling."*

That got a big laugh out of Collins and a major blush out of Eoin. Dr. Gogarty was delighted. "Speaking of whores," he said with a laugh, "Bernard Shaw just wrote me that he recently saw Churchill in London. They were at a dinner party, and he overheard Churchill say, 'Let the *Sinn Féiners* stop murdering and start arguing.'"

"There's been feelers," said Collins, "but nothing concrete—or should I say nothing *serious* yet." Collins rammed another cake into his mouth and washed it down with his sweet Irish tea. Collins had a penchant for cakes and sweets, and Eoin wondered if it was the sugar that was putting pounds on the Big Fellow.

The conversation was broken up by a terrible banging on the front door. All three men rose at once. The source of the noise was obvious—rifle butts being used as rams. "Quick!" said Gogarty. "Go into my surgery."

Gogarty watched Collins and Eoin disappear and then calmly went to answer the door, shooing away his maid. "What the hell!" he said, opening the door. "What's the meaning of this?"

"There are rebels in this house, and we want them," said the officer in charge.

"Rebels, my arse!" Gogarty shouted. "Lord French will hear about this. Do you know who I am?"

"Yes, sir," replied the officer, "and that's why we're here!"

"I see," replied Gogarty, a bit more calmly.

"We have orders to search the house. Who is here right now?"

"My servants, and I have a patient in my surgery."

"Show us to your surgery," the officer demanded, and he trailed Gogarty to his office in the back of the house. The door to the surgery burst open and Collins lay on the table, covered with a sheet. His eyes were covered by a cloth. Eoin stood by, dressed in white.

"This room is sterile!" said Gogarty, the foremost ear, nose and throat specialist in Ireland. "My patient is coming out of anesthesia. I just removed polyps from his throat. Advance no further. I don't want you infecting him."

Collins moaned appropriately, and the soldiers did not cross the threshold of the surgery. "Who's that?" demanded the officer.

"That my assistant, Eoin."

"He's awful young for a doctor."

"He's a medical student."

"Did you know Kevin Barry?" the soldier called out, but Eoin remained mute.

"He goes to Trinity," snapped Gogarty, "not University College, for God's sake. He's a fine Protestant lad from a fine Foxrock Protestant family. You soldiers are beginning to see rebels under every rock." There was a moment of silence. "Satisfied?" The officer stared for another moment before muttering under his breath. Then he turned and left, his soldiers right behind him. Gogarty followed them to the front door and closed it. "Jaysus, Mary, and Joseph," he muttered under his breath to his maid. "That was a close one!"

He went back to the surgery, where Collins was ebullient. "That was grand!"

"Oh, Mick," Eoin cried, white as his coat with fear. "You're killing me!" Gogarty saw that both Collins and Eoin had their guns in their hands, and he knew he had narrowly escaped a shootout. They followed Gogarty back to the parlor, and the good doctor poured three glasses of elixir—Jameson, neat. Eoin gave the toast: "God help us!" Gogarty and Collins erupted in laughter. The whiskeys disappeared in one drop, and Gogarty refilled them immediately. Eoin could see that Collins relished the danger of the situation.

"I hope you're wrong, Doctor."

"Wrong about what, Mick?"

"That we're all sterile here!"

"Have you ever heard a poem of mine called 'Ode to Welcome'?" asked Gogarty. Of course they hadn't, which gave Gogarty the opportunity to tell them about one of his great literary pranks. "I wrote it at the end of the Boer War, when all the Royal Dublin Fusiliers were returning to the city. The gist of the poem is, 'What does this *really* mean for Dublin?' So, without further ado, 'Ode to Welcome':

> *The Gallant Irish yeoman,*
> *Home from the war has come*
> *Each victory gained o'er foeman,*
> *Why should our bards be dumb?*
>
> *How shall we sing their praises*
> *Or glory in their deeds?*
> *Renowned their worth amazes,*
> *Empire their prowess needs.*
>
> *So to Old Ireland's hearts and homes*
> *We welcome now our own brave boys*
> *In cot and ball; 'neath lordly domes*
> *Love's heroes share once more our joys.*
>
> *Love is the Lord of all just now,*
> *Be he the husband, lover, son,*
> *Each dauntless soul recalls the vow*
> *By which not fame, but love was won.*
>
> *United now in fond embrace*
> *Salute with joy each well-loved face,*
> *Yeoman, in women's hearts you hold the place."*

"Not one of your best, Oliver," said Collins.

"Indeed," agreed Gogarty. "But it caused a scandal when it was published."

"Why?" asked Eoin.

"If you take the first letter of the first word of each line, you will know what the returning soldiers *really* mean to Dublin—THE WHORES

WILL BE BUSY!" Gogarty and Collins laughed, and Eoin realized he had learned more about whores in one hour with Gogarty and Collins than he had in his entire life.

"Yes," said Eoin absently. "The hoors will be busy." He wasn't thinking about the whores of Nighttown but of the British and Irish politicians looking to find their way out of this smoldering Irish morass.

130

EOIN'S DIARY

I *caught Mick daydreaming today.*

We were alone in the Mespil Road office, going over the National Loan books. I was banging away at the adding machine when I looked up and saw Mick staring off into space. I went back to the books.

"Have you ever been in love?" he suddenly asked.

"Only with *Cathleen Ní Houlihan,*" I said, cheekily.

"Oh, fook off," he said sharply, perhaps realizing that he had been caught in a dreamy state.

"I know nothing about women," I said. "You're eleven years older than me. You're the one who is supposed to know about the fairer sex."

Mick grunted. "There's nothing 'fair' about them." My guess is that he's having trouble with Kitty Kiernan or maybe with Harry Boland, who's just returned from America. Two into one won't go—at least not in Catholic Ireland. "I don't understand," Mick finally uttered.

"Understand what?"

"The women."

"You're not supposed to understand them," I said, slamming one of the ledger books closed. "Just like the Fenians, they're a secret society." Mick nodded. "Their biggest secret is their bodies. Róisín won't tell me anything. She just refers to her 'time of the month' and her 'cycle.' First time she talked about it, I thought she was talking about her bike."

Mick thought this was hilarious. "You don't know how lucky you are, Eoin," he said. "I wish I had your romantic problems. Róisín is the real thing." I didn't know what to make of that, so I just went about my business. I didn't want to pry. I put on my hat and coat and was about to leave when Mick said, "Where are you going now?"

"Back to Crow Street."

"We'll have our meeting at the Wicklow Hotel tonight. Seven p.m."

"See you then."

As I was about to go out the door, Mick called out. "Will you post a letter for me?"

I walked over the bridge into Lower Leeson Street and headed for the brilliant red postbox. I shouldn't have, but I looked at whom the letter was addressed to. It read: Kitty Kiernan, Grenville Arms, Granard, Co. Longford. I was about to pop it into the box when a tender filled with British soldiers came roaring across the Grand Canal, probably from the Beggar's Bush Barracks, and headed towards the city centre. I looked at the letter again and couldn't help but smile. The British and their £10,000 couldn't find Michael Collins, but Cupid and his little bow and arrow could.

131

Friday nights were Shankers Ryan's busy time. There was no rush to hit the streets, because the action really didn't get started until ten p.m. Shankers quietly had his tea served by his dutiful missus and then headed out to Hynes Pub for a few jars before he started working for the night. He had been hearing all the talk about the great Michael Collins and his notorious Squad, but here he was, more than two months after betraying McKee and Clancy, and nothing had happened to him. In fact, he felt that he was earning new respect in the neighborhood as he walked the soiled streets of Nighttown, for everyone knew that Shankers Ryan was the Brit's top spotter in the Kips.

After finishing his pint at Hynes, Ryan headed out to Sackville Street. Ten o'clock was the perfect time, because that's when the moving pictures and theatres let out and when folks started for home, getting their trams to beat the curfew. Shankers was on the prowl, looking for IRA men he could report to Dublin Castle and turn in for hard cash. A good tout could bring in up to £25 for a prominent rebel on a wanted poster. McKee and Clancy had brought him £250, but they were big fish. Tonight, he'd settle for small fry in the £1 to £5 range.

Shankers headed straight for Nelson's Pillar, right next to the GPO. Work was going slowly on the post office, but the Pillar still served as a terminus for many tram lines. Shankers examined faces as people began to queue up. He could strut and stare without hesitation, having no fear because, well, he was Shankers Ryan, the best British tout in Dublin City. What he didn't know was that Charlie Dalton and Joe Leonard were standing on the corner of Henry Street, taking Shankers's act all in. Tonight, he was the observed—and he was oblivious to that fact.

Shankers worked the street for two hours, but, as curfew came, he had found not one rebel. He turned tail and headed east back into Monto, like a rat into its hole. Usually, he might head over to his sister Becky Cooper's whorehouse for a nightcap, but, tonight, he didn't feel like it. He went home to his flat on Railway Street, slid into bed next to his snoring wife, and, within minutes, he was enjoying the sleep of the innocent. Dalton and Leonard watched the light go out in Shankers's bedroom and headed home, their work finished for the night.

"They say," said Eoin, "it gets easier after the first time."

"And what might that be?" asked Róisín, brushing her hair aside with a great flirt. Eoin could see she was in one of her teasing moods, but today he wanted none of it.

"Not *that*."

"Then what?"

"Murder."

Róisín suddenly felt guilty. She knew Eoin wasn't right. In fact, she hadn't seen him this way since the evening of Bloody Sunday. "I know, love."

"I hope this will be my last one."

"And I hope," said Róisín, "that this bloody war will be over soon, so we can lead normal lives."

"I hope I make it through."

"You will," she said. "Stop pacing. Come sit next to me," she added, patting the couch cushion next to her. Eoin did as he was told, and, as his bottom hit the sofa, Róisín took his hand. "I'll read about it in the papers tomorrow, won't I?"

"It will be there, alright. I can see it now: MURDER IN DUBLIN. I just hope you won't be reading my name in the story."

Róisín didn't say another word, but she did not let go of Eoin's hand. As a nurse, one who dealt with people when they were at their most vulnerable, she knew the importance of touch. Róisín knew there was nothing more important to one's spiritual, physical, and emotional health than the human touch. She knew that contact with another human being was the ultimate gift of friendship and love in its purest and simplest form. Soon, Eoin's head came to rest on Róisín's left shoulder, and his breathing became shallow, like he was going into a trance. There the two remained, wordless, for almost an hour. Róisín's touch had calmed Eoin, and, for a small time, he had been able to chase Shankers Ryan from his mind.

Eoin finally looked up at Róisín, and, when he did, she smiled that gorgeous smile of hers. Eoin noticed that, even in February, her nose was populated with fresh freckles. Her bright green eyes, born with a laugh in them, sparkled. She took his hand and put it to her mouth, giving it a long, solitary kiss. "A warm hand," she said, "can change your world!"

"I wouldn't be surprised," Eoin replied, with a newfound calm.

"Would you like something for your tea?"

"No, not tonight, my love. I have no appetite."

"Well," said Róisín, "will you come to bed with me?"

"No," Eoin replied, a bit regretfully. "I'll commandeer the sofa tonight. Very early start tomorrow. I don't want to disturb you."

"You're close to jeerin' me," said Róisín, lightly.

"You know what I mean."

Róisín nodded and kissed Eoin full on his lips. "I know exactly what you mean," she said, "but, tomorrow, there will be a command performance from you! There is no work for me at the Mater. It'll be *you* doing the work this time tomorrow!"

"Yes, ma'am," Eoin replied smartly, as Róisín headed for her bedroom. The slam of her door left him feeling lonely for a moment. But although Róisín was only in the next room, she quickly faded from his thoughts, replaced by the odious Shankers Ryan.

132

Saturday, February 5, 1921, dawned damp and miserable, and the Squad was on the make. They were going to make this kill quick and definitive. The shooting team would be made up of Eoin, Vinny Byrne, Paddy Daly, and Jim Slattery. A cover team of four would lend support.

Hynes Pub in Lower Gloucester Street was the destination. Shankers Ryan, the tag team had discovered, always needed a pick-me-up in the morning. Hardly a day went by when he couldn't be found gargling with a pint of porter first thing. Dalton and Leonard were back on station and reported the news to the Dump that Ryan had just marched into Hynes. At half-ten, two automobiles pulled up. The shooting team hit the street and pulled their guns as the cover team, in the second car, took their positions outside the pub.

Shankers had just taken his first taste of the day. He was putting his pint glass back down on the bar when the door burst open and the four men entered the room. He didn't even have time to turn around before Eoin stuck his Webley in the back of Ryan's head and commanded, "Hands on the bar!"

The barman had his mouth open and was about to warn Ryan when Paddy Daly hopped the bar and shoved a big Colt .45 into his gob. "Hit the deck," Paddy said, and the barman slammed onto the floor, flat as a pancake.

Vinny moved in and did a quick frisk, relieving Ryan of his Webley. "The Republic thanks ye," he told the chagrined Shankers.

Leo Flynn, Shankers's lone drinking crony this morning, felt the cold steel of Jim Slattery's gun at the back of his head. "Down," was the only command he was given, and he sunk to his knees like an altar boy at the offertory of the mass.

"John Ryan," said Daly, "you have been found guilty in the murders of Dick McKee and Peadar Clancy . . ."

"And Conor Clune," added Eoin.

". . . And Conor Clune," Daly continued. "Your sentence is death. Say your prayers."

Ryan cocked his head to the left, looked up at Daly, and gave a definitive, "Fuck you!"

They were to be the last two words of his life. Eoin shoved his Webley under Ryan's jaw and pulled the trigger. The bullet drove through his chin and exploded out of the top of his head, lodging in the ceiling. Ryan, his eyes still open, dropped to his knees, which made it easier for Daly to nail him with a shot to the left side of his head. Slattery came around and put one in the back of his head.

Slowly the three shooters started backing out of the bar. Vinny Byrne remained. "Now lads," he said to the barman and the lone customer, "just keep observin' that floor, and all will be well." Vinny was about to back out with the others when he decided he hadn't come all this way to do nothing. He went to the dead body of Shankers Ryan and saw that smoke was still coming out of his head from the three shots. "Jaysus," said Byrne with a laugh, "he should give up the faggots!" Vinny aimed his trust trusty Mauser, Peter, and blew the front of Ryan's face off with one shot.

Leo Flynn, only a few feet away from Ryan on the floor, felt the blood splatter on him. He thought he was next, and, out of the dark reaches of his brain, he managed to retrieve a prayer he hadn't uttered in donkey's years. "*Oh my God! I am heartily sorry for having offended Thee, and I detest all my sins, because I dread the loss of heaven and the pains of hell . . .*" Vinny, with a small laugh at the man on the floor imploring his Perfect Act of Contrition, backed out of Hynes Pub and joined his fellow shooters. "*I firmly resolve, with the help of Thy grace to confess my sins, to do penance, and to amend my life. Amen."* Leo Flynn looked up to find the room empty and discovered that, in his fear, he had peed himself.

The only thing that Eoin could think of in the car was that he was desperate to get the hell out of Monto. The cover team headed for the Northside, while Eoin's car raced for the quays and Butt Bridge. They crossed the Liffey, and Eoin jumped out at the corner of D'Olier Street, right across from the DMP stationhouse in Brunswick Street. He looked at his left hand, which was splattered with the blowback blood of Shankers Ryan. Against the wall of Trinity College, he took out his handkerchief and began wiping the blood off his shooting hand. He looked around cautiously, but no one was paying any attention to him. He put the handkerchief back in his pocket and thought about Shankers Ryan, with his final defiant, "Fuck you!" In the past Eoin had, in his own way, grieved for his victims, even the execrable Sebastian Blood. But Shankers was different. Maybe it did get easier the more you did it. But Shankers was now as dead as he would ever be, and Eoin felt absolutely no remorse.

All he could think about was Róisín and what she had said the night before: "A warm hand can change your world." Eoin waded through the Saturday morning shopping crowds, heading for Walworth Street, where Róisín O'Mahony and her healing hands were waiting for him.

133

MONDAY, MARCH 14, 1921

"This is fucking insanity!"

Eoin had had it, and he was giving Collins an earful in the Andrew Street office. "What's the purpose anymore? Nothing changes, and our lads are still being hanged by the British."

Collins only offered a feeble, "I know."

"Have you seen this morning's *Freeman's Journal?* SIX IRISHMEN DIE TODAY. That says it all. Thomas Whelan, 22. Patrick Moran, 26. Patrick Doyle, 29." Eoin could see Collins wince as he read off the roster of the condemned. "Bernard Ryan, 20. Thomas Bryan, 22. And Frank Flood, 19. Nineteen! He's even younger than I am, for Christ's sake! This has got to stop, and it's got to stop *now!*"

"Look, Eoin," said Collins quietly. "I did everything I could for those lads, but I couldn't get them out. We tried our backdoor channels, but the British are adamant about this."

"This country wants peace," Eoin insisted. "This country *deserves* peace. She has suffered enough."

"I know," Collins agreed. "Dev and Griffith are doing all they can with the British to get a truce."

But Eoin was having none of it. "They're not doing enough. Tomorrow, there will be six more men dead. They'll write songs about them and call them our 'heroes of renown'"—he stopped to laugh bitterly—"and for what? You told me it was over after Bloody Sunday, and yet we're still losing good men every day."

"It really is over," Collins said feebly, "but these things take time. Empires don't like being dismantled."

Eoin looked at Collins and did not speak immediately. "The problem with Ireland," he finally said, "is that we always say 'it's over.' But in Ireland, nothing is *ever* over."

Since the return of President de Valera to Ireland and the imprisonment of Arthur Griffith in Mountjoy Prison, Collins had learned the meaning of being a third wheel.

Before Dev had returned, there had been some movement in the truce negotiations. Archbishop Patrick J. Clune—ironically, Conor Clune's uncle—had come in from Perth, Australia, and had been shuffling back and forth between Dublin and London trying to find common ground. The Archbishop had reported to Collins that Lloyd George was "genuinely anxious" for peace, but Collins was not taken in and had no intention of letting up now that 10 Downing Street had been slapped awake by Bloody Sunday. Griffith—conveniently situated in Mountjoy, where the British could always find him—was the point man in the negotiations. Father Michael O'Flanagan, the vice-president of *Sinn Féin* (but without any portfolio), had also shot off to London, hat in hand, seeking out the Prime Minister. "Father Michael," remarked an annoyed Collins, "feels that nobody is able to handle things quite like he does himself." Collins's real fear was that the country would cave to Lloyd George and get terms short of what they deserved. Collins did not delude himself about the IRA's precarious situation, but this was not the time to buckle.

When de Valera returned, Collins was shunned to the back of the class by the grand marionette of deceit. Men like Austin Stack—the Minister for Home Affairs, designated by de Valera to be Acting President if anything should happen to Dev—and Cathal Brugha were getting all the attention from Ireland's President. Collins went about his business in finance and on his work with the Squad and the IRA throughout the country. Brugha, the titular Minister of Defence, came to Collins with his *one* idea. "I think we should assassinate the entire British cabinet."

"Cathal," said Collins, "didn't you come up with that idea about three years ago, during the Conscription Crisis? You've had three years. Think harder!"

"I may have to borrow some of your men," he persisted.

"You not getting any of *my* men," snapped Collins, "for *that* hare-brained idea. The Squad will not be compromised. We're finally getting some traction in London, and you want to destroy that? You're daft." Collins had made an enemy for the rest of his life.

De Valera was always worried about getting arrested, but he shouldn't have bothered. The British knew all about him and had no intention of detaining him. Right now, the British *needed* Eamon de Valera. Collins, however, was a different case. "Extremists must first be broken up," said Lloyd George, before truce negotiations could start in earnest. Collins had bested the British on Bloody Sunday, and their hatred—and fear—of him ran deep.

Collins had never seen Eoin this distressed, even after one of his shootings. "You're taking these hangings personally, aren't you?"

"You're damn right, I am."

"Why?"

"Do you know what they're hanging Thomas Whelan for?"

"Bloody Sunday."

"They are hanging him for the job *I* did!" Eoin exclaimed, gesticulating wildly from behind his desk. "I murdered Derek of Suez, not Tom Whelan."

Collins stood up from his desk and tugged his waistcoat down. "These things happen," he said. "They happened in the past, and they'll happen in the future. There's nothing we can do about them. That's why war is so random. We're lucky. Thomas Whelan isn't." Collins went to the front of his desk and sat down on its edge. "How long have we been together?"

Eoin looked up. "Five years next month."

"A long time."

"A full quarter of my life. T'ink about that. A long time, especially for a couple of rebels. We still *breathe*." Collins gave an appreciative laugh. "But this has got to stop."

"There will be a truce by summer," reassured Collins.

"Then the families of these lads," said Eoin, "will look back and want to know what their sons died for. On the day of the great truce, the lads in Mountjoy will get a reprieve. But there was no reprieve for these boys.

It makes no sense." Eoin paused, the events of the day weighing down on him. "Every day, I get up and say a Perfect Act of Contrition, just in case it's my last day. I'm no hero. I just want to make it right. I wish I could just throw this fucking gun of mine into the Liffey and be done with it forever."

"You will follow your orders," said Collins, with an edge to his voice.

"Yes, Commandant-General," snapped Eoin. "I haven't seen you pull any triggers lately."

Eoin was immediately sorry he had uttered the words, and he knew they had stuck in Collins's craw. There was a moment of silence before Collins spoke. "You're right," Collins admitted. "I wish I could be out with the Squad on every job, but I can't. That's not my job right now. I *hate* sending you guys out to do this terrible stuff, but there's no other way to do it."

"I'm sorry, Mick. I didn't mean that."

"Oh," said Collins, with a light laugh, "you meant it. And you're right to say it. The pressure on us in the last year has been incredible. Sometimes you have to let go." There was nothing but a heavy silence as Eoin got up and put on his coat. He then pulled his pocketwatch, Collins's Christmas gift, out by the fob and flicked open the lid.

"What time is it?" asked the Commandant-General.

"Too late for the Mountjoy lads. By now, they're all in Heaven."

"Where are you going?" quizzed Collins.

"Back to Crow Street."

Collins got up and put on his own coat. "Let's pay Peadar Doherty a visit before you hit Crow Street. Sometimes a drink is as good as a prayer."

"And sometimes," replied Eoin, "a drink is a prayer."

The two men walked out into Wicklow Street and headed for the Stag's Head, their love spat settled for the time being.

134

By April, Collins was in his full "bad cop" mode.

Eoin thought part of the reason was that the Big Fellow didn't like being number four on the Irish political totem pole, behind de Valera, Stack, and Brugha. Eoin knew Collins was smarter than the three of them put together, and that it was eating away at his boss. Any deference he may have had for de Valera was dropped. If Dev sounded conciliatory to Britain in the papers—playing his own version of the "good cop"—you could be sure that Collins would have a bloodthirsty retort in the same papers only days later.

Of course, this only served to further confuse the Prime Minister and his Minister for War. "We are getting an odious reputation," Churchill told Lloyd George.

"The question is whether I can see Michael Collins," the Prime Minister said, his olfactory system shut down years before. "No doubt he is the head and front of the movement. If I could see him, a settlement might be possible. The question is whether the British people would be willing for us to negotiate with the head of a band of murderers."

Lloyd George was clearly obsessed with Collins, and Collins couldn't resist teasing the Prime Minister. "Lloyd George," Collins said in a newspaper interview, "has a chance of showing himself to be a great statesman by recognizing the Irish Republic."

De Valera, with the help of Brugha, kept chipping away at Collins's power, casting doubt on his competence, even as Minister for Finance. Probably the ultimate insult was Brugha accusing him of misappropriating funds for buying ammunition in Scotland by redirecting it to his own family.

"That lying sonofabitch," Collins spat.

"Everyone knows," Eoin comforted, "that Cathal isn't the brightest bulb on the Bovril sign across from Trinity College." Collins grunted. "Don't dwell on it. You know the source. Or should I say, *sources.*"

"I don't know why the three of them are ganging up on me," Collins grumbled, showing how depressed he was over the whole thing.

"They are ganging up on you because you are dangerous to them," replied Eoin.

"To *them?*"

"Exactly."

"That's an interesting way to put it."

"It's the only way to put it," said Eoin, trying to put a little cheer into the downtrodden Big Fellow. "Besides," he added, "Dev found Brugha's charges to be 'groundless.'"

Collins laughed. "No one can pronounce charges 'groundless' like President de Valera," he observed, "and make them sound like a capital offense."

In all the years they had been together, Eoin had never seen this side of Collins before. It was obvious to Eoin that Collins had been hurt by the way he was treated by de Valera and his inner circle. And when he was hurt, Michael became either blustery or depressed. Years later, Eoin would realize that this was the bipolar side of Michael Collins. He would note that all great men—and women—had a little of the crazy in them, which separated them from the conforming majority and put them into the *sui generis* genius class.

Now Eoin sat looking across the room at Ireland's revolutionary genius, quietly doing his correspondence without enthusiasm or caustic comment, and wondered what it would take to get Michael Collins back where he belonged—leading, not following.

135

E oin and Collins were back at the Bachelors Walk office, working on Loan business, when Eoin suddenly said, "Have you read Yeats's poem about Easter 1916 yet? It just came out."

"No, I haven't," replied the Minister for Finance, tersely, without looking up from his ledger books. Collins wondered what was banging around in Eoin's young brain. Ireland was at the end of her rope, and all he wanted to do was talk about poetry.

"Pearse, Connolly, MacDonagh, and MacBride are mentioned in it," said Eoin earnestly, before pausing. "You're not." Collins leapt across the room and took Eoin to the floor in one fell swoop, his Webley flying out of his shoulder holster. "Jaysus, Mick, me gun!"

"Ya little bastard, ya!" Collins roared, as he pinned the lad to the floor with little effort. Eoin was too small to wrestle with. "You'll need a gun!" Collins was sitting on Eoin's chest, completely incapacitating him. "Do you know why I'm not in that poem?"

"No!"

"Because I'm still fookin' alive! Are ya ticklish?" Within seconds, he had Eoin howling.

"Uncle, uncle, uncle!" Eoin gasped, and Collins let him go, laughing himself as he tried to get his breath back.

"Speaking of uncles, how's your Uncle Charlie? Have you seen him lately? Is he still working at Guinness?" asked Collins, straightening his waistcoat.

"I had a drink with him a few weeks ago," answered Eoin, cautiously, reholstering his weapon.

"Does he have any more guns for me?"

"He's looking."

"He lives in Stoneybatter, right?"

"You know that," replied Eoin. "On Ben Edair Road."

"Near Aughrim Street?"

"You're in the right neighborhood."

"We could always use another safe house. Perfect cover, former British army. He married?"

"A widower. Auntie Margaret died of the influenza a few years ago."

"Perfect," said Collins, without emotion.

"That's cold."

"Do the right thing, Eoin, and *ask*."

"I will."

"As for Yeats, good God," said Collins. "Who put you up to that?"

"Róisín."

"I should have known."

"The Countess Markievicz is in it. And Róisín loves the Countess Markievicz!"

"Ah, Commandant Connie."

"'She rode to harriers,' Yeats wrote."

Collins laughed. "Harriers, my arse. Do you know why women ride horses?" Eoin shook his head. "Because it's the next best thing to ridin' a man!"

"You've a filthy mind."

"And I bet you can't wait to tell Róisín."

"Well," Eoin smiled. "I never did understand the attraction between women and horses—until now!"

"I'm gonna tell Róisín," the Commandant-General threatened.

"Don't you dare!"

"Did you know Yeats joined the IRB in London back in the last century?"

"Maybe you should call him to active duty!"

Collins roared at the inane thought. "Fookin' poets. I'm still cleaning up their mess."

"You shouldn't speak that way about Pearse and MacDonagh," said Eoin, earnestly.

"You forgot Joe Plunkett," replied Collins. "He liked to scribble, too."

"Yeah, poor Joe. I saw his widow, Grace Gifford, in Grafton Street the other day."

"How did she look?"

"Mournful. It's obvious she'll never recover."

"Don't get me wrong," continued Collins. "They were all good men, but they were not military men. The only men with a clue that week were Clarke, MacDiarmada, and Connolly. I'd march through hell for those three."

"Ah," said Eoin, "but the touch of the poet does add the romantic to the equation."

"You were there. There wasn't any romance in the GPO at all."

"Except me and Róisín."

"Ah, so it's finally 'me and Róisín' now, is it?"

"You know what I mean."

"Poets," mused Collins. "All poets are interested in only one thing—getting shagged!"

"Even Patrick Pearse?"

"Oh," said Collins, "for fook's sake, cut our first President some slack."

"But you said . . ."

"I say a lot of things. I don't know about poor Paddy and all that other stuff, but he was a good man, a brave man. A man who truly loved Ireland."

"But you said . . ." tried Eoin again.

"You know," replied Collins, "I bet that wall-eye of his must have had something to do with it. He was very self-conscious about it. Maybe that's why he was so shy with the girls. He didn't have many friends, maybe only MacDonagh and his brother Willie. He liked to give speeches, I'll say that. But there's a time to give speeches, and there's a time to make war. Sometimes I think Paddy confused the two. He was an odd duck. But he did his best. I feel sorry for him in a way. May God protect him."

Eoin couldn't get a word in edgewise. "But you said . . ."

Collins gave a low laugh. "My cynicism is having an adverse effect on you. You shouldn't believe everything I say."

"I don't—anymore."

Collins smiled—and, giving away his secret—replied, "I guess I've given birth to another 'terrible beauty.'"

136

"What we need," said President de Valera, "is some sort of big action in Dublin."

The President had gathered Collins, the phlegmatic Austin Stack, Cathal Brugha, and Oscar Traynor—another Dev man who had taken over the command of the Dublin Brigade from Dick McKee—at a safe house in Herbert Park. He was obsessed with his "big action," and he wanted it soon.

"We must bring worldwide public opinion to our side," the President said.

"It already is on our side," replied Collins. "We are David. The British are Goliath."

De Valera cleared his throat. "Exactly." He paused, as only Eamon de Valera could pause. "We must show the flag. We have to take on the Crown forces and show the world that we are capable of battling the British on equal ground."

"I don't think that is wise," said Collins.

De Valera remained silent. Brugha would do the President's lifting. "And why isn't it wise?" Brugha demanded.

"We are a small army," replied Collins. "We cannot afford big battles. If we have two big battles, we won't have an Irish Republican Army anymore."

"Nonsense," offered Stack. A wary Traynor remained silent.

Silence filled the room until the president spoke again. "We disagree."

"What do you have in mind?" Collins finally asked.

De Valera nodded at Brugha, and the blustery Minister for Defence took the floor. "I have planned out two areas of conflict. One, an attack on Beggar's Bush Barracks. And, alternately, the destruction of the Customs House."

"What do you mean 'destruction'?" asked Collins.

"Burn it to the ground."

Collins looked intently at Brugha. "Why?" he finally asked.

"Because it is the center of British administration in Ireland."

"But," challenged Collins, "how does that help us in this war?"

"It disrupts," replied Brugha.

"This country is so disrupted," shot back Collins, "that another disruption like this hardly makes any sense."

"Nevertheless," interrupted the president, "in the next fortnight, we shall settle on one of these two targets."

"We expect your help," added Brugha.

"Help?"

"The Squad could be of major help here," offered Brugha.

"There are other active service units," replied Collins.

"But yours . . ."

Collins cut Brugha off. ". . . Is the best?"

"They are efficient," said the president.

"They are the reason we're so close," snapped Collins.

"To what?" asked Stack.

"A fookin' truce," said Collins, rising from the table, his patience ebbing. "Let's stop fookin' around and get a truce done. It's going to come sooner or later. Let's make it sooner."

"Michael," said de Valera, drawing the name out. For a moment, Collins thought de Valera was going to criticize his language, but he didn't. "This big action will accelerate the truce negotiations."

Collins leaned forward and put his ten fingertips down on the table, his massive shoulders blocking out the light as he directed his words at the sitting president. "I hope you realize that we are almost done."

"Done?" asked the president, looking up. "What do you mean 'done'?"

"Done, as in finished," snapped Collins. "Our meager weapons have no ammunition. Our men are imprisoned. I am . . ." Collins stopped to correct himself, ". . . *we* are running this revolution on fumes. There's almost nothing left. Get the truce done—before we are done."

"You are expected to follow orders," shot Brugha.

Collins ignored Brugha and spoke directly to the president. "I know I am not the most popular man right now, but you're still my Chief. I may not like your orders, but I'll follow your commands to the letter." And, with that, the Minister for Finance turned and walked out of the room.

137

EOIN'S DIARY

I got an awful shock today.

Yesterday, Christy Harte up at Vaughan's Hotel rang to tell me that Uncle Charlie had been around looking for me. He told Christy he'd return today at five o'clock to see if he could catch me.

So I went up to Parnell Square this afternoon, and, as I was about to walk into Vaughan's, I turned left and saw Lord Nelson up on his Pillar, over the rooftops, keeping an eye on me from Sackville Street. Somehow, I took it as a bad omen. When I entered the lobby, there was Uncle Charlie waiting for me. What shocked me was that he had Frank sitting beside him. I shook Charlie's hand and gazed solemnly at Frank, who now looked like a young man, he had grown so much. I can be awkward in moments like this, and I didn't know what to say to Frank. "Aren't you happy to see me?" he asked.

"I don't know," I said, sorry that it had come out of my mouth. I have trouble lying, and that's one of my problems. Even in clumsy situations, I tend to say the truth. Sometimes I should just keep me gob shut. "Of course, I'm happy to see you," I finally blurted out. But my curiosity was on the march. "But what are you doing back in Dublin?"

Frank looked at the floor. "The rumor is there's some kind of big job coming up, and I was ordered to town." Frank looked up at me. "I hear you're a big shot now," he said, with a smile. "What the hell is going on?" I wanted to tell him nothing, either about my rank or the Customs House attack, which was planned for next week. "You still seeing that vixen from the canal? She's a nurse or something, right?"

"Róisín is not a vixen. A vixen is a fox. Róisín is a lady. Do you understand?"

"Yes," came the reluctant answer.

"You also ask too many fookin' questions for a Volunteer. Do you understand that?"

Frank gave a contrite nod and then asked, "Mary and Dickie still in the orphanages?" I nodded and wished there was an orphanage I could put Frank in.

The three of us stood facing each other, none of us speaking, when the door burst open and Mick unexpectedly came rushing through, his trilby pulled over his eyes. He stopped in front of us, turned to Christy, and nodded. "The three of yous," he said, gesturing with his attaché case, "upstairs!" We followed him up to the fourth floor. He stopped at the fire escape ladder opposite the door to his office. "If there's a raid," he said, gesturing, "up the ladder. Last man pulls the ladder with him." He opened his office door, and the three of us went in with him. "You must be Uncle Charlie," Mick said.

"I am," Charlie confirmed quietly. "And you must be the bold Michael Collins!"

Mick laughed. "I am. Your 'gifts' were most welcome!"

Mick turned to Frank, who stood stiff as he saluted. "General!"

Mick looked bemused, and I was embarrassed. "Frank," I began, but Mick would have none of it.

"Frank," he cut me off, "what are you doing back in town?"

"General," he stuttered, obviously shocked to be in Mick's presence, "I was ordered to town."

"Why?" Mick persisted.

"There's a big job coming up. That's all I've been told."

"Don't believe everything you hear, Frank," Collins said with a laugh. He then turned to Uncle Charlie. "Mr. Conway, I hear you served in the British Army during the Great War."

"I did, indeed," said Charlie. "In the Royal Field Artillery."

"Rank?"

"Corporal."

"The oldest corporal in the British army!" chided Mick to my uncle, who was twenty years older than him.

"Considering," Charlie replied, with a sly smile, "that I put twenty years in overall, I guess I was the oldest corporal in the field artillery."

"Twenty years!" said Collins, clearly interested. "Tell me about your service."

"There's not a lot to tell."

"There's twenty years," insisted Collins, and I could see that Mick had that look in his eye, like he had just stumbled on the Hope Diamond or something.

"Well," began Uncle Charlie, "I first joined the Royal Dublin Fusiliers reserves in 1885, the year my dear father died. We needed the money." This was all news to me, and I was fascinated to hear about my long-dead grandfather. "In 1888, I joined the regular British army, and they shipped me to India for seven years."

"What did you do in the army?" grilled Mick, as if this were an interrogation.

"I made saddles and was a horse handler," laughed Charlie.

"Ah," howled Mick, "a Jackeen horseman!" It wasn't that unusual, but it certainly wasn't the image I'd had of my Uncle Charlie.

"After India, I also fought in the Second Boer War before I came back to Dublin in 1902 and went to work for Guinness." I looked at Mick, and his eyes gave me a knowing look. The tales of Gogarty came to mind. Was Uncle Charlie one of Becky Cooper's clients back in 1902?

"Weren't you a little old for the Great War?" I asked.

"A wee bit," said Charlie. "My wife and your dear mother thought me daft, but I thought it was my duty to my country. I had to fight to get in. At first, they didn't want me."

"So you know what it takes to be a soldier," said Collins.

"I know too well," Charlie replied in a quiet voice.

"Where did you serve?"

"Gallipoli, and all over France."

"Gallipoli. Heavy lifting," said Collins. "Mister Churchill's adventure."

"Hernia heavy lifting," my Uncle Charlie said, dryly, before adding, "Churchill's adventure—our misfortune."

A knock came on the door. I pulled on the front of my jacket, revealing my Webley in its holster. "Yes?" I said.

"It's me, Christy."

I opened the door, and Christy had tea, cakes, and sandwiches. I closed my jacket but not before I caught the looks on Frank's and Charlie's faces. They were shocked that I was armed. The tray was placed on Collins's desk, and the tay was poured.

Collins, tea cup in hand, turned to Frank. "And what kind of soldier are you, Frank?"

Frank stood mute for a moment, before replying, "I hope I'm a soldier good enough and capable enough to die for Ireland!"

"Jaysus!" I spat. Uncle Charlie was obviously distressed at such fatalistic talk.

"Hush," snapped Collins in my direction. "I don't want any of my soldiers dying for Ireland," said Collins, pointing his index finger at Frank. "No one ever won a war by dying for his country, is that understood?"

"Yes, General," Frank said, meekly.

"Are you staying with Charlie up in Stoneybatter?"

"Yes, General."

"Is he giving you any trouble, Charlie?"

Charlie bit his lip before saying, "No, he's been a good lad." Charlie, like me, is a lousy liar. It must be a Conway trait.

"Well," said Collins, "if he gives you any problems while he's in town, let me know. I'll straighten it out." Frank was looking the most contrite I'd ever seen him. "So you're in town for the so-called 'big job,'" said Collins.

"I am, General."

"Well, remember, a good soldier should be seen and not heard. Is that understood?"

"Yes, General."

Mick turned to my uncle. "Charlie, I was talking with Eoin about asking you for a favor, soldier-to-soldier."

"Don't you mean general-to-corporal?"

Collins smiled. He was beginning to appreciate Charlie's ultra-dry sense of humor. "I always need 'safe' houses. You may have read in the papers recently how we lost two important offices, in Mespil Road and Mary Street. Would you be willing to help me out?"

"I might."

"Now," continued Collins calmly, "I know this must be a hard decision for you, being a member of the Dublin Fusiliers for these many years, but this is a very important time for Ireland." He paused to let it sink in to Charlie that he really needed his help. "Why did you give me those guns?"

"Because I don't like bullies," said Charlie. "That's why."

"I don't like bullies, either," said Mick, turning on that charming smile of his.

"Mr. Collins, I was willing to give my life for the Crown in two wars. I'm shocked at what they have done to my city. Half of it is rubble, and it's not safe to walk the streets without being searched by Auxies or Tans. I was regular British army. We were not thugs. I didn't fight in two wars to be a prisoner in my own city."

"We need the help of men like you," said Collins, and Uncle Charlie nodded his head.

"I was shocked when the Rebellion took place," Charlie whispered. "I didn't agree with the leaders, but they were men of conviction, and I admire that. I was a great admirer of John Redmond and the Irish Parliamentary Party."

"Good Jaysus," muttered Collins under his breath, trying not to reveal the full extent of his scorn for Redmond and his IPP.

"I was particularly upset over the hangings this past March," continued Charlie. "Especially young Whelan, who they say shot Derek of Suez. Everyone says he was innocent."

I cut in on Uncle Charlie. "He was."

Charlie had this look on his face, which prompted Collins to say, "Just take it as fact from someone who positively knows, Thomas Whelan had nothing to do with Bloody Sunday."

"So Thomas Whelan was a scapegoat," said Charlie, slowly.

"And there's no scapegoat," added Collins, "like a dead scapegoat."

Charlie looked at Collins, and another queer look crossed his face. "Hanged," he began. "I never liked that word. Pictures are hanged. It's such a refined word. So dainty. 'Hung' shows the necessary violence. In that word alone, you can hear the snap of the rope." Collins stared at Charlie, and Charlie stared back. "This is hard for me to comprehend," Charlie said at last. "These are not the fair English ideals I fought two wars for."

Collins got up from his chair and bent down over the sitting Charlie. "I hope you know that Ireland, not Britain, is now your country. Let that sink into your heart."

"You're right," Charlie agreed. "You can use my house anytime you need it."

"Thank you, Charlie Conway."

"Thank you, Commandant-General." Collins gave a loud laugh. "What's so funny?"

"It's nice being referred to as 'Commandant-General' by a member of your family who isn't jeerin' me!" I blushed and stared at the floor. Collins stood up. "It was lovely meeting the two of you," he announced, letting them know the impromptu meeting was over. "If you ever need anything, Charlie, let me know. You too, Frank."

"Yes, Commandant-General."

"Keep ya gob shut and follow your orders!" The two of them got up. We shook hands all around, and they left.

Mick sat down at his desk. "I like your Uncle Charlie. He's an honourable man. A straight shooter."

"My Mammy loved Uncle Charlie," I said. "She named my kid brother after him."

"As for Frank, he's a difficult child."

"He's a pain-in-the-arse," I replied.

"Ah," Mick exclaimed, "brotherly love!"

"Shite," says I. "Can you get him out of the Customs House job? He's not ready. He'll get killed."

"I can't do that, Eoin. Things have changed. I'm not running this thing. Dev and Brugha are. I have to be a good soldier. I have to do my part."

"And what part will that be?" I asked.

Collins gave a feeble smile. "I'm still trying to figure that out. They insist on using the Squad, and I don't want them compromised. It's insanity. Everyone in the Squad knows the inner workings of Crow Street. It's insanity to let any member of the Squad be exposed to or captured by the British. It would be a death knell to our whole intelligence operation."

"Well," says I, "why don't you put your foot down and say 'no'?"

"I can't. If I don't play along with this insanity, they will think I'm bucking them and the *Dáil*. I'm still figuring out what to do."

"A rock and a hard place," says I. "And you have only a week to figure it out."

"I don't know how to play this. I'm lost."

I was frightened. If Michael Collins was lost, so was Ireland.

138

WEDNESDAY, MAY 25, 1921

Michael Collins had personally sent out orders forbidding any
member of the intelligence staff from participating in the
Customs House operation. This put Eoin in an awkward
position, because he was the only member of Crow Street who also
worked with the Squad, albeit on a freelance basis. He took his case to
Paddy Daly, the Squad's leader.

Eoin knew the Squad would be assembling at the Dump, so he went
over to have a chat with Daly. "What are you doing here?" was the first
thing out of Daly's mouth when Eoin came in the door.

"I thought I was part of the operation," Eoin replied, as innocently
as he could.

"You know the orders," snapped Paddy.

"What orders?"

"Mick Collins's orders, backed up by Liam Tobin's orders—no one
from Crow Street is to be part of this caper."

"Can I come along?"

"Eoin," said Daly, "you're a great soldier, but do you know what
Collins and Tobin would do to me if you were captured? I'd be shot!"

"Oh," replied Eoin, "I don't t'ink it would be *that* bad."

Daly was forced to smile. "Against my better judgment, you can tag
along, but stick close to me. And, for God's sake, don't tell Mick!"

Well, at least Frank was safe enough, thought Eoin. He had kept after
Collins, and the Big Fellow had had a chat with Oscar Traynor about
Frank. It was decided that Frank would join the contingent that was to

guard the Tara Street Fire Brigade, making sure they did not leave their side of the Liffey and put out the fires in the Customs House. It was a simple holding operation, and much less dangerous than what would be going on just across the river.

The Squad left the Dump in twos and threes, covering each other as they made their way down Lower Abbey Street to the Customs House. They were to strike at exactly 12:45 p.m.

The Squad was to be nothing more than glorified concierges, covering the doors of the Customs House while members of the Second Battalion did the burning. They were to round up all personnel and visitors and keep them at bay. They would allow people into the building occasionally, so that no one would know what was going on until the place was actually on fire. Once the fires were started, they would shoo everyone in the building out and make their own escape.

It was a simple plan—and much too good to be true.

Eoin, Vinny, and Paddy Daly took the door on Beresford Place, opposite the bombed-out Liberty Hall, and, at once, Vinny was commandeered to go upstairs and help torch the place. Already things were going awry. Eoin was waving his Webley around to get people's attention and, happily, no one wanted to be a hero. Volunteers came in with cans of paraffin and rolls of cotton to start the blazes. Eoin stood by and detained individuals as they came through the door on their business. Eoin eyed his hostages warily and kept sniffing the air for smoke. "For Jaysus' sake, Vincie, hurry the fook up!" he muttered under his breath.

"Oh shite," Daly suddenly swore. Outside, a lorry full of Black and Tans stopped on Beresford Place. "Eoin," Daly shouted. "Come on. Get out!" He hated to leave Vinny, but, in this case, discretion was indeed the better part of valor. They put their guns away and casually walked out, looking as innocent as possible. The Tans were now standing in the lorry and getting ready to hit the pavement.

"Fuck this," said Daly, and he walked directly to the truck. He put his hand in his pocket, withdrew a hand grenade, pulled the pin, and dropped it into the back of the lorry. Then he took off at full speed, Eoin right behind him, and, as they approached Abbey Street, there was a terrific explosion that shot Tans into the air like acrobats.

Crowds were forming at the end of Lower Abbey Street, and Eoin and Daly blended into them, quickly making their way as far west as the Abbey Theatre. Then they made their way down Marlborough Street to the Pro-Cathedral and started moving back, advancing up Talbot Street towards Amiens Street Station. At Gardner Street, they turned right and came back down to the Customs House. Like the crowd in St. Peter's Square during a Papal Conclave, they looked eagerly for the white smoke, but were disappointed. "No *Habemus Papam!*" said Eoin, and even the dour Daly was forced to smile.

Inside the Customs House, on the second floor, Vinny Byrne was piling ledger books in the middle of the floor and pouring paraffin over them. He was supposed to wait for a whistle to start the fire. None was forthcoming, so Vinny reached into his pocket and withdrew a box of matches. A quick strike, and the place was an instant inferno. He scampered down the stairs and made his way to the Beresford Place exit. He was barely out the door when he was pulled aside by one of the Tans.

"What's your fucking business?"

"I'm a carpenter. I'm installing bookshelves here," Vinny replied.

The Tan slugged Vinny to the ground, and as he lay there, searched him for a gun, which Vinny had wisely left behind upstairs. "Get up," he commanded. "Stand over here."

"Yes, sir!" said Vinny, trying to sound contrite.

He was set in a line with other men. Tans, with hammers pulled back on their Webleys, looked for an excuse to murder someone. Soon an officer came to question each individually.

"What's your business here?"

"I'm a carpenter," Vinny repeated. "I was hired to build bookshelves."

"Prove it!" Vinny put his hand into his pocket and pulled out a sheet of paper with wood measurements on it. He also had a tape measure in his pocket. Vinny never left home without the two; it was part of his cover in case he got stopped. The Tan officer looked at Vinny's pink cherubic face, his ever-present Pioneer pin, and finally said, "Get going." Vinny started walking north towards Gardner Street and soon caught sight of Daly and Eoin.

"Jaysus, am I glad to see you lads!"

"You lucky sonofabitch," said Daly, and the three of them gave a huge laugh of relief. They looked at the smoke beginning to creep out of the second-floor windows and chimneys. There was no sign of the Tara Street Fire Brigade, and Eoin felt a certain amount of pride in his brother Frank. "Let's get the fuck out of here while the going's good," said Paddy Daly, and no one dissented.

139

"What a fucking fiasco!"

Three days later, the Customs House was still smoldering, but the smoke had cleared as far as Michael Collins was concerned. "Look at this," he said, waving a sheet of paper at Eoin and Liam Tobin, "eighty percent of the IRA taken! Six dead! More still in hospital. Well, Dev got his big battle, and I hope to fuck it didn't lose the war for us." They were sitting in the office at 3 Andrew Street, and the mood of the Director of Intelligence was most foul.

"What are you going to do about the Squad?" asked Tobin.

"Brugha wants to dismantle it," Collins snapped, "and consolidate the surviving members into a brand-new active service unit." Eoin didn't like the part about the "surviving members," so he decided, for the moment, to keep his gob shut, in case his part in the operation should leak out.

"What about Crow Street?" asked Tobin.

"You will continue as before," said Collins. "Eoin will brief me each evening. And continue to concentrate on our men of special interest."

The men of "special interest" were the contingent of British Secret Service agents that had inundated the country since Bloody Sunday. A lot had changed since that November day. Broy, finally compromised, was now on the run, and Boynton had, at Collins's suggestion, left the G-Division and joined the British Secret Service in hopes of gaining information. Bloody Sunday had been successful—the neutralization of the G-Division was complete—and now the big fish were in the Secret Service. A second Bloody Sunday was on Michael Collins's mind.

"Just how serious are you about these men?" asked Tobin.

"Very serious," replied Collins.

"There's a lot of them," interjected Eoin. "Maybe over sixty prime suspects."

Collins shook his head. "That's a lot. We lost a hundred soldiers in the Customs House." He stood and slammed his hand on the desk. "We're fooked. Fooked good." The frustrated Collins headed for the door and then turned swiftly and barked at Eoin, "How's Frank?"

"He did his job," said Eoin, with a little smile of satisfaction on his face.

"So he followed his orders for once?"

"Yes, he did," said Eoin proudly.

Collins stared hard at his young protégé. "Unlike some others I've heard about."

And with that, the omniscient Director of Intelligence was out the door, leaving Eoin Kavanagh with his gob dragging like an eejit in heat.

140

SATURDAY, JULY 9, 1921

Eoin was working at the Bachelors Walk office when he was interrupted by a terrific banging on the door. On instinct, he stood and drew his revolver.

"Open up!" demanded the female voice. "Eoin, Eoin, open the door!" Eoin pulled the door open, expecting the worst, and there stood Róisín, waving that evening's newspaper. "Look!" she said. The headline said it all.

TRUCE.

Eoin pulled the paper out of her hand and read the article. "It's official," she said. "By July eleventh. Two fookin' days. Imagine that!"

"I wonder what this will mean for Ireland?" said Eoin. "I wonder what this will mean for Mick?"

"Fook Mick. Fook Ireland," said Róisín, as she undid the top button on her nurse's uniform. She had other things on her mind.

The King had had it.

Negotiations had been going nowhere. Lloyd George was demanding impossible pre-conditions to truce talks—such as the disarming of the IRA—deliberate non-starters on the Prime Minister's part. He grew more stubborn with the burning of the Customs House, thinking that maybe the advice he was getting from the military about the diminishing capacity of the IRA was, perhaps, fallacious. De Valera's military fiasco had been misinterpreted in Downing Street. Weakness had become power. The status quo in Ireland would continue for the remainder of the summer, if not the rest of 1921. Things were hopelessly stalemated.

King George V was scheduled to open the new Northern Ireland parliament in Belfast on June tweny-second. He was tired of the black eye the Black and Tans had been giving Britain in the world press. He had told his prime minister he was not happy with the endless war in Ireland, and that something had to be done. In desperation, the King secretly collaborated with his friend, General Jan Smuts of South Africa, and the Prime Minister on some proposals. Lloyd George presented them anonymously to his cabinet, which reluctantly approved them.

With that endorsement, George V, in his Belfast speech, called on "All Irishmen to pause, to stretch out the hand of forbearance and concili-ation, to forgive and to forget, and to join in making for the land they love a new era of peace, contentment, and good will." Two days later, Lloyd George approached de Valera—who had been, in one of the great screw-ups of Anglo-Irish history, bizarrely arrested and then released—as "the chosen leader of the great majority in Southern Ireland," and a truce was soon in place.

"I never thought," Collins said, "that the Irish would have to depend on the fookin' King of England to get this truce business moving." He also added that he wasn't so sure about the "forgiving and forgetting part."

Eoin looked out the window, the summer sun still high in the sky even at eight p.m. From the quay below and nearby O'Connell Bridge, a buzz was rising around the city. A Guinness barge on the Liffey gave a joyful toot of its whistle in celebration of the coming truce. Across the river, he could hear the historic bells of his parents' church, Saints Michael and John's, chiming in jubilation.

"Poor Traynor, Maher, and Foley," he said.

"What?"

"Traynor, Maher, and Foley," repeated Eoin. "The last three lads hanged in Mountjoy for nothing. Nothing can bring them back."

"You're right," said Róisín. "Nothing can bring them back." She turned and closed the door, slamming the bolt hard.

At the bang of the bolt, Eoin turned around to see Róisín throwing her nurse's uniform onto Eoin's desk chair. "What are you doing?"

"I'm celebrating," she said, as she dropped her brassiere and slid her bloomers over her hips and onto the floor. "Take that fucker off," she said, and the Webley and its holster landed on the floor by the window. She undid his belt, and his trousers also dropped to the floor. She yanked his drawers to his knees and pushed him onto the couch. All Eoin was wearing was his shoes, socks, shirt, tie, and waistcoat—and an enormous erection. Róisín leapt on top of him and took him inside her. "My God," she said, throwing her arms around his shoulders and back and squeezing hard.

"A truce!" proclaimed Eoin.

"Yes," repeated Róisín, "a fookin' truce." She kissed him hard on the lips as she continued to ride him. It was joyous, uninhibited sex. "Fook the lot of them," repeated Róisín. "And their fookin' truce, save two—us!"

It had been a long time coming, and for this selfish moment in time, nothing else in Ireland existed except Róisín O'Mahony, Eoin Kavanagh, and their passionate love for each other.

141

"That wily old sonofabitch," said Johnny, laughing.

"What?" asked Diane.

"He's on his way to New York!"

"Of course he is. What's the big deal?"

"He's on his way to New York in 1921—not 1922—on a top-secret mission for Collins." Johnny was arranging Eoin's diaries in front of him on the dining room table. They held a big secret—one that Eoin would reveal only after death—but also some disturbing news about the relationship between Róisín and Eoin. "Róisín is going with him."

"Of course, she is," seconded Diane.

"Di, my love, this is 1921, not 2006," said Johnny. "Single women—spinsters as they were called then—and bachelors did not travel together."

"Spinsters," huffed Diane indignantly. "Did it stop Róisín?"

"Of course not."

"Ah, the lovely scandal!"

"Listen to this," said Johnny. "From Eoin's diary, dated July 29, 1921:"

Collins called me to the Mansion House, where there were meetings going on. He was brusque and seemed agitated. "You're going to America," he told me straight on. I asked him why. He said he wanted me to audit the books for the National Loan in New York. We had found discrepancies, and, as Minister for Finance, he wanted answers. I asked him why he didn't go to New York himself. "And leave Ireland at this junction of history? Are you daft?"

He told me that John Devoy would be my contact, and I immediately smelt a rat. Devoy hates de Valera, so I knew what was going on. "So I'm to get the goods on Dev?" I said. Mick grunted and said it shouldn't take me more than a month or so. I said, "What about Róisín?"

"What about Róisín?" he repeated.

"She wants to go on a long holiday. I guess America would fit that bill." Mick frowned at me. "Alright, she can go—but keep this to yourself." I asked who's paying, and Mick said, "The Minister for Finance."

"This sounds like quite an adventure for such a young Irish couple," said Diane.

"It was an adventure," admitted Johnny. "Imagine coming out of a little town like Dublin and going to the noise and excitement of the Big Apple." Johnny moved a few pages around before saying, "There are some terrific vignettes of New York City in 1921. Here's the arrival:"

We're roastin'! We arrived at the Cunard Line's Pier 54 at the foot of 14th Street in the Greenwich Village section of the city. It was 97 degrees and I was wearing long johns! I've never felt heat like this before, and I don't know how'll we're survive it. "It's the fookin' tropics," was all Róisín could muster. Aside from the heat, it felt like home, as all the dock workers are Irish and have the map of Eire on their faces. We disembarked from the Aquitania and were met by Devoy, who is terribly old. "I am delighted," said Mister Devoy, "to meet someone who works for Ireland's fighting Chief." Róisín looked at me and nodded. Mr. Devoy can't resist getting a dig in at the president at the first opportunity. In fact, he won't even refer to Dev by name; he just calls him "The Visitor," like some at home refer to the British as "The Stranger."

He took us to a flat on Barrow Street in the Greenwich Village neighborhood, which he keeps for visitors. I soon discovered that Devoy is as deaf as a haddock—and the squint of his eye told me he didn't see very well, either. Pretty soon I was shouting at the top of my lungs at him. I told him that Mick had sent us to go over the National Loan books, that Mick wanted an accounting. Devoy told us to come down to his office at the Gaelic American newspaper, which he runs.

He then handed us over to a young IRB man named Rory Holland, who is to be our escort around New York. "What can I show you?" asked Rory, who is from County Mayo.

"How about the inside of a public house?" shot Róisín, drenched with sweat. Rory laughed. "What's the joke?" demanded Róisín.

"Prohibition is the joke." Rory explained that they had just passed a law that made it illegal to drink.

"You're jokin'!" exclaimed Róisín.

"Remember, they've got more fookin' sour Protestants in this country," decreed Rory, "than in the whole of fookin' Belfast."

"At least the Orangemen like to drink," said Róisín.

"American Protestants have a starched Puritan strain," explained Rory.

"So we're dry?" I said.

"Not at 'tal," said Rory. "We new Americans think on our feet. There's a grand new invention—the speakeasy!"

He took us just down the street, to a little courtyard on the corner of Bedford and Barrow Streets, and knocked on the door. A little peephole opened, and then slammed shut. Then the door slowly opened. "Welcome to Chumley's," said Rory, and we spent the rest of the afternoon sippin' cold draught beer in the lovely new, cool American invention called the speakeasy.

"Remember in the 1970s, when I used to romance you at Chumley's?" Johnny asked.

"Yeah," replied Diane, "you didn't want some of your drinking buddies at the Lion's Head sniffin' around me."

"You were too good for that place. I wanted to keep your knickers pristine!"

"You were jealous."

"That, too," said Johnny, with a small chuckle. "Remember we used to double-date?"

"Yes," said Diane, "with Kevin Griffin—that big handsome Marine—and his Polish girlfriend, the actress."

"Cindy," clarified Johnny. "Cindy had a great ass!"

"You big moron!" roared Diane, swinging a damp dishtowel in Johnny's direction. "What were you looking at Cindy's ass for?"

"Because that's what men do!"

"Yeah, that's what men do—drink beer, watch baseball, and look at women's buttocks!"

"As American as apple pie."

"But," admonished Diane, "you were thinking of cherry pie."

"By the time I got to you, the cherry was long gone!"

"Incorrigible!" shouted his wife, as she dropped the towel around his neck and swiftly torqued it into a giant hug. "Just like your grandfather," she added, with a kiss on the top of his head.

"I wonder if they ran into Edna St. Vincent Millay?" Johnny pondered.

"Maybe," said Diane. "She lived right across Bedford Street during that period and drank at Chumley's."

"She would fit right into Róisín's world," added Johnny. "The kind of woman who thought like Róisín."

"So," said Diane, "how was Eoin's accounting work going?"

"In the inevitable direction," said Johnny, reaching for another of Eoin's notebooks.

We took the Ninth Avenue elevated train down to Devoy's office at the Gaelic American, getting on at the Christopher Street station, right next to St. Veronica's Church near Greenwich Street. I must admit I love the El, as the locals call it. You can look in windows at people and down to the docks and see the big liners coming in. And, as we got closer to the downtown area, we had a great view of the Woolworth Building, the tallest building in the world. We got off at the Warren Street station, and Rory left us with Devoy.

Mr. Devoy gave Róisín and me a desk, and he sat down with us. "Young lady," he said to Róisín, "do you work for General Collins?"

I thought we were in a real fix, but the question didn't faze your woman an ounce. "Yes, I do," she replied. "I am a member of Cuman na mBan, *and I met Mick in the GPO in 1916. Since that time I've been one of his agents, mostly working out of the Mater Hospital. I helped hide Dan Breen!"*

The old man's eyes brightened, and a slight blush came over his pale features, as if he were touched by Róisín's magic. "You are a true patriot, ma'am." With talk like that, he reminded me of an octogenarian Vinny Byrne! "So you'll be helping Eoin with this accounting?"

"On the orders of General Collins himself!" Róisín yelled out, loud and clear so Devoy could hear her, and I felt relieved.

Devoy brought over a small box, and it was filled with bank books. "This," he said, "is the National Loan money—in accounts all over the United

States." He explained that they had solicited $10 million and succeeded in collecting $5 million. As far as he knew, there was now less than $4 million in the accounts.

"Where's the missing million?"

"The Visitor spent it last year trying to convince the Republicans and Democrats to recognize the new Irish Republic."

"So we're short," I said.

"We are, indeed," said a resigned Devoy. "The spending of the money," he continued, "ought to have been available for military supplies and not in the work of disorganization here." He paused. "But the Visitor disagreed with me."

"How about Dev's expenses while he was here in America?" Devoy went into his office and returned with a folder of papers. He handed them to me, and I saw they were from some of the hotels that the president was so fond of. "Do you have an adding machine?" I added the pile up, and it came to $26,748.26—even more than I ever imagined—which I then announced to Devoy and Róisín.

"Jesus Christ," was all the old man could muster. Róisín's mouth remained open in astonishment. I locked the bank books and the bills in the desk drawer and told Mister Devoy we had other business to do.

"Won't you get lost without Rory?"

"We're Dubliners," I said proudly. "We can find our way around any city!" And, with that, we left Mr. Devoy and headed over to the Woolworth Building to do a wee bit of sightseeing.

"Twenty-six thousand dollars doesn't seem like that much," said Diane.

"In today's money, it would probably be close to half a million dollars! That's a lot of dough for hotels over an eighteen-month period. The president was living high on the hog. Remember, a subway ride in 1921 cost a nickel. And that's why Collins was so upset. He's sleeping in a different bed every night—as Eoin was—and de Valera is gallivanting around America like it's *his* money."

"What is all the mystery over the National Loan, anyway?" said Diane. "Collins is seemingly obsessed with it."

"The National Loan caused Collins more grief than any other part of the revolution—and that's saying something! Remember, without the

National Loan, there is no revolution. $5 million doesn't sound like a lot, but in today's money, that would be $55 million. That's a lot of Mausers, Lugers and Webleys, not to mention Thompson submachine guns. Even in insurrection, the piper must be paid!"

"I know," said Diane, "but this seems so unimportant eighty-five years later."

"*Au contraire*, my lovely. The National Loan money is the key to de Valera's hold on the Irish people for more than half a century."

"But how could that be?" asked Diane.

"It complicated," began Johnny. "The National Loan, the way it was set up in the United States, to meet legal standards, was basically a gift to the *de jure* government of Ireland. The 'investors' were promised interest if there was an actual country called Ireland someday. But for the moment, it was an investment in good faith in the future of Ireland."

"So how did this affect de Valera?"

"Well, after Collins was killed, Dev outfoxed President Cosgrave's Free State government in 1927 and managed to get his hands on a great portion of the American loan. At that point, he managed to persuade investors to sign over their donation certificates to guess who?"

"Who?"

"Eamon de Valera!"

"You're kidding!"

"No, I'm not," said Johnny, laughing. "Somehow the money of the Republic ended up in his pocket. He wasn't even serving in government at the time."

"So how did that alter the political landscape in Ireland for the next half-century?"

"He started his own newspaper called the *Irish Press*. It was kind of his version of Fox News—fair and balanced in favor of Eamon de Valera!"

"This is just unbelievable," said Diane.

"I'm sure Collins could smell it," said Johnny. "That's why he obsessed over the money. That's why Eoin is in New York. He just didn't trust Dev—especially when there was money lying around in banks more than three thousand miles from Ireland. When Eoin gets to New York, there is already over a million bucks missing from the amount collected. Where did it go? Hotels? Travel expenses? Lobbying? Who knows? If the National Loan was a charity, they'd close it down as non-functioning."

"What a conniver de Valera was."

"Oh, by the way," added Johnny, "did I tell you that Eoin loved baseball?"

Rory, Róisín, and I hopped on the Ninth Avenue El and headed for the Polo Grounds, where the New York Giants play a game called baseball. Mister Devoy was supposed to come with us, but he's not feeling well. It's so much fun riding through the various neighborhoods of New York. The west side of Manhattan, on the North River, is predominantly Irish, with many of the men working the docks. As we went uptown, we passed through the Village, Chelsea—where the White Star Line piers are—and on into Hell's Kitchen, the most frightening-named neighborhood I've ever heard of. We turned east and headed over to the Polo Grounds at 155th Street and the Harlem River. There are lots of Negroes in this neighborhood, and Rory told us it was the African capital of the world. We got off at the 155th Street station, and Rory said, "Welcome to Coogan's Bluff!"

I know the Polo Grounds because President de Valera gave a speech there just about the time Terence MacSwiney and Kevin Barry were murdered. It's a very big park with a middle field that is endless. We had seats right down next to the Giants' bench. The Giants have a big following of Irish, because their coach is a man named John J. McGraw, who everyone calls Mr. McGraw. I'm told Devoy and McGraw are friends, and these tickets are a gift from Mr. McGraw. McGraw stuck his head out of the bench—which they call a dugout here—and, when he saw Rory, he came out and greeted us. "Where's Mr. Devoy?" he asked. He was told that Devoy was under the weather. "Well, who are your friends?" Rory introduced Róisín and me, and, when Mr. McGraw heard our brogues, he quickly said, "Will the truce hold?"

"I hope so," I said.

"It'd better," added Róisín.

McGraw laughed at that and replied, "I don't know what you do in Ireland, but if you're friends of John Devoy, I know your work is important. Enjoy the game!"

We watched the game in the terrific heat, and, by the end of the first go-around, called an inning, I thought we'd die out there, it was so hot. A head popped out of the dugout, and three bottles wrapped in brown paper bags were handed to us by one of the players. "Thanks, Casey," said Rory, and the player gave us a big wink and disappeared. "That's Casey Stengel, a backup outfielder. Good guy. Mother Irish, father German." The bottles contained beer. I'm already beginning to like this American game, which reminds me of hurling so much. They use a bat, which is very much like a hurley stick, and a ball that looks like a hurley sliotar, *but with the seams sewn neat. Lots of Irish on the Giants. There's Rosy Ryan, Red Shea, George Kelly, Bill Cunningham, and even a fellow named Irish Meusel, who's not Irish at all. The sun, the beer, the smell of the grass, plus a Giants win over the Boston Braves makes me want to see more baseball.*

"Look at this," said Johnny, handing a yellowed Western Union Telegram to Diane.

CAPTAIN EOIN KAVANAGH

48 BARROW STREET

NEW YORK CITY

U.S.A.

RETURN AT ONCE TO DUBLIN.

I NEED YOU.

M.C.

"What does it mean?" asked Diane.
"It means he's going to London, but, first, there's a problem."
"With what?"
"With Róisín."
"Róisín?"
"Yes," said Johnny, "there was a spat when he told her he had been ordered back to Dublin."
"What happened?"
"She didn't want to go."
"Oh, my God," said Diane.
"Listen to Eoin's version:"

When Collins's telegram came, I told Róisín about it, and she immediately declared: "I'm not going back to Ireland." I was speechless, I was so shocked. "You have to come back," I finally muttered.

"I don't ever have to do anything," she snapped at me.

"What will you do here?" I asked.

"I visited St. Vincent's Hospital the other day," she said. "I'm a nurse in Dublin. I don't see why I can't be a nurse in New York."

"Do you want me to make an honest woman out of you?" It was my awkward attempt at a marriage proposal. As soon as it came out of my mouth, I knew I had said the wrong thing, because she went crazy.

"Honest!" she screamed. "I am an honest woman, and I don't need your help in anything—is that understood?"

"I didn't mean it that way," I told her, but that only got her hotter.

"Don't ever patronize me again!" she barked.

I put my tail between my legs and said I wouldn't—even though I don't know what "patronize" means. I'm a dunce.

"Oh," said Diane, "this is so sad." Then she gave Johnny a big smile. "But I know there has to be reconciliation."

"There was," replied Johnny, "that night."

I was sleeping on the couch when Róisín gave me a poke with her foot. She was standing above me naked. She took my hand and brought me to her bed. "I'm so hot," she said.

"Me, too," I replied.

"Not that kind of hot."

"Oh," says I.

We made love for hours.

"I'm coming home with you," she finally said. She could see the joy—and relief—in my eyes. "On one condition—we come back to America when all this truce business is over. I love this place. I was made for this city. I've had enough of Dublin, the Church, petty politicians, and that awful Irish weather."

"I thought you thought it was too hot here?"

"I'm getting used to it," she said, giving me that dazzling smile of hers. I think we're in love again.

"Well," said Diane, "I guess all's well that ends well."

"You have any other clichés you want to throw at me today?"

"Oh," Diane replied, with a drip of her own sarcasm, "how would the great writer handle this?"

Johnny laughed. "Not very well—as you may have noticed."

"So the American holiday is over."

"They did the work they had to do on the Loan," said Johnny. "But their last meeting with Devoy was disturbing to Eoin. Listen."

I looked at the newspaper on Devoy's desk. There was a picture of Eamon de Valera leading Arthur Griffith down a London Street on their way to a meeting with the British Prime Minister. "At least there's hope," says I.

Devoy squinted down at the photo. "Look at him leading Griffith along like a Judas Goat." Devoy allowed himself a laugh. "It won't be long before he has Collins in lockstep behind him, leading him to the abattoir as well."

"You really don't mean that, do you, Mister Devoy?" I couldn't believe he could really think such a thing. Devoy looked at me with that squint of his and said, "De Valera is the most malignant man in all Irish history."

"Judas Goat," laughed Diane. "I haven't heard that term in years."

"Leading the sheep to slaughter."

"Somehow I don't see Michael Collins as a sheep."

Johnny grunted. "Sometimes you have to play 'follow the leader' in politics. De Valera is the leader. He won't go to London to negotiate the treaty."

"That's a dereliction of duty," said Diane.

"Yeah," Johnny agreed, "for the *second* time in two years." He drew a breath. "He will poke and connive, and Griffith and Collins will follow their Chief's orders and trot off to London."

"Like lambs to the slaughter?"

"Dev was hoping for the 'Silence of the Lambs,' but, again, he underestimated Michael Collins—and our grandfather."

"An enormous, selfless accomplishment," added Diane, "that de Valera should have embraced."

"But he couldn't," said Johnny.

"Why?"

"Because it was the work of Michael Collins—and not the great de Valera."

142

The R.M.S. *Olympic*, the *Titanic's* sister ship, arrived at Queenstown, County Cork, at dawn on October 5. After disembarking, Eoin and Róisín took the train to Dublin and arrived by midafternoon. Eoin took Róisín and the suitcases to Walworth Street and then immediately headed over to the Wicklow Hotel in search of Collins. He was directed to an old address, 10 Exchequer Street.

Eoin walked down Wicklow Street into Exchequer and entered number ten. He went to the top floor and opened the door. The Minister for Finance looked up and said, "Nice of you to finally show up."

"And hello to you, too," Eoin replied. "Looks like we're back where we started."

"The circle goes round," said Collins. "This office was empty. We were still paying rent. So I commandeered it. I'm left alone here."

Eoin looked around at the familiar surroundings. "It seems like a century since 1917."

"It has been a century," replied Collins. "At least for Ireland."

"It's here you hired me," reminisced Eoin. "You gave me your cufflinks. We planned Thomas Ashe's funeral right here."

"That's all ancient history," Collins chided, always looking forward. "So, how did you two like America?"

"Róisín loved it. I had trouble getting her to come back to dear ould Ireland."

"She's a smart girl," replied Collins. "If you had any brains at all, you would have stayed with her in New York. What did you find out about the Loan?"

"It looks like there's about $1,500,000 unaccounted for."

Collins grunted. "Marvelous." Eoin could see that Collins was his cynical self, but he seemed distracted. "How's Mister Devoy?"

"Old."

"Does he still have his marbles?"

"More than he needs."

"What does he think of Dev?"

"He hates him."

"A wise ould Fenian, I think."

"So?"

"So what?"

"So," Eoin pressed, "why did you call me back?"

"The president has decided that I should go to London with Griffith to negotiate the treaty with Lloyd George."

"How did this come about? When I left for America, you were in Dev's doghouse."

"Doghouse!" sniffed Collins. "With Dev, Brugha, and Stack, it was like the fookin' Spanish Inquisition around here."

"What did you expect? You are, after all, a Fenian heretic." Eoin gave a small laugh, and Collins looked at him, exasperation painted on his face. "I'm going to London because the Chief likes to lecture."

Collins was referring to the summer of 1921, when the British Prime Minister and the erstwhile schoolmaster did not get along. "Negotiating with de Valera," Lloyd George had said, "is like trying to pick up mercury with a fork."

On hearing this, the president of *Dáil Éireann* responded: "Why doesn't he use a spoon?"

"These two eejits are having a pissing match," said Collins to Eoin, "so I end up having to go to London with Griffith. They can take their fookin' fork and fookin' spoon and shove them where Jack stuck the rusty shilling!"

"I take it," Eoin said, after a long pause, "that that place might be a dark place?"

Collins stared hard at Eoin before breaking out in a guffaw. "Only darker place," Collins roared, "is my heart!"

"I still don't understand," Eoin added, "why Dev won't go to London."

"Well," said Collins, a touch of exasperation in his voice, "Dev is claiming that as 'president,' he is superior to Lloyd George, who is only a 'prime minister.'"

"What?"

"He would only go to London if Lloyd George agreed that he was the superior official. The prime minister, of course, said 'no,' and I don't blame him."

"I'm still trying to figure out," said Eoin, "how the *Príomh-Aire* became president in the first place."

"No one else knows, either," said Collins. "He's apparently made himself head-of-state too. He's a combination of king and prime minister. Poor Lloyd George didn't have a chance!"

Eoin was forced to laugh. "But what does all this have to do with me?"

"I want you to come with me to London as my *aide-de-camp.*"

"Your aide-day-what?"

"My bodyguard, you hopeless eejit."

Eoin smiled. "Whatever you say, Commandant-General."

Collins finally smiled. "I missed your cheek." Collins gazed down at the floor and then finally looked back up at Eoin. "I have a bad habit—I visit my nastiness on my best friends." Eoin nodded, a stern look on his smooth face. "What's the matter?" asked Collins.

"Something Devoy said to me."

"What?"

"He said that de Valera was leading you and Griffith to London like a Judas Goat." For a moment, Collins did not speak. Finally, Eoin asked, "Do you t'ink he's right?"

"Someone has to go and negotiate this thing," said Collins. "It takes two to dance, and it takes two to negotiate." He was silent for a moment. "It's my duty." Eoin stood mute. "What do *you* think?"

"I t'ink the second mouse gets the cheese."

Collins stared long and hard at Eoin and then grunted, for he smelled a rat.

143

C ollins and Eoin arrived in London on October 10, Eoin's twentieth birthday.

Although Collins was deputy chairman of the delegation, he stayed at 15 Cadogan Gardens, while the rest of the delegates— Chairman Arthur Griffith, Robert Barton, Gavan Duffy, Eamonn Duggan, and the delegation's secretary, Erskine Childers—stayed at 22 Hans Place. This was Collins's way of showing that he would not be intimidated by de Valera and his merry band of Inquisitors, Brugha and Stack. Collins also brought his own staff, which, besides Eoin, included Liam Tobin and Ned Broy, now cashiered out of the DMP. Crow Street remained intact. Ironically, as Collins moved east, Harry Boland, on assignment from de Valera, was traveling to New York. Collins suspected that Harry was carrying a message from de Valera—forever the Machiavellian pessimist—warning the American Irish that hostilities were about to resume after Griffith and Collins failed in London. Meanwhile, Kitty Kiernan remained in County Longford, in love with Collins but still dealing with the quixotic Harry, who just wouldn't let go.

The delegation's orders from the *Dáil* were rather simple: "As Envoys Plenipotentiaries from the Elected Government of the REPUBLIC OF IRELAND to negotiate and conclude on behalf of Ireland with the representatives of his Britannic Majesty, GEORGE V. a Treaty or Treaties of

Settlement, Association and Accommodation between Ireland and the community of nations known as the British Commonwealth."

It was colder than a banshee's yowl inside the conference room at 10 Downing Street when the two delegations met for the first time on October 11. Both delegations were deeply distrustful of each other. Prime Minister David Lloyd George greeted and shook hands with each member of the Irish delegation. The British delegation remained stoic, refusing to shake hands with the murderers from Dublin. And, of course, the one murderer they couldn't take their eyes off was the man once again wearing his terrible mustache: Michael Collins.

Eoin was with Collins as they entered Downing Street but was shown to a side room shortly after they arrived. He figured he would be there for a while as the two delegations got to know each other. He sat down at a desk and found a piece of stationery. In the upper right-hand corner was the simple address:

10 Downing Street
Whitehall, S.W. 1.

Eoin heard himself laugh out loud. He couldn't help himself, and he took his fountain pen out of his inside jacket pocket—on station right next to his Webley—and scribbled:

My Dearest Róisín,
Look at the address!
Can you believe it!
Save this so we can show it to our grandchildren.
Love,
Your Eoin

He took an envelope and wrote the Walworth Street address on it and reminded himself to post it immediately.

"It's breaking up," a man said, sticking his head in the door. "You Eoin?"

"I am."

"The Irish delegation will be leaving shortly, and Mr. Collins wants you to get his car." Eoin rose and slid the letter into his pocket. "I'm Detective Sergeant W.H. Thompson," the man introduced himself. "I work for Mr. Churchill."

"Scotland Yard bodyguard?"

"Just like you," replied the older man.

"I have a bigger target," said Eoin, and the detective smiled.

"We both have big targets," returned the copper. "Let me show you out so you can get the car." As they were leaving the room, Thompson turned and suddenly said, "I bet you're a Webley man."

"And I t'ink you t'ink that this wee Fenian is going to give you an answer." Thompson laughed, and Eoin made note of it. "But you knew Jameson," he suddenly said, and Thompson stopped in his tracks.

"How did you know?"

"I know your phone number—Whitehall-1212." Thompson turned silent, having misjudged his young adversary.

The chauffeur brought the car to the front, and Eoin opened the rear door when he saw Collins coming through the door, swinging his square attaché case with intent. Collins shot into the backseat as the photographers blinded the crowd with their explosive flashes, and Eoin jumped in right behind him. He had no intention of questioning the boss right now, but he didn't have to, because Collins was heated.

"They're a cold bunch of hoors!" he spat.

"Cold?"

"Iceberg cold," said Collins, his blue eyes on fire. "This is not going to be easy. Now I know why I'm here. I have been sent to London to do a thing which those who sent me know had to be done but had not the courage to do themselves. The Long Hoor wants no part of this. But I'll warm them up. They're not dealing with de Valera now, you know." Then he went quiet and didn't say another word until they returned to Cadogan Gardens. Somehow, Eoin almost felt sorry for the British delegation.

144

"We have a problem with Mick," Liam Tobin said to Eoin.

"What happened?"

"This morning he went off by himself before anyone in the household realized he was gone."

"That's dangerous," said Eoin.

"Your job is to make sure it doesn't happen again. Be discreet."

"Aren't I always?" Eoin's response fractured the stoic-undertaker look on Tobin's gloomy face.

The next morning, Eoin rose at five and was dressed and ready before the rest of the staff awoke. He checked Collins's room, and the light coming from under the door told him the boss was up and already working. Eoin left the house and carefully surveyed the sidewalk. Over at Hans Place, someone had painted COLLINS THE MURDERER in red right in front of the building. The culprit probably thought that Collins was staying with the rest of the delegation and didn't know about the Cadogan Gardens site. As far as Eoin was concerned, no paint was good news. He crossed the street and stood in an alley as he waited for the dawn.

At half-six, he saw Collins come out, again alone, and start walking at an invigorating pace. Eoin trailed way behind, wondering where the Big Fellow was going alone at this early hour. The forced march ended in Maiden Lane, when Collins entered Corpus Christi Roman Catholic Church.

Collins went to the front nave of the church, genuflected, and stepped into a pew, where he knelt and blessed himself. Eoin went to the back on the opposite side and sat alone as a few parishioners arrived for the seven o'clock mass. The bell rang, and the priest came out to begin the mass. Eoin saw Collins rise, and he automatically rose in his seat. Collins went towards the altar and slid inside the altar rail to the sanctuary. He was going to serve as the priest's lone altar boy. Collins was soon ringing bells and belting out answers in Latin, and Eoin plopped back into his seat, a smile on his face.

Eoin kept a close eye on the handful of parishioners. They were an older, working-class lot, with women outnumbering the men. They were not what he was looking for. What he was looking for was MI-5, the British domestic intelligence service. A man had taken a seat behind Collins when he first arrived. Well dressed. Eoin kept a sharp eye on him, and soon the secret was revealed—your man was not a Catholic. He didn't know when to stand, sit, or kneel. Mass was grand exercise, Eoin always thought, and this guy couldn't keep up with the cadence.

Eoin rose from his seat and walked to that side of the church, taking a seat directly behind the confused mass-goer. The man never took his eyes off Collins, and Eoin knew he had a member of MI-5.

"*Dóminus vobiscum,*" said the priest.

"*Et cum spiritu tuo,*" replied Collins.

"*Ite, Missa est.*"

"*Deo grátias.*"

The parishioners began to shuffle out of the pews, but not the man in front of Eoin. Collins walked off with the priest to the sacristy. Five minutes later, he returned and headed to the back of the church, where a statue of St. Patrick proudly stood. The man stood up and slowly followed. Collins knelt in front of St. Patrick, and after dropping a copper, lit a candle. By now, the man was just a few paces from Collins.

Eoin thought it was time to stand and deliver. As the man approached Collins, Eoin picked up speed and gave him a terrific bump, knocking him to the floor and gaining the attention of Collins. "Oh," said Eoin, extending a hand to help the man to his feet. "I'm *so* sorry. I didn't see you." As Eoin pulled him up with his left hand, he allowed the right side of his coat to open, revealing his Webley. "Sorry about that," continued Eoin. "Next time, tell your boss to send a Catholic." Eoin stood his ground, and the agent, revealed and embarrassed before the assembled faithful, meekly retreated.

"What was that all about?" asked Collins.

"MI-5," was the succinct reply.

Collins chuckled. "Yes, I picked him out right away."

"Well," snapped Eoin, "why didn't you do something?"

"Do what? He was only watching me."

"That's not the point!"

"What are you doing here anyway?" quizzed Collins.

"Tobin and Broy were worried about your safety." Eoin paused as he looked upon the man the Tory press was headlining as IRELAND'S FOREMOST MURDERER. Collins turned and dropped another coin, grabbing a wick stick. "Now what are you doing?"

"Lighting another penny candle for Kitty."

Eoin grunted, and Collins ignored him as he returned to pray before St. Patrick. When he was finished with his devotion, the two men headed for the exit.

"A candle for Kitty?"

"Yes," said Collins.

"Why?"

"Because we've come to an arrangement."

"Arrangement?" asked a puzzled Eoin.

"We're engaged."

"Congratulations!" Eoin exclaimed, slapping Collins on his shoulder.

"It's not that simple."

"Why?"

"Harry."

"Tough decision?"

"For her it is," Collins said, exasperated. "Harry's absolutely mad about her, but she says she doesn't love him."

"Well, what's the problem then?"

"I think I sometimes frighten her."

Eoin laughed. "I'm sure you do!"

Collins cocked his head, disturbed by Eoin's retort. "I love her." He paused, before adding, "I think."

"You t'ink?"

"Oh," said Collins, "now you're the man who knows all about love."

"You want my advice about love?"

"Yes."

"Next time," Eoin said, "light a candle for yourself."

145

"Why do I have to go to this thing?"

"Eoin," Collins explained, with great but gentle solicitation, "we are now in the public relations business. We are trying to make friends for Ireland. This is one of the ways we do this. There are an awful lot of influential people going to these things, so try to be pleasant. Being nice to them may make it easier at the conference table when we get down to the nuts and bolts of the treaty. Have a few drinks. Enjoy yourself!"

The two of them got out of their taxi and advanced on the Bloomsbury townhouse of Lady Deametrice Churchill. A butler answered their knock, and they entered the foyer, where they were helped out of their overcoats. Eoin opened his coat to make sure his Webley was snug, and the butler's eyes grew wide. Collins gave himself a quick chuckle. He was delighted to be back in London.

The butler advanced to the entrance of the grand ballroom. "General Michael Collins and Captain Eoin Kavanagh of the Irish Delegation." All eyes fell on the Big Fellow and his pint-sized bodyguard. The room fell silent for a moment, but that was eclipsed with a great outburst of applause. Eoin looked at Collins and watched the General switch on his dazzling smile. He was immediately engulfed by admirers, who only a year before were calling him the most vicious murderer since Jack the Ripper.

Years later, Eoin would look back at that first cocktail party and smile. "Oh, how the rich and famous love their terrible terrorists," Eoin liked to remind the practitioners of "Radical Chic." He loved that wonderful phrase, coined by Tom Wolfe in 1970 about the cocktail parties that smug liberals like Leonard Bernstein used to give for members of the Black Panthers Party. "Old Lenny had nothing to worry about," Eoin once told his friend Joe Flaherty, as he bellied up to the bar at the Lion's Head saloon on Christopher Street, "because those clueless shites couldn't start a revolution if all they had to do was bang their hollow balls together!" Eoin's comments became front-page news in that week's *Village Voice* when Flaherty wrote it up: KAVANAGH: PANTHERS LIKE EUNUCHS.

"Joseph," Eoin said to Flaherty on the phone after the article was published, "you fucked me."

"I did, indeed, Deputy Kavanagh," said Flaherty, and the laughter on both ends continued for several minutes.

"Well, Joseph," Eoin said to the funniest man he had ever met, "I didn't mean it quite the way you put it. If I was black, I'd be in the Black Panthers too, but these guys are not interested in real revolution—they only want to be on the television. Remember, the Irish Republican Brotherhood was a *secret* organization. You don't win revolutions by going on TV and telling the enemy your carefully crafted plans."

"Are you getting many calls about the piece?" asked Flaherty.

"My erstwhile constituents on the Upper West Side are all *aghast* at my innocent comments, which you so viciously twisted. I gotta get outta town. Sometimes it's good to be Bi-Continental!"

"Bi-Continental!" howled Flaherty. "You fraud!"

"I am, indeed, and I'm going back to Dublin tonight. I'm fleeing the flaccid liberal hoors of New York City for the starched reactionary hoors of *Dáil Éireann*."

At the cocktail party, Eoin stood off to the side as his boss amused the gentry with his wit and stories of the London of his youth. He slowly sipped an Irish whiskey, never taking his eyes off Collins. Then, out of the corner of his eye, he saw her advancing on him, and Eoin was, frankly, stunned. She was wearing a silver dress that emphasized her oversized bust. The dress descended to just above her knee. Eoin thought he had seen bigger postage stamps. Her blonde bobbed hair was obscured by the cloud of smoke that her cigarette, in its smart holder, was making, not unlike a Great War dreadnought advancing at flank speed. So, Eoin thought, this is what a flapper looks like.

"Captain Kavanagh," the woman purred, "I've heard *so* much about you." Eoin nodded his head. In front of him stood this stunning woman, perhaps in her early forties, with the most bedazzling smile he had ever encountered. For a moment, Róisín didn't exist. She was old enough to be his mother, but Eoin's willie began telling him that things like age didn't matter in this case. "I'm Deametrice Churchill," she said.

"Yes, Lady Deametrice," replied Eoin. "Thank you for your hospitality."

"The pleasure is all mine."

Eoin knew exactly who she was. What was important was that she was the cousin of Winston Churchill, one of the head negotiators for the Crown. They may have been blood relatives, but Lady Deametrice, unlike her jowly cousin, had won the genes sweepstakes.

She was wearing a low-cut dress that made her buoyant breasts bubble to the top, and Eoin had to remind himself to lock his eyes on her blue eyes and not her swelling bosom. Eoin didn't know what to say. "The General," he finally blurted out, "really appreciates your hospitality."

"Yes, the General told me. He's an extraordinary man."

"He seems to t'ink so."

"What's that, Captain?"

"I said I t'ink the General might agree with your description of him." Lady Deametrice laughed, and Eoin saw what remarkable teeth she had. Eoin always checked out a woman's teeth. It was a subconscious part of his impoverished childhood that he couldn't escape. To Eoin, sound teeth were a sign of wealth.

"Captain Kavanagh," whispered Lady Deametrice conspiratorially, "you have a devilish sense of humor." She placed her hand on his, and Eoin thought she could probably see his willie begging for freedom in the front of his pants.

"This is a remarkable party, Lady Deametrice," Eoin said. "We don't have hooleys like these in Dublin."

"Hooleys!" she exclaimed, laughing. "You have a wonderful way with words—just like the rest of the Irish do! Thank you—I like to think I am just ahead of the social curve here in London. I like to think," she added, stretching out her neck like a proud swan, "of myself as the vanguard of the *avant garde!*" Eoin had no bloody idea what the fuck the *avant garde* was, but he politely nodded. Lady Deametrice gave him an unexpected peck on the cheek, shocking Eoin. "I have to go back to General Collins now, before all these shameless hussies hijack him. He has the most extraordinary blue eyes, don't you think?" Eoin grunted under his breath, and his willie slowly receded from what might have been a deadly ambush.

Collins stood in the middle of the drawing room, surrounded by women. One by one they dropped away, and Eoin saw Collins intently talking with just one woman, intensely lithe with sensitive, dark, mournful eyes. Later he would discover that this was Lady Lavery, wife of the famous painter. What he didn't know is that Collins had known Hazel Lavery, an American, during his previous life in London. They had been brought together by their mutual interest in all things Irish, both political and cultural. Now, less than a decade later, they had been reunited. It was an acquaintance that would have long-lasting implications for both Collins and Ireland.

Three hours later, the crowd of guests had diminished to just a few. Collins walked over to Eoin. "Lady Deametrice wants to show me her paintings upstairs," he said, almost in a whisper.

Eoin stared at the floor. "Do you want me to stay?"

Collins did not respond immediately. "Yes," he finally answered.

"Be careful," Eoin warned.

"I'm always careful with the enemy," Collins replied, with a sly smile.

Collins ascended the stairs behind Lady Deametrice, keeping an eye on her muscular arse and legs. She was rumored to be a superb equestrian, and Collins didn't doubt it for a moment. He wondered what kind of paintings she owned.

Once inside her bedroom, Lady Deametrice excused herself and went to the bathroom. When she returned, she was stark naked. She didn't say a word as she climbed on the bed and stuck her derriere out. Michael Collins, his own willie standing straight up now, stepped back, surveyed the scene—then gave a rambunctious laugh.

"And what's so funny?" said Lady Deametrice, stunned at the laughter, looking back over her left shoulder at Collins.

"Oh, I just thought you would make the most *perfect* British secret service agent."

"Oh," said Lady Deametrice, seemingly insulted, as she came to a sitting position on the bed. "Don't be ridiculous." Immodesty became her, thought Collins.

"Lady Deametrice," Collins said smoothly, "one can never be *too* careful of the machinations of the British Empire." Collins then leaned over and kissed her gently on the lips. "Perhaps another time," he said, as he headed for the bedroom door.

"General Collins," she called out, panting slightly.

"Yes?"

"You have tremendous self-discipline."

Collins laughed. "In your case, Lady Deametrice, the discipline is not easy to enforce. You were made for temptation."

Lady Deametrice laughed. "Thank you," she said, before adding, "I'll give your *passionate* regards to my cousin, Winston."

Collins nodded and smiled. "I'm sure you will." And with that, the elusive Dublin Pimpernel, along with his devoted bodyguard, soon disappeared into the London night.

refer to Collins as "The Arsonist," much to Tobin's and Broy's amusement.) Sometimes, Collins thought negotiating with Lloyd George was easier than negotiating with Kitty. She could be an awfully odd girl, as she herself admitted, calling herself, at various times, "moody," "childish," "peculiar," and "silly."

Collins, ever the businessman, reminded her in his letters of their "arrangement" or "contract." Perhaps their attraction to each other was based on the fact that they were complete opposites. Kitty was emotional, displaying her heart on her sleeve, while Collins was the master of compartmentalization and organization. It was through this compartmentalization that Collins could be Minister for Finance, TD, Director of Intelligence of the IRA, head of the IRB, a Commandant-General of the IRA, and now a chief negotiator of the treaty—and do a superb job in all of them.

Now he added romance to his portfolio, probably neatly tucking it in somewhere between Finance and Intelligence. Maybe because Collins was approaching marriage the way he approached collecting dossiers on the British Secret Service, Kitty always seemed to be wavering. Collins was in such a rush that it seemed he treated Kitty, whom he genuinely loved, like he would treat Eoin or Batt O'Connor. It seemed that, even in love, he wanted his orders carried out to the letter. Not surprisingly, Kitty had trouble turning the other cheek, as Eoin or Batt often did. "My one ambition is to have you like me—in the right way," she wrote Collins. "All will yet be well if I was sure that you won't be getting into those fits of temper with me and hurt me so much and make me feel that we are most unsuited. Otherwise, dear, I love *you*, but the other will count a big item to my happiness."

She also worried about Collins's fidelity. She had seen the photographs of Collins in London and heard the rumors about other women. "I hope I have the pleasure of gazing on you (among all the beauties)," she wrote to him.

"I never said any such thing," he would earnestly protest in denial. "Newspapermen are inventions of the devil."

She was jealous when a friend of hers innocently commandeered Collins's knee, reminding him that her friend "had the loan of *his* knee." Then the apologies would follow: "And I do hope it pleases you well to know this, and that you are really not fickle, and will love me all the more if I devote my life to you only." But, in her own way, she was very direct with Collins, telling him what was in her heart and not sugar-coating it. "I'm very sensitive, will always be looking for a pinhole to reproach you if I noticed anything, and there's where the trouble lies."

And, of course, there was always the trouble with Harry. By November, the Harry situation seemed to be finally, albeit glacially slowly, resolving itself. To put it mildly, Harry was *desperately* in love with her. "I'm wondering if you are ever a wee bit lonely for me," Boland wrote Kitty on his way to America, "and are you longing as I am for the day when we shall meet again? Won't you send me a wireless and say you have made up your mind? If you have done so, cable *yes*, and if you are still in doubt, then for God's sake, try to make up your mind, and agree to come with me . . . I would just love to have you come to America, where we will spend our honeymoon in perfect bliss!" He signed it, "Your devoted lover."

Harry was pulling out all the stops. He had half the Irish Republican Brotherhood sending notes to Kitty, encouraging her to marry him. "And if only Harry—and his friends—would stop storming Heaven with his prayers," Kitty wrote Collins, "I wouldn't be getting unhappy and such mixed and peculiar feelings." Finally, Kitty declared the truth: "I told Harry I didn't love him."

But how Harry loved her, as his pleading letters from America resolutely declared. Would she come to America, marry him, and then honeymoon in sunny California? No, Harry, she would not. Her heart was with the other rebel, now entrenched in London with the most thankless job in the history of Ireland. "I may be wrong, but I think Harry is capable of deeper affection for me than most men," Kitty wrote Collins, "but he also knows that I don't love him—it's no effort for him to be a great lover, and, of course, he gets no thanks." Finally, it seemed, Harry had come to comprehend the bad news. "Must really write Harry soon. Poor Harry, he's getting used to me at last and seems quite happy now, thank God."

And if her Michael was playing the field of young beauties in London, Kitty could dangle the thing that women always dangle—sex—in front of her "Elusive Pimpernel": "I love to have you here, but we must be really good, no bedroom scene, etc., etc, etc. . . . I'm wearing my old long frock, black and very low! Of course *you* would be shocked!"

And, finally, she reveals that she has given her all to Collins: "I've given you what I've never given any other man; indeed, it's not much, I suppose, but you have it anyway."

So as Collins was working on the torturous negotiations of making a nation, Kitty was working equally hard on the difficult questions of love and marriage and her ultimate decision to be "married to a gun." Even as she succumbed to Collins's love, she had an odd way of expressing it: "Here was I—a victim, actually—to a man. Don't laugh—that's not exactly it, but my way of putting it!!"

Finally, she surrendered to Michael Collins: "How anxious I am to secure your love really well. It is too bad that our little romance should have such ups and downs. Sweetheart, wouldn't you like me to be more sensible and not be silly? Whereas it's so good to know that you have someone who won't forget you. Your trouble is hers. One not complete in anything without the other. That's my conception of love, and you are the first who made me believe in love, and that's why I wouldn't like to be ever disappointed in you. You will forgive me for saying this, won't you?"

"Bring the car around," Collins said to Eoin.

"Where to?"

"Sir John Lavery's house. He's going to paint me."

"What's the address?"

"5 Cromwell Place."

"Cromwell," repeated Eoin, as Collins raised his eyebrow. Eoin kept his lip buttoned shut and did not say what this omen might mean.

Lavery was painting all the players in the treaty drama, and, now, it was Collins's turn. The two of them went to the Cromwell Place address, and Collins removed his overcoat. "It's heavy," he said, handing it to Lavery. "Don't drop it. There's a gun in the pocket." Lavery handled the coat gingerly, and Collins looked around the room for an appropriate seat. Out of habit, he took a seat facing the door. There would be no surprises. Eoin nodded his approval, and Sir John began sketching as Collins, uncomfortable, fidgeted like a child in his chair.

The sitting had been arranged by Lavery's wife, Hazel, known to all as Lady Lavery. She interrupted her husband's work once, and Eoin recognized her as the woman who had commandeered Collins atten-tion at Lady Deametrice's party. Lady Lavery couldn't take her eyes off of Collins, but Sir John paid no attention. Perhaps the thirty years' separation in their ages had some impact. "They are a queer lot," Eoin said to himself. Eoin's suspicions increased when he would accompany Collins to eight o'clock mass at Brompton Oratory, the Church of the Immaculate Heart of Mary, where Lady Lavery would be waiting for him. Collins may have been lighting candles for Kitty, but he was reciting the *"Mea Culpa"* with Hazel. Perhaps *"mea máxima culpa"* was more appropriate.

"I don't understand this," Eoin told Róisín, when he was back in Dublin with the General.

"Don't be naïve," she said to him, and then added a devilish laugh. As usual, Róisín was about ten lengths ahead of Eoin in life experience.

Kitty was right to be a little suspicious of "the famous M.C.," as she called him. For, while women like Lady Deametrice Churchill would literally throw their bodies at him—Eoin joked that the pulchritudi-nous London ladies hell-bent on seducing Collins lent new meaning to the term *"body*guard"—it was finally becoming obvious to Eoin that there was one woman in London who had caught the eye of the noto-rious gunman.

Collins was coming to learn that he could always depend on Hazel Lavery for a supportive ear and to serve his needs as a back-channel communicator with the British establishment. His thoughts may have been with Kitty, but the person who had his ear in London was the sad-eyed Hazel.

Lady Lavery's life story reminded Eoin a little bit of Erskine Childers. They were born outside the sphere of Irish nationalism—Hazel in America, Childers in Britain—yet both had converted to the cause of Irish Republicanism. Hazel had actually gone one step further, in that she had converted to Roman Catholicism. But while the stoic Childers took an antagonistic approach to the treaty talks, Lady Lavery did all she could do with her social contacts to help Collins and Griffith close the gap in the negotiations.

After talking with Róisín, Eoin couldn't help but wonder what was going on behind closed doors with Collins and her ladyship. Even while in London, the rumors had started. The two of them were often seen riding together to a function, and the London press—brutally yellow long before the advent of Rupert Murdoch's filthy pseudo-journalism— started referring to Hazel as Collins's "sweetheart." Kitty, back in Longford, was not amused, and Collins would try to joke his way out of his tight fix, always blaming the antagonistic English press. Although he would never tell Kitty, London afforded Collins a separation—and a sense of privacy—that a parochial city like Dublin could never provide. Soon Collins had nicknamed Hazel "Macushla," and friends of hers, such as George Bernard Shaw, began referring to Collins as her "Sunday husband."

But the compartmentalized Collins managed to stay several steps ahead of the rumormongers. They would have been shocked if they knew he had been trying his hand at poetry, directed not at his fiancée, but to Lady Lavery:

> Oh! Hazel, Hazel Lavery:
> What is your charm Oh! Say?
> Like subtle Scottish Mary
> You take my heart away.
> Not by your wit and beauty
> Nor your delicate sad grace
> Nor the golden eyes of wonder
> In the flower that is your face.

Years later, when asked about the Collins-Lady Lavery relationship by historians, senior statesman Eoin Kavanagh struck to the script. "Sure, General Collins was too busy working on the treaty. I was with him every minute, and I know there was nothing inappropriate. Everybody knows that. He was devoted to Kitty Kiernan."

But if his interviewers had looked closely, they could have seen the jolly dance in Eoin's eyes, for he remembered the very words of Michael Collins himself: "All poets are interested in only one thing—getting shagged!"

Although Kitty and Hazel may have preoccupied Collins's heart during the negotiations, perhaps the most important female on his side that fateful fall was the wife of the Secretary of State for the Colonies, one Clementine Churchill. She was known to all as "Clemmie," and she was one of the great beauties of her time. As she cared for the growing Churchill clan—without much help from Winston, who was constantly away on government business—she also kept up with the news, especially when it concerned her husband. The thing that caught her eye, interestingly enough, was the assassination of Alan Bell in 1920. Collins meant to send a telegram with news of this assassination, and, apparently, Western Union delivered it to the right people in London.

"This new Irish murder is very terrible," Clementine wrote her husband.

"Really getting very serious," Winston responded. "What a diabolical streak the Irish have in their character! I expect it is that treacherous, assassinating, conspiring trait which has done them in in bygone ages of history and prevented them from being a great responsible nation with stability and prosperity. It is shocking that we have not been able to bring the murderers to justice."

Churchill's career was marked by a visceral bellicosity. His first instinct was to always go to the whip. This had not served him well in Gallipoli, and it had not served him well in Ireland, where his solution to a popular revolution was to send in the Black and Tans and Auxiliaries, thereby exacerbating the situation, playing into the hands of Collins and rallying the Irish people behind their rebels. He ranted about revenge. "It is monstrous," Churchill declared, "that we have some two hundred murders, and no one hung."

Clementine was well aware of her husband's sanguinary instincts, and she tried to temper him. "Do, my darling," she wrote him, "use your influence now for some sort of moderation, or at any rate, justice in Ireland. Put yourself in the place of the Irish. If you were ever leader, you would not be cowed by severity, and certainly not by reprisals which fall like the rain from Heaven upon the Just and upon the Unjust. It always makes me unhappy and disappointed when I see you inclined to take for granted that the rough, iron-fisted 'Hunnish' way will prevail." Churchill would huff and puff, but he could not fool his wife. "You know that if the situation was reversed," she chided, "your heart would be with the rebels." For once, Winston Spencer Churchill was speechless, for he knew his wife was right.

148

On Christmas Eve 1941, Congressman Eoin Kavanagh was trying to get out of Washington and catch the train back to New York so he could have a quiet dinner with Róisín and their son. But as he was leaving the office, he got a call from the White House. The operator asked him to hold, and Kavanagh was surprised when the president himself got on the line. "Eoin," said FDR, "could you possibly drop by this evening for a drink? There's someone I'd like you to meet."

Eoin's heart sank. "Of course, Mister President." He immediately called Róisín and told her he would catch a later train.

"Oh, for God's sake," Róisín snapped on the phone.

"I know," apologized Eoin, "but it's the president, and this is a time of war."

"It's always a time of war with this family," returned Róisín, as she hung up the phone. She was terribly disappointed, because Eoin Jr. had just enlisted in the United States Navy, and this might be the last Christmas they would ever spend together as a family. Silently, she cursed FDR and all the famous people they had known through the years. Power, she decided, just brought misery, especially to this family.

Eoin knew exactly what the president was up to. Everyone was talking about it. Winston Spencer Churchill had taken the nation's capital by storm. The prime minister was in town for a strategy conference with the president about the priorities of the war. In their meetings over the years, Eoin had told FDR all the stories about the treaty negotiations between Collins and Churchill, and, now, thought Eoin, the president was going to have a little fun at the expense of the British prime minister and the representative from New York's seventh congressional district.

When Eoin arrived at the White House, he was shown to the president's private quarters on the second floor. The president was in high spirits, playing bartender to the prime minister. His wheelchair was in high gear, shifting between the bar and the couch where the PM was planted. The room was filled with smoke from Churchill's big Cuban cigar and the president's holdered cigarette. *Ah, the fog of war*, thought Eoin to himself.

"Congressman Kavanagh," beamed the President, "I'm glad you could make it on such short notice."

"*Nollaig Shona Duit!* Mister. President and Prime Minister Churchill. Happy Christmas to both of you. But you, Mister President, are in Róisín's doghouse."

The President laughed. "I'll make a note to personally apologize to the beautiful Mrs. Kavanagh. Now, I want you to meet our special guest. Winston, you remember Eoin Kavanagh, don't you?" said the president mischievously, as he raised an eyebrow.

The prime minister rose and took Kavanagh's hand to shake. He looked at the young man, who now wore a brilliant red beard. Eoin stood mute. The ball was in Churchill's court. "Ah, you look familiar," said Churchill. "But I can't place you. Should I know you?"

"How's Lady Deametrice?"

"Lady Deametrice?" repeated Churchill, raising an eyebrow of his own. "Lady Deametrice is fine."

"What an intriguing name, Deametrice," interjected FDR.

"My cousin," said the PM. "But I still can't place you, young man," Churchill conceded.

"Downing Street, December 1921."

"Twenty years ago," snorted Churchill. "What was going on twenty years ago this month?" Suddenly it hit him. "The Irish treaty delegation! General Collins! You were his little bodyguard, were you not? Captain Kavanagh!" Eoin nodded his head.

The only difference in Eoin's appearance in the last twenty years was the red beard, which he had worn since he arrived in America. The contrast between it and his dark brown hair—almost black—was stunning.

Eoin thought Churchill very sharp to have recognized him. "Yes, Prime Minister, I was Mick Collins's bodyguard and general factotum."

As he sat with two of the most famous politicians of the twentieth century, the last days of the treaty negotiations seeped back into Eoin's mind. Things had not been going well, and it was decided that Griffith—despite his poor health—and Collins would break into subgroups and try to hammer out some kind of compromise to the stickiest problems: whether the Royal Navy would still have control of the Irish ports; the question of tariffs; the partition of Ulster; what part the new Irish state would play in the British Empire; how much Ireland would contribute to Britain's war debt (a sore point with the Minister for Finance, already outraged that Britain had been super-taxing the impoverished island for centuries); and the trickiest problem of all—the question of allegiance to the king. Sitting with his martini, and with the smoke of the president and prime minister almost smothering him, it came back in all clarity—Churchill's townhouse in Sussex Gardens, Hyde Park, London.

He was bodyguarding both Collins and Griffith that day, as the work at 10 Downing Street crept towards the evening. Everyone was tired. Finally Churchill said, "Let's go back to my place and have a drink." Before he realized it, Eoin found himself piling into one car with Collins and Griffith, while Lloyd George, Lord Birkinhead, and Churchill piled into another. When they arrived, the prime minister and Griffith headed upstairs, while Collins, Churchill, and Birkinhead remained in the sitting room on the first floor. Eoin, along with Detective Sergeant W.H. Thompson, headed for the kitchen.

"Want a drink?" asked Thompson.

"I'd better pass," answered Eoin. Thompson and Eoin had worked with each other for more than a month now, and they had an easy relationship. Thompson was old enough to be Eoin's father, but he never treated him as a subordinate. They had a professional relationship, and Thompson knew how dangerous Eoin's job was. Few wanted to shoot Churchill; it seemed *everyone*, English and Irish, wanted to take a shot at Collins. Privately, he worried about Eoin's safety, because he knew how dedicated Eoin was to the General.

The kitchen door opened, and Churchill's head popped in. "Ice," he said, "we need ice!" Seeing Eoin, he stepped into the kitchen. "You're General Collins's bodyguard," Churchill said, pointing at him.

"I am, Mr. Churchill."

"Well, my lad," he said, with a twinkle in his eye, "you're doing a fine job, because he's still breathing and causing trouble—both here in London and, from what I hear, back home in Dublin!" A maid filled a bucket with ice and was about to exit the kitchen when Churchill stopped her. "Give that to me, Elizabeth. I'll take it back out." But he placed the bucket on the kitchen table and advanced on Eoin. "I hear you're a Webley man." Eoin nodded. "Can I ask where you got it?"

"It belonged to a spy."

Churchill laughed. "Any particular spy?"

Eoin's eyes turned cold. "The spy who murdered my father."

Churchill was taken aback, embarrassed that he had asked the question. "I'm sorry," he finally said. "Was your father a rebel?"

"On occasion."

"I see," said Churchill, as if he had just learned something important. "Did you shoot the spy to get the gun?"

Eoin thought. "No, I didn't." As soon as he spoke, he was sorry he had replied to the enemy's interrogation.

Churchill picked the ice bucket up and headed for the door, but turned before he went through. "Did you ever shoot anyone?"

This time Eoin did not answer.

"Alan Bell?" asked the minister. Churchill was still obsessed with the Crown's unlucky bank examiner.

Eoin remained mute but allowed a small smile.

"You don't say much, do you?" Churchill finally said.

"Mr. Collins," Eoin said deliberately, "has all the answers you want."

"Ha!" Churchill retorted. "You're as hard to pin down as General Collins."

"Thank you," Eoin replied.

Churchill shook his head. "Tough little sonofagun, Tommy," he said, with a wink to Thompson as he exited, clutching the ice bucket like a rugby ball.

Thompson laughed. "I think the minister likes you."

"How can you tell?"

"You have the 'rogue factor.'"

"The rogue factor?"

"The minister loves men of action," said Thompson, "and I think he thinks you are one, otherwise you wouldn't be here protecting the General. After a few drinks, he can't stop talking about his adventures in the bloody Boer War."

"Well," Eoin replied, laughing, "he has the head rogue at his disposal this evening. I t'ink we're in for a long night."

And a long night it would be. In the sitting room, the drinks were poured, and the chatter had nothing to do with the business of the Treaty. Churchill hated Collins before he had ever laid an eye on him. To him, he was a guttersnipe and murderer. It was only after he saw him in action around the conference table at 10 Downing Street that his opinion began to shift. He saw a big, handsome farm boy, self-educated, who was not afraid to mix it up with the scions of Eton and Oxford. He gave as good as he took, and could facilely display either great contempt or extraordinarily good humor in making his arguments. He soon realized that Collins was not a ruffian after all, but a brilliant tactician in guerrilla warfare. Churchill thought him the sharpest tack in the room. From the moment of that epiphany, he always referred to Collins as "General," and, years after his death, whenever speaking about the Big Fellow, it was always "General Collins." Clementine Churchill also had great influence in changing her husband's attitude. Her comments about "Hunnish" behavior on her husband's part had also hit the mark with Winston. Before, he was part of the Irish problem; now, he tried to be part of the solution.

Collins's initial reaction to Churchill was also one of contempt. He knew that Churchill was instrumental in getting the Auxies and Black and Tans into Ireland—and keeping them there. Collins wrote that Churchill "will sacrifice all for political gain . . . Inclined to be bombastic. Full of ex-officer jingo or similar outlook. Don't actually trust him." But he soon found that he could work with him, that he was a fascinating raconteur and drinking partner, and that he was a man who, like himself, knew how to make a deal.

"Now, General," said Churchill, refilling Collins's glass, "how did you save yourself?"

"What?"

"How did you save yourself? How did you avoid capture? Was it sheer luck?"

"Not at 'tal," said Collins modestly. "I had some very good people watching out for me. You can't match the Dubliner for loyalty."

"There must be more to it than that?"

"I always watch the other fellow," said Collins, "instead of letting him watch me. I make a point of keeping the other fellow on the run, instead of being on the run myself. That is the secret of success that I have learned during the past year or two."

"Extraordinary," exclaimed Lord Birkinhead, who was taking it all in.

"Well," said Collins, "I shouldn't have told you that."

"Why not?"

"Because if we don't get this Treaty done, I'm going to be on the run again—and this time, I don't think I'll be that lucky."

"We will get this Treaty done," proclaimed Churchill, "and you will live to be an old man—both of us will live to be old men!" They clinked snifters. "More cognac?"

"Indeed," said Collins. "Do you have any Curaçao?"

"Curaçao?" repeated Churchill. "My God, man, you do have a sweet tooth!"

Collins laughed. "As me big hoor of a belly will attest to."

The three men shared a laugh, but the cognac and Curaçao shortly began to cast a black spell over Collins. "What, General, do you think will be the big sticking point on the Treaty—if we ever get it done—back in Dublin?"

"Allegiance to the king," said Collins, without hesitation.

"Hmmm," mused Churchill, glancing at Birkinhead. "That will be a sticking point on our side too, I'm afraid. I don't see us shifting much on that one."

"Well," said Collins, "you better find a way to 'shift,' as you say, or there will be no Treaty."

Collins suddenly turned on Churchill in such a threatening manner that Churchill, years later, wrote that, "He was in his most difficult mood, full of reproaches and defiances, and it was very easy for everyone to lose his temper."

"After seven hundred fucking years," shot Collins, "you'd think you people would come to your senses—or, out of simple guilt—would just get the fuck out of Ireland."

"Now, now, General," said Churchill, "there must be a way to resolve this problem."

But Collins was having none of it. Eoin could hear Collins's voice rising, and he looked at Thompson with trepidation. He got up without saying a word and peeked through the kitchen door, which gave him a clear view of Churchill and Collins going at each other.

"You hunted me day and night!" Collins shouted, gesticulating with his snifter. "You put a price on my head!" Birkinhead was afraid that blows were about to be struck.

"Wait a minute," countered Churchill, "you are not the only one." With that, Churchill took Collins's wrist and pulled him from his chair. He walked him to the other end of the living room and pointed out a framed poster on the wall. Collins put his nose almost to the glass. It was a poster from the Boer War for the recapture of one Winston Churchill. "At any rate, it was a good price—£5,000. Look at me—£25 dead or alive. How would you like that?"

Collins was silent before shouting out, "£5,000 my arse! It was £10,000!"

"Whatever pleases you, General Collins." Both men laughed a good drunken laugh, and Eoin let the kitchen door close, the crisis concluded. It was the moment that finally broke the iceberg that existed between the British and the Irish, and, now, for the first time, a Treaty was possible.

———

"Yes, Prime Minister, I was Mick Collins's bodyguard and general factotum." A shocked Churchill embraced the congressman, but Eoin did not return the hug. "You look well, Prime Minister."

"I am well," said Churchill. "And this time, we're going to be on the same side!"

"You're lucky Hitler is such a dunce," said Eoin. "Only someone that stupid would declare war on the United States of America."

"Well put," said the president. "Let's drink to victory!"

The three martini glasses clinked together. "To our three great countries," said Eoin.

"Three?" said Churchill and the president, together.

"You're not forgetting about poor little *Saorstát Éireann*, are you?"

"The Irish Free State," sniffed Churchill. "Very difficult person, that de Valera."

"Yes," said the president. "Charles De Gaulle thinks he's Joan of Arc. Eamon de Valera thinks he's St. Patrick."

The two leaders—who had their hands full with de Valera's neutral Ireland—laughed, but Eoin did not. "Perhaps," counseled Eoin, "but if Britain didn't habitually condemn Irish patriots to death, there might be more cooperation from those you didn't get around to shooting—namely Eamon de Valera. You condemned this man to death! You expect him to kiss you now because you're in trouble?" This was not going the way the president had expected. "You know de Valera is difficult. It's no secret. That's why Michael Collins negotiated the treaty."

"De Valera is insignificant," said the Prime Minister.

"Then why did you cable him on the night of Pearl Harbor, December seventh?" The president's ears pricked up in surprise.

"Where did you hear about that?" snapped Churchill.

"Maybe my intelligence network is *still* better than your intelligence network," laughed Eoin, but there was no smile in the laugh. "Remember who I worked for—the DOI of the IRA."

"DOI of the IRA?" echoed Roosevelt.

"Director of Intelligence of the Irish Republican Army," said Churchill. "Michael fucking Collins."

"Yes," said Eoin, with a sly smile. "Michael fucking Collins." FDR blew smoke out of his nose and turned on that dazzling smile, showing he was enjoying the match. Eoin's intelligence network was Jack Lemass, who had fed him the information. "I hear you're a great fan of Thomas Davis?" Eoin said to Churchill.

"Thomas Davis?"

"He's the man who wrote "A Nation Once Again." If I recall your exact words in that de Valera telegram: 'Now is your chance. Now or never. A nation once again. Am ready to meet you at any time.'" Eoin was polite enough not to mention that Churchill's cable-writing was cognac-fueled.

"Is that true, Winston?" asked FDR.

Churchill harrumphed and straightened out his dickin-bow before Eoin came to the rescue. "And you did the right thing, Prime Minister." Even Churchill looked stunned at that. "If Dev had any wit, he would have shown up the next morning at 10 Downing Street. Now, Michael Collins would have made a deal with you!"

Churchill smiled at the congressman. "Yes, General Collins would have made a deal. As always, he would have done what was right for Ireland." He paused for a second. "He would have done what was right for everybody." The prime minister took a slug of his cigar. "I'm mildly shocked that you are defending the *Taoiseach*," surprising Eoin, in that he knew the relatively newly minted Irish term for "prime minister."

"I am not defending Eamon de Valera," said Eoin. "I am defending the right of Ireland to have her own say—no matter how different it may differ from that of Britain or the United States of America—in this war that is about to engulf the world." He turned to the president. "You t'ink this man de Valera—who I don't personally like or admire, for that matter—is a troublesome wart. But he can be dealt with."

"How?" asked the president.

"A pet will get more of a positive reaction out of him than a threat. Remember, he sent the Dublin fire brigade to Belfast to put out the inferno from the *Luftwaffe's* bombing campaign last spring. It was Irish generosity at its best. He can be stroked."

"He did do a good job there," admitted Churchill.

"So realize, gentlemen, that the wily old rebel now in Dublin, the *Taoiseach*, can be *gently* maneuvered. And I can help you with that." Eoin had stood his ground between two of the most important men of the twentieth century, talked common sense, and proved that he was no one's pawn. And with that, Eoin Kavanagh said his goodbyes and rushed to catch the train back to New York City, hoping that Róisín had kept his dinner warm—and was still in the mood to talk to him on this strange Christmas Eve.

It was early on the morning of December 6, 1921, at 10 Downing Street. The Irish Delegation had just signed the Treaty, and they were being photographed by the British Pathé Newsreel cameramen. Collins, considering the ordeal and stress he had been under, looked remarkably fresh and handsome, even with his awful "Charlie Chaplin mustache," as Kitty called it. He even smiled and laughed for the camera.

He came out of the room, and his smiling face went completely blank as he motioned to Eoin to follow him into the cloak room. "This morning I signed my death warrant."

Collins's words rang in Eoin's ears. "My God," he said, "what are you talking about?"

"My life is forfeit."

"Twelve months, sixteen days," said Eoin to the distraught Collins.

"Now what are *you* talking about?"

"It's exactly twelve months and sixteen days since Bloody Sunday." Eoin grabbed Collins by his two arms. "You did it, Mick. You did the impossible."

"I did fuck all."

"Don't you say that to me after all we've been through." Eoin released his grip on Collins and stuck his index finger right under Collins's nose. "The delegation birthed a nation this morning, and you and Mr. Griffith were the midwives."

"I hope it won't be a stillbirth," replied Collins. "But that's up to those back in Dublin. I don't think Dev will receive this well. But I'll do my best to get it through the *Dáil*. It's my duty. If I don't, we'll be back to the killing again. Even if we do get it passed, we might be back to the killing again."

"A civil war?"

"A hell of a civil war."

"Led by Mr. de Valera?"

"It wouldn't surprise me," said Michael Collins. Then he laughed.

"What's so funny?"

"I was just thinking about your mouse."

"My mouse?" said a confused Eoin.

"You said the second mouse gets the cheese."

"Oh," Eoin replied, shaking his head as though he were in terrible pain, "don't say that."

Collins smiled an exhausted smile. "I guess I'll never see the cheese, will I?"

And he would never see the cheese, because, in an act of total self-lessness and total love of Ireland, Michael Collins threw himself into the trap and sprung his country free of seven hundred years of British oppression.

Eoin's Diary
January 7, 1922

1922

That was the vote in the Dáil today. In favor of the Treaty 64 yeas, 57 nays. It's hard to believe that, after seven hundred years of British occupation, fifty-seven Irishmen actually voted against getting out of this mucking country, including Dev, Brugha, Stack, the Countess Markievicz, and the rest of that gang. Mick was beside himself. "I'd rather instil to concede victory," he snapped at me. "I'm apparently in the blood."

They're outraged that the six Ulster counties are not coming into the new Free State. They never consider what the Orangemen think. If the situation were reversed—if the new government were to be run out of Belfast—how would all of us Catholics feel about that. We'll have enough trouble setting up a government that works. The Orangemen would only complicate the situation. Anyway Mick thinks that this will work its way out, because of the boundary commission, which, he hopes, will bring Catholic Tyrone and Fermanagh into the Free State.

And if it suit the North, they're never about, it's the loyalty oath to the king. With these people, there will always be an excuse. And that's than, as Mick would say.

I am very disappointed over the whole vitriolic tone of the debate, but I'm more concerned with Róisín. I think the whole Treaty debate is beginning to get under her skin. She knows the sacrifices that we have all made, and she's had enough. The Countess na mBan has voted 419–63 against the Treaty and she is livid about that. I think her romance

535

150

EOIN'S DIARY
JANUARY 7, 1922

I s toil *64*. Ní toil *57*.

That was the vote in the *Dáil* today, in favor of the Treaty. 64 yeas. 57 nays. It's hard to believe that, after seven hundred years of British occupation, fifty-seven Irishmen actually voted against getting the British out of this fucking country, including Dev, Brugha, Stack, the Countess Markievicz, and the rest of that gang. Mick was beside himself. "The Irish inability to concede victory," he snapped at me, "is apparently in the blood!"

They're outraged that the six Ulster counties are not coming into the new Free State. They never consider what the Orangemen think. If the situation were reversed—if the new government were to be run out of Belfast—how would all of us Catholics feel about that? We'll have enough trouble setting up a government that works. The Orangemen would only complicate the situation. Anyway, Mick thinks that this will work its way out because of the boundary commission, which, he hopes, will bring Catholic Tyrone and Fermanagh into the Free State.

And if it isn't the North they're upset about, it's the loyalty oath to the king. With these people, there will always be an excuse. And that's that, as Mick would say.

I am very disappointed over the whole vitriolic tone of the debate, but I'm more concerned with Róisín. I think the whole Treaty debate is beginning to get under her skin. She knows the sacrifices that we have all made, and she's had enough. The *Cumann na mBan* has voted 419-63 against the Treaty, and she is livid about that. I think her romance with the Countess Markievicz is over. The Countess called Collins and Griffith "oath breakers and cowards" in the *Dáil*. "I can't believe," Róisín said in disbelief, "that she could talk to Mick that way, after all he has done for the country."

Róisín is beginning to talk about New York nonstop. "Let's just leave," she said to me last night. "I've had enough." I told her we couldn't leave now, because the job wasn't done. Mick is feeling very down about all this nonsense, and I couldn't leave him at this time. "Mick will survive!" she snapped at me.

"So you want me," I replied, "to leave him in the dust, just like the Countess Markievicz?" She had no reply. I told her what Mick said to me the day the Treaty was signed in London, about predicting his own demise, but the bold Róisín told me it was just nonsense. I don't think it's nonsense. I wish we weren't in this mess, but we are, and I'm determined to ride it through so we can, finally, have our own little country.

But Róisín, at the bottom of it all, is right. It's despicable shite we're going through, after all the hard work Mick and Mr. Griffith did in London. Róisín talks always of "America," but it's New York she means. It has come to mean paradise to her. And she may be right, because New York and its speakeasies look very appetizing right now. But, for the time being, I shall remain here in Dublin at Mick's side. God help us all.

151

"**I**'m shocked," said a dead-serious Diane, "that such sexual hijinks
were going on in London during this important time."

"You're a regular Captain Renault from *Casablanca*," replied
Johnny. "Just shocked, *shocked* by it all!"

"You're such a wiseass," hissed Diane. "I'm surprised at Michael. At
least Grandpa wasn't gallivanting around."

"Eoin was getting his from Róisín back in Dublin."

"I still don't like it. I expected more from Michael Collins—fidelity
to Ireland!"

"Oh," shot back Eoin, "and this from Miss Nude New Jersey of
1973!"

"Will you stop it!" Diane screeched.

"Love, there's no one else here."

"Oh," said Diane, relieved, "I keep expecting to see the kids coming
into the room and learning of my little adventure." Then Johnny started
laughing, hard. "What's so funny?"

"You," said Johnny, his face aglow. "The family enforcer, the scourge
of your children—no credit cards, no tattoos, no piercings. How would
they react if they knew their mother was an exhibitionist?"

"Yeah," said Diane, "I always get to be the bad cop to your good
cop." She straightened up and stared hard at her husband. "I should
never have told you." In one of their many breakups on the way to
marriage, Diane—apparently "just because I wanted to"—landed in a
nudist colony on the Jersey Shore. "If I recall," said Diane, changing

the subject, "you were under indictment or something in Dublin at the time, when you should have been courting me."

"No," corrected Johnny, "that was Grandfather. He was indicted. I was his *unindicted* co-conspirator."

"Big difference."

"Grandpa needed help. I was his legs. I was young and innocent."

"Young and innocent my ass," countered Diane. "But we did some nutty things when we were young and foolish—and so full of hormones."

"I didn't consider helping my grandfather foolish," replied Johnny, solemnly. "We forget what old, conservative fucks we have become. We forget how it was when our hormones were raging, and the only thing we could think about was getting naked and screwing."

"I know," said Diane. "We should have saved some of those hormones for middle-age! I see the girls, and I just want to borrow some."

"Jesus," said Johnny, "I don't want to hear anything about my daughters' hormones."

"They are young women, don't forget, with the needs of young women. In fact, our Róisín is just about the age I was when you first met me."

"Don't give me any of this 'needs of a woman' crap," said Johnny, deadly serious. "These are my little girls!"

Diane suppressed a laugh and patted Johnny on his hand. "There, there, Daddy."

"My daughters can have all the sex they want," spat Johnny, "after I'm dead!"

"You hypocrite! You had your hands down the back of my pants on our first date!"

"That was different."

"Sure it was."

"Well, maybe Michael Collins had the same idea with Lady Deametrice and Lady Lavery," said Johnny. "And maybe even Kitty Kiernan."

"But, in his situation, it wasn't right."

"Who's being the hypocrite now? Michael was a man. With the needs of a man. He wasn't saving it for *Cathleen Ni Houlihan.*"

Diane laughed. "You know," she said, "I told only one other person about that nudist camp—Grandma Róisín."

"You're kidding," laughed Johnny. "What did she say?"

"'Good for you!'"

Johnny laughed out loud. "Typical Róisín. Rebel to the end."

"She was great," Diane reminisced. "I was all upset at your reaction—you were totally disgusted!—and so I tearfully told Róisín. She said, 'Dearie, Johnny is an old, moralistic stick-in-the-mud like his grandfather. They are like all Irishmen—seemingly horrified at the sight of a naked female body, except when it's under them *assuaging* them!' She went on to say, 'Do what you want, you're only young once.' Then she added: 'I would have *loved* to have gone with you!' I felt so much better after talking to Róisín. She had you Kavanagh men pinned down perfectly."

"Grandma didn't miss a trick," agreed Johnny. "It's amazing that she and Eoin took to each other like they did; happy to the end, they were."

"Well," said Diane, "they did lead very separate lives. Eoin in Washington and Dublin, Róisín in New York with her feminist friends. Róisín said she always admired Eoin for his earnestness and steadfastness. Something you just didn't see in other men. I'll never forget what she said to me about Eoin. She said, 'He was such a good person, taking care of his Mammy, Daddy, and siblings. You know what impressed me most of all? The absence of greed. He wasn't interested in power, money, bullying people. And even with all the terrible work he did for Collins, he was, in a very sweet way, very gentle. He was just a good man—and I found that sexy.' She then gave me this devilish laugh and added: 'He was also a great little fuck in bed!'"

"She didn't say 'fuck,' did she?"

"Yes, she did," laughed Diane. "Róisín was such a great broad."

"It's a wonder," laughed Johnny, "that she didn't fall in love with Michael Collins herself."

"Not Róisín's type," said Diane definitely, as Johnny looked on, doubt on his face. "Women know these things, husband dear. Their Type-A-driven personalities didn't match. She came to love Collins, but I think that was because of Ireland and Eoin and what he was doing. That poor man. 1922 doesn't look promising."

"Well," said Johnny, holding up Eoin's diary for January 1922, "you can see it didn't start off well."

"It's beginning to look like a disaster."

"Well," said Johnny, pensively, picking up a book and looking for the right page, "you're pretty close to the truth. Collins brings the Treaty back with him from London, with the admonition to the *Dáil* that he did 'not recommend it for more than it is. Equally I do not recommend it for less than it is. In my opinion, it gives us freedom—not the ultimate freedom that all nations desire and develop to, but the freedom to achieve it.'"

"Wise words from General Collins," said Diane.

"Well," continued Johnny, "to some extent, he had Dev, Brugha, and the rest of them cornered."

"How?"

"The people were tired of war. The people were *for* the Treaty. It was the dead-enders—Brugha, Stack, etc.—who were against it. They couldn't buck public opinion, except by scurrilous deeds in the *Dáil*, and that's what they were trying to do in the early part of 1922." Suddenly, Johnny laughed.

"What's so funny?" asked his wife.

"At one point in the debate, de Valera was trying to use all kinds of parliamentary tricks to subvert the Treaty, and Collins shouted at him and his cohorts in the *Dáil*, calling them out as 'bullies.' He went on to say, 'We will have no Tammany Hall methods here. Whether you are for the Treaty or whether you are against it, fight without Tammany Hall methods. We will not have them.'"

"Tammany Hall!" laughed Diane.

"Yeah," said Johnny, "it was like Collins was telling Eoin where his future was—in New York, with Mayor Walker and Tammany."

"It's funny how this old world works, isn't it?"

"It's diabolical, that's what it is."

"Seven months," said Diane.

"Seven months?"

"That's all Collins has left." Johnny put his hands to his face and rubbed his eyes. A tear escaped his paw. "What's wrong?"

"It's this fucking book," said Johnny. "It's tearing at me. The emotional toll is still overwhelming, even nearly a hundred years later. Can you imagine how tough it was to live through the period that Collins and Grandpa did?"

"What's that old Chinese saying?" said Diane, with a wistful smile. "'May you live in interesting times'?"

Johnny shook his head. "It's really a curse, because sometimes, you die in them."

152

Róisín had just dropped off a friend at her nurse's job at St. Vincent's Hospital on St. Stephen's Green when she looked up to see the Countess Markievicz advancing on her. The *Dáil* was meeting at University College Dublin in Earlsfort Terrance just down the way. There was no mistaking the Countess, with her big feathered hat and that determined walk. Strangely, thought Róisín, with all the focus on the *Dáil* and the Treaty debates, she was without an entourage.

"Connie!" Róisín called out, interrupting the Countess's concentration.

"Róisín? Is that you?" Markievicz asked in surprise, as she stopped in her tracks. They embraced as the early January darkness descended on Dublin like a lid closing on a coffin. "How have you been?"

"Oh," replied Róisín, "things are pretty much the same. I'm still up at the Mater."

"Well," said the Countess, "we in the *Cumann na mBan* must stay together during these tumultuous times. That was quite a vote by the *Cumann*—419–63."

Róisín stared at the sidewalk. "I was one of the nays," she said quietly.

The Countess looked shocked. "But why, dearie? We must be adamant at this crucial time."

"I've had enough," said Róisín, bringing her eyes back up to the Countess's face.

"But we must fight for the Republic!" the Countess declared. "We can't let cowards and English deceivers like Collins and Griffith seduce us with this false Treaty. Walk with me," continued Markievicz, "I have a meeting at the Shelbourne."

Róisín, mouth agape, starting walking with the Countess, when it hit her. "Wait," she said, stopping Markievicz by taking hold of her arm. "Cowards? What cowards?"

"Collins and Griffith."

Róisín had a quizzical look on her face. "Cowards? Mick Collins is not a coward. Mick Collins won the war. Mr. Griffith said so in the *Dáil* just the other day."

"Collins did no such thing. Poor man. He's now starting to believe his own press. The 'Dublin Pimpernel' and all that rot. Some soldier. Brugha said he was just one of his subordinates. A very minor subordinate, at that." The Countess starting walking again, leaving Róisín alone by the fence of the Green.

"Connie," said Róisín, running after Markievicz, "that's not true. Brugha's a fool. Everyone in Dublin knows that. A little man with a big chip on his shoulder. He's jealous of Mick."

The Countess stopped in her tracks. "Cathal Brugha is one of the most courageous men in Ireland."

Róisín moved her head closer to the Countess. "He may be brave, but he is a fool."

"How can you talk like that? What has gotten into you?"

"Sense," replied Róisín. "Sense has gotten into me. We have our own country. The English are leaving. What more do you want?"

"We want a Republic!"

"You'll get your Republic in due time. That's what Mick said."

"Mick, Mick, Mick. I thought you didn't like the ruffian."

"Mick Collins is not a ruffian. He is a patriot. Unlike de Valera, he is selfless. He didn't go hide in America when things got sticky."

Róisín saw Markievicz's face go as dark as the approaching dusk. "You don't know what you're talking about," said the Countess, as she turned the corner of the Green and started galloping towards the Shelbourne.

"I know very well what I'm talking about," snapped Róisín. "I've been in Dublin for the last six years, when you and de Valera weren't."

"I was in prison in England."

"I know you were, but I was here. I saw the Black and Tan terror, and I saw Bloody Sunday, too. Mick did that, you know. Not Brugha. Not de Valera. He wiped the English scum out in one morning."

"I always thought Bloody Sunday was overblown," countered the Countess.

"Overblown? I know the men who did this," Róisín said, thinking of her Eoin, Vinny Byrne, and Jack Lemass. "This was an act of supreme national courage." She subconsciously gestured towards Baggot Street, where two of the shootings had taken place. "Bloody Sunday drove the British to the truce. Without it, we'd have a Black and Tan stationed on every corner in Dublin today." The Countess always knew that Róisín was direct, but she had never seen her so impassioned. "Yes, Connie, Mick's men eliminated the scum, and who shows up immediately, after two years of sitting on his arse in America? Our esteemed president. He knew the truce was coming, and he had to have his hand in it."

In front of the Shelbourne Hotel, the Countess stopped and looked at her erstwhile acolyte. "I stand with the president. His work in America was important, raising funds and bringing the struggle of Ireland to world attention."

"And I stand with the General," replied Róisín. "Raising money before Legion of Mary breakfasts in Columbus, Ohio, is not the same as taking out British spies."

The line was drawn, and the two women just stared at each other. "Róisín," the Countess finally said, trying to bring Róisín back to her side, "think of our martyred heroes. Think of the unborn generations of Irish children."

"How about us?" retorted Róisín. "The living. Do we not get to have a say?"

"But look who's against the Treaty," implored the Countess, as she started the litany of prominent names. "Kathleen Clarke, Mary MacSwiney, Grace Gifford Plunkett, Mrs. Pearse."

"I don't want to belittle their martyred dead," said Róisín quietly. "But they are dead, and I am alive. Don't I get any consideration? I want a free Ireland—now—for my own unborn children."

It was no use. "Goodbye, Róisín," said the Countess. "We have nothing further to discuss." With that, she turned and walked into the Shelbourne.

"Goodbye, Connie," Róisín called after Markievicz, realizing that their friendship, like the country, was forever fractured.

153

Eoin and Collins rode in silence in the Crosley tender. They were coming from the Portobello Barracks, where they both now lived and worked. The tender rolled through the infamous Dardanelles, turned left at Dame Street, and sped by Dublin Castle and Christ Church, on its way to Lower Bridge Street. As they got to the Liffey River, they could see the two eighteen-pounder field artillery the British had lent the new National Army.

A lot had changed since the *Dáil* voted for the Treaty. In fact, things were moving so fast that, by June, the situation was changing day-to-day, if not hour-to-hour. In January, de Valera had stepped down as president, replaced by Arthur Griffith. De Valera, followed by Brugha, Stack, and the Countess Markievicz, had also walked out of the *Dáil*. On June 16, the Irish people had voted overwhelmingly for the Treaty. It was now time for the Provisional Government to act. "If we are not prepared to fight," said President Griffith, "and preserve the rights of the ordinary people, we should be looked on as the greatest set of poltroons that ever had the fate of Ireland in their hands." Trying to keep up with the deteriorating situation in both Dublin and Munster, it was decided that Griffith was to take over the political reins, and Collins would run the army that was so crucial to the survival of the new nation, which was nearly stillborn.

The effect that all this had on Eoin was that he was conscripted into the National Army and given the rank of Commandant-Colonel. It did not sit well with the twenty-year-old. It did not sit well with Vinny

Bryne either, who also ended up a Commandant-Colonel and, irony of ironies, had been placed in charge of Richmond Barracks by Collins himself. Eoin's job really hadn't changed. He still worked in intelligence and continued his work on the National Loan, as Collins had also remained Minister for Finance. His bodyguarding duties also came with the package.

"I don't want to go into the army," Eoin had initially protested.

"You have no choice," snapped Collins. "Half the IRA is anti-Treaty, and they have deserted. I have to raise an army to run this country. You are in, and you will like it." Eoin was wise enough—and knew Collins well enough—to know that this was not the time to argue. He knew Collins was under intense pressure, not only from his pro-Treaty comrades, but also from the anti-Treaty forces he was trying to placate. Not to mention from London, where the Brits were looking at the deteriorating situation with immense concern.

The Four Courts had been taken over in April by Rory O'Connor and two hundred of his men. For two months, the standoff had been rather quiet, as Collins decided not to push the issue, hoping for a peaceful solution. Then two things happened. Sir Henry Wilson had been assassinated in London by IRA agents, and Free State General J.J. O'Connell had been kidnapped by the anti-Treaty forces. The phone lines between London and Dublin had been hot. Mr. Churchill was not at all pleased.

"Enough of this shite," were Collins's last words to Eoin before they climbed into the tender.

No one loved Dublin the way Eoin did. And he especially loved the architecture, be it the façade of Trinity College, the beautiful Georgian squares, or the quirkiness of Henrietta Street. He had often thought that the British may be brutes, but they really knew how to lay out a city. Now his beautiful city was in ruins. They were still rebuilding the GPO, and he had helped burn the Customs House. Now, as he stood next to Collins at the foot of Lower Bridge Street and viewed the patina-domed Four Courts on this beautiful, tranquil June afternoon, he suddenly realized that he was to have a hand in the destruction of all three.

"What do you think?" asked Collins.

Eoin didn't know if it was a rhetorical question or not, but he replied anyway. "I hear Jack Lemass is second-in-command." Collins shook his head and bit his lip. "My brother Frank is in there, too," Eoin added.

Collins pulled at the collar on his tunic and drew his hat down over his eyes. "It can't be helped."

General Emmet Dalton, Charlie Dalton's brother and a veteran of the Great War, was the man Collins had put in charge. "Mick, Eoin," Dalton said, "how are you?"

"You ready?" asked Collins.

"As we'll ever be."

"So these are our English cannons," said Collins. "Nice of Mr. Churchill to make them available to us." He patted the barrel and grunted at Dalton, "Fire when you're ready." Then both Collins and Eoin backed away. The eighteen-pounder shot, and the recoil almost took it back into Collins, as if it were a warning. Collins stubbornly retreated further down Lower Bridge Street. Then, from Winetavern Street, at the other end of Merchants Quay, they could see shells flying over the Liffey and hitting the Courts. The cannons at both ends of the quay couldn't miss. The Four Courts were a sitting duck. Soon dark smoke rose up, and patches of fire could be seen. The pounding continued as shell after shell was fed into the artillery. Eoin winced as each one exploded.

He looked behind him and saw that he was only a few yards from the Brazen Head, the oldest pub in Dublin. "I need a fucking drink," he told Collins, and didn't wait for an answer.

He was sipping a Jameson when he felt a big body next to him. It was Collins. "I'll have what the Commandant-Colonel is having," said Collins to the barman, who stood, mouth agape, when he realized who his new customer was.

"How can you do this?" Eoin asked.

"Because it's my duty, that's why."

"The beautiful Four Courts."

"Full of anti-Treaty forces."

"Let the British do it."

"This is our country now," replied the General. "This is our business. We are not going to turn around and plead with England to come help us when things get messy. This is our mess, and we are going to clean it up. That's what independence means. Do you understand?"

Eoin was quiet for a moment. "Yes, I understand," he finally said. "But I still don't like it."

"I don't like it either, but it's my job."

The two men, in their brand-new Free State Army uniforms, stood next to each other not saying a word, slowly sipping their whiskeys. "You should have let me do that Wilson job, instead of those amateurs you sent," Eoin finally said. "Me and Vinny could have done the job and been back in Dublin before they knew Wilson was dead."

With all the trouble in the Free State, Collins still had his eye on the "Black North," as he was wont to call it. It had been open season on Catholics, especially in Belfast, and Collins had gotten no satisfaction out of Sir James Craig, the Northern Ireland premier, nor Churchill or Lloyd George on the matter. He finally said to Churchill, "There is a pogrom going on in the North against Catholics, and if you don't stop it, I will." But nothing was done, and refugees had flooded into Dublin. Collins was aware that Wilson, from the safety of London, was proud of the murder work his men were doing in Belfast. Collins decided that if he couldn't help the Catholics of the North, he would make a statement—and Wilson became that statement. His mistake was that he did not send the Squad, but two local Irishmen who were soon apprehended. It had all become the perfect political storm, and, now, the eighteen-pounders were doing Collins's talking. Some were saying that that talk was actually from the ventriloquist Churchill in London.

"I can't afford to have men like you and Vinny out of the country at this time," said Collins. He paused and pursed his lips. "Maybe I should have just let it go, but Wilson had it coming to him. Maybe Craig and Churchill will heed me the next time I have a protest in the North."

"I hear Robert Emmet used to drink here," said Eoin, suddenly changing the conversation.

"And plot rebellion!" added Collins.

"He'd probably be in the Four Courts if he was alive today."

"I wish I was in the Four Courts myself," added Collins, wistfully.

"We're not rebels anymore, are we?"

"No," replied Collins. "No, we're not. We are now the government. All my life I have fought government, and now I am the government."

"God has a cruel sense of humor."

"He has," agreed Collins.

"We are living a fookin' disaster, aren't we?"

Collins drained his Jameson, looked at Eoin silently for a minute, and then laughed. "We are indeed, Commandant-Colonel. It is a fookin' disaster. But it's *our* fookin' disaster!" Eoin smiled at Collins's gentle jibe at his rank and followed his boss back outside to witness more obscene destruction, which they hoped, eventually, would help build the new nation.

154

"Welcome home," Eoin said to Jack Lemass. Lemass smiled wearily and took a seat to the side of Eoin's desk. They were back at Richmond Barracks, which was under the command of Vinny Byrne. "Can you believe it, Jack? Six years later, and we're both back in the same prison we started out from."

"Yes," said Lemass, "we were baby rebels then. Now Vinny's the boss man, they tell me."

"It seems so long ago." The two friends were having a hard time getting their conversation going. Neither wanted to talk about why they were there. Neither wanted to utter those two dreaded words: "civil war."

"You need a shave," said Eoin, with a small laugh. Lemass looked particularly sinister unshaven. It seemed his five o'clock shadow started at about nine in the morning.

"Beautiful uniform," Lemass said to Eoin, giving a gentle gibe. Lemass himself was a mess; his own clothes were filthy with grime and soot from the fires inside the Four Courts. His appearance reminded Eoin of their escape from the GPO into Moore Street, dragging the poor, stranded Jew, Abraham Weeks, with them.

"You can blame Mick for the uniform. He conscripted me."

"How is Mick?"

"How do you think he is? He's worn out—thanks to you guys." Lemass shrugged his shoulders. Funny, thought Eoin, it was a similar question he heard from a lot of the Four Court rebels, "How's Mick?" Ernie O'Malley had asked. So had General Tom Barry from County

Cork. This was the cream of the crop of the Republican movement, and somehow, they had lost them. All of them were great Irishmen.

"What do you want to see me for?" asked Lemass.

"Paperwork," replied Eoin. "I'm supposed to interview you."

"Interview away."

Eoin got up without speaking and went to the door. "Bring me Frank Kavanagh," he told the sentry.

"Where are you sending me? Mountjoy?"

"Home," said Eoin to the surprised Lemass. "You're no use to me locked up."

"You'll get in trouble."

Eoin gave a small smile. "So what can they do to me?"

"What do you want from me?"

"You'll see."

The sentry returned with Frank. "Commandant-Colonel, how are you?" jeered his brother, cheeky as ever.

"Just shut your gob. Do you know who this is?" Eoin said, pointing at Lemass.

"Commandant Lemass."

"You are to do exactly what the Commandant tells you to do. Do you understand?" Frank nodded his head affirmatively.

It was Lemass who was confused. "What . . . ?" wondered Lemass.

"Jack," interrupted Eoin, "take this eejit out of here and get him out of the movement. I don't want him on the pro-Treaty side or the anti-Treaty side. I just want him out of the movement. And out of the country."

Eoin reached in his pocket and pulled out a twenty-pound note. "Here, Frank, this is for you," holding it in front of Frank's face. He then gave the money to Lemass for safekeeping. "This is my life savings. Take it, and get the fuck out of this country. North Wall. Tonight. Jack, you make sure. Now both of you get out of here, while the getting is good."

Still confused, Lemass got up to leave. Frank looked at Eoin hard before he spoke. "You know you have no right to tell me what to do."

"I have every right," snapped Eoin. "You have never been anything but trouble. It's all about you, Frank. You're nothing but a narcissist. You do things just to spite me. If I was anti-Treaty, you'd be in the Free State Army right now." Frank gave Eoin an idiot's smile of acknowledgement.

The next thing Frank felt was Eoin's fist exploding against the side of his head, knocking him face-first into the floor, which was soon covered with Frank's blood. "Pick him up and get him out of here."

As Lemass and the sentry helped Frank to his feet the, intense hate between the two Kavanagh brothers was palpable. Hate that only the Irish can comprehend. Lemass saw a change in Eoin. He was no longer the idealistic boy he had known in the GPO. He figured it must have been from constantly working with Collins for the last five years. Lemass was a part-time Republican, called upon only when there was a job to be done. He knew the intense pressure Eoin had been under working for Collins, first in finance, then in intelligence. And Eoin was not one to shrink from duty. Not only did he find the bad guys, but he was also a freelance member of the Squad. *If I had Eoin's job*, thought Lemass to himself, *I'd probably hate Frank, too.*

"I'll get even. I swear," muttered Frank, as he pressed a handkerchief to his bloodied face. "If it's the last thing I do."

"Get even in England," said Eoin, now back to his usual calm. "Even better, get even from America." And with that, Jack Lemass—more of a brother to Eoin than his own sibling—guided Frank Kavanagh out of Richmond Barracks.

155

J uly brought chaos to Dublin—and death was beginning to claim the players.

The anti-Treaty forces had taken to the streets, and bands of armed men in trenchcoats marched straight down Grafton Street in defiance of the Provisional Government. After the shelling of the Four Courts, the Irregulars—reinforced by the *Cumann na mBan*—had retreated to make their stand on Upper Sackville Street, taking over the Gresham Hotel and the areas adjacent to Parnell Street. Eoin had stood at the Westmoreland Street end of O'Connell Bridge with hundreds of other Dubliners and watched the scenario play out, as if in a film. "Where, in God's name, were all these heroic shites when the Black and Tans were terrorizing Dublin City?" he said aloud, but no one was listening to him.

"Flush them out," Collins had ordered, and the Free State Army systematically, building-by-building, finally pushed the rebels out of the city centre. Among the Irregulars in Sackville Street were de Valera, Austin Stack, and the Countess Markievicz. They had the good sense to escape. Cathal Brugha did not. On July 5, Brugha, pistol in hand like Billy-the-Kid, came out into Sackville Street firing. He was hit in the leg and died two days later from massive blood loss.

"Poor Cathal Brugha, R.I.P.," wrote Kitty Kiernan to Collins from Longford. "A pitiable ending for a fruitless gain."

"Good riddance," was Eoin's reaction, which made Collins wince.

"Show some respect for the dead," said Collins quietly. "Because of his sincerity, I would forgive him anything. At worst, he was a fanatic. At best, I number him among the very few who have given their all that this country should have its freedom. When many of us are forgotten, Cathal Brugha will be remembered."

Eoin was shocked by Collins's words. He could not forgive Frank for his stupidity, yet Collins could forgive Brugha for his many transgressions. Eoin was embarrassed into silence by Collins and his seeming serenity in the face of tragedy after tragedy.

"I'm sorry," Eoin said at last.

"That alright," replied Collins. "We have to learn from all this. I don't want this nation to be born in hatred." In fact, Collins was showing the Irregulars that he would not be cowered by their belligerence, and, conversely, he hoped that his measured approach to provocation would be seen by the rebels as an opportunity for compromise, not as weakness. Collins even went so far as to contact Boland and make amends: "Harry—it has come to this!" he wrote. "Of all things, it has come to this. It is in my power to arrest you and destroy you. This I cannot do. If you will think over the influence which has dominated you, it should change your mind. You are walking under false colours. If no words of mine will change your attitude, then you are beyond all hope—my hope."

And as bloody July turned into an even bloodier August, Eoin received a phone call at the Portobello Barracks that turned his stomach. Harry Boland was dying at St. Vincent's Hospital after being shot up by Free State troops in Skerries.

"Do you want to go and visit him?" asked Eoin.

"I don't think this is the time or the place," said Collins. "I think the last face the Boland family wants to see right now is mine."

Collins sat at his desk and stared straight ahead, not seeing anything. "Remember," Collins suddenly said, "the Joe McGuinness campaign up in Longford? The three of us stealing that election?"

Eoin had fond memories of his first adventure outside of Dublin, chauffeured by Boland and Collins, his two big Fenian brothers. "Yes," said Eoin smiling, "our 'felon candidate.'"

"Put him in to get him out," laughed Collins. "That was a long time ago."

By this time, Collins and Eoin were spending close to twenty-four hours together. Kitty was up in Longford, and the Dublin situation was

not a salubrious one for her. The passing of Harry Boland had intensi-
fied the feelings of Kitty and Collins, with Boland serving as the unlikely
catalyst. "Last night I passed Vincent's Hospital and saw a small crowd
outside," Collins wrote to Kitty. "My mind went out to him, lying dead
there, and I thought of the times together; and whatever good there is
in any wish of mine, he certainly had it. I thought of him only with the
friendship of the days of 1918 and 1919. They tell me that the last thing
he said to his sister Kathleen before he was operated on was, 'Have they
got Mick Collins yet?' I don't believe it so far as I'm concerned, and, if
he did say it, there is no necessity to believe it. I'd send a wreath, but I
suppose they'd return it torn up."

"Naturally I feel Harry's death," Kitty replied to Collins, "but I would
never have believed that I could feel it so much. The whole thing's so
tragic that today I almost wished I had died, too. Poor Harry, may he
rest in peace. I murmured little aspirations all day yesterday to Our
Lord, to have pity on the dying. I had an idea he might die, strong and
all as he was. When the hour comes, Oh! Vain is the strength of man.
I realize I have lost a good friend in Harry—and no matter what, I'll
always believe in his genuineness, that I was the one and only. I think
you have also lost a friend. I am sure you are sorry after him."

Death or not, after the Battle of Dublin, Collins concentrated on
pacifying the countryside, particularly in the south, where the Irregulars
had control of what they called the "Munster Republic." He sent
Commandant Paddy Daly, erstwhile leader of the Squad, to Kerry, and
can-do General Emmet Dalton was put in charge of subduing Cork.
And he did just that, with a miraculous amphibious landing. Things
were beginning to look up. On August 12, Collins and Eoin were in
Tralee when the telegram came that President Griffith had died of a
stroke. He had been in poor health since the Treaty negotiations and,
against the stern advice of his physician, Dr. Gogarty, had worked
himself to death. Gogarty was bitter, saying Griffith's death was caused
by "envy, jealousy, and ingratitude."

Collins looked like somebody or something had pulled the guts out
of him. "There seems to be a malignant fate," he told Eoin, on their way
back to Dublin, "dogging the fortunes of Ireland, for, during every critical
period in her story, the man whom the country trusts is taken from her."

Now, Collins stood alone, the only man capable of stopping complete
chaos. He instinctively knew that this was not the time to show fear.

So, on the morning of President Griffith's funeral, he looked powerful and utterly handsome in his General's uniform. The supreme actor in Collins had taken over. He would play to the Pathé Newsreel cameras and reassure the nation. That morning, at Government Buildings on Merrion Street, he talked on the phone to his various commanders in the field and prepared to travel to the Pro-Cathedral for Griffith's solemn requiem high mass. As they rode to the cathedral in Marlborough Street, he told Eoin, "After we're done with Arthur, we will be traveling to Cork to see how Dalton's doing down there. He seems to have the situation in hand." He paused before mysteriously adding, "I hear that Dev might be in the area."

Fook Dev, Eoin thought to himself, as he reached into his pocket and handed Collins a letter. "This came this morning from 44 Mountjoy Street," he said.

He knew it was a letter from Kitty, and Collins hungrily tore it open. Eoin saw him nodding his head and heard him grunt once or twice. Then he gave a quick laugh, which was quickly shut off as he thought again about what Kitty had written to him. "Do you know what she said to me?" Collins said, gesticulating with the letter. "She said, 'I am always thinking of you and worrying, and, just tonight, somebody said that, if you go to the funeral tomorrow, you'll be shot, but God is very good to you.'"

"Jaysus," said Eoin, the concern on his face.

"Don't worry, Eoin. Remember what Kitty said. God is very good to me."

"I don't like stuff like this."

"Don't worry," replied Collins, "I don't think I'll die today." Then he suddenly laughed. "There will be plenty of time to die tomorrow or the next day. And as my ould daddy used to say, 'You'll be a long time dead.'"

"You will, indeed."

"I will," echoed Collins, as he climbed out of his limousine, pulled on his leather gloves, and waited for the coffin of his friend Arthur Griffith to arrive. As he greeted mourners and well-wishers in front of the cathedral, only one thought kept running through Michael Collins's mind: Whose coffin would be next?

156

Róisín had just finished her shift at the Mater Hospital on the day after President Griffith's funeral. It was four p.m., and, although the day was still bright, it had begun to turn cold, unusual for this time of August. It was the harvest, but the weather was beginning to feel more like November. She paused to say hello to her fellow nurse, Christine Reynolds, who was running late for her own shift. As they exchanged quick pleasantries on Eccles Street. an automobile pulled up in front of them.

"Róisín!" the voice called out.

Róisín peered into the car. "Frank," she said, surprised. "Is that you?"

"It's Eoin, Róisín," Frank said. "He's been shot. He sent me to get you."

"Oh, my God!" exclaimed Róisín, suddenly flushed and aggrieved as she gave a quick wave goodbye to Nurse Reynolds. Then it hit her. "What are *you* doing in Dublin?"

With that, Frank pulled out a Mauser and said, "Shut ya gob and get in." He gave her a good shove in the back with the gun, and Róisín, infuriated, did as she was told. "To Stoneybatter!" Frank said to the driver, as he got into the back seat alongside Róisín. The car pulled out with a screech, and Christine gasped at what she had just witnessed.

"Sister, Sister," Christine said to the white-habited Sister Aloysius, the head nurse, as she entered the hospital. "Róisín's just been kidnapped!"

All day, Collins had been holding meetings at Government Buildings with his various commanders and the proposed new president of the

Dáil, William T. (Willie) Cosgrave. Although Cosgrave was only forty-two years of age, he looked older because of the way he dressed. With his signature bowler hat, winged collars, and little mustache, he looked like an aged version of Charlie Chaplin's Little Tramp. Collins and Cosgrave made an odd couple, Eoin decided. Cosgrave was holding onto the nineteenth century with his old-fashioned dress, while Collins was advancing as fast as he could into the twentieth century with his beautifully cut suits and military uniforms. Collins had served time with Cosgrave in Frongoch after the Rising and apparently trusted him. Eoin wasn't as sure. He knew that Ireland was going to miss Arthur Griffith and miss him tremendously. Little did Eoin know that fifty-two years later, Cosgrave's son Liam, the new *Taoiseach*, would indict him for running guns to the Provisional IRA in the North.

Collins came out of his office with Cosgrave and suddenly said, "Willie, do you think I shall live through this? Not likely." Suddenly, he turned on Eoin. "How would you like a new boss?"

"Mick," said Cosgrave, "stop. Don't frighten the boy."

"He's no boy," replied Collins. "He's a commandant-colonel in the National Army."

Cosgrave exited, and Eoin winced. Collins was putting the finishing touches on his plan to visit Cork the following week. After exchanging telegrams with General Dalton in Cork, Eoin didn't think it was wise to venture south. "The situation is stabilizing down there," he told Collins, "but it's still somewhat unpredictable. The security is perilous."

"What are you saying?" asked Collins.

"I don't think you should go."

"Yerra," Collins snapped, "they'll never shoot me in my county."

"I'll make the arrangements," Eoin acquiesced, not feeling right about the whole thing. As he sat at his desk, his phone rang. "General Collins's office," said Eoin.

"Eoin?" said a female voice. "Is that you?"

"Yes. Who is this?"

"It's Christine Reynolds. I work at the Mater with Róisín. Are you alright?"

"I am, Christine," said Eoin, confused. "And why wouldn't I be alright?" There was silence on the other end of the line. "Christine, are you still there?"

"Your Róisín's been kidnapped," she finally blurted out.

"What?"

"Two men in a car took her at gunpoint."

Eoin was stunned into silence. He managed to compose himself as Vinny Byrne went by. "Vinny, wait!" Then he returned to the phone. "Christine, did you know who these guys were?"

"No, but Róisín knew one of them. She addressed him as 'Frank.'"

A cold chill went through Eoin, and Vinny noticed that he had turned as pale as a newly whitewashed wall. "Frank?"

"Yes," replied Christine. "A young fellow. Couldn't be more than fifteen or sixteen. Very handsome."

"Christine, I'll be up there as soon as I can. Don't go anywhere."

"What's up?" asked Vinny.

"Róisín's been kidnapped."

"My God!"

"By Frank."

"Frank?" asked Vinny. "I thought he was out of the country."

Eoin didn't say a word. He got up and walked across the room, retrieving the thin Dublin phone directory, which really wasn't anything more than a glorified pamphlet. He hit the Ls and searched for J.T. Lemass of Capel Street. He relayed the number to the operator, and, finally, the voice said, "Hello, J.T. Lemass, Hatter and Outfitter. How may I help you?"

"Can I speak to Jack Lemass?" It took a moment, but Jack got on the phone. "Jack, it's Eoin. I have a question for you. Did you put my brother Frank on that boat to England?"

"Yes," replied Lemass, "I did as you told me. I bought the ticket and gave him the rest of the money. I saw him get on the boat."

"Well, he apparently got off again."

"How do you know?"

"He just kidnapped Róisín at the Mater Hospital."

"Mother of God. I'm sorry, Eoin, I'm awfully sorry. I should have waited until the boat sailed."

"It's not your fault, Jack. The little shite is always up to no good."

"Can I help?"

"No, I don't think that's such a good idea. I don't think you want to be seen with Free Staters like me and Vinny."

"Well," said Lemass, "God speed to you. If I hear anything from my side, I'll let you know."

"Thanks, Jack. I'll handle it from here." With that, he hung up the phone. "Let's get a car and get up to the Mater," he said to Vinny. "I'm going to kill him if I have to." He went to a coat rack and put on the holster that held his Webley.

"Who are you going to kill?" asked Collins, entering the room. Since their trip out west to Kerry, Collins had been ill. His stomach was at him, and he was having trouble keeping food down. Eoin also noticed that he was listless. A lion for work, Eoin saw him shuffling papers without interest. The robust rebel now looked like he was going through the motions. He had managed to pull himself out of it for Griffith's funeral, but he was playing to the cameras, the supreme actor-politician he was. Somehow, impossibly, Ireland had sucked the energy out of Michael Collins. Eoin was distracted by Collins's appearance, and, once again, the General asked him, "Who are you going to kill?"

"My imbecile brother Frank."

"What did he do now?"

"He kidnapped Róisín at the Mater."

"Well," said Collins, "let's get moving."

"Hold on, Mick," said Eoin, holding up his hand like he was stopping traffic. "Me and Vinny will handle this. You have no business getting involved in something like this. The Irregulars see you on the street, and someone will take a shot at you."

"I will not be held captive in my own country," snapped Collins. "I'm the General. You two are colonels. A general still outranks two colonels. And that's that. Let's go." It seemed that Róisín's kidnapping had pulled Collins out of his phlegmatic state.

Eoin found himself in Collins's Rolls-Royce Silver Ghost automobile with Vinny and the driver. Even with all the Free State troops stopping traffic at security checkpoints, they got to the Mater in record time. It was amazing how the presence of Michael Collins could expedite things.

At the Mater, the presence of Collins started a buzz. Eoin saw the distraught Christine Reynolds and went to her. "Are you alright?" The handsome young woman, about the same age as Róisín, had closely cropped hair, sensitive yet lively eyes, and a smile that, when she felt like it, could dazzle. But right now, this minute, she looked like she was in shock.

"I can't believe it," she said. "I just can't believe it."

"Is there a place we can talk privately?" Collins interjected.

She looked up at Collins and numbly stuttered, "Yes, yes, Sister Aloysius's office."

Inside the office, Eoin said, "Now, Christine, tell me everything from the beginning."

She told them what she knew.

"Anything else?" asked Eoin.

"No, that's it."

"Are you sure?" asked Collins. He put his right hand to her elbow and, with his thumb and index finger, gently massaged her funny bone, as if to soothe. "I know it was a terrible shock to you, but was there anything else said between the three of them?"

Christine pursed her lips in thought. "Stoneybatter," she finally said.

"Stoneybatter?"

"'To Stoneybatter,' That's what the gunman said to the driver. Then they left."

Suddenly Collins gave a bright smile to Christine, and she could see the gap between his two front teeth. "Christine," the General said, "you're brilliant!"

"Not much in Stoneybatter," said Vinny, not getting it.

"Yeah," said Eoin. "Nothing there but my Uncle Charlie, twenty-year British army veteran."

"He thinks Charlie is a fellow confederate," said Collins.

"I guess he doesn't know," replied Eoin. "As the man said—'to Stoneybatter!'"

The three of them jumped in the Rolls and continued the journey to old Stoneybatter, one of the quirkiest neighborhoods in Dublin. Its history went back to the time of the Vikings—its narrow, winding roads and small one- and two-story buildings (it seemed that every building in Stoneybatter was off-balance and about to topple over) gave it the appearance that maybe, once, Lilliputians had lived there.

Their destination was 47 Ben Edar Road. *Ben Edar*, Eoin knew, was the Irish for Howth, but this Howth was in Dublin's inner city. As dusk fell, darkness began to blanket the Northside of Dublin. It was eerie being in this neighborhood, so close to Arbor Hill, where all the executed 1916 Kilmainham rebels shared one quicklime grave. It didn't take long to get lost, as the streets wound into unexpected cul-de-sacs. Finally they came to a long, narrow street lined with small, one-story structures. In fancier neighborhoods, these would be called artisan cottages. Here, they were just working-class homes. Stoneybatter was especially popular with Guinness employees because of its easy access to the brewery via bicycle—a quick, downhill run across the Liffey to work.

Collins's car stopped at the bottom of the street. There was an old Ford parked in front of number forty-seven. "How are we going to handle this?" Vinny asked.

"What's the point of this?" Eoin wondered. "To hurt me? To hurt Róisín? And why would Uncle Charlie help him?"

"He thinks he's doing something that would embarrass the government," said Collins. "That's his point. Frank never plans anything out. He's a kid with fantasies, and right now his fantasy is that he is some kind of heroic revolutionary out to bring the Provisional Government down. It's not exactly biblical."

Eoin disagreed. "Oh, yes, it is!"

"How so?"

"Cain and Abel. And there can be only one result."

"Are you your brother's keeper?" chided Collins.

"Jaysus lads," interjected Vinny, exasperation in his voice. "Let's get Róisín out of there. Continue your Bible study later."

"Vinny's right," said Collins. "Let's go get Róisín. I'll go in first."

"You will not!" protested Johnny. "He could blow your brains out."

"Or I could blow his brains out."

As quick as that, Collins was out of his Rolls, heading for the house with Eoin and Vinny trailing behind. Eoin had seen this reckless behavior before. He remembered Collins defying the British by dressing in his general's uniform at the Mansion House, and also the time when they were cornered by a British squad at Dr. Gogarty's surgery. Collins seemed to relish these occasions of danger, rejoicing in the adrenaline high. Eoin did not. Collins was enjoying it all, Eoin realized. "Wait!" he called out.

Collins stopped in his tracks. "What?"

"We need a plan here," said Eoin.

"Somebody has to go through the door first," Vinny counseled. "Then the shooters follow, ready to shoot."

"I'll go first," Collins repeated.

"No!" Eoin protested again.

"I'm the biggest," Collins insisted. "I can take someone down and clear the way for you lads." Eoin was in agony. He wanted to save Róisín without losing Collins.

"That's an order—and that's that!"

They instructed the chauffeur to stand back and make sure there was no escape. Eoin decided that he would do the talking. He rapped hard on the door and waited. "Who's there?" came a voice from behind the door.

"Eoin Kavanagh."

They could hear bodies moving around inside. The door opened a peek, and Collins put his shoulder to it and flung it wide open, almost tearing it off its hinges. He knocked Charlie Conway to the ground and bulled straight ahead to Frank, who stood there with his gun in his hand, pointed straight at Collins. He never got a shot off as Collins, running like a Gaelic footballer possessed, hit him squarely in the chest with his head. The gun flew into the air, and Frank landed squarely in the middle of the floor. While Frank was still looking up at the ceiling, Vinny Byrne cast a shadow on him as he put the nozzle of his Mauser semi-automatic flush in the center of Frank's forehead. "You move, and you're dead," Vinny said calmly, as if he had done this before.

Eoin had his Webley trained on Frank's confederate, who was sitting on the couch next to Róisín. She was tied and gagged. "What's your fookin' business?" he said to the young fellow, who was maybe sixteen years of age.

"I want to die for Ireland!" he said excitedly, which elicited a great laugh out of Collins.

"What's your name?"

"Seamus Crowley."

"Hit the floor, Seamus, and I may let you live."

Seamus did as he was told, and Róisín was red in the face as she struggled with her gag and rope. Collins went over to her and patted her on the head, like a favorite pet. "Cat got your tongue?" he said to her, as he removed the handkerchief from her mouth.

"I'm going to kill you, Mick Collins!" she said, much to the amusement of the General. As soon as the rope was removed from her hands and legs, she advanced on Frank, who Vinny had cornered in a corner. She hit him with a roundhouse blow to the face, which knocked him onto the floor, spilling blood. "You fucking eejit!" she said. "And if you ever touch my breasts again, it will be the last teat you'll ever touch in your life!" Vinny's look turned dark, and Frank began to wonder if he would make it out of Stoneybatter alive.

"Are you alright, Captain Conway?" Collins asked Charlie.

"Captain!" spat Frank.

"National Army, you fookin' eejit," said Eoin to his brother.

"Now, Frank," said Collins, "if you want to be a successful Irregular, I suggest you not enlist one of my trusted advisers."

"We didn't have a chance," muttered Seamus Crowley with disgust.

"Since when?" asked Frank.

"Since March," said Charlie. "General Collins convinced Guinness to give me a leave of absence so I could train Free State troops at the Royal Barracks. It's a short commute for me," Charlie added, with a sly smile.

"You should have told me," said Frank, blood running down his chin from Róisín's battering.

"Frank, son," said Charlie, "you had the gun. I didn't think the truth was the correct option for Róisín and meself at the moment."

"Rope, Charlie," said Collins. "Give me rope, lots of rope." Within minutes, Frank and Seamus had their hands tied behind their backs. "Frank," said Collins, "you're a mess! And you, Seamus Crowley, should get some sense."

"Yes, General Collins," Seamus said, meekly.

"Vinny, they're all yours. I'm sure you have enough room at Richmond Barracks for these two wee lads." The two young Irregulars were marched outside to Collins's Rolls-Royce. "No, not this one," said Collins. "I don't need Frank's blood all over my brand-new Silver Ghost."

The two were marched back to the car they had come in. "I'm sorry, Eoin," said Frank, blood still dripping onto his shirt.

"No, you're not," replied Eoin. "And the one you should be apologizing to is Róisín."

Róisín stepped forward and instinctively reverted to nurse. She put her fingers to his split lip and nodded. "You'll live," she said, before adding, "you little shite."

"Forgive and forget!" joshed Collins.

"You fookin' men are all alike," Róisín fumed.

They sat Frank and Seamus in the back seat of the Ford, with Vinny riding shotgun next to Collins's chauffeur. As they drove off towards Richmond Barracks, Collins said, "Let's get a drink, the four of us."

"Not me, General," said Uncle Charlie. "I have to be at the Barracks at reverie."

They said their goodbyes, and Collins headed to his Rolls. "Who's going to drive?" asked Eoin.

"I am," said Collins.

"Since when do you drive?"

"Since spending my youth in London. I've been driving for more then ten years."

"Your talents *amaze* me," said Róisín, not amazed at all, as she needled the man who had rescued her. Her cynicism quickly turned to terror as Collins, despite the now-blinding fog, put the car into third gear and tore down the Northside quays before crossing the Liffey at Gratton Bridge.

Ten minutes later, they were parked outside of the Stag's Head. Silent Peadar Doherty was delighted to see them and offered them the back room.

They made their way past stunned patrons at the bar. Every eye was on Collins. Life was odd, thought Eoin, as he made his way through the bar crowd. Two years ago, no one knew what Collins looked like. Now everyone in Dublin knew his mug. He was, without a doubt, Dublin's biggest celebrity.

Once seated, Doherty took their order. "Pony of Jameson," said Róisín, and Eoin and Collins asked for the same. When the whiskeys arrived, Collins proposed a toast. "To Róisín, one of our bravest!"

Róisín responded to the General. "To Michael Collins, who gave us our country!"

Eoin, exhausted and thankful that Róisín was unharmed, added a third toast, "To our comrades, living and dead."

"Even those who went against the Treaty," said Collins, as he sipped his whiskey. "Just think," he added, "two years ago, we'd be looking over our shoulders for the Cairo Gang. Now Dublin Castle, just down that lane, is populated with people dedicated to our new Irish nation."

"It's really a miracle, when you think of it," said Eoin.

"Well," Collins replied, "Let's hope we have a few more miracles left in the bag. Maybe I can track down Dev in Cork next week and perform the miracle of miracles . . ."

"Yeah," interjected Róisín, "turn him into a true patriot, and stop this fookin' insanity."

"We'll see," said Collins good-naturedly, before turning serious. "You know what I hate?" he asked. "I hate Glasnevin Cemetery. I couldn't believe I was up there yesterday burying another patriot, Arthur Griffith. I went by the Republican Plot and saw the fresh graves of Harry Boland and Cathal Brugha, and I didn't know what to make of it. All I could think was, 'Who's next'?" The three of them sipped in silence. "Do you know what Bishop Fogarty said to me yesterday after we planted the president? He said, 'Michael, you should be prepared—you might be next.'"

"That clerical sonofabitch," said Róisín, rising up from her seat. "How dare he!"

"It's alright, Róisín."

"He had no right," snapped Róisín. "No right at all."

She plopped back down in her seat, and the three of them sat in silence, the air gone out of their balloon. Róisín looked down at the table and was suddenly filled with guilt. She remembered her earlier threat, "I'm going to kill you, Mick Collins!" Even as a figure of speech, it seemed threatening, because Ireland was filled with people who really wanted to kill Mick Collins. The queue was growing by the day, and Collins knew it. As the three of them finished their whiskeys, they knew who was going to be next. It was only a matter of time.

157

The next morning, Eoin was up especially early, so he could figure out what to do with Frank. After sleeping on it, he had decided that Frank had to go—to America.

The first thing he did was wire John Devoy in New York that Frank would be visiting soon and that he should take care of him. Eoin took a car from the Portobello Barracks to Dublin Castle and secured a passport—one of the new Free State passports—for Frank. "He'll need a photograph," the clerk had said.

"I'll use his mugshot," replied Colonel Kavanagh.

From the Castle, he pulled up to Cook's Travel Bureau, where he had transacted a lot of travel business for Collins and himself in the past. "When's the next boat to New York from Cobh?" he asked.

"Sunday evening," came the response. "RMS *Celtic* of the White Star Line."

"I'll take a steerage ticket."

"They don't provide steerage anymore," the clerk replied. "It's now called 'third class.'"

"Whatever," replied Eoin, and the deed was done.

He took the car to Government Buildings to meet up with Collins. "So," said the General, "what are you going to do with Abel?"

Eoin shook his head at the Biblical reference and Collins's attempt at humor. "I've decided, with your permission, to send him to New York. I've already wired Devoy to take care of him."

"Thanks for waiting for my permission," said Collins, lightly.

"The ship leaves from Cobh on Sunday evening. There's a boat going down to resupply General Dalton on Saturday, and I think I'll hitch a ride for Frank and myself. Then I can put Frank on the ship at Cobh and meet up with you in Cork City. I can't trust the roads or the rails with the way the Irregulars have been behaving."

"Sounds like a plan," said Collins.

"It's the best I can do. After this, I'm finished with the little bugger."

Collins gave a staccato laugh. "You are never finished with people like Frank. They are the family gift that keeps on giving."

Saturday afternoon, Eoin arrived at Richmond Barracks to pick up Frank.

"I've sent for him," said Vinny Byrne. "How do you want to have him 'dressed'?"

"In handcuffs and leg-irons," Eoin responded without hesitation. "Tight ones," he added.

Vinny laughed. "You really have it in for the lad, you do."

"Believe me, Vincent, if I didn't have the power of Collins behind me to do this, I'd just shoot the bastard. I have had enough. Can you spare two men?"

"Anything you want," said Vinny. "Are you getting used to your new uniform?"

Eoin looked warily at the sleeve of his military tunic and laughed. "I hate the fooker. If it wasn't for Mick, I never would have put it on. I miss my blue three-piece suit. I feel like an eejit in this thing."

"I'm with you," said Colonel Byrne. "Only for Mick would I do this."

With that, Frank entered the room. "Oh, it's you," he said to Eoin, as causal as could be.

"Handcuffs and irons," Byrne said to the two soldier escorts. "This time we're going to make sure Frank Kavanagh leaves the country."

"What do you mean 'leaves the country'?"

"You're a lucky man, Frank," said Eoin. "You're about to embark on an all-expenses-paid trip to New York."

"But I don't want to go."

"Too bad," replied Eoin. "You're going."

The restraints were brought in, and Frank found himself handcuffed with a chain running down his front from his cuffs to his leg-irons. He looked like the most dangerous man in the world.

A car took them to the North Wall, where supplies, including artillery, were being loaded on an old tramp steamer that the Free State had chartered. During the ride, Eoin told Frank the facts of life and warned him that this was his last chance. "Devoy won't put up with any of your shite. He'd shoot you as quick as look at you. They'll find your body floating in the Hudson River," Eoin told his brother. Frank had a look on him that showed he might actually be listening for a change. The two Free State soldiers brought Frank to the hold, where they took turns guarding him.

The journey down the Irish coast was slow and monotonous. The only amusement for Eoin was Frank's screech when a rat ran across the hold. *Tough ould Frank*, thought Eoin, and a laugh followed. As they approached Cobh Harbor, Eoin took in the sights—from the high tower of St. Colman's Cathedral to the surreal quiet of Spike Island, still full of British soldiers and Royal Navy personnel. As part of the Treaty, Britain got to retain several Irish ports for use by the Royal Navy. It infuriated Eoin, but he realized it was all part of Collins's master plan for the future of Ireland. The RMS *Celtic* sat anchored in the middle of Cobh harbor. To Eoin, it was a mini-*Titanic*—not as big, but bigger than anything he had ever seen before. It had two smokestacks and the pronounced Harland & Wolff bow that was common on all White Star liners.

The old steamer tied up at the dock, and Eoin, Frank, and the two escorting soldiers made their way to the *Celtic*'s tender, which would take them out to the ship. As he prepared to board, Eoin buttoned the collar on his tunic and pulled his hat over his eyes. When he got on deck he said, "Take me to the Captain."

The four Irishmen were taken to the bridge, where Eoin met the ship's master, Captain Reginald Cowgill. Eoin immediately saluted the captain, shocking even himself. Cowgill sharply returned the salute. "Captain, I'm Commandant-Colonel Kavanagh of the National Army. I have a prisoner here whom I want you to contain in your brig for the crossing. He will be picked up by Free State personnel in New York."

Cowgill looked like he was about to blow a gasket. "Of all the impertinence!" he exclaimed. "Coming on one of His Majesty's liners at Queenstown and dictating to a White Star master."

"Look, Captain," said Eoin, eyes narrowing, "you are not in Queenstown anymore. You are in the ancient Irish harbor of Cobh. Right now, your ship is sitting in Free State territorial water, and, if you don't follow my orders, you will sit right here until I say you can go. Do you understand me?"

"How dare you!"

"You're not listening. I work for Michael Collins, and this prisoner is sailing to America under General Collins's orders. Do you want me to get General Collins onto your business? He's in Cork right now." The mention of Michael Collins had the magical effect Eoin was hoping for, and Cowgill backed off. "Very well," said Eoin, "here's the prisoner's papers. All is in order. Here's his ticket and Free State passport. He is not to leave your brig until he is fetched in New York. Is that understood?" The fight had apparently gone out of the captain. Taking Frank by the arm, Eoin presented him to Cowgill. "He's all yours." Frank didn't say a word, but Eoin could see he was seething. They took Frank away to the brig without a goodbye, and Eoin took in the panoramic view of Cobh Harbor from the bridge. It was magnificent. As he waited for his two soldiers to return, he noticed a plaque on the wall of the bridge. It was dedicated to Captain Smith, the master of the *Titanic* and former captain of the *Celtic*. When his two soldiers returned, Eoin pointed out the plaque to them. "Captain, I hope you're a better sailor than that eejit." Eoin was the only one who laughed. As he left the *Celtic*, he felt the weight of the world come off him with the removal of Frank. He figured the job of bodyguarding Michael Collins would be the easiest part of this trip to County Cork.

158

After returning to shore, Eoin headed for the Imperial Hotel in Cork City, where Collins was scheduled to show up Sunday evening after his business at the Curragh Barracks in Kildare and then Limerick. He was expected mid-evening, but there was no sign of him. The lobby was busy with people anticipating his arrival. Free State troops were all about, but Eoin's instincts led him to look for Irregulars, possible assassins. Eoin felt his National Army uniform was nothing but a hindrance to his security work.

As midnight approached, the lobby emptied. Two Free State sentries were behind the night desk, still awaiting Collins's arrival. Eoin found an easy chair and slipped into sleep. His nap was soon disrupted by squeals coming from the sentries. Collins had arrived and, seeing them asleep at their posts, had grabbed them by their hair and slammed their heads together, eliciting painful howls. "Fookin' eejits," screamed Collins. "You two are good for nothing!"

Eoin was delighted to see that the General was feisty again. "How was the trip?"

"Educational," said Collins, before he started coughing violently. "Fucking cold," he said. "First my stomach, now my chest. This fookin' country has damned near destroyed me. Let me get to bed. We'll talk in the morning."

But by morning, he wasn't much better. At least the itinerary for the day wasn't too bad—mostly meetings with army brass and banking officials. The Irregulars had been getting their hands on Free State money, which was infuriating the Minister for Finance, who also happened to be the Commander-in-Chief of the National Army. "I'll murder these fookers for stealing the nation's wealth. I've even sent some bank examiners to London to put a stop to them hiding the money in accounts there. The nerve of them."

The irony was not lost on Eoin. "Too bad we shot Alan Bell. He could have been some use to us on this." Collins was about to respond, but a violent cough overtook him. "You should get to bed," Eoin told him.

"Too busy. Too busy," was Collins's only response.

Tuesday, August 22 broke cold and gray. By 6:15 a.m., they were on the road. Collins and General Dalton sat in the back of an open tourer car, with the driver and Eoin in the front. Their itinerary was insane, thought Eoin. Macroom, Coachford, Kilmurry, Ballymichael, Crookstown, Newcestown, Bandon, Clonakilty, Sam's Cross, Skibbereen, Rosscarbery. Even with the accompanying Crossley tender and other vehicles, Eoin felt powerless because he was in foreign territory. The streets of Dublin were Eoin's friend; the back roads of Cork were not. He knew it was a security nightmare.

Collins was outfitted in a heavy overcoat and, despite his chest cold and dyspepsia, seemed to be enjoying himself among his own people. At every stop along the way, they entered the local pub or small hotel, and Collins would start buying drinks. He talked to everyone, often retiring into a corner with an old acquaintance. Eoin knew exactly what he was up to—he was trying to feel out intermediaries to the Irregulars. It was dangerous business, because Eoin didn't know who he could trust. Christ, he had a hard time even deciphering the terrible County Cork brogue. He knew his Squad skills were no use down here, because they were up against some of the best Flying Column soldiers in the world. These IRA men had annihilated the Black and Tans in the field, and he knew his Webley was not in their league. Eoin also didn't like the idea of the drink. This was business, not a hooley. But Collins kept buying, and the thankful local peasantry kept drinking.

The tour went on all day, and, as dusk fell, Eoin felt as miserable as the weather. The entourage had a motorcycle scout, who was reconnoitering the road ahead. Now, here he was, flying back towards them. They were somewhere outside Clonakilty, but they might as well have been in Timbuktu, as far as Eoin was concerned. The scout and his motorbike pulled up to the tourer car. "Trees down," the scout told Eoin.

They advanced slowly down the road until they came to the obstruction. "Let's clean it up," Collins shouted to his men. "This is not an accident," he said to Eoin, the look on his face just awful with fatigue. For the first time, Collins looked like he was a defeated man.

"No kidding," was all Eoin could muster.

Collins heard a click, and he reached for his Colt. Eoin also drew and was shocked to see that it was only a local with a little box camera, taking a photo of the celebrity in their midst. Apparently, *everyone* in the county knew that General Michael Collins was visiting them this day. It was the last photo ever taken of Collins, looking vicious as he reached for his gun.

Collins lent a hand, and, in about a quarter of an hour, they had cleared the trees. They all piled back into their cars, and the slog began again as they made their way back to Cork City. At a bend, known to the locals as *Béal na mBláth*, sniper shots were fired on the cars. "Drive like hell!" Eoin yelled to the driver.

"No!" shouted Collins. "Stop! Jump out, and we'll fight them."

Eoin couldn't believe the driver had actually stopped. "Go! Go! Go!" he shouted, but they had stopped on the General's orders. It was obvious that the driver was terrified of Collins and had no intention of disobeying him as Eoin would have. "Oh, Jesus," Eoin said, realizing they were in the eye of a perfect ambush. They all jumped out of the car, and Dalton, a decorated veteran of the Great War, took cover behind the tourer car and started returning fire. Eoin had his Webley out, but he knew it wouldn't be of much use because the snipers were situated above them and too far away. These were country marksmen; Eoin knew he was a back-alley Dublin fighter. Out of the corner of his eye, he saw Collins standing, firing away with his Colt. "For fook's sake, get down!" he shouted. Then he heard a dull thud and saw Collins drop violently, as if his legs had been cut off at the knees. Eoin ran to him and put his hand to the General's shoulder to pull him onto his back. He then saw that his hand was covered with blood. He turned him around and saw that the back of Collins's head on the right side was gone.

"You fookin', fookin' eejit!" Eoin screamed at Collins, who was now on his back, eyes wide open, blood gushing out of the hole in the back of his head. Eoin punched him in the chest and continued to berate him. "You eejit, you fookin' eejit! How could you? How could you?" Collins just stared at him, not seeing anything anymore. There was only one thing more the Commandant-General demanded of his young charge—a Perfect Act of Contrition. Eoin put his mouth to Collins's right ear and spoke: "*Oh my God! I am heartily sorry for having offended Thee, and I detest all my sins, because I dread the loss of heaven and the pains of hell. But most of all because they offend Thee, my God, Who art all-good and deserving of all my love. I firmly resolve, with the help of Thy grace to confess my sins, to do penance, and to amend my life. Amen.*"

The firing stopped as suddenly as it had begun, as if the Irregulars knew their job was done. Eoin stood and looked down at his fallen friend. He knew his work for Ireland was over. He could tell by his tears, which would not stop.

159

Róisín was late for work, and she was racing her bike as she made the turn into Westmoreland Street. As she approached Fleet Street, she realized that there was a queer quiet to this Wednesday morning rush hour. Something was wrong, and she couldn't figure it out. As she got closer to Bewley's, all the noise of the city just disappeared. People were standing right in front of the tea emporium. They were surrounding a sobbing Black Terry O'Neill, who was on station. The sign around his neck hawking the morning extra edition was in huge letters:

COLLINS

SHOT

DEAD.

Róisín dropped her bike in the gutter and ran towards Black Terry, whom she knew through Eoin. She looked at Black Terry and heard his wail, as if he had been possessed by a banshee. The boy stood, possessed by uncontrollable grief. "Mr. Mick is dead," he said and kept repeating, "Mr. Mick is dead!"

Róisín embraced the lad, and soon their wails were united. She never even thought of her Eoin, only Collins. She knew this was the end. Ireland had deserted Michael Collins, and now she would desert Ireland.

160

It was impossible to move Collins's body to Dublin over land, because the Irregulars were playing havoc with the roads and rail system. Back in Cork City with Collins's coffin, Eoin had had enough of the indecision of the hierarchy. "We'll take that old tub I came down from Dublin on," he finally said. The old boat was still tied up in Cobh Harbor, and they quickly took the coffin down to the docks. Eoin was thankful to get out of Rebel Cork while still breathing. He sat alone with the coffin in the hold, trying to figure out the future for both Róisín and himself. Right now he didn't give a fuck about Ireland.

The old tug finally arrived at Dublin's North Wall after midnight. President Cosgrave and General Mulcahy met the boat, but the man Eoin was most happy to see was Dr. Gogarty. "Are you alright, Eoin?"

Eoin shook his head. "I should be in that box," he said. "Not Mick."

"No," Gogarty chided, "stop it. Mick died the way he wanted to. A heroic death! Just like Collins, unhesitating to attack, regardless of odds. Just like Collins, to send his enemies flying before the terrible exhibition of his courage. One of constituents of courage is contempt. And Collins's contempt for the men who turned on him was heroic!"

They were bringing the casket up from the hold. "Where to now?"

"They're taking Mick to the City Hall for the time being," said Gogarty. "I'll embalm him in the morning."

"I'll stay with the body tonight. He shouldn't be left alone." Eoin thought of the hapless Conor Clune and how he and Collins had spent the night with the boy's body before they shipped him home for burial.

When they got to the City Hall, Eoin found a chair and spent the night sitting at the foot of his boss's coffin, fast asleep.

The next morning, Gogarty arrived, and they took the body to the Anatomy School of Trinity College to be embalmed. It was difficult to see who was in worse shape, Eoin or Gogarty. This was Gogarty's second embalmment in a week; he had also prepared President Griffith. They opened the coffin, and General Collins lay there, still clutching the crucifix they had stuck in his hands in Cork. They removed the body to an examination table and slowly began to strip it. Eoin went through Collins's pockets and found Gogarty's latchkey to 15 Ely Place, where Collins often spent the night. He gave it to Gogarty. "He won't be needing this anymore." Gogarty, a white apron covering his suit, began his gruesome work. Eoin thought about how this scene was so familiar. How many times had he spent in Dublin mortuaries with dead rebels, dressing them for their funerals so Collins could make public-relations props out of them? He thought back to that time in the morgue of the Mater Hospital, when the corpse was his own father. Eoin promised himself that this was the last time he would ever do this. A messenger arrived from the Portobello Barracks with one of Collins's fresh uniforms. Slowly, they began to repackage the General. Then the simple casket arrived from Fanagan's, and they gently placed the body in the box. The last thing they did was rewrap the General's hands around his Cork crucifix.

Their first stop was St. Vincent's Hospital on St. Stephen's Green. There would be a viewing there until the body was brought back to the City Hall for the official lying-in-state. Crowds began to assemble, running all the way to Lower Leeson Street and around the corner. Wasn't it something? Eoin thought. Only three weeks ago, Harry Boland lay dead in this hospital, and now it was Collins. Eoin looked at the crowd and felt better. Mick wouldn't be alone anymore. Eoin decided to head back to the Portobello Barracks and catch some sleep.

Early the next morning, Róisín brought both Dickie and Mary to the City Hall. People were lining up to pay respects, but Eoin wanted to have a quiet moment with his brother and sister before the general public was allowed in. Eoin remembered how impressed he had been when his father took him to see Jeremiah O'Donovan Rossa lie in state in 1915 and how he'd thought then that Rossa might be Ireland's

Lazarus, because he'd been dead so long but didn't stink. Tom Clarke and Padraig Pearse had indeed performed a Fenian resurrection. That was only six years ago, but it was a century in the history of Ireland. How many dead did this country need to be free?

Róisín had fixed Mary's hair up in a pretty bob, and she was so glad to see her big brother that she hugged him and wouldn't let go. Then she looked into the General's coffin and blessed herself. Now it was Dickie's turn. He wasn't tall enough to look down into the coffin, so he put his hands on the side of the box and pulled himself up to take a peek at the General. Eoin half-expected Collins to snap to life and say "Boo!" "Is he asleep?" asked Dickie.

"Here," said Eoin, lifting the lad up so he could see Collins. "Yes, Dickie, the General is sleeping. He's sleeping with Jesus in Heaven. Say goodbye to the General."

"Goodbye, General Collins," the child said, before adding, "and thank you."

"Yes," repeated Eoin. "Thank you, General Collins."

161

Róisín didn't go to Collins's funeral because she was so distraught. When Eoin returned, he looked like he was going to collapse. "How did it go?" she asked.

Eoin laughed, his bitterness evident. "Like all Fenian funerals, it was a grand success. All had a grand time, excluding the corpse."

"How did Kitty Kiernan hold up?" asked Róisín.

"I thought well, considering."

"Considering what?"

"Well," began Eoin, "Lady Lavery showed up from London dressed all in black—like she was the widow woman or something."

"Jesus," said Róisín, shaking her head.

"But there's more!"

"Guess who else showed up draped in black?" Róisín had no idea. "Lady Deametrice!"

"Go 'way!" said Róisín. She knew all about Collins's "London Ladies," because Eoin had told her the stories. "Did she bring her bosoms?"

Even Eoin, on this terrible day, had to smile. "Handsomely displayed under black mourning lace!"

"Some people have no shame," said Róisín, and Eoin knew she was right on the money. "Were you a pallbearer?"

"Not even that," replied Eoin. "They had me bodyguarding General Mulcahy and President Cosgrave. They're all afraid they're next."

"I don't blame them."

"I did have a nice chat with Dick Mulcahy," said Eoin, as he opened the tunic on his uniform. "He wants me to continue on in the same position, working for him now that he's the Commander-in-Chief of the National Army."

"Oh, God," muttered Róisín.

"But I heard there's a few jobs open in America, in New York. Diplomatic jobs."

"I don't care if it's a charwoman's job," shot Róisín. "Anything to get out of this godforsaken country."

"I put in for the job," continued Eoin. "I think I can get it. And we can get the hell out of here." Róisín rushed to him, giving him a big kiss and holding him closely, hoping for some relief from the terrible torment she was feeling. First Eoin took off his holster and his Sam Browne belt. Then he began peeling off his uniform. "This is the last time I'll ever wear this fucking thing," he swore.

"Let me help you," she said, as she began unbuttoning his tunic. Then she undid his buckle, and his pants dropped to the floor. After the boots came the socks. Then she jerked his underwear down. She rubbed his flat belly and he began to stir. "I think I was just saluted!" said Róisín, and they both laughed.

After undressing Eoin, Róisín slowly began to peel her own clothes off, garment by garment. Soon she was nude as well. She took Eoin by the hand and led him to the bedroom.

Men and women grieve differently, and Róisín was wise enough to know the difference. For men, sexual release can calm and relieve. For women, touch and feel and the warmth of a body can help abate grief. What occurred for the next six hours satisfied them both—a savage, animalistic, relentless lovemaking session. Except for guttural sounds, they hardly spoke. The long lovemaking session went by as fast as a snap of the fingers. Near midnight, near exhaustion, they stopped.

"Chumley's," Róisín said, with a light laugh.

"Prohibition."

"Baseball."

"At the Polo Grounds."

"Mister John J. McGraw."

"Casey Stengel."

"America."

"New York City."

"Are you ready?" asked Róisín.

"I am," said Eoin, and he knew the two of them—and the child they had just conceived—had found their new home.

EPILOGUE
NOVEMBER 2006

162

EOIN'S DIARY
OCTOBER 10, 2006

I've lived too long. And, thank God, I'm coming to me end. The one thing I've learned is true in life is that, when you're young, everything is pure. When you're old, everything is rancid.

My dear grandson and Diane, today is my 105th birthday, and I think God is still getting even. If He had any compassion, I would have died years ago, as my dear Róisín did. But He keeps me going. I think for penance. For my terrible work for Mick.

You know, when I was forty, they were already calling me "that old Irish rebel." That was over sixty years ago. That's not funny. When I was in my seventies, I used to wake in the morning and check to see if everything was working—my eyes, my knees, my old wrinkled willie. Now it even hurts to take a piss. I won't mention the havoc that taking a shite entails.

So this is it, my final entry. I've tried to keep all the notebooks in their proper boxes. Now they're your problem, Johnny, not mine.

I've outlived my lovely, feisty, impossible Róisín. She died in 1981 at 82, a good, solid age to die at. Of course, I have no sense, so a quarter of a century later, I'm still here, very alone. I've outlived my only son, Eoin, by over a half a century. He was conceived in grief, and we never took to each other. He was a walking reminder of my failure at *Béal na mBláth*. I know he felt it. Son, I'm sorry. I hope you and your mother are reunited somewhere in the great galaxy beyond, and maybe, someday, I'll join you.

I outlived my entire family, except for you, Johnny. I buried Mary, Dickie, and Frank. I must say that I'm not a great one for wakes, but it felt good to look into the box and see Frank just lying there, his gob sealed shut—for once—and out of my fucking life forever. He made all his siblings suffer and, I think, took a twisted delight in doing it. Well, I've outlived the bastard by fifty years, and I'm proud of that fact, at least.

I've outlived my friend and mentor Vinny Byrne—but not by that much. In old age, Vinny became a television fixture and a Fenian celebrity. His stories about the shootings, even that one in Mount Street on Bloody Sunday, were stunning. The general reaction was: I can't believe this lovely little gnome of a man was a cold-blooded killer! Shite, he was—and so was I.

Mick is loved by 99.9 percent of the Irish, not only here in Ireland, but worldwide. Of course, now there are the revisionists, as they call the guys who make up their own versions of history. I was amused by a recent article in the *Irish Independent* by this young shite of a columnist named Kevin Mayes or something—the latest member of the Conor Cruise O'Brien wing of the Royal Society of Irish Eunuchs—who wrote that the men of the Squad were "a bunch of serial killers." Apparently, he was shocked that we had to shoot the British to make them leave Ireland. All I can say is, he's lucky this old serial killer is short his Webley. And then there's that Joyce fraud, the creampuff of a Senator, whatever his name is, who is now claiming Mick was gay—the Micheál Mac Liammóir of revolutionaries! It's bad enough they won't leave poor Roger Casement alone—now they're after Mick. As we used to say in days gone by, yeah, Mick was a bugger, but he wasn't that kind of bugger! And after seeing him in action with Kitty Kiernan and Lady Lavery, I think I can safely vouch for his heterosexuality. It's all silly nonsense.

I've outlived Jack Lemass by thirty-five years. Of all the treacheries that de Valera did, I think keeping Jack from becoming *Taoiseach* for at least a decade was the most costly to Ireland. He was a talented executive with a vision and, I'm proud to say, my good friend. And a fellow conspirator on Bloody Sunday.

Now people want to have their picture taken with me when I travel into town to make an appearance at the *Dáil*, or when I venture into the Stag's Head for that now-rare pint. People actually want to touch me. I've turned into a (barely) walking national monument. I'm reminded of de Valera working that crowd at the Gresham Hotel months before he died. But I don't extend my hands like Dev did, doing his impression of the Blessed Virgin Mary standing on the globe, the serpent underfoot. Let them take their pictures. I was only a soldier doing my duty.

I've outlived Mick Collins by eighty-four years. Wherever Mick ended up—heaven, hell, purgatory—I want to join him there. If we burn, at least we burn together.

As I look back on my long life, I have to admit that everything I was told as a child was a lie. My religion was a lie—full of abuse directed at children and adults alike. History will look at the Catholic Church in the latter part of the twentieth century as nothing but a cadre of pedophiles in Roman collars, led and protected by sixteenth-century reactionaries in miters. I've decided that God—if there is a God—does not have a master plan but a recycling plan that consists of doing the same ould shite over and over again, century after century. Life on earth is basically God's serial insanity. As it was in the beginning, is now, and ever shall be: world without end. Amen. I will not be checking the reincarnation box when I get to the pearly gates and they hand me my application form.

My country—the country I helped to create—is also a lie. Born in hope and idealism, it has become the captive of greed—crooked politicians, bankers, and real estate developers—all deserving of Squad attention. Oh, the politicians—praising Patrick Pearse with one hand, and pocketing the cash with the other. The greed is given a fig-leaf by superb propaganda—the heralded "Celtic Tiger." And the Irish, cynical bastards that they are, somehow bought it hook, line, and sinker. God help them, because they are about to pay.

I wonder if all the things I did for Michael Collins were worth it? Would we have fared any worse under the English? Did I sell my soul to a false prophet? For a false idea? Maybe, but I make no apologies.

So this is it, Johnny Three. I'll be gone very soon, and this is your big surprise. See what you can do with it. You're a lucky man, surrounded by the beautiful Diane and those wonderful girls of yours, Róisín, Aoife, and Aisling, all beauties with great Irish mugs and matching names. May they live in interesting times—but they'll be hard-pressed to outdo their great-grandfather.

And, as Mick might have said, "That's that!"

I love you all.

Slán agat!

Granddad

163

Six weeks after Eoin's funeral, it was time to go home to New York for Thanksgiving.

Johnny walked across the room and laid a kiss on his wife's forehead. "I'm going out to Glasnevin tomorrow. I want to see the old man one more time before we go home. Would you like to come along?"

"I wouldn't miss it."

The next day they took the DART into Tara Street and then walked over to Westmoreland Street to catch the bus to Glasnevin. When they got to the front gate of the cemetery, Johnny stopped and bought three red roses from a vendor. "How's business?" he asked, as he received his change.

"Steady," said the woman, and the three of them shared a laugh.

Johnny took Diane by the hand and walked through the front gate and then straight ahead to the new graves of some long-dead Fenians. "There's Sir Roger," he said, pointing out the tiny headstone of Roger Casement. "It only took the British forty-nine years to return his bones. There's even a rumor that they aren't Sir Roger's bones. Could be that wife-murderer, Dr. Crippen. Both were buried in the same prison yard in England. Hard to tell after fifty years. No DNA then."

"A wife-murderer?"

"Yeah," said Johnny, "I thought they were a bit heavy with the death sentence for poor Crippen." Diane gave him a playful punch in the arm. "Look, here's Kevin Barry. Finally dug him up out of the yard at

Mountjoy and planted him here where he belongs." Barry was buried next to other young rebels who had been executed in Mountjoy Prison as pawns in the time leading up to the time of the Truce in July 1921. Johnny read the names aloud: "Thomas Whelan. Patrick Moran. Patrick Doyle. Bernard Ryan. Thomas Bryan. Frank Flood."

"My God," said Diane, "those were the young fellows Eoin challenged Collins about."

"Yes, Grandpa's 'This is fucking insanity' moment. I feel particularly bad about Whelan, because he was accused of doing the job that Grandpa and Vinny Byrne did."

"It's so sad," said Diane, beginning to tear up. Johnny took Diane by the hand and walked her around Dan O'Connell's tall monument. They settled into the well-named Republican Plot, where many great Fenians were buried. Johnny pointed out Jeremiah O'Donovan Rossa, only four graves away from John Devoy, Collins's great friend in New York City. "There's Cathal Brugha!" said Diane. "Apparently *anyone* can get in here!"

"Here are the Countess Markievicz and Nurse Elizabeth O'Farrell, who Eoin met in Moore Street at the time of the surrender." Johnny pointed to the ground and a tiny headstone. "Harry Boland," he said.

"Poor, poor Harry," said Diane, thinking of a lost love and a lost life.

"Do you want to see de Valera's grave?"

"No!" said Diane. "Definitely not."

"Well," said Johnny, "you're going to see it. There's something special about it. But before we visit Dev," said Johnny, "let's say hello to Róisín and my daddy. They're right over here." The marker contained only two names:

Eoin Kavanagh Jr.	**Róisín O'Mahony Kavanagh**
1923-1960	**1899–1981**
	Cumann na mBan
	Author

"They seem comfortable together," said Diane.

"I know Róisín is," replied Johnny. "I just hope my poor father found peace once he got off this planet." Johnny felt tears coming on, and he put his hand to his eyes, covering them. "Oh, Róisín, you were such a great grandmother. No, you were really my mother." Then he started reciting:

"Thee have I loved, for thee have roved
O'er land and sea;
My heart was sore, and ever more
It beat for thee;
I could not weep, I could not sleep,
I could not move!
For night or day, I dreamed always
Of Róisín Dubh!"

"That's lovely," said Diane.

"'The Dark Róisín.' James Clarence Mangan, from the Gaelic," Johnny explained. He quietly placed a rose on the grave. "A rose for Róisín and her only son, Eoin, my daddy," he said. He turned to his wife. "'When you name a child,' the old man once told me, 'you should always think how that name will look on a tombstone.' The old man was appalled that someone would name their child 'Treat' or some such name. 'What's his twin named?' he would say, 'Trick?' It's a very Irish sentiment."

"It's a very Catholic sentiment," corrected Diane.

They walked the short distance and stood before the simple marker of Eamon and Sinéad de Valera, and other members of the de Valera family.

"So?" said Diane.

"What do you see?"

"Nothing."

"Yeah, it's the most naked grave in the cemetery," said Johnny. "They all voted for him, but no one really loved him. And now it shows."

With that, he led her down the short path connecting de Valera's grave to Collins's. Unlike de Valera's, Collins's grave overflowed with colorful flowers and notes of thanks that had been left by admirers, brightening the bleak November morning. There was no mourning at the grave of Michael Collins, just a celebration of his extraordinary life.

"Well," said Johnny, a bit choked up.

"It's beautiful," replied Diane. "The people absolutely love this man. Even all these years later."

Johnny added his own rose to the flowers. Eoin Kavanagh was just to the south of General Collins, buried among Irish soldiers who had been killed in the Congo on a UN mission in the 1960s. The inscription was simple, just as the old man had wished:

EOIN CHAOMBÁNACH, IRB, 1901–2006

"It's in Irish," said Diane.

"That's the way he wanted it. Didn't even mention he was a Commandant-Colonel or a TD." Quietly, Johnny placed the last rose in front of the marker and blessed himself.

It was so quiet now, unlike the day of the burial. Then the grave was surrounded by the politicians of Ireland. The *Taoiseach* had to be there, but there was a lack of other *Taoisigh* because so many of them had disagreements with Eoin, especially on the North. The only other former *Taoiseach* to show up was Albert Reynolds, who had had a close relationship with Eoin, and who was responsible for setting the foundation for the Good Friday Agreement.

The graveside that October day had been surrounded by the Irish president, Mrs. McAleese, Gerry Adams, Eoin's friend from the North, and the American Ambassador, a grumpy, rich old Republican who worried that there might be some kind of gunplay, and he might get shot by mistake. Former U.S. Ambassador Jean Kennedy Smith was there, but Teddy Kennedy was a late scratch. The twenty-one-gun salute was followed first by the Star-Spangled Banner, and then by *Amhrán na bhFiann*, "The Soldier's Song," the national anthem of Ireland. It was over in fifteen minutes.

Johnny took out his grandfather's pocketwatch—which he now carried with him at all times—and flipped the lid open. "Lunchtime," he said. "Let's get out of the cold and find a drink." They walked past the Angels Plot, where all the unnamed babies were buried, and exited through the south gate, which was right next to John Kavanagh's, "the Gravediggers Pub."

"My God," said Diane, "this place is great."

"And appropriately named!" added Johnny. Kavanagh's was an old spirit-grocer and public house. Behind the bar they had spice boxes, jugs, and glass cabinets. The pub was painted a permanent nicotine brown. "I haven't been here in more than thirty years," said Johnny, "when grandmother died. In those days, you had to piss on the back wall." Diane looked concerned. "I bet they've installed plumbing since." The barman approached, and Johnny said, "Two pints of Guinness, please." The jars were pulled in proper time, and the two of them clinked their glasses together.

"To the memory of the great old Fenian, Eoin Kavanagh," said Johnny.

"To Grandpa, God bless him," replied Diane. She took a gulp and licked her stout mustache with her tongue.

"Watch that," said Johnny. "I can think of a better use for that thing."

"What thing?"

"Your tongue."

"You Kavanagh men are incorrigible! You really are. Sex, sex, sex. That's all you think of."

"Hey," protested Eoin, "I have the work of two to do now—myself *and* Grandpa!" He then gave her a gentle pat on her bountiful booty, eliciting first a smile and then a peck on the cheek.

"What's the thing that impressed you most about Collins?" asked Johnny.

"His compassion at the end," said Diane. "Not only to his friends, like President Griffith, but also to his opponents. Like Brugha and Harry Boland."

"He wasn't your typical Irishman," agreed Johnny. "He wasn't vindictive. He may be the only Irishman who didn't hold a grudge."

"Yes," said Diane, "the Irish and their never-ending grudges."

"Darling," said Johnny, "love may make the world go around, but hate gives you a reason for living!"

"Do you think you can make something out of Grandpa's diaries?"

"I think I can make it into a book," said Johnny. "Set it in historical perspective and add some clarifying text, and I think it will make a fine book." He again took out the pocketwatch, which he was beginning to think might actually contain parts of the souls of Eoin and Collins.

"What will you call it?"

Johnny thought for a moment, as he slowly massaged the watch between the palms of his two hands, like a pitcher rubbing a baseball. "*The 13th Apostle*," he finally said.